QUEEN OF MONSTERS AND MADNESS

QUEEN OF MONSTERS AND MADNESS

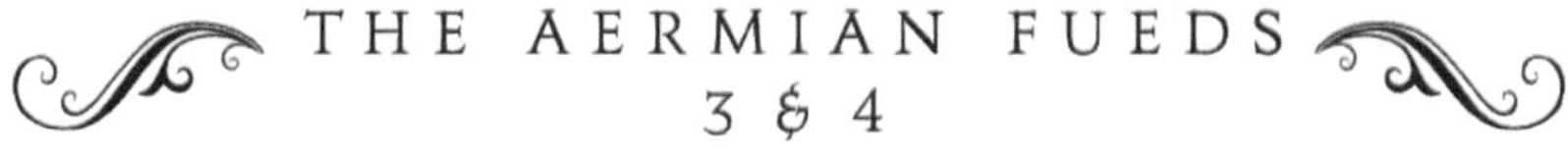

FROST KAY

QUEEN OF MONSTERS AND MADNESS

First Edition

Cover by Covers by Combs
Interior formatting by We Got You Covered Book Design
Copy Editing by Madeline Dyer
Proofreading by Holmes Edits

ALSO BY FROST KAY

TWISTED KINGDOMS

FAIRYTALE RETELLING

The Hunt

The Rook

The Heir

The Beast

DRAGON ISLE WARS

FANTASY ROMANCE

Court of Dragons

DOMINION OF ASH

POST APOCALYPTIC FANTASY ROMANCE

The Stain

The Tainted

The Exiled

The Fallout

The Chosen

MIXOLOGISTS & PIRATES

SCI-FI ROMANCE

Amber Vial

Emerald Bane

Scarlet Venom

Cyan Toxin

Onyx Elixir

Indigo Alloy

ALIENS & ALCHEMISTS

SCI-FI ROMANCE

Pirates, Princes, and Payback

Alphas, Airships, and Assassins

THE AERMIAN FEUDS

DARK FANTASY ROMANCE

Rebel's Blade

Crown's Shield

Siren's Lure

Enemy's Queen

King's Warrior

Warlord's Shadow

Spy's Mask

Court's Fool

To the people in my life who have survived their own monsters and demons, and come out the other side scarred, but beautiful.
Your strength and courage are not unnoticed.

I see you. I accept you.

I AM AWE INSPIRED BY YOU.

Thank you for sharing your stories with me.

THE Five Kingdoms
Rooi
NAGAL
the Mort Walls
Janem
CASPERNAE OCEAN
the Mort Walls
SCYTHIA
AERMIA
Salvren
the Dregs
Sanee
the Blessed Beach
THALASSIAN SEA

N
Devil's Cage
Skigara
Laos
METHI
Sirenidae
the Wyver

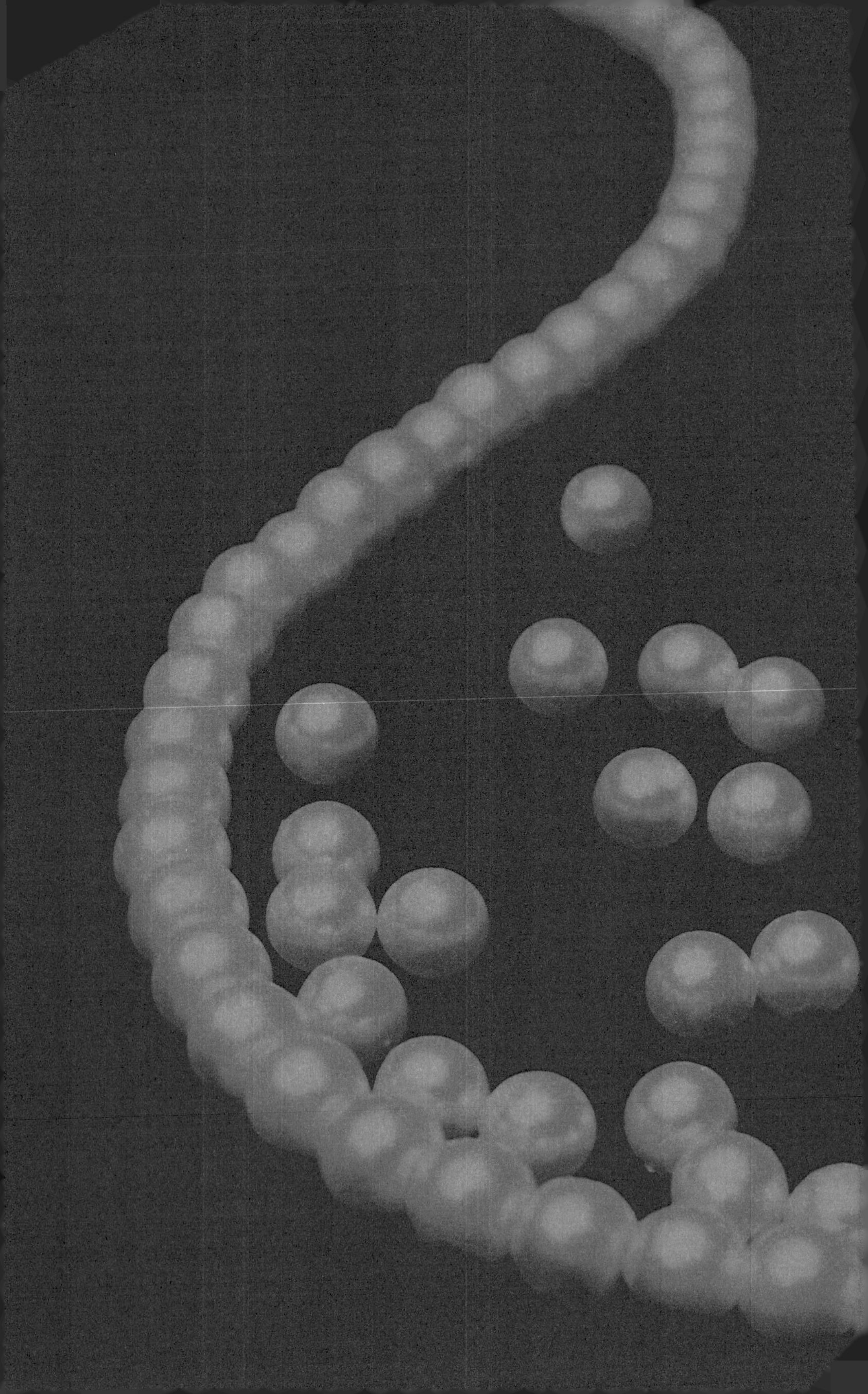

PART ONE

THE ENEMY'S QUEEN

PROLOGUE

THE STORYBOOKS HAD IT WRONG.

Prince charming wasn't always perfect, and monsters weren't always ugly.

The deceptive thing about monsters is they're never what you expect them to be. They're not always the shadows underneath the bed, but the hero expected to save you.

Those are the most dangerous.

Those devils are so beguiling that your breath catches when they look at you, and your heart flutters when they grace you with a smile. But therein lies the rub. They're the type of monster you want to hide from. The ones you pray never notice you.

Beware of the winks, and innocent touches. It's nothing but deception, an intricate trap. And remember, beauty and perfection have a price. Nothing is free.

Sage's monster was everything and nothing like she imagined, and this time there was no escape.

The devil had come to collect his dues, and Sage was short.

ONE

JASMINE

"JADE, WE WON'T CATCH A thing if you don't tread more lightly. How can you make so much noise?" Stephen complained.

"Shhhhh...," Jade's tiny voice admonished, her fawn-colored eyes narrowed. "You'll scare the animals."

The young boy huffed. "Suuuurrree. *I'm* the reason we'll go without meat."

Jasmine smiled as she glanced over her shoulder at the young boy helping her niece through the underbrush. Each day, Jasmine checked the traps, and each day, she'd bring along either Jade or Ethan, the three-year-old twins. In the meantime, the other would stay with the widows of her village. Today was Jade's turn. Her niece was trying to walk quietly, but it seemed that the harder she tried, the louder she became. As Jade loudly snapped yet another twig under her feet, Stephen met Jasmine's gaze, exasperation clear on his face.

"At least the animals in our traps can't run away," she offered, grinning.

Stephen rolled his eyes and shifted an overly-large bow onto his shoulder, looking dejected. "I know."

Pain lanced her heart. The poor thing. He wanted so badly to have a chance trying out his new bow. She sighed. It had been months, yet, in many ways, the Scythian attack still affected them as if it had happened only yesterday. Stephen was but one of the many children to lose his father. She frowned, some of the pain in her heart giving way to anger. None of them would be in this situation if the Scythians hadn't been such monsters.

Jasmine tried to do what she could for the village, and Stephen was one whom she happened to be in a position to assist. He needed archery lessons and she needed help caring for the twins, so their arrangement was a win-win.

A small hand slipped into hers, jarring her from her thoughts. "Okay, Auntie?"

Jasmine blinked several times, focusing on her niece's round face as she forced a smile. She squeezed Jade's hand three times, reminding the little girl that she loved her—one squeeze for each word. It was something her family had always done. A toothy grin split the small child's face as she returned the three squeezes.

She pulled her gaze from her niece to scan the forest. At the edge of a meadow, a small plant sporting small, bright green leaves caught her attention. Dropping to her haunches, she brushed Jade's dark brown hair from her eyes and widened her own at the small girl. "Guess what I just spotted?"

"What?"

She leaned in conspiratorially and whispered, "I found strawberry plants!"

Her niece squealed and bounced on her toes. "I *love* strawberries!"

"Yes, I know." Jasmine pointed to the strawberry patch on the left. "They're right over there, so I need you to stay in the patch and do some picking while I help Stephen with his bow. Okay?"

"Okay!"

Jasmine released the child's hand and Jade rushed over to the patch where she immediately flopped down, her hands already searching for the sweet, plump fruit.

Jasmine shook her head and turned to her other charge. "You ready?"

Stephen smiled and nodded as he yanked his bow from his back. "Where can I shoot?" He skipped over to a flat spot.

She chuckled. "Slow down a second. You need to calm down, and be still."

"But I can't," he said, bouncing on his toes.

Jasmine smiled and wandered over to the boy. "Just close your eyes and breathe. In through your nose, and out from your mouth. Try to calm your mind, still your limbs."

He slammed his eyes shut and breathed in rapid succession. She hid a smile at how excited he was and repeated, "Slowly, Stephen, slowly."

At her admonition his breathing slowed and, as she was hoping, his body relaxed.

"Perfect. Now, open your eyes and take up your stance."

Stephen planted his feet shoulder-width apart, rotated into a closed stance, and straightened. Jasmine eyed his stance. "Good, very good. Beautiful form. But don't forget your sequence. You need to perfect this form as well as the movement, so you can effortlessly repeat it each time." Adjusting his grip, she continued, "You must also remember to grip exactly here."

She stepped back, briefly glancing back to Jade. Her niece was happily munching on strawberries, oblivious to the rest of the world, with her face already stained crimson.

Jasmine turned her attention back to Stephen. "Draw."

He wobbled only a little as he pulled back on the bowstring, though his form mostly held.

"Excellent job."

The boy smiled at the praise and his cheeks pinked. She stepped forward to tap his hip where it stuck out a bit, and he quickly straightened into a smooth line, accepting the silent critique.

"Lower your bow."

He did as she said and looked at her expectantly. "Now what? Can I try it with an arrow now?"

"Yes."

He let out a joyful whoop and snatched an arrow from his quiver.

"But," she added, "you must first replicate that stance perfectly ten times."

His nose wrinkled, and he returned the arrow back to its quiver. "Okay."

Leaving the boy to his practice, Jasmine found a comfortable tree, leaned her back against it, and slowly closed her eyes. She took the moment to enjoy the peace and quiet of the forest. She'd always been drawn to the almost magical stillness it offered, and now, like a plant in the desert, she soaked it up. It was something she needed.

After a while, she cracked an eyelid, checking on Jade. She was hardly surprised to note her niece hadn't moved, but she couldn't help checking on her all the same. Ever since the death of her brother, and the subsequent transfer of the twins to her care, she couldn't help but be overprotective of them. They were her only family now.

Her eyes had just closed again when a sound reached her ears, faint but familiar—thundering hooves. Her brows drew together as the sound grew closer. The hooves weren't slowing down.

Jasmine's eyes snapped open. The only reason for a rider to be charging in such a reckless fashion through the forest was if they, firstly, were guilty of a crime or secondly, were being chased by something terrible. Neither scenario boded well for herself and the children.

"Stephen," she barked, "we're leaving." Rushing to Jade's side, she urged, "Get up, sweet girl. We need to go."

"I'm still hungry."

"I know. You're always hungry. But I promise to make some lunch when we get home." Scooping up the little girl, she threw her on her back and instructed her, "Hold on."

As the sound of the rider drew even closer, Jasmine spun on her heel and swept toward the little boy, who was still struggling with his bow. "Let's go," she ordered, grabbing his hand as she passed him. It seemed like his feet were dragging behind her. "Hurry up!" Before they got anywhere her arm jerked, and he cried out.

Jasmine released his hand and turned to him, finding his clothes caught on a branch.

"I'm stuck," he said, pulling at his clothes.

Her heart picked up speed. The thundering hooves were much closer now. They were almost out of time. She frantically scanned the trees around them. She finally spotted a tree hollow behind a bush and sprinted toward it. She then pulled Jade from her back and pushed her through the bush and into the hollow. "Stay here. I'll get Stephen, and then we're going to play hide and seek."

"Okay."

She rushed back to Stephen and tugged on the bow. Somehow, he'd got it hooked in the limbs of a bush and it wouldn't budge. "We don't have time for this," she growled. Pulling a small dagger from her sheath she cut the bowstring.

"My papa made that," he cried, appalled.

"I know, and I'm sorry. I can fix it when we get home, but for now, we need to hide."

Desperation filled her voice. The rider was so close, she could hear the horse's ragged breaths. She yanked Stephen to her and shoved him in the hollow as well—it was just big enough for the two children. Carefully, she sank down behind the bush, sheltering the hollow entrance. "I need you both to be silent. Can you do that for me?"

Whispered yeses reached her ears as the horse and rider broke into their meadow. Sweat poured down the flanks of the horse, its chest heaving as the rider dug his heels into the poor creature's sides. The tall rider held a struggling woman in his arms and Jasmine hissed. If the woman wasn't careful, she'd fall. A fall like that could kill a person; she was surprised he could even ride like that. Almost as soon as the thought ran through her mind, the woman flung herself from the man's arms, and narrowly missed the horse's hooves as she crashed to the ground. Clutching one arm, she struggled to stand. Just as quickly, the man pulled the horse back and dismounted in one smooth motion, storming toward the woman. When he reached her, he yanked her up by the hair and Jasmine had to muffle her gasp of alarm.

"How stupid are you? Did you really think you could get away? And now all you've done is hurt yourself."

The young woman slammed her head into his nose and spat blood in his direction. He dropped her hair and clutched at his face, cursing. The woman collapsed to the forest floor, heaved, her face pale, and began to crawl away.

"Oh, no, you don't," he growled. "I think you need to be taught a few lessons."

Jasmine's stomach dropped when he pinned her to the ground. Oh God, she couldn't sit there and watch. She had to do something. She glanced back to Stephen and Jade, their small faces pale and frightened. "Don't watch, loves." She swallowed. "I need to help the woman, but you two do *not* leave this hollow unless I come and get you. Understand me?"

"Yes," Stephen whispered, voice shaking.

"I need you to keep Jade calm and quiet, Stephen. Can you do that for me?"

"Yes."

"Even if I get hurt or look like I'm not okay, do not come get me. You take Jade home and get help. You must not approach that man." Turning to Jade, she whispered, "Auntie loves you so much, but I need you to be a good girl and listen to Stephen, okay? Once I'm done, we'll go home and make lunch. Okay?"

"Okay."

She kissed both the children's faces and pulled in a breath before slipping quietly from her hiding place. The man had flipped the woman onto her back and was now holding her down with his weight and pinching her chin between his fingers. The rumble of his voice filled the air, and Jasmine could only guess at what disgusting things he was saying. Anger burned beneath her chest. It was men like this who made the world an awful place for innocents. She glided through the forest on silent feet, drawing closer to the man and woman.

"You'll learn your place," the man threatened as he slapped the woman across the face, her eyes falling shut. She wanted so badly to charge across the meadow and teach him a swift lesson, but she knew better, so she did the opposite. Inhaling quietly, she continued her careful trek.

When she'd almost reached them, the woman's eyes popped open, revealing vibrant green eyes. The green eyes widened, and she opened her mouth to speak just as a hand clamped over Jasmine's lips. While keeping her gaze on the woman, she raked her nails down the arm detaining her. Her captor cursed, and the huge dirty hand pressing against her face pressed harder, now covering her nose. When she tried to breathe, no air would come. She thought frantically, trying to recall any of the things her mama had taught her to do in such a situation. She needed to offset her attacker. Jasmine threw herself down, becoming dead weight, hoping to upset his balance. Her move did little to aid her, however, for all he did was grunt and heft her against his body. Dizziness overwhelmed her, but she refused to give up. As a last resort, she bit down with all her might. She gagged as a metallic taste filled her mouth, but she didn't dare let go. When she felt a blow to her side, she was forced to release his hand as she gasped. Then, something knocked her in the head, and she found herself on the ground, staring at the raven-haired woman.

"This wench drew blood," a male growled.

"Well," a deep, smooth voice answered, "at least she has fight. That's exactly what we need. Are the men here?"

"They're waiting at the border with Blair. He was getting antsy, because you were late, my lord."

Border? She thought, *What border?* The treetops swirled together above

Jasmine. *The only border close is … No!* Jasmine tried to sit up, to escape, but the world lurched when she made the attempt and then she was right back on the ground.

"There were a few complications," the smooth-voiced male answered.

"Like abusing the master's woman, my lord?"

"She needed to be taught a lesson."

"He'll be displeased with what you've done, my lord."

"We'll see. Let's move. It won't be long before the Crown figures out she's missing."

Right before the world went black, the green-eyed woman mouthed something to her.

Fight.

She didn't need to be told. That was something she would always do.

TWO

TEHL

TEHL SIGHED AS HE SNUGGLED deeper into the blankets, relishing the sunlight warming his back.

Wait...Sunlight?

Tehl squinted at the window. The sun was high. When was the last time he had slept in? He couldn't remember. His stomach growled. It was most definitely past breakfast. He stretched out a hand to touch the empty spot beside him, a smile on his face. Sage had slept beside him last night of her own volition and that was truly a victory. Her words from the night before came back to him, and his smile widened further as he rolled over to stare at the ceiling.

You have a loyal heart. That one statement changed everything. It meant she cared.

Finally, after everything they had been through, she was warming up to him. Admittedly, he had thought for quite a time that she never would. And after last night's misunderstanding, he'd expected her to cut him off completely, or possibly even stab him. But he was very surprised when, instead, she'd opened up to him and they'd been able to communicate freely and honestly for possibly the first time ever. At last, it seemed there was true hope for a friendship with his wife.

He clutched his stomach when it, once more, rumbled its displeasure. It was well past the time he usually ate. Tehl glanced again to the windows and Sage's empty spot. He had slept better last night than he had in a long time. Normally, Sage's nightmares woke up both of them frequently. It gutted him each time he had to reassure her that no one was hurting her, or when he had to hold her so she wouldn't hurt herself or him. What a cruel hand they'd been dealt.

Tehl shook off the glum thoughts and rolled out of bed, stretching his arms above his head. No matter what had happened in the past, today would be a good day.

He shuffled to the vanity and brushed his black hair, splashed water on his face, smoothed his rumpled shirt, and finally, pulled on his boots. It was well past time to get his day started, but first…breakfast.

Pulling the door open, Tehl paused, looking between the guards. Addressing the redhead, he asked, "James, do you have any idea where the princess is?"

"Garreth took her for a walk a while ago, but they've not returned."

"Probably training already," he mused. After nodding to the two men, he moved down the corridor and to the stairs where his brother lounged carelessly against the banister. Moving past him, he began to descend the steps, slapping his brother's shoulder good-naturedly as he passed.

"How are you this morning?"

Sam followed him. "Not as good as you, it seems. Why, you seem downright chipper this morning."

He raised a brow and smiled. "It's going to be a good day."

"I take it things went well with your wife last night?"

"She forgave me," he said simply.

A choking sound came from behind him. "She didn't make you grovel or anything? Or attack you?"

"She's not that type of woman."

Sam sniggered. "Uh, yeah… she is. She would definitely stab you."

"That's not what I meant. I meant she isn't a petty woman."

"Then you're a lucky man," his brother said.

Tehl stopped at the bottom of the stairs and turned to his brother with a smile. "I am. Last night resolved itself better than I ever expected. She can be so emotional at times, and yet, she can also be extremely rational. It's remarkable and confusing."

Sam grinned. "You act like you're surprised. Of course, Sage is remarkable."

Something in his brother's tone gave him pause. There was an intimacy there that he hadn't expected. His brows furrowed as he tried to work it out. When Sam caught his expression, he slapped the back of his head. Tehl rubbed it and glared. "What was that for?"

"Don't be stupid. You know I consider Sage my sister. I have no feelings for her, save the sort of love and admiration a brother usually has, so stop looking at me like I'm about to steal your wife."

"You've been known to steal women." His brother's lack of expression pulled a sheepish smile from him. "Sorry," he offered, continuing to rub the back of his head.

"Apology accepted. It happens to the best of us."

Now *that* made him snort. "Like you've ever been jealous. You don't keep company with the same woman long enough to become envious."

It was Sam's turn to furrow his brow as they began descending the arched, airy corridor. "Well… maybe one day, I'll find the right woman."

Tehl stumbled, gaping at his brother.

"What?" Sam shrugged. "I'm just saying one day it would probably be nice to have a family."

"Who are you and what have you done with my brother?"

"Very funny," his brother said, rolling his eyes. "I'm not saying right now, just… you know, in the future sometime."

"And what brought on this change of heart? You've always told me you're not a one-woman man."

"Things change."

"*Things?*" he asked incredulously. "What sort of things?"

Sam entered the private dining room and closed the door behind them before responding. "Sage," he said, with a shrug.

"Sage?" he repeated plopping into his chair.

His brother paced back and forth with his hands behind his back before placing himself in the chair across from him. "Well… She's interesting."

Tehl waited a beat before prompting, "And?"

Sam tilted his head back to stare at the ceiling. "She's strong, hardworking, loyal, funny, sweet, smart…" He paused. "She's a good person. She's even warm and empathetic, which is hard to find. Being her friend has brought me to the conclusion that, perhaps, marriage wouldn't be so bad after all."

"Because of Sage..."

"Yes, she's helped me realize that all women aren't the same."

Tehl plucked a grape from the table and tossed it into his mouth while studying his brother. He agreed that Sage certainly was unique. Like his mother. That thought stopped him mid-chew and a lump lodged in his throat. He forced himself to swallow. "Do you ever think about Mum?"

Sam smiled softly and dropped his head to meet Tehl's gaze. "From time to time. Sometimes, Sage snarks something at me and it reminds me of Mum. I think she would have liked Sage."

"Father said that, as well."

Both men fell silent, lost in their thoughts. His mum would have welcomed his wife with open arms, he was sure. She'd always wanted a girl in their family. Tehl pulled himself from his thoughts and asked, "Have you seen Sage this morning?"

Sam blinked and shook his head. "Not this morning. She's probably skulking around somewhere. I heard her ladies-in-waiting wanted to go to the market this morning, so I bet my horse she'll hide out all day, just to escape the horrors of shopping."

The brothers exchanged a look and burst out laughing. "I've never known a woman to hate shopping more than Sage. I tried to have new dresses commissioned, but she about ripped my head off, spouting off about 'ridiculous and unnecessary things.'"

"Let me guess, she wanted you to use the money to fund some cause?"

"She's predictable in that way, isn't she?"

"Well, at least she isn't a power-hungry money spender."

Tehl swallowed a bit of honey cake and nodded. "She's special." He blinked, surprised at his own admission.

Sam grinned. "I'm glad you think so."

"What do you mean by that?"

"You're finally seeing her worth."

His brows wrinkled in confusion. "I've always seen her worth."

"No." Sam shook his head. "Not her worth as a consort, her worth as a *woman*."

Tehl's mind conjured up her sweet smile, the glint in her eye when she was about to do something crazy, and the curves she hid beneath linen and leather. "She's beautiful," he blurted. "My wife is beautiful."

"Inside and out," Sam said.

"Indeed," he muttered, staring at the table. He definitely appreciated her appearance, but he had to admit it was the person she was on the inside that had finally won him over. Sage had done many things for his family, but she'd received very little in return which benefited her personally. Maybe he could change that. But what could he do for her? Despite living with her, he didn't know her very well. All he knew was that she didn't care for extravagant gifts and she liked weapons, but, as she was a blacksmith, she liked to make her own, so that was not an option. What did women like?

"Sam…" He eyed his brother. "What do women like as gifts?"

"Jewelry, flowers, romantic dinners, things from the heart. Sage is a little different from the typical woman, but she still appreciates things from the heart."

What was in Sage's heart? Her friends and family. It was that thought which sparked an idea. He smiled. "I've a plan," he declared. "I'll set up a dinner with our families at her parents' home."

Sam slapped a hand on the table, excited by the prospect. "That'd be a perfect gift."

Echoing his brother's excitement, he expounded on the idea. "I want this to be a surprise. It can be Father, Gav, Isa, Lilja and Hayjen, her brothers, her parents, and the two of us. We can spend the evening together as one united family."

Sam leaned forward on steepled fingers. "Tehl, I must say, I think this is one of the best ideas you've had in a long time."

A moment of uncertainty plagued him. "You think she'll like it?"

"She'll love it."

He stood up and pushed back from the table. "I need to go see her parents and Lilja."

"Right now?"

Tehl felt like his smile couldn't get any wider. "Yes, right now. I want to get this underway as soon as possible, before the summer ends."

"Well, best of luck. Give Gwen and Colm my love."

"Give it to them yourself. You're coming with me."

Sam's face dropped. "I don't know. I haven't seen them since we discovered Sage at the forge, and I'm not sure they'd welcome my presence."

"Then it's about time to talk it out. Stop being a coward."

"Very mature."

"What can I say? Communication does wonders. Last night is proof of that."

Sam sidled up to him with a wolfish grin on his face. "What indeed did it accomplish, brother of mine?"

He punched his brother on the arm, ignoring the question, and headed toward the doors to the training yard. "None of your business. What happens with my wife is private."

"Your wife? Not Sage?"

He smiled. "Yes, my wife."

THREE

SAM

SAM TILTED HIS FACE TOWARD the fading sun and soaked in the last rays of warmth, reveling in the feeling of sand between his toes. Dropping his chin, he began scanning the beach as he walked, reminiscing. He'd spent innumerable hours here as a young boy, playing with his brother and his mum. A smile softened his features at the memory. His mum had cared nothing for propriety; everything had been about their family. He knew she must have ruined countless gowns by wading into tide pools just to gather sea treasures or to show her sons some of the little sea animals.

Catching sight of something small and shiny, he moved toward a pool surrounded by porous rocks. He reached into the water and plucked the shell from the sand, holding it up to the light. The iridescent abalone was a mural of swirling blues, greens, and purples. It was just the right size to be made into a necklace, one his sister-in-law was sure to love. His sister-in-law had a love for sea baubles that almost rivaled his mum's. Grinning to himself, he pocketed the treasure and moved toward the entrance of a cave which lay hidden among the rocks. Just before entering, he paused. The large, arching cavern was still a source of wonder for him; it was a study in contrasts. Some spots had been so worn by the ocean's waves that it felt as smooth as glass, whereas others were sharp enough to cut your hand.

Just past the hidden entrance was a staircase carved into the stone walls.

Sam stopped to pull on his socks and boots and grimaced. The sheer number of steps combined with the steep gradient made the hike a brutal one. Putting one foot in front of the other, he began the long trek up.

As he walked, his mind wandered to their recent reunion with the Blackwells—how his stomach had been in knots when Gwen had answered the door. How, much to his surprise, she'd looked him over, and before he understood what was happening, hugged him fiercely. She had then ushered them into her kitchen, where Colm stood. The four of them had awkwardly stood there until Gwen forced them to all sit down. As was his way, his brother had forgone any small talk and launched straight into his idea for their families to spend an evening together. That particular moment had amused him since, by the looks on Colm and Gwen's faces, they had yet to adjust to Tehl's straightforward manner of speaking.

But, what bothered him the most was when they'd discreetly catch his eye. The questions lurking in their eyes had him wanting to squirm in his chair. He knew he deserved it for lying to them for years. They were owed an explanation for his behavior.

After Tehl had talked everything through, he sat back and eyed all of them for a moment. Sam got a little nervous when he'd noticed a glint in his brother's eye. His brother had flashed them a smile before excusing himself to 'get some fresh air' while Sam had glared at Tehl's retreating back. The traitor. He hadn't even been subtle about it. Taking a deep breath, he'd then turned to face the only people that had given him one thing it was hard to find at the palace after the death of his mum. A sense of normalcy.

"I'm happy to see you, my lord. We appreciate your visit," Gwen had murmured.

The way she had spoken held a note of respect, but he detected wariness as well. He had felt his heart sink in his chest a little more, hating that he'd lied. His lies almost always hurt someone and he hated that, this time, it was someone he cherished. Carefully, he had reached out a hand and taken one of Gwen's. "There's no need for such formality. You still know me."

"Do we?" Colm asked.

That one question had felt like a punch to the gut. "Yes," he paused, then amended, "Well, part of me."

"And who is the other part?" Gwen asked.

"Brother, prince, commander. Take your pick."

"Those are merely descriptions of your roles, Samuel, not who you are. Your lot in life does not define you. Your actions do."

Gwen's words had struck him. The concept was both powerful and foreign to him. His roles did not define him?

"So, again, my lord, who are you?"

Sam had met her eyes, imploring her to believe him. "A boy looking for a family when his own fell apart, and please, call me Sam. That's who I am to you, just Sam."

At his response, Gwen's expression had shifted from that of wariness to understanding. "You'll always have a family here."

Sam had swallowed several times over the lump in his throat. He'd never expected them to be so understanding and forgiving so quickly. "Thank you."

"I've heard Sage's side. Now I want to hear yours," Colm interjected.

Sam had straightened and met the older man's serious gaze squarely. "First of all, we never meant for her to be harmed in the prison. That's not how we treat even the worst of our prisoners."

Colm nodded his head. "Sage said as much, but I would like to hear what you have to say on the matter."

He had then taken a deep breath and started the long story of how Sage had entered their lives.

Something crunched beneath his boot. Sam blinked, pulled from his thoughts. His brows lowered as he truly saw the stairway around him. Seashells, sea glass, and sand dollars were strewn everywhere, as if the sea had vomited trinkets all over the place. He squatted and fingered a particularly dark piece of sea glass. Odd. The only persons to travel these tunnels were members of his family. It was unlike Sage to leave her sea treasures, especially so strewn about like this. If she couldn't carry them all up, she would have piled them safely in a corner somewhere, so she could come back to get them.

He stood and ascended a few more steps to a platform with intersecting hallways. Had a servant found the passages and dropped their stuff when they got scared? He scanned the area for clues, freezing when he thought he heard something unusual. Trying to identify it, he turned to face a hallway to his left, holding his breath and listening, but he could identify nothing except the sound of wind.

Shaking his head, he returned to the staircase. He was being daft. Perhaps it was the creepy, old tunnels getting to him. He should know better. After all, it was here that, over the years, he'd frequently played tricks on both his cousin and brother.

"Sam." The word came from one of the tunnels. He spun toward it, his cloak flaring around him, as he pulled a dagger from his waist. That was *not* the wind. "What do you want from me?" he demanded.

Silence. He stared into the dark, trying to decipher any human shapes. It was dumb to go in blind, but he couldn't let a threat escape up into the palace. "If I have to come get you, you won't like it."

Something shuffled forward, and he kept his gaze focused ahead. Slowly, bloody fingers became visible, then an arm, and finally, a face. Sam blanched. The face was a familiar one. Rushing forward, he pulled Garreth into the dull light. As he did so, his friend cried out, his entire body seizing. "What the hell happened to you?"

Garreth tried to speak, but with his lips swollen and bloody, the best he could manage was a croak.

"Never mind, we'll get you some help." He tried to stand, but one of Garreth's bloody hands latched onto his forearm. Sam sank down to his haunches and ran his worried gaze over the member of his Elite. "What is it?"

"Sage," Garreth whispered.

Sam squinted at his friend, his heart picking up speed. "What about her?"

"Gone."

His blood turned to ice. "Gone?"

Garreth coughed, and it wracked his whole body. "Taken."

"By whom?" Garreth's eyes started to roll back in his head. Sam shook him hard, jarring his entire body. "No dying on me. Who took Sage?"

His friend's eyelids fluttered. "Rhys."

"No," he breathed out, horrified. How could that monster have gotten to her? He'd spent months hunting the man, but could find nothing, absolutely nothing. It was like he had vanished into thin air.

Sam grabbed Garreth's chin and looked him in his one good eye. "What's broken?"

"Ribs, but there are other wounds. I've lost blood," Garreth gasped.

He winced. That didn't sound good. "I'm sorry, old friend, but this will hurt." He grabbed the Elite's arm and slid it round his neck, maneuvering Garreth until he was draped over Sam's back and shoulders. Sam shifted until he had a good grasp on Garreth's arm and leg hanging over each shoulder. "I'm gonna try to lift you. Be ready," Sam warned, before he pushed up from the blood-smeared ground. Both men bellowed, one from pain, the other from strain. Garreth's body trembled hard against Sam's back.

"Just hold on. We'll get you some help. Maybe even from sweet Mira. Don't think I haven't seen the way you look at her."

"She wouldn't have me," Garreth tried to shake his head and wheezed. "I'm too bitter for the likes of her."

"She said that?"

"No, but I've known women like her."

Sam just nodded and slowly trudged up the stairs, his muscles protesting. He stumbled near the top when Garreth's body suddenly went completely slack. "You better have passed out and not died on me, you bastard!"

At long last, he came to the secret door and crashed through it, catching his boot on the rug. The motion had him crashing to his knees in the royal wing hallway. An Elite standing outside his brother's door only gaped a moment before moving into action and pulling Garreth from his shoulders.

"Get him medical attention," Sam gasped. The door to Tehl's suite opened, his brother's dark head poking out. Spotting him, he immediately rushed over.

"That better not be your blood," Tehl growled.

"No," Sam said as he stood, willing his legs to keep him up. He closed his eyes, gathering the strength to tell his brother the bad news. When he opened them, he met eyes which perfectly mirrored his own and forced himself to just say it. "She's gone."

His brother's face scrunched up in confusion. "Why? I thought we worked everything out last night. Why would Sage leave? She makes me so insane.

Why can she say what—?"

"No," Sam interrupted, "She was taken, Tehl."

Tehl's features hardened. "What do you mean *taken*? Where is she? Where is my wife?"

The menace in his voice gave even Sam a twinge of fear. He held his hands up. "I don't know, Tehl. I found Garreth in—"

Tehl moved around him and powered down the hallway, no doubt to find out for himself. Sam groaned and spun around, sprinting after his brother. He caught up as they ran down the stairs and toward the infirmary, startling the staff. He touched Tehl's shoulder, but he was shaken off as Tehl crashed through the infirmary door, where he skidded to a stop, causing Sam to plow right into him.

He watched over Tehl's shoulders as the healers buzzed around the bloody, unconscious Garreth. His gaze moved to his brother's profile, attempting to gauge his reaction. Only horror and rage were readily apparent.

"Will he live?" Tehl asked Mira.

The healer glanced up from her work, her face pinched. "He'll live, but only time will tell if his mind is still stable. He's taken a terrible blow to the head."

His brother nodded and pushed past him back into the hallway. Sam kept quiet, merely observing his brother as he paced the hall, tugging on his hair the way he did when he was thinking. Finally, Tehl paused to look at him. "What information do you have?"

Frustration bubbled up inside him. "Just what I told you. I took a walk along the beach to think..." Sam lowered his voice, "and entered through the cave to the stairs." He placed a hand over his mouth and focused on remembering each of the details. "There were sea trinkets scattered everywhere, and blood. That's when I found Garreth. If I hadn't taken that route, he would have died."

Tehl placed his head in his hands. "So, no sign of Sage?"

"I didn't examine the hallway, but most of the blood seemed to come from Garreth."

"Whoever came for them knew when to strike. She doesn't go for a walk every morning, she trains. Someone was watching her."

His stomach soured, and he had to force the words out. "I know who it was."

"Who?"

"Rhys."

Tehl stared at him blankly, then shouted a black oath. "How?" he demanded. "How did he get into my home? How did he take *my wife*? I promised Sage I would protect her! I looked her father in the eye and swore she would never have anything to fear." His fists clenched and his whole body shook. "Damn it!" He darted a look to the floor and back to Sam's face. "Why couldn't you find him? You swore to me you would do so!"

Although Sam knew in his head that Tehl was merely reacting to the situation and lashing out because he was worried, it still hurt to hear his brother hold him responsible. "I just couldn't," he replied, trying to keep calm. "I used every asset at my disposal … and nothing. It is like the man's a ghost. I'm sorry."

His brother shook his head. "No, I'm sorry. I'm not blaming you. I just—when I think of her in his hands, it…" Tehl shook his head, as if to rid himself of the thought. "It makes me want to retch and strangle him at the same time. But blame and pity won't find her. Send the Elite into the city. Make sure they leave no stone unturned," he commanded. "Also, call the council together, and retrieve Lilja. We'll need her. Sage has been missing for far too long already. We need to find her. Now."

FOUR

SAGE

EVERYTHING BLOODY HURT.

Munching on a stale cracker, Sage eyed the surrounding jungle, attempting to ignore the pain in her feet. Four days in the jungle of Scythia had taught her this: touch nothing.

That first day, Sage hadn't questioned why Rhys and the other Scythian warriors had left her and the other woman untied. She and Jasmine coordinated an escape, but they only made it thirty paces before stumbling upon a black feline creature that had been feeding. The creature had what looked to be human remains strewn across the ground. Golden eyes had clashed with green, and in that moment, she'd welcomed death. If the beast had attacked her, at least that way it would have been her choice and saved her from the horrors to come. But that was snatched out of her hands by an arrow. She had glared at the dying creature, feeling absurdly jealous.

A shudder moved through her body as she noted movement at the base of a nearby tree. She shuffled carefully forward, her eyes never leaving the enormous snake coiled around its trunk, the reptile's beady, black eyes observing her quietly. Sage hadn't been afraid of snakes until very recently, when one tried to make off with a horse two nights ago.

The rope which bound her wrists was suddenly yanked taut. It bit into her already tender skin and sent her cracker to the forest floor. She bent down, attempting to retrieve it, only to be pulled off her feet. She crashed into the foliage and cried out when the horse, to which the tether was attached, just kept moving forward, dragging her behind it.

"Sage, must you keep slowing us down? It's a wonder I even keep you around."

She scrambled to her feet and limped after the horse, ignoring the surrounding sniggers. Bastards. All of them. The warriors were as cruel as they were cold. She glared up at the monster on the other end of her leash.

Rhys.

Everything inside her rebelled at being near him. Her skin hadn't stopped crawling since he'd first kidnapped her, nor had she been able to sleep. Each time her eyes finally closed, before she could drift off, a sensation of being watched would creep along her skin, jerking her into awareness. And she knew it was his dark eyes that roved over her. This was the only reason she was actually grateful for the other warriors. Without them around, he would no doubt have already tortured and raped her.

"Come now. Surely, you want to end your punishment?"

Sage clenched her teeth together to keep her scathing retort in her throat. Perhaps if she'd had only herself to think of, she would have spouted off, heedless of the consequences, but her actions wouldn't hurt just her. Each time she misbehaved, it was Jasmine who suffered the punishment. She craned her neck to check on the woman and grimaced. She looked as bad as Sage felt. The young woman's brown hair hung in limp strands, and every inch of Jasmine's skin was covered in bruises, even her face, a result of the fight left in her friend.

"Admiring your handy work? It's your little rebellions which created her pain, you know."

Sage pulled her eyes from Jasmine to stare straight ahead, forcing herself to look calm. Men like Rhys thrived off their victims' reactions and enjoyed blaming others for his cruelty. But no matter how hard it was, she would not allow him to gain any sick pleasure from seeing her react. It was one of the most difficult things she'd ever done.

She tensed when his horse slowed, and he moved right next to her. Her hands trembled slightly and sweat pooled between her shoulder blades as she forced herself not to move away.

"Look at me when I'm speaking to you."

Bile burned the back of her throat. She had no desire to look upon the face which still featured in her nightmares. But for Jasmine, she had to. Slowly, she pulled her eyes from the forest and up to his face. The satisfaction she saw in Rhys' eyes was enough to make her want to stab him, repeatedly. Her eyes dipped briefly to the dagger sheathed at his chest before quickly moving back to his chin.

Rhys' lips formed a smirk. "I can read you. You think you're hiding your thoughts, but they're written on your face for all to see. Take it, Sage. I know you want to."

Her gaze didn't waver from his chin. She wouldn't play his games. The last time she'd grabbed a weapon and attacked Rhys, he'd batted it away like it was a child's toy. He moved faster than anyone she'd ever seen, and her entire world had shifted in that moment. The Scythians were something unusual. Something unnatural. Something that, unfortunately, she couldn't outrun.

From that point on, she'd watched the warriors under the guise of examining the jungle. They all looked eerily similar, and they prowled in the same dangerous way she'd seen the large black felines move. One time, a warrior seemed to disappear, only to emerge a few feet from her. The Scythians also heard and smelled things she couldn't. She shivered. What sort of creatures were they?

"Given up already? I thought you had more fight in you."

She did, but fighting just excited him. So, she did the opposite; she didn't react at all. Not until a calloused fingertip caressed the shell of her ear did she flinch and jerk away, losing all composure. The rope jerked again, pulling her closer to the monster. Panic seized her body and tugged back, but she wasn't strong enough. Soon, she found herself leaning against the horse with her arms held painfully above her head.

Rhys leaned down until the tip of his nose brushed hers, as if they were lovers. Fear paralyzed her as she stared into the mud-brown of his eyes.

"If you weren't property, I would've torn you apart already." His eyes ran over her face, an unholy glee plain on his face. "Maybe I already did."

It disgusted her that he was right, but she couldn't let him see that. Pushing through the fear, she whispered, "Filth like you won't ever break me." She regretted the words before the blow even came.

Pain radiated from her face, and she tasted blood in her mouth. She blinked several times. Stupid. That wasn't brave, it was just plain stupid. It was good, though, that he took it out on her and not Jasmine. Before she collected herself, Rhys grabbed her chin and forced her to meet his gaze. His eyes were lit with a demented kind of excitement, and beneath that, lust. The latter was more disturbing than the former. "You always thought yourself so much better than everyone else, so righteous, so honorable. But where's your honor gotten you?" He grabbed her hair and hauled her up higher. She sucked in a deep breath as the pain had tears pricking the corners of her eyes.

"When the warlord has had his fun—"

"Watch yourself, Rhys. She does not belong to you," a deep voice called from behind, moving closer.

Rhys' expression morphed into a sneer; he released her roughly and straightened in his saddle. Sage dropped to the ground in a heap, breathing hard through the pain, the damp dirt soaking through her pants.

"You don't command me, Blair. My uncle would hate to hear of your disobedience."

Uncle? Sage stared at the crushed plants beneath her knees, listening. Was Rhys' uncle someone important to the Scythians?

Cautiously, she picked herself up, standing on shaky legs. She peeked at the warrior from beneath her lashes. Blair. He was a huge man with broad shoulders and a wide, muscled chest. Sage had named him the leader in her mind, for all the warriors followed his lead. What he said went. He wasn't as cruel as others, but he wasn't a saint, either; both she and Jasmine had received a cuff or two from him. But overall, from what she'd observed with his men, he was fair. And Rhys hated him, which made Sage inclined to tolerate him slightly more than the others.

He spared her a glance through his long black braids before looking back to Rhys and bowing his head. "You're right," he rumbled. "Your uncle *does* hate to hear of disobedience."

Sage dropped her eyes to the forest floor. That was a threat if she'd ever heard one.

She snuck a glance at the two men as they stared each other down. Rhys with anger, the leader with tolerance. Rhys cracked first, shifting his eyes to the surrounding men, his feelings flitting across his face: embarrassment, no doubt that he'd been chastised, anger, from humiliation, and finally, hatred. She took a small step back, the wet earth and leaves squishing through her toes. She had been on the other side of his hatred. It wasn't a place anyone wanted to be, yet the leader didn't even blink.

"We camp here tonight," Rhys barked as he swung off his horse, clipping her in the ear with his boot in the process.

The blow disoriented her, and she stumbled into a warm, muscled chest. Horror dawned as two large hands curled around her biceps. Sage jerked from his grasp and put as much distance between herself and him as possible. She eyed the leader's blank face and rubbed her throbbing head. He was dangerous. His beauty couldn't hide what lurked beneath the surface. Beneath the skin of his perfectly symmetrical face was a killer. He was just humane enough for her to give him a little trust.

Rhys yanked on her bonds, knocking her off balance, and threw the rope at the leader. "It's your turn. I tire of her." He stormed off through the camp, yelling at a warrior about a tent.

Tension in her body eased as he moved farther away. She watched the exchange between Rhys and the other warriors, once again noting the differences between them. All of the men were extremely tall, but that was where the similarities ended. The warriors were flawless, like they were sculpted from stone. High cheekbones, cut jawlines, coal-black hair, smooth olive skin, and deep brown eyes. She'd always thought Rhys unremarkable, but here among the flawless warriors, he was downright ugly. A perverse sense of delight bubbled up in her. *He* was the damaged one here.

"Stop smiling or someone will notice your disrespect, woman."

Sage cleared all expression from her face and blankly stared at the bone and feathers woven into Blair's raven-colored braids.

"You'll have to do better than that if you want to survive us, woman. You need to have self-control."

Self-control? Anger pushed through the icy fear still gripping her. If she didn't have self-control, she and Jasmine would have been dead already.

A grunt left his lips when she didn't answer, and he stepped closer to her, cupping her chin. Her body froze when he tipped his head forward, his braids falling around their faces like black silken curtains.

"Look at me, Sage."

She met his deep brown eyes at the soft tone. It unnerved her that, up close, he didn't appear so harsh.

"Stop baiting him," he breathed. "You're owned by the warlord. You're his possession."

"Possession?"

"All women are possessions of the warlord." The leader shook his head. "If you keep baiting Rhys, he will lose control of his berserker rage. He'll kill you before he knows what he did. You're putting all of us in danger."

Sage mulled over the information. Rhys was on the edge of losing it. She could see it and so could his warriors. "What do you want for that little bit of information?" she whispered back, just as softly. No one gave information away for free. It was every bit a currency as gold.

His eyes ran over her face, softening a little, almost friendly. If possible, her body stiffened even more. He was not her ally, and she was not a woman to be passed around. "No. My body is not payment." She'd die before she let them use her like that.

"It's not what you think."

A snort escaped her. "Then what? Are you my friend now?" she asked, trying to keep the sarcasm out of her voice. The last thing she needed was another beating. She was sure there had to be something wrong with her mind from all the blows to the head she'd recently received.

"I'm not your friend, and never will be. I'm just trying to save my men."

That was truthful. He may have been the enemy, but he did care for his men.

He leaned back and gestured to the men setting up camp. "They die if you die."

That disturbed her. "Why?"

To her surprise, he answered her: "Because we would have failed to complete our task. The warlord does not have time for things that are not useful."

Disgusted, she grimaced. No one should use a person like that, but in the back of her mind, an idea took root. If she died, they died. It was simple.

"I know what you're thinking." He shook his head. "You're not selfish enough to do it."

"You don't know me."

"I've known people like you. Despite what you know of us, you wouldn't sacrifice all these men. It wouldn't be something you could shoulder. It would destroy you."

"Perhaps, but none of you are *men*." His eyes narrowed, but she hurt too much to care. Maybe if he hit her, she would black out for a bit and find some relief.

He raised a brow. "Then what are we?"

"Monsters," she said, not losing eye contact. They were. They weren't human.

"Always remember that," he said as he tossed the end of the rope at her feet. "Tend to the other woman."

She let out a sigh of relief as the frighteningly intense warrior turned from her and prowled toward his men. She winced as she gathered up her leash and picked her way to Jasmine, who sat on the ground glaring at all of the surrounding men. Sage slid down the tree next to the feisty brunette and watched as a camp emerged among the trees.

"How are you?"

Jasmine scoffed. "Well, that's obvious. I am damn peachy."

The reply pulled a smile from Sage, despite her split lip. "What's the worst of it, Jas?"

Jas grimaced and pulled in a painful breath. "The cracked ribs. I think they may have broken one yesterday."

"Did you bind it?"

"Sort of."

Sage moved onto her knees. "Let me see it."

Jasmine shifted to the side. "Lift my shirt, please. My shoulder's not working."

Sage gently pulled up the woman's shirt. "Beasts," she hissed. Jasmine's skin was mottled purple, blue, and green. She glanced at her friend's pained face. "I'm sorry for this, Jas. This is going to hurt."

"Do what you must."

She sat back and stared at her shirt. There wasn't enough fabric. "Swamp apples," she cursed. "I will have to ask them for supplies."

Jasmine gripped her thigh as she moved to stand up. "Don't. They'll just taunt you."

She met her friend's remarkable blue-gray eyes. "I've no other choice. You can't go on without healing."

She squeezed Jasmine's hand once and forced herself to stand on her cut feet. Once again, she squished through the mud and leaves toward the men forming up camp. It discomfited her greatly, but it was better than being in Rhys' arms. She scanned the camp and caught sight of the leader. "Blair!"

The camp seemed to freeze at her shout. The large man turned, his mouth turned down. "What did you call me?"

Hell. She'd broken some sort of protocol. "Your name."

The black slashes of his brows rose as the whole camp seemed to hold their breath. "This is not Aermia. You may not speak to me as you wish."

Gritting her teeth, she calmed herself at his mocking tone. She needed supplies for Jasmine. Time to play nice. Sage dipped into a deep curtsey, humiliated. But it was worth it for her friend.

"My apologies. What shall I call you?"

"My lord."

She pulled herself from her deep curtsey and met his eyes. "My lord… I need supplies for Jasmine. Her injuries need care."

He eyed her. "Do you not have fabric?"

Sage blew out a breath. Obviously not, since she was asking him. "No, I do not."

Rhys sauntered back into camp, his gaze dipping to her shirt. "Seems to me you do."

Her lips thinned. "There's not enough material," she replied as calmly as she could. "And its filthy."

Lazily, Rhys smiled at her. "You do, but you're being selfish. Would you really let your friend suffer for the sake of modesty? Take it off and help her."

The blood in her veins froze; her heart seized painfully in her chest. He wanted her to strip in front of everyone. She looked over her shoulder at Jas, who was glaring daggers at all the men. Sage turned back to the leader and Rhys, meeting his gaze. They held a taunt and a dare. He might think to humiliate her, but she'd gone through worse things. If he wanted to punish her, so be it. She'd not cower.

Despite her resolve, her hands trembled and her cheeks burned as she began unbuttoning her shirt. Sage held her head high and locked her eyes on the leader. It was easier looking at him than the demon at his side.

The dirty linen slowly parted to reveal the half-corset she wore underneath. Her sleeves slipped down her arms, exposing her damp skin to the humid air. She peeled the soiled fabric from her wrists, one at a time, hung it over her bicep, and held her hands out, her body completely on display for the silent group of men gawking at her. "Anything else, my lord?"

Even though she tried to ignore the heavy stares of the surrounding men, she couldn't help the goosebumps that broke out across her arms. That one piece of linen was protection. It hid her curves from them; it was at least a barrier they would have to get through to get to her.

Or, at least, it had been.

The leader broke their stare-off and scanned her body, his brows pulling together. "So many scars."

Sage kept silent and swallowed the retort on the tip of her tongue. Her sarcasm was a way to protect herself. One more defense that the Scythians had stripped her of.

The leader crossed his arms and tipped his head, his raven braids sliding over his shoulder. "What happened to you?"

Surprise filled her. He didn't know?

"I did," Rhys boasted.

Stillness settled over the camp. The hair on her arms rose, and she shifted on her feet, wanting to hide from whatever was coming.

"You marred her?" the leader asked, his tone sharp as a blade.

"It was punishment."

"That's disgraceful," a lanky warrior said, venom clear in his voice.

"Silence!" Rhys snarled, a promise of vengeance on his face. The warrior immediately shut his mouth and stared at the ground, no doubt pondering his future punishment.

Sage shivered and brushed at her filthy corset, needing to do something with her hands. "Woman…" Something about the leader's voice scared her.

He was not one to be trifled with.

She lifted her eyes and stared at his chest.

"You have your fabric. Go take care of the woman."

Her spine stiffened at the command, but, as it gave her the chance to escape being the center of attention, she simply nodded. Turning her back to the leader and Rhys, ignoring the gazes of the surrounding men, she started to leave. Her steps faltered as the leader issued a command:

"The prior rule stands. If you touch her or the other woman, your life is a forfeit."

Picking up speed, she reached Jas just as her legs gave out. As she fell to her knees beside her friend, every muscle in her body hurt. She studiously kept her eyes from Jasmine's face.

"I'm so sorry, Sage."

"Me, too," she whispered as she tore long strips from her shirt. Tears blurred her eyes, turning her task into a watercolor of greens, browns, and creams. She hated crying; it made her feel weak. A small hand halted her jerky movements, causing her to look up. She blinked repeatedly, trying to clear the tears from her eyes.

Jasmine's stormy gaze met hers. "Truly. If I could move right now, I'd go give them an earful."

Sage scanned her face, noting the sincerity, but right behind it lurked fear. "I won't let them do this to you. I'll protect you."

Her friend's lips curled. "We'll protect each other, sis."

The casual use of 'sis' about knocked the wind out of Sage. Jas had just claimed her as family. For the first time in four days, warmth bloomed in her chest. She held her hand out, and Jas clasped it. "We'll protect each other, sis." She'd found a friend and an ally in the most unexpected place.

Dropping Jasmine's hand, she plucked a strip of her shirt from the damp ground and said, "Hold still. This will hurt."

FIVE

TEHL

DESTROY HER.

It didn't seem possible for anything to destroy Sage. She conquered everything that came her way. But Lilja would never say something like that unless she meant it.

"We can't know for sure that's what he plans for her," William offered.

Hayjen glanced at William, his expression grave. "We've seen this time and time again. Lilja's not the only one to have had such an experience. You should be afraid for the consort."

The gravity of the situation settled heavily over the group.

"Then what do we do? We can't leave her there," Gav barked.

"But what can we do?" Zachael asked. "If we cross the border, it will mean war. We have no idea what is on the other side of that wall. We cannot take them on."

"What about a small rescue team?" Lelbiel offered.

"I have sent some of my best spies over that wall. None have come back. None. We would send the men to their grave."

"So…what?" Rafe snarled. "We leave Sage to die? To be used as a broodmare of their young? I'll not do it! She's been hurt enough to last many lifetimes. I won't let her live in that hell where she'll be raped until she dies."

Tehl felt the same way. Their gazes met and understanding passed between them. For the first time since they'd met, they agreed on something. "I'll not leave my wife there."

"So, what do you propose? You can't go traipsing through the jungle to retrieve her. Aermia needs you here."

He glared at his brother. "You don't think I know that?" His swept the men with his glare. "You're all aware of how Sage came to become my wife. I did my duty, and so did she. I will honor my duty to Aermia, but I also have a duty to Sage, not only because she's my consort, but my friend."

"What about a treaty?" Jeren suggested.

"What?" William gasped. "You want to make a treaty with those monsters? They deserve to rot where they are."

"No, listen…" Jeren leaned forward in his chair. "Scythia has been preparing for something for a long time. Presumably to invade Aermia. But what if we threw them off balance by offering a peace treaty? Scythia has been excluded from other kingdoms for hundreds of years, and we have what they need. Women."

"Clever," Lilja mused. "But the warlord would see right through that. He's cunning, ruthless, and arrogant. He would see the treaty for what it was, a final attempt to keep them from invading our kingdom. He'd strike before you had a chance to rally your men, but his weakness is arrogance."

"So, we use that," Sam proposed. "We don't want them anywhere near Aermia, but if the warlord is as arrogant as Lilja claims, he'll want to meet. If only to flaunt his army and Sage in front of us."

"That's a huge risk to take," Tehl said, then glanced to Lilja. "Would that work? Would he fall for it?"

The captain pursed her lips before speaking, "He would suspect a trap, but it would be an enticing lure that he'd likely engage. The warlord would meet with you, but no doubt have his army at hand."

"We'd need to have ours ready," Zachael remarked.

"How much time would that take?" Tehl asked.

"We could be ready in four months."

"Make it two," Tehl commanded. "Every moment we linger here is another moment the princess suffers in Scythia." He turned back to Lilja. "Would the warlord bring her to the negotiations?"

A bitter smile graced Lilja's face. "He wouldn't miss the chance to bait you. He'll bring her, but you won't be able to rescue her."

Silence filled the room.

"Why?"

"You don't understand the enemy you'll be engaging. The warlord is not like you or me. He has plans, and then plans to cover those plans, and plans to cover *those* plans. He would never leave Sage open. She'll be so heavily guarded, you won't be able to breathe in her direction without a blade to your throat."

"Then, why the ruse?" William asked. "The whole point is to retrieve Sage."

Understanding dawned. "Because we'll coax him out into the open. For the first time in years, he'll be out of his fortress. He'll be vulnerable. Vulnerability means mistakes."

"We will never be able to get to her if she's locked away. We may not be able to get to Sage *at* the negotiations, but afterward..." Lilja eyes held a predatory gleam, "she'll be coming home."

Tehl fought a shiver at the bloodthirsty expression on the captain's face. Once again, he was happy she was on their side. She'd make a formidable enemy.

"So, we plan an assault for after the negotiations?" Sam asked, a faraway look in his eyes.

"Yes, but we also plan for one before and during," Rafe interjected. "If he's as brilliant as Lilja says, we need to have a backup plan and expect the unexpected."

"Indeed..." a deep voice said from behind Tehl.

The men around the table stilled, and then, in a flurry of movement, all stood and bowed. A heavy hand landed on Tehl's shoulder and gave a squeeze. "Always expect those who act treacherously to be treacherous."

Tehl peered up at his father, shocked at his presence. It had been years since his father visited the war room. "My king," he said respectfully, and began to stand. The hand on his shoulder tightened and pushed him back down into the chair.

"This seat is yours, Tehl," his father murmured. "I won't take it from you. You have earned it."

He blinked as he sank back into his chair, sifting through his emotions: pride, dread, and relief—mostly relief. It was reassuring to have his father by his side. Gav stood from his chair and pushed it over to the king. Tehl's father smiled and patted Gavriel on the back before sitting. His white-blond eyebrows lowered over his blue eyes as he took in the group.

"So, what is being done to get my daughter back?"

There was a beat of silence before Sam, Zachael, and Jeren began explaining their plan. Tehl sat back in his chair and watched his father as the plan was laid out before him. The king rubbed at his chin after the explanation finished. He let out a long sigh. "Two months? That's the best we can do?"

Zachael's face screwed up. "I wish we could get our men together sooner, but we'll have to collect the Guard from all over Aermia, gather weapons and supplies." The combat master shook his head. "That will take time."

"I understand. Thank you, Zachael, for your service." The king scanned the group once more. "Thank you. You've all been fine advisors to my son. Those of you who are new, welcome."

It still awed Tehl how his father could command people and bolster them. He smiled at the king, then addressed the group: "Start planning our assault. I would like to go over it tomorrow afternoon. Thank you, and good day."

At his dismissal, his advisors began to remove themselves from the room.

"Captain Femi, would you please stay?" the king called over the thumping of booted feet against stone.

Lilja glanced at the king in surprise, and then to Tehl. He offered a slight shrug and eyed his father with curiosity. What did he want with the captain?

The king stood as Lilja glided to his side, Hayjen following behind. To Tehl's shock, his father bowed low and kissed the captain's hand. "My lady, I'm honored to host you in my household. It's been a long time since the Sirenidae have graced these hallways.

Lilja's eyes pinched. She yanked her hand from the king's grasp and Hayjen pulled several daggers out. Tehl shot out of his seat and in front of his father. "What do you think you're doing, Hayjen?"

"Protecting my own," the big man growled.

Sam and Gav circled, letting their presence be known.

Tehl's eyes snapped to his father and back to Lilja and Hayjen, tension filling the room. "What in the blazes is going on?"

His father responded without looking from Lilja. "Her kind are very rare and are to be treasured. The fact that she's Sage's guardian is beyond special."

"Sirenidae?" Tehl repeated. "You're not making any sense."

"Your mum used to tell you tales of them."

"Some say they were real at one time," Sam said from his left.

"They are real, Samuel. Your mother has Sirenidae family."

Tehl's eyes rounded. Just when he thought his father was sane. Tehl shook his head in disappointment, then scrutinized the man and woman in front of him. He didn't miss how, throughout it all, Hayjen and Lilja kept backing away from them. "Everyone needs to calm down. Obviously, there's been a misunderstanding."

"There's been no misunderstanding, son." His father moved past him and held a hand out with a dagger resting on his palm. Tehl shot a look at Sam. Where did he keep getting blades?

His brother shrugged and crowded in closer.

His jaw dropped in shock when his father knelt and held the dagger out to Lilja. "My family and I mean you no harm. I did not unveil your secret to all the council, just to my family. My wife made sure I knew the original stories, not the propaganda that Scythia began spreading years ago. You're welcome in my home, not for what you can offer, but for the service you've done my family already. We are in your debt."

Lilja's unusual magenta eyes locked in on the king kneeling before her. She was quiet a moment before she plucked the dagger from his hand and handed it to Hayjen. "Friends should never bow to one another," she said softly, helping his father up.

"Are we at peace?" his father asked, equally soft.

"We are." Warmth filled her eyes when the king kissed her hand once again.

"Is no one going to explain the Sirenidae comment? Or the family part?" Sam demanded.

Tehl crossed his arms and raised an eyebrow. "Who are you, Lilja?"

A laugh bubbled out of the woman. "I'm many things: captain, pirate, survivor, guardian, wife, aunt, friend, lover, ally, Aermian, and…Sirenidae."

"What does it mean to be Sirenidae?" Gav asked, silent up until now.

"It means I'm different from you, yet your eyes mark you as my family."

Gav's jaw dropped.

Tehl ignored his cousin and took a step closer. "Different how?"

She pulled in a breath, releasing it once Hayjen placed his large hands on her shoulders. "I grew up in the fifth kingdom."

"Fifth kingdom? The underwater kingdom of legends?" Sam asked.

"Indeed."

"How…?" Tehl blinked, trying to wrap his mind around the idea. "You're telling me the myths are real?" He eyed the woman. The stories painted Sirenidae as bloodthirsty, dangerous people.

Lilja observed his expression before answering. "Some myths are real, even the bloodier ones, but as a whole, Sirenidae are not killers."

"You look so…" Tehl drew out, looking for the right word.

"Aermian?" she supplied.

"Normal."

Sam sniggered. "That wasn't rude…"

Heat crept into Tehl's cheeks. "I meant that she looks like a woman."

Lilja's eyes filled with mirth. "Am I not a woman?"

"That's not…" He heaved out a sigh and ran a hand through his inky locks. "I always imagined the Sirenidae as something akin to fish."

There was a beat of silence before Lilja threw her head back and let loose a husky chuckle. "You have a way with words, my lord."

He rubbed the back on his neck, embarrassed. "That's what my family is always telling me." He blinked, a thought occurring to him. "Does Sage know?"

"Yes," Hayjen answered.

Tehl scoffed. "Of course she bloody well knew. Nothing escapes that woman."

"She's a smart one," Sam muttered, plopping into a chair. "This is my question: how were they caught unaware?" Sam glanced at them. "Sorry for changing the subject, but I can't figure it out. Garreth is one of the best Elite I know, and Sage, well, her sneaking and self-defense skills are excellent. How did Rhys surprise them?" Frustration tinged his brother's voice.

Lilja propped a hip against the table. "I believe I can shed light on this as well. The Scythians are enemies like you've never faced before."

"You've said that," his father said. "What makes them so different? We vanquished them before."

"That was before they were flawless."

"They've always strived for perfection," Gav reasoned.

"True, so are you saying now they've accomplished it?" Sam asked skeptically.

"Not in the truest sense, but in the ways that mattered most to them. Unparalleled beauty and an exceptional thinking ability are two."

"Beauty is hardly dangerous," Tehl said.

"It is when used the right way," Sam said.

"Your brother's right, but there are more deadly qualities. Enhanced hearing, increased speed, and inhuman strength."

"That seems impossible," said Gav.

Tehl glanced at his cousin. "So did the annihilation of the Nagalians, and the existence of the Sirenidae."

Sam quirked a brow. "Are you so quick to believe in this madness? You who never believes in anything but logic?"

Tehl tipped his chin at Lilja. "She's all the proof I need. Her story does not conflict with any of my knowledge. It makes sense the Scythians would be enhanced. They've had hundreds of years to do God-knows-what to their people."

"How did they accomplish such a thing?" his father asked.

"Science."

Tehl wrinkled his nose at Hayjen. "That's dangerous."

Lilja shrugged. "It's only dangerous in how it's used. They've discovered and manipulated different essences from their jungles, the ocean, and from the red caves of Nagali. If used the right way, the plants could heal many in the kingdoms."

"I don't want any of that here," Tehl barked.

"That's your prerogative as crown prince. But I would like to leave you with this thought: would you let your people suffer because of your own prejudice?"

He blinked. When she put it like that, it made him feel like the villain. "We've done just fine until now."

Lilja cast a glance at his father and he followed her gaze. The king stared at the floor with his shoulders slumped.

"Have you?" Her question was soft.

Anger burned in his chest at her cruel question. "That was a low blow."

"Everyone has lost someone, Tehl, especially those of us who have lived long lives."

He met her gaze and saw understanding and loss there.

"Why let others suffer when you have the power to bring about change for the good? Change will happen, with or without you. Don't you want to shape it into something great for your people?"

His gaze dropped to the floor as he mulled over what she said. Change for Aermia and for him had happened even if he didn't want it to—his mum's death, his father's mental breakdown, picking up the pieces of the kingdom, and marrying Sage. Many unexpected things had befallen his family and himself, but it was because of their choices that things were still going well. He lifted his head and nodded.

"I will think on it."

"That's all I ask." She clapped her hands together and pushed off the table. "How do you think your advisors will react to the news of the Scythians' advancements?"

"Disbelief, anger, bloody panic, and a steeling of themselves for what is to come," Sam drawled.

"Very astute for someone so young," Lilja said. "No wonder Sage likes you. You're very similar."

"You hear that, Tehl? You married the female version of your brother," Sam joked.

Tehl began to retort when Lilja cut him off. "You think you're cloaked in shadows, Samuel Ramses. But just as Sage sees who you are, so do I. Just remember that playing so many roles can blur who we are, even to ourselves. If you wear too many masks, you may forget what you *really* look like."

"Spoken like someone who knows something of it," Sam replied, his tone serious.

Lilja strode toward Sam and clasped his hand in both of hers. "I've lived a long time in the dark, hiding who I am to protect the ones I love. I know something of it. You and I are more alike than you realize. Call on me for anything."

Sam blinked and shifted a hair closer to Lilja. Tehl rolled his eyes, already knowing what was coming. His brother smiled seductively down at the woman.

"Call on you for anything?" he purred.

"Hey now," Hayjen objected.

Lilja leaned closer to Sam. In a move meant to seduce, she ran her hand up his arm and to his cheek. "You're out of your league," she whispered, and then patted him on the cheek twice, hard enough to sting. She spun on her heel, wearing a grin that spoke of vindication, and sauntered back to her husband.

Tehl sniggered at how his brother cupped his cheek and stared after Lilja with both admiration and fear.

"Now that that's over, how do you propose we move ahead with our plans, my lady?" his father asked.

The smile on Lilja's face was positively devious. "We run circles around the Scythians."

"How will we do that?" Gav jumped in.

"With the promise of women, of course."

SIX

SAGE

SWEAT DRIPPED BETWEEN HER BREASTS as she struggled to place one foot in front of the other. Each breath was wet, like she was breathing water—the air seemed saturated, heavy.

She glanced to Jasmine. Her friend's face pinched with every step. A curse burst out of the brunette's mouth as she stumbled, her knees buckling. Sage reached out and caught her roughly, stumbling and almost going down herself. She strained and locked her knees, barely keeping them both upright.

"You're slowing us down. Pick up your speed or I'll drag you."

Sage clenched her teeth and turned to glare at Rhys.

"He's not worth it," Jas wheezed in her ear. "Just help me, Sage."

She swallowed back her rage and slid her bare arm around Jasmine's back. "Can you still walk?"

"Yeah. It's just my damn ribs. They hurt in the back, too."

"You need more exercise," she said, trying to lighten the mood.

Blue-gray eyes narrowed on her. "You're hobbling as much as I am."

"It's my bloody feet. There's not much skin left." And it was the truth. The soles of her feet were always soft from the rain, so they shredded and cut easily. Each evening, she attempted to clean the wounds and bandage them, but they were always caked with black soil, so it was mostly futile.

She shivered as a drop of water splashed between her shoulder blades and ventured into her half-corset.

"He's watching you again."

Her jaw clenched. She didn't even need to look to know who Jas was referring to. When she'd sat with Jasmine after his forced disrobing, Rhys' eyes had locked on her like she was his prey. At that moment, she'd frozen as he glided across the camp toward her. Jasmine had shaken her out of her stupor, and she had stood to face the monster. His eyes had slowly traced the curves of her body. Sage had forced herself not to back away when he had leaned close to whisper, "Soon…"

It was only one word, but it was enough to keep her on edge for the next two days. She blinked, and the memory disappeared as Jasmine's face swam into view. "I know."

"You need to be careful."

"I know, Jas," she whispered harshly.

"Even if you have to beg protection from one of the other men, like the leader, do it."

She scanned the circle of men surrounding them, pausing on the large roguish-looking warrior. He lifted his head and glanced her way as if he could hear their conversation. For all she knew, he could. Not looking away from him, Sage whispered, "They're not our friends. They're our enemies."

"Yes, but some men are worse than others."

"Indeed."

Both women fell silent, as it took all their focus to keep painfully trudging on. Sage kept her eyes on the ground to avoid anything sharp that could damage her already severely abused feet even more. She suppressed a shriek when a spider the size of her fist scuttled across the forest floor. Jasmine wasn't so discreet.

"Swamp apples!" she hissed in disgust. "That's nasty."

Sage tuned her friend's grumbling out while scanning the surrounding jungle. Her brows slammed together. Something wasn't quite right. The trees were duller, and the ground had begun to slant downward. The soil between her toes even felt different, scratchier. She dropped her chin, her wet hair flopping limply into her face. With care, she examined the surrounding men. The warriors still walked with a purpose, but something in their stance had changed. She scrutinized it for a moment before deciphering what it was.

Excitement. There was a spring to their step now. Her stomach dropped. What were they excited for?

Her gaze swept the jungle again, searching for the source of their excitement. She blinked. Somehow, she'd missed that somewhere along the line, trees had been thinning. A large, dark hill rose just a stone's throw away. Whatever excited them rested on the other side of that hill.

"What is it?" Jasmine murmured.

"What?" she asked absently, still trying to figure out where the men were taking them.

"Your arm tensed, and you squeezed my ribs."

Immediately she loosened her grip and glanced at her friend, holding her panic at bay. "Whatever is over that knoll is the end for us."

Jas squinted at the dark hill, little lines appearing on her forehead, before she turned back to Sage. "Once we enter where they are taking us, there won't be any escape."

"No," she agreed.

"Then you need to escape now," Jasmine said, only loud enough for her ears.

She jerked. "I'm not leaving you."

The brunette's jaw set. "I can't run. I can barely walk. You can make it, Sage. You have to try. For the both of us."

Everything inside her ached to just run, to escape. Her hand opened and closed against Jasmine's back. "I can't leave you." Guilt threatened to swamp her at the angry expression on her friend's bruised face. "You wouldn't be here if it wasn't for me."

"That's not true," Jas whispered harshly. "I would have tried to help anyone. It just happened to be you. I should have checked the forest better. I wasn't cautious enough. That's on me. Now run. I'll distract them."

Her gaze darted around as she debated the outcome. Could she make it? The answer slapped her in the face as her eyes connected with Rhys. "No," she said, tearing her eyes away from him and back to Jas. "Even if I could escape the warriors, I would still have to get through a week of jungle without food, water, and a direction in which to run. Not to mention the deadly creatures the warriors had to battle back there. The black felines are still hunting us. I wouldn't make it. I'd be dead by morning."

Jasmine visibly wilted. "You're right, I wasn't thinking."

"You weren't thinking."

They both stiffened at the deep, accented voice behind them. Sage craned her neck and was met by feathers and coal black hair. The leader.

"You're wise not to run. You wouldn't survive in our jungle. Now put all childish dreams of escape and freedom from your mind."

"Freedom is childish?" she questioned. "I thought your people would appreciate—" Pain slammed into her face, causing her to lose her balance and topple Jasmine. She crashed to the ground, the wind knocked from her. Rolling to her hands and knees, she swayed, trying to see past all the stars swirling across her vision. A metallic tang invaded her mouth. Someone had made her bleed. Again. If it was the last thing she'd do, she'd—

Sage jolted out of her thoughts at Jasmine's cry. Her gaze cut to Jas, lying flat on her back and clutching her ribs while a boot rested on them. Sage looked up and glared at Rhys. Her vision turned red and all she could see was him and his smug face.

Enough was enough. It was time for him to die.

"Rhys! You've had your fun," the leader admonished.

Sage's hand ran along the forest floor, seeking a weapon. Anything to protect herself and Jasmine. A grim smile tugged at her lips as her fingers closed around a sharp rock. That would do. Slowly, she shuffled closer.

"They need to be punished for plotting an escape," Rhys said.

"They were speaking nonsense."

"I think you've grown soft in your old age. The men see it. You've been soft on these girls. Do you think they'll be handed to you for your obedience?"

She froze at the beat of silence, taking the utmost care not to attract attention.

"The warlord will grant you nothing," said Rhys. "You are nothing."

"Those are large words from a flawed."

The forest seemed to still at the leader's words. Sage watched Rhys through the curtain of her hair, his face turning almost purple. His fists clenched, and his arms began to shake. She closed her eyes, pulled in a deep steadying breath, and prepared herself. A large hand rested on the top of her head, causing her eyes to fly open. Boots she'd become familiar with stood right in front of her. She hadn't even heard Rhys move.

Sage obeyed the tug on her hair as she was forced to meet his cruel, soulless gaze. "This is how you should always be. On your knees."

That was it. She couldn't move because of the hand in her hair, but she still had use of her hands. Clutching her rock, she licked her bloody lips, knowing he'd follow the motion, and slammed the pointy rock into the side of his knee. His eyes widened, and his mouth parted in a bellow right before she received a kick to the gut. She flew backward, her breath rushing out of her. Her shoulders slammed into the ground, and her feet tumbled over her head.

She coughed, trying to get air into her screaming lungs as she brushed her hair from her face. Pain was everywhere. Sage pushed up from the ground and grimaced as a large hand snaked around her waist and pulled her from the forest floor. Rhys struggled with three warriors, trying to get to her. She bared her bloody teeth at him in a smug smile.

He strained harder against the arms restraining him, the veins in his neck bulging. "You're dead! I'll kill you! You're dead," he screamed.

A crazed laugh bubbled up from her belly. "I died in that cell. There's nothing left to kill."

"You shouldn't have done that," the leader muttered next to her ear. "Look at what you've wrought."

Sage's smile faded as she truly *looked* at Rhys. His whole body shuddered, and it was almost as if he had grown in size. Something had shifted in his eyes. She slammed into the hard chest behind her when his bloodshot, feral eyes clashed into her own. The rage-filled man she'd come to know was nothing like the wild beast in front of her now.

His teeth gnashed, spittle flying through the air as he bellowed, "Mark my words, you'll pay."

One of the warriors pushed a flask against his mouth and another pinched his nose. He fought harder, spewing the brew everywhere. Sage watched in horror as liquid and drool dripped down his chin, and he mouthed, "You're mine."

She trembled in the leader's arms for a few minutes as the wild glint in Rhys' eyes died and his usual soulless gaze returned. He growled at the men and jerked his arms from their grasp. Rhys shook himself and sneered in her direction, before limping to his horse and swinging up into the saddle like nothing happened.

"Let's go," he commanded, like he wasn't losing blood each second.

She turned her face and leaned her cheek against the warm chest behind her, shuddering. What *was* he?

"I warned you not to push him."

"Not well enough," she pushed out between chattering teeth. They always did that when she became scared or excited. "What was that?"

"Berserker rage. If those men had not held him back, he would've torn you apart, woman. I keep thinking you've learned your lesson, and yet you keep rebelling. You're lucky today. If you try that with the warlord, he'll kill you. No one will stop him. Your death will be senseless. Be smart. Try to survive."

Sage pulled herself from the leader, took shaky steps away from him, and turned to look at him with a raised brow. "Why?" Why was he looking after her?

He shrugged his wide shoulders. "Women are rare. You're worth more alive."

"Indeed," she muttered, and turned her back to the leader. Jasmine had managed to stand, but still clutched her ribs, her face a map of pain.

"Are more broken?" Sage asked with worry.

"I'm sure. I got kicked by my brother's horse when I was younger. I know what it feels like."

"Beasts," she spat.

"After that display, I don't doubt it." Jasmine's voice wobbled on the end, betraying her fear.

Sage slipped her hand into her friend's, giving strength as much as receiving it. It was a comfort to have someone in which to share the poor circumstances. "We're in this together."

"Together."

She thought they were going over the hill.

She was wrong.

She stopped, confused as to why they weren't moving up the hill. Her confusion doubled when the warriors stopped next to an enormous rock and pushed. Her eyes rounded as they revealed a black hole in the side of the hill, a gaping maw which could devour them.

"Where does that lead?" she asked. No one answered. Wherever it was, it was not somewhere she wanted to be.

One by one, they entered the black hole and disappeared. A calloused hand wrapped around her bicep. She winced at the tight hold and leaned away from its owner.

"Don't cause trouble or you'll regret it," Rhys threatened.

Her skin prickled at his proximity, and her heart galloped. He was unhinged; it was boiling right under the surface. Sage dipped her head in a respectful way, she hoped, and wished he would release her throbbing arm.

"Good."

He let go of her abruptly, almost upsetting her balance, but she'd prepared for it. Rhys had a way of being predictable when it came to his abuse. She lifted her eyes to catch the leader's; the small dip of his chin sparked anger inside her. She neither needed nor wanted his approval. She just wanted to stay alive.

The warriors took up formation, surrounding and ushering them toward the opening. Jasmine's hand clenched in Sage's.

"I don't like this. It's a cave!"

"Me neither."

They fell silent as the opening loomed before them. Sage finally let go of any hope she'd harbored for a rescue as they entered the dark.

No one would find them here.

SEVEN

SAGE

THE GRATING SOUND OF STONE against stone etched into her mind.

There was no escaping the inky darkness.

She blinked repeatedly, trying to help her eyes adjust. Someone pushed her from behind and her right shoulder slammed against something cool, wet, and rough. She pressed her hand to the cave wall and ran her fingers over its surface. Porous stone, similar to that which was beneath the Aermian castle. Were they close to the sea here?

Another shove forced her to abandon her exploration and shuffle forward in the pitch black, every step a gamble.

"It's so dark in here, I literally cannot see my hand in front of my face." Jasmine's voice grumped from her left.

Sage's lips twitched. Jas seemed to have an uncanny ability to lighten the mood without trying.

As they trekked through the dark, the air of what she assumed was a passage slowly heated from the press of so many bodies and sweat. She paused for a moment to help Jasmine, only to have a very large, hot, sweaty body press against her back. She skittered away, dragging the brunette with her. Deep masculine laughter rumbled around them and her cheeks heated further, both in embarrassment and anger.

Jas squeaked in outrage. "Who was that?" the brunette demanded.

"What?"

"Someone touched me."

More laughter.

The women huddled closer together as the dark seemed to escalate their fear. The dark was both oppressing and unnerving. It made them too vulnerable.

"Enough."

One word, and the laughter stopped. The press of bodies around them seemed to lessen. Her breath whistled out from between her clenched teeth; she was thankful the leader had command of his men.

After walking for a while, she lost all sense of direction as well as time. The only thing she could discern was that they seemed to be descending, her legs and thighs burning from the slope. Her brows furrowed when she detected faint traces of light, which brightened their surroundings bit by bit. She blinked a few more times as the outlines of the men surrounding her became visible. Something cracked underneath her foot. She paused and squinted at the floor.

Bones.

Jasmine followed her gaze and yelped, pulling them to the side. "Is that…a skeleton?" she asked, her voice shaking.

"It's what happens to those who run away." Rhys' voice slithered over them.

Sage grimly stared at the skeleton. That had been *someone*. It had once been a living, breathing human being, maybe even with a family. Before she could stop herself, she asked, "Why?"

"He was hunted down, hobbled, and then let free," the leader replied.

She finally tore her gaze from the bones. "Free?"

"Free to run until the leren caught him."

"Leren?" Jas asked.

"The man-eater that almost killed you that first day in the forest."

Chills ran up Sage's arms when she thought of the giant black jungle cats that had tracked them through their entire journey. "You let them run free here?"

"No," Rhys whispered in her ear. "We ration their food until another source presents itself."

"You starve them until you want them to hunt someone?" she asked, her tone flat. Just when she thought they couldn't get more barbaric, they got worse.

"They love to hunt prey that runs from them," the leader supplied. "Let's move on."

Sick to her stomach, Sage carefully stepped over the bones with Jas plastered to her side. She shivered at the thought of being hunted in the maze of dark tunnels. Disgust gave way to hysteria, and a giggle slipped out. How fitting. The stone was as black as the Scythians' souls.

Jasmine looked at her askance.

"Nothing," she muttered, and stamped down the hysterical thoughts bubbling up inside her. If she let go now, she'd probably come unhinged.

The group snaked around a corner, and her steps faltered as light poured through a wide doorway. When she saw what lay beyond it, she stopped short. It was a phenomenon unlike anything she'd ever seen. The doorway led to a massive open cavern that hosted what looked to be an entire city, carved from the black stone. Sage squinted, barely able to make out the filthy people scuttling about the curved lanes, carrying all sorts of tools. Lanterns cast a sickly, yellow glow over them and she suppressed a gasp. Were those chain slaves?

"Move on."

The leader jostled her forward, and just like that, she was swept away from the strange underground city. A thousand questions were at the tip of her tongue, but she kept her mouth shut. It wasn't like they would answer her anyway.

The stone hallway twisted left then right, and at the far end were two enormous wooden doors into which symbols had been charred. Four giant men guarded the door, their bare, muscled skin painted with those same symbols. She shivered as their dark eyes zeroed in on her and Jasmine. It wasn't sexual, but they looked at the girls with unveiled curiosity, as if they were some sort of exhibit.

In unison, the guards bowed and pulled open the doors. Her lids slammed shut at the sudden burst of light. One eye at a time, she cracked them and forced herself to move through the doors.

She squinted, the bright light blinding her. Everything was white. The walls, ceiling, and floor were made from white stone polished so brightly she could practically see her reflection. The bare walls sloped into high arched ceilings and the entire place felt cold, empty.

Sage looked behind her just as the doors thudded closed. She blinked. From this side, the door was invisible. The only thing that gave it away was a fine line where the stone didn't quite touch, allowing the doors to glide smoothly.

Her attention was pulled to the floor when she noticed garish scarlet footprints that marred the pristine beauty of the floor behind her. Something about it raised the hair of the back of her neck. She tracked the bloody footprints to her own feet.

"Rhys," a woman greeted.

Her head snapped up. She hadn't heard the woman arrive. She couldn't afford slips like this. Time to focus.

The woman's body was cloaked in furs, with daggers strapped to her thighs. When combined with her lithe, toned body, she was even more a warrior than Sage ever was. She scanned the strong features she'd learned were typical of the Scythians: sharp cheekbones, straight nose, and coal black hair. She paused when she met a shrewd, caramel gaze.

"This is the one?" the woman asked as she moved through the warriors and to Sage, stopping a pace away. Her eyes scanned Sage from head to toe, then back up. She cocked a hip and pursed her lips in a way that betokened disapproval.

Sage tipped her chin up. She'd be damned if she let some random woman intimidate her. Her body was in bad shape, but no one would make her feel ashamed for it; it wasn't even her fault. She eyed the woman as she circled her, and turned just enough to keep her back from the woman.

The Scythian female paused and raised a brow. "You're smart not to turn your back to me. Although…" She scanned her body again. "It seems you were not always smart."

Jasmine shifted by her side, an aggravated gesture. Sage grabbed her friend's wrist and squeezed. They couldn't afford rebellion.

The woman noticed the gesture and grinned. "It seems she has manners."

Sage stiffened.

"She needed training," Rhys replied, his face a mask of smugness.

"Indeed," she drawled in her slight accent.

"Where is he, Maeve?"

"The throne room, where else?"

"Of course."

The woman smiled with fondness at Rhys. Sage blinked, surprised. No one liked him.

"If you release the women into my care, I'll clean them up before you present them to the warlord."

"No, he needs to see them now."

The woman's eyes widened slightly before she schooled her reaction. "Do you think that wise?"

"You think to counsel me?"

Sage shifted closer to Jas when Rhys moved around her to tower over the woman.

"No, my lord," she replied. "But you know how he is."

"I have to agree with Maeve, Rhys," the leader added, stepping into the circle they'd formed in the hall.

Rhys cackled in his deranged way. "You live to disagree with me, Blair." He stepped back and wrapped a hand around her bicep. "*I* brought her here. *I* delivered her. *I* won't have this honor taken from me."

She kept her face blank even though he was pinching her arm.

"You shouldn't hold the Aermian so tightly. Even I can see you're hurting the girl," Maeve admonished.

His cold eyes locked onto her face, and she had to force herself not to run in the only way she could: by retreating into her own head. As appealing as it seemed, however, it was not something she could afford.

"There's beauty in flaws," he whispered near her cheek.

Her stomach heaved. Lord, how she despised him.

His face soured as if he read the thoughts she fought to hide. "We go now," he snarled. "Move!" He released her arm and spun around to stalk away, the warriors seamlessly parting for him.

The men straightened, forming a ring with Blair, the Scythian woman, Jas, and her at the center. Sage stepped forward, only to be tugged back. She met Jasmine's blue-gray eyes.

"I can't move," Jas whispered.

"What?"

"My legs, they've seized."

Sage released her friend's hand and tucked the brunette into her side. "Put your arm around my neck."

Jasmine grunted and did so. "God, that hurts," she hissed.

"It's going to hurt more before it gets better. Brace yourself."

A small cry fell from Jas' lips as Sage held her tightly and began moving.

"You have one extra," a feminine, accented voice spoke from her right.

"She…inserted herself where she didn't belong, and we had no choice but to bring her. We always need more stock."

Stock? What did that mean? She tilted her head down, focusing on carrying Jas and listening at the same time, her ear cocked toward the woman.

"The last few did well."

There was an undercurrent of jealousy in the woman's tone. Interesting. Why would she be jealous of stock? Her foot slipped, and she jerked, jarring her friend.

"Hell, Sage," her friend cursed through clenched teeth.

"Sorry," she mumbled, adjusting her grip. She glanced at the floor and grimaced at the trail they were leaving. If by some miracle they could escape, at least they'd have their own trail of dirty, bloody footprints to return by.

Looking ahead, she caught sight of a set of twenty-foot-tall, engraved, white doors adorned with curling black handles carved from wood. The warriors stationed outside them bowed to Rhys and then immediately looked at her. Was she that different? That odd? To her, *they* were the odd ones, all looking the same.

She was pulled from her questions when Rhys appeared before her. "You will not speak unless spoken to. You will stare at the floor unless addressed, and you will not embarrass me." He then spun on his heel and disappeared past the ring of warriors.

"He's right," the leader whispered. "Be careful, both of you."

The immense door pushed inward.

Sage took a deep breath and looked to Jasmine. "Are you ready?"

"As ready as I'll ever be when walking to my death," she wheezed.

Sage briefly quirked a smile at her before shuffling along with their procession as it moved through the doors and into the room. Upon entering, her eyes widened and she barely managed to keep her jaw from dropping.

The room was large and domed, its walls at least four stories high, with glass ceiling tiles sprinkled here and there. The white stone floor was broken up by large trees that stood like giants surveying their kingdom. They reached up through the dome and disappeared into a sea of greenery above them.

She was jerked from her inspection when something touched her cheek. Her lips thinned. It was a reaching fern. Nothing else. Just a plant.

She plowed ahead, trying to keep her wits about her, but she still felt like something was off.

"There are no birds," Jas whispered.

The hairs rose on Sage's arms. That's what it was. There wasn't a sound in the throne room except for their own shuffling footsteps. The feeling of being watched had the back of her neck prickling. She scanned the surrounding trees, but found nothing, at least, nothing she could see. That's what worried her the most. It didn't dissipate as they moved on, but intensified.

The trees opened up and formed a half circle, which butted up against the biggest stone wall she'd ever seen. In the center, a strip of the black porous rock ran from ceiling to floor. She peeked between two warriors to get a better look and caught a glimpse of stairs which led to what she suspected was the dais.

"Nephew, it's been some time since I've seen you in the flesh."

The deep voice rolled over Sage like thunder in a storm, all power. She'd always thought Tehl's voice held power, but his was nothing compared to this.

She stilled when it was Rhys who answered the warlord. "My lord, I'm humbled to be in your presence."

Her insides quivered in fear. This was going to be worse than she thought. The warlord was Rhys' *uncle?* "Oh, God," she breathed.

"He can't help you here," the leader whispered.

She whipped her head around to stare into the solemn eyes of the leader.

"Blair…" the deep voice commanded.

If Sage hadn't been staring so hard, she would have missed it. Just for a moment, hate flashed through Blair's eyes at the sound of the warlord's voice, but it was gone as quick as it came. He broke their stare-off, then pushed through the ring of warriors.

"My lord," he responded, his tone respectful.

"You've done your job well. Thank you for bringing my nephew home safely."

"It was nothing."

"Untrue." A pause. "Did you accomplish your task, nephew?"

"I did," Rhys replied.

"Excellent. And what of your guests? I wasn't expecting you to bring anyone home."

Jasmine sucked in a breath and began to tremble.

Rhys' voice drifted closer. "I've brought you a gift."

"Intriguing."

Sage's heart raced when her enemy pushed through the circle of warriors. He captured her gaze and held his hand out. She stared at it as if it were a venomous snake.

"Come now, Sage, don't be foolish. And mind your manners," Rhys spoke through gritted teeth.

Inwardly, she steeled herself. She didn't have any other choice. Things would go very badly for them if she offended the warlord. Sage turned to the woman, who was currently watching the spectacle, and gestured to Jasmine. "She can't stand on her own. Will you help me?"

Maeve eyed her with annoyance but moved to Jasmine's other side.

Sage squeezed her friend's hand once more, and then placed that same hand in Rhys', her jaw clenching when his thumb rubbed against her wrist. The warriors parted, and she dropped her eyes to her dirty feet as her own personal demon led her like a fine lady toward the dais. Her gaze snagged on his limping gait. Despite the horrible circumstances, she had to hide a grin at his shuffling pace. The bastard deserved that and then some.

Blair's instructions ran through her head. *Don't speak unless spoken to. Keep your head down. Don't make eye contact.* But she wouldn't be led to the warlord like a lamb, cowering and staring at her feet like she was in submission to them. Using her last vestiges of strength, she raised her head and stared ahead.

Gasps surrounded her, and Rhys' hand tightened on hers, but all she saw were warm, black eyes. It shocked her. She'd expected soulless, cruel eyes. The smile lines around the man's eyes spoke of something different. His inky hair hung around his angular face, just brushing his bare, muscular shoulders. He was beautiful. Everything about him called to her, from the straight, proud line of his nose to the stubborn chin and almond-shaped eyes. But it was more than his features; it was how he wore them. Sage kept her face schooled and lifted her chin. Never in her wildest imagination did she expect him to be so stunning, or so young. Her eyes told her he was beautiful when her mind told her he featured in the nightmares of many. It wasn't right that evil could don such an alluring mask.

Her gaze strayed to the lounging felines on either side of him, and she barely contained a gasp. Leren: the man-eaters. Their golden eyes latched onto her as they flicked their tails in her direction. With her head still held high she surveyed the Scythian court; they were every bit as beautiful and cold as she expected. They eyed her with shock and disgust, but also a flicker of fear. Why did they fear her?

"What have you brought me?"

Her eyes snapped back to the warlord, who had sat up from his lazy sprawl, now leaning forward, one elbow resting on his knee.

Hell, he was flawless.

She'd spent time surrounded by handsome men—Tehl, Sam, Gavriel, and Rafe—but this man was regal in a way that left her in awe, rather like a fine painting or well-carved statue.

Rhys tugged her close, pulling her from her gawking, but when he tried to brush a tangled strand out of her face, something inside her snapped. She slapped his hand away and jerked out of his grasp. In an instant, both man-eaters sprang from the dais and to the floor, growling in a way that had fear clawing at her belly. Her instincts told her to run, but she knew that would only sign her death warrant. She reached for her belt and clasped air. Again, she cursed Rhys for taking her weapons. She was now completely defenseless. Slowly, so as to not startle the beasts, she settled into a defensive position, hands held out in front of her.

"Who's this?" the deep voice purred.

She shivered, but didn't pull her gaze from the giant midnight felines.

"This is Sage Blackwell, the rebellion's blade, and…princess of Aermia."

"Princess?"

"Yes," Rhys replied, pride in his tone.

There was a beat of silence, and then, "Sage, I'm so happy you're able to visit my court."

Visit? What a joke. "It wasn't much of an invitation, my lord." It took all her energy to hold still and remain calm. In reality, she couldn't hear anything over the pounding of her pulse and the ringing inside her head.

More curses and murmurs erupted around them. Inwardly, she winced. Probably not the best idea to disrespect the warlord. She felt his gaze hot on her face, but she still didn't look away from the beast that had just licked its lips.

"She's feisty."

"More than you know, my lord."

"Why are you limping?"

She swore she could almost hear Rhys' teeth grinding.

"She fought me and landed a blow," Rhys rushed out.

"Interesting," the warlord drawled. "And her injuries?"

"Earned."

She bit her lip to keep herself from lashing out, but still kept her eyes on the beasts stalking back and forth in front of the immense throne.

"My loves, come back," the warlord cooed.

She studied the felines as their ears flicked back and forth before slinking back to his side, settling like shadowy pools that stained the white dais. Her hands trembled, and she had to clench them to hide it. At least she would not be torn apart by beasts. For now.

The warlord stood from his throne made of stone and thorns. She blinked at his bare, chiseled chest, which also seemed to be carved from stone, and again wondered why he didn't wear clothes. In her mind, a warrior would want as much protection as possible. Sage studied him as he glided down from the dais and toward her. He truly did glide, each movement of his body flowing into the next. She shivered. Only highly trained warriors and assassins moved like that.

Tipping back her head, she maintained eye contact as he approached, halting less than an arm's length away. Stars above, the man was enormous. He had to be well over six feet tall, maybe close to seven.

He completely threw her off balance when he bowed slightly, murmuring, "My lady."

She dipped her chin in acknowledgement. The Scythian warlord straightened, and raised a black brow like he was waiting for something. If he expected her to curtsey, he would be sorely disappointed. She'd crash to the ground if she attempted such a thing.

Rhys stormed to her side and jerked her arm, crushing her skin in his hand. She winced as pain shot through her arm. Black eyes caught hers, and she masked her expression. But he'd seen it.

"Kneel," Rhys demanded.

She locked her knees, not losing eye contact with the warlord. "No."

Before she knew what happening, her knees cracked against the stone, her palms slapping the unforgiving floor, stinging. Much to her frustration, a tear squeezed out of one eye. It dripped off her face and splashed onto the white floor, mixing with the blood and dirt she'd tracked in. Glaring at the black boots of the warlord, she prepared herself for the beating that was sure to come.

EİGHT

THE WARLORD

HE THOUGHT IT WOULD TO be another day of dealing with petty bickering, but then his nephew reappeared, and with him, a girl.

The voices inside him quieted the longer he stared at her. The moment she lifted her head and met his gaze, he jolted. Images of the past assaulted him: sad, green eyes, a kiss, brown hair wrapped around his fist, and blood. He blew out a deep breath as the memories faded.

The voices whispered that they wanted her. That she was different. That she was *his*.

The resemblance was striking, and yet, she was unlike the women he'd surrounded himself with. By all accounts, he should've been disgusted by her, offended and repulsed by her green eyes and scars, but he was intrigued. Ensnared. The flawless Scythian women scattered around the room and the dangerous, broken creature before him created an almost laughable contrast.

But as enchanting as her body might be, it was her face that captivated him. It looked sweet, innocent, and honorable. Everything he was not.

She wore a mask of calm, but again her gaze betrayed her. Flames burned behind her eyes; she was dangerous. But what piqued his interest was the small glimmer of fear he detected. It was an interesting combination: fear, hate, and feigned innocence. He had killed for less than the expression she wore, and yet the voices stayed his hand at her insolence. Death clearly didn't scare her, but he did. He both liked and hated that.

Before he really knew what he was doing, he descended the dais, almost desperate to be closer to her. Her obvious hate for his nephew warmed him to her even more. Rhys had always been a pathetic excuse for a Scythian. The moment Rhys struck her, something snapped inside Zane. Only knaves and cowards hit women. It was despicable, and no one touched what was his. Ever. It was an act which was not to be borne. His nephew had signed his own death warrant right then and there.

His gaze never strayed from the woman as he drew closer. Could she be the key to what he sought, or would she be the key to his destruction?

NINE

SAGE

A LARGE, CALLOUSED HAND WEARING several rings entered her vision. She stared at it. What kind of joke was this? He couldn't mean to help her up.

"Take it, please," his smooth voice said.

With no other option, Sage slipped her hand into his. He lifted her from the floor, and she swore she heard her bones creak. She met his gaze and dipped her chin as she pulled her hand away. "Thank you."

A nod. He scanned her face slowly, taking all the time in the world. Then, he moved down the rest of her body, stopping here and there to examine a scar, a cut, a bruise. Was he admiring his man's handy work? Looking for ways he could hurt her? She held herself stock-still as he walked around her as if he was inspecting chattel.

"What happened to her clothing?" he murmured, only loud enough for Rhys to hear.

"The other woman needed medical attention. Sage had to use her shirt as punishment for insubordination."

The warlord hummed and paused by her side.

"Is she still pure?" The question lingered in the air.

"Of course, my lord. We wouldn't dare touch what is yours."

She forced herself to hold still when he caressed a scar along her hip, and then her wrist.

"How did she come by the scars?"

"She and I had…a disagreement, if you will," Rhys replied smugly.

Her stomach churned at his lies.

"And the rest? She's been beaten badly."

"All deserved, I can assure you. She brought them on herself. She never stopped fighting."

Another hum. "What do I cherish most in the world?" the warlord asked conversationally.

"Perfection." Rhys' response was automatic.

"What comes second?"

"Our line."

"True," the warlord answered, circling her again. "And who bears our lines?"

"Our women," Rhys drawled.

Sage turned her head to follow the prowling warlord. All his pacing had her on edge. He stopped between Rhys and herself.

"Do we *ever* hurt our women?"

"No," the monster replied, his mud-brown gaze darting from her to the warlord.

He glanced at her arm, and the warlord's lips thinned just a touch. Slowly, he began circling her again. This time, she turned to keep her back from him. She was finished with his inspection.

A small smile tipped up his sensual lips. "I wondered when you would give up your submissive pose. You don't have it in you to bend to someone else's will."

She bared her teeth at him, countering his movements. "You know nothing about me."

"On the contrary, I know everything." The warlord slid behind Rhys and whispered, "You shouldn't have marred her. You know how I feel about that, and yet you disobey me."

One moment, Rhys was staring smugly at her, and the next, he was gurgling on the floor, scarlet liquid slipping from his neck.

Her body flashed hot and cold, and a high ringing filled her ears. A tremor rippled through her body as Rhys gasped and writhed on the floor. Even as death claimed him, he managed to choke out something that would surely haunt her dreams.

"I'll always be on your skin," he coughed, and the light in his eyes dimmed.

She blinked. *No.*

Sage scrambled toward Rhys and dropped to her knees next to him. Carefully, she held a hand over his parted lips, shaking. Not one breath. "No," she uttered as she frantically grabbed his wrist to feel for a pulse. Nothing. "No, no, no, no, no, no!"

Her eyes darted back to his face, and she gagged at his empty, unseeing eyes. He was gone. Dead in a matter of heartbeats.

No pain. A clean death. No suffering.

An ember of rage caught flame in her gut. How dare he die! "You bastard!" she screamed and slammed her fists on Rhys' unmoving chest. "You don't get to die! Breathe, damn it."

Still, his chest didn't move. He was dead.

He didn't deserve a quick death. He didn't deserve death at all! He deserved to rot and suffer in eternal hell like she did *every day*. A wail came out of her that didn't seem physically possible. "Death was too good for him!"

Sage pulled her hands back and held up her shaking palms. They were red. Covered in blood. She retched, bile burning her throat and flooding her mouth. In a frenzy, she scrubbed her hands over her pants and half-corset, sobbing. She didn't want him on her. Pushing up from her knees, she tried to stand, only for her feet to slip in the gore. Again, she gagged and scrubbed harder, but only succeeded in making it worse. Her body now looked like a garish painting of red, brown, and black.

Even in death, Rhys seemed to win.

Another sob broke loose as she lifted her head. The warlord was observing, completely calm, utterly unaffected by the murder he'd just committed.

"You," she accused. "You killed him!"

A shrug. "He deserved to die for his actions."

"He deserved to *suffer*," she choked out as the warlord's form blurred from her tears.

"My justice is swift. No one breaks my laws without punishment."

"His life was mine!" she yelled. "Mine!" Sage flinched as her voice echoed in the room.

"Was it?" the warlord questioned softly, returning his blade to the sheath at his hip. "Is anything really yours? Every decision you've made has been guided or forced from you. Your life, your body, and even your children will not be yours. He was mine, my subject to deal with."

She had begun shaking during his little speech, tears still pouring from her eyes.

"It was justice." He gestured at Sage. "He had no right to touch you. For that, he had a price to pay. You're too valuable to ruin."

She scoffed and sniffed, looking for Jasmine, while holding her arms out. "Your men have proved otherwise."

The warlord barked, "Blair."

The leader stepped away from the group of silent Scythians. "My lord."

"Is what she says true? Did the men harm her?"

The leader stilled and flashed her a look that asked, *Can you handle our deaths?*

She swallowed, and tried to think through all the madness swirling inside her. She held many lives in her hands. Part of her wanted them all to die, but did they deserve to die because Rhys happened to be part of their party? No.

"Your men did not permanently harm me. They followed orders." The words tasted like ash on her tongue.

"And the other woman?" the warlord asked.

"Anything that befell us was at the order of Rhys." Her nausea rose up again. She'd just defended the enemy. What was wrong with her? She blankly stared at the grisly scene on the floor, no longer seeing anything.

"Indeed." He addressed the leader: "Blair, make sure both women are cleaned, healed, and fed. Also, notify my sister that her son has died."

A large hand touched her arm and something squished underneath. Sage pulled away and stared at the bloody handprint overlapping the silver scars of her forearm. The sight sickened her. She hunched forward and expelled what little there was remaining in her stomach, and watched it splash all over the dirty, bloody floor around her. She wiped the bile from her mouth and stood on wobbly legs, only to come face-to-chest with the warlord. When had he moved? She lifted both crimson-stained hands, and pushed against his chest while stepping back. But she was stopped short and hauled back when his hand wrapped around the back of her neck.

She began struggling, but it felt like she was moving through sap. All her movements were slow and uncoordinated.

"It's easier this way," he whispered.

She darted a look up at him as his finger pressed into her neck. His sensual mouth and black eyes were the last thing she saw before darkness swallowed her.

TEN

TEHL

"SHE WON'T SAY A DAMN thing!" Sam paced and ran a frustrated hand through his hair. "I've tried everything, and nothing! Nothing works. She's silent as the grave. If I didn't know better, I'd say she might be deaf. All she does when I ask her a question is stare at me expressionlessly, as if she can't understand the words coming out of my mouth." He cursed. "We don't have time for this! Sage is enduring God-knows-what circumstances and—" Sam broke off and swallowed hard. "I worry for her."

Tehl closed his eyes and held the bridge of his nose. "We have to get her to speak."

"What do you expect me to do? Torture her?" Sam snarled.

The anger that had been simmering beneath his skin finally bubbled over. "I don't know!" Tehl exploded. He shot out of his chair and threw a bottle of ink at the wall. "My wife has been missing for over a week in enemy territory. I have no way of knowing if she's even alive." He watched the ink drip down the wall like black blood. "Some part of me hopes she's already dead. Then, she would be spared from Rhys," he admitted. "Do you understand how messed up that is?"

Jeffry, Gav, Sam, and Rafe all stared at him in silence like he'd lost his mind. Maybe he had. Since Sage had been taken, he'd had nightmares every night. She always died in his dreams, mouthing something he couldn't understand with accusing eyes.

"You don't want that," Gav said with sorrow clinging to him. "Mourning a loved one is not something I'd wish on my worst enemy."

A loved one.

Somewhere along the lines, Sage became not just someone foisted on him, but part of his family. She got under Tehl's skin, just about drove him crazy, and ribbed him mercilessly, but that made him like her all the more. He loved her; not like his father loved his mother, but she was a loved one. The realization startled him.

Rafe uncoiled from his spot on the wall and rolled his neck. "Let me have a turn at her."

"Do you think you'll do better?" Sam asked.

The rebellion leader shrugged. "Maybe, maybe not. But I'll try until we get something we can use."

Tehl tipped his chin at Rafe. "I'll go with you."

"Is that wise, son?" Jeffry asked.

He smiled sharply at the Keeper. "No."

The Keeper blinked his eyes dangerously slow. "You're not planning on anything you'll regret, are you?"

"The only thing I would regret is the death of my wife," he said over his shoulder. He then stormed down the winding hallways that made up the labyrinth of cells.

"Do you have a plan?" Rafe asked from beside him.

He sent the rebellion leader an irritated look. "How do you move so quietly? If I didn't know any better, I'd say you were related to Sam."

A small smile played about Rafe's mouth. "I can't help it. It's how I was raised. You didn't answer my question."

"I will study her, and maybe read," Tehl answered.

"Read?"

Tehl pulled a small book out of his pocket and brushed his fingers over the silver filigree. "*The History of the Mort Wall.*"

"You're going to give her a history lesson?" Rafe asked skeptically.

"The last time Sam and I spoke with her, she was a staunch believer of all things Scythia. Sam seems to think she was indoctrinated with their beliefs. If

I belittle her kingdom, maybe she'll start speaking. When we captured Blaise, she was the most emotional of the warriors. She had a temper."

"That's brilliant."

Tehl shot Rafe a startled look. "We're agreeing on something again?"

A shrug. "It was bound to happen sometime. We've always had Sage in common."

Guilt churned his stomach. He should've protected her.

"It wasn't your fault," Rafe murmured.

Tehl's jaw tightened, hating that the rebellion leader was reading him. "It was my task to protect her. I promised her family she'd be safe."

"You're not the only one. She's been mine to protect for the last few years, and all I've done is send her into one bad situation after another for the greater good," Rafe scoffed. "What the hell is the greater good? Is there really any good left in the world?"

"Sage and people like her are the good in our world."

"Very astute for someone so young."

Tehl's brows wrinkled. "You're not that much older than I am."

Rafe's lips thinned. "Indeed."

Both men fell silent, lost in their own thoughts. Tehl slowed to a stop at the Scythian woman's cell. Her hair fell in dull strands over her slumped shoulders, her eyelids closed. Even dirty, the woman was extraordinarily beautiful.

The rebellion leader sucked in a sharp breath. Tehl glanced at him and his lips twitched. "Have you never seen a Scythian?"

"I have, but I've never seen one of their women. They're guarded jealously. I can now see why. She's, she's—"

"Flawless," Tehl finished.

Rafe scowled, his scar puckering. "Indeed."

Tehl turned his back on the gawking man and moved to the stone wall across from the cell. He sank down to his haunches, then sat and pushed back against the wall. Tehl ran his fingers over the butter-soft cover of the book, remembering how his mum used to read it to him and his brother growing up. When he was little, it seemed like a bedtime story, but as he grew, he discovered the real value of the book. History meant everything.

He ignored Rafe as the rebellion leader plopped down several feet away and tipped his head back against the stone.

Tehl focused, opened the book, and began reading.

In the beginning, there were five kingdoms with very different peoples: Aermia, Methi, Nagali, Scythia, and Sirenidae. Each people had something very special to offer the world.

The Nagalians had the ability to communicate with the red dragons of the realm by singing. Their bonding led to working in the caves to retrieve rubies.

Methians were a courageous, regal people who lived in the mountains despite their somewhat temperamental neighbors—the griffins.

The Sirenidae lived in the sea, and graced all the peoples with treasures from deep below. They kept fishermen and traders safe on their passages.

The Aermians were a clever, kind people whose borders touched all other kingdoms and became the hub for trade. They welcomed all to their land.

Last were the Scythians, a brilliant, resilient race of people who lived in the harsh jungles, and could create the most amazing healing draughts from their plants. They were healers and warriors by nature.

Tehl read for hours, describing what each kingdom traded, how the people intermarried, how time passed. He read until his throat went dry. Licking his lips, he glanced at the lightly snoring Rafe, and prepared to start reading again.

"Must you drone on and on?" a husky female voice asked.

Casually, he placed the book in his lap and lifted his eyes to the woman in the cell. "Do you have anything else to do?"

She stared stonily at him.

Tehl shrugged. "If you don't mind, I'll continue." He plucked the book from his lap and picked up where he left off.

Unbeknownst to the other kingdoms, Scythia's warlord had grown increasingly obsessed with perfection, and began to covet something that was not his. A woman. One who was promised to another.

Rafe sniggered. "Sound familiar?"

Apparently, the rebellion leader wasn't asleep.

Tehl raised a brow but kept reading. "*Time passed, and the warlord's experiments continued from just healing his people to attempting to alter them so they would never get sick. And he succeeded. His people never became ill. But that wasn't enough; he kept searching for ways to fix his people, to perfect their race.*

When the other kingdoms became aware of his tampering, they immediately sought the warlord of Scythia. He smiled and placated the kings with lies and promises of healing draughts from their lands. But slowly, the Scythian people stopped marrying into any other race, worried that their children wouldn't be healthy. They began to distance themselves, withdrawing back into their jungles, fearing imperfection would infect them.

That was the first sign of danger. The Sirenidae saw the danger and calamity ahead, but no one paid them any mind. So, they pulled back into the ocean and disappeared altogether.

After years, it seemed normal that the Scythians didn't leave their kingdom, and the Sirenidae became a myth. But there was still peace.

As time passed, the warlord became more obsessed with perfecting the world. He hated the bond shared between the people and dragons of Nagali. It was unnatural in his mind that the death of a beast would break a person and change them forever. So, he offered the Nagali king a draught that would heal and alter his people, but the king refused. This angered the Scythian warlord, so much so, he decided to cleanse the Nagali people from the land."

A snort.

Tehl ignored her and kept on.

"Scythians crept into Nagali like thieves in the night. They swarmed the land like locusts and destroyed everything in their path. In a matter of days, an entire race had been murdered, down to the last ruby dragon. Aermia and Methi rallied and moved to meet Scythia in battle. But Scythia never planned to battle them. They had created a sickness that would spread through the people. It was only because of one man that this didn't happen."

"The traitor," Blaise spat.

"Many consider Alexander a hero."

Somehow, she managed to look down her nose at him whilst sitting down. "He betrayed our kingdom. I assure you, he was no hero. Every year, we celebrate his death by dancing on his grave."

Rafe tipped his head forward and looked at Tehl. "They're more demented than I expected."

A mocking laugh poured out of the woman. "The only thing demented here is you. Don't think I can't smell what you are, Methi."

Tehl froze, keeping his face schooled. *Methi?*

The rebellion leader smiled arrogantly at the woman. "With senses like that, you're no better than an animal like me."

Blaise lunged to her feet, only to be jerked back by her cuffs. "I'm nothing like you."

"Don't be so sure. Who do you think your warlord was trying to imitate when he started experimenting on his people? He was jealous of everyone else's abilities."

She spat at him and sat on the floor again, her chest sawing heavily.

"Charming," Rafe remarked.

Tehl watched her as she tried to calm herself down.

She pulled in one final breath and opened her eyes. "Even in this kingdom, staring is considered rude." A pause. "You won't break me."

"I'm not trying to break anything."

"Liar," she hissed.

He crossed his arms and cocked his head. "Truly, nothing broken is useful."

A long blink. "Agreed." Another pause. "Where's the woman? I enjoyed her last visit. She's interesting."

"Come now. Surely, you can use her name?" Rafe needled.

"Sage. I want to see her."

Then the Scythian woman wasn't aware. "So do I," Tehl replied.

Two little wrinkles appeared in her forehead. "What do you mean?"

"You know what I mean, Blaise."

Her attention jumped from Rafe to himself and back again. "Is she dead?"

"No, she's been taken by a man I originally met as Serge," he explained, then took a risk. "A man you're acquainted with. A man named Rhys."

She didn't fidget or look around. She just froze. But her gaze held a glimmer of fear.

"Are you familiar with him?"

Silence.

"Answer me."

Anger, frustration, and panic churned in his gut. All he wanted were a few answers. He didn't want to play the bad guy. He hated it.

He uncoiled from his spot and walked to the bars, never losing eye contact.

"Do you know what happens to political prisoners like yourself?" No answer. "Let me tell you. We marry them off." She pulled in a sharp breath through her clenched teeth. Good, she needed to understand the stakes here. "It hasn't been done in many years, but don't think I wouldn't marry you off to the highest bidder. That is your future if you don't speak."

"Do you think I would betray my kingdom because of a threat?" she whispered, disgust clear in her tone.

"No, you're too honorable for that. But I'm not asking you to betray your kingdom."

"Lies, but for the sake of the argument, what do you want from me?"

"Why did he take Sage?"

"I don't know."

"Lies," he repeated her words.

"I don't. If he did, no good will come from it."

"Who ordered her kidnapping?"

She hesitated.

"Tell him, or I swear I'll come in there and rip your tongue from your throat," Rafe growled.

Tehl frowned at Rafe. "Enough."

The rebellion leader snarled but kept quiet. He turned slowly back to the prisoner to lock eyes with her. Her gaze bounced between them, and a half-smile curved her lips. "You're both in love with the princess."

"You're right," he allowed. "She's part of my family."

"The beast and the prince," she murmured. "How scandalous."

"Why has he taken her?"

"If he's taken her, it could be many things. Someone may want her, or…he could have taken her for himself."

"Why?"

"He needs a reason?"

"You're being obtuse." Time for a different tactic. "Blaise, you owe me nothing, but you owe Sage something. She's made sure that your safety and health were a priority. You've been in this prison, but you've been well taken care of. No men have touched you. You haven't been starved or tortured. She has been your champion. I understand Scythians have their own code of honor. Would you really leave your debt unpaid?"

Her fists clenched, and she tipped her head back to stare at the stone ceiling. "You don't need me to tell you why she was taken. It's common sense. She's valuable. She was the most valuable thing in this entire castle." Blaise rolled her neck and peeked at him from under her lashes. "She's not in immediate danger, but she'll wish she was dead."

"Why is that?"

"Scythia is not kind to chattel."

"Chattel?"

She looked him dead in the face. "The women used to birth our young."

Rafe cursed and slammed a hand on the bars. "Why would they even want her? Scythians hate outsiders. She's not one of the flawless."

"There are ways to make sure the young she carries are flawless, even if she isn't. Plus, one can always close their eyes..." A hint of revulsion colored her words.

A wave of disgust washed through Tehl. "That's sick."

She turned away, hiding her face from him. "Flawless or not, no one should be used like that," she admitted.

"I agree," Tehl said, trying to keep his emotions locked down. "Thank you for speaking with us. When Sage returns, I'll send her to you." He pushed away from the bars and strode away.

"Don't expect the same woman," she called after him. "The woman you knew as Sage is dead."

He sped up and wound through the hallways, trying to sort out the conversation in his mind and keep himself from killing the spy striding next to him.

"That woman's toying with us," Rafe growled from his right.

Tehl skidded to a stop and stared at the rebellion leader. "She's not the only one."

"What do you mean by that?"

He snatched his dagger from his waist and slammed his forearm against Rafe's chest, pushing him into the stone wall. "Do you really think I would forget what she said? You're a damn spy."

Amber eyes narrowed on him. "Are you going to trust what that lying wench said?"

"She wasn't lying, but you have been. Why are you here, *Methian*?" he demanded, pressing the blade against the rebellion leader's throat.

"I'm here to help Sage, and make Aermia stronger."

He snorted. "That's utter rubbish. You started the first successful rebellion in Aermia's history. Enough with the lies. What's in it for Methi?"

The large man stared at him and then sighed. "I'm not here to cause trouble."

A sarcastic laugh burst out of Tehl. "What makes you think I would believe anything that comes out of your lying trap? First, you're the Methian prince, then you were the leader of rebellion, and now you're on my council. How convenient." His own gaze narrowed at a thought slithering through his mind. "Is she aware of who you are?"

Rafe held his gaze. "Yes."

"Damn it," Tehl yelled, and pushed back from the spy. He glared at the stone wall and pointed the dagger at Rafe. "How long?"

"The night before you wed."

"Of course." He laughed. "You were hoping to spirit her away."

"She refused me."

"Only because she has more honor in her little finger than most in their whole body."

A bitter chuckle rumbled out of Rafe. "That's what attracted me to her in the first place. She was so loyal and dedicated to her family. Then I saw her practicing in her meadow. She was glorious."

Something flashed across the rebellion leader's face that made an unfamiliar emotion stir in Tehl's gut. It felt suspiciously like jealousy. "Why does she keep protecting you?" Tehl asked, feeling completely at a loss. "You've done nothing but put her in harm's way, and betray her time and time again. And yet, she forgives you."

The rebellion leader scoffed. "That woman hasn't forgiven me for anything. I have fought tooth and nail for her. I even bribed her with what she wanted most in life, and she still wouldn't leave with me." Rafe glanced to the floor, and ran a hand through his wine-colored hair. "She was mine before she ever met you. *Mine.* If Rhys hadn't betrayed both of us, she never would have been your wife."

Tehl arched a brow. "Rhys wasn't the only one to betray her."

"You're right," the rebellion leader growled. "She was everything I ever wanted, but duty demanded I take care of my responsibilities before my feelings. You understand that."

It was something Tehl understood well. "Duty is important," he acknowledged. "What were these responsibilities that kept you from her?"

Rafe blew out a breath and ignored his question. "She says she forgives me, and yet she holds me at arm's length. I can't help but feel that if I listened to her the first time, none of this would have happened."

"We can't go back. It's useless to dwell on the past, unless it's a lesson to be learned."

"Very wise."

Tehl smiled. "My father used to say that when we were growing up."

Rafe cracked a smile. "He's an interesting old man."

"That he is," Tehl said. "What are you doing in my kingdom?"

The rebellion leader studied him for a long minute. "The Methi have never forgotten the stories of old. They are even part of our education for our young. We've watched Aermia for a long time, and then things started to change in your kingdom."

"The kidnappings," Tehl said.

"Among other things," Rafe answered vaguely. "Then your mother died."

A sense of loss filled Tehl. It had been years, but the loss was still there.

"Your father, in his grief, lost his grip on your kingdom, and things became worse. It was then decided that something had to be done."

"Why? Why meddle in Aermia's affairs?"

"Your kingdom is all that keeps the Scythians from us. If your kingdom falls, Methi is vulnerable. To keep the Scythians at bay, you needed a leader to take charge."

Both Tehl's brows rose. "And that's you?"

"No, it just wasn't your father. We needed someone who would fight for your kingdom and unite it."

"Sage."

Rafe dipped his chin. "One of several possibilities. Everything was going according to plan until you captured Sage. Even then, I thought it would be great for information, but then…"

"Rhys."

"Rhys," the rebellion leader hissed. "That double-crossing son of a whore. He destroyed everything."

"He needs to suffer."

"Indeed."

Both men stared at each other, wearing matching grins, and, for the first time, it seemed like there was no animosity between them.

Tehl took one step closer and held his hand out to Rafe. "This is not the path either one of us planned on traveling, but tragedy, unexpected events, and Sage have shoved us together. For the sake of my wife and the woman that you love, do you suppose we can get on together? For her?"

Rafe eyed him, then clasped forearms with him. "For the woman we love."

"For Sage."

ELEVEN

SAGE

SAGE GROANED. EVERYWHERE HURT.

When she finally got up the strength to crack her eyelids, she blinked, and then blinked again. Was there something wrong with her eyes? She saw only darkness, not even a sliver of light. Sage ran her hands along the rough surface upon which she lay. The familiar rough texture of stone met her fingertips. Where was she? A dungeon?

She tried swallowing and found her throat burned as if she were swallowing fire. After a moment, she was able to croak out, "Jasmine?"

"Here," her friend's voice was a whisper, and it came from somewhere on Sage's right.

"Are y— ?" She broke off, seized by a sudden coughing fit. "Are you alright?"

"Well, I haven't really moved around, but my ribs don't bother me as much, so I guess there's that."

Sage shifted to sit up but stopped short, cool air caressing her skin. She gasped and grabbed at the soft cover around her. What the hell had happened? "What happened to my clothes?" she grumbled out loud.

"They took them and washed you. I watched the whole time. Nothing horrid happened."

She shuddered as the image of Rhys' hungry, soulless eyes flashed through her mind. Shaking her head, she rubbed at her forehead, as if the motion could somehow erase both the memory and the fear it created. "So where are we now?"

"My guess? Some sort of cell."

"How long have we been here?" she asked, turning toward the sound of Jasmine's voice.

"No clue. I've slept on and off, and there's no light. No one's visited us since they left us here. If I go by my throat and belly, I'd say it's been at least a day." A pause. "I'm so glad you're okay. When the warlord grabbed you, you went limp. I fought to get to you, but that Scythian wench held me back. I thought he'd killed you." Her last words were a broken whisper.

"I'm so sorry, Jas. That must have been horrible for you."

Jasmine sniffed. "There was nothing I could do! I've been so damn helpless this entire time!"

Sage sat up and clutched her head as a wave of dizziness washed over her. Once she'd regained her equilibrium, she tugged on the edges of the fabric covering her and tied them into a knot. Even if Jas couldn't see her, there was no way she was going without clothes. Sage scooted in the direction of Jasmine's voice, and paused as something smooth and cool on her ankles halted her. Her breathing quickened as she ran a shaking hand toward the object brushing her skin. Her fingers discovered cool metal encircling her ankle— a manacle.

No…

She was chained… trapped....

"Sage?"

No, no, no, no, no! The words echoed over and over in her mind. This couldn't be happening, not again.

"Sage!"

The harsh tone snapped her from her trance. Pushing her now-dampened hair from her brow, she gave voice to her thoughts. "We've been caged and bound," she whispered, her heart galloping. "We're trapped."

"I'm so sorry."

She started tugging on the iron. "There has to be a way out."

"I already tried."

She pulled harder and pain shot up her fingers.

"Sage…"

She stopped pulling. Suddenly, she felt faint. Why was there no air in the room?

"Sage!"

"What?" she yelled.

"You need to calm down."

"I c-can't breathe, there's no air!" she wheezed. "I can't breathe!"

"Yes, you can. You just need to calm down first." She heard metal slithering across stone just before she felt a hand grasp her arm. "Sage. Inhale through your nose and out through your mouth. I'm going to do it, so you just copy me, okay?"

Clasping Jasmine's hand, she tried to do as her friend instructed, breathing in and out. In and out. She focused solely on accomplishing those two things, and how long they sat in the dark, just breathing, she didn't know. Slowly but surely, her breathing slowed. Sage patted Jasmine's hand when she finally managed to speak without wheezing. "Thank you."

Sage felt her friend shrug beside her.

"My nephew has had episodes since his parents died in a Scythian raid a few months ago. I've since taken charge of their care, so I've had to learn how to calm him down."

She shifted and pulled her sheet tighter around her. "Your nephew?"

"My brother and his wife had twins, a boy and a girl, but I'm raising them now. Or at least, I was…" She trailed off.

"I'm so sorry." She squeezed Jasmine's hand. "You will see them again."

"And you're a damn liar."

"Nothing is impossible."

A snort. "You know how ridiculous that sounds?"

She did, actually. A chuckle slipped out, and then another. Sage laughed and laughed and laughed, until tears streamed down her cheeks and her belly cramped.

"It wasn't that funny."

She wiped her eyes and stared into the darkness. "It's this ridiculous situation. Everything about it is surreal."

"I understand what you mean."

She opened her mouth to continue when she heard what sounded like a shoe scuffing against stone, followed by the scraping of stone as a door was pushed open, and the two girls were left blinking in the newfound light. Sage rubbed at her eyes and then squinted as her eyes tried to adjust. She was barely able to make out the two masculine shapes standing in the doorway. "What do you want?" she demanded.

They ignored her and moved into the room. As her eyes began to adjust, one of the men approached Jasmine and knelt beside her, removing the chain connecting her feet to the floor. The girl attempted to scramble back away from him, but was held immobile by a large hand wrapped around her ankle.

"What are you doing?" Jasmine yelled.

Sage's hand tightened on Jasmine's when the warriors remained silent, trading a look. This didn't bode well.

"Get your hands off me!" Jasmine commanded.

In a coordinated move, the men placed themselves on either side of her and plucked the small woman from the ground, holding onto her arms and feet.

"No!" Jas yelled as she fought.

Sage surged to her feet still holding tight to Jasmine's hand. "Let her go!" Her fist struck out, smashing into the taller of the men. He grunted but didn't release her friend. Sage's sheet fluttered to the ground, leaving her body exposed, but she didn't care about her nudity.

Jasmine let out a pained cry when the shorter one wrapped his arms around her damaged ribs.

"Careful," the taller warrior warned. "Don't hurt her. Can you handle her?"

"Yes."

The taller warrior dropped her flailing feet to the floor and turned to Sage. "Do not make this difficult. We do not want to hurt you."

Sage wrapped her other hand around Jasmine's arm and gave him a defiant look. "Let her go."

"I'm sorry," he said, before he pushed her and tore her grasp from Jas.

"NO!" she screamed as the shorter warrior hauled her friend, kicking and screaming, into his arms. She lunged toward Jas, only to be jerked back by large arms.

"Sage!" Jasmine screamed and reached for her just as the warrior disappeared through the door.

Sage spun on the taller warrior when his arms released her, and sprang at him, only to be tripped by her shackled feet. Her bare knees slammed into the stone, her teeth clacking together at the impact. Tears sprang to her eyes. "Bring her back!"

His lips turned downward. "Forget about her." He picked up her sheet from the floor and tossed it to her. "Cover yourself. Not all are gentlemanly."

She caught it with numb hands, still unable to believe they had stolen Jasmine. "What will happen to her?"

"She will be disposed of."

Disposed of? Her panic doubled. "What are you going to do?" He gave her a sad look and moved out the door. "Tell me, damn it!"

"She's never coming back," he said and closed the door, shutting all light out once again.

"Bring her back!" she screamed, completely blind. Without hesitation, she started wrenching at her shackles. "Come on, you bastards! Bend, break, something!"

No matter how hard she screamed and pulled, they didn't budge. It was perhaps hours that she went on like that, but to no avail. Her breath seesawed from her chest, and her hands throbbed in time with her heart when, finally, she collapsed against the cool floor, tears streaming down her face. They'd taken her friend. She should have fought harder. Done something.

And now they were both alone.

She cried and cried until there were no more tears, and exhaustion claimed her.

Sage woke up, still naked and on a stone floor. She groaned and rolled onto her back, a tear leaking from her eye as she stared up into the darkness above her.

"I'm so sorry, Jas. Sorrier than I could ever tell you," she whispered, her heart so heavy it felt difficult to breathe.

She swiped her eyes with the back of her hand and lay her cheek upon the cool floor. She ached all over at the loss of her friend. It felt like someone had reached into her chest and squeezed her heart. Another tear snuck out. She'd only known Jasmine for little more than a week, but they'd bonded in an extraordinary way, having supported one another through the most gruesome of circumstances. She'd chosen to stand and fight, and Sage admired her for it. Even when she was badly beaten, she stood back up. That endurance and grit had made Sage feel like she could fight harder, too...

But now, her friend was gone, and she was alone. Hadn't they just been laughing together, comforting each other in spite of their circumstance? How could she just be ripped away? Tears welled up in her eyes. It wasn't fair, to either of them.

"Jasmine," she whispered, her tears spilling over. "What did they do to you? How can you be gone? I need you. I need your iron will to keep me going. I, I-" Her throat felt tight, her voice raw. "I'm sorry I couldn't save you and-" She let out a sob. Her breath stuttered as tears streamed down her face, her words barely intelligible. "I'm s-s-sorry that your babies have to grow up without their momma a-a-and now you." She wiped at her nose with the back of her hand. "I'll miss you so much. I'm sorry. I'm so, so sorry." She was choking out breaths now, her cries echoing around her in the darkness. For the second time, she cried her heart out for her friend, her grief overwhelming her.

After her tears had mostly dried, she lay on her back, staring once again into the darkness above, just thinking. She thought of her friend and how it seemed so unfair that no one would know of the enormous sacrifice she'd made just to help a stranger.

"But I do," she said softly, "and I'll never forget it, just like I'll never forget you." She also thought of those two tiny children, the ones no doubt missing their auntie, with no one to care for them. She would do it if she could. She would give those children the love and care they needed and deserved. "And if, by some miracle, I get out of here alive, I'll see to it your babies don't, either." Those children deserved to know about their aunt, and Jasmine deserved to be remembered.

A sense of calm came over her. The pain didn't diminish, but the hopelessness did. She realized she still had a reason to fight and to live. She wasn't just fighting for herself but for those babies who'd already lost so much. When she escaped, Sage could fully mourn, but first, she had to survive.

She was a survivor, not just a victim. Now she had to act like one.

Her tongue felt swollen in her mouth, and her lips were cracked. Her arms shook as she forced herself to sit up and lean against the wall. She was wasting away in here. A meager amount of bread and water were delivered each day, but it wasn't enough to sustain her. It was just enough for her to die slowly. That she felt she could handle. It was the darkness that was bound to drive her insane. Her eyes roved the darkness, seeking any sort of light. How long had she been here?

"You've been here for five days, Sage."

She jumped and glanced around, shocked to hear the sound of Tehl's voice.

"Tehl?"

"You're just having a nightmare. Go back to sleep."

Sage blinked slowly. "I was dreaming?"

A grunt. "You have nightmares almost every night. It's a miracle I haven't been stabbed yet."

"It seemed so real," she said.

"Nightmares usually do. Now, go back to sleep. I'll protect you."

"But I…" Something wasn't right.

She ran a hand along the bed and froze when cool air whispered across her chest. Her bare chest. She jerked the sheet over her body and slammed her eyes closed. What was happening? She'd never slept naked in bed with Tehl. Why was she naked?

A masculine laugh rippled through the dark, causing goosebumps to rise on her arms. "You can sleep naked anytime you like, love."

Sage tucked the sheet under her armpits, and pressed her palms to her forehead. She was hallucinating.

She felt a touch on her arm and jerked, opening her eyes only to find she was still surrounded by darkness. "Who's there?" she croaked.

"Just me," Tehl replied.

"You…you can't be!"

"Why not? Think about it logically. How many times have I had to wake up and convince you that you were just dreaming? Thirty? Forty?"

This was starting to freak her out. Where was she?

"You're at home."

"Stop speaking to me! I can't think," she yelled. Sage wrapped her arms around her belly, and rocked back and forth. What had Gav said to do when she had nightmares? "Say what is truth," she whispered. "My name is Sage. I am a blacksmith. I'm the crown prince's consort. Lilja and Mira are my friends. I've never slept naked with Tehl. Rhys kidnapped me." She swallowed. "Rhys is dead. You're not real."

"Very good."

"You're not real."

"I thought we established that."

"My mind is making you up."

"Seems likely."

Sage shook her head. "Why in the world would my mind create you?"

A snort. "Don't ask me to decipher a woman's mind. I almost never know what you're thinking anyway."

"But why?"

"I'm thinking that's a question only you can answer."

"Why couldn't I have imagined my mum, Lilja, Mira, or Gav? Why choose you?"

"I don't understand it, either."

"But you're me," she pointed out. "I'm talking to myself."

"It does seem that way."

She slumped against the wall as her stomach cramped painfully.

"You need to eat soon."

"That's not helpful," she retorted. "I can't control what they give me."

"You'll die soon."

"Not soon," she whispered. "Slowly. At least they've given me enough water," she whispered, curling up into a ball. As hungry as she was, it wasn't enough to keep her awake. Her eyelids were so heavy they closed of their own volition and she shifted her sheet so she was cocooned inside it. "Tehl?"

"Yes?"

Tears burned the backs of her eyes. Just hearing his voice was a comfort, even if his presence was imagined. She slid her hand out of the sheet with a faint tremor. "Will you hold my hand?"

Silence. It was a ridiculous question. She needed the comfort of human contact, but it was ridiculous to ask her hallucination to do so. She started to pull back when she felt Tehl's hand slip into hers and squeeze three times. Tears filled her eyes. Jas did that every night they fell asleep in the jungle. Sage pulled his hand closer and swore she smelled his spicy scent.

"Thank you," she said, grateful.

"You're welcome, love."

Then, she slept.

TWELVE

SAGE

"I'M DYING."

"No, you're not," argued Tehl.

Sage twisted her neck to face the direction of Tehl's voice. "I'm not even strong enough to move anymore. It won't be long."

"You have to fight."

She laughed weakly. "I can't fight starvation."

"You're giving up." It was an accusation.

"What do you expect me to do? I can't do anything."

"Don't give up hope."

"How exactly? There is no hope. I'm in enemy territory with no hope for rescue, no hope for escape, and no hope for recovery. The situation is hopeless."

"So, you're going to give up? Just like that? You're going to let Jasmine's sacrifice be in vain? That's selfish and weak."

Her anger flared. "Shut up, Tehl! Why can't I be selfish and weak, just this once? I'm dying, for heaven's sake!" She blew out a frustrated breath. "Just let me go in peace. I can't be strong *all the time*. Why do you expect me to be?"

"Because I'm you."

She blinked. In that moment something occurred to her. She was holding herself to a higher standard than she held everyone else. It was she who never allowed *herself* to be weak. *She* never allowed herself to be taken care of. *She* was harder on herself than anyone else, and *she* made excuses for others when they made mistakes, but for herself, she accepted none. Tears pricked her eyes at the thought.

And then she made another realization. "I don't have to be the martyr."

"No, love, you don't."

"Will my parents be disappointed in me?" she asked.

"No, Sage, your parents are beyond proud of you. They worry, though."

"That's what parents do."

"Indeed, it is."

"What about your father? I worry about him."

"He's not beyond helping. You're proof of that."

Sage thought about Sam and Gav. She never thought she'd want more brothers, but after living with them, she found she didn't want to live without them. They'd become her family. Then there was Tehl. Painfully, she shifted onto her side. "And what about you? Do you need me? Will you be okay?"

"I won't lie and say I don't need you. Even you must be able to see that."

She snickered and then winced when her stomach cramped. "I never know what will come out of your mouth. You make me laugh." A small smile tightened her dry cheeks. "I didn't expect that when I married you. Surprisingly, your awkwardness is somewhat charming."

"Call me 'Prince Charming.'"

"Never," she retorted, and curled up tighter.

"But back to before, I will be okay, you know. I'm a survivor, like you."

She closed her eyes. "I never thought about it that way."

"We're a lot more alike than you realize."

She snorted. "I realize it. I'm just not sure I like it." A yawn. "I need to sleep now… I'll talk to you when I wake up."

"Okay. Sleep sweet, love."

"M'kay."

"You need to wake up," Tehl urged.

"I'm too tired."

"Open your damn eyes!"

Her eyelids sprang open at his demand, only to slam shut. Stars dotted her vision, and tears leaked out.

"What have you done to her?" someone snarled. "You almost killed her! What were you thinking? You weren't thinking! Get out of my sight!"

Someone moved into the room and knelt beside her to brush the hair from her face. "Oh, wild one," a deep and smooth voice whispered. "What have they done to you?"

She cracked an eye, only to be blinded by brightness, and immediately squeezed it shut again.

"Close the door!"

She sighed in relief when the darkness returned.

"Sage? I need to move you. Can you open your eyes for me?"

Flopping her head toward the voice, she forced her eyes open. The room was dark, but one sliver of light shone from the door, giving just enough light that she could make out a face in the darkness. "Hello," she whispered.

The face leaned nearer. An extremely handsome face. A perfect face, with eyes as dark as pitch. "Are you here to steal my soul?" she asked.

Her heart stuttered in her chest with the breathtaking smile he gave her. "No. I could never steal something like that, nor would I want to. If I were to keep a soul, it would have to be given to me."

His words didn't make sense, but it was such a pleasure to see something after being in the dark for so long. Not to mention being with someone so stunning. It was almost too much. His dark gaze roamed from her face to the sheet covering her nude body. By the darkening of his face, it was apparent that, as he looked on her, he found no pleasure in it. His face hardened, and she flinched back when he met her eyes.

"I'm sorry." He bowed his head for a moment. "What hurts?"

"Everything."

A nod. He lifted his head and pushed shiny black hair from his face. "I need to move you somewhere I can take care of you. Is that okay?"

Hope fluttered in her chest. "You'll take me out of here? I would love to see the world again before I die."

"You're not going to die," he said with conviction. "I'll make sure of it."

"Okay," she whispered.

He eyed her sheet. "I'm going to lift you and wrap the sheet around you. Can you hold on to it while I lift you?"

She didn't think so, but she wouldn't admit that. "Yes."

A whimper escaped her when he wedged his arm underneath her back.

"I'm sorry," he whispered, and lifted her to her feet.

Pain hit her like a wall, but she managed to keep the sheet barely clenched in her fist, the fabric draping down her front. Cool air chilled the backs of her thighs and back. She swayed into a firm chest as her knees buckled. The warm arm pressed against the bare skin of her back, anchoring her to his chest.

She clenched the sheet tighter in her fist when he tugged on it.

"You need to let go, so I can wrap it around you."

She still didn't let go. It was like her fingers wouldn't unclench.

"I promise I'll not look," he said in a gentle voice. "On the count of three, let go. One, two, three…"

Sage let go, shaking. She hissed as he wrapped the fabric around her sensitive skin, and tucked the ends around her, still holding her against him.

"Brace yourself, I'm going to lift you."

Her nostrils flared as the pain stabbed at her from all over when he swept her off her feet and into his arms. Her arms trembled as she wrapped them around his neck. Everything hurt, and all she wanted to do was go to sleep again.

"Close your eyes. The light will be too much for you."

She took one last glance at the space she had expected to be her coffin, and then peeked up at the man studying her. "Thank you."

"Don't thank me. I'll never be your hero. Now, close your eyes."

His words didn't make any sense to her, but she obeyed as he began moving toward the door. "Open the door."

She hid her face in his shirt when the light draped over them like a long-lost friend. She wished she could open her eyes.

"You'll be able to see soon," he murmured over her head. "But you've been in the dark too long. Your eyes need time to adjust." He shifted her in his arms, but at her sharp breath, he paused. "What?"

She shook her head, his linen shirt caressing her forehead. "It hurts."

"I know. Soon the pain will all be over."

He picked up his pace and the bright light soon faded; even the air cooled.

A creak of leather. "My lord," a masculine voice said then.

"Fetch broth, Maeve, and have Ezra create a draught."

"It will be done."

Silence. Not fading footsteps. Had the other man left?

A door opened and slammed shut. The air heated, and it was like she was breathing steam.

"Everyone out. When Maeve arrives, send her in. Also, close the curtains."

There were more people in the room? She strained to hear any sound, but nothing. Damn Scythians and their sneaking.

"I'm going to set you down. Don't open your eyes."

He placed her on something soft. She sank into it, reveling in the luxury. She heard the rustling of cloth just before large arms plucked her from her new bed. She growled.

"Hush. I'll let you sleep soon enough."

The sounds of lapping water reached her ears, and then they were descending. Warm water soaked her feet, shocking her, and her eyes flew open. It was dark enough that she could just make out a large room with a massive hexagonal pool in its center. And they were in the pool. "Wh-what are you doing?" she squeaked.

"Getting you cleaned up."

"No!"

She blinked up at him. His expression was firm, with a stubborn set to his jaw; apparently, this was happening with or without her consent. His gaze roved her face.

"I'll not ravish you in the pool, if that's what you're worried about. But you need to be cared for."

A blush heated her face. "It's my body."

"True, but it won't be your body if you're dead."

He had a point. "Isn't there a woman who can help?"

"No. I've helped many women birth babes. The female form is nothing new to me. Your modesty has no place here." He descended further, submerging her body in the warm water.

Her jaw clenched when he sat on a submerged pool ledge and pulled her body into his lap, tugging the sheet from her.

He hissed, and Sage squinted down at her bare body. She couldn't see much, but what little she could make out looked like a collage of colors accented by silvery slashes, but that wasn't the worst of it. It was like her skin was too big for her body. She looked like a monster.

"You're not a monster."

She'd said that out loud? Fatigue hit her hard, and she collapsed against the warlord's bare chest.

"That's it. Just relax," he crooned. "I'll take care of you."

A warm, sudsy cloth started on her hand and carefully moved up her arm. Sage kept her eyes closed, blocked out everything happening to her, and focused only on the warm water and the comfort it gave her. She checked in when he washed her stomach and the tops of her thighs, but his hands never strayed to her important bits.

His hands moved to her head, and she hummed, soothed by the soft touch of his hands through her hair. His hands stilled.

"You like that?"

"Mmmhmm… My mum used to wash my hair and brush it for me. I love it," she said, not knowing why she gave a stranger that information.

"I'll remember that," he rumbled and began washing her hair again.

A few times she hissed as he untangled her matted locks, but for the most part, it was the best thing that had happened to her in a very long time. It was the last good memory she'd have before she died. "Thank you."

"My pleasure," he hummed.

She let herself drift and was almost asleep when a knock jarred her.

"Enter," the warlord called.

"I have everything prepared, my lord," a female voice answered.

Sage pressed against his body, both embarrassed and scared that she still couldn't see the woman speaking. The warlord hugged her closer and ran a hand down her wet hair. "I'll bring her out."

A door clicked softly shut, and the warlord turned toward her. She could feel him regarding her. "Can you wrap your arms around my neck?"

She shook her head, all strength gone.

"No matter," he said and he picked her up, sloshing water around, and ascended from the pool. He placed her feet on the floor and wrapped his arm around her back. A fuzzy towel rubbed against her head and then gingerly wrapped around her body. Once again, she was swept into his arms and moved into another dark room where she was then placed on the softest bed she'd ever felt.

"I can take care of it from here, my lord," the female voice offered.

"No, Maeve."

"Do you think that's wise? You're on edge."

"It's not your concern," the warlord responded and ran a hand over her head again. "I'm going to remove your towel, Sage, but I'll cover you with blankets."

She nodded, not caring as long as she didn't have to move from this spot. The wet towel disappeared, and warm blankets were smoothed over her. She sighed and snuggled in deeper.

"You don't get to sleep yet. You have to eat."

"I'm not hungry."

"You'll eat." His tone brooked no argument. His palm cradled her head, and something was placed at her lips. "Drink."

She opened her mouth, and something warm and savory met her taste buds. She gulped down more and cried out when it was taken away.

"You have to drink slower, or you'll get sick."

Sage nodded. She'd have agreed to anything as long as he brought back the delicious broth. She forced herself to take small sips, but before long, she turned her head away. "No more."

"You hardly ate anything. Just a little more," he coaxed.

"No," she moaned, her stomach cramping painfully.

"Let her be," the female said gently. "It'll take time."

A hand smoothed the damp hair from her face. "Sleep sweet, wild one."

She sighed and did so.

She shivered, hearing voices while heat licked inside her veins.

"She needs more," a dangerous voice snarled.

"If I give her more, she'll change," a soft male voice answered. "Do you think she'll follow you meekly when she doesn't even recognize the girl in the mirror? She's just a breeder anyway."

"She's *mine*. I'll do with her what I want."

Why was it so hot?

"But—"

"I didn't bring you here to challenge me. Obey me or suffer the consequences. You know what's on the—"

Stars above, it was bloody hot. She was burning. She whimpered and rubbed at her skin.

A cool hand touched her brow. "Sage?" a deep voice crooned.

"Burning," she whispered.

"I've got you," the voice whispered.

Something pressed to her cracked lips, and blessedly cool liquid coated her tongue. Instantly, the burning began to dim, and the darkness sidled closer, like an old friend, an old friend Sage welcomed with open arms.

THIRTEEN

SAGE

SAGE AWOKE TO A POUNDING in her head. Her limbs felt heavy, and she thought about just going back to sleep when she noticed dull light dancing behind her eyelids. Light? Could she really be seeing light? Or was this another trick of the mind? She bolstered herself and cracked one eye.

It was real.

She lay in a giant room with couches and chairs scattered in cozy nooks. Wanting to see more of the room with its luxurious rug and woven tapestries, she turned her head but immediately regretted it. She brought a shaking hand to her throbbing temple. It was as if there was someone inside her head ringing a gong over and over. Carefully this time, she turned to the right and then froze. A man held her hand, and he was fast asleep in a chair that was far too small for him. It was the warlord. Her eyes ran over his shiny raven hair that had fallen over his face and down his bare chest. Sage blushed and returned her gaze to the hand clutching hers. Maybe if she pulled just right, she could extract her hand. She loosened her grip and tried gently tugging her hand from his.

"What are you doing?"

Startled, she looked up at the man now staring at her. "Moving my hand. It fell asleep." The lie fell easily from her lips. Thank goodness for quick thinking. He ran his thumb over her wrist and let go, still watching her with his onyx gaze. She wet her lips and asked, "Why are you here?"

"Someone needed to care for you."

Her brows slashed down. "Why?" What did the warlord want?

"Because you were sick."

"Because of you," she whispered.

"I never meant for you to be there. To be locked in the dark."

She flinched as the memory of blindness slammed into her.

He leaned closer, his hands laced with his elbows on his knees. "I promise."

She stared at him. Everything told her he was the enemy and a liar, but he couldn't fake the dark circles rimming his eyes. He certainly had been concerned for her. She decided she believed him, but still didn't trust him.

"How long have I been out?"

"Fourteen days."

Panic slammed into her. "I've lost fourteen days? Fourteen? How long have I been here?"

"You've been in my home for six weeks."

Unbidden, tears sprang to her eyes. She'd been locked in the dark for twenty-eight days? She blinked repeatedly and turned her stare to the ceiling as the tears dripped down her face.

"I'm so sorry. I came to you as soon as I became aware of what happened. I didn't order your imprisonment. Someone betrayed me." His tone took on an edge. "They've been dealt with."

A pool of crimson flashed through her memory. "Like you slayed the monster?"

He paused before answering. "Yes."

"They killed my friend," she choked.

"They paid dearly for it."

Fatigue weighed heavily upon her, and she felt her eyes begin to droop, despite her mind whirling with questions.

"Here…" Something was placed at her lips. "Drink this to gain your strength."

She obeyed, not even tasting the broth, just sipping until none was left.

"I'll let you rest."

Sage turned, putting her back to the warlord.

"I'm sorry."

"Sorry doesn't bring Jasmine back," she whispered.

"No, it doesn't." His hand softly brushed her shoulder. "Good night, wild one."

She ignored his touch and stared vacantly at a covered window. Vaguely, she noted a door closing, but she was leagues away in her mind. Six weeks. She'd been gone for *six weeks*. What was happening in Aermia? Were her parents okay? What about the alliance between the rebellion and the Crown? Would it still be honored in her absence? What about Tehl?

"What about me?" he asked, sitting on the bed.

Sage smiled, more tears springing to her eyes. For the first time, she could see him. Black hair, sapphire eyes, and broad shoulders.

"You're here." Her heart stopped when he smiled at her. It was rare for him to full-on smile; when he did, it was a thing of beauty.

"I never left." He looked around the room. "It seems you've moved up in life."

She darted a second glance around the room. "It seems I have."

"The warlord has taken fine care of you."

She dropped her gaze to the coverlet and traced the pattern. "It seems so. He said it was a mistake. That he didn't know."

"Do you believe him?"

"I'm inclined to say no, because of what I've been told about him. But he's different," she admitted. "I can see, but I'm still blind."

"Well, remember we judge on actions, not on hearsay. Examine what you understand to be true. Start from the beginning."

"People have been kidnapped by Scythians. Rhys hurt me." She shuddered and moved on. "He kidnapped me and abused me more. The warlord killed him. I was thrown into prison. Jasmine died," she choked out. "I thought I would die. The warlord rescued me. He has taken care of me."

"Indeed. There might be more beneath the surface than what appears. Could it be that our council has been blind because of prejudice? Possibly. But have you been led to see something that isn't really there?"

That pierced her. Rafe had lied and lied, and she had gobbled up everything he said. The world wasn't black and white. She understood that now. Her eyes started to slide shut. "I'm tired."

"Sleep, love. I'll watch over you."

The next time she woke, a Scythian woman sat next to the bed, reading a book. Cinnamon eyes met hers over the top of a page. The woman snapped the book shut and raised a brow. "It's about time you woke. Your stench is enough to make my eyes water."

"I beg your pardon?" Sage blurted.

"You shouldn't smell like that."

The woman pushed from the chair and yanked back her covers. Sage wrapped her hands around her bare body. How long had she been naked? What had happened to her while she slept all that time?

"Stop looking so scandalized. No one's touched you but the warlord himself."

Her eyes widened. That didn't make her feel any better.

The woman rolled her eyes and helped Sage sit up, then stand. "As if he would take advantage of you looking and smelling like you do. Honestly, you Aermians assume everyone wants you."

Sage blinked and locked her knees when they threatened to buckle. "I meant no offense," she drew out, feeling off balance.

The woman swiftly lifted Sage into her arms, and strode to another room with a rectangular, steaming pool in the middle. They moved to the edge, and the woman plopped Sage in like she weighed nothing at all. Sage's bottom rested on a stone ledge, and her fingers weakly grasped the side of the pool. She glanced at the beautiful woman who was watching her like a hawk.

"Don't drown. I'm not crawling in there to take care of you like the warlord."

Sage gasped. "He bathed me?"

The woman tsked. "It was nothing untoward, child. You would have died without his care. Do you understand?"

The woman's rebuke had Sage feeling about a foot tall. She nodded her head.

"Now, don't let go of that edge, girl. I need to grab supplies."

What happened? She had bathed naked with that man? Her stomach sank. She was an adulteress. Wait, why did *that* of all things come to her mind? All the slurs which had been thrown her way after she'd escaped from the palace, they now applied.

"You're not at fault."

Sage peeked at Tehl lounging by the pool, looking almost as carefree as his brother.

"I know who you are. I know you would never break our marriage vows."

"But I did..." She blinked at the stone edge, feeling violated. "I bathed with another man."

"Not of your own choice. You were on the verge of dying."

"I'm sorry."

"What was that?" the woman asked as she came bustling back in. Sage glanced to where Tehl had been a moment earlier, only to see the bare stone floor. "Nothing," she muttered. God, had she lost her mind in that cell? Had she died? Was this even real?

"You're thinking out loud you know, and this *is* real. Just wait until I have to untangle those snarls in your mane. Then you'll know it's real. Now hold still."

She submitted to the vigorous scrubbing and ignored the muttering and cursing coming from the woman. And, stars above, she was right. At one point, she may have begged for the woman to simply cut her hair rather than keep yanking on her head so. "We'll get there," was all she said.

When she was finally permitted to leave the pool, she was utterly exhausted. The woman dried her and slipped a linen shirt over her head that was much too large, but Sage didn't care. She was just happy to be wearing a garment. She sat Sage in front of a mirror, and whipped out a pair of scissors from God knows where. She lifted a hand and grabbed the woman's wrist, meeting her cinnamon gaze in the mirror. "I may have been a bit hasty when speaking about cutting it."

"I'm only going to trim off the dead."

Sage eyed her suspiciously but relented. It was hateful, really, to place her in front of a mirror. Her skin was sallow, and the shirt hung off her bony shoulders. She brushed aside the collar and glared at her protruding collarbone. Her gaze travelled to her face. She looked half dead. The black bags underneath her eyes were the most prominent part of her face. When she couldn't stand to look at herself anymore, she watched the graceful woman behind her. It was obvious that she found taking care of Sage distasteful.

"What's your name?" she prodded, hoping to break the silence.

"Maeve."

She jerked.

"Hold still," Maeve chastised, fingering her hair. "It's uncanny how similar you look to my mother," she muttered, absently.

This was the same woman who'd eyed her with disgust when she and Jasmine were first brought in? Blinking, she scrutinized the woman wielding the scissors. Maeve looked so much younger than she had first thought. She frowned. The Scythian woman spoke in a way that portrayed age, but the woman could hardly be a handful of years older than her.

"If you keep frowning like that, your face will be stuck," Maeve said, never looking up from her task.

Her frown deepened. That was something her mother would say. It was odd, to say the least.

True to her word, Maeve only trimmed her hair, and then plaited it simply. Once she was finished, she wrapped an arm around her back. "Back to bed with you, missy."

She helped Sage back to the bed, but 'helped' was probably a generous word. Sage gritted her teeth while she was basically carried back to bed. It was horrible having to rely on a stranger for her basic needs, but she was grateful nonetheless. Sage was the enemy to them, and yet the woman took care to help her. As the woman tucked her in, Sage caught her hand and offered a smile. "Thank you, Maeve. Truly. I won't forget your kindness."

The woman stared at her for a long time, like she was looking deep inside her. "It was my pleasure, my lady." She patted Sage's hand and left the dim room.

Finally alone, Sage allowed herself to fall back asleep.

Hands tore at her clothes, and cruel, brown eyes glared down at her. "You're nothing. You'll always be nothing."

She struggled, and the monster pressed harder down onto her.

"No!" she screamed.

"I'll always be on your skin. You'll never get away from me," Rhys whispered into her neck.

She struggled harder, unable to breathe.

"Sage."

"Always on your skin."

"Sage!"

She jerked awake, her entire body shaking. Disoriented, she tried to roll over, only to come into contact with a masculine chest. "No!" She struggled, but her body wasn't fighting like it should. Her movements were sluggish and weak.

"Sage, it's just me. It's just Zane," the warlord murmured in her ear. "Rhys can't hurt you. He's gone forever. He'll never hurt you again."

She collapsed against his chest and cried harder. "He's not gone. He's still haunting me." She trembled, her skin crawling. It was like Rhys' breath was imprinted on her neck.

"They're just nightmares. It's not real." He placed her curled fist over his heart. "Count my heartbeats."

She flexed her fingers, pressed her palm against his chest, and began to count. She reached 562 when her heart stopped racing, her breathing evened out, and she realized exactly where she was and whom she was with. Sage pushed upright, and scooted away from the warlord, pulling the covers around her tighter. What was he doing here? She met his black gaze.

"Thank you, but I would appreciate it if you got out of my bed." She held her breath and inwardly winced. Even she could hear the tremor in her voice. She could not afford to appear weaker than she already was.

He studied her, then climbed out of the bed and stood with his hands in his pockets. She breathed a sigh of relief and ran her eyes over his moonlit-haloed figure.

"You're in my room," she stated.

"Well, technically it's my room, but it's yours until you heal," he replied.

That startled her. "Why?" What was he after?

"Because I can protect you here."

She didn't believe that for one moment. People always have ulterior motives. "Why do you want to protect me? I'm the enemy." She squinted harder, trying to gauge his reaction.

"Are you my enemy? Have I treated you as one?"

"No," she said slowly, "but I can't help feeling there will be a price for your generosity. It's the way of the world. What do you expect of me?"

His laugh danced through the air, raising goosebumps on her arms. She scowled at him while trying to rub them away. What was so funny?

He shook his head. "So suspicious. Here…" He pulled something from his waist and held it out to her, the edge of a blade glinting in the low light.

Sage eyed the dagger, and then the warlord. Was he trying to bait her? What trickery was he weaving?

"It will not bite you. Take it. It's a gift. A warrior should never be without a weapon." He held it out farther.

Sage reached out and hesitated, her hand hovering over the blade. She glanced at the warlord again and decided to just take it, since he was offering it. Pulling the dagger from his grasp, she held it to the light, examining it. It was a simple design, but the hilt fit well in her hand. She balanced it on her palm and smiled. It was balanced well, perfect for throwing. A sense of comfort blanketed her as she palmed the dagger and set it on her lap. Having a means to protect herself meant everything to her. Her gaze flicked back up, and her comfort fled at the intense interest on the warlord's face. She needed to remember that, even with a weapon, she wasn't safe here.

He cocked his head. "What made you this way?"

"What?" His question caught her off guard.

"It's like you expect me to attack you at any moment. What made you so suspicious?"

She thought about lying, but from what she'd seen of him so far, he seemed like someone to see through untruths. So, she led with the ugly truth. "Rhys," she said flatly.

His jaw clenched, then loosened. "Not every man or Scythian is like him."

"True, but not every man is as good as my father," she pointed out.

"I find it interesting that you say your father, not your husband. From what I hear, you have a love match."

Her fingers clenched in the bedding when the warlord glided around the bed before sinking into a chair placed next to the mattress. He moved with an inhuman grace, and with restrained power. She shivered. He was dangerous. She had to stop forgetting what he was.

"Tehl's an honorable man with a good heart," she said softly, inconspicuously pulling the blade from her lap and into her hand. The warlord seemed to miss nothing; he tracked the movement, but said nothing of it.

"Do you trust him?"

"With my life," she replied without hesitation. She did. Tehl had many qualities she didn't care for, but loyalty and honesty were two of his best traits. She trusted him.

"Does he love you?" the warlord asked.

"He does," she said carefully. What an odd question. Where was he going with this? Her sluggish brain couldn't figure it out. Already, fatigue was weighing her down.

"Then why hasn't he come for you?"

That was a punch to the gut. She brushed aside her feelings and focused on logic. "A crown prince has many responsibilities. Running after his kidnapped bride into enemy territory would be foolish. And Tehl is not a fool."

Leather creaked as he leaned closer. "I sent word that you were safe but sick. That your health made it impossible to travel home without an escort. I even sent word that I would bring you to the border."

Home? Her breathing stuttered. He had to be lying. He was playing a game.

"His reply was not what I expected." His voice hardened. "A peace treaty and a threat."

She bowed her head to hide her expression. Tehl threatened the warlord of Scythia? That was a bold thing, but peace? It seemed farfetched. "Is peace such a bad thing?"

"No, but the crown prince's actions suggest otherwise."

"I don't follow," she replied, her brows slashing together.

"Instead of jumping at the chance to retrieve you, he countered with the offer of your skills as a mediator. He said they were unparalleled."

Her heart fell to her stomach. Tehl wanted her to stay here? "What else did the letter say?"

"That as long as you were healthy and whole, he'd bring back his Scythian prisoner in the same condition."

What prisoner? Then it came to her. "Blaise," she whispered.

"What did you just say?"

She cleared her throat. "He used Blaise?"

"Yes." He plucked a mug from the side table and handed it to her. "His wording was quite strong."

"To what end? That doesn't sound like the crown prince at all."

"Men will do whatever is necessary to accomplish their will."

She took a sip and watched him over the rim. "And you?"

He smiled. "I'm no different. But here is my concern. It may not sound like the crown prince, because he's being manipulated."

"By who?" she mused.

"I have my suspicions."

"Humor me," Sage replied.

"I believe it's the Methian running things."

Her fingers tightened on her mug. How did he know Rafe was Methian?

"Excuse me?"

"You heard me, Sage. Don't play coy. You're not unintelligent. You know of the one about whom I speak. He's been manipulating everyone from the beginning." The warlord leaned forward to make his point, energy seeming to teem around him. "Ask yourself this: why would he stir Aermia into a rebellion? How would that really help Aermia at all?"

"We needed a new leader."

"But stirring up a rebellion? Surely, there are better ways to bring about change than a bloody rebellion? Why would he want Aermia weak?"

"I haven't the slightest idea," she deflected.

"Come, now, you're a brilliant woman. Aermia is the central kingdom. It holds all the power."

"True, maybe." She raised a brow. Time to bait him as he'd been doing to her. "What keeps you from going after it, if it's *that* valuable?"

"I've never desired to leave my jungle. We're self-sufficient. I don't need your kingdom, so it has no appeal."

A small laugh escaped her. "The power kingdom has no appeal? I'm sorry, my lord, but I don't believe you."

"It's just Zane."

She ignored his correction, and steeled herself for what she would say next. "Your kingdom has been known for being power-hungry and covetous of others. What you're saying is the opposite from everything I know to be true."

He lifted a hand and tugged at his hair. "Do you like to be held accountable for your family's actions? Or people you don't even know? That's what it's like. I have been held accountable for the sins of a deranged madman with a god complex who died hundreds of years ago. We can't leave this place without being scorned."

The anguish in his voice did something to her. She knew what it was like to be judged by rumors.

"Do you want peace?" she echoed again. The warlord didn't seem evil. If he truly wanted peace, maybe she was exactly where she needed to be.

"I want absolution," he murmured. "I want the voices of the past to quiet."

"I can't give you that, but—" Goosebumps broke out on her arms at the way he stilled at her words, like a predator reading for the hunt. *Be brave, Sage. Brave.* She swallowed and continued: "I can give you a chance to make a difference."

"Be careful," Tehl whispered in her ear. "You're playing a game you don't know the rules to."

She blinked and ignored him, watching the man who held her future in his hands, and quite possibly, the future of her kingdom.

"Do you really think you can erase hundreds of years of bad blood and animosity?"

She chose her words carefully. "No. As much as I would like to say that prejudice will be a thing of the past, it's not possible. Since the beginning of time, man has found a way to label each other, and then judge those labels. There have always been divisions, and there always will be."

"So, what are you saying?"

She stared straight into his handsome face. "I'm saying that I can't change the past, but we can change the future. Together," she added.

His head cocked. "Together?"

"Together."

She flinched when, in a single fluid motion, he stood and leaned toward her, the ends of his hair tickling her cheeks.

"I accept your proposal, my lady."

Her eyes were huge when he kissed each of her cheeks. He smiled at her reaction, his white teeth flashing.

"In Scythia, we seal a deal with a kiss."

She pursed her lips.

"Once you do this, there's no going back," Tehl warned in her ear.

Sage leaned closer, not losing eye contact, and kissed one cheek, then the other.

"It is done," he whispered, his breath washing over her face.

"It's done," she repeated.

For better or worse, she'd just made a deal with the warlord of Scythia.

FOURTEEN

SAGE

"YOU'RE GOING TO SLEEP THE day away, Sage. Get up."

She yawned and ignored Tehl's voice, snuggling into the bed. When was the last time she'd slept in?

"Remember whose bed you're sleeping in. How are you so sure he won't come and join you?"

A tingle ran up her spine and she stiffened. She wasn't so sure, but the warlord had yet to try anything. "I don't believe the warlord will harm me," she muttered. "He wants peace, I can tell. Now go away."

A voice as smooth as whiskey washed over her. "Now, that's just rude."

Sage jerked up, slipping her dagger from beneath her pillow, gritting her teeth as her whole body screamed with the unexpected move. She blinked repeatedly, her eyes still not focusing right, and frowned at the warlord sitting beside her bed.

"What are you doing here?" Her tone was a little harsh, but this was the second time in a handful of hours he'd shown up in her room, silent as a wraith.

Zane blinked at the dagger and sniggered. "I think that was the weakest threat I've ever received."

A grimace pulled her lips down as she glared at her shaking hand.

"Put your dagger down, wild one." He stifled his smile when she turned her glare on him. "Sorry," he said, not sounding sorry at all.

"I'm sure," she muttered.

"Who were you speaking to?" he asked, changing the subject.

"No one," she responded automatically. How much had he heard of her conversation with Tehl?

"It didn't sound like no one."

"It was a dream." That was partially true. She hadn't been dreaming, but Tehl certainly was not real.

The warlord cocked a brow. "You're lying."

She kept her face impassive. "No, I'm not. My husband can tell you I talk in my sleep."

He shifted his hulking figure in the small chair and steepled his fingers. "Sometimes, when someone suffers a traumatic event in their lives, they experience certain things that are not healthy. These can be nightmares, flashbacks, being on edge, paranoia, and hallucinations. These things happen when your mind can't handle what you experienced. Sometimes, your mind will block those memories to protect itself. I've seen it with my men." A pause. "Blair reported to me what your journey was like."

She pulled her gaze away from his knowing eyes and stared instead at the wall over his shoulder. She'd do anything to lock away her memories of Rhys.

"I've also seen your scars. All of them."

Her spine straightened. "Excuse me? What do you mean, 'all of them'?"

He ignored her question. "I have someone I want you to speak with."

She rubbed at her head. It was like he was speaking another language. "What do you want from me? Speak plainly."

"I want a healer to assess you."

"Why? What are you looking for?" she asked.

"Nothing. He is going to speak with you. That's all."

"That's it? He won't touch me?"

The warlord stood. "He won't touch you. In fact, he's waiting right outside. May I send him in?"

She blinked. The warlord had asked. He hadn't demanded or done what he wanted. He'd asked.

"I guess that's okay."

He smiled at her and nodded to the cup next to the bed. "Drink your broth."

She reached out and took a sip from the mug.

Satisfied, he strode to the door and whispered something to someone out of sight before an extremely tall man entered. It was almost an impossible task for Sage to keep her mouth from hanging open. His white hair shone like a beacon in the dim light. She sucked in a sharp breath as his magenta eyes met hers.

A Sirenidae.

"This is Ezra," the warlord said. "He will visit you every day from now on." He cast a glance at her and walked backward toward the door. "I'll visit you later in the day, and Maeve will be by to help you bathe."

Sage nodded, noting the warlord's departure, but refusing to take her eyes from the man now staring at her. He moved to a divan at the end of the bed and sat down, just observing. Her gaze darted to the door and back to him. She wet her lips, not sure what she should say.

"It's a pleasure to meet you."

His eyes tilted up at the corners when he smiled, making him even more handsome, if that were possible. She patted at her hair, self-conscious of her state of dress.

"It's a pleasure to meet you, too, Sage. But that's not what you were going to say, was it?" He arched a brow.

"You have unique eyes," she said slowly, gauging his reaction.

His head tipped to the side as he studied her. "You know what I am. Intriguing. So, you've been in the company of a Sirenidae before. Well, a story for another day, I'm sure."

She blinked. She didn't expect him to be so candid about it. "How did you come to be here?"

He waved a hand at her. "My story is short and boring, but I would very much like to learn about you."

Immediately, she was on guard. What information was he after? "My name is Sage Blackwell, and I'm the daughter of a swordsmith."

"A humble beginning."

"A perfect beginning," she corrected.

"Indeed. There's nothing better than being raised in the country with a family who loves you."

The affection in his tone bespoke of a similar life.

"You speak from experience."

Ezra smiled softly. "You're now a princess. Why did you leave your happy home?"

"Because it was the right thing to do." Her generic answer.

"That's a large burden for you to bear."

"It had to be done."

"But surely someone would have stepped up to protect the kingdom?"

She shrugged. "Maybe, but how could I take that chance with so many lives on the line?"

"You protected them."

Glancing down in her mug, she swirled the dark broth. "It's my duty to, if I'm able."

"Who protects you?"

"What?" She frowned at the Sirenidae.

"You heard me. Who protects you? Who has shielded you, when you could not shield yourself?"

Her eyes dipped toward Tehl, now sitting in the chair next to her, his face serious.

"My family."

Ezra nodded. "True, but that's not who you see." He jerked his chin toward the chair. "Who are you seeing?"

She startled, and her lips thinned. "No one."

He held her gaze, his face stern. "Do you know what happens when we push our minds too far?"

She stayed silent. He would tell her whether she wanted to hear it or not.

"They break, and there's no coming back." He paused, his face a mask of seriousness. "If you indulge your hallucinations, your mind will fracture. Can you honestly tell me you could rule a kingdom and protect your people with a fractured mind?"

Marq flashed through her mind. "No," she replied honestly.

"Then you need to let your hallucinations go. Don't encourage them, and don't speak to them." He stood from the couch and bowed to her. "I wish you a speedy recovery." His long legs quickly ate up the distance to the door and he disappeared, the door clicking shut quietly behind him. He was gone as quick as he came.

"He's right, you know," she murmured, not looking in Tehl's direction. It was unhealthy to indulge her hallucinations.

"I know, but you can't wish me away just like that," Tehl said, his tone solemn. "I'm part of you."

"It doesn't matter. I have to," she whispered to the empty room.

FİFTEEN

SAGE

TEHL DIDN'T DISAPPEAR. HE WAS stubborn, that one. He still spoke to her, but now she ignored him.

The Sirenidae had made a good point that first day they'd met. She wanted a healthy mind, and a future. If she kept going the direction she was, she'd end up like Marq, broken and half crazy, hurting the people around her.

Each day came easier, and slowly she settled into a routine. Ezra would visit her in the morning for a brief time. Sometimes they would talk, other times they would sit in comfortable silence. Each day, she grew a little stronger. The warlord always made sure to help her walk, and let a little more light in each day, so her eyes would continue to adjust. It was frustrating to be cooped up in the room, though. She wanted to explore, to get to know the people here.

Maeve's visits, though, slowed to a trickle and eventually stopped. When she asked about the woman, the warlord joked, "Am I not enough?" and that was that.

Days went by, each of them like a dream. She didn't really have a perception of time or even reality anymore. So, one day she shared this with Ezra.

"Do you ever feel like your life is one big dream?"

He set his cup down and watched her in his gentle way. "How so?"

"Like you're not sure what's real. Like the world is moving around you, but you can't see it. You just have a vague feeling that things are changing."

"You feel disconnected."

"Exactly. I'm stuck here in this bed with no way of knowing what is going on. I can barely walk. I'm so frustrated I could pull my hair out. I long to see the sun." She sighed. "I miss my home. Do you understand that? Everything I do seems empty. The only joys I have are when you and Zane visit."

Ezra jerked. "Zane?"

She blushed. "He gave me leave to use his name."

"I see. He's a good friend to you."

Was he her friend? Sage smiled. "He is."

"The warlord has sacrificed much for you. I hope you realize what an honor it is to be held in such esteem."

"You mean because I'm not Scythian?"

"Yes. There's a reason only myself and the warlord visit you. There have been many attempts on your life. We've managed to thwart all of them, but it's been a bloodbath since you arrived." He smiled and shrugged a shoulder at her horror. "The things we do for peace, right? And the ones we care about," he tacked on.

"It's worth it."

"Indeed. Now…" He slapped his hands against his thighs. "Would you like to take a turn about your room?"

Her body was riddled with fatigue, but she wouldn't turn away a chance to move. She hated being stuck in the bed. "Yes, please."

She'd lost some of her self-consciousness over the last few weeks. It wasn't ideal to rely on someone else, but Ezra and Zane had been extremely gracious about assisting her.

She peeked up at the Sirenidae as he helped her from the bed. "We've been speaking for some time now, and I still don't know much about you. How did you come to be here?" she asked.

He stiffened for a moment before continuing their shuffle around the room. "My family was taken from me, and the warlord offered me a chance to help others, so I took it."

"I'm so sorry about your family." Losing her own family, even if temporarily, was extremely painful.

His gaze intensified as he looked down at her.

Was there something on her face? She lifted a brow in question.

He smiled at her and tightened his grip on her waist. "Sage, you're a special girl. I'm sorry for the tragedy in your life."

She nodded, accepting his sympathy, and they both fell into silence, finishing their walk. Ezra helped her into bed and left her with a small bow, his shoulders stiff. When he closed the door, she wanted to slap herself, and, to her horror, cry. Obviously, bringing up his family had been a mistake, and she hoped desperately that it wouldn't ruin their new friendship. She was short on friends these days.

The warm water lapped at her skin, relaxing her. Sage had come to love the hexagonal bathing pool. It was a luxury to be able to swim and bathe at the same time. A smile turned her lips up. Maybe she could convince Tehl to install one.

"Sage, wake up."

Speak of the devil. She kept her eyes closed and ignored him while attempting to float in the pool.

"Woman, listen to me. You're not alone."

She smoothed her arms along the water. *He's not real, Sage. Ignore him.*

"You're going to die."

Her eyes snapped open, her gaze seeking Tehl. Sage sputtered, flailing in the water, and wrapped her arms around her breasts.

Ezra knelt beside the pool, his face looking infinitely sad as he leaned toward her.

"Wh-what are you doing here?" she screeched, blinking water out of her eyes. "Get out!"

He dipped his finger into the water and drew a pattern. "You're too good for our world, Sage. You shouldn't be here."

She took a tiny step away from him. Something in his voice was off. It sounded as if someone had died. "Thank you. If you give me a moment, I'll get dressed and come out to you."

His lips tipped up, but he didn't look up from his water drawings. "Do you remember when we spoke of peace?"

Chills erupted along her arms. Something wasn't right. Why was he bringing that up now? She glided back another step, eying the stairs that led out of the pool. She darted a look to the open door. No guards. Could she make it out of the pool to the outer door? Unlikely.

"Yes," she said, slowly twisting toward the Sirenidae. She jerked when her gaze clashed with his.

"I want to give you peace," he whispered, and something akin to determination altered his expression. "I'm going to help you end your suffering."

She balked and opened her mouth to scream, but he lunged. Water closed around her face as he shoved her under. What the bloody hell? Her feet touched the bottom, and she propelled herself to the surface.

Gasping for air, she pushed toward the stairs, panic building in her breast. All she needed to do was make it to the stairs. Her foot landed on one stair, then two, and then three. Hope blossomed. Maybe she would make it.

A shriek flew out of her as a hand grabbed her ankle. Her palms slammed against the stone, and her chin cracked against the step's edge, clicking her teeth together. Dark spots dotted her vision, and the room swirled. She dug her fingers into the stone as she was pulled back, and kicked at his hand.

"Let. GO!"

He jerked harder, and her nails broke, her hands slipping. She sucked in another breath and screamed, the sound piercing the air, and echoing around the empty room.

She scrambled forward when the hand released her ankle, but she didn't make it far. Ezra's arm wrapped around her torso, and his hand slapped across her mouth, cutting off her screams. He towed her back into the pool kicking and screaming.

"Don't do this," she pleaded from behind his hand.

"I'm sorry…" His voice broke. "I have to save you from him. I won't let you be used. You deserve peace after everything you've suffered. I'm going to grant you at least that."

Her eyes widened. He was really going to do it. Ezra was going to drown her.

She pulled in a deep breath through her nose when he kissed the top of her head and pulled her under. All sound disappeared except for Ezra's soft humming. She struggled against him, bit at his hand, raked her broken nails down his arms. But he didn't budge. Panic filled her as her lungs burned, begging for air. She flung her head back and crashed it into his face in a blind panic. She needed air. Now. But even that didn't help. It earned her a hand around her throat.

Unable to hold her breath any longer, she sucked in a breath and choked. Her body spasmed at the invasion in her lungs. It burned. Stories said drowning was peaceful, but those were lies. Her body seized, trying to get rid of the fluid. She tried to claw her way to air, the surface of the pool just above her, taunting her. She gazed at her hair floating around the pool, and closed her eyes. This was how she would die.

Suddenly, something slammed into her, breaking the vise around her torso and throat. She was free. She tried to swim, to move, to do anything, but her body wouldn't obey. How unfair. Freedom was just an arm's reach away, and yet she would still drown.

Something smashed into her chest and pain radiated into her ribs. Why did she have to feel pain? Why couldn't she go in peace? It hammered into her chest, and she choked out water, coughing. She tried to breathe, but all she did was spew water. Sage gasped, gagged, and coughed. God, it was painful. She cracked open her eyes to find Scythian warriors dragging Ezra away. Her ears were ringing, so she couldn't hear what he was screaming, but she caught the last words on his lips before she puked up more water: "Don't drink it!"

She shook her head and panted, staring in shock at Ezra.

His wild magenta gaze latched onto hers. "He'll be the end of you. You're just a pawn. Don't trust—"

Zane lunged from behind her, and, in a move too quick to follow, slammed his fist into Ezra's face, rendering him unconscious. Her muscles locked up at his speed. She stared, wide-eyed, at the warlord's wet, heaving back. *Inhuman.*

She squeezed her eyes shut as another bout of coughing racked her body. A hand soothed down her back as she expelled the rest of the water and collapsed on the floor. Her body trembled, her cheek pressed to the tile. Ezra had tried to kill her. She'd almost died. She shuddered at the thought, and vaguely noticed someone draping a towel around her. She forced her eyes to open.

Zane leaned over her, rage and worry battling for dominance of his features. His hand cupped her cheek, his thumb running along her cheekbone.

"Wild one, are you okay?"

Her gaze wavered as tears filled her eyes. "No. No, I'm not. He tried to kill me. Why?" she cried. "Why, Zane? Ezra was my friend. I don't understand."

"I don't know," he murmured, brushing the tears from her face. "I don't know."

She hiccupped and cried harder, snot mingling with her tears. "I-I-I just don't understand."

"People do things beyond reason all the time."

Zane slipped his arms around her wet body and carried her to the bed. He tucked her in, then snuggled behind her, one arm draping over her waist. That small act of comfort broke her. She sobbed and clutched his hand while the shock and betrayal ran torrents of tears down her face. "He was my friend…"

"I know, love. I know."

She cried until there was nothing left, exhaustion immediately claiming her.

Sage blinked her eyes open, and for one blessed moment, she felt peace, until memories of the prior day slammed into her. She sat up and swung her legs to the side of the bed, and placed her head in her hands. Maybe if she squeezed her head hard enough, she could erase the memories. She pulled in a shuddering breath and lifted her head, staring sightlessly at the wall across from her. What had possessed Ezra to attack her? She thought they were friends. Had she been blind to his true feelings the entire time? She shook her head and blew out the breath she was holding. Sometimes, people were impossible to understand.

Her stomach pinched, reminding her that she hadn't eaten or used the bathroom. Sage pushed her tangled hair from her face and stood on wobbly legs. She frowned. When would her strength return? She hated being weak. She rolled her shoulders back and carefully made her way to the vanity, plucking the long linen shirt from the top and continuing into the bathing room.

Her skin prickled uncomfortably when she entered the room. Sage kept her focus on the doorway to the chamber pot. She quickly relieved herself and tugged off the old shirt, each move stiff and painful. She winced when she lifted her arms above her head to slip on the new one that Zane had left. She blinked, her pain forgotten for the moment. When did she start thinking of him as *Zane* and not the warlord? Her brows slanted downward as she stared at the swirling stone tiles beneath her bare feet. She couldn't pinpoint when it changed, just that it had. Her heartbeat quickened at the thought. What else had changed that she hadn't noticed.

She shook her head and smoothed her hands down the shirt in an attempt to calm herself. Change was a part of life, and it wasn't something to be afraid of. Her fists clenched in her shirt when her eyes snagged on a particularly wicked bruise. God, that was ugly. Her lips thinned as she began to notice all the other cuts and bruises on her legs. She didn't even remember how they'd happened.

Without her permission, her gaze darted to the placid pool. Her breath seized, and her heart pounded in her chest. Her friend tried to kill her. Drown her. Her stomach rebelled, and she dropped painfully onto her bruised shins, heaving over the pot.

She trembled as the heaving subsided, then wiped her mouth with her shirt sleeve. Sage panted as the room tilted around her and warped. Her fingers bit into the chamber pot edge as she fought to control the panic that threatened to swallow her whole. She had to get out of there. On clumsy legs, she clambered to her feet and lurched forward, skirting around the pool as quickly as she could and racing for the door.

She burst into her room, and the fist around her lungs loosened. She couldn't be in there; it made her feel like the walls were closing in on her. Her breath sawed in and out of her chest, and she jumped when she caught the reflection of a girl with wild green eyes. The girl was wild, and on the edge of breaking.

Sage closed her eyes and gulped air. She needed to follow Jasmine's advice and slow her breathing. Each breath was a challenge, but with every breath, her heartbeat slowed a touch. She opened her eyes and stared at the mirror. The girl looking back at her was her, and yet, it wasn't. Cautiously, she approached the mirror and lifted a hand to her cheek. The girl mimicked her. She jerked back, startled. How could she reconcile this strange, frightened creature with herself?

She stepped closer to the mirror and touched the cool surface. It *was* her. She couldn't believe how much she'd changed. Her eyes were a deep green, her skin practically glowing and smooth; even her nose seemed straighter than it had been. Her brow furrowed. That wasn't possible. She ran a finger over her nose and gasped when she couldn't find the little bump from where she'd broken it at nine years old. What was happening to her?

She shrugged her left shoulder out of the linen shirt, and shifted to the side to inspect the giant bruise across the back of her shoulder. God, it was ugly. Purple and green, it just looked angry. The door creaked, but she didn't look away from the mirror. She already knew who it was. Zane's reflection moved across the mirror and paused behind her. She watched him watch her, but it wasn't awkward. His presence brought her a sense of comfort. Despite the horrors of the day before, she wasn't alone.

Zane leaned closer, his eyes staying on hers as he ran a hand down her arm before clasping her hand. "How are you feeling?"

She gave him a forced and lopsided smile. "Like my friend just tried to kill me." She gestured to her shoulder. "And like these stupid cuts and bruises are a reminder of that."

His dark eyes studied her before he leaned over to place a soft kiss on her bare shoulder. "You're strong. Each of these is proof of that. The scars and bruises are beautiful." His heated breath slithered across her skin.

She shivered and stepped forward, unease churning in her belly. "But I'm not flawless," she joked.

His hand tightened on hers, and he bridged the space between them, hugging her from behind. His arms were wrapped around her, and rested his chin on her shoulder. "You may not be a Scythian beauty, but as I've aged, I've come to realize that knowing what's inside a person is just as important as what you see. I've seen beauty which disguises rottenness and depravity, but yours isn't that kind. To me, your beauty is flawless."

Her throat tightened at his words, and the back of her eyes burned. "That's one of the nicest things anyone has ever said to me. Thank you."

"No need to thank me for the truth."

She smiled, and her attention shifted her face. "I've changed."

"You have been through much."

"No..." She gestured to her face. "I mean, yes, but that's not what I was talking about. I mean, I broke my nose when I was nine, and I've always had a bump on the bridge of my nose...but it's gone now. Why?"

His eyes scanned her face. "You were given some of our special herbs to heal the damage to your body. This is just a byproduct of that herb. Are you angry?"

"I'm not sure." And she wasn't. It didn't feel like a violation; it was just strange to look at her own face and see someone slightly different than she was used to. "I don't look like myself."

"Yes, you do. The same luminous green eyes framed with dark lashes, the same heart-shaped face, and the same honey brown hair. You're still you."

When she continued to squint at her reflection, he squeezed her, pulling her attention back to him. "If you hadn't received that herbed broth, you would've died."

"I don't doubt that."

They stood there together, simply staring into the mirror. For how long, she didn't know. It was only when her legs began to tremble with the effort that Zane pulled her away and tucked her back into bed. She stared into his stunning face and reached a hand out to touch his wrist.

"Thank you for saving my life. I feel like I'm continually in your debt."

"There's no debt." He hesitated. "But I will need you to attend the execution."

Bile crept up her throat. "Execution?"

His face hardened. "Ezra attempted to kill you, and he almost succeeded. You are royalty, and you are my friend. He's earned his death."

"But execution? It seems so..."

"Barbaric?" he supplied, his body tense.

She bit her lip and answered carefully. "I don't believe murder is the answer."

"Really? And Rhys?"

She flinched.

"Was his death okay with your moral code?"

"That was different."

"Was it?"

Her lips thinned, and she looked away.

"Things here are not the same as in Aermia, but that does not make our customs wrong. If you're not careful, you'll let your prejudice color your perception of the world. Don't judge people by your own standards without considering theirs, or you will give them leave to do the same with you."

She swallowed but didn't relent. In her mind, this wasn't a matter of prejudice; it was right and wrong.

"Think about what I have said, Sage. Even if you don't agree with it, your presence is needed there. You don't have to watch, but you need to be there, so he can stand trial. I'll not let him go free. This is my right as his ruler. You may be willing to forgive everyone, but you must remember some people don't deserve forgiveness. They deserve judgment." He placed a soft kiss on her cheek. "I'll check on you later. Don't forget to drink your broth. You need your strength. Sweet dreams, wild one."

He began to stand, and Sage looked up into his face and squeezed his hand once. "Thank you, again."

The hard expression on his face softened a touch. "Anything for you."

SIXTEEN

SAGE

SHE GLARED AT THE CURTAINS covering the window, a single sliver of light having escaped through the crack between them, cutting a swath of light across her room. Every part of her longed to throw back the curtains and see what lay beyond, but her hand hovered above the velvet cloth as she wondered, was it worth the risk to her sight? Her eyes had not fully healed yet, and she knew it was dangerous to expose them to too much light until they were. It had been *so* long though, so long since she'd seen anything outside of these walls. Her rooms had become a prison.

Her hand shook, and she clenched it into a fist. Leaning forward, she let her forehead press into the curtain.

No, she thought, *I can't risk it.* She might enjoy the view, but it'd be short-lived and the action could irrevocably affect her future. The dark fabric tickled her face, and the smell of vanilla teased her nose. It smelled like its owner: Zane.

With an angry huff, she pushed from the window and shuffled toward a divan piled high with pillows, her thoughts on the warlord. Zane had been quiet since Ezra's attack on her. He cared for her and was extremely tender, but once his duty was finished, he left rather quickly.

Sage winced as she sat on the couch and got comfortable, tucking her feet up under her. Did he blame her for what happened? Tipping her head back, she stared at the ornate ceiling. She wouldn't blame him if he did. Ezra had been his friend for many years, and now, because of her, he had to execute one of his closest companions.

The door creaked, and she flopped her head to the side. Speaking of the devil, Zane stepped quietly in, pausing when he caught her staring. "I thought you would be asleep."

That comment cut her. Was he sneaking in while he thought she was asleep, so he wouldn't have to deal with her?

"I'm sorry," she whispered.

His dark gaze moved to her face. "For what?"

"For killing your friend."

His hand clenched on the doorknob, and the door groaned. Again, she was reminded that he wasn't like her. More powerful. Stronger. The idea should've frightened her, but it didn't.

He glanced at the door and stepped away, prowling toward her. He grabbed an enormous chair and placed it in front of her as if it weighed nothing. He sat down and studied her face.

"Why do you think you killed that traitor?"

She frowned and looked to the side, avoiding his searching gaze.

"Look at me, Sage."

She stubbornly kept her face turned, giving herself time to rein in her emotions. She was one comment away from crying. A finger touched under her chin.

"Please talk to me."

"It's my fault you have to execute Ezra. If I wasn't here, this wouldn't have happened." She looked back at him. "I'm sorry. I didn't mean to cause trouble."

"You have nothing to apologize for. He was the one to break our trust. He was the one to attack you. You didn't force him to do anything. He made his choices."

"Then why?" she paused. "Why?"

Zane cocked his head. "Why what?"

"Why are you avoiding me?" She blushed at her blurted question and stared at her clenched hands. She sounded like an affection-starved idiot.

His hand reached out and stroked her fingers. "You think I'm avoiding you?"

"It's just that, you've been gone, and you're not speaking…" Her brows furrowed. "You sneak in and out. I assumed it was something I did."

He heaved out a sigh. "It's not you, Sage. I wanted to give you time to process what you've been through. I assumed you would want to be alone, that you wouldn't feel comfortable with me around. You've suffered much from men. That sort of trauma doesn't disappear in days, sometimes not years. I figured you would need time."

Her gaze flew to his. "I don't blame you for any of this, Zane. You're my only friend here. It's been…lonely without anyone to speak to."

His smile was blinding, with just a hint of triumph, and just as attractive as everything else about him. She blinked. Who knew teeth could be so attractive? It was distracting.

"I'll make sure to bother you more often." His smile slipped a bit. "On a more serious note, though, we do need to discuss the execution."

The air flew from her lungs. She pulled her hands from his and smoothed the dressing gown across her thighs. "What about it?"

"Are you prepared?"

She'd had time to think about it over the last few days, and had come to a conclusion. "I'm not going." Sage met Zane's gaze as steadily as she could. "I'm sorry."

"You're going."

She blinked at his stern tone. "Excuse me?"

"I told you four days ago that I need you there."

"You told me to *think* about it," she pointed out. "And I did."

He pursed his lips. "That was more of…'think about it and get used to the idea,' because as I said, you have to be there."

"I don't want to go."

"And I understand that, but there's no other option."

"Murder is wrong," she said.

Something angry flashed through his eyes. "You're right. Murder is wrong. So is *attempted* murder. Did you forget that Ezra tried to kill you? That he tried to take you away?"

Pain, and her lungs burning, and watery silence assaulted her mind. Ezra's betrayal wasn't something she'd soon forget. She traced one of her jagged fingernails with the pad of her finger. "I haven't forgotten."

"Then why are you being so difficult?" Exasperation colored his tone.

"Because something is not right!" She stood on shaking legs and ignored the hand he held out to steady her. "Ezra never acted like that. Not once. Something was wrong with him that day. He was speaking nonsense, and he was so sad." The look on his face still wrenched her heart. She paced the floor, leaning her hand against the wall for balance. "We shouldn't be executing him, but examining him."

"There's nothing wrong with him."

"How?" She spun and walked back to Zane. "How do you know?" she asked, staring at his upturned face.

"Because he was interrogated, and I know crazy." He sighed and pulled her down to sit on the divan. "It was another plot to kill you."

"*No.*" She wilted in her seat.

He squeezed her hand. "Yes. You're different and unwelcome to some of my people. You're a threat. One they will do anything to eliminate. I'm so sorry."

She went numb. "This was his plan all along? Ezra planned to kill me the entire time?"

"Our intelligence says yes, this was the plan all along." Zane stood up and then sat next to her. He pulled her into his arms and held her. "I'm sorry, but he was never your friend. He was a spy and a murderer."

Sage stared vacantly at the fur rug beneath their chair. "Murder does not condone murder, though." The arms holding her tightened. She peeked up at Zane from under her lashes, and her breath caught in her throat. It was as if Rhys was looking down at her with his disturbing, soulless eyes. She blinked, and it was Zane staring at her, lines between his brows.

"Are you alright?"

She shuddered and pulled from his embrace. Zane was nothing like Rhys. She couldn't keep comparing every man she met to him. "I'm fine."

She wasn't. Not even close.

"I'll send a dress for you tomorrow and have the women help you with your bathing. Then, I'll fetch you for the execution." He pressed a kiss to her temple and tipped her chin up. "It will be okay, love. I promise."

It was not okay in the least. Actually, it was awful.

When the women came in to help her bathe, she nearly punched one in the face when they tried to force her into the bathing room. She had been avoiding the bathing room since her attack, and there was no way she was going in there. She had kept the door closed all week with the hope that it would stop the memories from bothering her. It didn't.

After some heated debate, Maeve barged in and ordered a bathing tub to be brought into her room instead. Quickly thereafter, the women got her scrubbed and into her dress. It was a black silk dress that sat off the shoulders and dipped into a low back. A black fur and a leather belt hugged her waist with a sheath for her dagger, and the skirt followed the swell of her hips, which had finally begun to fill out again.

Sage sat on the stool in front of the mirror, staring at herself. The Scythian women hadn't even applied any cosmetics, yet she still barely recognized the woman before her. She pulled her gaze from her own face and looked over her shoulder at Maeve.

"What should we do with my hair?"

What was one supposed to do for an execution? Her stomach cramped.

Maeve frowned and dipped her head. "The warlord has something special planned. I'll take my leave." A shallow bow and she was gone.

She returned her gaze to the strange woman before her. How had she changed so much? Surely, the broth couldn't have changed her this much?

"Lovely," Zane's deep voice purred.

She slowly turned to him. "It seems like too much for…" She swallowed. "An execution."

He sauntered toward her. Part of his hair was braided back from his face, highlighting his sharp cheekbones and strong jaw, and he had an earring made from obsidian and ruby in one ear. She scanned the black shirt, leather pants, and boots he'd donned, noting the numerous daggers strapped in various places on his person. She had to admit, she was impressed. He looked good. Better than good—he looked perfect.

He smiled at her perusal and placed the parcel he carried on her bed.

Stepping behind her, he laid his hands lightly on her shoulders. "Not too much for a consort."

She twisted back around to stare at the mirror. "This feels wrong, like I'm celebrating his death."

"No, it would be a dishonor if we wore rags."

She gestured at her hair and joked, "Well, my hair is enough of a dishonor."

Zane pulled a shiny lock from her shoulder and rubbed it between his fingers. "Nothing this beautiful could ever be a dishonor." He caught her gaze and kissed the lock of hair.

Heat suffused her cheeks. He was always affectionate, but this was something more, something she couldn't give.

She broke the moment and looked away, trying to ignore the way his stare seemed to burn into the top of her head. Sage startled when his fingers wound through her hair. "What are you doing?" she asked, watching him in the mirror.

One side of his mouth quirked up. "Fixing your hair?"

"You?" She arched a brow.

"I had sisters."

"I didn't know." She didn't know much about his family. He kept that to himself, mostly.

"They died a long time ago."

"I'm sorry."

She sensed the conversation was over, so she closed her eyes as his hands worked through her hair. There was nothing better than having someone play with her hair. She stayed quiet and prepared herself for what lay ahead.

Death, that's what lay ahead.

"Open your eyes."

She peeked at the mirror and was pleasantly surprised by what he'd created. Her hair was braided back from each temple, forming ropes, and twined behind her head like a crown. She turned her neck and smiled at how the rest of her hair tumbled down her back. It was simple but beautiful. "Thank you."

His grin reached his almond-shaped eyes when he held a finger up. "That's not all." He turned and opened the parcel and pulled out a crown.

Her eyes widened. Its base was black metal, shaped into roses and thorns. Rubies and obsidians sparkled, catching the light. He settled the heavy crown on her head, and placed his hands on her shoulders.

"Do you like it?"

"It's beautiful, and deadly," she remarked in awe. "But it's too much."

"It's not enough, wild one. I had it made just for you. It shows your two sides."

She swallowed back her emotions and twisted around to peer up into his inky gaze. "It's stunning."

"It's not the crown, it's the wearer."

Warmth infused her at his compliment, but it quickly cooled. She wasn't going to a ball, she was attending an execution. How she looked was inconsequential. Sage dipped her chin. "I'll wear it proudly."

He offered her an arm and she took it, her dress rustling gently as she moved. At Zane's sharp breath, she looked at him with raised brows.

He blatantly eyed her figure, his eyes roving first up and then back down. "Beauty, where you lead, I shall follow."

She tried to figure out what to say to that. "Thank you for the dress and crown," she said lamely. Her breath stuttered when his burning gaze met hers.

His eyelashes lowered, shuttering his eyes. "My pleasure."

Zane swept her from the room and she blinked hard, her eyes watering at the brightness of the hallway. Warriors snapped to attention and bowed deeply as they passed by. Sage tried not to shrink away from their lingering stares.

"They're just curious," Zane said, under his breath. "You're unusual."

She snorted, finding that somewhat amusing, and she felt some of the tension drain from her body. She continued with Zane down what seemed like an endless stone hallway until they finally veered into a luxurious room. She froze when she caught sight of the creatures which came to greet them. Two black felines slunk from their pillows and rubbed against the warlord and herself.

"Breathe," Zane soothed. "They'll not hurt you."

She released her breath, never taking her eyes from the golden-eyed beasts brushing against her. Her hand clenched in her skirt as one pushed its nose up to her fist.

"She only wants a good scratch."

Her fist clenched tighter. Zane moved behind her and smoothed a hand along her arm and down to her fist, prying her hand from her skirt. He entwined their fingers and placed both their hands on the feline's head. A loud rumbling erupted from the beast, making Sage jump.

"She's just happy. She's purring."

Sage pressed her back into his chest and marveled at how soft the feline's coat was. "What are their names?"

"Nege and Nali."

"Beautiful."

Zane pulled his hand from hers, and moved to stand before her. He jerked his chin at the door behind him. "Through that door is my throne." He let that sink in. "Once we leave this room, I'm no longer Zane to you, but 'my lord.' Do you understand?"

"Yes."

He scanned her face. "This is just a formality. Nothing can make me look weak in front of my people. We can't be familiar."

"I understand." It was an execution. It was to be solemn.

"I will prompt you through everything you need to do."

Panic clawed at her throat. "What will I need to do?"

"Nothing much. You'll basically sit next to me the entire time."

"You'll warn me when it's time?"

He stepped closer and ran his fingers along her face. "You won't have to watch. Are you prepared to see him again?"

She swallowed. "Yes."

"You'll be a spectacle to my people. Prepare yourself for the gawking."

She nodded. "I'm ready."

He scrutinized her, and she watched as he slipped into the role of leader. He was a warlord once again. It disturbed her. He looked the same, and yet everything about him was colder. She took his offered elbow, and clenched her dress in her right hand as both felines flanked them. The immense door caused her to shiver.

Beyond it lay a people who hated her and a traitor.

Beyond it lay death.

SEVENTEEN

SAGE

THE DOOR OPENED, AND SHE barely managed to keep a tranquil expression in place. The door led to the warlord's dais, but that wasn't the most disconcerting thing. It was the thousands of eyes upon them. She'd never felt so naked in her entire life.

He led her around his throne to a small, but equally ornate, wooden chair. He guided her to sit, and gasps reverberated through the crowd. Did she do something uncouth? Sage glanced at Zane for assurance. With his back to the crowd, he allowed a ghost of a smile to cross his face, but it quickly disappeared. Her momentary panic faded until he moved over to stand in front his own throne. Then it came surging back.

Suddenly, she was staring at the vast crowd. Every eye was on her, and not in a friendly way. She forced a sense of calmness she didn't feel. She was Sage Blackwell and she had been through much in her lifetime. She could do this.

The warlord stood in front of his throne with Nege and Nali sitting regally on either side of him, looking for all the world like a warrior god who'd come to prey on humanity. "Let it commence."

A door opened, and a group of warriors dragged out Ezra. The crowd booed and threw food. Sage barely kept her mask in place at the sight of him. His pale white skin was covered with dried blood and bruises, his face so swollen he could only crack one of his magenta eyes. It was as though he felt her stare, for his eye found hers and stayed upon her. She was shocked to see neither anger nor sorrow, but pity in his face. Did he pity her? Why?

Her breath hissed out of her, and she opened her mouth to object to Ezra's treatment when she felt Zane's large hand settle over hers. Ezra, too, took note of the action, and his gaze slid to the warlord, his expression so filled with hate that it felt like a punch to her gut. Why did he hate his friend? He was the one who committed a crime.

Something was wrong. What was she missing? She shifted uncomfortably beside the warlord when he pressed closer, and Nali pushed against her skirts, rubbing against her knee. She glanced to the feline and back to Ezra, her heart pounding. None of this felt right.

"How do you plead for the crimes of which you have been accused, Ezra of the Sirenidae?"

Ezra stared straight at the warlord. "Guilty."

She swallowed hard.

"Do you have any last words?"

"No one lives forever. Your time will come." He turned to Sage. "But until then, don't be blind, be smart."

Her brows slanted together. It was a warning, but what was he talking about? And why? "Ezra…" she began.

"Enough," the warlord cut her off. "It's time."

Her throat tightened when Ezra's sad eyes met hers, and he mouthed a single word: *Sorry.*

"Proceed." Zane motioned with a bored gesture to a warrior with a large sword.

The man stepped forward and forced Ezra to his knees.

"This isn't right," Sage whispered.

"She should be the one to end his life," a man piped up from the crowd. "It is our law!"

Others cried out their agreement.

Sage stiffened. *What?*

The warlord stilled, and the room seemed to cool. "You wish to challenge me?"

A behemoth of a man stepped to the front of the crowd and dropped to his knees. "I've no desire to challenge you. The woman is not from here and does not know our laws. If she is to understand what it is to be Scythian, it does not make sense to coddle her, my lord."

"And that is for you to decide?"

The warlord's tone made her want to hide underneath her seat, and, wisely, the man stayed silent and shook his head.

Zane's boot entered her vision, and he lifted her chin with gentle fingers. "I'm inclined to agree with him. It is our custom."

"You would like me to do what, my lord?" she asked calmly.

"In our land, the victim exacts justice for the crime." He released her chin and gestured for her to stand.

Sage stood on wooden legs and placed one hand on Nali's head. Zane held a hand out toward the warrior, who strode to them and knelt, holding the sword up. The warlord plucked it from the warrior's hands and held it out to Sage.

"My lady…"

She stared at it like one would a poisonous snake. Did he expect her to pick up the sword and cut Ezra down? He knew her better than that. But when she looked into his black gaze, it held no friendship, no emotion, and it eerily reminded her of the look she often saw in Rhys' eyes. But it had to be her imagination; they weren't at all alike…were they? She shuddered at the idea, but her thoughts were interrupted when Zane prompted her, "Take it, my lady."

With trembling fingers, she carefully pulled the large sword from his hands, but much to her surprise, it took everything she had to keep the sword steady in her hands. She gritted her teeth. How had she lost so much strength in such a little time? A babe was no doubt stronger than she!

Zane swept his arm out, pulling her attention back to him. "After you."

Her legs weak, she barely managed not to stumble as she approached Ezra, halting before him with the large sword swaying slightly, as her arms strained. The Sirenidae was a shadow of what he used to be. As he looked up, his eyes seemed to plead with her, but she hadn't a clue what for.

Zane raised his voice above the din of the crowd. "As our laws command, it will be done."

Sage's jaw clenched. She couldn't do this. It was wrong.

"I can't do this."

"You have to," the warlord whispered in her ear, his warm breath tickling her neck.

Her stomach rolled. "You misunderstand me. When I say I can't, I mean I won't."

"You must, Sage. You have no other choice. This is the first step to securing peace, to prevent *more* death. This is why the crown prince wants you here, for us to work together. To do that, my people need to accept you and see that you understand them. We need them to see that we are not so different as they think."

But they *were* different, she and Zane. She'd never executed a man, nor forced someone to watch their friend die. It was unthinkable to her, yet here Zane was, calmly demanding she do so. Was one man's life worth the countless deaths of others if she refused? Was her taking of Ezra's life worth a chance at peace?

She stared at Ezra kneeling before her. Tears burned at the back of her eyes, but she wouldn't let them fall. Now was not the time for tears. She hefted the sword and held it to Ezra's neck, wavering slightly. None of this was right. She didn't know why Ezra had done what he'd done, but she was sure he was not so terrible he deserved the death to which he'd been sentenced. Yet could she really let this chance to end hundreds of years of hate and prejudice pass by, merely because of her personal feelings?

"Do it quickly. Right at the base of the throat. He won't experience any pain that way," the warlord coaxed her. "The worst is almost over."

A tear fell from her eye and rolled down her cheek. The worst is almost over? What a ridiculous statement. She'd be tormented with the memory and guilt of this long after this single moment, and she would deserve that torment. This was wrong. Was there a way to escape this choice without inciting a riot—or worse, a war?

"It's okay, Sage," Ezra whispered. He leaned closer to the blade, the sword kissing his neck, his eyes understanding, his voice forgiving. "It's okay."

It was his forgiveness which undid her.

She simply would not do something which violated her moral code, and it was wrong of him to try to force her. She would do her utmost to secure peace, but not at the price the warlord was asking. The cost was too great.

Peace gained by murder was no peace and she would not give up another part of herself to appease someone else.

Throwing her shoulders back, she stood taller and smiled at Ezra. "I'll not do it," she said loud enough only for Zane and Ezra to hear.

Her brows furrowed as her words wrought a range of emotions skittering across Ezra's face, which she found difficult to interpret, but very quickly, they disappeared. His eyes met hers and she was surprised to see a determined look in them. She had just begun to pull away the sword when the Sirenidae did something that would haunt her until she died; he smiled sadly and brought himself down onto her blade.

A cry stuck in her throat. She was paralyzed as he fell to the ground, crimson staining the white floor. Numbly, she let go the sword, allowing it to fall from her fingers and clatter to the stone floor.

"No," she breathed. She tried to drop to her knees to help him somehow, but a large hand kept her from doing so. "No!"

"Calm yourself before you ruin everything," Zane commanded, steel in his voice.

The Sirenidae writhed for a moment, then stilled. He was there one moment and gone the next. A dull roar filled her ears, and her knees threatened to buckle.

"Look away."

For the life of her, she wanted to, but she couldn't. The world took on a dream-like quality, and everything blurred around the edges.

He'd killed himself. Her chest heaved. Ezra had taken his own life.

"*Why?*" she whispered. Why would he do such a thing? She lifted her hands and stared at her shaking palms. What had she done?

Vaguely, she was aware of Zane leading her from Ezra's body and toward the dais. She craned her neck and watched as the warriors collected the Sirenidae's limp form. It wasn't right. He should have still been there.

"You've done well, love. You've secured peace."

She slowly spun to the warlord, his praise turning her heart cold. "If it was done, it was by no action of mine," she replied woodenly.

"But the people believe it was, and that's all that matters." He smiled.

Sage looked past him to the Scythian crowd and realized that the thundering in her ears was actually cheering. Bile burned the back of her throat. How could they be *applauding* death? It was disgusting. Somehow, she ended up on her chair next to the warlord's throne. She blinked at how Zane's olive hand held her creamy one. Both different, but both stained by death. Chills erupted over her arms, but she didn't bother to rub at them. The sea of celebrating people warped into swirling colors, Ezra's beautiful magenta eye blank at the forefront of her mind.

A tug on her hand turned her attention to the man at her side. Zane gave her a searching look. "I'm sorry."

A seed of bitterness took root at the empty words. Sorry? Well, so was she. He stood and guided her from her seat and down a few steps to a table piled high with all types of food. She simply stared. The aromas, normally enticing, upset her stomach even more.

"We're to eat?" she asked, incredulous.

The warlord glanced at her. "It is our custom," he said sharply.

They expected her to eat after...

She pulled a breath through her nose and pressed her lips into a firm line, hoping it would prevent her from vomiting all over the table. Zane placed her in a seat and took the one beside her. What she assumed was the warlord's inner circle surrounded them and took their places at the table. People in power always surrounded themselves with other powerful people.

The warlord gave some sort of speech, but Sage tuned it out, thwarting each of his subsequent attempts to pull her into his conversation. She couldn't focus her own scattered thoughts, let alone carry on a conversation, most especially during this barbaric and morbid celebration.

Relief filled her when the feasting finally seemed to consume most everyone's attention. The questions and blatant stares decreased as they focused on the bounty of food. She scanned the table and paused when she met a familiar gaze. Blair. He looked much the same as when she'd last seen him except that tiny wrinkles appeared between his brows when his dark eyes met hers.

She stared back, blankly, before noticing the woman in the seat next to him. The shock of red, curly hair pulled Sage out of her dream-like state. Hazel eyes peeked out from a freckled face as the woman arched a brow at her. Sage blinked, but continued staring. The woman wasn't Scythian.

Her round cheeks and soft pink lips lent her an air of youth, but the fine lines bracketing her eyes betrayed her age. The woman pushed back from the table and placed a hand on her belly. Sage glanced down to the redhead's belly. A very pregnant belly. Sage's stomach soured even further. A pregnant woman came to an execution. Did the redhead have a choice? Or had she been conned into attending as well?

The woman's other brow accompanied the first as she placed her fork down. Some of Sage's disgust must have been apparent. She wiped all expression off her face and ignored the woman's questioning gaze.

Sage's forehead wrinkled as something occurred to her. The only women present besides herself seemed to all be in some stage of pregnancy. Odd. She shifted in her chair and picked at the food the warlord had placed on her plate. Was that too some sort of strange custom? Community birth planning? A snort escaped her.

"My lady?"

Sage tried to keep her thoughts from showing on her face when she glanced at the speaker, a beautiful Scythian woman with a headful of raven braids. "Yes?"

"When are you due?"

"Due?" She searched the Scythian's face. What did she mean?

"When is the child due?"

Child? The idea was so out of place, it struck her as hysterical. She laughed aloud and shook her head. "I'm not with child." At her words everyone at the table stilled and quieted, their eyes moving from her to a spot behind her. Did she say something wrong?

An arm slid across her shoulders, Zane's cedar scent tickled her nose. "It's much too early to be speaking of children. You've barely met her." The censure in his voice was clear.

The Scythian woman blanched and stared down at her plate. "Forgive me."

"There's nothing to forgive," Sage said with as much feeling as she could manage. The Scythian woman gave her a weak smile and picked at her food, while her warrior husband was stiff, his eyes glaring at his wife. Again, odd. Why would he be angry about a simple question?

She thought dinner would be the end of it, that she'd be able to flee to her room and grieve, but boy was she wrong. Drinking and desserts followed, and as each hour passed, it became more unbearable. All she wanted to do was escape, to mourn the loss of her friend. Maybe scream and throw things a bit. The surrounding depravity sickened her. These people were celebrating like this had been the grandest of events and not an execution. It was as if his death fazed them not at all. She swallowed thickly and sipped water from her cup, trying to ignore the gruesome commentary on Ezra's death that was currently taking place at her table.

A heavy furry head landed in her lap, and she did her best not to jump. Sage looked down to find large golden eyes peeking up at her. She set down her cup and slipped a hand underneath the table, praying the beast wouldn't bite it off as she scratched Nali's soft ears. The big cat let out a rumbling purr, but none of the revelers reacted.

They were most likely too deep into their cups. Disgusting.

"She likes you," Zane murmured into her ear.

Sage ignored his proximity and continued to pet the beast, tucking her thoughts away. "She's beautiful."

"She is," he breathed the words against her skin.

His nose skimmed her jawline and then something wet touched the lobe of her ear. Sage jerked away and gaped at the warlord. "What are you doing?" she demanded, her hand sinking into Nali's fur.

His smile was lazy. "Tasting what's mine."

She stiffened and then leaned closer to stare into his eyes. Zane misunderstood the action, and leaned in even closer, triumph lurking in his eyes. Sage placed a hand on his chest. "Are you drunk?" she asked, infusing her voice with as much disdain as possible.

"Not at all," he scoffed, plucking her other hand from the arm of her chair and nipping at one of her fingers.

She yanked back her hand and closed it into a fist. She glared at her fist for a moment, seriously considering punching him. He caught the gesture and something akin to anticipation crossed his face. Her nose wrinkled. He was drunk.

"I'm leaving."

His hand snaked out and clutched her skirts. "You're needed here."

Leaning forward, she whispered in his ear, conscious of the advanced hearing of the others. "I am not needed. This display of celebration over a man's death is disgusting. I've done what you've asked me."

"He wasn't a man. He was Sirenidae."

He said it so matter-of-factly that she almost missed it. The prejudice. The hate for Ezra's race. She pulled back and searched his face, his eyes confirming what she suspected.

"You actually believe that? That Ezra wasn't a man because he was Sirenidae?"

A shrug and a haughty look was all the answer she received. She waited for some sort of emotion to bubble up inside her at his response, but there was nothing. Apparently, everything inside her was numb. Sage tugged at her skirts in his hand and then touched his fist when he didn't release them.

"I'm done. Let go."

He just stared at her.

"Allow me to leave, or I'll make a scene," she hissed, and she meant every word. She'd create a scene so fantastic that it would go down in Scythian history.

His black eyes traveled to her face, then he nodded. "Goodnight." His fist released the crumpled silk of her skirt, dismissing her like a servant.

If he thought to humiliate her, she didn't care in the slightest. She'd endured much worse and she was much too numb to care anyway. All eyes moved to her when she scooted her chair back and stood. "Goodnight..." She dipped her chin and spun on her heel, her black silk dress flaring with her every stride.

The thrones loomed before her, seeming to grow with every step she climbed up the white stone dais. She skirted around the thrones and moved to the door behind them. Her hand paused on the handle as she took one more look at where Ezra had died. It was pristine, the shiny white stone glaring at her, showing no evidence of what had happened earlier. It was wrong. Like they had wiped away the crime. Like it didn't exist. The air in the room seemed to evaporate the longer she stood staring.

Hurrying through the door, Sage almost closed it on her feline shadow. Nali slunk through the door behind her and traipsed out into the hall. Using her memory, Sage navigated the hallways, not surprised when warriors materialized and followed her. Sage glanced down a side hallway and skidded to a stop, not believing her eyes.

"Jas?" She blinked, and the hallway was empty. Her heart pounding hard in her chest she stared at the empty space. She could have sworn she'd seen her friend standing in the hallway. Oh no. Would she start hallucinating Jasmine, too?

She shook herself and spared the silent guards a glance before continuing on. The sadness and anger she'd been waiting for crashed into her, and she gasped at the force of it. She picked up her speed and shoved the emotions down for the moment. There was no way she would cry in front of the warriors. They turned a corner and her door came into view. She hustled through, slammed it in the warriors' faces, and placed her back against it. Her chest heaved, and angry tears spilled onto her cheeks. Everything was so muddled. The Scythians' display was barbaric and revolting, and yet she'd been forced to participate. What kind of person did that make her?

She pushed through her door and Nali jumped onto her bed, circling a few times before snuggling down, but Sage could not lay down. The emotions coursing through her had her feeling on edge and she began pacing the room. She ran a hand through her own hair and winced when one of the crown's metal thorns pricked her finger. She'd forgotten it was there. She glanced to the mirror and examined her reflection. She was shocked to realize she looked like a queen, but not an Aermian queen—the enemy's queen. She stormed up to the vanity and placed her hands on it, staring into her reflection.

"Who are you?" she asked herself. "What are you doing?"

"You're surviving," Tehl answered from her side.

Sage stared at him. His visits had become less frequent ever since she'd stopped speaking with him over the last couple weeks. "Am I really?" She returned her attention to the face in the mirror. Was she doing what she had to in order to survive, or merely following along because it was easier than fighting?

"You're being hard on yourself and it's partly because you lost someone today. Your legs are shaking so hard, I'm not even sure how you're still standing."

Now that he mentioned it, she realized her legs were shaking and she was on the verge of collapsing. She let out a scream of frustration. "Why am I so weak? I should be healing, or healed!"

"I don't know."

The crown glinted in the low light; it seemed to taunt her the longer she looked at it atop her head. In a fit unlike her, Sage yanked the obsidian crown from her head, along with a few hairs, and lobbed it across the room.

"Do you feel better?" Tehl asked drolly. "Anger won't help, you know. It'll make you vulnerable and prone to mistakes."

He was right.

A deranged chuckle burst from her. "Tehl, you're not even here and you're right. It's uncanny and it's unfair." She dropped her chin to her chest and glared at her clothes. It sickened her to have anything Scythian touching her skin.

"The dress is beautiful," he said. "Keep in mind, though, men generally only have dresses made for women they feel belong to them."

She bit her lip. It was time to stop talking to her hallucinations. It was dumb to keep lapsing. "I can't speak to you, Tehl." She glanced at him. "I appreciate that you helped me survive, but you're not real, and it's unhealthy to speak to you."

His face was serious, watching her. "I know, Sage. But I'll be here when you need me."

She turned from him and stepped toward the bathing room. Her feet stumbled, and her hands clenched as memories assaulted her of her drowning. Her eyes turned to slits. She'd let fear rule her too much as it was. It was time to fight. Her fear ended now.

EIGHTEEN

SAGE

SHE WAS PROUD OF HERSELF. At least one positive thing had happened in this nightmarish day. She had changed and washed the cosmetics from her face in that cursed room; she'd never taken her eyes from the pool, and her heart was still pounding from it, but still, she'd done it.

Sage knotted her dressing robe over her body, still feeling naked. The lack of underclothes was something she just couldn't get used to. It made her vulnerable and she hated it. Her eyes wandered over to where the crown lay on the floor. It was beautiful and skillfully made, but she could hardly bear to look at it, as it brought gruesome memories to the forefront of her mind. Its beauty would be forever tainted by the stain of death.

Quickly, she plucked it from the rug and returned it to its box. She then placed it by the door with the black dress neatly folded atop it. They were beautiful, to be sure, but she could not bear to keep them.

She moved to the end of the bed and leaned a hip against it, eyeing the enormous ball of fur occupying that space. "Where am I to sleep?" she asked Nali. "You take up the whole bed." She wanted nothing more than to crawl under the covers and sleep.

Nali cracked an eye before slowly stretching out onto her back, her belly up. Sage's hand flew to her mouth as she gasped. Nali's belly was crisscrossed with silver scars. "Oh my, you poor thing. What *happened* to you?" Who had done this to her?

Carefully, Sage placed her hand in front of Nali, waiting to see how the beast would respond. The feline's ears flicked to the side and she sniffed Sage's fingers and bumped them with her nose. Sage smiled and scratched under Nali's chin, feeling a sense of kinship with the powerful creature.

"You and I are the same, it seems; both of us scarred. What a pair we make. I have to admit, I didn't think we'd be friends. I was sure you were going to eat me." Sage laughed to herself, and Nali let out a little chuff when Sage slowed her scratching. Her door swung open and she dropped her hand to her lap, any sense of peace evaporating through the doorway. Sage felt like a cat with her hackles raised; there were so many things she wanted to say to Zane, the fury and confusion from earlier welling back up inside her. But who would she receive, Zane or the warlord? She gasped when he came straight to her and pulled her off the bed and to him, his arms encircling her waist. She stood frozen as he buried his face into her neck and hair.

"I'm *so* sorry, Sage. This was never meant to happen. What a hellish day."

Sage remained stiff in his arms. "You're right, today was a day from hell."

He pulled back and clasped both of her cheeks, his gaze darting over her face. "You're angry?" It was a question.

She shook off his hands and shoved at his chest, though she couldn't even move him an inch. "You lied to me," she accused. It wasn't as eloquent as what she'd been rehearsing in her head, but it was a start.

He sighed heavily. "I did not lie to you."

"You *said* I wouldn't have to watch! That all I would have to do was sit by your side and it would be over." She stepped away from him and pointed a finger in his direction. "How could you subject me to that? You knew how I felt about the execution already, and yet, at the behest of your people, you forced me not only to watch, but *participate!*"

"What did you expect me to do? Cave to you in front of my kingdom? That would've made me appear both weak and inept as a ruler. Doing so would have been dangerous, not just for you but for me as well!"

"Are you serious?" she yelled. "Standing up for what is right is not weak!"

"How was it wrong? It was all according to law."

"But it's barbaric!"

His face turned to stone. "And what of Aermia's hangings?"

"We don't personally have to hang them ourselves."

"Well, maybe you should," he retorted, "Perhaps you'd consider it more carefully, then."

She tugged on her braids, realizing he had a point. She'd never been comfortable with that particular aspect of her government, but that was not the whole of it. "It wasn't only the manner of execution – it was your reaction. You practically held a festival!"

"Be reasonable here. There's one less murderer in the world. Shouldn't that be cause for at least *some* rejoicing?"

Sage gaped at him. "He wasn't a murderer, and you know it. He was sick. He attacked *me* and yet, I saw it plain as day. His attack made no sense. But, that aside, even if he was just a murderous person, his life was still precious." She narrowed her eyes at him. "Death should never be celebrated."

Zane held his hands out placatingly. "I know you're having a hard time accepting what happened and that's natural. You've been through some tragic experiences in the last couple weeks, Sage. But you have to realize: abuse, murder, ravishment; none of them make sense. So, stop trying to make sense of his actions." He gave her a pitying look, "Sometimes, you just have to accept that someone is bad and move on. I've done it, and so can you. If you don't, it will eat you alive inside."

That spiked her anger. "Don't you dare! How dare you just chalk this up to some 'poor, broken Sage' situation. I'm not blind. I know what I saw, and he wasn't a murderer. Something was wrong that day! And you–" she jabbed a finger in his direction, "don't you talk down to me about 'letting go'! Of course, I understand letting go. You know how much I've already done so!"

He tossed his hands in the air. "I don't pity you. I'm trying to explain something to you, but you're so focused on your anger that you won't listen. I'm trying to help you understand that some people are just evil."

"First of all, like I already said, that doesn't justify your people's rejoicing over that fact! You don't get it, Zane! What happened today was horrible. It was wrong for so many reasons."

"No. It's you who's missing the point. You're skewing the situation." He ran a hand through his hair and blew out a frustrated breath, "I don't understand why you can't just be reasonable here."

"Zane, I am being reasonable. You can't say that just because I don't agree with your opinion I'm unreasonable. That's tyrannical and unfair!"

He began pacing the room, his hands clenching and unclenching as he gestured wildly to punctuate his sentences. "But *your* opinion is wrong, so yes! You do have to agree with mine! What is *wrong* with you right now?!"

Sage didn't even know what to say to that. What exactly did he expect her to do? She opened her mouth to say just that when he stopped abruptly, his attention snagged by the neatly packaged crown and dress sitting by the door. Slowly, he strolled to it and bent down, opening the box and pulling out the crown.

"Why are these by the door?"

If she could have thrown the gifts in his face, she would have. "I will not accept such generous gifts, *my lord*," she bit out, knowing he hated when she used his title. "It's too much."

He narrowed his eyes at her. "I told you to call me Zane, and you *can* accept them. They were made specially for you." He pulled the crown from the box and frowned, first at it and then at her.

She pulled her lips into a tight smile "And as much as I appreciate the thought, I will not accept it. I cannot. It–"

"It what?!" His hand tightened on the crown. "Isn't to your liking? After everything, you would scorn my gifts, my generosity?"

"That's not what this is about, I–"

"What then?! You spite me out of anger? Have I not done my best to care for you? To meet all your needs? Why isn't it enough?"

He suddenly seemed more agitated than the situation merited and he was starting to make her nervous. "Zane," she said soothingly, "That's not what I meant. It *is* enough. And that's why I won't accept these. You've taken care of me, protected me, and even given me your room. I can't possibly take anything more from you."

He seemed not to hear her words. "I should've known better. None of this was enough. It's *never* enough," he whispered heatedly. He turned to face her, still holding the crown. "Wild one, what game are you playing with me?"

Something about the query and his posture raised the hair on the back of her neck. A strange glint had entered his eye; whatever was going through his head made her heart pound. He seemed different, dangerous. He cocked his head and, almost offhandedly, remarked, "You obviously have a keen mind, yet you still give in to the weakness of your kind. Why do you refuse logic and why do you refuse me? I admit I find it both infuriating and fascinating."

She frowned at him. Now, that just didn't make sense. Her gaze bobbed to the crown. What was going on? And why did her refusal of the dress and crown upset him so much?

Sage stepped behind the bedpost and held onto it to keep her hands from shaking. Her movement backward seemed to propel him forward. Step by slow step, he prowled toward her, unnaturally fluid. She'd told him how nervous and unsettled she felt when he did that, so after that first week, she'd rarely seen him move with his Scythian grace. Why was he doing it now? Was it just to unnerve her, because she'd irritated him?

She looked into his face and her stomach dropped when she met his eyes. They were lit with anger and lust, but it was the lust which scared her the most. He'd never looked at her like that before. A little voice in her head told her to run; she wasn't sure if it was Tehl or herself, but she felt for a certainty that Zane was very dangerous right then. She'd have to tread carefully.

"Everything's okay," she said in a smooth, calm voice, hoping to soothe whatever was going on with him. "You can put the dress in my wardrobe if that makes you happy. I didn't mean to be offensive."

But there was no change in his posture. He still eyed her like a predator. Her instincts were screaming at her to run, and run now. Ever so carefully, she gathered her robe in one hand and moved a step back, then another, and another until she'd moved around the end of the bed's other post.

The warlord ran his hand along the opposite bedpost. He studied the wooden frame like it held all the answers in the world and then seemed to speak to it. "Each time I expect you to break, you become stronger. It's beautiful. I…" he turned to face her, "I actually find myself wondering how far I can bend you."

"Excuse me?" His words made her shudder. Something was very wrong here. Even the cadence of his voice had changed, and his speech was almost lilting. It was as though a different person inhabited his body. She placed a hand on Nali in an attempt to steel her nerves. "Are you drunk?" she asked again.

"No, my dear wild one. I'm in agony."

"What do you mean?" Maybe if she kept him speaking, she'd have time to get closer to the door.

"Because I want—no, need—something I shouldn't. When I contemplate the idea, it infuriates me, even makes my gut churn." His eyes narrowed and his lips compressed. "The two of you are far too alike."

Her fingers tightened in Nali's fur, earning her a chuff of indignation, but Sage paid it no mind. She snuck a glance at the door. She knew there was possibility she was blowing the situation out of proportion and overreacting, but her gut told her something wasn't right. He wasn't in control of himself. A memory flashed through her mind of Rhys in his berserker rage. It was possible the warlord was almost at his edge. He wasn't between her and the door yet, though. He was faster than she, so she might only have one chance. She needed to tread with care.

She took a step toward him and channeled the real concern she felt for her own safety into false concern for him. "What can I do to help? You've helped me so much already." The words she spoke were true. Despite their horrid day, he'd been nothing but attentive and kind up until this point. But if he *was* going to lose it, she would not be a casualty. It was time to get out until he calmed down or got over whatever seemed to be taking him over.

"You can do nothing, Sage," he replied, and then sighed.

She took another step toward him and almost faltered when she saw his eyes track her progress with hawk-like focus. She steeled herself, though, and moved steadily forward.

"Nothing?" She was only a few steps from him and about fifteen steps from the door. She could make it, but she needed to surprise him.

"No. You can't change your imperfections or your heritage."

She stilled. Imperfections? Heritage? The words echoed in her mind, familiar. She'd heard almost those exact words from Rhys when he'd been tormenting her. The memory flashed through her mind: *Inferior heritage, disgusting imperfections...* The air froze in her lungs as something unsettling occurred to her. *Stars above, no...* Had Rhys' insanity been a product of Zane's influence? Could Zane be the originator of those barbaric ideas? But how could that be true? Truth or not, she had to escape *now*.

She lunged for the door, her quivering muscles screaming. Her heart galloped in her chest as she wrenched open the door, but there wasn't enough room to slip into the hallway before he hooked an arm around her. Sage let loose a scream and caught the calm expression of one guard before Zane pulled her back against him and landed a hand on the door, slamming it closed.

Then his breath was in her ear. "You can't run from me. It's only fair, really, as I haven't been able to run from your memory for years."

Memory? She screamed again and lifted her legs to the door, pushing against it with all her might. Just as she hoped, it upset their balance enough that they crashed to the floor. Sage pulled herself to her feet and lunged for the door again. Zane stepped in front of her and held his arms out, a smirk on his face.

She skidded and turned toward the draperies. Maybe she could make it out the window. She zeroed in on a lamp. That would break the glass.

But she wasn't fast enough. Again, the warlord's arms encircled her. "Why are you trying to run, wild one? There's nowhere to go."

"Let me go!"

"Never." He punctuated the word with a bite, latching onto the skin between her neck and shoulder.

She cried out, pain pulsing from the spot he'd bitten. "Please stop, Zane. You're not yourself."

"I am, actually. I finally am." He tightened his grip on her body and dragged her backward, away from the window.

Sage jerked her head to the side, her eyes widened in fear. "No! You're drunk. You don't know what you're doing." He didn't slow down. She clawed at his arms and fought harder. She had not survived the jungle and Rhys only to be ravished today. She'd die first. "Zane, stop! Just think about this first!"

"I'm afraid that's all I've been doing. All day, every day. My control can only last so long."

She screamed again when he pushed her face down onto the bed. She tried to scramble away, but his hand closed around her ankle and jerked her back. She pulled the dagger he'd given her from its sheath and then gasped as he dropped his weight down onto her, pinning her arms and legs, his hand closing around the dagger.

"No," she cried desperately, straining with all her might to hold on to her only weapon.

He dug his finger into the web of her fingers, and like magic, her hand released the blade without her consent. She twisted her face to the side and arched her neck, so she could breathe and keep herself from suffocating in the pillows. "Please don't do this. I'm Sage Blackwell, your friend. Don't do this," she pleaded. "I'm your friend. Work through your berserker rage. This isn't what you want."

"That's where you're wrong. You've never seen what I've wanted and you still haven't a clue." Suddenly, she felt cool metal bite into her neck as he held something to her throat. She jerked, and a sharp edge of metal pierced the fragile skin where her pulse hammered.

"Hold still or you'll hurt yourself," he commanded.

"Go to hell."

"I own it, and I'll make you queen of it. You'll suffer as much as I have."

As he said these words, she felt him squeeze the metal around her neck until it encircled her like a collar. She wheezed at the pressure, choking on her pain and panic. The warlord yanked her back off the bed as she coughed and tried to catch a breath.

"Help!" she huffed, but it was barely audible.

He spun her to face the mirror, one hand banding around her waist and arms, immobilizing her; the other lifted her chin to display what was constricting her breathing. She gasped and tried to look away, but his bruising grip held her still.

It was the crown. Roses and thorns. Obsidians and rubies. Death and Blood. It wrapped around her neck like a beautifully-crafted animal collar.

"Lovely," he purred, watching her reaction in the mirror. "For so long, I've wanted my crown on your skin, it's been unbearable." One finger slipped from under her chin to caress her lips. "Do you like it?"

Sage tried to bite his wandering finger. "Don't touch me!"

He smiled, looking pleased. "It's too bad you don't share my appreciation, Sage."

How was she to get away now? Letting her legs buckle beneath her, she dropped her entire body weight. If he had been any other man, it would've worked. But she should have known better; he wasn't just any man. She hung in his grasp while he simply smiled at her like she was an indulgent child.

"I guess if you insist on misbehaving, you'll need to be restrained."

"No!" She struggled harder. If he tied her, there was no escape. She ignored the thorns biting into her neck as she fought him. She cried out and threw her head back into his face, stomping on his instep. It did nothing. He simply picked her up and carried her to the wall where he yanked down a tapestry. Her horror doubled as she discovered chains behind it, secured to stone. She screamed bloody murder. *"Help!"*

In a move both smooth and painful, he secured her hands above her head, then stepped back, rubbing his chin as though admiring his work. Her breath see-sawed in and out of her chest, and her legs quivered with exhaustion. She strained against the manacles, and the familiar feeling send a wildness through her as she flashed back to the dungeon and Rhys.

"I'm not him," the warlord said quietly.

How did he know what she was thinking?

"You're everything like him." How had she been so blind? But why trick her into trusting him? He had her weak and sick when he discovered her in the cell. Or was that a lie, too? Her mind spun, but she couldn't untangle anything with the panic riding her. "Why?" she shouted.

The warlord rushed toward her and pushed her into the wall, both of his arms caging her in. "Because you're too alluring for your own good!" His eyes darted between hers. "I should be disgusted by your imperfections, by your green eyes." He ran a hand along her exposed collarbone. "By your creamy, scarred skin—but I'm not."

Rage flashed across his face; he slammed his hands against the wall, making plaster from the ceiling rain down around them. She cringed back from him. Just how strong was he?

He stepped back and jerked his shirt into place. "I should just take you and get this over with."

Revulsion overwhelmed her, and she pressed herself hard into the wall. "No."

"No?" he scoffed and took a step closer. "Nothing but 'yes' should come out of your mouth. You'd be lucky if I took you." His gaze dropped to her body and stayed there. "You'd love it, revel in it."

She gagged. "That's exactly what it would be: *taking*," she replied, trying to gain his attention from where it was currently fixated. "I would never consent."

"I doubt that," he whispered. Carefully, he reached out a finger and ran it over her chest.

She hunched her shoulders forward in an attempt to make her breasts smaller.

"There's no need to hide. I've seen it all before, Sage. Every inch of your skin has been bared to me." He moved closer, pressing his body along hers, his lips brushing her temple. "I promise it will be so good, but I'll wait. It will be all the more sweet when you cave in to me."

She panted harder, his excitement making bile flood her mouth. "I'll make it terrible. That is *my* promise."

He ignored her comment. "And lucky for me, I can introduce to you all the pleasures of intimacy. In this way, you're different. She was never innocent."

She froze. Who was he talking about? Another woman he'd been with? "You will introduce me to nothing."

Zane chuckled, his voice rough as his hands roamed down her body and wedged between the wall and her butt. "I can tell when you lie, wild one. Something tells me that the crown prince did not touch your flesh." His hands traced from the back of her around to the front, and his fingers slipped inside her robe to caress her bare thigh.

Her breath hitched as he continued his journey upward. She snapped her teeth at the warlord, a smug smile on his lips, his pupils dilated. "Get your hands off me!"

"I've never appreciated our garments, or lack thereof," he murmured, his eyes never leaving hers, as though enjoying her reaction. "I suspect Aermia is different in this way. You have too much modesty. It's useless."

Her panic increased as his hand inched higher. She bucked against him. "Stop!" When that didn't work, she used her last resort. She spat into his face.

The smirk on his face dissolved; he pulled his hand from inside her robe and placed it over the juncture of her thighs.

"Don't test me."

Sage's breathing was shallow. She was very aware that only a flimsy piece of barely-tied linen protected her.

Zane pressed his forehead to hers and kept eye contact. "I can feel the heat of you," he growled and then licked his lips.

"You're vulgar," she spat, turning her head to the side.

"And barbaric. So you've told me," he purred.

He removed his hand and pressed against her, his hips snug with her, and she shuddered, disgusted. She didn't know which was worse, his hands or his body.

He placed a small kiss behind her ear like a lover, not a ravisher. "Sage," he groaned. "What am I going to do with you? I should have just had you bred, but when I saw you in my throne room covered in dirt, grime, and blood, glaring at me with your emerald gaze, I knew you were special. You were the one."

Sage had tuned him out and was staring at the curtains covering the window. Her escape had been so close all along, and yet she had never even dreamed of running. Stupid. Her stupidity never ceased to amaze her.

"You're not stupid, Sage. Far from it, actually. I'd never say this to your face, but it's one of things I like about you," Tehl whispered.

Relief filled her at the sound of his voice. She wasn't alone. Fingers touched her chin gently and forced her gaze back to Zane's face.

"You have no more energy to fight him off. The time for fighting is over, love. It's time to hide, okay? It's alright to let go. You need not be aware for this. I'll protect you."

The warlord watched her as he pressed his lips to hers. Sage didn't fight, didn't respond. He pulled back and cocked his head, frowning. "Kiss me once like you mean it, and I shall leave you unmolested."

It took her a moment to process what he was saying. She barely had any energy left. "Forever, or just tonight?"

"Forever."

She narrowed her eyes. "I don't believe you."

"You know me, Sage. Have I ever taken anything that wasn't offered?"

The question confused her. Had he ever taken anything? No. But he wasn't in his right mind. Or was he? Was he crazy, or did the berserker rage work differently with him? She mentally slapped herself. Why was she trying to find an excuse for him?

He must have seen her thinking about it and pounced. "I want you willing.

I will not force anything from you. It's barbaric and disgusting. Any man can force a woman, but seduction? That takes skill. Come to me willingly and life will continue as it has." He smiled beautifully as he spoke and she hated it. It was so unfair that the rot in his soul wasn't evident on his face. "It's just one kiss. Be reasonable."

It was more than that. It meant her surrender. It would be *her* choice.

"Sage, he's telling the truth," Tehl whispered again. "Protect yourself at all costs. Just imagine me when kissing him."

She squared off with the warlord. "One kiss."

Anticipation flashed across his face. "One."

She expected him to maul her right away, but instead, he paused, his eyes softening as he simply looked at her. He then crooked a finger beneath her chin and raised her face toward his, his thumb tracing the curve of her lower lip.

"Flawless," he whispered and touched his mouth to hers. He drew his hand down her neck to the hollow of her throat just below where he'd forced the metal collar. His breath caressed her skin and her entire body tensed. This was so wrong. She didn't know if she could do this.

"Just breathe. It'll be okay, love," Tehl murmured.

One muscle at a time, she tried to force her body to relax. His arms wound around her so tightly she could hardly breathe. His hands spanned her back before leisurely exploring her curves, their trailing path leaving her skin crawling. He held her securely against him and tangled one hand in her loose tresses, cupping the back of her head as he first brushed his lips across the bow of her top lip, then her full bottom lip, his touch feather-light. When he began softly nibbling at it, she started shaking. This was too much. *I'm sorry, Tehl.* Everywhere he touched felt dirty, and guilt pooled in her belly.

He pulled back, his fingertips touching her chin and tracing her jaw, catching the wet trails of tears she didn't know she'd shed. "It's all right, love. Open for me."

More tears burned in her eyes, but she closed them to keep them from falling. This was her choice, no matter how sick and twisted it was. He cupped the side of her face gently, and kissed her like he could consume her. One tear squeezed out when he moaned quietly. She sucked a deep breath when his hand slid down, fingers brushing across the tender skin under her jaw, then trailing over her abused neck.

Stars above, she couldn't do this. It was too much. She turned her head to the side to break the kiss. His mouth traveled across her jaw and along the side of her neck, following the path of his hand. His fingers caught the edge of her robe and pushed the fabric off her shoulder. The cold air made her shiver, and her eyes slammed open as he nipped at her collarbone.

Tehl stood behind the warlord, staring at her over Zane's shoulder. He gave her a tender look. Sorrow rose, howling inside her, choking her. All that time she spent fighting Tehl, making him the villain, blaming him, and yet he wasn't the monster of her story, he was the hero. He'd always been the hero, albeit an awkward one.

Zane lifted his head, his hooded gaze scorching her. "That was as exquisite as I imagined it to be."

Sage stared at him, knowing he'd taken something from her she'd never get back. His hand slid down into her robe to cup her bare belly.

His fingers caressed the skin, and his smile was all male satisfaction. "Just imagine what you'll look like when you're swollen with my child."

All of her muscles locked down. "Excuse me?"

He graced her with one of his heart-stopping smiles. "You'll make a wonderful consort, and our children will make the most powerful warriors. Just imagine Aermia and Scythia ruling together."

"You're out of your damned mind," she blurted. "I'm married."

"No, I promise you, you are not." His smile was sin and the devil rolled into one. "Wild one, do you remember when I saved you from that hole? Healers were necessary, and so was an examination."

"What?" she asked through numb lips. He couldn't mean…

He cupped her cheek, a tender look on his face. "I had to be sure. I couldn't make you mine if you'd been used. Imagine my excitement when my healers informed me you were pure. Your marriage is void if not consummated. You, my love, will be my queen. And make no mistake, I won't make the same mistake as the Aermian prince."

"I will never marry you. I'll die first." She meant it.

He chuckled like she was amusing him. "There are a great many things that you, my love, will do for those you love."

"You're just like Rhys," she whispered. "He said something similar to me once."

The warlord scoffed. "He's nothing like me, but a cheap imitation. I'm the original."

"How could I be so blind?" she muttered.

"It's not your fault. You're young and naïve still. Time hasn't jaded you or turned you into a suspicious shrew. It's a good thing."

"You disgust me."

"Disgust can turn to love."

He was delusional. "You can take many things from me, but my love will not be one of them."

The warlord studied her. "I have plenty of time, but I think you need a visit from the dead to inspire you to action."

Dread filled her. "The dead?" she croaked.

"Yes, I think Jasmine needs to visit."

NINETEEN

SAGE

SHE SHIFTED PAINFULLY FROM ONE aching foot to the other. Stars above, everything hurt. At one point in the night, her legs had collapsed. The metal manacles had bitten into her wrists, and it'd taken everything she had not to break down. She didn't, though, and she wouldn't. She wouldn't give him that satisfaction. After several torturous hours, she'd finally found the strength to stand again.

She tilted her head back against the stone to stare at the dark ceiling, thinking of the previous night. For hours, she'd berated herself and examined each of her conversations with the warlord. After his display last night… Sage shuddered. When she'd looked into his deranged eyes, she'd felt her soul grow cold. She'd been scared in her life before, but something about last night had been worse than anything she'd ever experienced. What kind of monster's lair had she wandered into? Even now, she didn't know, and there was a part of her that still hoped Zane would walk in nursing a hangover. She hoped he wasn't truly evil.

She banged her head against the wall at the last thought. That part of her was foolish but insistent, and she didn't quite understand it. It was like she wanted him to be… What *did* she want him to be? Her friend? A good person? In the light of day, Sage could see it for what it was. It was a longing. She longed for safety, for home, for her family, for her friends, and for Tehl, but in lieu of those things, it seemed her mind sought those things in Zane. Something was wrong with her.

The door slammed open and cracked against the stone wall. She swallowed hard when the warlord sauntered in and smiled boyishly. He moved toward her, her customary breakfast in his hands.

"Good morning, wild one. I hope you slept well."

Inwardly, she quelled. Everything was normal about him—well, the normal she'd come to know up until very recently. Gone was the hard, imbalanced, and calculating man from last night. However, neither did he rush to her side with apologies, nor help her down from the wall. That in and of itself told her something. Was this some sort of game to him? Or was he truly not well in the mind?

He placed her food on the nightstand and then pinched a piece of bread from the loaf, holding it out to her. "Are you hungry, Sage?"

She eyed the proffered food skeptically. "Is it poisoned?"

His deep chuckle washed over her, and she dared to peek at him. What she saw made her gasp. He was smiling at her with love and adoration. What in the world? Was he normal again?

He popped the piece of bread into his mouth, never losing eye contact, and brushed the back of his fingers along her cheek. After he'd swallowed, he asked, "Will you eat now?"

"Will you unchain me?" she ventured.

"Not right now. As much as it pains me to have something so wild and exotic chained like a slave, it's really in your best interest. You'll have to stay this way for your protection." He actually had the audacity to look hurt by it, as if he was not in control of the situation.

"In what world is this protection?"

Rather than respond, the warlord pinched off another piece of bread and placed it at her lips. Sage took the morsel from his fingers and chewed slowly, confused by the brilliant smile he gave her. Had the kingdom been turned on its head? Everything felt off-kilter.

He held the broth to his lips and sipped, then offered it to her. She placed her lips on the cup and slurped, watching him over the rim. What was his game?

A hand brushed her collarbone and then her chest. Sage sputtered and jerked back, knocking the broth from his hand. It crashed to the floor and stillness filled the room, as if awaiting violence.

Sage coughed and glared at the warlord through watering eyes. His reaction, though, wasn't what she'd anticipated. Instead of responding angrily, he let loose a heavy sigh, gathering the broken pieces of clay into his hand.

"One day, Sage, you won't fear me as you do now. You'll accept my kindness without question, and my touch without shuddering. This, I vow."

Not in this life. But she kept her thoughts to herself, staring at the broth that had soaked her robe, rendering the thin fabric translucent. Color heated her cheeks when she realized the fabric was translucent. The warlord stood and stilled as he, too, seemed to notice. Her breath froze in her lungs when he moved closer.

"Goddess," he whispered. "Lead, and I will follow." He looked into her face and touched one finger to her blush. "Do not be ashamed of such beauty. It's a gift many covet, and yours is natural. That's rare. It's a treasure."

"One that is mine," she whispered.

He leaned closer, his words whispering over her skin. "One that is *mine*. This time it will be my choice."

She went rigid at his statement. "You're mistaken…or just deranged." She inwardly winced. She needed to tread carefully. If she needled him too much, there could be a repeat of the night before.

He took a step back and studied her, amusement touching his face. "I like this side of you, Sage. The warrior queen I met in my throne room all those weeks ago is starting to peek out again."

"My lord?" A warrior stepped into the doorway with a bow.

"Yes?" Zane answered, glancing over his shoulder.

"We have what you requested."

"Ah, yes!" The warlord turned back to her and clapped his hands. "I've arranged a gift for you. Bring her in."

A warrior swung into the room, toting someone Sage had never dreamt she could see again. "Jas?" she whispered, tears springing to her eyes.

Jasmine stared at her and lunged forward. "Sage!"

The male holding her jerked her back. "Do not speak in the warlord's presence unless asked. And bow to your betters." He tossed Jasmine to the ground. She landed on her hands and knees. That had to be painful, but her friend didn't utter a sound of complaint as she knelt before the warlord.

Zane stepped up to Jasmine, and a sound of protest escaped Sage's lips. He glanced back at her with a raised brow. Some of her distress must have shown on her face, because he gave her a warm, reassuring smile which did nothing to reassure her. It rather did the opposite. He turned back to Jasmine and leaned down, tipping up her chin. Sage ran her eyes over her friend's face. There weren't any bruises or cuts, just what seemed to be evidence of lack of sleep.

"Aermia has a way of creating enchanting creatures, despite their imperfections, don't they, Phoenix?"

The warrior nodded and watched Jasmine with a look that spoke a bit too much possessiveness. "Indeed. If nothing else, their spirits are to be admired."

"I agree," Zane murmured, turning Jasmine's face from one side to the other. "Her blue eyes are off-putting, but her facial structure and build are amenable. She'll do nicely."

Nicely for what? Sage stifled her question for fear of his reaction while handling her friend.

"Stand, woman," the warlord commanded.

Jas stood and kept her gaze pinned to the floor. He spun her around and led her by the hand until she stood an arm's length away from Sage. Jas' eyes met hers and tears dripped down her face.

"I'll give you a minute. Enjoy your gift, wild one." The warlord let Jas go and moved to speak with the warrior.

Jasmine rushed to her and wrapped her arms around her. "Oh, God. I never thought I'd see you again."

A sob escaped her. "You died," she choked out. "I was told you died. I lost you, Jas. I've mourned you this whole time!"

Jasmine pulled back and clasped Sage's face. "But I'm fine. I'm here, you see? I'm here! Are you okay?"

"I'm fine."

"I saw you at the execution."

Sage's stomach dropped. "You did?"

"You look different."

A chill ran down Sage's spine. "Is it bad?"

The skin around Jasmine's eyes tightened. "Not bad, but," she hesitated, "you're starting to seem… flawless."

The idea sickened her. "It wasn't by choice," she whispered.

"I don't doubt you. The power to choose is a rare commodity here."

Sage caught movement over Jasmine's shoulder as the warlord made his way back toward them. Panic filled her. "I love you, sis."

"Love you, too, sis," Jas croaked.

The warlord closed a hand around Jasmine's arm and pulled her from Sage. "That's enough." In a quick move, he drew a dagger from his side and placed it at her friend's throat. His gaze captured Sage's. "Do you love her?"

"You know the answer."

"I fear you will be unruly without something to hold you in check."

Sage's gaze wavered to Jas and back to the warlord. "Have I been unruly?"

"No, but I can sense rebellion building within you. I've dealt with rebellion before, so I know what it looks like." He frowned and blinked as if willing a memory away. "I need your compliance in all things."

"I promise," she answered quickly.

His smile became bitter. "I know you, and I've told you not to lie to me." He slashed the skin of Jasmine's shoulder, making her cry out and try to pull away from him.

"No!" Sage jerked forward with a cry, only to have her chains pull her back. "Leave her alone! She's done nothing wrong."

"You're right, Sage, she hasn't. But you have. Look at the price of your lies." He pressed his finger into Jasmine's wound and her friend's face turned white. His face was a mask of anger when he returned his gaze to her face. "Look what you made me do, Sage! I hate this! Now, answer me."

"I didn't lie!" she shouted, continuing to tug on her manacles.

"More lies!" He moved the dagger back to Jasmine's throat. "Swear to me you'll be obedient, or I'll slit her throat where she stands. Choose carefully. Her life is in your hands."

"I'll obey. I'll obey. Just let her go!"

He observed her. "I believe you, this time. Phoenix! Grab your woman and send for a healer."

The warrior glided forward and took her pale friend from the warlord.

Jasmine stared at her and didn't even bother to struggle.

"Don't take her away! Please!"

But the warrior paid her no mind and slipped out the door with Jasmine in tow. Sage tore her gaze from the door after it closed to glare at the warlord.

"Damn it!" He wiped the blood off his hand, his agitation apparent as he jerked his fingers across the fabric. "I hate this."

She wanted to hit something. "Why?" she whispered, knowing he could hear her.

Zane cocked his head. "I can see your anger, Sage, and that's only natural. But, remember what you promised. How you act in the future will affect Jasmine. Your transgressions will result in punishments for her, and I'd hate for you to witness that."

"You're sick."

He gave her a tender look. "You think that now, but I think, in time, you'll understand." He reached for the bread and held it out to her. "You need to eat."

She wanted to refuse, to spit at him and shout obscenities, but she didn't. Like a good little captive, she bit into the bread and ate every bite.

The warlord lifted a lock of her hair and rubbed it between his fingers. "Adjustment periods are always difficult, but don't worry. It'll get easier." He pursed his lips and stared at her wrists. "You're bleeding," he said flatly.

Sage blinked and looked up at her hands. Sure enough, blood was dripping down her arms. She hadn't even noticed it.

"You must not harm yourself, or I'll have to take drastic measures. Do you remember your first cell?"

Terror overwhelmed her. Darkness.

He nodded. "I see that you do. I'll be back later to clean your wounds, but I'd like you to think about what your actions have wrought today. I hope you choose to do better next time. I don't want our lives to be like this. I desire peace. This fighting gets old."

Peace? What a joke. The promise of peace is what he'd lured her in with the first time. He might utter pretty words and make fine promises, but that was all they were. "I meant what I said," she said softly. "Did you, Zane?" Something glinted in his eyes. Pleasure. She thought back to what she'd said. Zane. She'd used his name. Sage filed that away. That information could prove useful later.

"I always mean what I say. Have I broken my word?"

"No."

"Show a little faith, wild one."

"Do you think you deserve my faith and trust?"

"Have I ever hurt you?" he countered.

She glanced up to her bloody wrists and back to him, saying nothing.

"You did that to yourself. Think about it, Sage. Have I ever really hurt you? Have I left scars on your body, or ever taken a hand to you?"

"No," she drew out. "But you've wounded me just the same."

He cocked his head as he regarded her. "You are the crown jewel of my accomplishments. I have a feeling we will change everything."

"Change everything how?" Unease rolled in her gut.

"By ripping apart the world, piece by piece. Then, once we're done, we'll reshape it into something better."

TWENTY

TEHL

SWEAT DRIPPED DOWN TEHL'S FOREHEAD and into his eyes. He swiped a quick hand across his brow, his eyes never leaving his opponent. It took only one moment of distraction to lose your life.

His arms screamed in protest as he met his attacker head-to-head, their swords flashing in the morning light as they crashed into each other. Tehl clenched his jaw and pushed against their crossed swords, hoping to upset the other's balance.

"You'll have to do better than that," his brother heckled.

Tehl spun out from their lock and retreated, his teeth bared in a ferocious smile. He kept his steps light as he maneuvered around Sam and met each thrust and cut of his sword. Every move was calculated on his part for, slowly but surely, he was wearing his opponent out.

"You have enough yet?" Tehl taunted him.

Blue eyes, so like his own, narrowed on him. "Big words for the man who passed out after yesterday's bout."

He glared at his brother, but didn't take the bait. He knew better than to let anger take reign over his actions. Giving into anger made you sloppy; it made you lose. Instead, he coolly assessed his brother's form as they sparred. The spymaster had been favoring his right side for the last five minutes.

Having ascertained what he needed to, Tehl lunged. As he moved in a sequence of attacks, Sam dropped to the ground and slid under Tehl's arm, only to pop up behind him and place his sword on the back of Tehl's neck.

"You lose."

"Swamp apples," he muttered. The crown prince's chest sawed in and out as he fought to catch his breath. He slid his sword into his scabbard and yanked his sweat-soaked shirt over his head. A whistle had him turning his neck and arching a brow at his brother. "What?"

"By the time Sage gets home, she won't even recognize you with all those muscles and bruises."

Tehl scowled and shrugged on the clean shirt an Elite had handed him. He didn't bother with the buttons and crossed his arms over his chest, self-consciousness striking him.

His brother barked out a laugh. "Only you would be embarrassed by that comment." Sam took on a thoughtful expression. "Maybe I should have my wife kidnapped…then I could be motivated enough to look like you."

His levity disappeared. It was like his brother had thrown cold water on him; as if he needed a reminder of his worries. "And you say I never watch *my* mouth."

Sam's smile faded. "What would you have me do? If you can't laugh about it, why live?"

"Well, it's not funny," he growled back.

"You're right, it's not, but it's how I handle things. You know that."

Tehl shook his head. "Well, this time it's not right."

Sam scrubbed a hand down his face. "What then? Ought I to deal with this situation like you? Work constantly, hardly eat, and spar while you're supposed to be sleeping? How's that working for you, huh? You know you're at the end of your rope, so you tell me which of our coping methods is healthier."

Tehl dropped his head to stare at the sand beneath his feet. His brother had a point, but it didn't make this any easier. He was occupied enough with his duties as ruler during the day that he simply forgot to eat, but at night… Well, at night he found he just *couldn't* sleep. His dreams frequently featured Sage these days and in them, he was always searching for her, but she always died right before he reached her. He rubbed his chest. Her scent had even begun to fade from their room. He swallowed hard and met his brother's sympathetic gaze.

"It troubles me… more than I'd like to admit." That wasn't something he'd planned on sharing, but it was true.

Sam crossed the circle and clasped his arm. "I know. The black bags beneath your eyes attest to that. When was the last time you had a decent night's sleep?"

His response was automatic: "The night before she disappeared."

His brother sucked in a breath. "As long as that?"

Anger sparked inside him and he shook off Sam's hand. "How can I sleep, knowing she is suffering or she might be…?" He couldn't finish the thought.

"She's not dead. We have to believe in that."

"It's been over two months." He paused, his face sober. "Honestly? There's a part of me that almost hopes she is," he confessed, though the admission caused a familiar pang of guilt. He watched his brother's expression, awaiting judgment for his words, but none came. He blew out a relieved breath. It seemed his brother understood that in some situations death was a mercy and a kindness.

"She's strong. She'll make it through this," Sam assured. When his brother didn't seem relieved, he added, "She will… She has to."

"Even if she does, in what condition will we find her, Sam? Will she still be Sage, or will she be a shell? Or perhaps worse?"

"We can't know and it's better to leave the *what ifs* alone. You can't worry over something that might never happen."

"I know." And logically, he did. But since Sage had snuck into his life, things weren't as clear and logical as they used to be. His attention shifted to Garreth, who was striding in their direction at a clipped pace, his limp barely noticeable.

"News, my lord. We've finally received news!"

He exchanged a shocked look with his brother, before they both ran toward the man.

"What news?"

"We've received a letter from Scythia. It's awaiting you in the war room."

"Make sure Lilja and Hayjen are notified," Tehl commanded, already heading that way.

"They're here already."

Tehl simply nodded and sprinted into the palace. The hallways and doors blurred as his mind focused on one thing: getting to the war room and reading the contents of that letter. He burst through the doors and scanned his council as he took his chair. "Where is it?"

"Here, my lord." Gav held out a sealed letter.

Tehl stared at it for several heartbeats, slightly afraid of the information it contained. He took a breath and commanded, "Please read it, Gavriel."

His cousin nodded and cracked the seal with his dagger. Gav first scanned the document and then began reading:

"'To the lord of the Aermian kingdom, the warlord of Scythia sends his greetings.

It was somewhat of a shock when we discovered one of your messengers bearing a missive. It's been a long time since Scythia's been in contact with the outside world, so please excuse my manners if they offend.'"

Gav pulled in a breath and continued: "'Many years have passed since the atrocity my ancestors committed against Nagali, yet my people continue to suffer for crimes which they did not commit. It has been hundreds of years. I understand that a crime of that magnitude can never be wiped away, nor should it. But I offer to make atonement in the way of restoration. I want to restore what was lost in Nagali. With time, we can honor those who have fallen.'"

Jeren scoffed. "How could one atone for that? Bring all those dead back to life? Even with the use of science, I'm sure that isn't possible."

Tehl ignored his outburst and nodded to Gav. "Please continue."

"'Most of my people have never been outside Scythia, nor encountered someone of a different race. The beliefs of our ancestors have slowly faded over the years, leaving us an isolated people with a bloody, shameful history. But I believe my people deserve to experience life beyond our kingdom, so I will accept your olive branch. It is our desire to reach an understanding that will bring both our kingdoms into lasting peace and prosperity.

"'However, I'm a cautious man, and I can't help but feel suspicious of the fact that this treaty coincides with the arrival of a certain female in my kingdom. She has assured me, though, of your good intentions, and I must say it is only by her counsel that I accept your offer, albeit somewhat blindly. She has also advised me that, as neither side will feel safe in each other's territory, I should find an alternative. Therefore, I propose we do so in the middle, or, in this case, where it all began. In Nagali. There's a palace near both our borders where we can begin negotiations. It's prudent to let you know that Sage Blackwell is very well looked after. Our interactions have become a special part of my day and I admit, I cherish our intimacy. In fact, one would be remiss in not seeking her stimulating company whenever possible. I have, of course, offered to bring her to the Mort Wall for your retrieval but, dedicated as she is to peace, she has thus far insisted on staying.'"

"Lies," Lilja hissed, her eyes flashing. "My Sage would never stay there! Especially not without consulting her family!"

Gav nodded and began again. "'Also, I hope you've shown the same consideration to my woman, Blaise. It's important to me she continues unharmed and well cared for.'" Gavriel's hand tightened on the letter. "'I'm sure you can relate to my concern, as, it would be likewise unpardonable if Sage were to fall ill or be hurt during her stay in our nation.'"

"That's a blatant threat," Zachael snarled.

"'But have not a care, I'll do my utmost to keep her safe, warm, and loved during her time here. My messengers will be on their side of the Mort Wall and are instructed to wait until they receive your response. I send my best wishes and hopes that you continue on in health and prosperity. Your humble servant, Zane Ziy, Lord of Scythia.'"

There was a beat of silence before his council erupted.

"You can't trust a word of that document!" Lelbiel stated.

"He wants us to meet him in Nagali? Where the man-eaters roam unchecked? Surely, it's a trap!" William shouted.

"It would be a terrible place to wage war," Zachael retorted.

"And he presumes to threaten us! *Us*!" Jeren yelled.

"Silence!" Tehl's father commanded over the din.

Tehl looked to his father, who'd been silent until that moment. "What say you, my king?"

His father's face was stern. "The warlord mentioned some valid concerns. We don't know what's been happening over there, thus we cannot say for a certainty that he was the one to sanction the attacks and kidnappings which have been taking place."

"I respectfully beg to differ, my king," Lilja said softly.

His father looked over to the Sirenidae. "Can you be sure that the same man is leading?"

Her lips thinned. "No, I cannot. I lost my contact within Scythia fifteen years ago, but I believe they are the same. I can't give you proof, only my experience and my observations."

The king dipped his chin. "Thank you. We need to be cautious, but we must also have our minds open." He turned to William. "Is Nagali such a bad middle ground? From his letter, I know of the place he speaks. It's just beyond Scythia and Aermia's borders, at the base to the Kugami Mountains."

Old William's face scrunched up as he thought. "I need to study the area to be sure."

"I have extensive maps of that area," Lelbiel added. "They might need some updating, but it's nothing the scouts couldn't take care of."

"Good," the king remarked. "Son, your thoughts?"

Tehl stared at his father, the air around him seeming to turn to water. *Safe. Warm. Loved.* Drowning, he was drowning. "Did no one miss the statement of 'safe, warm, and loved'? Or his use of the word 'intimacy' when he spoke of their interactions and his enjoyment of her 'stimulating company'?" Silence descended as his voice echoed around the room. "What is he doing to my wife?"

"We can't know for s—" Sam began.

Tehl stabbed a finger in his direction. "Don't you placate me. You're the spymaster and the trickster of words. Was that not blatant verbiage for sex?"

Sam snapped his mouth shut and his eyes shuttered. "It was."

"Do you have any doubt of her having been abused at his hands?"

"No, I don't," Lilja whispered, answering for Sam. "Even if she looks whole and beautiful when we see her, we won't know what she's suffering inside."

The very idea brought on a flood of unknown emotion. He'd always been awkward when it came to feeling so, because he didn't know how to react; he packed his feelings away in a box. But today, the box would not close. Rage, anguish, and frustration all poured out of him. He slammed his hands against the table and let out a roar. He ignored the shocked looks on his councilors' faces as he shoved back from the table, his chair clattering to the ground behind him. "Why do we need to accommodate this monster?"

"Because it means Sage's life."

Tehl swung his gaze to Rafe. "What?"

"If we do not accomplish this and put on the most amazing show for the Scythian warlord, she will die." The rebellion leader paused, staring him in the eye. "Or worse, he'll keep her."

Tehl inhaled deeply, getting his anger under control. His emotions had been getting more and more out of hand the longer he went without news of Sage. He sparred and it helped; the energy he expelled calmed him for a time, but it wasn't quite enough. He righted his chair and took a seat. One by one, he scanned the council, pausing on Zachael. "Our army?"

"Close, but I'm afraid we still need more time."

He nodded and tucked that away. "Then I guess that leaves us one option." His voice took on a dangerous edge. "We accept the good warlord's invitation and prepare to give him hell."

TWENTY-ONE

JASMINE

HER SHOULDER BURNED, AND THE men hovering around her weren't helping the situation.

"What did you do to anger the warlord?"

"We told you to keep your mouth shut! Why can't you do what you're told?"

"She's reckless, Phoenix. She'll get us all killed."

"Enough," Phoenix growled, lifting her arm to clean the wound.

Jasmine winced and stared past the men crowding her. The image of Sage chained to the wall in a translucent robe was frozen in her mind. What had the warlord done to her? She looked like herself…but not. She winced when Phoenix probed her arm.

"Careful," she growled. "That hurts."

The gigantic warrior glanced at her and then back to his task. "It was necessary."

"What happened?" Mekhl demanded.

"You know I can't reveal that," Phoenix rumbled as he began to bind her arm.

"He used me," she replied flatly.

"For what?" Orion asked, crossing his arms.

"To control—"

"As a demonstration." Phoenix cut her off with a glare, then turned it on the others. "Don't risk all our lives and positions for something as petty as curiosity. Others have disappeared for less." He pinned her with his cinnamon gaze. "And you should know better. It's time to keep silent."

She bit her cheek and looked away. It rankled her that when he demanded her silence, she gave it. She had to admit, she felt guilty for it, she felt like a coward. But she knew she was also being smarter. She'd fought at the beginning. Oh, how she'd fought. But all it led to was punishment. The beginning was the worst. Nightmares still plagued her of the examination forced upon her, and the subsequent drugging that ensued afterward. She'd awoken here, with Phoenix, Mekhl, and Orion staring at her. A tug on her arm pulled her from the memories.

"All done," Phoenix murmured, and then began to clean up his healing supplies.

"Thank you," she said and stood with a stretch. "I think I'd like to go on a walk now."

"No."

She blinked at Phoenix's hard tone. "No?"

He stood to his full imposing height and stared down at her without any emotion. "You've been confined to our home."

"Confined?"

"You're too important to let wander."

His statement didn't comfort her; it did just the opposite. Up until this point, she'd played her part, and in return, they'd allowed her a certain amount of freedom. For instance, she could go for walks, as long as she was escorted. It was the only time she was free of fear, guilt, and self-loathing.

"This is because of our little trip today?"

"Yes. Don't think of sneaking out. The warlord stationed his personal guards outside our door."

Her stomach dropped.

"Is he interested in her?" Orion asked, a hint of worry in his tone.

"No, he's busy with his Aermian consort." Phoenix shook his head. "But Jasmine's a means to an end."

Anxiety churned in her gut. What an apt phrasing: a means to an end. She was an exhibition, a slave and a broodmare already, but now she was to be a means by which a maniac would control Sage. She cast a glance to the men speaking quietly. She hated that they wouldn't hurt her. At the beginning, she'd expected them to beat or torture her, but instead they'd included her in their lives: they spoke with her, took her for walks. But it wasn't because they cared for her personally, not at all. Rather, she was their property, and, as their property, their responsibility; rather like a well-cared-for animal.

She swallowed hard and stared blankly at the wall. The worst part was the night, not because of what she remembered, but because of what she *couldn't* remember. Her breath came heavier as she thought about each night. Apart from the first night, every night since she'd been taken from Sage was a giant blank. No matter how hard she pushed, the veil of darkness wouldn't lift. She could only guess what happened in those blank spots.

The first night still plagued her during daylight hours. She'd been frightened and curled up in a corner. The two walls to her back had brought her a little comfort, while three huge warriors had stood and studied her like she was some sort of animal in a menagerie. They hadn't moved forward to touch her, nor had they spoken. They'd just watched. She'd stared back, terrified to take her eyes off them for even a second, lest one of them attack her.

It had shocked her when, after a few hours of their staring contest, her eyes began to droop. Sleep hadn't come easy when she didn't know what would come next, but her exhausted body won out and demanded sleep, if only for a second.

Apparently, that second turned out to be the whole night, for when Jasmine had blinked her heavy eyelids open, she was no longer in her corner. She iced over when she realized she was in a bed, and not alone. She'd jerked to the side and tried to scramble away. A heavy hand had landed on her thigh, halting her escape. She'd stared at the hand and the warrior sprawled out next to her. He had regarded her in a quiet way and then, slowly, pulled his hand from her leg before wordlessly getting up. He then simply strode away.

She had shivered and leapt from the bed, taking the sheet with her. Her body had not appreciated the maneuver. She hissed, the pain from her ribs robbing her of breath. How did she end up in that bed? She hadn't been able to sleep a full night in days, for every little sound woke her, yet she'd slept through being moved?

When she'd taken another step from the bed, she'd felt an ache in her lower body and the world came to a screeching halt. Her hands trembled, and her lip quivered. That could mean only one thing. Her innocence, had they stolen it? She'd pulled in a deep breath, and bravely pulled the sheet back to examine her body: her old clothing was gone, replaced with a simple nightgown that reached the knee. She had swallowed at the notion that someone had cleaned and changed her, and she never even felt it. What else had happened? Her hand had lifted the hem of her nightgown and paused.

"You can do this, Jas. Don't be a coward."

She'd sneaked a glance to make sure none of the warriors were watching her, and then yanked up her nightgown. Nothing. No blood, no bruising. She had then jerked the nightgown down, shivering, and moved back into the corner, the familiar comfort of the walls to her back. Nothing seemed amiss, yet her body told her something was different.

Jasmine blinked at the hand on her arm and pulled herself back to the present. She looked up into Mekhl's face with a raised brow.

"How are you feeling?"

"Tired," she replied automatically. It was like she couldn't get enough sleep, but that was to be expected with all the healing her body had had to do the last couple months. *Months.* Her heart squeezed. She had been away from the twins for so long. How much had they changed? Did they still miss her? Were they being taken care of?

Orion's soft voice washed over her: "Where do you go when your gaze glazes over?"

"Home," she whispered without thinking.

"This is your home," Phoenix stated, taking a step closer.

"No." She shook her head with a sad smile. "This is my prison."

Phoenix scoffed. "Your prison? Do we have you chained to the wall like the warlord has his woman?"

"She's not his woman."

Orion slapped a hand over her mouth and stared at their door with hard eyes. "You cannot speak like that, Jas. You need to control your speech."

She pried his hand off her face, one finger at a time. "It's never stopped me before."

"You've seen what it's like in the obsidian pit," Mekhl said. "If you cannot control yourself, we will be banished or executed."

Death didn't scare her, but the obsidian pit did. She'd barely managed to catch a glimpse of it before the warriors had taken Sage and herself before the warlord. Curiosity had led her to take her walks there. It wasn't as beautiful close up. Slaves lived in abominable conditions, starved, filthy, beaten and bloody. The depravity and sin in which the Scythians conducted themselves was sickening. Any woman was considered fair game there by the barbaric warriors. She'd had a few close calls herself. If it hadn't been for one of the men, she'd have been raped, or worse. Regardless of how bad it was down there, she kept visiting. It was like she needed to see the terrible conditions to keep herself from doing something stupid—like attempting an escape. Plus, it was one of the few ways she could do something to help. Only Orion knew that she smuggled food down there to feed some of the people.

She turned to Phoenix with her arms crossed and stood tall as he regarded her. "I would choose death before that."

"Brave, but you may not have a choice. You're now part of the warlord's circle. If he comes for you, there's nothing we can do."

A chill skittered down her spine. The way the warlord had examined her with his cold, calculating eyes had pulled the warmth from her body. He was every bit the monster she'd imagined him. But it was when he spoke she saw that he was also insane. Her heart ached for her friend. Had Sage been with him the entire time? What had she experienced at the hands of such a man? Goosebumps broke out on her arms. Her friend looked so different. So foreign. She'd touched Sage's face, needing assurance that her friend was still there. Sage's beauty had become something almost unreal. She resembled the warlord in that way, and it frightened Jasmine.

Rubbing a hand over her arm, she eyed the men, each observing her. It was times like these that she felt guilt. She could be suffering so much more, and yet she wasn't. Even though she hated being a captive, she appreciated the men she'd been sold to. They could've been like that bastard Rhys who'd just enjoyed inflicting pain, but they tended her wounds, spoke to her, fed and clothed her. Really, they didn't ask anything from her except obedience when in the public eye. Yes, it could be much worse.

Times like those were the most trying. She hated acting the slave in front of other warriors, it was demeaning. But it was then she remembered the twins. This wasn't about her anymore. They needed her, so it was her responsibility to do everything she could to survive and eventually get back to them.

"You could always let me go." At their silence, she tried another tactic. "Do any of you have children?"

"No, but by the stars, we hope to in the near future," Mekhl said, his voice holding reverence.

"Before your people took me, I was a mother."

The three men stilled.

"I have twins in Aermia, ones that I desperately miss and adore. I want to go home. They need me."

Phoenix strode forward and lifted her chin. "Lying about children is despicable. They're rare in Scythia and precious. How dare you use them as a way to sway us!"

"It's true. Their names are Jade and Ethan and they're three years old."

His lips thinned. "We know you lie. The healer certified your purity after your examination."

She jerked her chin out of his hand and glared at him. "They are mine, but they're not from my womb. Your people attacked my village, killing my brother and his wife, leaving the twins alone in the world except for me. They became *mine* from that point on."

Phoenix dipped his chin. "Apologies."

She didn't want to acknowledge it, but rarely did they apologize for anything. "Accepted."

"So, you have children?" Mekhl asked.

"I do, and I miss them so much. I worry about them constantly."

"Why are you just telling us of them now?" Orion demanded.

She looked from one man to the next. "Because you need to know what your kingdom's crimes have wrought, and what sort of place and people you expect me to embrace as home."

"You will never go back there," Phoenix said, softly. "Even if it was possible to grant you escape, you wouldn't survive the trek through the jungle. You barely survived the first time. The best thing you can do is put those children out of your mind. I'm sure your village is taking fine care of them." Something warmed in his eyes. "I'm sorry for what you suffered, but we can't change what's happened. If children are something you want, I'll give them to you. There would be no greater joy in the world than for me to have my own young."

Jasmine choked on her retort as he finished. Phoenix was offering her something that he thought she wanted. He was trying to help, even though it did the opposite. "Could you forget children you'd left alone and helpless?"

Phoenix glanced to the side, his jaw ticking.

"With the way you speak of children, I know the answer is no. Please don't expect me to forget them. They're everything to me. And, as for your offer, I appreciate it, but the answer is no. I don't want to bring more children into this world. It's too dangerous."

"If that's what you wish," Mekhl murmured.

All Jasmine's energy seemed to abandon her, leaving her with a headache and a desire for a nap. "I need to lie down," she muttered and left the group behind her.

She climbed onto the bed and stared at the wall. She had too many problems to solve. Maybe life would look a little simpler after a nap.

TWENTY-TWO

SAGE

SHE'D SPEND THE REST OF her life chained to the bloody wall.

She hung against the chains, not caring about her wrists. They were scarred already. What was a little more?

The warlord had left her strung up for five days. *Five days*. By day three, she'd pleaded with him to let her down, her arms numb and her legs feeble. The memory of his response still nauseated her.

He'd kissed her on the temple and cupped her face gently, gazing at her with affection. "This hurts me as much as it hurts you," he had said. "It kills me to have you tied up like this, but it will be better for us in the end. Soon, you'll long for my company." His nose nuzzled at her ear. "To crave my affection." His hand drifted from her cheek to her pulse beating wildly at the base of her throat. "To beg for my touch." Another soft kiss against her temple. "To come to grips with what it means to be *mine*."

To her everlasting shame, she'd told him exactly what he wanted to hear.

But he'd stared right through her with a sad smile. "They don't sound like how I imagined. One day, though, you'll mean those words. Until then, we both must suffer."

And suffer she did.

Each day, she submitted to him wiping her down with a cloth, feeding her from his hand, and conversing with her like they had before. Upon waking today, she was filled with a hopelessness she'd never before experienced. Sage wanted to close her eyes and just sleep forever.

The bathing pool was just in sight, and she had a sudden revelation. She now understood why Ezra had tried to kill her. Somehow, he had seen this coming. In the only way he could, he had tried to save her. Even now, staring at the pool, she wished he had succeeded. That peace Ezra promised? She longed for it and didn't even have the energy to be ashamed of her thoughts.

The door banged open, admitting the savior-turned-tormentor.

His wide, handsome smile should've put her on guard, but at this point, she didn't care what happened.

"I have news I'm sure you'll love."

She hung her head, tuning him out.

A finger slipped under her chin and lifted it up. Black eyes met hers. His smile slowly faded as he studied her. Minutes or hours might have passed as he gazed at her face. "It's done," he whispered in awe.

It took her a moment to realize he was smiling at her—not his normal smile, but the smile that made her heart flip and her chest warm. Despite everything that had happened, when he smiled at her like that, it made everything a little better. Shame filled her. Stars above, she was pathetic.

"It's time for you to come down, wild one."

A slow blink. She couldn't even rouse herself enough to get excited. What if he was just playing with her, only to snatch away her hope?

"Send for Maeve," he commanded.

The warrior who stood just inside his door spun on his heel and disappeared through the door.

"Okay, my lovely. It's time."

Zane moved in close and wrapped an arm around her waist. He lifted her, taking all her weight off her wrists and feet.

Tears sprang to her eyes at the instant relief, and pain swamped her. Her forehead landed on his shoulder as she breathed heavily. A small cry escaped her when he moved her arm from the one manacle and placed it around his neck. Hell, it hurt so bad.

"I know it hurts, but it will get better. I promise."

Her body trembled against his as he removed the chain from the wall and laid her down on the bed. His hands circled her arms and rubbed at them. More tears blurred her vision.

"It hurts."

"Patience. This will help."

Sage bit her lip to keep her cries of pain locked away as he worked feeling back into her arms.

"You sent for me, my lord?"

The familiar feminine voice had Sage searching for its owner. Maeve was as beautiful as she remembered—and just as disapproving. The woman's gaze scoured her and rested on the warlord's back. Something flickered across Maeve's face, and quick as lightning, disappeared. But Sage had seen it. It was an emotion with which she'd become very well acquainted over the years.

Hate.

Sage dropped her eyes to the warlord before the other woman saw the surprise on her face. Maeve had sung the warlord's praises the last time she'd been here, so what had changed these last few weeks?

"I need you to have a bath drawn for Sage."

Maeve started for the bathing room.

"Not in there. Bring one for the room."

Maeve paused and muttered, "It will be done, my lord."

"That's not necessary, my lord," Sage whispered, knowing even then Maeve heard the words. "The pool in the bathing room is adequate."

When he lifted his head and pushed his hair from his face, she forced herself not to cower. A coldness emanated from him, giving his face cruel lines.

"You'll never bathe in that pool again."

"Why?" she whispered.

He reached out a hand and brushed her cheek so softly that his touch could have been a butterfly's wing. "He almost took you from me. I'll never forget, and I don't want reminders. You'll not bathe in there again."

She swallowed and nodded her head in understanding. Some tension in his broad shoulders fell away, and he went back to rubbing her arms. Sage glanced over his head to the woman staring at her with an unreadable expression.

"Maeve?"

"Right away, my lord."

Sage stared at the covered window, listening as a tub was brought in and then the hot water, one pail at a time. The window was so close. If she could walk the fifteen paces, it would be within her grasp. But as close as it was, it was plenty far away. She'd never escape through there. Plus, part of her was afraid of opening that curtain. She had no idea what she'd find on the other side.

A finger traced her brow. She turned to Zane and stared up at him, silently accepting the touch.

"Are you ready for your bath?"

"Yes."

Even though he'd cleaned her as she hung there, she only felt dirtier. Maybe if she scrubbed hard enough, she could scrub away the last five days.

He took her hand and helped her slowly sit up the rest of the way.

"If you'll give us privacy, I'll make sure she's well taken care of," Maeve said.

"I'll stay." The warlord's tone left no room for argument.

Maeve gaped for a second, and then her expression hardened. Even her feet widened like she was getting ready to physically fight an opponent. "It's not proper, my lord. I assure you, I'll take the utmost—"

"No." His icy tone doused the room. "Do not tell me what's proper, sister. I'll not take any chances with her. Now, please do as I command. Help her undress and care for her, but I'll not leave."

Sage swallowed and stared at Maeve over the warlord's shoulder. She was Zane's sister? The woman looked ready to retort, but she inhaled deeply and seemed to forgo any further argument.

"It will be done."

"Thank you, Maeve." He stood and moved toward the pool room. "I'll give you privacy to change," he called over his shoulder.

If she could muster a grain of humor, Sage would've snorted at that. The man hadn't given her privacy in days. He'd been the one to bring her a chamber pot in which to relieve herself, for God's sake. Sage turned to the Scythian woman, scrutinizing her. She didn't care for the haughty look Maeve was giving her. It wasn't her fault she was in this situation.

"Quit scowling at me and help me up, please."

Maeve shook her head and strode to her side. Her nose wrinkled as she got a good look at Sage's robe. "You stink."

She shrugged, not offended in the least. She did stink.

"Can you walk?"

"I cannot," Sage replied without shame.

Maeve mumbled something under her breath and slipped an arm behind Sage's back. "I'm not carrying you."

Sage nodded and painfully shuffled toward the bath.

"Place your hands on the tub's edge, and I'll help you out of your robe."

Sage did as she was told and shivered as the Scythian woman stripped her of the soiled cloth. Maeve sucked in a sharp breath. Sage peeked over her shoulder to catch Maeve looking like she'd bitten into a lemon. Sage ignored her and managed to slip into the tub. A sigh slipped out as warmth caressed her aches. Fingers lifted her hair over the tub's edge.

"This will need a good brushing before I can wash it. It's a mess."

Sage's eyes slowly closed, and she hummed deep in her throat as Maeve began to brush her hair. There was something so soothing about it. In that moment, homesickness slapped her so hard she lost her breath. She wanted her mum, wanted to be hugged and held by someone who loved her.

She opened her eyes and stiffened. The warlord knelt by the bath, watching her with an intensity that made her gut clench. How long had he been watching her? She crossed an arm across her chest and one to the juncture of her thighs. "Wh-what are you doing?"

"Watching my consort bathe, as is my right."

She shrank deep into the tub, wishing to disappear from his heated gaze.

"My lord, you're making my job difficult. No doubt you wanted her to relax during her bath?"

"Indeed," he murmured. He smiled, all seduction, and skated his fingertip across the top of one of her breasts. "So beautiful."

Everything cried out at the violation. There was nothing she wanted more than to slap his hand away, but she didn't. She let him touch her. She had to.

He sighed, and his midnight-black gaze flickered above her head. "I know what you're alluding to. I'll leave you, but just know that if anything happens to her, there will be consequences. I'm leaving the door cracked so the guards can listen." He glanced back at her face. "I'll see you soon, wild one." Zane pushed from the floor and glided on silent feet out the door.

Sage stared at the closed door, wondering if it was a trick. Was he just waiting on the other side for her to get comfortable, so he could lunge back in?

"You can breathe now," Maeve murmured, her accent lilting.

The breath she was holding rushed out in a torrent of air. Her pounding heart didn't slow, though. How often did he sneak up on her without her knowing?

"He's gone now."

"What?" Sage asked.

"The warlord. I can no longer hear him."

It unnerved her that she was surrounded by people so much more powerful than she was. Here in Scythia, she was the prey. A shudder worked down her spine at the thought.

Maeve poured water over Sage's hair and began to wash it. Minute by minute, Sage's unease abated. A calm quiet settled over the room, giving her a small sense of safety and comfort.

"Thank you," she whispered, while staring blankly at the wall ahead. "I know this isn't something you'd wish to do, but I appreciate it nonetheless." After spending days chained, she was sure she couldn't have washed her own hair even if she'd been given the option, and the idea of the warlord doing it made her sick.

The fingers in her hair paused. "You're welcome," Maeve said gruffly. She finished up with Sage's hair and moved gracefully around the tub. Holding a rag, she sank to her knees in one fluid movement. "Your wrist, please," she asked, holding her hand out.

Sage pulled her hand from the scented water and held her abused flesh out for the Scythian. Maeve's lips tightened, but other than that, she said nothing. The Scythian woman took painstaking care of her arms, washing the wounds until they were clean. Sage startled when Maeve's hand clenched against her wrist. Her yip of pain made the Scythian woman loosen her grip, but the glint in her eyes and thin lips spoke of anger. Sage followed her gaze. Ah, her scars.

"They're not as bad as they seem," she murmured.

"How did you come by them?" Maeve whispered, her tone

uncharacteristically soft.

"A Scythian thought he'd have fun with me." Her words were slow and lifeless, even to her own ears. "I'm sure you know him." Sage arched a brow. "You were there when the warlord executed him."

Maeve paled, her normally olive skin turning a sickly color. She dropped Sage's wrist into the water and clutched the side of the tub. "No," she breathed, anguish on her face.

Sage's brow furrowed at the intense reaction. "I'm sorry if he was your friend." Her brows furrowed when one tear dripped down Maeve's face. Was he more than a friend? A husband or lover? She searched her mind for something to say to soothe the woman, but she came up with nothing. Rhys was a monster.

"All of them, were they from—" Maeve stuttered.

She pitied the woman, but she wouldn't lie to her. "He personally etched each and every scar into my body himself."

Maeve placed a hand on her own stomach and panted. "I had no idea. I—" She shook her head. "How can a little boy grow into such a man?"

She blinked and tried to make sense of Maeve's words. A little boy? She hadn't noticed it before, but Maeve looked familiar. She studied her a moment.

No, she thought. It couldn't be possible. The Scythian woman looked hardly older than she and yet... when she thought of it, she couldn't remember seeing anyone that looked older than 30 at the execution or the feast. Could it be possible? She *was* the warlord's sister, but the mother of Rhys? That seemed too far-fetched. "Were you his mother?" she whispered.

"I was," Maeve whispered back, staring at her neither with malice nor friendliness.

A thousand questions flashed through Sage's mind, but only one came out. "How?" she breathed. "You're too young."

Maeve gestured to her face. "I'm older than I look."

A product of Scythian tampering? Likely. "Like the Sirenidae?"

A bitter smile twisted the woman's lips. "Something like that."

Stars above, what kind of creatures did the Scythians create? Panic squeezed her chest. Had they been experimenting with her, too?

"What has he been giving me?" she demanded, grabbing Maeve's wrist.

Maeve's gaze shuttered. "I don't know."

"Don't lie to me," Sage said desperately.

"I'm not. You think he shares his plan with me just because the same blood runs through our veins?" The Scythian woman shook her head. "You're still so young and naïve. You've no idea what you're doing."

"I'm surviving," she said simply.

"No one survives him, child. No one."

That she could believe. "And you, how have you survived?" Sage asked. Maeve might be abrasive, but Sage was sure she wasn't insane like her brother.

A mirthless laugh burst out of the woman. "I didn't. I gave up pieces of myself until all that remained was this perfected shell."

Sage stared hard at the woman, who stared back evenly. "If that were true, you'd have killed me already."

"How do you know I won't?"

"You fear him," she said simply. Maeve's expression didn't change much, but the tightening around her eyes betrayed her. "You wouldn't risk his wrath, not for yourself, but for the ones you love." Sage leaned her chin against the tub, never taking her gaze from the Scythian woman. "You have shown me kindness."

Maeve scoffed.

"You can pretend all you want, but I see the good you try to hide under your rough persona. You're kind to me in spite of everything. I'm not Scythian, your brother wants me, and…" She paused and continued in a soft voice, "I'm the cause of your son's death… I'm sorry for it." It wasn't his death she was sorry for, but that it caused this woman pain. No parent should ever have a child die before them, let alone witness it.

The Scythian woman studied her. "Why apologize? You hated him. I saw it the moment you looked at me when we first met. Surely, his death pleases you?"

A part of her, the dark twisted part, was happy he was dead. But that part also sickened her. She should never rejoice in the death of someone, no matter how depraved they were. A life was still a life.

Sage pushed her thoughts away and answered, "Because no matter what he was to me, he was still your son and that means something to you."

Maeve's brows rose in surprise, and then her face settled into its normal stoic expression. "How?"

"How what?"

"How are you so…so good?"

A dark chuckle slipped from Sage. "There's nothing good about me."

Maeve shook her head. "You should hate me, based on association alone."

"I could say the same about you. But that's the type of thinking that got our kingdoms into this situation in the first place."

"He doesn't deserve you."

Sage's eyes widened.

The Scythian woman stiffened and shot to her feet. "Enough of this conversation." She blurred from the room in a burst of speed, then was standing before Sage holding a towel out for her in less than five seconds.

"Get out. He's coming."

Using all her strength, Sage heaved herself up, water sluicing off her body. Maeve held a hand out and helped her from the tub, wrapping the towel around her just as the door burst open.

"I've wonderful news."

Sage turned carefully and clutched the towel tighter to her body as Zane's gaze heated, slowly running over her barely-clad form. Time for a distraction. "Good news?"

He lifted his hand, holding a letter, and grinned. The boyish smile softened his foreign, otherworldly beauty into something warm and approachable. Shame washed over her at the errant thought.

"Aermia has responded!"

"Responded to what?"

"My letter, of course."

She forced herself to not step back when he pushed into her space and clasped her face between his huge hands.

"Soon, we'll have peace."

His smile was positively infectious, and she had to force her mouth flat to keep it from answering his. What was he really up to? He didn't desire peace, he desired control. So, what was his game?

The warlord seemed to know her thoughts, and his smile turned a little dangerous. "Oh, dear Sage, I long for peace. Peace of mind that no one can steal from me, that my line will continue, and that the Aermian dogs won't interbreed with my people."

She swallowed hard, very aware that he could crush her skull between his hands as easily as cracking an egg. Still, she spoke her mind, "I'm Aermian."

His eyes darkened, and a fevered light entered them as he stared at her. "Much to my chagrin." He pressed closer, his nose touching hers, his breath puffing across her lips. "You are my greatest crime against my people," he whispered. "I hate that I want you. It would be easier to kill you. Believe me, I've mulled over the idea at great length."

Stars above. Her insides were quivering with fear. He had said it so matter-of-factly, like he was speaking of the weather, not that he'd pondered murdering her, all the while holding her like a lover. Something dangerous crossed his face and then cleared the next second, leaving her shaken.

"But I cannot do it." A disappointed sigh escaped him, ruffling the hair at her temple. "Despite your inferior birth and flawed genes, I want you, and I hate you for it. Yet, there's something about your scars and green eyes that calls to me."

There was nothing to say to that. It was the ramblings of a madman. A madman who somehow managed to sway her emotions and who she was still inexplicably drawn to. A dangerous madman.

He kissed her forehead and then stepped back to address Maeve, who stood next to the mirror, still holding the brush. "This is good news for you. It means you will see your daughter sooner than we thought. You shall have her back in your arms by the end of the month."

Maeve looked like he had slapped her. "My lord?"

He waved a hand toward her. "It's been too long since I've seen my niece. Her punishment is over. I'm sure she's learned her lesson. Now, leave us."

Maeve placed the brush on the vanity and quickly left the room, leaving the warlord and Sage alone. He turned to her and reached out to brush a finger along her bare arm, leaving goosebumps in its wake.

"How was your bath?" he asked, strolling slowly toward the vanity.

"It was refreshing," she said.

He picked up the brush and jerked his chin toward the bed. "Put on your new robe and then come and sit. I'll brush your hair."

She glanced at the semi-translucent robe he'd brought in and back to the warlord. "Will you give me privacy?"

"I've been generous enough for today."

Sage swallowed and slowly stepped up to the bed. She peeked over her shoulder to find the warlord leaning against her vanity, legs crossed, watching her. Turning back to the robe, she inhaled deeply and picked it up. He expected her to wear that?

"You still aren't changing. I think someone wants me to dress her myself."

Panic fluttered in her chest at his softly-spoken words. Carefully, despite her shaking hands, she slid her arms in without dropping the towel, and closed the robe before letting the towel fall to the floor. As fast as her shaking fingers could move, she tied it closed and smoothed the fabric.

Turning, she almost stumbled when she caught sight of herself in the mirror. The robe reached the floor and trailed behind her, but that did not mean it was modest. It clung to her curves in a way that was seductive; the fabric was just see-through enough that it gave tantalizing peeks of what was underneath. Sage pulled her hair over her shoulders to cover her chest.

Zane tilted his head as he studied her face. "Come to me, consort."

Rafe would have been proud at how she kept her mask in place, not reacting to the heated way the warlord gaze at her, or his use of 'consort.' She put one foot in front of the other and sank onto the stool.

He pushed off the vanity and moved behind her, all grace and danger, and began to brush her hair. She avoided watching him in the mirror, his perfection almost too much to look at. What sort of sick game was he playing? One moment, he was cutting her friend open, and the next he was brushing her hair. Everything inside her was muddled, leaving nothing but confusion.

Her jaw flexed as he gathered up the hair falling over her chest. She might as well be naked for all the good this robe did. Light fingers brushed her hair over one shoulder, and his lips ran along the skin of her neck in an unhurried way.

A shudder worked through her body.

He peeked up at her, his eyes glittering, his hair tickling her collarbone. "Kiss me."

She shook her head.

"Remember the cost of your rebellion, wild one."

If Tehl were there, he'd tell her to fight the warlord, no matter the cost. But friends protected each other, so that's what she did. She protected Jasmine.

She twisted her neck and met the brush of his lips.

Her stomach churned, and she willed her mind to go blank. *Wrong, wrong, wrong*, her mind screamed. The warlord softly touched her chin and skated his fingers down her neck to rest above her heartbeat. The kiss lasted far too long, and she felt dirty from the inside out. No amount of scrubbing would remove the guilt and taint from her soul.

Finally, he broke away; she gasped out a breath as his lips left hers. He looked stunning, and innocent, which was the farthest thing from the truth. There was nothing innocent about him or the way he was gazing at her.

"This pleases me, wild one."

Another piece of her heart shriveled in her chest. She just bet it did.

His thumb traced her lips. "One day, you'll look at me like you did before. You'll see reason. We just need to be patient until that day comes."

He'd wait a long time.

He pulled her up from the stool and led her toward the bed. He sat and tugged her onto his lap. Her heart jackknifed in her chest and she squirmed, uncomfortable. Hands landed on her hips and squeezed. Sage peeked up at him.

"You need to stop squirming, wild one," he said through gritted teeth, "or I will forget my promise, and eating will be the last thing we will be doing."

Hell. She froze like a deer scenting a predator.

Zane plucked a grape from a platter sitting on her bed and held it to her lips. "Eat, consort. You must keep up your strength, so you can heal."

Her lips parted, allowing him to push the grape into her mouth. She chewed slowly and stared blankly across the room. A healing that she wouldn't need if he hadn't chained her to the wall for five days. Another grape entered her vision, and she glanced up at him, hoping her feelings were well hidden from the monster wrapped in this deceiving package. How could she ever escape him?

Her answer was clear. There was no escape.

TWENTY-THREE

TEHL

TEHL STEPPED INTO HIS STUDY and examined the draperies, his brows furrowed in confusion. It seemed that his curtains were giggling. He closed the door and cocked his head, listening. Well, it certainly couldn't be an assassin, or even a lady come to seduce him; the giggle was much too childish. The corner of his mouth twitched at the small purple shoes peeking out from the bottom. If he had to venture a guess, he would say there was a certain small girl hiding herself behind the material.

Feeling mischievous, instead of just whipping back the curtains as he might normally do, he began speaking to himself in a loud voice, affecting bewilderment. "My, my, it seems as though my study is full of humor today."

Another soft snigger slipped from the draperies.

"I wonder, could there be someone hiding in this room?" He crossed to his desk and peeked underneath it. "Well that's odd. No one is under my desk. Where else might someone be?"

He stomped dramatically to a tapestry, which hung on the far wall, and yanked it back. "Huh. No one behind my tapestry." Tehl then crept quietly toward the curtains and whipped them back. "I found you!"

The girl let loose a screech loud enough to burst his eardrums and then fell into a fit of giggles.

He smiled to himself. "Isa?"

She pushed a shock of fiery red curls from her face and looked up at him with enormous violet eyes. She grinned and jumped to her feet, wrapping her delicate arms around his leg. "Uncle!" she squealed, "I surprised you!"

Tehl pulled her up and swung her into the air, landing her in his arms for a bear hug. "Isa, darling. It's been so long since I've seen you!" His heart warmed when she wrapped her arms around his neck and squeezed. It didn't even bother him that her unruly curls were tickling his nose. "I've missed you so much! When did you arrive?"

"Today. Papa sent for me and now I get to live with you! In the castle!"

He stared at his three-year-old niece, slightly shocked at how different she looked from the last time he'd seen her. Her limbs had slimmed, her face was sharper, and it occurred to him that he had already missed a lot of Isa's life. He didn't like that idea.

He was pulled from his thoughts when a small finger tried to smooth out his brow.

"Uncle, did I make you sad?"

It was incredible that, even at her age, she was so aware of the feelings of others. He brushed a curl from her face and smiled, cupping her cheek. "Of course not, Isa. You could never make me sad. Is your papa aware of where you are?"

She glanced to the ground and then looked up at him sheepishly. "No."

Tehl rolled his eyes. Of course, the little rascal had escaped notice. She was infinitely more devious than any of them had been growing up. Turning on his heel, he opened the door and addressed the guard stationed outside: "Inform Gavriel that his daughter is with me." The guard nodded and bowed before striding off down the hallway.

"What would you like to do, Isa?" he asked as he closed the door and moved toward his desk.

"Can I paint?"

He kissed the top of her head and sat her on his desk as he took his own seat. "Sadly, I don't have any paints. Can you use a quill?"

"Uh huh."

Tehl eyed his niece in doubt. "Are you sure?"

Her little nose wrinkled. "Nurse's been teaching me. I can do it."

He had to hide a smile at the indignation in her little voice. "I'll make sure to have colors brought to my desk, so the next time you visit, you can paint."

She grinned and snagged the quill out of his hand. "Okay, Uncle."

There was something magical about having her here with him. He'd always loved children. They were so honest in their affections and full of vivacity. Reaching out a hand, he ran it over her curls. When was the last time he'd felt so light, so happy? He couldn't remember. He banished the glum thoughts and began working on his own paperwork. The two continued that way for quite some time. Every once in a while, she'd ask him a question that he would answer, and then she'd go back to her swirls.

"Uncle?"

"Yes?" he answered, continuing his correspondence.

"Where is Auntie?"

He jerked and shot her a questioning look. "Auntie?"

"Aunt Sage. Papa wrote in his letter that I would get to meet Auntie and that she'd teach me how to use a dagger." Her eyes widened comically. "But Nurse said that wasn't proper."

For the life of him, he couldn't figure out how to respond. His mouth opened and closed a few times as he thought about explaining what kept him up most nights. "Your auntie…" he drew out, "isn't here right now."

Isa's pixie face fell. "When will she be back?"

"Soon," he deflected. Hopefully soon, but hope was never on his side.

His door burst open and in stormed Gav. When he spotted the two of them at Tehl's desk, he skidded to a halt and a small smile replaced the scowl he'd been wearing. "I see you've acquired a helper."

"Papa!" Isa grinned and held up a paper with squiggles all over it. "Flowers!"

"Those are beautiful pictures, darling," Gav said.

Tehl squinted at the paper she held up. Nothing in that even closely resembled flowers, but when she held it up for his inspection, he just smiled and nodded as well.

Gav strode to the front of the desk and lifted Isa to the edge. His cousin's face turned serious as he gazed down at his daughter. "Isa, what did I say about staying by Nurse?"

Isa ducked her chin.

"Look at me, Isa." The little girl peeked up at her father. "What did I say?"

"Not to run off?"

"And what did you do?"

"I wanted to see Uncle."

"I understand that, but I asked you to do something, and you disobeyed me."

"But I wanted to—"

"Isa," Gav admonished. "Don't argue with me. I told you we would visit later. You scared your nurse and me. It's not safe for you to wander the halls like you did at home. Because you disobeyed, you're going to bed early tonight."

Isa's shoulders slumped forward. "Sorry, Papa."

"I know." He wrapped his arms around her and hugged her to his chest. "I appreciate you apologizing, and I love you."

"Love you," she sniffed.

"Nurse is going to take you for a snack and then a nap."

"No nap," Isa complained.

"Not a choice." Gav turned toward the door. "Mrs. Clairette!"

An ancient-looking woman opened the door and stepped inside. "My lord?"

"Isa is in need of a snack and her nap."

The older woman nodded and held her hand out. "Isa? Come, child."

Isa hid her face in Gav's shirt. "I don't want to go, Papa." She peeked up at Tehl. "I want to stay with Uncle."

He was about to assure her she was welcome to stay when he caught Gav's expression. "Well, the quicker you go and eat your snack and take a nap, the quicker you can wake up and have dinner with me. Maybe we'll have cake for dessert."

His niece's eyes rounded. "Cake?"

"Yes."

Isa squealed and wiggled down from his desk, all but sprinting to the nurse. She waved to them over her shoulder as she left. "Bye, Papa! Bye, Uncle!"

Gav blew her a kiss while Tehl simply waved, the little girl now following the old woman without a complaint. He closed the door behind them and turned to his cousin, smiling. "You finally brought Isa home! Why didn't you tell me?"

"We were going to surprise you tonight, but," Gav scowled, "apparently

Isa couldn't wait. I wish that Mrs. Clairette could keep a better eye on her."

"By the way Mrs. Clairette squinted around this room, it seemed as though she couldn't see," Tehl said. "How old is she now?"

Gav ran a hand through his raven hair. "She's old. And sadly, old enough that I now need to find someone else to take care of Isa."

"But hasn't Mrs. Clairette taken care of Isa since birth?"

"Yes, but Mrs. Clairette can't live at the palace. Her husband is older than she, and her children and grandchildren live around my keep. I can't uproot them all just for my daughter. The journey here has already worn her out. I'm not saying they're unwilling. I'm sure that if old Will was healthy enough to make the journey, they would do it, but honestly? It's just not possible."

"What are you going to do, then?"

"I'm not sure. I hate the idea of trying to find another suitable companion and caretaker for Isa."

"Have you told Isa?"

"No," Gav grimaced. "It will break her heart, I'm sure."

Tehl opened his mouth to answer when the door slammed open. He rolled his eyes at his brother. "Will you ever learn to knock?"

Sam powered to his desk and held out an envelope. "Not when there's news."

He plucked the envelope from his brother's grasp and brushed his thumb over the black wax seal. This was it. Everything hinged on the contents of this letter. He glanced up at his brother and then Gav.

Pulling in a deep breath, he snatched the letter and ripped it open. All the air rushed from his lungs. It was just three sentences.

We are in accord. Your letter pleased me. We will meet in one month and embark on something our kingdoms haven't experienced in hundreds of years: peace.

Tehl's jaw hung open. This was unreal. He turned to the two men at his side. "He agreed. We're set to meet in one month."

Sam moved around the desk and pulled him into a hug. "Just one more month, brother, and then we'll have Sage in our arms. She'll be safe."

Emotion clogged his throat. They were almost there. Only thirty days until he had his wife and advisor back. "I need to tell her parents," he said absently.

"Do you think that's a good idea? To give them hope?" Sam asked.

Tehl ran a hand through his hair. "I've got no other choice. I can't keep this from them. And even if I don't say anything, I'm certain Lilja will. Honestly, though, I'd rather…"

"You want it to come from you," Gav supplied.

"Yes, and I'm due for a visit anyway." He blew out a breath and handed Sam the letter. "Alert the war council. We'll meet this evening." He rounded the desk and clapped Gav on the shoulder. "Tell Isa I'll be back for dessert."

His cousin nodded and, just as he was exiting the room, his brother called out, "Give the Blackwells my best."

Tehl tensed as the door swung open, revealing Sage's father. The man looked fairly healthy, but also very tired.

The older man stepped up to him and wrapped him in a hug. "Welcome, son."

He released Tehl and stepped back. The heat of the forge enveloped him, the warmth draping over him like a warm blanket. A small smile pulled at his lips as the older man sat him down and poured him a drink. Tehl sank onto the bench and took the cup of ale with a muttered, "Thank you." Colm sat and sipped his ale, all the while watching him over the rim.

"What's eating at you?"

"Is it that obvious?"

"Yes, though I've also come to know you a bit over the last couple of months."

Tehl swallowed. "I've had word."

Colm paled and placed a bracing hand against his workbench. "Sage? Is she…is she all right?"

"She's alive."

Tehl shot to his feet as the older man leaned forward, visibly sagging. "Colm!"

The older man grabbed Tehl's hand and yanked him to his knees before pulling him into another hug.

"So, she's really alive?" Colm rasped, his eyes full of tears.

"She is."

Sage's father let loose a heavy sigh and pulled back. He quickly wiped his face and stood, extending a hand to his son-in-law. "We need to tell Gwen."

Tehl clasped his hand and pushed off the floor, looking the other man in the eye. "Is she strong enough to bear it? We may be getting her back, but I'm not sure in what condition we'll find her."

The older man's face hardened. "Condition?"

"She's been in Scythia this whole time. Specifically, with their warlord," he finished softly.

"No," the older man breathed, looking green.

"He's assured us that she's been well taken care of and is in good health, but…"

"It's damn Scythia. You can't trust a word they say!" Colm thundered.

"I know, but what other choice do I have?"

Colm's face fell. "You've none, I know."

"I have to balance my feelings for Sage with the good of the whole kingdom." He slumped onto the bench and hung his head. "I'm tired, so tired. Each day I awake only to find myself stuck in the same nightmare from the day before."

A large hand settled on his shoulder, and his father-in-law's deep voice washed over him: "We don't blame you."

"How could you not? I'm the reason she's gone."

"Do you really think that's true?"

A bark of laughter escaped him. "No, I suppose not. Somehow, she still would have found a way to be in the middle of this mess."

The man chuckled. "She never could stay out of trouble."

Tehl sobered. "I worry."

"We all do."

He nodded. "Where's Gwen?"

"She is sewing by the fireplace."

"Are you sure she can handle this?"

He nodded once. "She's stronger than most."

TWENTY-FOUR

SAGE

TIME STRETCHED AND BLURRED, ONLY measured by the warlord's visits. It sickened her how easy it was to fall into a routine with him. It was now second nature to accept the food he offered from his hands, his kisses, and his care. The night he released her from her punishment, he moved back into his suite.

She had tried to sleep on the couch, but all it took was a reminder of his threat for her to trudge back to the bed. Her skin had crawled when he'd slipped into bed, but he had left her untouched. She hadn't thought she'd sleep, but exhaustion had pulled her under. The next morning, she'd awoken in a panic, barely able to breathe. A close inspection, however, revealed that he'd left her unmolested. He'd left her to the silence of his empty room.

The silence was the worst.

Her thoughts ran in a continuous loop in his absence. Day by day, she was losing what was left of her mind. She reflected on her mistakes, her misjudgments, her unnatural attraction to the warlord, dying, and back to the warlord. He consumed so many of her thoughts.

After being starved of human interaction for so long, she looked forward to when he'd visit, to the gentle touches bestowed upon her. One day, she realized that she wasn't scared when he came to bed, and that his side had slowly encroached onto hers, until he slept curled around her. It disgusted her that sadness blanketed her when he left in the morning. She craved his company, but didn't understand why. It was wrong, depraved, and yet she couldn't help it.

"Wild one?"

Sage blinked and glanced over her shoulder to catch the warlord watching her. "Yes?"

"Come here."

She pulled her fingers from Nali's fur, earning her a chuff of discontent, and moved to stand in front of him. He leaned forward and brushed a kiss across her lips with a smile.

"I have news for you."

"News?"

"It's time for a trip."

"A trip? You mean, I get to leave this room?" Even she could hear the desperation and excitement in her voice. She was pathetic.

"Yes, we leave now."

"Now? So soon?" Her heart raced. What brought this about?

"It's safer to travel."

"Where are we going?" she asked. Maybe he'd tell her.

"To another one of my castles."

She hid her frown at his evasion. How would she ever escape if she didn't know where she was?

"I need to pack." She scanned the room. It held nothing of hers. The only thing she truly cared for was the black feline staring at her through a slitted eye. Turning back to the warlord, she shrugged. "I have nothing to pack."

He cupped her face with a grin. "I've already arranged clothing to be packed for you. Something befitting a queen." She stiffened as he caressed the crown collar around her throat tenderly before settling his palm on the side of her neck. "I don't understand how you do it, but you bewitch me. Something about you ruins all of my best-laid plans."

"Ouch." Sage pulled away from him and rubbed her neck. "A thorn poked me," she explained. The collar stopped bothering her after the first couple weeks, but every so often it would hurt something terrible. Her brow furrowed as the room spun. "I don't feel so good." Zane's arms wrapped around her as her stomach plummeted, and she stumbled.

"Are you alright?"

"I'm exhausted." Her temple pounded, and she lifted a hand to her head, blinking. Just barely was she able to focus on his face. Concern was evident in his expression, but his eyes spoke the truth. Calculation. Her heart sank. This was planned.

"Did you drug me?" she asked weakly.

Zane swept her feet out from underneath her and carried her to the bed. "I had to. You wouldn't be reasonable about traveling. I can't risk you trying to escape and getting yourself hurt. This is for your own protection."

"Zane," she whispered, struggling to sit up. "But I promised."

"I know. That's why Jasmine is coming as well."

She shook her head to keep awake. "You're bringing my friend?"

"I couldn't rely on you being logical with what's ahead of us. I don't plan on hurting her. I'm bringing her to protect you, really."

"How does bringing her protect me?" she mumbled, the words becoming hard to form.

"It protects you from doing something stupid." He pressed a kiss to her lips. "I will explain it all when we arrive."

"Liar," she whispered, her eyelids too heavy to keep open. He didn't explain his plans to anyone. He was too suspicious. Too cautious. Too controlling.

"Goodnight, wild one."

He'd lied. Again. Hurt her. Again. Tricked her. Again. When would the deception end?

Never.

TWENTY-FIVE

SAGE

WHEN SAGE CAME TO, EVERYTHING was blurry.

She blinked several times before the world came back into focus. When it did, she found herself in a massive tent with tiny lanterns hanging from its ceiling. There were furs covering the floor, and the lanterns cast a soft glow over the space, casting deep shadows in the corners. Where was she and why couldn't she move her limbs? What had Zane given her?

She felt movement on her right and, when she turned her head to inspect it, found herself nose-to-nose with Nali. The black feline swiped her rough, long tongue from Sage's chin to her temple. She scowled at the beast.

"Nali! No kisses!"

If Nali could have rolled her eyes, Sage was sure she would have. She was about to scold her further when the murmuring of voices caught her attention. She lifted her neck, attempting to see farther. One tent flap was tied back, giving her a view into a connecting room.

In it, the warlord stood, hands braced against a table, surrounded by warriors. Even after everything he'd done, something about him called to her. Was it his unearthly looks? His charisma? Whatever it was, it disturbed her, deeply.

Almost as if he heard her thoughts, his dark gaze cut to hers, entrapping her. A shudder rolled through her. Everything about him was all sorts of wrong. A stunning smile curled his sensuous lips at her blatant stare, and she jerked her eyes away, staring instead at the canvas wall. Her eyes traced the flickering shadows in an attempt to calm her beating heart.

The murmurs died down, and she had to force herself not to glance in his direction again. She could feel his attention on her, but maybe if she paid him no mind, he'd leave her alone.

"Consort," his smooth, deep voice called.

She was never that lucky. Sage continued to stare at the wall, her fingers tightening in Nali's fur.

"Look at me, wild one."

Sage stared harder at the shadows.

She heard him sigh before he moved to kneel before her, cutting off her view of the wall. She focused on staring at the laces of his shirt.

"I know you're angry with me."

Angry didn't even begin to describe how she felt.

Another sigh. "You needed protection, and this was the only way I could protect you."

"By drugging me?" she whispered, still not looking up.

"You know the dangers of jungles. I needed to transport you safely. The risk is too high, and you're too important."

Her gaze flew to his face. He was serious. His expression showed tender emotion and something deeper than passing affection. She hid her dawning horror at this revelation and forced herself to remain still as he cupped her cheek. "Don't hide from me. I hate it."

"I'm right here," she whispered.

"Don't lie to both of us. You're a thousand leagues away, Sage. I know the symptoms. I invented them."

She swallowed and focused back on his laces. "I can't move my arms," she said, changing the subject.

"It will be a while until you can."

He pushed back from the bedroll and began unlacing his shirt.

"What are you doing?" she asked in a high voice.

"Undressing. It's time for bed."

Panic fluttered in her breast, and her breathing turned shallow. She was completely at his mercy. She couldn't fight back even if she wanted to. He stilled and cocked his head.

"Hell…" He dropped his hands with a scowl. "I'm not going to accost you. Have I not told you that? I will never take from you!"

She didn't believe him for one second, and her expression must have shown it, because he let out an irritated huff as he jerked off his boots before stomping to the bedroll, pulling back the fur covering her, and sliding in. Her heart pounded as he rested on one elbow and leaned over her, earning a growl from Nali.

He glared at the beast, then looked back to her. "I've not *ever* taken from you, have I?" he demanded.

"No," she whispered, conscious of the fact he had complete control. Now was not the time to challenge him.

He scanned her face and brushed a stray hair from her cheek. "I regret what happened that night. I've never been that close to losing myself. It sickens me when I think of it."

Sage didn't regret it, not one bit. It had shown her who he truly was, and she now understood that the other person she'd come to know was merely a persona, one invented for her benefit.

"I hate that it was necessary," he whispered. "Do you think I liked seeing you chained to my wall?" He shook his head, his hair brushing her face. "I hated every moment of your punishment. It hurt me as much as it hurt you."

Sage doubted that, but still she remained silent. She was getting good at that these days.

"One day, you'll understand. I wait for that day," he whispered and pressed his lips to her cheek. He pulled back, a tender smile on his face. "Until then, I can content myself with only holding you."

Zane wiggled his arm underneath her head, twisted her to face Nali, and pulled her into his arms.

She squeezed shut her eyes as he curled his large body around her, holding her like she was precious, even though she already carried scars from his cruelty. She inhaled sharply when his other arm snaked across her waist and rested against her stomach. Her moment of alarm passed quickly, though, as the warmth of his body cocooned her and fatigue settled over her.

"Are you hungry?" His breath moved the loose hair around her ear.

The idea of food did not appeal. "No."

Warm lips brushed the skin below her ear. "All right, love."

Goosebumps broke out along her arms at the whispered endearment. His hand moved from her stomach and passed along her arm, soothing her goosebumps even as he caused more to erupt. Her skin prickled, hyperaware of him as he intertwined his fingers with hers, the metal of his ring kissing her. He turned her hand and brushed his fingers along her wrist.

"Sleep, wild one."

She hissed as something pricked her wrist. "Again?" she asked, not even shocked that he'd drugged her.

"For your protection. When you wake, we'll be at the palace."

"You mean the prison," she slurred as Nali faded into a black blob.

"*My* prison," he whispered, and darkness once again claimed her.

Awareness came to her in the form of warmth. Sunlight filtered through her eyelids and warmed her face. Her fingers twitched, and then brushed over the material under her. A bed. It was a real bed, so they weren't still traveling. Sage took stock of her body, flexing her fingers and toes. Her muscles were stiff, but at least she could move them this time.

With care, she rolled to the side and scooted just out of the light. Cracking her eyes, she took stock of her new prison. Two huge doors were opened toward her, revealing a sprawling red stone balcony that boasted a view unlike any she'd ever seen. She stumbled to her feet, lurching toward the balcony. Pain stabbed at her temples and her stomach heaved, but none of that mattered. She gasped, and tears poured down her face when the cool breeze wound around her. She was outside, *finally.* So many emotions coursed through her. She blinked several times, trying to remember the last time she'd seen the sun.

Smiling, she leaned on the intricately-carved railing to get a better view and then gasped. The balcony hung in the air, a two-hundred-foot drop below her. Pine trees stood like giants on the mountainside below, and red sand peeked out between them.

They had to be in Nagali.

She craned her neck. Above her, similar balconies adorned what seemed to be a castle, and the structure itself had been built into the mountainside. It amazed her how seamlessly the castle blended into the rock. Her gaze traced the exotically-upturned roofs, and the way each story of the castle was smaller than the last, reminding her of a tall, castle-sized cake.

Prying her eyes from the architectural marvel, she turned back to the view. It was stunning and foreign. Part of her mourned for the land. How no one now enjoyed its beauty. Part of her was in awe that she'd get to experience something that she'd only read about in books.

Her eyes still watered at the bright light, but she didn't care. She was outside. She didn't realize how much of her longed for the outdoors, craved it. Dark green forest and red sand gave way to more familiar trees and golden fields. Her heart squeezed in her chest, and another tear slipped down her face for another reason entirely.

Aermia. Home was so close, and yet so far away. It was a cruel joke.

She shot a glance at the open doorway. She could spare herself the pain and go back inside, not force herself to gaze upon what she'd lost, but she didn't. She craved the view. While she felt pain and loss, she also enjoyed the beauty and the freedom of being out there, and it was more than she'd had in a long time. So, she sank to her knees and took it in, sitting until her butt went numb and the sun had moved across the sky.

The air was colder now, and a shiver worked through her, though she still didn't move. The sunset was the most beautiful thing she'd ever seen, the sky painted with rich reds, oranges, and purples.

"It's beautiful, isn't it?"

Sage barely kept herself from jumping at the sound of his voice. Slowly, she turned to the warlord. He stood, arms and legs crossed, one shoulder leaning against the stone wall. The wind ruffled his inky hair, giving him a softer, tousled look. But it was a lie, just like everything else about him. Her traitorous heart flipped when he gave her a lopsided smile and pushed off the wall, holding his hand out for her. She slipped her small hand into his large one and allowed him to pull her to her feet.

Zane spun her to face the sunset and wrapped his arms around her, his chin resting on her head. "You like your view?"

She swallowed and nodded.

"Did you sit out here all afternoon?"

"Yes. It's beautiful."

"I hoped you would." He paused and hugged her tighter. "There's something wild and exotic about this land that makes it easy to lose yourself in it." Zane lifted a hand and pointed to the far-off river. "Our company will arrive soon."

Sage squinted and then gaped when she spotted what he was pointing at. It was an army. "Who is it?" she asked, her heart pounding in her chest.

He pulled his hand back and rested it on her beating heart. "The Aermian council."

Her pulse kicked up another notch. "Why?"

"The time has come for treaty negotiations."

"A treaty?" She all but choked.

"Rather boring business, but something we must discuss nonetheless. Come."

She took one last glance at the fading sunset and followed him in. Sage took in the rooms as he went about closing and barring the doors.

The walls were a soft cream fresco, accented with a few colorful mosaics. One particular scene was of a red dragon drawn on the wall across from the bed. She walked up to it and ran her hand along the dragon's scales, fascinated. Had they used jewels to create this picture?

"I should've known you'd be enticed by the dragons."

Sage jerked her hand from the mosaic like she had been caught doing something naughty. Spinning on her heel, she eyed the warlord. "It's beautiful."

He shook his head ruefully and began rolling his sleeves up. "Out of all the pictures that caught your eye, it was the abominations that drew your attention."

"The stones caught my eye," she said, knowing it was only half the truth.

"They're rubies," the warlord said. "The palace is filled with them."

The room fell silent, the only sound the crackling of the fire.

The warlord let out a sigh and moved to one of two large chairs placed beside the fire. He turned them to face each other and then sat down. He glanced at her and held out a hand. "Please sit."

His serious tone turned her blood to ice. Cautiously, she moved to the seat across from him, doing as he requested. She clasped her trembling hands together and held her breath, waiting for him to speak. The intensity of his gaze made her want to squirm, but instead, she straightened and lifted her chin. If things were going to be bad, she wasn't going to cower in her chair.

"Tomorrow, the Aermian delegation arrives."

She stayed silent.

"And along with them, the crown prince."

Tehl was coming with them? How stupid. Sage kept her face carefully blank as the warlord scrutinized her reaction to his words.

"You will need to be on your best behavior when they arrive."

"I'll see them?" she asked.

His smile held a dangerous edge. "Yes, from my side."

His words settled in. She was going to stand at his side, like a traitor, like the consort he was always calling her. Bile burned the back of her throat, but she held herself in check. "Is there anything else I should know?"

The warlord leaned forward and pulled one of her clenched hands from her lap, lacing his fingers through hers. She stared at their hands and prepared herself for what would come.

"Know that attempted escape will result in quick and violent retribution." His hand squeezed hers. "Look at me."

She lifted her eyes at the command and felt as if the world had dropped away. Heat simmered in his gaze, but his expression was all calculation.

His lips curled up on one side. "If you make a mockery out of me, I will destroy your friend, then the Aermian delegation, and then everything you hold dear."

He said this casually, as if he were merely speaking of the weather. It chilled her to the bone. He meant every word. She could see it in his eyes.

Sage swallowed past the lump in her throat and spoke in a low tone, like she was trying to soothe a dangerous beast. "And what do I tell my husband?"

He jerked her out of her chair and onto her knees in front of him. Her knees stung as he traced her face with one fingertip.

"He's not your husband, wild one." His hand skimmed up to the thorn collar and settled around her throat. He squeezed once gently, just enough for her to know he had complete control and held her life in that moment. "Do you know what this collar represents?"

She forced out a soft, "No," and was pleased with how her voice didn't shake.

"In Scythia, it is not just a method by which women adorn themselves, it is a statement of ownership. Of marriage." His nose rubbed against her temple. "Where do you think your cuff custom originates from? Scythia," he breathed. "You may have been married to the enemy, but it was never consummated. But my claim…" His lips curled against her hair. "It's been validated by a doctor."

Sage gasped and jerked back, staring into his dark eyes. "That's a lie!"

A lazy grin spread across his face. "Is it? How could you prove otherwise? You've been unconscious for five days. And if any of the delegation ask about your room arrangements, they'll be made aware of the fact that you've been sleeping in my bed for months."

Horror filled her. He was right. To anyone on the outside, it would seem like everything he was saying was true. And then, something dawned on her. The execution. It had been for show, for his people to bear witness that she was standing at his side. If anyone from the Aermian council looked at the evidence, it would seem very much like she was a traitor. A bitter laugh escaped her, causing surprise to flash across the warlord's face.

"That was disgustingly ingenious. You are a monster after all."

He smiled. "A monster to some, a hero to others. Who's to say what I am to you?"

"My death," she breathed.

"And your life," he whispered.

TWENTY-SIX

TEHL

THE DAY HAD COME.

He patted down his horse, murmuring soft words to the beast. "We have a long way to go, Wraith, and this time, we'll have a companion." He flicked a glance at the mare behind them. "But I need you to act honorably, okay? We don't have time for your attitude. Sage's mount will be spending a lot of time with us, so just get used to it." Wraith nickered and nudged his pocket. Tehl pulled out the apple piece he'd placed inside it and held it out. "Be good."

Tehl spun and faced the mare creeping up on him. She was tall, around sixteen hands, with a bold face and an off-center stripe on her face. He plucked the other quarter of an apple and held it out to her with a smile at how her ears perked. "You and I are newly acquainted, but I promise you'll like me once you get to know me." The mare stepped forward and lipped the apple, crunching down happily. He stroked a hand down her neck and patted her chest. "There's a good girl. You'll like your new mistress. She's a little like you. Beautiful, smart, and spirited."

"We're ready," Sam said, striding toward him. Right behind him were Rafe and the Scythian woman, scowling at his side.

"Is she secured?" he asked his brother.

"As much as possible. Lilja and Rafe will ride next to her. I doubt she'll give us much trouble. We're taking her home."

Blaise shifted her glare from the rebellion leader to Tehl. Something about her troubled him. It was obvious she hated them, but it also seemed like she was afraid. But why? What was she afraid of? Going home?

"Are you ready?" Sam said, interrupting his thoughts.

Tehl shook his head and patted the mare once more, and then moved to Wraith. "Let's ride."

He was about to hop into the saddle when a familiar voice stopped him from doing so. He glanced over his shoulder to catch Gwen pushing through soldiers and warhorses. He released the saddle and turned toward her as she barreled into him. Surprise, then affection, blindsided him as the petite woman wrapped her arms around him in a fierce hug.

"Bring her back to us," she muttered into his vest.

Tehl squeezed once and then released her. "I'll do my best."

Gwen scanned his face and then cupped his cheek. "Take care of yourself. You're part of the family now, too."

Emotion clogged his throat. "Thank you."

She graced him with one last smile and wrapped Sam in the same fierce embrace. The Blackwells were an unexpected gift that Sage had brought with her into their marriage. Determination filled him as he swung up and into the saddle. He'd bring Sage home. If for nothing else, for the sake of her family.

Tehl squatted by the Potam River and stared at its dark surface, reflecting on the last few days. They'd been long and exhausting as they rode hard toward the Kugami Mountains. The small army that followed his retinue slowed them down considerably, which kept Tehl in a foul mood. He scowled at the water. If it had been just him and a smaller party, they would have arrived in a few days, not eight. He glanced at the silent, dark mountains which grew larger every day, and prayed they'd arrive soon. Time was of the essence.

A sharp puff of air left his lips as he splashed the icy water over his face and across the back of his neck. If it weren't so cold, he'd be tempted to bathe, but he could see his breath. It wouldn't be long until fall waned and gave way to winter.

He cast a glance over his shoulder at the camp of men. Scattered fires were burning like fireflies in the night, illuminating the outlines of the faithful protectors of his kingdom. He shouldn't be so negative about their presence. They were heroes in their own right and were necessary for this plan to work.

He turned back to the water's edge, his reflection shining in the moonlight. He peered at himself. It was a rough, hardened stranger who gazed back at him. Black bags had permanently made camp beneath his eyes. During the day, he put what could be happening to Sage out of his mind, focusing on what he could control, but at night, there was nothing to occupy his mind. His lips pulled downward, and he stood, kicking at his watery reflection. He needed to stop moping and focus on what was most important.

Spinning on his heel, he strode toward his tent and tossed back the flap. His advisors stood around a table, strategizing with maps of the Nagalian palace and Kugami Mountains.

Rafe acknowledged him with a lift of his chin and continued speaking: "The Nagali favored open floor plans, so a frontal attack from the Scythians is unlikely."

Tehl stopped next to the Methian and scanned the map as Rafe pointed to lines representing an underground system.

"This is where the danger lies. Even with William's maps, we're not familiar enough with the tunnels to actually use them, and that's risky."

"Then why bring them up?" Jeren asked.

"Because the warlord chose this place for a reason. We may not know the tunnel systems, but I've no doubt that the warlord and his men do. We need to keep in mind that with their enhancements, they are faster than anyone you've ever fought, and their sight, hearing, and sense of smell are superior in all ways. We need to tread carefully."

"How will we beat such an opponent?" Lelbiel asked. "By all accounts, we are inferior."

"Only in physical ways," Lilja said, her white brows furrowed in concentration. "That doesn't mean we can't outsmart them. Their warriors do what they're told and don't deviate from their commands. We can use that to our advantage. Surprise will be our greatest weapon."

"But surely, the warlord has planned for such attacks?" Madden said.

"No doubt. One so corrupt does not keep power without calculation and skill, but he is at a disadvantage as well." Zachael smiled with a hint of malice. "He may be familiar with Aermia, but not us. It's a weapon we can wield."

"And Rhys?" Tehl asked. "He was in our midst for quite some time." He cast a glance to Rafe. "How much information does he possess?"

Rafe's arms crossed and his eyes narrowed. "Enough to be dangerous, as you well know."

Tehl gnashed his teeth. He expected nothing different, but even talking of the traitor made him want to kill something. "Sam..." He turned to his brother. "If the warlord does not let her go, what of Sage?"

Sam scanned the group. "We'll get her out..."

"That's it?" Zachael asked.

His brother stared down the weapons master. "The more people aware of the plan, the more likely it will fail. It's safer if only a few of us have pieces of the information. That way, if one of us is captured, our whole plan won't fall to pieces."

The weapons master dipped his head. "Understood."

"Should I be worried?" Tehl asked.

"You should always be worried when it comes to the spymaster," Gav grumbled while scrutinizing one of the maps.

Old William growled and pushed away from the table. "I hate that we're going into this blind." He gestured to the table. "We can't plan anything until we know where we'll be staying. At least he can't surround us with his army," his advisor grumbled. "The Nagali chose well when they built their palace into the Kugami Mountains."

"My question is, why this place?" Sam asked out loud. "Sure, it's a fortress, but Scythia hates all things Nagali. So why not somewhere else? Yes, the mountains hobble us, but they hobble him as well. What's so special about this place? I feel like we're missing something."

"He's proud of his accomplishments, and he enjoys mind games," Lilja offered. "He could have chosen it for the purpose of showing us what Scythia is capable of, to remind us of what they've conquered, or maybe just to keep us guessing. We can't know. The best we can do is stay alert and plan for anything and everything."

"Indeed. We've discussed all we can for the evening," Tehl said with a hint of finality. "I'll see all of you tomorrow morning."

His council bowed and left his tent one by one, until only Lilja, Hayjen, Gav, and his brother remained.

"May I speak to you privately, my lord?" Lilja asked.

Tehl nodded, fatigue riding him hard. Hayjen clasped him on the shoulder, kissed his wife's cheek, and then led Sam and Gav out of the tent. Tehl and Lilja stared at each other, both silent and unmoving. Her unnatural stillness unnerved him.

"Out with it, Lilja. You're never one to beat around the bush." He pulled a pouch from his waist and took a swig of the spirits, ignoring her stare. When Lilja still didn't answer, he pulled a chair over and sat in it, gesturing to the one across from him. Holding out the pouch, he offered, "A drink?"

The Sirenidae glided to his side and pulled the pouch from his hand, taking a swig. He wasn't surprised that she didn't cough at the liquid that burned like fire. Nothing surprised him anymore.

She sank into the chair across from him and leveled a look he couldn't decipher. "You're tired."

He chuckled at that. "That's nothing new."

"Are you prepared for Sage's return?"

"Yes. I didn't fathom how much of an impact she had on my life," he answered honestly. Lilja smiled at him, and something loosened inside of him. He never had to put on a pretense with her. He could be blunt and honest, maybe even to the point of being rude, but she never judged him. "I miss her."

Lilja's magenta eyes misted. "I do, too." She blinked a couple times and took another swig of spirits before handing it back to him. "When I asked my question, I meant something different, Tehl. That place…" She pulled in a sharp breath and looked at the rug. "It strips you down until you don't know who you are anymore."

"Sage is strong." She was. He truly believed she could survive whatever came her way.

"She is, and I still worry for her." Lilja pinned him with her gaze. "I worry for you."

"Me?"

"Yes."

"Why?"

"Because when you finally see her, it will break you."

"I'm not that easily broken."

"Indeed." She leaned forward, her face very serious. "How will you handle it if she's pregnant?"

Her words slapped him in the face. "Pregnant?" he croaked.

It was possible, but it wasn't something he even wanted to contemplate. Lilja reached out and touched his clenched fist.

"Will you be able to accept another man's child?"

"Children are blessings." He meant it. Children were precious. Tehl glanced up when Lilja squeezed his hand.

"That is admirable, but really look inside of yourself. This won't be just any child, but that of your enemy. Can you accept your enemy's offspring as your own?"

He opened and then closed his mouth. A 'yes' was on the tip of his tongue; his throat worked, but no sound came out. Could he really raise a child that wasn't his? Yes. But his enemy's?

Lilja squeezed his hand once more and sat back. "This is not an easy task, but it is one that falls on your shoulders. She will need you; your support, your strength, your acceptance, and your love. Are you prepared to give those things to her?"

"Yes." That was easy.

"And the child?"

Tehl exhaled and nodded. "It doesn't matter how a child was created. Scythian or no, the child is an innocent, one that I will welcome into my home and raise as my own, no matter how difficult it may be."

A smile lit up Lilja's face. "Then you're a good man."

He shook his head and ran a hand over his face. "If I was a better one, we wouldn't be in this situation."

"Do you really believe that?" the Sirenidae asked.

Guilt weighed him down. "With my whole heart."

"Maybe Sage isn't the only one who needs support, strength, acceptance, and love."

"Do you think that is possible for us?" he asked, holding his breath as he waited for Lilja to reply.

"Do you think her parents, or Hayjen and I, would've allowed your marriage to take place if we believed you'd be unhappy forever?" She smiled at him like she held a secret. "We all care for Aermia, but if you think for one moment that we would have allowed our girl to attach herself to an unworthy man for the kingdom, you're daft."

Her statement struck him as funny. He chuckled, which turned into a full laugh. Lilja looked at him like he'd lost his mind, and maybe he had, but her expression just made him laugh harder. His stomach cramped, and tears blurred his eyes. With much effort, he managed to get control of himself and wipe the tears from his eyes.

Lilja grinned at him. "Laughing is good for the soul, isn't it?"

"My mum used to say that."

"What was so funny?"

"Your statement. After spending time with the Blackwells, I should've realized this was part their decision, too. It seems I have many more people to be thankful to."

Sam pushed into the tent, interrupting them. His gaze darted between the two of them. "Gav," he shouted. "I told you it wasn't Tehl laughing. Lilja made him cry."

Tehl scowled at his brother and rubbed his eyes hard. A hand on his shoulder pulled his attention up.

Lilja's eyes were sparkling with mirth. "I've brothers, too," she mock-whispered just loud enough for his brother to hear. "They never grow any less bothersome."

"My lady! I'm wounded."

The Sirenidae rolled her eyes and strode toward his brother. "I'm sure nothing could wound you on account of your battle prowess."

Sam's eyes narrowed playfully. "I get the feeling you're playing with me, Lilja. What a cruel thing."

She sniggered and swept around him. "You haven't seen my cruel side yet." She paused before the tent flap and swiveled to look at Tehl and his brother. "We'll reach the castle tomorrow. Sleep well. I'm sure it will be the last time any of us do so until we leave that accursed place." She glanced through the flap. "I better relieve Rafe before he kills the Scythian wench. They squabble like crows."

With that, she disappeared outside, leaving the brothers to stare after her.

"She's a magnificent woman," Sam commented.

"Lilja's certainly unique," Tehl answered and shifted into a more comfortable position, waiting for his brother to sit and have his say. "How much did you hear?"

"Not much. Only your deranged cackle." Sam plopped into Lilja's vacated chair, swiped the spirit pouch, and stared at it. "It's been a long time since I've heard you laugh like that."

"It's been a long time," he admitted. His mind then turned to the possibility of a pregnant Sage.

"Your serious face is back," Sam noted. "Will you share your burdens with me?"

Tehl leaned forward, his elbows on his knees, his hands clasped. "What if…" His voice cracked. He cleared his throat and tried again. "What if she is carrying a child?"

Sam stilled and then took a swig of the spirits before answering, "Then you do what you do best."

"And what is that?" Tehl really didn't know. Everything was falling apart around him. Nothing seemed to go the way he planned.

"You care for her and the child."

"Care?" he scoffed. "Gav is better suited for it than I am."

"Not true. You're stunted when it comes to understanding others' emotions, I'll grant you that. But you care for those close to you. You've been caring for all of us for a long time. Just keep on doing what you're doing."

Tehl shot to his feet and began pacing the tent, his brother watching him.

"Speak, brother, I'm listening."

"I can care for the child, but what of Sage?"

"What of her?"

He stopped pacing and pinned his brother with a look. "How do I heal rape? I don't know how to deal with that. When I think of it…" He broke off as rage filled him. He glared at the chair, wanting to throw it. "I want to kill him. I want to tear things apart."

His brother's face clouded over. "If he has, he will pay."

"That's my point!" Tehl exploded. "How can I care for her with all this hate and rage inside of me?" His hands curled into fists at his side. "How can I get her back if I'm this out of control?"

"You're not out of control, brother." Sam stood and clasped him on the shoulder. "You've borne this better than anyone."

His jaw clenched, and he looked to the side, his fears spilling out of his lips. "What if we can't get her back?"

"We will," Sam said resolutely.

"And what if we do and the Sage we love died in Scythia?"

Sam grabbed him into a rough hug. "Then we'll welcome her home and get to know this new version of her."

Tehl nodded and thumped his brother's back a few times before pulling away. "Thank you."

His brother clasped his forearm. "I'm with you. You're not alone." Sam scanned his face. "Get some sleep if you can. Tomorrow is the big day." He slapped Tehl on the shoulder and then moved to his bedroll.

A new sense of strength filled Tehl. They would get Sage back.

He glanced at his own bedroll. It was doubtful he'd get any sleep, but he needed to try. Tomorrow, they would change history.

TWENTY-SEVEN

TEHL

IT WAS MORE BEAUTIFUL THAN he expected. Golden grass gave way to rich, green pine forests; the earth shifted from a deep brown to an intense red. He scanned the castle looming in front of them, anxious. Somewhere inside was Sage. She was so close.

"Breathe, my lord."

Tehl glanced at Zachael. "I am."

The weapons master scoffed. "Not evenly. Remember your training."

He nodded and pulled deep breaths in and out as they ascended the mountainside toward the castle. It was eerie how pristine the Nagali palace still was. Not a single tower or wing looked run down or in any need of repair. It was exactly how it looked in history books.

His men circled nearer on their horses as they moved ever closer to the palace. He couldn't see the Scythians, but he knew they watched. Everyone was on edge as they crested the mountain path, finally arriving at the palace gate.

Silence met them.

Tehl scanned the area, hyper aware of his surroundings. It was like the mountains also held their breath, waiting. His gaze snapped to the metal gate when it groaned and swung inward, a group of dangerous-looking Scythian warriors just inside it.

The largest one stepped forward. It was the same warrior they'd encountered all those months ago outside of Sanee. The one who'd shot down his own men. Tehl schooled his face, one hand tightening on his reins, causing Wraith to toss his head. He loosened his grip and straightened in the saddle, his other hand on the pommel of his sword.

"My lords and ladies," the warrior's deep voice boomed, echoing off the surrounding stone. "Welcome to Palace Kamugi."

Tehl dipped his chin but shot a look at Lilja, who had let out an uncharacteristic gasp. He blinked at her odd behavior. She never let anyone know they'd surprised her. He turned back to the warrior who was staring at the Sirenidae. Was this the warrior Lilja had been given to? He pushed the thoughts away and focused on the warrior.

"It's our pleasure to join you in negotiations. Where is your warlord?" Tehl asked.

The warrior bowed and then stepped to the side. "Unfortunately, he's been detained and could not greet you himself, but accommodations and refreshments have been arranged, so you can refresh yourselves and rest until dinner is served, where my lord will later join you." He gestured to the other stoic warriors. "My men will care for your mounts."

So, that was how it was going to be. "Indeed, send my thanks to your lord," Tehl said, his voice ringing clear. He swung off his horse, his men following his lead. The warlord refused to greet them? What sort of game was he playing? He lifted the reins over Wraith's head and pulled him forward, keeping his gaze sharp.

Sam sauntered up to Tehl's side and smirked at the warrior. "It's a pleasure to see you again," he said to the large warrior. "I didn't get your name the first time we met."

The warrior stiffened, the feathers in his long-braided hair fluttering in the air. "It's Blair."

"Our thanks, Warrior Blair," Lilja purred in a voice that had Tehl glancing in her direction.

At that moment, everything about her screamed unearthly. Her hips swayed as she sashayed up to the warrior, drawing all the eyes of the Scythian men. Even in disguise, she was the most sensual creature he'd ever come in contact with.

Tehl snuck a glance at the warrior and didn't miss the flash of interest in Blair's dark gaze as the Sirenidae glided to a stop in front of him, her hip cocked and hand held out. The commander carefully took Lilja's fingers in his gigantic hand and kissed the back of hers prettily, his gaze locked on the woman.

"My pleasure, my lady," he rumbled against her skin, then straightened and held an arm out.

Lilja flipped her hair and handed her reins to a warrior standing to her left. "I believe it shall be," she murmured, taking his arm.

How did her husband feel about the warrior lusting after his wife? Tehl glanced at Hayjen, who stood behind, watching his wife with a blank mask. Whatever he was feeling, it was deeply hidden.

Tehl's gaze moved to Blaise, standing proudly in the middle of the Aermian delegation.

"Are you not going to welcome me home, Blair?" her question hung in the air.

The Scythian warrior bowed shallowly and straightened. "It is a happiness to see your face again, Blaise. Your mother has missed you dearly."

"And my uncle?"

Blair froze for a second. "I'm sure he'll rejoice in your return as well."

Her cheeks sucked in, and she glanced to the side. "Where is my mother?"

"In her suite, I assume."

Blaise nodded and strode from the group and into the palace.

He shot a look at his brother. The first piece was in play. Sam slid his gaze away.

Tehl handed his reins to a Scythian warrior and kept his face pleasant as the warrior glared at him. The air was taut with unease, hostility, and suspicion. Their peace accord was already going well.

The palace courtyard was like nothing he'd ever seen, and he had to force himself not to gawk.

"Shall we?" Blair asked, staring at him, with Lilja's arm tucked into his.

"Lead the way."

The warrior spun on his heel, and he and the Sirenidae led the procession upstairs and into the palace.

The inside was even more beautiful than the outside. The high, cream, arching walls created a long tunnel, scattered with tall windows that illuminated the ancient art on the walls—ruby dragons sleeping amongst children, Nagalians riding on dragons, people singing and working alongside their beasts. Each mosaic was more beautiful and fantastic than the last and just as heart-wrenching.

"What a tragedy," Gav muttered under his breath.

Sadness blanketed him as well. An entire people gone. He pulled his eyes from the depictions of the past, disgusted. Scythia had destroyed everything. Tehl stared at the warrior's back, trying to get himself under control. It wouldn't do to hurl accusations around at peace negotiations. His lips curled at the thought. Negotiations. There wouldn't be any negotiations if he had anything to say about it.

Time. They needed more of it to discover what the Scythians plotted, as well as to move their own soldiers into play, but it seemed to be the one thing they lacked.

They trekked up level after level of the castle, each unique. He ignored the murmurs of their party. He was sure the historians and scribes were soaking up the rare chance to see the art of the extinct culture.

Finally, Blair stopped and moved them to a hallway that looped back on itself, creating a circle of doors. Tehl eyed the "servants" stationed outside his door and muffled a snort. If the men standing outside the doors were servants, he'd eat his horse. They were warriors, through and through. So, the question that begged to be asked was, were they there as jailers, protectors, or spies? Definitely two of the three.

Blair nodded to two warriors who stood at attention outside two large doors and flung the doors open, gesturing to him with a bow. "Your rooms, my lord."

Tehl cast a glance at his party, who were all being shown into their own rooms, before moving into the suite. It was beautiful, designed in a way he'd never seen. Rich colors decorated the curtains bracketing the large balcony window, lush rugs carpeted the red stone floor, and exotic art complemented the walls.

"Is it to your liking?" the warrior asked.

"It is." He paused and noticed Sam meandering off into another room.

"My delegation?"

"They will all be housed in this same corridor."

"And the warlord?" Tehl asked, the question hanging in the air.

"He hopes you and your delegation will join him for dinner this evening."

"We accept his invitation with thanks," Tehl murmured in an attempt to be respectful. He clamped his lips shut from asking about his wife. If the warrior had any information about Sage, he doubted the Scythian would share it with him.

With one last bow, the commander strode out of the room and closed both doors behind him, leaving Sam, Gav, Rafe, Lilja, Hayjen, Zachael, and Tehl in the room.

"That went as well as I expected," Gav said while walking around the perimeter of the room.

"Indeed," Rafe added, inspecting the balcony. "This place, it smells like death."

A shiver worked up Tehl's spine. There was something eerie about the abandoned palace. No, not abandoned, just empty. He shook it off and shot a glance at his brother, who was peeking underneath the bed. "What did you think of it?"

"Tactically, it's a brilliant place to stage a massacre."

Everyone's attention snapped to Sam.

His brother stood and tapped his temple. "Think about it. It's the perfect place to corral people. Looping walkways, narrow stairways, and every passageway looks identical. It would be easy to get lost if you're not familiar with the place." He shrugged and shoved at the bed, only budging the colossal piece of furniture but a few inches. "Some help, please."

Hayjen and Tehl both stepped forward and heaved the bed over. His brother smiled and flipped back the rug, revealing a hatch in the floor.

"But if you know where the tunnels are, well…" Sam's blue eyes glinted dangerously. "We won't be so difficult to corral."

Zachael dropped into a squat, his black-and-silver hair falling into his face as he ran his hand along the door. He lifted his fingers, his eyes narrowing. "No dust. What does that tell you, Sam?"

"It's been in use. Recently."

The weapon master's lips thinned. "We should be prepared for company." He flicked a look to Tehl. "Also, consider everything said in this room to be public knowledge. Even if they don't attack, there's no way to know who's listening."

Tehl stared at the hatch. "We need to station someone down there."

"I'll do it."

He clashed eyes with Rafe. The rebellion leader let a ruthless grin take over his face, puckering his scar so that it looked even more fierce. "Don't you want to be at the delegation?"

"Yes, but I can guard during the night."

"And when will you sleep?" Gav asked without snark. "You will need rest, or we will all be in danger."

"They won't get past me," Rafe responded with confidence. "During the day, I'll station several men down there."

Tehl noticed Lilja staring blankly out the window. Hayjen stood silently behind her, his hands rubbing her arms. They both were uncharacteristically quiet.

"Lilja," he called softly.

The Sirenidae glanced at him with a sort of sorrow in her eyes.

"Thank you," he murmured. "I know this is painful for you and I wish you didn't have to bear it, but I'm thankful you're here, for Sage." He stepped closer, lifted her icy hand, and kissed the back of it. "I'm in your debt."

He began to pull away when she wrapped her arms around him in a fierce hug. "I'd do anything for Sage, but know I do this for you, too, Tehl."

Tehl squeezed her once and smiled at Hayjen, who stepped forward and hugged him with a lot of back-slapping. He was warmed by the gesture. He'd always had his family for his friends, but since Sage came into his life, his friends seemed to expand day by day, and he couldn't be more grateful.

"What's next?" Rafe asked.

"Now, we wait."

TWENTY-EIGHT

TEHL

HE HATED WAITING.

Tehl paced the room as the sun set, blazing pinks and oranges splashed across the sky. "Are we supposed to go down unescorted?" he growled, tugging on his blue velvet vest, eyeing the sinking sun.

"Calm down, brother, or you'll tire yourself out. The night is still young."

He pulled in a shuddering breath. "I need some air." He strode across the room and joined Rafe on the balcony. The rebellion leader's head was tipped back, eyes closed, his wine-colored hair lifting in the breeze.

"Have you worn out your boots yet?"

Tehl wrapped his hands around the banister and rolled his shoulders back. "Not yet, but I'm on my way."

An amber eye peeked at him. "You need to calm down."

He scowled at Rafe, his jaw clenching. "I'm trying. It's like I'm trying to burst out of my skin," he confessed. "I want it to stop."

"It's being so close that is difficult," Rafe commiserated.

"What a sad pair we are," Tehl said dryly, scanning the other balconies in view. None were close, but in a pinch, he could possibly maneuver down if the need arose. Was Sage trapped in one of those rooms? He tore his eyes from the windows below. "Does the worry ever end?"

A bark of laughter escaped the rebellion leader, only to be carried away in the wind. "It only gets worse the longer you love someone."

Tehl mulled over that, scowling. He worried over his father, his brother, his cousin, but nothing compared to the agonizing pain and worry he carried over Sage. Was that what love involved? He caught Rafe observing him from the corner of his eye. "What?"

"You are the only one I could ever deem worthy of her. You've sacrificed much for her." The rebellion leader leveled him with a look. "Things your family doesn't even know."

Tehl straightened, knowing exactly what he referred to. "How?"

"The how doesn't matter right now, only that my respect for you has grown." Rafe held out his forearm. "I promise, from this moment forward, I will leave your mate alone."

"My mate?" he repeated, to make sure he'd heard correctly.

"Your mate," Rafe reiterated without so much as a blink.

Tehl took the offered forearm. "Thank you." And he meant it. He knew how much the rebellion leader loved Sage, even if he had a poor way of showing it.

Rafe smiled, but it was bitter. "Just take care of her, or there will be consequences."

He smiled back. "Naturally."

A knock at the door had everyone straightening.

"Let's go get our girl," Lilja whispered.

Zachael pulled open the door, admitting a different warrior. The man bowed and gestured to the side. "Dinner is served. If you will please follow me…"

Tehl strode forward with Rafe and Zachael at either side. In the hallway, the rest of his delegation stood in their finery and bowed at his entrance. He nodded, but kept up with their escort as they were led through a series of twist and turns, finally arriving at a gigantic black door painted with golden dragons. The Scythian pushed the door inward and it split in half, revealing it was in fact two doors instead of one.

Tehl glanced at his brother and nodded as if to say, *Here we go*. He threw back his shoulders and stepped into the room just as the servant's voice rang out:

"Crown Prince Tehl Ramses and the Aermian delegation."

The dining room was immense. To say it was opulent was an understatement.

Rubies the size of his fist hung from black metal chandeliers that highlighted the elaborate paintings on the ceiling. But that wasn't the most interesting part. What was more intriguing were the exotic people staring at his group, completely silent. A chill ran down his spine when he noted just how similar they all looked to one another. A man stood at the head of a table and held a hand out to the woman next to him.

Tehl's breath seized in his lungs as he got a clear look at the woman. "Sage," he mouthed.

His wife sat serenely next to the warlord, her face a pleasant but placid mask. His heart jumped, beating so hard he swore everyone could hear it. She was alive. Whole.

A pinch on his arm pulled his attention from Sage to Sam. His brother's lips lifted in a smirk, but his eyes held a warning.

"Steady," Lilja whispered. "Calm."

Tehl barely registered her words, but he gave a curt nod in acknowledgment and centered himself. Tonight wasn't for reunions, no matter how much he wished it. Tonight was for battle. A battle that involved words. A moment of dread gripped him at the thought. He was terrible when it came to speaking pretty words, but Sage's life depended on it. He pushed the thought away and focused on his wife.

She rose gracefully and placed her hand in the warlord's. They moved around the table gracefully, step by step, and Sage never looked more like a queen than in that moment. Tehl froze as two gigantic man-eaters sauntered after the couple. *Stars above.* His mind told him to run from the predators prowling their way.

"That's the biggest cat I've ever seen," Sam breathed. "How in the blazes did he acquire those?"

"With skill, I'm sure," Lilja whispered.

Tehl tore his gaze from the felines and back to Sage. Her expression was pleasant, pleased even, but he knew what that really meant. She was scared. He squinted, but otherwise kept his expression schooled. Her court mask wasn't the only thing that looked different. Sage looked like an altered version of herself, more polished than the wild woman he'd taken as his wife. She looked… flawless. That thought caused unease to churn in his gut. Was it simply his being away from her so long that meant perhaps his memory was inaccurate, or could it mean something more?

With great pain, he pulled his gaze from her and met the pitch-black eyes of the man escorting her. It felt like he'd been slapped in the face. He'd always considered himself a good judge of beauty, male and female alike. But the man—if you could call him that—was beyond anything he'd ever seen. Tehl had never felt more disheveled and self-conscious. The warlord smiled at him, and the hair rose on the back of his neck. Tehl knew a predator when he saw one.

In that moment, Tehl put aside any faint but fanciful notions of peace. The man escorting his wife did not want peace. But what did he want? He'd find out soon enough. Tehl straightened and pulled himself together as the warlord and Sage halted just out of reach.

The warlord's deep voice washed over him, both powerful and smooth with a hint of accent: "Welcome, Crown Prince Ramses."

Tehl dipped his chin. "I thank you for the invitation to join you. I also look forward to our new endeavor for peace."

"I likewise look forward to our future." The warlord's dark gaze swept over the group and paused on someone behind Tehl before coming back to him. "I can't wait to meet your delegation." He turned and smiled at Sage. "I trust you know my companion."

His thoughts stilled at the look the warlord gave Sage. There was too much heat in his smile to just be polite. Far too much.

The warlord lifted Sage's hand, and she glided forward, her green gaze meeting Tehl's. His world tilted on its axis and righted at the sight of her whole. She was here, safe. He kept his feelings shuttered and took her offered hand, placing a chaste kiss on the back of it instead of pulling her into his arms for a hug like he wanted to. "My lady…"

"My lord," she murmured, her voice music to his ears.

It was ridiculous. Since she'd disappeared, he'd almost forgotten how beautiful her voice was. He breathed in and smiled that she still smelled like herself. She looked different, but still was Sage. "Thank you for taking such good care of my wife. I cannot tell you how much she's been missed," he murmured against her skin.

Sage smiled and gently tried to pull her fingers from his grasp. He tightened his grip for several seconds before he allowed her to step back. The light in her eyes dimmed and her mask slipped into place. The hope he held inside died at her reaction. She appeared whole on the outside, but he knew the inside would tell a different story. He forced his hand to keep from clenching and smiled pleasantly at the warlord studying him.

"It was my pleasure." The warlord lifted Sage's hand and turned it over, kissing the inside of her wrist.

Tehl didn't react to the sexual gesture and kept his façade in place, but inside, he was seething.

"She's been an absolute treasure to have in my home. Now, let's eat," the warlord said. He wrapped Sage's arm in his and spun on his heel.

A flash of rage burned through Tehl at the manner in which the Scythian ruler held his wife. He blinked, surprised at the strong emotion. He couldn't risk showing his hand and endangering everyone, so he shoved his feelings aside. With forced casualness, he followed them to the table littered with Scythians.

Two chairs sat at the end of the table. The warlord sat Sage at one and stood in front of the other. "Please, sit, and let dinner begin."

Tehl placed himself on the other side of his wife and sat at the same time as the warlord. His brother glided to his other side and sat with a flourish all his own. For once, Tehl was thankful for his brother's antics as they pulled much of the attention off of Tehl and onto Sam. He glanced across the table and nodded to Gav, who sat beside the behemoth of a warrior who had escorted them to their rooms earlier. Blair, the commander. Tehl acknowledged him and then eyed the servants placing tray after tray of food on the table. Traditional Aermian, and what he assumed to be Scythian delicacies, littered the table, the spicy, savory, and sweet aromas wafting temptingly through the air.

He nearly jumped when a rumbling sound erupted next to him. Tehl glanced down to the floor and caught the golden gaze of a feline. The hair rose on his arms. If he so much as moved his hand he could touch the beast's fur.

"That's enough," Sage whispered softly and placed a hand on the feline's head.

Tehl blinked, and swore he saw the feline smile smugly before pressing against Sage's leg. He eyed the leren for only a moment more before forcing himself to turn back to the table. He inhaled the spices teasing the air and placed a few foodstuffs onto his plate, then turned to the warlord with a practiced smile, not surprised to find the Scythian ruler was studying him. "The fare looks delicious. I thank you for the hospitality shown to my men and myself, Warlord Zane. Our rooms are exquisite, and the view, breathtaking."

A twinkle entered the warlord's eye as he plopped a piece of fruit into his mouth, flashing white teeth. "It was my pleasure, Your Highness. And I might thank you for returning my niece home safely. Not everyone is so honorable."

Tehl nodded. "It was my pleasure. Blaise was no trouble at all."

The warlord released a booming laugh. "I wouldn't go that far. She's a handful and enjoys causing mischief wherever she goes. Isn't that so, niece?"

Tehl glanced down the table to Blaise.

She set her spoon down prettily, dipped her head. "As you say, my lord."

"Cheeky," the warlord mumbled, eyeing his niece. He raised one eyebrow before dismissing her and returning his attention to his plate.

Tehl turned and peeked at Sage next to him, who was picking at her plate. "Are you not hungry, my lady?" he asked, wondering if there was something wrong with it. Was it poisoned?

Her bowed head lifted just a touch; her gaze flitted to his for a fraction of a heartbeat and then back to the food on her plate.

"I'm afraid my stomach is unsettled, my lord."

"Wild one, why didn't you tell me?" The warlord sat forward, a flicker of concern on his face.

Wild one? Anger heated his gut. The warlord had a pet name for his wife? That didn't bode well.

"It's nothing," Sage murmured.

The warlord scanned his plate and plucked up a little yellow fruit and held it out to her. "Here, this will help."

Tehl expected her to take the fruit from the warlord, but the air in his lungs froze when she scooted closer and ate the fruit from his hand. From the corner of his eye, he caught Gav gawking for only a moment before he recovered. The warlord smiled, brushed her lip with his thumb, and caught a drop of juice. Tehl watched as the Scythian leader sucked it into his own mouth. The move was blatantly sexual, and completely inappropriate. His hands clenched into fists under the table.

The warlord's obsidian gaze wandered from Sage to Tehl, a small smirk on his smug face, like he knew what the crown prince was thinking. Sage's small hand slid over Tehl's and squeezed once before retreating. He kept his expression schooled into something polite. Sage continued to eat like nothing had happened, so he followed her cue.

He sipped his savory pumpkin soup while scanning the table. It was ridiculous. The entire group, Aermians and Scythians alike, was silent, each pretending they weren't all sneaking glances at the other. The dislike and mistrust were evident with each glare or false smile. He met Gav's purple gaze before dropping his eyes back to his soup. No one wanted to be here, including himself.

"Is the soup to your liking?" a deep voice rumbled.

He glanced at the warlord. "It's delicious."

"Not a man of many words, are you?"

Tehl leaned back into his chair and cocked his head. "I've found that people like to dance around a problem with too many fine words and end up accomplishing nothing. I hate wasting time. Why not say what you mean the first time?"

"Why not, indeed?" The warlord swirled his wine in his goblet and dipped his chin. "I, too, believe in being straightforward and honest. So, I'll say this..." His dark gaze intensified. "I desire peace. My people deserve more than being punished for the sins of their ancestors, but prejudices long ingrained are hard to remove. This won't be easy, but I believe it possible."

Tehl regarded him thoughtfully. His words didn't seem false, but that made him wary. The best lies were ones rooted in truth. He turned to Sage, who was listening intently, but had remained silent. "And what of you, Sage? What do you think? You've lived with both our peoples."

She twisted and stared him dead in the eye. "Peace is always possible. It just depends on how much one desires it."

"A wise observation, my lady," Zachael murmured, pulling her attention. "May I also say you're looking well."

"Thank you," she said with a small smile.

"Your presence in the ring has been missed."

"The ring?" the warlord asked.

"It's where we train," Sage explained.

Zachael smiled, faint wrinkles creasing around his mouth. "She's a tough opponent. Our men nursed battle wounds and wounded pride daily."

"What a fierce little consort," the warlord said.

Sage stiffened.

Tehl frowned. Nothing the warlord said was offensive that he could note, so why was she upset?

His heart beat a little faster as Sage pushed back from her chair and stood. Tehl was on his feet, along with all the other men out of respect. She curtseyed to the table and caught his eye just for a second before she turned to the warlord.

"I find myself fatigued. I must beg your forgiveness for my early departure."

The warlord plucked her hand from the table and kissed the back of it, lingering far too long. "As you wish, wild one."

Sage pulled her hand from his grasp and glided away from the table without a backward glance.

His fingers clenched around his fork.

What had the warlord done to his wife?

TWENTY-NINE

SAGE

SHE HUFFED OUT A BREATH as she exited the dining room, Nali quick on her heels. Four warriors materialized from the dark, surrounding her and leading her back to her prison. The tension in her body increased as they wound their way through the abandoned palace. Tehl kissing the back of her hand flashed through her mind. He looked every bit as handsome as she remembered, and his eyes just as kind. Heat built behind her eyes. Little did he know what a traitor she was…what an adulteress.

The pressure built in her chest, and Sage grasped at every last thread of strength she had. She wouldn't cry in front of these men. They'd report it to Zane, and that was the last thing she needed. All she had to do was make it back to the room. There, she could release her feelings.

The warriors led her around a corner, and the double doors to her room became visible. It was both a relief and pain to see them. Sage ignored the warrior who opened the door and moved into the dim room. The door slammed behind her, and the sound seemed to echo, although it was probably just in her broken mind. Her shoulders hunched forward, and soundless sobs burst out. She stumbled toward a chair and gripped the back of it.

It killed her to ignore her friends and family. Tears dripped down her face, remembering the smile Zachael gave her. The weapons master was like family to her, and while the situation couldn't be worse, she was grateful to see him.

Her hands tightened when she thought of how Lilja had stared. The woman attracted attention everywhere she went, but tonight she'd dressed somberly, her hair covered, and her eye color changed. Fear had gripped Sage when she'd spotted her Sirenidae friend. If the warlord figured out what she was, there was no telling what he'd do.

The pain in her chest increased as she reflected on Tehl's expression when the warlord had made her eat from his hand. Shame and humiliation scorched her cheeks and her hands shook. The entire dinner had been a farce, a test to see if she could be trusted to play her role when the talks began on the morrow. It was sick and demented, just like him. Rage flowed freely through her veins, and a giant crash had her blinking. She stared at her outstretched hand to the vase that had shattered into a million tiny pieces at her feet. When had she picked that up?

The bedroom door slammed open, and Sage spun to face the warriors bearing down on her. Nali released a hair-raising growl and loped to her side, making the warriors halt. They eyed the mess and the man-eater. One brave warrior edged closer and placed a gentle hand on her arm, pulling her away from the broken vase.

"I dropped it," she said.

He stared at her for a moment, disbelief on his face. He obviously didn't believe her lie for one second. She hissed an angry breath when he brushed his hand along her legs, and then her arms.

"I'm not hurt," she said.

"I'm following my commands, my lady." He finished his search, satisfied, and jerked his chin toward the other men. As quickly as they entered, they exited, leaving her behind with only her regret, the black feline, and a broken vase for company.

A shiver worked through her body as a cool breeze blew into the room. She snagged the blanket off the bed and threw it over her shoulders before moving out to the balcony. The black beast pressed into her side, and Sage laid a hand on her head, gazing at the night sky. Bright stars twinkled like gems on velvet. A shuddering breath escaped her when she caught sight of fires burning in the distance.

The Guard. Aermian soldiers.

So close, but so far away. It was cruel, really, to see her escape and not be able to attain it. It could have been seconds, minutes, or hours that she stood gazing out into the dark.

A warm chest pressed to her back; muscular arms wrapped around her, fingers digging into the blanket and her hips.

"Are you going to stand out here all night?" the warlord's deep voice whispered in her ear.

It was unfair how musical his voice was. It could corrupt the most prudish maiden. He was the devil, plain and simple.

He took her hand and tsked. "Your hands are as cold as ice. Come warm them by the fire."

She allowed him to pull her from her sanctuary—one last glance at the encampment. Even though escape was improbable, the Aermians' presence still comforted her, inspiring hope.

The warlord drew her to the fire, where Nali had curled up for the night. Sage sat on a low bench in front of the heat, still cocooned in her blanket. The flames hopped from one side to another in a happy dance of orange, yellow, and red. Her skin prickled, and she pulled the blanket tighter, trying to ignore the huge man studying her.

"You did well tonight."

Sage jerked and craned her neck to meet his eyes. "I did nothing tonight."

"Precisely. You played your part remarkably. You should've seen the expressions of the Aermian delegation when you ate from my hand." An amused chuckle rumbled out of him. "Thank you."

"I didn't do it for you," she muttered. She tensed and dropped her gaze to the swirling rug beneath her feet, wishing she could take back what she had said. Her words were careless. Careless words killed people.

The warlord sank to his haunches and lifted her chin. Bravely, she met his gaze, not flinching at the way he scrutinized her face. One finger traced her eyebrow, then down her temple and cheek.

"I suppose not, consort," he rumbled, leaning forward to press his lips against hers in a kiss so gentle it made her feel like weeping. "Some days, I feel like I could forget the past," he said, his words whispering across her skin.

What past? It threw her when he let her glimpse his softer side every so often. It was just enough to make her second-guess herself and look for something good.

He held his hand out. "Let's go to bed, love. Tomorrow marks the beginning of our future."

Trepidation filled her as she once again followed him to the bed. When she got to its edge, she stared at it like it might bite. Each night went this way. She feared what might happen in that bed, but soon the fear gave way to exhaustion, and she'd find herself wrapped up in Zane's arms come morning. With a huff, she flung the cover off her back and tossed it onto the bed. Sage crawled into the bed and turned onto her side to watch the warlord strip off his boots and shirt. It made her feel like a lecher, but she'd rather stare at him while he undressed than turn her back to him. No use in making herself more vulnerable than she already was.

He caught her eye as he shrugged his shirt off, the moonlight highlighting his muscles, which rippled with his every move. Despite everything that had occurred, he was still the most beautiful thing she'd ever seen. He crawled into bed and scooted closer, never losing eye contact, and placed his hand in the curve of her waist.

She glanced down at his arm and shivered, pulling the cover tighter, unsettled that the heat from his hand burned through the fabric and seemed to imprint itself on her skin like it belonged there.

"Wild one?"

Sage peeked up at him from underneath her lashes. "Yes?"

"You touched him tonight."

Licking her lips, she attempted to calm herself. His tone might have been casual, but it was anything but. It was the calm before the storm.

"It wasn't anything."

"The way he looked at you wasn't just *anything*, consort."

"Do you want peace?"

Her question must have startled him, because his intense expression melted into confusion.

"Have I not made that clear?"

"I was securing peace."

His gaze shuttered. "Is that what you think you were doing?"

"I know him," she said, avoiding using Tehl's name. "Your display upset him. I didn't want the peace accord to be destroyed before it had a chance to succeed." Sage meant every word. Her people didn't understand the kind of creatures they were dealing with. 'Deadly' was the word that came to mind.

His expression was unreadable as he lay there staring at her, searching for something. He must have found it, because he smiled at her and brushed her hair from her cheek.

"I believe you, Sage."

A breath she didn't know she was holding leaked out of her.

He hitched his arm around her, pulled her against his chest, and rolled onto his back. She stiffly held herself against his side, her ear over his heart. Sage hated him in that moment, because he was so human. His heart thumped in his chest just like hers, steady and calm, the calm she craved when everything was so messed up and confused.

"Sleep, wild one."

Almost against her will, her body softened and her eyelids grew heavy. But she wouldn't fall asleep until he answered the question that had been plaguing her since he pointed out the Aermian camp in the distance. "Zane?"

"Yes, love?"

"Will you harm my people?"

Silence.

She lifted her head and met his dark gaze. He lifted his hand and cupped her cheek.

"As long as they don't harm me or mine, I'll leave them unharmed. I want to make the kingdoms a better place."

By what means? she wanted to ask, but instead she whispered, "Do you promise?"

"You have my word, consort, and you know I keep my word." His heated eyes bore into hers, making it clear what he was speaking of. He hadn't taken her yet. He'd kept his promises, all of them, even the one she didn't want to remember.

"Thank you." She placed a hand on his heart and leaned closer to brush a kiss along his cheek. The small intake of his breath clued her into something she hadn't expected. She affected him, but it was more than lust, more than his insane need to control her.

A small part of him might care for her.

Sage pulled back and curled up by his side. The thought startled her and gave her a little seed of hope. Somewhere, deep down inside him, he had good qualities. No one could be completely bad. But she wasn't his salvation, a way to fix his wrongs in the past. Without him knowing it, he'd just given her the key she'd need. It was a dangerous risk to take, appealing to his heart, but if it succeeded, it might mean her freedom.

His hand curled around hers, and his lips pressed to the top of her head.

Freedom. She dreamed of freedom.

The morning came too fast, and before she knew it, she was standing before a mirror dressed like a queen. She grimaced at her reflection. With its rich red silk and black fur, her dress screamed Scythian royalty. Her gaze slid to the warlord buttoning his black vest over a black silk shirt. It shouldn't have surprised her; black seemed to be his signature color.

As if feeling her gaze, his almond-shaped eyes peered up at her from impossibly thick eyelashes. "Yes, wild one?"

She shook her head and turned back to her own outfit, her eyes snagging on the collar around her neck. Anger buzzed in her veins. It wasn't right that something so beautiful could represent something so disgusting.

"Something wrong?"

Sage wiped the look from her face as the warlord sidled up behind her and placed his hands on her shoulders. She wanted to test her theory, but baiting him before the peace talks wasn't beneficial for anyone. "No." She shook her head. "Just tired."

He squeezed her shoulder and squinted at her head. A smile pulled one side of his mouth up. "Well, your hair is wide awake," he commented wryly as he brushed down a stray hair.

The moment was surreal. It was times like these that confused Sage. They were so mundane, so human. It scared her how easy it would be to stop fighting, to let go, to let the warlord devour her. He'd been her friend at one time. He could be that again if she let go.

He placed a quick kiss on her thorn collar. "This looks so beautiful against your skin."

Her heart fell. And that's why she would never comply. When he let his human side out, it was brief and beautiful, like a shooting star, but the darkness that raged after it was brutal.

He straightened and held an arm out. "Are you ready to change history?"

Sage nodded and ignored her sour stomach. What sort of changes was he planning?

Tables and chairs had been placed in a loose square, while unshuttered windows allowed the mountain breeze to pass through a ballroom. It didn't escape her notice that she didn't quite sit in the middle of the group as the position of mediator dictated. Her chair was slightly to the left, closer to the Scythian side.

The Aermian delegates, the Scythian delegates, and leads were given seats, their places marked with nameplates of onyx inlaid with silver. Pitchers of water, juice, and ale were at all the tables. Scythian scribes she'd never seen before sat on lush pillows against the wall, ready to take notes, while the Aermian scribes sat at a table behind the crown prince.

She scanned the Scythian side, only knowing three of the nine delegates: the warlord, Maeve, and Blair.

Her heart squeezed as she twisted to the right and stared at all the familiar faces. Zachael, Gav, Tehl, Sam, Hayjen, Lilja, William, and Jeren. Even the stodgy Jeren was a welcome sight. But it was the man with golden eyes and wine-colored hair that pulled her attention. Rafe sat watching her, his face blank, but in his eyes, she detected a familiar look.

Sage smiled inwardly. The warlord was a master tactician, but he'd never met Rafe. If there was a way to escape, he'd figure it out. She scanned the group once more and moved back to the man she'd skipped. His dark blue gaze nearly knocked the wind from her lungs. He was more beautiful than the phantom her imagination had conjured.

"Good morning, wife," Tehl murmured softly.

She swallowed hard, ignoring how the warlord stilled at the crown prince's soft-spoken words. "Good morning, my lord. I trust you slept well?" she said, her tone polite, nothing more.

"I did. The accommodations were excellent, thank you."

She nodded and tore herself from his intense gaze only to be ensnared by the warlord's. He looked cool and collected, but Sage saw something different. She saw rage brewing beneath the surface, one she didn't know if she could survive a second time. He looked to Tehl and then shot her a look; she blinked. Had that been hurt in his eyes? What was he thinking? She tore her gaze from the warlord and pushed aside her thoughts. She had a duty to do.

With care, she rose from her chair. "I welcome all to the peace delegation that will change the very fabric of our kingdoms," she recited from memory. "Today, we'll embark on something historic that has not been attempted in one hundred years. Today, we strive for peace."

Silence settled over the solemn group of men and women as her words died in the echoing space. She curtseyed to the table. "It's my honor to mediate this peace accord. It is my hope that we can reach an understanding that will benefit both our lands and peoples." She held a hand out toward the warlord and the crown prince. "Please step forward to begin our discussion."

Tehl moved to her right side, and the warlord prowled to her left. "Please repeat after me: I pledge to seek the advantage for both our peoples as lord and ruler of my kingdom." Both men repeated after her, and she held a hand out to each man. A measure of calmness settled over Sage when Tehl placed his hand in hers, combating the fear that the warlord's grip instigated in her. She placed the men's hands together. "Let it be done."

Tehl and the warlord shook hands in the Aermian custom and then kissed each other's cheeks in the Scythian custom before moving back to their seats.

Sage swept an arm out and sank into her chair, her wobbly legs grateful for the support. "Begin," she announced.

Relief washed over her. Her part was done for now. Now, she listened and watched.

Her worry was for naught.

The morning had started off awkward for everyone seemed reluctant to speak, but after an hour of stilted speeches, Sam had managed to crack a joke that broke even the most stoic Scythians' demeanors.

Each Aermian delegate had a speech prepared that was eloquent and overly polite, and each of Zane's delegates followed by making a speech of their own. The first day was wasted on pretty words that were anything but sincere, but at least they'd gotten the ball rolling.

She rubbed between her brows. A throbbing pain in her head made itself known just as the Scythian at the end of the table, Phoenix, finished his speech. The delegates had spent all day speaking, yet nothing seemed accomplished.

"Are you all right, consort?" the warlord asked. Tehl and Lilja's gazes turned to Sage.

"My head hurts," she said, offering a weak smile. All the stress of the day had led to rising pain that stabbed her eyes.

"We're finishing up here," the warlord murmured. "Why don't you retire to your room until dinner?"

She glanced at the window, noting the sinking sun. "I will." Sage stood, curtseyed, and slipped from the room. She stumbled a step and placed a hand against the rough red stone wall. The hallway lurched, causing her stomach to do the same, and the grapes she'd nibbled on for lunch threatened to make a reappearance.

"My lady? Are you all right?"

Sage glanced to the warrior who was watching her with trepidation. "No, I need to rest."

He nodded, and she forced herself upright and lurched after him. She managed to stumble into the room and crash onto the bed, the pain so overwhelming that stars dotted her vision. Nali grumped, but otherwise didn't move when Sage cuddled up to the big animal.

"Do you need anything, my lady?"

"The curtains," she mumbled, burrowing into the coverlet and pressing her face into Nali's fur.

A rustle of cloth reached her ears, and then blessed darkness closed over her. "Thank you," she whispered.

Silence, and then, "You're welcome."

The door clicked closed.

She grimaced and prayed that sleep would claim her quickly.

Cool skin touched her forehead, and she followed it, seeking comfort. Her hand shot out and wrapped around the wrist, moving it back to her forehead.

"Wild one, I need you to let go, so I can give you something for your head."

"No," she moaned. "No draughts." A whimper escaped her as another wave of pain slammed into her.

A curse reached her ears. "You're so frail! Every time I turn around, there's something wrong with you! Let me help. I can heal you."

A large hand slipped behind her neck and something cool was placed at her lips. Sage pushed through her pain and opened her eyes to stare at the warlord's angry face.

"What is it?"

"Something for your pain."

"Are you telling me the truth?"

His face darkened even more. "I'm not poisoning you."

"That's not what I asked," she croaked.

"It's only for the pain."

She searched his face, not sure if he was lying.

"Drink it, or I will make you. Stop choosing to suffer when I can fix you."

And there it was, the threat to take away her right to choose. But even if she did choose, it wasn't really a choice. Another wave of pain crashed into her. Attending the talks in this state wasn't possible, and she needed to be there. It was an easy choice. By way of answer, she opened her mouth and drank the draught.

He laid her down and brushed her hair from her face. "Not terrible, was it?" He placed a kiss on her cheek and rubbed his fingers along her scalp. "Why do you have to be so stubborn? You make no sense sometimes. Women are such fickle creatures."

She breathed a contented sigh as his fingers released some of the pain assaulting her.

"I can't miss dinner, but I'll make excuses for you." He stroked her cheek and then disappeared without a sound, leaving Sage to snuggle back into bed.

THİRTY

SAGE

SAGE WOKE UP, TINGLING WITH awareness. She curled her hand around the dagger underneath her pillow. It was comical that the warlord let her keep it as she'd tried to use it on him once, yet he'd disarmed her so quickly that the dagger was more of a symbol of her helplessness than anything else. She was, however, thankful to have it this night—because there was someone in her room.

Listening intently, she kept her eyes closed and her breathing even. She forced herself to stay calm and to not move a muscle. A Scythian assassin would be stronger and faster, and she was virtually blind in the dark. She needed to keep still and lure the assassin toward her. It was a risk, but at least if the intruder was close, she could attack first and catch them by surprise; then maybe she'd have a chance.

Blessedly, the pain in her head was gone, so she could really focus. One breath, two breaths, three breaths, and there it was. The scent of mint. She snapped her arms out, clutching a shirt, and jerked with all her strength, throwing the assassin over her head. With speed she didn't know she still possessed, Sage rolled onto her knees and threw a knee over the intruder. She grabbed a handful of his hair and yanked back, holding her dagger's tip to the assassin's throat.

"Give me one reason why I shouldn't kill you right now?"

"Because I'm your brother, and I love you."

She stilled and let the dagger fall from her hand. "Sam?"

"And I'm much too handsome to die so young."

Sage scrambled backward, across the bed, her eyes darting across the darkness, seeing nothing. "You can't be here," she whispered urgently. If the warlord found him here, he'd kill Jasmine without thought and perhaps slaughter the entire Aermian delegation. She jumped from the bed and skirted around the furniture by memory to get to the window, pulling it back so just a touch of moonlight entered the room.

Sam sat on her bed, watching her.

"I've missed you."

Those were the last words she expected to hear. She both cherished and loathed them. He stood and held his arms out. Sage was ready to step into them but, thinking better of it, halted after only a pace.

His brows furrowed, and he snuck a glance toward the door. "You're right. We don't have time for a reunion right now." He stalked on silent feet to a trapdoor beneath the rug in front of the fire. "Let's go."

She swallowed hard and clenched her fists. Every part of her wanted to go with him, to just leave this place and the horrid memories, but she couldn't leave Jasmine. And even if that was not an issue, the warlord was too cautious. If Sam was here, it had to be by design.

"No," she whispered.

Sam froze and flew back to her side. "What do you mean 'no'?"

"No," she said, watching emotions ripple across his face. Sam rarely let his emotions show. Sam clasped her cheeks in his palms and his eyes darted between hers. He dropped his hands and wrapped his arms around her in a fierce hug. "I don't know what he's done, or what you've had to do to survive, but none of that matters. All that matters is going home to your family and friends who love you. Don't you want that?"

More than he knew, but he hadn't had to live like she did. "I won't go with you."

His embrace loosened and slowly, he released her and stepped back; this time, his spymaster's mask was in place. He reached a hand out and fingered her gauzy robe. "What is he holding over you?"

She slapped his hand away, stared him in the eye, and lied. "Nothing that concerns you, my lord. Now, please leave."

"I'm not leaving until you explain yourself." He gestured to her state of dress.

She slid a glance to the closed doors and back to Sam, shame coloring her cheeks. "I owe you nothing."

Sam cursed, his jaw clenching. "You owe the kingdom everything, and the warlord nothing."

"I owe him much. He saved my life and has taken care of me." The words tasted like ash on her tongue, partly because part of her believed that.

"He's using you."

"No more than the rebellion or the Crown did. Now, leave." Before the warlord stormed inside.

His face was a stone mask. "We can't protect you from him if you don't leave with me, *right now.*"

A sad smile touched her lips. "No one can protect themselves from him." Her words lingered in the air as Sam stared at her in silence. After a moment, he turned on his heel and snuck back to the trapdoor.

He glanced over his shoulder, the moonlight turning his hair silver. "You're playing a dangerous game. One that could destroy you." He smiled carelessly, pulling the trapdoor down. "Be seeing you soon, sis."

Her heart dropped to her feet as he disappeared down the dark hole, the trapdoor closing soundlessly. She fell to her knees, the pain so acute she couldn't breathe.

She'd let her chance to escape slip away. Sage allowed herself a moment to mourn and then pulled herself to her feet. Wallowing served no purpose, and she needed to calm herself before the warlord arrived. She needed to have a clear head when he arrived. Muddled thoughts led to poor choices in words, and bad decisions.

Sage stoked the fireplace and slid the rug over the trapdoor Sam escaped through. Not that it would make a difference. Zane was almost impossible to hide things from. She wilted into a chair and picked at her robe, pondering if she should change or not. The warlord would smell Sam on her like a bloody animal. There was no hiding his visit. She might as well just wait.

Two hours passed before the warlord sauntered into the room, closing the door behind him. Sage ignored his entrance, staring into the flames as he moved to stand across from her.

"How are you feeling, Sage?"

"Better," she said, still not looking in his direction.

The crackle of the fire filled the silence that descended between them. Not companionable or comfortable silence, but the kind that is brewing with tension and unsaid words.

"I'm proud of you, consort. You've done well."

She glanced at him, her face schooled. "Why are you proud?"

He glided toward her, all Scythian grace, and cupped her upturned face. "You didn't betray me."

Her suspicions were confirmed. "You knew he'd break in."

"I did."

She scanned his unearthly face and reached up to pull his hand from her face. "Why?"

"I needed to know where your loyalties lay." A breathtaking smile burst across his face. "I needed to know who you belonged to."

"I belong to myself."

"No," he breathed, leaning closer. She could smell the wine on his breath. "I *own* you."

She shot to her feet and rounded the chair, putting it between them. "You made me lie to my family."

The warlord chuckled. "Your family? That boy isn't your family."

"Do you even know the meaning of family?" she spat.

His face soured. "Family means nothing."

"I understand that after what you did to Rhys." Sage snapped her mouth shut, not able to take the words back.

"There are consequences for betrayal. Family is no exclusion."

"What made you like this?" she whispered.

"A sick old man and a twisted woman."

He sprang and grabbed her around the throat. Her hands pried at his as he lifted her and pushed her against a low dresser, the wooden top biting into the back of her thighs. He forced himself into the cradle of her thighs and met her gaze.

"You're a reminder of what's wrong in the world."

Sage gasped when the warlord squeezed the collar, the thorns digging into her skin. He released his grip slightly, so she could pull in a breath.

His gaze scanned her face, softening slightly. "And yet, you're all that's good."

"I don't understand," she whispered.

The warlord's chuckle chilled her. "You wouldn't. No one could understand the deranged old man's obsession with perfection or his covetousness of things that didn't belong to him."

"Who was he?" Sage ventured, trying to keep him talking.

His dark eyes emptied of all emotion. "My father."

She swallowed hard at the way he stared right through her.

"Everything was flawed in his mind, except for a Nagalian beauty he managed to steal and take as his wife. She was his prize, his goddess. She became pregnant. He anticipated the birth of his son—surely, he'd be as flawless as his mother! But the son was born resembling himself, and looked nothing like his goddess. So, the experimenting began." His empty black gaze focused on her. "Now, his mother had always hated the boy. He was a symbol of all that she had lost, all that was taken. But as the boy aged, he changed and grew into a striking figure, one who had no equal, except for his mother. And she took notice."

Her stomach sank. She hoped he wasn't saying what she thought he was saying.

The warlord smirked. "She couldn't help herself. It was only reasonable she'd be attracted to him. He wasn't really her son anymore, or so she told herself and the boy."

She thought she might throw up.

"He didn't know it was unnatural until his sister told him. Shame battered him every time she touched him, and he reacted, but his mother consoled him with logic. They were family. Naturally, they would love each other."

"Oh, Zane," she breathed, nausea threatening to overwhelm her. "I'm so sorry."

He jerked, his hand tightening around her neck briefly. "For what?"

"For your pain."

Anger darkened his face. "I don't need your pity."

"It's not pity. It's sympathy."

He leaned closer, his eyes darting between her eyes. "I can see that."

"What happened to your family?" She needed to know.

"They died, all but his beloved sister who protected him when no one else would."

"Maeve?"

"So smart," he murmured and trailed a hand down her bleeding neck. "Remember this, wild one, science doesn't lie or manipulate. It is truth." His hand skimmed down to her belly and caressed it. "But it does have consequences. Even I couldn't anticipate how it would affect our women and their birth rate."

Oh God. The room swirled around her in a kaleidoscope of color. All the pregnant women at the execution flashed through her mind. *When are you due?* Bile burned her throat.

"You look so much like her," he whispered, still staring at her flat belly. "This time, it will be different."

His mother. Sage swallowed, trying not to gag. "I'm sorry," she choked out.

"It was long before your birth."

"How long?" she ventured to ask, terrified of the answer.

"Since the purge."

The room spun. It couldn't be. It wasn't possible, but as Sage stared at the warlord, his dark, knowing gaze searched her face. The beautiful monster in front of her was far more dangerous than she ever realized. How was it possible for a man to live that long?

"Why?" she croaked. "Why would you do such a thing? All those people."

"They wouldn't let me cleanse them." His gaze traveled to her neck. "You're bleeding," he said, as if he'd just noticed the damage he'd caused.

She wanted to scream when he plucked her from the dresser and carried her to the bed. Her skin crawled at his touch. Sage panted hard as she tried to sort through her emotions. She'd been sleeping with the most notorious war criminal her land had ever seen. She'd let him touch her skin. Every part of her felt defiled.

The warlord uncorked a vial, poured it into a cup, and held it out to her. She stared at the cup and weighed her options. Did she drink it to appease the creature of death and darkness before her? Or did she fight an ancient monster who had once been human? Her gaze lifted to the warlord's, and what she saw there killed her. Not only could she see the monster, but she could also see the abused little boy.

"No."

His hand clenched on the cup, cracking it.

Sage shoved all the emotions down and reached out, touching the warlord's trembling hand. "I'm not something to be fixed, Zane." He stilled at her use of his name. She lifted her other hand to her throat. "You did this. It's not fair for you to erase it like it never happened."

"Life's never been fair, consort."

"True, you and I both know that." As much as she loathed to admit it, they had something in common. They were survivors. She pushed his hand down and dug deep for her bravery. Slowly, she rolled up onto her knees, so they were at the same eye-level, and cupped both his cheeks. "I'm sorry for what you've suffered," she whispered. "Truly, I am, but that doesn't condone what you've done." He began pulling away from her, but she tightened her hold and lied. "But I will help you change."

"Change is impossible for me."

She agreed. But she said, "Change is never impossible. And I will help you."

He pulled her hands from his face and rubbed his thumb along her cheekbone. "Wild one, you may look like her, but you are nothing like her. She was sick and selfish. You are honorable and kind." He pressed a kiss to her temple. "I'll call for Maeve and have her see to your wounds."

Sage nodded, trying not to puke. As soon as he closed the door, she ran for the railing and released all the contents of her belly. Tears streamed down her face. How could everything go so wrong? A knock had her swiping at her tears and turning to the door.

Maeve opened the door and paused when she caught sight of her. She carefully closed the door and strode to the balcony, carrying a basket. Her cinnamon gaze swept across Sage's face and neck, and her lips pulled down. "Come with me, child."

Sage followed Maeve back into the room, all her emotions raw.

Maeve pulled her to a chair and knelt before her.

She swallowed hard and turned to stare at the fire as the Scythian woman cleaned her wounds.

"Where else does it hurt?"

She pointed to her hips. "He grabbed me."

Maeve brushed aside the robe and hissed.

Sage glanced down at the angry purple bruises already forming.

"What did you do?" Maeve muttered.

"What did I do?" she hissed. "This is clearly your brother's doing."

"Well, you must have set him off."

"Because I look like your mother?"

Maeve jerked. "What?"

"You heard me," Sage whispered. "How can you want your daughter to return to this? How?"

"I can protect her here."

"Can you?" She stared straight into Maeve's eyes. "Can you protect Blaise from him?"

Silence.

"He's more dangerous to her than anything else she could possibly encounter."

"What do you expect me to do? Leave her as a prisoner in Aermia?"

"No." Sage clasped the woman's hands. "I will protect her. I could keep her away from here, keep her safe."

Maeve scoffed. "You can't even protect yourself."

"If you help Jasmine, Blaise, and I escape, I can."

Time seemed to stand still as the Scythian woman stared at her, thinking. After a moment, she glanced at the door and then back to Sage. "You want me to betray him, then?"

"I've seen the emotions you keep hidden from him. Don't lie to yourself or to me. He may be your blood, but we both know he's more a monster than a man, a murderer."

Maeve pulled in a breath and squeezed Sage's hand, something shifting in her eyes. Sage didn't know how she hadn't before noted the ancient wisdom in the woman's eyes. "Can you promise me you will do everything in your power to keep my daughter from here? And to keep her safe with you, wherever you go?"

"I will," Sage vowed.

"Then I will retrieve your friend and Blaise…and I will help you escape. I can't promise you will live, but you won't die by his hand, and you'll be free."

Hope fluttered in her chest for the first time in a long time. Sage leaned forward and kissed both of Maeve's cheeks.

The Scythian woman stood and smiled down at Sage. "Thank you."

She grabbed Maeve's hand before she left. "Will you be okay?"

Maeve's smile turned dark. "Zane's not the only one who's been around a long time. Don't worry about me, child. All will be well. Prepare yourself, for the journey will be both difficult and dangerous."

She stood and strode to the balcony, filled with nervous energy as she anticipated what was to come. Gazing at the fires of the army burning in the distance, she took a calming breath. *Soon.*

Soon, she'd escape this hell.

Soon, she'd be home.

And soon, she'd be hunted by an ancient master hunter.

Soon couldn't come fast enough.

THIRTY-ONE

TEHL

TEHL SWIRLED THE PUNGENT AMBER liquid in his cup, mulling over the day's events. It had gone smoother than expected. Part of him wondered if the warlord really did want peace, though. The talks seemed legitimate, but then again, it could have been well-orchestrated play-acting to cover the warlord's true agenda.

He threw back the contents of his drink, his eyes watering as the spirits burned the back of his throat and warmed his belly. Dinner had been another horrid affair, both groups merely staring at each other, occasional whispers echoing in the giant room. More upsetting than their people's inability to communicate was the empty seat beside him.

In the past, it had been difficult to control his emotions, but manageable. But when Sage didn't show up for dinner, he had to employ every trick he knew to keep his feelings locked away. Panic was the first one to grab hold of him, then helplessness. Luckily, Gavriel had asked after Sage, leaving Tehl time to compose himself and pulling the warlord's attention elsewhere.

He frowned into his empty glass. Even when the Scythian leader wasn't watching him directly, the warlord seemed very aware of everything Tehl did. What almost tipped him over the edge wasn't the fact that Sage didn't come to dinner, but the way the enemy referred to his wife. It was intimate, and Tehl hated it, hated how he didn't know if it was the truth or simply a means by which to manipulate him. His hand tightened on the cup. It was probably both.

Tehl glanced over his shoulder as Sam entered his room, shutting the door only to fall heavily against it, his shoulders slumped.

"Sam?" Lilja called, rising from her perch on the divan.

"Music," Sam whispered. "I need music."

Tehl turned and placed his cup on the table near the fire. "Why? What for?"

His brother lifted his head, devastation clear on his face. "I need it."

Short. No explanation.

"Hayjen?"

The tall man met his wife's gaze, disappeared into the adjoining room, and reappeared with a fiddle. He lifted his bow and began to play a haunting tune that rose the hair on Tehl's arms.

Lilja eyed Sam. "Now speak."

Sam dragged a hand over his face and pushed from the door. His stride was clipped as he approached the silent group of people lounging around the room. "We have a serious problem."

That got Tehl's attention; Sam must have needed music to prevent their conversation from being overheard. "What is it?" he asked in a low voice.

His brother opened his mouth and then closed it, shooting a glare at the door behind him. Sam strode to a desk situated in the corner and poured whiskey into a cup. He tossed it back and then pulled in a deep breath before speaking. "She refused."

It was only two words, but they knocked the wind from Tehl's lungs.

Hayjen missed a note, but quickly continued playing.

"Why?" Zachael breathed, devastation clear on his face.

"I don't know. I—" Sam shook his head. "Why would she do this?"

"Did she give you any hints?"

"Nothing." Sam cursed and kicked at a log. "Absolutely nothing."

"She's been with the warlord for months," Lilja murmured, almost hesitant. "She could be under his influence somehow."

"That's nonsense," William retorted. "She seems not the kind of person to be unduly influenced."

"That's the problem, though," Rafe rumbled. "It's not always something one can control."

"How did she act with you?" Lilja asked.

Sam tugged at his hair. "She attacked me." A goofy smile flittered across his face and disappeared. "To be fair, I did sneak up on her when she was in bed. But when she recognized me, she embraced me. I saw Sage, or a glimmer of her, before she locked her old self away and then disappeared." Sam's fingers curled into a fist, his arms shaking. "She…she told me that she owed the warlord everything, and that he was using her as much as…" His brother hesitated. "As much as the rebellion and Crown."

He froze. She thought he was using her? She compared him to the Scythian warlord? Tehl clenched his hands, trying to ward off the pain those words caused him. Something wasn't right. Sage could be reasoned with despite her emotions. Those words weren't reasonable at all. They were nonsense.

Hayjen played straight into another song, his fingers flying over the strings.

"That's not what Sage believes," Lilja reasoned. "I know, because we've talked about it. Those words aren't her own; they have to be someone else's." She shot a glance at her husband. "Hayjen and I have rescued girls who have been inflicted with this type of torture. They're manipulated into believing things that make no sense at all. It seems crazy to us, but seems absolutely real to them."

Jeren stepped closer, his head bowed. "So, you're telling me that our consort has been deceived by our enemy?"

Lilja nodded gravely.

Tehl's advisor, Jeren, glanced around the room and held up his hands. "You all know that I have not hid my dislike for Sage, but in the time she was with us, she changed things for the better. It's with a heavy heart that I say this, but someone needs to." He pulled in a deep breath, looking very old. "Sage is a wealth of information for both the Crown and rebellion. If the warlord has accomplished what you suspect, Captain Femi, then it is logical for us to examine those consequences."

"No," Gav growled.

Tehl met Jeren's gaze. "You think she's working with him. That she's a traitor?" Tehl didn't attack the man for the accusation. It was logical. If the warlord wanted information, Sage was his key.

Jeren glared around the room. "The crown prince believes me," he uttered softly.

All eyes swung to Tehl. "It makes sense. Think of it. She's the perfect piece for him to use in his game."

"So, you're naming her a traitor?" Zachael asked calmly.

"No," Tehl glanced at Lilja. "I am just saying that he's hurt and manipulated my wife. We don't have any idea what information she may have unwittingly given him."

"What a brilliant idea," Sam hissed. "Even if she was able to reason through all his lies, her actions would be proof of treason. The warlord has created an intricate trap." Sam's brows slashed downward. "We're still missing something. Sage was afraid."

Sage never let anyone see her fear. That in itself was disturbing.

"What kind of fear?" Rafe questioned.

Sam squinted at the ornate ceiling. "Fear for me." He dropped his chin down, blankly staring at the group. "She wasn't afraid for herself. Sage was protecting me."

"That sounds like my wife," Tehl muttered. His brows furrowed when something tugged at the back of his mind. He blinked. The girl from the village. "Sam. The girl." Sage would never leave the girl behind.

"What girl?"

"The girl from the village."

"Of course," Sam exploded. He glanced at the door and continued in a lower tone. "Sage would never leave anyone behind."

"Do you think she's protecting the girl and so not being manipulated?" Jeren asked.

"I'm sure he's manipulated her, but if Jasmine is alive, Sage wouldn't leave her behind. What better leverage for the warlord to have? Sage would probably risk her own life, but the life of a friend?"

"What do you suggest we do?" Rafe asked, watching Lilja.

The Sirenidae scanned the group as Hayjen's song came to a crescendo. "We play our parts. We must be content to watch and wait for her signal."

"And you believe there will be one? A signal, I mean?" Jeren asked.

"I would stake my life on it."

"Then, we wait," Tehl said.

"We wait," Lilja echoed.

THIRTY-TWO

SAM

AND THEY WAITED.

Five days passed in a flurry of pretty speeches, veiled threats, and reluctant compromises. Each day, he prayed that Sage would give them a signal: a look, a cue... anything really. But she didn't. She sat at the end of the table, a ghost of her former self.

Sam glanced at his brother from his seat at the dining table. Tehl sat in his chair, sipping wine from a goblet, looking regal, as if the world were there only for his amusement. But Sam knew what lay beneath the surface of that façade. It was evident in his brother's gaze resting on Sage, the tightness of the skin around his mouth whenever the warlord needled him, and how tightly he clenched his goblet. His brother was worried, angry, and dangerously close to losing his temper.

Sam sighed, lazily scanning the table. A pair of cinnamon eyes snagged his attention. They were perusing him with interest, so he cocked his head and smirked at her. The one called Maeve didn't simper, flush in embarrassment, or look away. She simply held his gaze and raised a goblet of wine to him. That wasn't something he experienced every day. For once, he felt like the prey, not the predator.

She broke their stare-off and whispered something in her daughter's ear. Sam glanced between mother and daughter, discreetly observing them.

Things rarely shocked him anymore, but seeing two women who looked like twins, but were mother and daughter was an eerie experience.

Maeve glanced at him from beneath her dark lashes, a sensual smile curling her lips.

"I'll take my leave," the warlord said as he stood. He held his hand out to Sage. "Consort, would you like an escort to your room?"

Sam schooled his expression as Sage placed her hand in the other man's and swept out of the room with the Scythian.

Her room? Liar. The warlord didn't let her out of his sight.

His gaze shifted to Tehl. His brother stared in the direction of the couple before tossing back the last of his wine emotionlessly. It seemed like his brother fractured a little further as each day passed. They didn't have much time before Tehl broke and did something that got them all killed.

He turned back to Maeve as she daintily dabbed at her mouth and stood. She turned on her heel and sauntered out of the room. At the last second, she peered over her shoulder and met his gaze, winked, and disappeared from view.

Intriguing. She was flirting with him, but why? He swirled his wine and sniffed the fruity liquid while scanning the table. Both delegations were still watching each other apprehensively, though some of the tension had departed the room with the warlord. Sam caught the eye of Blaise and smiled widely, knowing his dimple was on display. It was a smile that always worked for him.

Her lips thinned as she bared her teeth.

Well, almost every time. Apparently, she still hadn't forgiven him for his interrogations.

Sam pushed back from the table and bowed to Blaise in a courtly fashion, earning looks from many at the table. He strode from the room, keenly aware of the attention he drew. He kept smiling as he exited the room, keeping his stride lazy while examining the hallway with a sharp gaze. One never knew who was lurking about.

He sauntered past a curtained window when something grabbed the back of his vest and yanked him back. Sam pulled a dagger from his waist and spun, using the momentum. He blinked in shock as his dagger was plucked from his hand, and he was yanked into the dark and slammed against a stone wall. He tried to surge forward, but the body pressed against him held him in place.

"Calm down. I'm not going to kill you."

A soft, flowery scent curled around him in the dark space. A woman.

"I find I must warn you that I like being taken captive, my lady," he purred as his mind scrambled for an explanation. He blinked, his eyes adjusting to the dark space. *A secret hallway. How unoriginal. Where did this one lead?*

"I don't doubt that, Prince."

His eyes narrowed at the voice as he focused on the woman holding him, just able to make out the shape of her face. Maeve. "I'm flattered, but I must say that you have me at a—"

"Enough," she whispered. "Time is short. Do you wish to take your princess home safely?"

Sam stilled, sensing a trap, and answered carefully. "We all wish for our loved ones to be safe."

A small growl from below his chin. "We don't have time for pretty words. Sage is in danger. If she doesn't escape, he'll kill her."

His body tensed. "Why tell me this?"

"Because I'm going to help her escape our warlord and put his tyranny to an end."

He forced a chuckle out while he ran through the possible reasons she'd really approached him. "That sounds an awful lot like treason, my lady. The Aermian delegation is here for peace. We'd never jeopardize our endeavors."

Maeve scoffed and released her arm from his throat. "Please, we all know why you're here, but you'll not succeed."

Sam almost reached for a blade, but thought better of it. The woman had been able to restrain him in seconds. Plus, he didn't know if her superior eyesight included some form of enhanced night-vision. He straightened his vest. "This has been exciting, but I must be returning to my room. It's been a long day that I'm sure we'll repeat tomorrow."

"She said you'd be difficult. I don't expect you to trust me, but I do expect you to trust someone you've sworn yourself to."

He stilled. "What do you mean?"

"She said to tell you that when you helped to arm her, you promised to support her even against your own blood; you became her brother in truth."

His mind flashed back to Sage sobbing while trying to attach her dagger sheaths before her wedding, and how she shook so hard she couldn't clasp them. He'd never shared that with anyone. He was also sure Sage and Gav wouldn't have, either. This was Sage's sign. "What do you need from me?"

A sigh of relief. "You need to pick a fight tomorrow."

"That sounds dangerous."

"Not a physical fight, but you need to raise an issue that the warlord will never accept, and that Aermia will never budge on."

"And that is?"

"His experiments."

A chill ran through him. "He's still experimenting?"

"That's neither here nor there, but he'd never agree to give up his perceived rights. It'll be an insult he won't be able to ignore."

"He'll have to change his game," Sam murmured. "That's dangerous."

"It'll be enough to ensure the delegations escape from this place, and also allow me time to get the girls out of this hell."

"Girls?" he asked.

"Be prepared to rescue three girls. Span your men along the Scythian border. They won't be able to cross near the Nagali border. There will be too many warriors roaming the area."

"It'll be done." Sam's mind raced, thinking on all the things he needed to put into motion in order for this to succeed. It would be difficult, but not impossible. "And you promise to get her out safely?"

"I promise nothing but freedom."

"And what does that mean?"

"If I cannot free her, she'll die a clean death. I won't allow her to suffer another moment more."

His lips thinned. He hated it, but he didn't understand what Sage had suffered, so perhaps that was the best she could offer. If his sister-in-law was willing to die rather than suffer any further by the warlord's hand, it must be unimaginable. "And what do you get out of this situation?" No one did anything for free.

"I judged you to be an honorable man, so I'm trusting you with a piece of information precious to me. One of the women who will be escaping with Sage is my daughter. You know her by the name of Blaise."

He blinked. The Scythian woman they'd returned. It was a possibility she was a spy. But even if that was the case, he'd welcome her with open arms if it meant having Sage safe at home.

"She's the only light in my world." Maeve's face snapped to the side. "Our time for speaking has ended. I hope her trust in you is warranted." She popped up on her toes and kissed both his cheeks. "Take care of the girls and keep them safe." Her hand curled around his arm, and she pushed him out of the dark and into the window alcove.

Sam spun and caught a glimpse of her face before the door closed silently, only showing a wall of stone where the door once was. He breathed heavily, panic tugging at his gut. It was a gamble trusting her, but ignoring her words was a bigger gamble.

He sucked in a huge breath. No matter what, the peace talks could only end one way. In war. The delegation would honestly risk little to go along with her plan. It was Sage who risked everything.

They had nothing to lose, and everything to gain.

He entered the room and caught Hayjen's eye. "I would love some music."

Lilja grabbed the fiddle and handed it to her husband, her gaze never leaving Sam. Rafe, Gav, Zachael, and Tehl all focused on him as Hayjen began to play.

"We have our sign," he whispered.

Tehl shot to his feet. "What?"

Sam shook his head. "I can't tell you the specifics, but I have a plan set in motion. I'll need everyone's cooperation. You each have a role to play."

"What can you tell us?" Rafe asked.

"I'll speak with each of you personally, and Lilja?"

Her serious eyes met his. "Yes?"

"I'll need your help."

She nodded.

Tehl strode over to him, his face displaying heavy fatigue, worry having created shadows underneath his eyes.

"What do I need to do?" Tehl asked.

"Ruin the peace talks."

A dangerous smile crept across his brother's face, making him resemble a mercenary more than a prince. "With pleasure."

Sam released a breath. "So, we begin."

THIRTY-THREE

SAGE

IT WAS ANOTHER DAY OF speeches and promises she knew would never come to fruition. It was a pretty little play. She'd been discreetly yawning behind her hand when Jeren snarled something at Blair.

"We will *never* accept your tampering in Aermia. Your monstrosities end here," the Aermian counselor hissed.

She still felt the shock of his words in the pit of her stomach. How had they gone from trade to this? The room seemed to drop in temperature as the warlord leaned forward in his chair, the lines of his body rigid.

"I suggest you leash your delegate before he says something he'll regret," the warlord growled.

The crown prince eyed the warlord and straightened. "I apologize for his utter lack of tact, but not for his intent. I understand that your people's crimes are in the past and should stay there. But my people's fear and hate for the way you use science has not. If we are to obtain peace, then we need assurances that all your tampering has ceased as well."

The warlord cocked his head. "Haven't I already done so?"

"So you say."

"Are you implying I lied?" the warlord asked casually.

The hair on the back of her neck stood. She knew that tone intimately. It spoke of danger and pain.

"No, I am not," Tehl said. "But we're concerned not about your past deeds, but rather your draughts used for healing. They go beyond what is natural."

The warlord's brows arched. "You don't want me to heal my people?"

"In order to forge our peace alliance, we require all altering to cease. We want no part of your tampering in Aermia."

"You presume to command me?"

"No." Tehl shook his head. "But from leader to leader, you understand what it means to protect your people." His gaze hardened. "And I will protect my people. I will not allow Scythian draughts in Aermia."

"Even if we could heal the disease that plagues your people?" the warlord asked tightly.

"Even so. We will not risk the danger and corruption. This is non-negotiable."

The air seemed to leave the room as the warlord stood. He flung his arm out in her direction.

"Does Sage look corrupted? She's alive because of those draughts. I'd venture to say she's even healthier now than when she was under your roof."

Sage inwardly winced at the warlord's dig and held her breath when Tehl stood. He turned and pinned her with his sapphire gaze. She blushed as he leisurely scanned her before turning to the warlord.

"You're right. She looks healthy, but she also doesn't look like my wife." He flicked a disgusted look in her direction. "She dresses and speaks like a Scythian, not an Aermian." His teeth clenched together. "And apparently, she sleeps in a Scythian bed, too," he growled.

The floor seemed to fall out from below her, and the room swayed. She begged him with her gaze to look at her, to let her explain, but all her words caught in her throat. Their lives hinged on her silence. She swallowed down her explanations and focused on the two men staring each other down. One smug, the other disgusted.

The crown prince lifted his chin and stared the warlord in the eye. "Will you comply for peace?" The question hung in the air.

The warlord stared at her with an unholy glee in his eyes just before turning to the crown prince and replying, "I will not."

"Then we are at an impasse," Tehl said.

"No, we are at the end," the warlord said.

Both men watched each other for a tense second before the crown prince dipped his chin. "So be it. Let the record show that Aermia and Scythia did not come to a peace agreement. The laws of our forefathers will still be upheld." He glanced at Sage. "You have no place among my household. Traitors usually receive death, but since you are my wife, I will grant you mercy. You shall be exiled."

Her heart cracked into a million pieces, but her mask was as flawless as ever when Tehl turned and strode from the room. Heat built at the back of her eyes as the delegation left, refusing to even look in her direction.

She blinked constantly, the stars wavering around her.

Six hours.

It had been six hours since the last of the peace talks began.

It had been three hours since the Aermian delegation had named her a traitor.

It had been one hour since they closed negotiations and abandoned her.

She stared into the dark, the wind whipping her clothing around her and chilling her tears. A muffled sob slipped out when she remembered Tehl naming her an adulteress, nothing but condemnation and disgust on his face.

Sage lifted her robe and scrubbed the tears from her face, all the while trying to catch a glimpse of the fires burning in the distance. Before, they shone brightly, beacons of hope, but now they wavered like mirages, false promises. Even now, thinking over the day, she couldn't believe that Tehl thought her a traitor. He was smarter than that. Despite the evidence, he knew her, knew she would never betray him.

But you have already, haven't you?

Sage swallowed down the pain and focused on what she knew to be true. Her name was Sage Blackwell. She was married to the crown prince who was brave, honorable, and intelligent. She had four brothers, and that included two sworn brothers. Sam, the cunning spymaster, and Gav, the warrior with a heart of gold. Neither one of those men would hurt her.

Sage welcomed the cold air as it helped to clear her thoughts. Sam had tried to rescue her six days ago. He knew where to find her. Her brows furrowed, and she pulled her robe closer to her body. He already knew she was in the warlord's chamber. Not only that, but she'd sent Sam a message. So, why did Tehl name her an adulteress and traitor today? It didn't make any sense.

"Wild one, are you going to stand out there all night? I can't possibly keep you healthy if you keep putting yourself at risk."

Rubbing at her arms, she spun to face him, then meandered into the room ever so slowly. The warlord lounged in a chair by the fire, eyeing her with an emotion she couldn't decipher.

"Have you been crying over those fools?" he asked softly.

She forced her hands to stay by her side instead of scrubbing at her face like she longed to. "I'm a woman. We're emotional creatures," she said with a half-smile.

He set his goblet down and stalked in her direction before clasping her face in his hands. She tilted her head back to meet his black gaze.

"If I didn't have any morals, I would have cut them all down where they stood for what they did to you," he whispered. "I have half a mind to hunt them down."

Fear shot through her at his words. "But you won't?"

He scanned her face. "No, I won't, but not only for you. When Aermia bows before me, it will be because they were weak and they failed."

His words incited a shiver. She pulled her robe tighter and gently pulled from his grasp. "It's been a long day, and I'm tired."

"Of course, consort."

She shuffled to the bed and turned her back to him, afraid he could see all of her thoughts and feelings swirling in her mind. He released a sigh and strode around the bed to tug the draperies across the window. Her skin prickled when his belt jingled and his clothes rustled. Her eyes slammed closed as his weight sunk into the bed, and a heavy arm curled around her.

"Sleep, wild one. Tomorrow will have its own worries."

"Wise," she whispered, very aware of how his hand slipped into her robe and pressed against her bare stomach. "It must be because of how old you are."

The warlord stilled and then chuckled, shaking her body. "Sage, you never stop surprising me. Never change."

"Change is inevitable."

His laughter died off, and a light kiss caressed the back of her neck. "True. You and I will change the world."

She stayed silent and forced her body to relax. He was right, each day had its own worries. She had to focus on one thing at a time. Now wasn't the time to decipher Tehl's actions; now was the time to escape.

Sage jerked away, her heart pounding. She blinked furiously and sat up, the warlord's arm slipping into her lap. She scanned the room, but nothing looked out of the ordinary. She frowned and glanced at the warlord. He was asleep.

It must have been a dream.

She released a heavy sigh and stared at his handsome face. Awake, he was devastatingly handsome, but asleep, his face was a mask of serenity and peace, angelic. She traced one of his eyebrows and brushed his dark hair from his cheek. In that moment, she could almost forget his atrocities. The thought sickened her. Did a pretty face sway her that much?

"Sage."

She jerked and rolled out of the bed, glaring at the source of the voice.

"Maeve." Sage glanced at the warlord and back to the Scythian woman. "Is it time?"

Maeve slipped all the way through the curtains and shook her head. "It's time. No questions."

Her eyes rounded as she glanced at the warlord.

"Now, Sage. He won't wake for some time. The drug will keep him down."

She swallowed hard and climbed onto the bed. The part of herself that she hated most mourned leaving him. She pressed a kiss to his temple and placed her forehead against his. "I know there's a shred of good inside you, I've seen it, but I cannot stay here with you, hoping I can coax it out. You're too broken, and you'll break me. I'm sorry."

Sage crept from the bed and shivered as she moved through the curtains and into the cold night air. Maeve smiled sadly and glanced toward the room.

"Wait here. I need to secure him."

The Scythian woman slipped away, silent as the night. Meanwhile, she wrapped her arms around herself and waited for Maeve to return. It seemed like an eternity before the woman emerged, just as silently as she left.

They both moved to the balcony and Maeve lifted a rope. "I need you to secure this under your armpits."

Sage nodded and took the rope from her, securing it around her body with numb fingers. Maeve tugged on it and then tied it around her waist.

"I'm going to lower you down first and then follow. Blaise has secured our weight. Make sure to hold on, or the rope will bite in painfully. This is the most tedious part of our plan."

Sage nodded and placed her hands on the railing. She'd never been afraid of heights, but putting her trust in another to keep from falling hundreds of feet was no simple thing.

"Breathe in and out. You can do this, Sage. You're strong," the Scythian woman whispered.

She could do this. She had to do this.

Carefully, she slipped one leg over the railing, and then the other, spinning so she was facing the railing, her bare toes clenching the stone ledge.

"Slide down to your knee and edge your body off."

Gritting her teeth, she did as she was told. Her legs dangled below, and her fingers bit into the railing.

"Let go of the railing and grasp the rope."

Sage counted to three and released the railing. For a breathless moment, it felt like she was falling. Then the rope bit into her underarms. She snatched the rope and pulled upward. The pain receded, but her arms began to shake as she swung below the balcony. She glanced up to catch Maeve slipping over the edge, lowering them. Sage's stomach lurched as she dropped a foot and then another.

It shouldn't have surprised her that Maeve held their weight so easily, but it was still amazing to see the petite woman using just her arms to lower them. It was faster than she liked, but even that felt too slow. Every second they were in the air, she felt like the warlord would lean over the railing and haul them back up.

They passed seven levels when Sage caught sight of Blaise. The Scythian woman was holding the other side of the rope. The curious side of Sage's mind was intrigued by the pulley system that they'd rigged, but all of that was forgotten when Blaise locked eyes with her and whispered, "You need to swing toward me. I can't reach you."

Sage nodded and steeled her nerves. She couldn't think about it, she had to just do it, so she began to swing. Her stomach twisted as the rope creaked and groaned, but it held. When Blaise wrapped her arms around Sage's legs, she offered a little prayer of thanks. She then clambered down to the balcony, her legs shaking, and tugged at the rope tied around her.

A flask entered her vision. "I told Mum she was crazy. I've never seen anyone attempt that."

Sage grabbed it and took a large swig. The spirits burned away some of the jitters and the cold. She wiped the back of her mouth and handed it back. "Thank you for not dropping me."

A grunt.

Toes landed on the railing above her head and then Maeve dropped into view, landing without a sound. "Pull the rope, Daughter." She turned and offered Sage a hand up. "We need to get you changed."

Sage shivered and followed her into a much smaller room. Leather trousers, boots, a linen shirt, and a fur vest were laid out on a trunk.

"I think these will fit you."

"Thank you," she whispered and stripped off her skimpy nightgown and robe. She'd lost most of her sense of modesty. All she wanted was to feel *real* clothes against her skin.

"One moment," Maeve murmured. She poured some sort of oil in her hands. "We need to oil your entire body. It will change your scent."

"Okay."

Heat burned her cheeks as Maeve left no inch of skin untouched. Maeve grinned at her reaction for only a moment before sobering. "This is not a time to be shy. This is life or death. You've never faced a foe such as he."

Again, her stomach twisted. She knew.

Once Maeve finished, Sage yanked on the trousers, socks and boots, and then laced her half-corset. She threw on her shirt and quickly buttoned up her vest. Maeve handed her a ring. Sage eyed it. "What's that?"

Maeve flipped back the top of the ring revealing a sharp needle. "This holds a poison that will paralyze a Scythian." She flipped the top of the ring closed and held it out to Sage. "This is a last resort."

She pulled the ring from Maeve's palm and slipped it on the middle finger of her right hand. "What next?" she whispered, feeling a little more like her old self.

"We disguise you. Come here."

She turned and sat on the trunk as Maeve instructed her to do. The Scythian woman quickly did her hair in a Scythian braid.

"If anyone possibly sees you, you'll look Scythian. They won't look twice." Maeve stood and glanced at the silent Blaise. "Are you ready, Daughter?"

"Yes, Mum. I removed any trace of our footprints."

"Thank you." Maeve moved to the wall and pressed on a red mosaic tile piece. A door swung inward soundlessly. "Time to go."

Sage stood, but paused. Both Scythian women glanced at her with raised brows. "Where's Jasmine?"

"Safe," Maeve answered. "She's waiting for us."

"You swear?" Sage scrutinized the woman.

"I do. I would not leave that poor girl to the warlord's wrath."

Sage believed her and so she moved into the dark hidden passage. She turned and watched with rising dread as Blaise wiped off everything they touched and threw her clothing into the fire. Blaise scanned the room once more and moved into the hallway, closing the door.

Darkness surrounded them and blinded Sage.

"From this moment onward, you mustn't say a word until I give you permission. Do you understand?" Maeve said, her tone grave.

"Yes, but I can't see."

"Hold on to my belt until your eyes adjust."

Each step, each breath was torturous. They felt too loud. Panic swirled in her belly at being in the dark. It reminded her too much of how she ended up here. She stifled a hysterical laugh. Well, the warlord had done something for her. Her eyes were still used to the dark, so it was easier to see at night than it used to be.

They took endless twists and turns, descending staircase after staircase. Her ears popped, and she shook her head to dislodge the fuzzy feeling it created. Her mouth dropped open as the hallway opened up into a cavern. Sage scanned the area once and followed Maeve around its rocky edge.

"Blaise, I need light."

A few seconds later, a soft glow came from a bitty lantern in Blaise's hand.

Where did that come from?

Maeve took the lantern from Blaise and weaved around the precarious rockface. Now, Sage knew why they needed the light. She almost wished it was dark again; then she wouldn't have seen the jagged rocks below, looking like giant teeth ready to swallow them.

She trod softly behind Maeve and into the next cave where she skidded to a stop, her mouth hanging open. Something enormous slept in the middle of the cave. A red, scaled mountain breathed.

"Wh-what is that?" she stuttered, knowing exactly what it was, but not believing her eyes.

"It's sedated."

"How?" she breathed as she pressed her back to the cave wall glittering with rubies.

"The warlord."

Two little words. But enough to make her hair stand on end. She could scarcely pull her eyes from the myth slumbering on the floor, its massive wings curled against its sides, tail tucked around it. It reminded her of how Nali slept. "But it's a *dragon!*"

Maeve eyed her and picked up her speed. "It is, but we don't have time for explanations. Let's move."

Sage forced dragons from her mind and ran, her boots thumping on the floor. They ducked into another tunnel and weaved until they reached another room. She stumbled as Jasmine pushed from the wall and ran toward her. They crashed into each other, hugging.

"You're here, you're really here," Sage whispered.

"You got away," Jasmine cried.

Sage pulled back and smiled at her friend. "I can't believe it." She glanced at Maeve who was hugging Blaise fiercely.

She released her daughter and pulled Sage into a huge hug. Maeve pulled back and looked to each girl. "You all are strong in your own way. From here, you rely on each other. You have no one else. If you don't work together, you won't survive. The warlord will hunt you relentlessly, so you must get over the border as quickly as possible. There will be help waiting for you." She glanced to the side. "Nali."

Sage's eyes widened as the black feline slunk out of the dark and brushed against her hip. She ran her hand over the cat's head and glanced at Maeve.

The Scythian woman smiled. "Nali bonded with you, so you're now her mistress. She'll protect you from danger and ward off other predators who might normally try to hunt you. Heed her warnings and watch her reactions closely. I promise you, she will save your lives." She scanned the group of girls again. "Live long, happy lives. Fight, love, and live."

Blaise stepped closer and wrapped her arms around her mum. "Let me stay. I can help."

"No," Maeve murmured. "He'll destroy you. I couldn't take it if he took you from me, too. I love you, Daughter, more than anything."

"Love you, Mum." Blaise pulled back from her mum and wiped her eyes. She glanced at Sage. "Are you ready?"

Sage sank her fingers into Nali's fur and slipped her hand into Jasmine's. "Hell, yes."

For better or worse, she'd be free and, at the very least, she'd die that way.

THIRTY-FOUR

TEHL

HE KEPT HIS MASK IN place as they entered the camp. His guard moved from their tents and bowed low as their party rode by, their gazes scouring the group for the one person missing. The one person he was supposed to bring home. But he did the opposite. He condemned her and left her in that snake pit.

Pressing his heels to Wraith's side, he urged him forward and shot a glance to his brother, who was as collected as ever. He trusted him, but it was all he could do not to wrap his hands around Sam's throat and throttle him until he spilled the plan.

A relieved breath passed his lips when his tent came into view. He slid from his mount, gave the faithful beast a good pat, and nodded to the elite stationed outside his tent. Pushing through the flaps, he maneuvered around the table and chairs scattered about the room and snatched a bottle of spirits from a pack on the floor.

"Drinking?" Sam's voice said. "That's a poor tactic to deal with life."

He spun on his brother and defiantly took a swig.

Sam just arched a brow.

The whiskey burned his throat. Tehl slammed the bottle down and began pacing. His hands trembled by his sides, pulling a laugh out of him.

"What's so funny?"

He held his shaking hand up. "I've always been in control, had things planned. But this?" He waved his hands in the air. "I can't tell up from down. All I feel is anger." Even now, his rage boiled, seeking a target.

"I understand."

Tehl froze, his eyes narrowing on Sam. "How could you?"

"How could I what?"

"How could you possibly understand what it's like to leave your wife to her death?"

Sam wisely stayed silent.

He ran his hands through his windswept hair, guilt and fear rolling in his gut. "We left her there." Sage's pale face flashed through his mind. "I condemned her."

"It was only a show," Sam reasoned.

"But she didn't know that!" he shouted. "You can't pretend you didn't see the despair in her face. Sam..." His voice broke. "She looked at me like I'd signed her death warrant."

Sam strode to his side and pulled him into a rough hug. Tehl stiffened, shock radiating through him. It was like Sam was attempting to hold the pieces of him together. His brother thumped him on the back and released him.

"I understand it was difficult, but you played your part perfectly." Sam eyed him seriously. "Are you ready to hear everything?"

"Yes," he said gravely. "Gather the others."

His brother studied him a bit more and nodded.

Tehl collapsed into a chair and ran a hand down his face. He couldn't fall apart right now. Too many depended on him. Sam had never steered him wrong. He needed to trust in his brother, his people, and himself.

Lilja pushed through the tent, followed by Hayjen, Rafe, William, Gav, and Zachael. The Sirenidae took one glance at the whiskey and grabbed the bottle. Tehl smiled as the willowy woman took a deep pull and passed it along to her husband. She grinned at Tehl while wiping her mouth with the back of her hand. She patted his knee, moved around him, and plopped into a chair to his right.

The group kept silent as they found places to sit while whiskey was passed around. Sam murmured something to the Elites stationed outside the tent and let the flap fall. He walked to the table and placed both hands on it. "Where do you want me to start?"

"How about the beginning?" Rafe said sarcastically.

Lilja scowled at the rebellion leader. "Hush, Rafe. We don't have time for your sass." Rafe's eyes narrowed, but he stayed silent. The Sirenidae turned her attention to Sam. "How did Sage give you her sign?"

"By means of Maeve."

Tehl frowned. "The warlord's sister?"

"Yes," Sam said.

Zachael held his hands up. "Wait, you trusted the warlord's flesh and blood with Sage's life?"

"No, *Sage* entrusted everyone's safety to Maeve."

Tehl kept silent as that soaked in. If it was a trap, surely they would have been cut down before they reached their army. "How did she contact you?"

His brother smirked. "She pulled me into a darkened hallway, quite forcibly I might add… I always like a woman with a little spirit."

William snorted and ran his fingers along his grey mustache. "She'd break you, boy."

Sam shook his head, his expression sobering. "Of that, I have no doubt."

"What was her sign?" Gav asked. "Sage could have shared any information with them. How do you know this woman was legitimate?"

"She spoke of our time right before the wedding. Our promises."

Understanding passed between the two princes. Sam met Tehl's stare.

"Sage would never divulge something like that to anyone."

Tehl only knew of what Sam and Gav had done for her, because he had stood outside the door. His wife was a strong woman who didn't like anyone to see her weak, thus it was unlikely she would have shared something so personal. The Scythian woman must have been telling the truth.

"What did the Scythian woman have to say?"

"She had a plan." Sam tipped his head back to stare at the canvas ceiling. "I did everything in my power to devise a way to bring Sage home with us." He dropped his head. "Every outcome led to death for someone. Maeve's offer afforded us ignorance, escape, and safety, to some degree."

"And what of Sage?" Hayjen rasped.

"Her fate lies in the hands of Maeve."

Tehl's stomach plummeted. He had a hard time allowing himself to trust the woman, but prejudice did no one good. No one was completely evil, just as no race was completely bad. His hands clenched and unclenched. He would have to accept her help and trust her.

"We've followed your directions as you asked. What is the next step?" With Sam, there was always a next step.

"We keep moving."

"Because we'll be watched," Rafe supplied.

His brother nodded. "The warlord is a shrewd man. It would've been stupid not to send scouts and patrols to roam the borders, especially with a third of the Aermian Guard camping outside his border."

"Where do we rendezvous with Sage?" William asked.

Sam winced. "That's the hitch. I don't know."

Tehl blinked at his brother. "That complicates things."

"Indeed."

"When were they to attempt escape?" he asked.

"Tonight." Sam said.

"They won't make it across the border," Gav growled. "It's too dangerous."

"That's why we need to keep moving," Zachael supplied. "If it was me, I would stay near the Scythian border, but move as far down as possible and then cross."

Rafe cursed. "That's only if she can survive the Scythian jungle. Did you see how pale and soft she looked?"

"It's the drugs," Lilja growled. "They give women drugs to keep them docile and weak."

Tehl's jaw clenched. "Bastards."

She reached over and clasped his hand. He didn't know if it was for her benefit or his.

"The journey will be difficult, but she won't be alone, and she has a guide."

"Who?" Gav asked.

"Blaise."

"You mean our former Scythian captive?" Zachael asked.

"Yes."

"Why would she do anything for Sage?" William jumped in.

"Because her mother doesn't want her in Scythia," Tehl whispered to himself. It made complete sense. Maeve was Blaise's mother. All eyes turned to him. "Blaise is the warlord's niece, so it stands to reason Maeve is her mother. Am I correct?"

Sam dipped his chin. "She fears for her daughter, so she aided us to aid her kin."

"That's not possible," William argued. "They're the same age!"

"Things are not what they appear in Scythia," Hayjen murmured.

"Downright unnatural," the old man grumbled, lacing his fingers across his stomach.

"So, she has a guide, and a protector of sorts. How will she make it past all the patrols?" Rafe growled. "Two women won't survive against a dozen warriors."

"Three women," Sam corrected. "Jasmine is with them as well."

"I have that covered," Lilja spoke. "I have someone on the inside who will protect our girls."

"How?" Sam demanded, his eyes like chips of sapphire.

"It was a long time ago."

"That's not a damn answer! I've lost so many spies. And you've had someone on the inside the entire time?"

Lilja lifted her hand placatingly. "I wasn't aware he was alive." She glanced around the room. "What matters is that the girls will have some protection."

Tehl blew out a breath and stood, lacing his hand behind his head. "So, we keep moving. We stay close to the border, and we leave men discreetly behind, watching closely for sign of them."

He hated the idea of someone else finding her.

"It's the only way, brother. We can't be everywhere at once," Sam reasoned.

"If we pace ourselves, we might be able to keep up with them. It's too dangerous to traverse the jungle at night," Rafe said. "So, we travel when they travel, and sleep when they sleep."

Tehl spun in a circle, scanning the group and finally meeting the rebellion leader's amber gaze. "So be it."

"We'll get our girl back," Zachael said with confidence.

How did he end up with such amazing people at his side, guiding, supporting, and helping him? Some of them, he knew, were due to his wife. A debt he wouldn't soon forget. "Thank you," Tehl said. "I will never forget what you've done for the crown, myself, and for Sage."

"Our pleasure, my lord," Hayjen answered.

"We are all with you," Gav added.

"Together," Rafe murmured.

"Together," Tehl echoed.

THIRTY-FIVE

SAGE

HER ADRENALINE HAD LONG SINCE worn off. Fatigue weighed her down, but she couldn't slow their pace. There wasn't time. She glanced up through the leaves, noting golden streaks of dawn chasing away the dark velvet of night. She worried. How long until the warlord awoke and discovered her gone?

Not long enough, she was sure.

Sage picked up her pace, her weak muscles protesting the use. A branch caught her foot and she stumbled, catching herself against a tree. Deep breath heaved from her lungs, and her nails dug into the smooth trunk beneath her palm. She had to move, but she felt like she couldn't.

Jasmine paused, glancing behind her. "You okay?" She whispered the words, as if the jungle itself was listening and reporting.

"Yes."

Blaise halted, scanned the area, and strode toward them. She pulled a draught from the pouch at her hip and held it out.

"Drink it."

Sage eyed the concoction. "What is it?"

"Something to help keep up your stamina," Blaise darted a look in Jasmine's direction. "Only drink half. You must share."

She didn't want to drink it, but she did want to escape the warlord.

Gingerly, she pulled the vial from Blaise.

"Thank you," she said and uncorked the draught.

A pungent odor filled the air. Hastily, she gulped down half. Her eyes watered, and she fought not to gag at the bitter taste. *Disgusting.* Swallowing quickly, she handed it off to the wide-eyed Jas. Her friend eyed it with disdain.

"Drink it," Sage commanded. "We don't have time to dally."

Jasmine threw back the rest of the draught and coughed, her face screwing up. "What's in that stuff? That's worse than my mum's carp and onions."

Blaise took the empty vial from Jas and tucked it back into her satchel. "A bit of this and that. Can you continue?"

Sage rolled her shoulders and assessed her body. She felt stronger. "How fast does that react?"

"It's immediate, but it will wear off. We need to move. You move slower than our people and that's a major disadvantage."

"Lead the way," Jas said, waving her hand.

Blaise took the lead and began to jog, followed by Jasmine, and then Sage. The jungle seemed less daunting in the daylight than the night, but Sage knew that was a deception. The daylight predators were more cunning and better disguised.

A flash of black pulled her attention. Nali slunk through the trees just out of sight. Their silent protector reassured her. Last night, the beast hadn't left their sides. Several times, her feline protector warned them of danger or scared away other predators. If it hadn't been for Nali, Sage was sure they wouldn't have been able to travel; they'd have been dead within the first few hours.

There was something both peaceful and intimidating about the silence broken up by their boots thumping against the damp earth. The jungle blurred around her as they ran. Sweat poured down her back and between her breasts as they moved deeper into the jungle. Every once in a while, Blaise would pause and cock her head, no doubt listening to sounds Sage couldn't hear. It was in those times, she was thankful for the Scythian woman's guidance. She knew escaping the warlord would be difficult, if not impossible, but after traveling with both Nali and Blaise, she realized she never would've made it out of the palace on her own.

Blaise wove around a tree and stopped. Sage slowed next to Jas and crept closer. Blaise held her hand up, stopping her. Her heartbeat pounded in her ears and she held her breath. The Scythian woman's shoulders relaxed, and she peeked over her shoulder back at them.

"It's past time we ate. Come on." She waved them through the fronds, disappearing from view.

Sage quietly followed, licking her cracked lips as the babbling of a brook reached her ears. Water. She was so thirsty. She could probably drink a whole lake and still, her mouth would feel dry. Surprise and delight brought a smile to her face when she pushed through the lush green foliage. Fronds, orchids, vines, and trees of all sorts wove together and arched over the brook, creating an arbor over the water. It was one of the most beautiful things she'd ever seen. It was a hidden paradise.

Blaise knelt, cupped her hand, and dipped it into the water, scanning the area even as she drank. Sage moved to her side, impressed with the woman's foresight. She was so thirsty that all she wanted to do was dunk her head in the stream, but despite their paradisiac surroundings, she knew that was dangerous. It was one of the first things her papa taught her when hunting in the forest: you never let your guard down. It only took one mistake to die. The cool water soothed her parched throat, and she heard Jasmine's contented sigh as she wiped water onto her heated face.

Jas pulled her pack from her back and dug through it. She pulled out dried meat, berries, and bread, and then began distributing some of it to Blaise, Sage, and herself. It was a little hard but delicious, and before she knew it, she'd finished her small meal. She groaned as she forced herself up from her crouch and stretched her back. Blaise also stood, twisting side to side to stretch, as Jas packed everything back into her sack.

Sage tipped her back and squinted. The trees completely blocked out the sun, but dim light that surrounded them suggested that darkness wasn't far off. Her brow furrowed. Whatever was in the draught was a miracle. All the water she drank seemed to crash down on her at once. She would be vulnerable when relieving herself.

Sage eyed Blaise. "Will you watch my back? I need to go to the bathroom."

Blaise jerked her head toward the steam. "Go in there. It will carry your scent away." The Scythian woman turned her back to the stream.

Jas gaped. "You're going right here?"

Sage smiled and shrugged a shoulder. "Would you like to go into the jungle by yourself?"

Jas sobered. "Point taken." Her friend spun around to give her privacy.

She quickly finished up and stood guard as each woman followed her example.

Blaise shouldered her pack and glanced at the brook. "We have only a few more hours of light. I would like to hide our scent and tracks, so we'll be traveling through the stream."

She glanced between Jas and Sage.

"The water will disguise your steps, but you still need to move quietly. We don't want to attract any unwanted attention."

Sage nodded and waved to her friend. "Jas, you move in the middle."

The girl snorted. "You're weaker than I am."

"But I'm trained in weaponry."

"If I only had my bow," Jas grumbled as she fingered her dagger. "This won't do much good. If whatever predator, whether beast or Scythian, gets this close, I'm dead."

Sage stepped into the stream, the rocks slippery underneath her boots, and moved forward without a word. There wasn't much to say. Jas was right. If a predator got that close, it was probable they'd die.

Her senses went on high alert as she entered the arbor that arched around the stream. It was a double-edged sword. The foliage afforded them great coverage, but it also hid danger from them. The progression was slow, which rankled her, but she understood the necessity of it, for the warlord had abilities she'd never dreamed on. Just the thought of him hunting her raised the hair on her arms.

She glanced behind her as the feeling of uneasiness intensified. Nothing but the calm stream. She faced forward, her hands clenching two daggers. Something was off. "Blaise," she whispered.

Blaise paused and peered over her shoulder. "What?"

"Something's not right."

The Scythian woman frowned and scanned the area. "I hear nothing."

Jasmine spun and stared at her. "I don't-"

Something scaled slammed through the arbor above them, crashing into Jasmine. Shock prevented Sage's scream as a giant snake pulled Jasmine under the shallow water with its girth. Blaise leapt onto the snake, straddling its slick green flesh. "The head," she shouted.

Sage blurred into action, scrambling through the water. She stabbed her daggers through its skin and the head whipped up, hovering in the air with its beady eyes locked onto her. Jasmine jerked upward, coughing up water, and screamed as it coiled around her. Sage shifted to the side, the serpent mimicking her. What was she supposed to do? If she killed it, its weight would still pin Jasmine. "Blaise," she called.

The Scythian woman stabbed again and the snake twisted and struck at her. Blaise rolled away just in time.

"What attracts it?" Sage shouted.

"Blood!"

"Jasmine?"

"Yes?" Jas croaked, her nails scrabbling at the snake coiled around her.

Sage adjusted her dagger and pressed the point to her forearm. "Get ready." The blade bit into her skin and pain radiated from the wound. She squeezed her hand close and let the blood drip down her arm. It was like the world slowed. The snake stilled, Jasmine screamed, and Blaise froze. The serpent's attention snapped to her and all she could see was its gem green eyes with black vertical slits. She caught Blaise's gaze and nodded once before all hell broke loose. Time sped up as Sage spun and began sprinting along the water's edge, keeping her focus on the ground in front of her. Everything inside her demanded she look back, but she didn't. She kept her gaze ahead. One, two, three steps, fou—

A screech flew out of her as the serpent crashed into the back of her knees, knocking her into the stream. Sage flipped onto her back and scrambled backward as an enormous serpent head hovered above her. She swallowed back her scream and held her bloody arm out to the side. The snake locked onto it and slid forward. Its scales hissed as they scraped along the rocks. Her whole body trembled as it neared. *Stars above, it could probably swallow her head whole.*

She pulled in a deep breath as its heavy weight crashed onto her legs. One, two, three seconds- Blaise leapt onto the snake and slammed her sword through its skull. It thrashed for three heartbeats and then fell to the ground, unmoving. Sage scrambled back, pushing the snake off her.

"Is it dead?"

Blaise climbed off the snake and kicked it in the head. Nothing.

"It's not coming back from that," Blaise muttered.

Sage trembled and skirted around the snake's carcass and ran toward Jasmine. "Jas? Jas, are you okay?"

Jasmine moaned, still pinned beneath the dead snake. Sage tried to push it off, but barely moved the cursed serpent.

"Blaise! I need your help! I can't move it. It's crushing her."

The Scythian woman appeared by her side and hauled the snake off like it weighed nothing.

Jasmine's face was white and she was panting, obviously in pain. Sage's hands hovered over her friend, not knowing what to touch. "What's hurt?"

She cracked her eyes, tears flowing down her face. "My ribs. Broken."

"Swamp apples." Sage grimaced and smoothed Jasmine's hair from her face. "I need to find out how many."

"Do it," Jas said between clenched teeth.

Carefully, Sage began prodding her ribs. A sigh of relief slipped out when she finished the right side. All of them were intact. She'd counted six ribs when Jasmine cursed and cried out. Sage met Blaise's serious, dark gaze.

"Two are broken."

"Damn it," Blaise growled. "That will slow us down."

"Sorry," Jas wheezed. "It wasn't my plan to almost get squeezed to death and eaten today."

A surprised chuckle burst out of Blaise. "Well, next time you should plan better."

Sage blinked as the woman smiled at her friend. That was shocking. She was stunning when she smiled; it completely transformed her face. Blaise raised a brow at her staring.

She shook her head and mumbled a quick, "sorry," while scanning the darkening jungle. "We need to find shelter."

"We also need to dispose of that snake. It's like an arrow pointed to where we've traveled."

An idea struck Sage. "Would Nali eat the snake?"

Blaise grinned. "She would indeed."

She eyed the thirty-foot snake. "Can you haul that?"

"Its weight won't be a problem, but it will get caught on rocks."

Sage winced at the mental picture that inspired. "How much farther until we leave the brook?"

Blaise pointed. "Only about fifty more paces."

"Okay."

Sage stood, her wet clothing clinging to her body, chilling her. "I'll carry Jasmine, you get the snake."

"I can walk," Jas argued.

She squatted and placed her hands under Jasmine's armpits. "Yes, you will, 'cause you're going to have to. Brace yourself, though. This will hurt."

Jasmine growled and spat curses as Sage helped her upright, wrapping an arm around her. Jas shivered, her teeth clacking together.

"Bloody hell," Jas snarled.

"You'll be better in no time. Only fifty paces until we leave the stream. We can do this." Sage moved in careful steps, trying her best not to jar Jasmine while scouring the plants caging them in.

Blaise grunted behind them. "This beast stinks." A pause. "I hate snakes."

"I have to say, I'm with you on that one. I now hate them, as well." Jas muttered.

Five paces till they reached a gap in the arbor, Sage stopped and pressed her finger against her lips. She propped Jasmine against the greenery and pulled her daggers from her sheaths, creeping forward. A hand touched her shoulder, halting her progress.

She met Blaise's gaze. "Let me go ahead."

"We go together."

The Scythian woman studied her and nodded. Both women crept forward and peeked out into the jungle. Birds chatted their goodnight songs, but apart from that, nothing stirred. Sage jerked when a rumble came from above. Her gaze flew to the trees and a familiar pair of golden eyes peered down at her.

"Nali," she breathed. The feline stretched and jumped from the tree to the ground, sauntering toward them.

Blaise stiffened.

Sage glanced at the woman from the corner of her eye. "What is it?"

"Nothing."

"Nothing?"

Blaise scowled and crossed her arms, never taking her eyes from the beast. "I'm still not sure that beast's not going to eat me."

"Nali? She's a lamb."

Blaise chuckled. "You know nothing of her kind. They're vicious man-eaters. I've only ever known of a handful to bond with humans."

"Huh. Interesting." She shrugged. "If you're worried, I'll let you present the snake to her. I'm sure she'll appreciate it."

"I'm sure." Blaise eyed the area. "Darkness is approaching. We need to get up into a tall tree, and rest." Her lips flattened as she stared at Jasmine. "Tomorrow will be worse for her, but we are going to have to push harder."

"I understand," Sage breathed.

Urgency thrummed in her veins. Each moment they dallied was another the warlord gained on them.

Blaise scuffed her boot in the soil. "Are you prepared for the next leg of our journey?"

Translation: are you prepared to die?

"I am," Sage said solemnly, and lowered her voice. "I want you to get Jasmine out first, and then you go with her if it comes to that."

The Scythian woman's dark gaze met hers. "You would sacrifice yourself for me? Your enemy?"

"Hopefully, it won't come to that, but," Sage stepped closer and held her forearm out, "I haven't survived this long by hoping for the best. I'm shrewd. You are our best asset if you decide to help Aermia once we arrive. I'm a symbol, nothing more. You hold real power. Your life is worth more than mine."

Blaise studied her. "And if I don't want any part of the coming war?"

"Then, that's your choice." Sage held Blaise's stare. "But know this, women of power, honor, and courage, women like us, are never on the sidelines. We are drawn into the thick of it. I won't force you into anything, but I predict you will be an intricate part of our kingdoms' future."

Blaise shook her head, a small smile on her face. "My mother was right."

"About what?"

"The warlord cannot have you. If he did, the world would tremble at your feet."

Sage scoffed to hide the chill that ran up her spine. "He will never have me."

"Are you sure of that?"

All the air seemed to be pulled from Sage's lungs. Did he possess part of her? The broken, twisted part of her whispered yes, but the sane portion understood it as manipulation. She rubbed at her chest. She felt like a war waged inside of her. But despite that battle of her emotions, she knew two truths: he was the enemy, and Tehl was her home. She had to keep that in mind.

She pushed back her shoulders and lifted her arm again. "I know what's right. That surpasses all else. I won't allow his tyranny to continue."

Blaise clasped her forearm and then kissed each of her cheeks. "I believe you, Sage Blackwell. You make a fearsome queen. Your prince has no idea who he appointed to share his throne, does he?"

Sage walked over to Jasmine and helped her from the ground. "He doesn't know the half of it."

An infectious chuckle burst out of Blaise. "I'm sure."

THIRTY-SIX

TEHL

HE STOOD FIFTY PACES FROM the crumbling Mort Wall, his quieting camp behind him. A cool breeze ruffled his hair as he examined the tall grass blades. Nothing moved, but the creaking jungle trees on the other side of the wall sent chills up his spine.

He eyed the crumbling stone barrier. The wall was a joke, really. After learning about the Scythians, something as common as stone would never keep them out if they were truly determined. So, why had they been kept apart for so long? Was it because of their radical ideas? How had the warlord kept the people complacent? It was human nature to be curious, to want to explore.

A snort escaped him. By fear, no doubt.

He was man enough to admit that the warlord gave him chills. A leviathan seemed downright docile next to the hulking man. He scanned the swaying grass, his hand resting on his sword. Where was Sage? Was she running right now? Hiding? Fighting?

"If you don't sleep soon, you're likely to collapse," Lilja's silky voice called.

Tehl turned toward the woman perched on a rock just to the right of him. She'd sat there in silence for the last few hours. His designated escort. Part of him took offense that his council assigned him an escort, but the rational part of him knew they were right. Scythians were powerful, and he needed someone equally powerful on his side to protect not just himself, but Sage as well.

"I can't sleep," he admitted. "My decisions repeat in my mind. I can't help but wonder if I had done things differently, would we be in this situation?"

"I understand." Lilja tossed a small rock into the silvery grass. "But we can't go back, no matter how much we wish we could."

"I know."

Logically, he did. But emotion wasn't logical.

"Do you have any regrets?" he found himself asking. He cringed at the personal question he'd just lobbed at her.

"Many things," she said. "I've seen much sorrow in my life, but much good. I can't regret the good things that came from the bad."

"That was one way to—" he cut off his words as Lilja held her hand in the air.

Her magenta gaze cut to his as she slid off the rock and into a crouch. Ever so slowly, she raised her finger to her lips. His muscles tensed, his gaze scouring the area for whatever put the Sirenidae on edge. His eyes narrowed as two large shadows shifted on the other side of the wall. Shadows much too large to be Sage.

Lilja shot him a glance and held her hand up, signaling for him to stay. She slunk into the tall grass and disappeared from view without a sound. Tehl released his breath and pulled his sword from his scabbard with care. The blade slipped free with naught but a soft hiss. Yet somehow that slight noise was loud enough that the shadows creeping through the gap in the wall froze.

One heartbeat, two, and then they rushed him. He shifted his stance and braced himself. The two Scythian warriors rushed him, their movements fluid. He blinked as one disappeared into the grass with a muffled yelp. The other warrior paused, noting his fallen comrade, and that was his undoing. He also disappeared without a sound.

The hair on the back of Tehl's neck rose as silence descended. He strained his ears, but he could hear nothing unusual. His gaze ran over the wall and the grass, searching for danger. His breath stuttered as Lilja stood from the tall grass a mere five feet away, looking like an avenging goddess. Her white hair haloed her exotic face that looked like it was carved from stone. It took a few times for him to find his voice.

"Are you alright?"

"I'm fine," her lyrical voice washed over him. She turned toward the wall.

"Why are you here?"

Silence. Who was she speaking to?

"Answer me. Old friend or not, I will cut you down if you mean harm."

Only years of practice, and thanks to many of Sam's pranks, kept him from jumping when a deep voice answered the Sirenidae.

"Lil, you always had a way with words."

A warrior materialized from the grass to their left. He made no move in their direction, though. Instead, he lifted his hands up.

Tehl lifted his sword, but didn't move from his spot. His eyes cut to Lilja who glared at the enemy with such anger, it inspired fear even in him.

"You didn't answer me. What are you doing here?" Lilja repeated.

"Helping."

"Helping," Lilja growled. "You're playing a very dangerous game, Blair."

Tehl stiffened and narrowed his eyes on the man. Why was one of the warlord's closest men on his land? And where was his wife? Lilja's hand landed on his chest. He frowned at the arm holding him back. When had he moved? He glanced at the Sirenidae eyeing him.

"You good?" she asked.

"Yes," he said as he planted his feet, glaring in the Scythian's direction.

Lilja turned her attention back to Blair, waiting for him to speak. The warrior held her stare for what felt like minutes until he cursed and pushed his midnight braids from his face.

"You know I couldn't help you."

Lilja's jaw clenched, but she said nothing.

Tehl glanced between the two. What was going on?

The Scythian dropped his hands and crossed his arms over his bare chest.

"You're not being rational about this. I know you, Lil. Calm down and listen to what I have to say."

Tehl winced. There was something he learned while living with Sage, and that was not to tell a woman to calm down when she was upset.

"Listen to you? Are you serious?" Lilja hissed. She wildly gestured to the grass with her daggers. "You brought warriors to my home."

"And you're also aware that if I didn't want to be discovered, we wouldn't have been. I wanted you to catch them. Why would I want that, Lil?"

"Twenty years," she whispered.

The Scythian hung his head. "Twenty years," he said softly.

"Why?"

"I couldn't risk it."

"Nothing?" Lilja's voice wavered, surprising Tehl. "It wasn't possible to spare one moment and let me know you lived?"

"No, it was not."

"I loved you!" Lilja's voice rose. "Mourned you every day for years. I even went into Scythia in search of you. I almost died! If Hayjen hadn't pulled me out, I would have." She chuckled bitterly, tears dripping down her face. "A part of me died when you didn't come home."

"I have a family, Lil. I couldn't leave them." His tone pleaded for understanding.

Lilja gasped, her face crumpling and her hands curling into fists. "How could you after everything we went through?"

"I did what I had to."

She scoffed, wiping her tears from her face. "I guess my Blair really did die in that jungle. He would never have agreed to something so sick."

The warrior's hands clenched. "I didn't force her. Why would you think that?"

"I don't know you," she said, her face hardening. "I'm thankful Gem isn't here to see what you've become."

"Lilja Femi, don't you dare say that! I've loved you longer and better than anyone else in this world. Don't you dare bring Gem into this." He stabbed a finger at Lilja. "You know what's in my heart. Every day we've been apart, I've fought to right the wrongs of so many years ago. I've sacrificed, so that others might have freedom and the life we weren't afforded. I've suffered, so I can remove that monster from Scythia. You and I are the same, so don't you tell me you don't know me."

His gaze shifted to Tehl.

"You're lucky the warlord hates an easy battle, or you'd be dead by now, and your wife in his clutches forever."

"What do you know of my wife?" Tehl growled.

"That he'll never stop hunting her."

"So, she's alive?" He braced himself for the answer.

"Yes."

Relief surged through his body until Blair spoke again.

"But she'll wish she was dead if he catches her."

"Why are you here?" Tehl asked, suspicion in his tone.

"I'm here to offer help."

"And what do you require in exchange?" No one did anything for free.

"The warlord's death."

"Why now?" Lilja asked.

"Because it's time."

Tehl cocked his head and studied the warrior. The way he said the words meant he was resolute… they also meant a rebellion. "You're organizing a rebellion."

Blair lifted his chin. "For someone so young, you're astute."

"I've dealt with rebellion members. I can spot a rebel when I see one."

"You speak of your wife."

"She's taught me much." Tehl said.

"I'm sure. She's a fierce woman."

"Indeed."

"The warlord doesn't trust you," Lilja murmured.

Tehl glanced at Lilja askance.

"He trusts no one, Lil."

"That's why you didn't seek me out."

"One reason."

"And the others?"

"I have four daughters."

"Four?" Lilja croaked.

Blair smiled, his teeth flashing in the dark. "You'd love them, Lil. They're my life." His smile faded. "But they're coming of age."

Lilja's face turned to horror. "He would take your daughters?"

"They're not mine according to the warlord. He gave me my woman, and he can take her away at any moment, along with our daughters."

Tehl's gut churned. No one should have that sort of power.

"That's sick," he muttered.

"I agree," Blair growled.

Tehl's mind ran over all the information Blair had revealed, and then to Lilja's comment a few nights ago about her man on the Scythian side. "Is this your spy?"

"Yes."

"And do you trust him?"

Lilja glanced up at Tehl and back to the warrior watching their exchange with interest. "I do."

"Will he protect Sage?"

"I already have," Blair said. "And I will continue to do so."

Damn Scythian hearing. "How so?"

The warrior gestured to the surrounding grass. "We're supposed to be hunting your wife ahead of the warlord. I caught your wife's trail a day ago. It was very faint and hidden well. It was easy to miss, so I led the men astray. I will protect her as best as I can..."

"So long as it doesn't reveal your true intentions," Tehl finished.

Blair nodded. "Like I said, the best I can."

"You better," Lilja growled. "She's what's left of my family."

"Family?" Both men echoed.

Lilja flashed Tehl an apologetic smile. "She's Hayjen's niece."

He blinked and then blinked again. Hayjen looked nothing like Sage. Tehl's forehead wrinkled. But Sage looked like her father. Her brothers, on the other hand, looked like their mother and… Hayjen. He shook his head. He'd deal with that revelation later. "What do you need from me, Scythian?"

"Peace."

Tehl laughed. "Peace? There's no such thing."

"Deal fairly with the Scythians when this is through. Don't let your prejudice cloud your judgment. The people have suffered far more than you, and the warriors are only following orders."

That was fair.

"I can do that." Tehl threw his shoulders back and strode toward Blair, Lilja hot on his heels. He halted before him and held his hand out. "If you're honorable and do what you say, then I will likewise honor our agreement. You risk much to protect my family, so I will extend the same courtesy. If your family needs safety, send them to the palace. I will make sure they're taken care of."

Blair studied him and clasped his arm. "Thank you."

Blair kissed both of his cheeks and stepped back, gaze sweeping the grass to his fallen warriors.

"I didn't kill them," Lilja muttered. "I knocked them out."

"Thank you, Lil. I'll retrieve them and be on my way. May luck be with you both."

"Not luck—skill," Tehl said.

"Indeed," the Scythian warrior said and turned to leave.

"Blair?" Lilja called.

He paused and opened his arms.

The Sirenidae flew into the Scythian's arms. He pulled her off the ground and buried his face into her neck, mumbling words too low for Tehl to hear. Tehl backed away, feeling like the world had turned on its head, with a million questions running through his mind. He glanced at the couple embracing one last time before turning around. If the Scythian had planned to kill them, he'd have already done it. And from the looks of things, it didn't look like he'd be letting go of Lilja anytime soon.

He eyed Hayjen, who was now leaning against the rock Lilja had vacated. The big man nodded to him briefly before his attention moved back over Tehl's shoulder.

"I take it you're also acquainted with Blair?"

"He's a friend," Hayjen said.

"Just a friend?" Lilja and Blair's conversation seemed like it was a lot more.

"Her best friend."

Hayjen saw the doubt he was obviously not hiding well.

"He brought Lil and I together, and he also helped her escape Scythia. They have a bond that words cannot describe."

"Apparently, we too share a bond – one that no one told me about, Uncle."

Hayjen's gaze sharpened. "She told you?"

Tehl chuckled. "Not on purpose."

"Everything Lil does has a purpose."

He sobered and glanced at Lilja. "Good point." The Sirenidae had a brilliant mind. Tehl turned his attention back to Hayjen. "I guess I should welcome you to the family. I take it you're the younger brother?"

Hayjen shook his head. "No, I'm older by several years. Do you understand why we kept such a thing a secret?"

Tehl frowned. Hayjen didn't look more than ten years older than himself, and yet he claimed to be older than Gwen? He squinted at Hayjen while he calculated the man's age. Logically, the man would be over 50 years. Something wasn't right. "How?"

"Lilja. The sea offers many wondrous things."

He rubbed at his eyes while he mulled that over. "Are you telling me Lilja is in possession of something that can grant immortality?" Saying those words felt comical, like something from a bedtime story.

"Not immortality, but a greatly-lengthened life span."

Something like that would be highly sought-after if word ever got out. Lilja would be hunted, and anyone in association with her. People did dangerous things when they thought something could lengthen their life. "You kept this from Sage to protect her."

Hayjen nodded, his face serious. "Now, you understand why that information has been kept a secret. Many would harm my family, or Lilja and me, just to retrieve it." He pushed off the rock and held out his hand. "We didn't keep this from you for lack of trust."

"I understand." And he did. Tehl reached out and clasped Hayjen's hand. "But I hate secrets. They have a nasty way of backfiring. Is there anything else I need to be aware of?"

Hayjen shook his head. "Not that I know of." He released Tehl's hand and glanced at his wife. "I'll make sure that anything important gets passed along."

"I appreciate it," Tehl murmured and pulled back his hand. He blinked and his eyes burned. The lack of sleep was catching up with him.

"You have the next watch?" he asked tiredly.

"Yep," Hayjen said.

"I'll see you in the morning."

"Goodnight."

Tehl strode away from his newly-discovered relative, still reeling from the information he'd learned tonight. Lilja had a warrior spy at her beck and call, a rebellion was brewing on the Scythian side, Hayjen was Sage's uncle, and he'd sealed an accord with the warlord's right-hand man. He barked out a laugh and ran a hand down his face. Sage wouldn't believe this. He wished she was here, so he could tell her about the craziness that had become his life.

The smile slipped from his face. If the Scythian didn't keep his end of the deal, then Tehl might not ever get the chance to.

THİRTY-SEVEN

SAGE

SAGE'S ARMS AND LEGS WERE screaming in pain, but just a glance at Jasmine's pained face was enough to do her best to shove the pain aside. After all, it could be worse; she could have broken ribs.

As they made their way through the jungle, a spider the size of her fist skittered across their path, but she didn't care. It didn't harm them and soon would be off terrorizing someone else with its hairy appendages. The creature hunting them was truly something to be afraid of.

She stopped in her tracks when Blaise paused, listening to the jungle. In the last two days, she'd been doing that more and more often and Sage couldn't help but feel that a noose was tightening around their necks. Each moment of rest, each minute of sleep was disturbed by the fact that it only meant the warlord was gaining on them. They were losing time. It was a miracle they'd lasted this long.

"Damn it," Blaise cursed softly, casting a glance in their direction.

The blood in Sage's veins iced over at the look on the woman's face. Sheer terror.

"What is it?" Jas whispered, her breathing labored.

On silent feet, Blaise strode back to them. "They've caught up with us." She shook her head in frustration. "We can't avoid them. My only hope is that they aren't a part of the hunt, just a border patrol."

"And if they are?" Sage let the question hang in the air.

"Then we'll have to fight." Blaise eyed Jasmine. "We need to get to the river. The wall is close here." She met Sage's gaze. "We need to cross it today. If we don't, he'll catch us before night falls."

Her legs trembled. "How close is he?"

"I'm not sure. If I was to venture a guess, I'd say he was not farther behind than a few hours. The hunt moves much quicker than we do."

"It's my fault," Jas said, hugging her arms around her waist. "I slowed you down."

"No." Blaise shook her head. "We could not have anticipated the attack, but you've handled the pain better than expected."

"I can survive pain. I can't survive captivity," Jas murmured.

"That, I understand well," Blaise whispered. Her lips pursed as she eyed them. "You both look Scythian from far away, but your eyes will give you away. Keep your gaze down and keep silent. Your accents will give you away as well." Blaise pulled in a deep breath. "We're almost there. We can do this."

"I'm not dying here," Jas said with conviction. "My little ones need me."

"Let's move," Sage said.

Blaise nodded turned around, taking off to the left. "Keep a sharp eye. I may have heightened sense, but it doesn't mean I have eyes on the back of my head," she called over her shoulder.

Sage glanced at Jasmine. Her face was pale, but determined.

"Are you ready?" Sage asked.

Jasmine smiled at her and grabbed her hand. "I've been ready for months."

She squeezed Jas' hand once and stepped aside for her friend to pass. Chills skittered down her spine and her shoulders tightened. Her stomach clenched; she couldn't help having a sense of foreboding. Slowly, she spun, her eyes wide as she examined the surrounding trees. Nothing unusual, and yet...goosebumps dotted her arms. It was like the jungle held its breath. But for what?

She swallowed hard and backed away before spinning on her heel and sprinting to catch up to the others. Blaise shot her a questioning look, but quickened her pace now that she'd joined them. The greenery blurred as they ran through the jungle, leaves and vines grabbing at them like unwanted suitors. Panic ate at the pit of her stomach. Time was slipping through her fingers.

She skidded to a stop as they neared the edge of a clearing. Sage's brow furrowed. Why had they halted? She didn't see anything, but that meant nothing in Scythia.

"Warriors," Blaise breathed.

Sage dropped her chin, her eyes glued to the jungle floor. She pulled in a deep breath. She had to maintain her calm.

"My lady," a deep voice answered. "It's a surprise to see you so far from a village."

Her heart galloped in her chest. Hell. She hadn't even heard them approach.

"We were scouting the area," Blaise replied.

"For what?" A gruff voice asked.

Sage stared at the decomposing leaves beneath her boots and stained her ears to hear the surrounding sounds. Were there only two men?

"A man-eater. We'd all like the right to choose our betrothed."

"A lofty goal indeed," the deep voice commented. "I must say that it's rare to find so many women together. Your companions are quite beautiful."

Jasmine shifted next to her, but otherwise kept quiet.

"Their mothers were of…" Blaise trailed off. "Unusual birth."

"Indeed."

Sage sensed a touch of disdain in the warrior's tone. That was something. Disdain she could work with; it was actually a step up from lust. Footsteps moved closer, and a hand smoothed down her braid. Sweat beaded on her forehead as boots entered her vision. Calm, she had to maintain her calm.

"Are you on patrol?" Blaise asked, her tone neutral.

"Yes, we are," the gruff voice supplied.

A finger ran along her jaw and pressed under her chin. Sage clenched her teeth and looked up at the warrior. His dark eyes studied her face as she stared at him. One finger wandered up to trace the bow of her lip. Sage snapped her teeth at him, not able to handle his exploration any longer. "Get your hands off me."

A slow smile spread across his handsome face. "So much light, so much fire in your eyes," he murmured. "No wonder the warlord kept you."

Horror moved through her. She whipped her knives out and slashed at the warrior. His hand snapped out, grabbed her dagger by the blade, and tore it out of her hand. Sage dropped to the ground, sweeping her leg out. The warrior avoided her kick deftly. She gritted her teeth. She was slow. As Sage regained her position, the warrior disappeared. She stumbled in surprise and then shouted when an arm wrapped around her throat.

"Weak," he whispered. A hand traced her side. "But alluring."

She. Was. Not. Weak.

Sage dug her nails into his arm and tilted her face forward, biting down. A growl filled her ears as a metallic tang filled her mouth. A hand fisted in her hair and yanked. Pain bit at her, but she didn't let go. He jerked her head back again, tearing her teeth from his arm with a bellow. She cried out when teeth bit into her ear.

"How do you like it?" he hissed. "Just wait until the warlord—"

An earth-shattering roar deafened her a moment before something crashed into her. She slammed into the ground, her face pressing into the damp earth. Sage choked on dirt and leaves and almost cried when the weight crushed her.

She scrambled upright, coughing. She spit dirt out and glanced to the side. She froze, terrified, when she spotted the man-eater tearing into the Scythian. Her hands shook as the beast's golden gaze met hers, its lips pulled back from its crimson stained teeth. Stars above, Nali was fearsome.

A scream pulled her out of her stupor just in time to watch Jasmine sneak up on the Scythian pinning Blaise. Her fiery friend swung her arm and smashed a rock into the warrior's head. He yelled and seized a handful of Jasmine's shirt. Sage's eyes connected with Jasmine's right before the Scythian threw her. A scream caught in her throat as Jas tumbled through the air and crashed into a tree. She didn't get up.

Rage exploded inside her. That was it. She was done with people hurting her friends. Ignoring the beast, she forced herself upright and crept on silent feet toward the warrior beating Blaise into the ground. The beast's snarling was hair-raising, but a blessing. It hid her movements. It hid the warrior's death. He raised his fist one more time, and it was his last. Sage struck. He stiffened and then, like a puppet with its strings cut, he collapsed.

"Blaise," she panted. Her breath sawed in and out of her, and her hands trembled as she tugged on the huge man. He wouldn't budge. Sage scrambled to the side, dropped to her butt, and used her feet to push him off Blaise. Pushing to her knees, she knelt next to Blaise. Her heart flew to her throat at the state of her friend. Every inch of skin Sage saw was damaged. Carefully, she placed two fingers at the base of her neck. A pulse. A sigh of relief escaped her before the panic came rushing back in. How were they supposed to cross the river?

She glanced around the area, skipping over Nali and her meal. Emotion clogged her throat as Jasmine limped toward her. "Are you okay?"

"I'm alive," Jas croaked. "Is Blaise alive?"

"I am," Blaise rasped.

Sage whipped back around. "What is broken?"

"I don't know. It all hurts, so probably everything."

"Can you move?"

"Not without help."

Sage breathed hard while she thought over their options. There was only one. They had to cross the river. They weren't far from it. She could hear it from here.

"Leave me."

She focused back on Blaise. "No."

"Those were part of the hunt, not the patrol. You have to leave now! There's no time."

"I know," Sage growled and slipped an arm under Blaise. "Jas, I need your help."

Jasmine hobbled around Blaise and slipped an arm under her other side, a moan of pain escaping her thin white lips. Her broken ribs must have hurt horridly.

"What are you doing?" Blaise cried as they forced her upright. Tears poured down the woman's face as they began hauling her across the meadow.

"Saving your life," Jas grunted.

"Nali," Sage called. "Leave your meal. I need you."

She didn't know if the feline would follow, but she hoped she would. Every step they took felt too slow. It was like the warlord was breathing down her neck. They broke through the trees, and she about collapsed in relief when Nali loped past them and to the bank.

"I can't swim," Blaise whispered in a pained moan.

Sage glanced from Nali to Jasmine to Blaise and back to Nali, an idea forming in her mind.

"Nali."

The feline eyed Sage, her ears twitching and laying back, a low growl rumbled in Nali's throat.

Sage's stomach dropped. Something was coming. Her urgency doubled. "Nali, I need you to take Blaise across the river."

"Are you mad?" Blaise hissed as they dragged her into the freezing water.

Sage placed a hand on Nali and scratched behind her ears. "Nali, I need you to be kind to Blaise. Take her across the water. Protect her."

Nali strode deeper into the river and paused.

"Jas, help me lift Blaise onto her back. Hurry!"

They managed to get the Scythian woman onto the beast. Sage wrapped Blaise's arms around Nali's neck and met her gaze. "You hold onto Nali with all you have. Trust her. She'll protect you."

"It was an honor knowing you," Blaise whispered.

"We'll meet again."

Sage slapped Nali on the rump, and the beast strode deeper into the water and began swimming. She cut through the water like she was a fish. "Be safe," Sage whispered.

She grabbed Jasmine's hand and ran along the bank.

"What are you doing? We need to cross!"

"Do you see how wide that part was? We'd drown before we made it halfway. Plus, the water is too cold."

Sage sprinted harder and crashed through some trees near the river. Branches slapped at her face, but she didn't register the sting. Panic and fear were ruling her now. Her breathing was rough and she ached to stop, but she tugged on her friend when she slowed. "We're so close, Jas. Just a little bit further."

Jasmine clutched her side, sweat pouring off her forehead. "Sage, I won't be able to swim across the river. I can't do it. There's something wrong with my other arm."

Tears of frustration filled Sage's eyes. They were so close, they had to make it. She sucked in a deep breath and pulled harder. "We make it together or not at all. I will swim us both across." She wouldn't go back to that hell, but neither would she condemn Jasmine to it.

They weren't going back.

With strength she didn't know she still possessed, she propelled them forward. "Jas, just think, the twins are just across the river. Think how happy they'll be to see you."

Jasmine sobbed and stumbled behind her. "I will hold them and never let go."

They crashed through the trees onto the Scythian side of the bank. Sage gasped for air, staring at the impossible challenge ahead of them. The water was so swift. How would they survive? She swallowed hard and glanced to Jasmine, who was simply staring at the river. It seemed like an ocean before them.

Every hair on her body rose when the forest quieted behind them. Hell. He was near. She met Jasmine's wide eyes. "We have to swim now."

Jasmine nodded, and they both scrambled to the water's edge. "Have you ever swum someone across a distance like this?" she panted.

Sage shook her head and kicked her boots off while wading into the cold water. Jas' trembling arm seized her bicep. She met her friend's eyes, trying to emulate a calm she didn't feel.

"You need to swim pulling me. I'll use my legs as much as I can."

"Okay." She wrapped an arm around Jasmine's chest and pushed back into the current. Sage gasped as the cold water wrapped around her body painfully. The river pulled on her, trying to suck them down. Sage gritted her teeth and fought against the current and the cold, keeping her eyes on the Aermian bank. They were so close.

"Sage!" Jasmine's horror filled voice pulled her attention from her strokes.

Sage glanced back to the Scythian bank, and fear clogged her throat, her strokes faltering. Scythian warriors lined the jungle's edge, silent. Her heart stopped in her chest as she locked eyes with the most devastatingly handsome man she had ever laid eyes on. The warlord strolled to the water's edge with his hand tucked into his trouser pockets, completely casual. Somehow, that frightened her even more.

"Did you think you could escape me, wild one?" he asked, smiling softly.

Her breath seized in her lungs. No, she didn't.

"Swim harder, Sage." Jasmine whispered.

Sage pulled her eyes from the master of her hell and pushed with everything she had. She couldn't let him mess with her mind.

Masculine laughter sounded behind them, deepening her anxiety. She knew that laugh. It was gloating, triumphant. She flicked her eyes back to the bank in time to catch him stepping out of his boots and pulling his sword free from its scabbard.

"You know I love a good game of chase. Keep running. I love the hunt."

She battled the panic threatening to consume her. If she panicked, both she and Jasmine died. Sage cocked her head back and gauged the distance to the other side. They were almost halfway, but her energy was waning. She glanced back to the warlord, who was carefully rolling his pants up, as if that mattered when swimming. If he got into the water and they were still swimming, it would be over for them. She knew how fast he moved. They wouldn't have a chance.

Sage kicked harder and stared at Jasmine's honey brown head. Perhaps one of them did. Jas had children waiting for her to return. What did Sage have? Her family was well looked-after, the treaty was in effect, and the crown didn't need her. She breathed out and made one of the easiest decisions of her life. "Can you swim if I get you to the slow part of the river?"

"I think so."

Sage swallowed and forced her numb legs to kick. "I am going to push you into it and then you have to swim."

"No," Jasmine gasped, her cold breath clouding around them.

"Yes," Sage forced out. "Once he enters the water, we won't make it."

"Then they'll take both of us. I won't leave you."

"You don't have a choice. Think of the twins. They need you. You are their only family."

Jasmine's face was grieved. "I don't want to leave you."

"You must." A calm settled over her. This was the right thing to do. She could repay Jasmine for all the pain she'd endured on her behalf. A splash sounded, pulling Sage's eyes to the Scythian bank. The warlord waded into the water, his face a mask of concern.

"This water is too cold, my love. You need to get out, or you'll get sick. Come back to me, and all of this will be forgotten."

"No way in hell," she hissed between clenched teeth.

He tapped his ear. "I can still hear you."

"I know."

"So that's how it is to be." He shook his head, his dark hair waving in the breeze. He pushed forward and cut through the water like a leviathan.

"It's time, Jas." Sage flipped them onto their stomachs still swimming with everything she had. "Tell my family I love them, that I forgive Rafe, and tell the princes that I'll miss them." Sage shoved Jas with all her might and never stopped swimming. Jasmine pushed toward the Aermian bank clumsily, but at least she wasn't drowning.

Terror strangled her when a hand wrapped around her ankle, jerking her backwards. She clamped her lips together holding in the scream in that would only serve to distract Jasmine. Large burnished arms wrapped around her, hauling her into a solid chest. She stared straight ahead, ignoring the giant body behind her as tears of relief pricked her eyes. Jas had made it to the bank.

"You've led me on a merry hunt, Sage."

Her eyes slammed shut as the warlord's voice curled around her. A nose ran along the column of her neck as they bobbed in the river.

"Cinnamon," he growled, "How is it you haven't bathed in days and yet you still smell like cinnamon?"

She remained silent, her body trembling against him as she ignored him. It was so cold. Everything was numb.

His hand slipped up her chest and to her throat. He pulled her head back and tipped it to the side. "You know how I feel about being ignored. Look at me, Sage."

Part of her wanted to obey him. The thought caused bile to burn her throat.

He spun her around and pulled her flush against his body as he treaded water in the river like it was nothing. The warlord scanned her face. "You've been hurt." She hissed when he brushed a wound on her cheek. "If you hadn't run from me, you wouldn't have been hurt." His hand dropped to her waist and kneaded the flesh. She cringed at his attentions.

"Have you nothing to say?"

"I would do it again."

His face transformed into a proud smile that made her stomach drop. "And that's why I love you, despite the unfortunate line you were born from. You have a fire I want to claim."

"There shall be no claiming."

He brushed a wet strand of hair from her face, tenderly, like her father used to do. "You and I both know that's not true." He dropped his forehead to hers and stared into her eyes. "No matter where you go, I will be imprinted on your soul, and in your dreams. We will always be part of each other."

The sick part was that his words were true. If she survived, he would haunt her nightmares for life. "You're right," Sage murmured. She lifted her exhausted arms and laid them around his dark olive shoulders. With careful movements, she spun the ring on her finger that Maeve had given her and flipped the lid. "But in death, you can't haunt me."

"I'll never let anything hurt you."

"You already have." Sage slammed her hand around the back of his neck holding on tight as his eyes narrowed.

"What have you done?" he growled as he ripped her arm from his neck. The warlord yanked her hand up and examined the ring, his grip going lax even as his eyes burned hotter with rage.

"Nothing that will kill you." She leaned closer and placed a kiss on his cheek. "I freed myself from you."

Sage shoved away from him with the last of her strength, managing to break his grasp because of the toxin. The water tore her from him, clawing at her legs and trying to pull her under. She fought it, knowing that drowning was not a peaceful way to go, but she wasn't strong enough. The last thing she saw was the warlord's panic-filled gaze before the river claimed her.

Water tugged her left and right, up and down. Darkness surrounded her as her lungs began to burn. Her body flailed as she clawed at the water, desperate for air. Her body slammed into something, forcing the rest of the air from her lungs. Her face broke the surface, sputtering and gasping for air. Sage blinked at the bank not ten feet from her. How? She heaved in painful breaths as the freezing water beat at her body. It would be so easy to close her eyes and sleep.

She jerked, her eyes springing wide, when a growl roused her. A dark, furry head bobbed up next to her. Sage let out a sob and sunk her fingers into Nali's wet coat. "Help me," she whispered through numb lips.

She was certain her nails were digging into the feline's skin, but it didn't stop Nali from propelling them toward the bank. Slick stones bumped against her knees and feet as they entered the shallows. Her hip dug into the sand, and she couldn't hold on any longer. Sage collapsed into shallow water, her teeth chattering. Nali quickly moved to her side and bit into the back of her shirt, tugging her from the water. Stone scraped her palms as she did her best to aid Nali, clawing her way up the bank. When her hands sunk into sun-warmed sand, she collapsed with her cheek pressed to the earth, water dripping into her eyes.

She didn't drown. She didn't die.

Sage didn't know how long she laid there, savoring the air filling her lungs, the sand and gravel beneath her hands. Only when her body began to tremble so hard her teeth clacked together, did she gain awareness. Painstakingly, she pushed to her hands and knees and took in the surrounding land.

Forest.

Aermian Forest.

She sat on her calves as a sob tore from her. Tears blurred her eyes and dripped down her face. "I made it," she whispered to herself, relieved beyond words.

For a moment, she had thought the river spat her back upon Scythian land, but to be back again was overwhelming. She never thought she'd truly make it. Great, heaving cries broke free, wracking her body. She hunched forward and sunk her fingers into the sand.

She'd made it home. She was home.

Time blurred as bone-weary fatigue set in. Sage studied her bluish fingers, and something inside her head said she should be worried. But for the life of her, she didn't remember why she should worry.

Nali released a heart-stopping growl that finally pulled Sage from her muddled thoughts. The feline hunkered down in front of her, the feline's jet-black fur puffing up menacingly. Fear penetrated the fog hovering over her mind. There was only one reason Nali would growl like that. He'd found her.

Her heart galloped and her stomach rolled. She kept her blurry gaze on the sand beneath her scratched hands. Why was life so cruel? Hadn't she suffered enough? What more could she give?

"Sage."

Her eyes closed, more tears seeping out of the corners. "Tehl," she whimpered. Even after she'd banished his presence from her mind, still he rescued her when she most needed him. He'd give her a reprieve from the awaiting horrors. "You didn't leave me," she choked out.

"Love, I will never leave you."

Her fingers flexed in the gritty sand. "I can't live this life." She gasped for breaths which seemed unwilling to come. "I can't go back to him. I'm not strong enough."

"You will never have to go back. He will never touch you again."

A sad smile tugged at her lips. If only that was the truth. Tehl knew what she had to do. He was part of her mind after all. She sucked in a shuddering breath. "Thank you for keeping me company. I'll always love you for that."

Her shoulders tensed as Nali snarled louder, protecting her from her dark fate. It was only a matter of minutes before everything she loved would disappear forever.

"Sage, you're shivering. I need you to call off your beast, so I can get you warm."

She frowned at the ground. What was he talking about?

"Call off your beast, please. There's no time to waste."

Another snarl. "Look at me, Sage."

She raised her head at the command and every part of her stilled. Nali stood in front of her, snarling with her lips pulled back, exposing huge canines as she warned the enemy away, but it was not who she expected.

A group of men surrounded her, but one stood apart, his hand held out to the man-eater. His tense form suggested fear, and yet he whispered soothing words. Sage attempted to decipher his words, but she couldn't hear anything over the ringing in her ears. His blue-black hair waved in the breeze as he glanced in her direction and spoke a little louder.

"Sage, love, please calm your beast," he begged. "You need a healer."

She jolted and fell onto her bottom, desperately blinking the tears from her eyes. It couldn't be Tehl. What trickery was this? Had she gone insane?

"You're not insane, but you are ill."

Her lips trembled as her gaze traced his beautiful face. He wasn't real, he couldn't be. Her mind must be broken. That was the only logical explanation that or… "I died." No fear, just numbness. A sense of peace settled over her. She could handle death.

Tehl stepped closer, earning another snarl from Nali. "You're not dead. I need you to trust me and trust yourself. I'm real."

She swiped her arm across her face, her tears smearing across her cool skin. Sage focused on him. "Don't placate me with lies, Tehl. I can't stand any more lies. Just be honest with me."

"I am." He shook his head, his face a mask of frustration.

She smiled as he jerked his hands through his hair. The gesture was so familiar, so human.

He eyed Nali and then Sage, his eyes narrowing. "You stubborn wench. It's me."

"My lord, calm down," a deep voice chastised.

Sage blinked slowly. Her thoughts sluggish. Wench? When was the last time he snapped at her? She couldn't remember. She rubbed her sandy hand across her forehead, the rough grit biting into her skin and grounding her. Could he be real?

"Sage!"

Her heart squeezed as she glanced in the direction of the voice. Jasmine stood bedraggled at the front of the group. She was bruised, dirty, and slightly blue, but there wasn't anything more beautiful in that moment than her friend. "Jas?"

"We made it. We're home."

She pointed a trembling finger at Jasmine. "How do I know you're real?"

Jas rolled her stormy eyes. "Bloody hell. Trust us. Trust your husband."

Sage's eyes slid to Tehl, standing patiently on the other side of Nali. Trust. She'd trusted him the entire time she was in Scythia. Why was she doubting him now when he might be real?

"Fine," she growled. Her friend would only badger her until she complied anyway. She tried to stand, only to have her legs collapse underneath her.

Nali's growl grew louder.

"No, Nali," she whispered, and placed a soothing hand on the feline's side. "It's okay. These are friends." Nail's ears flattened, but she held still, her flesh quivering under Sage's hand. "You're going to have to help me stand, girl."

The beast chuffed and held still as Sage wrapped her arms along her neck and back. Painfully, she hauled herself to her feet with Nali's aid, wavering slightly. Her fingers sunk into black fur as she studied the man standing fearlessly on the other side of her man-eater. He looked real, but could it be?

He smiled at her and held a hand out. "Take my hand."

She stared at his outstretched hand. What if she was dreaming? Sage reached out and paused, her hand suspended in the air. Could she handle the disappointment?

"Don't be a coward, Sage," Jasmine called.

She clenched her jaw and eyed her trembling hand. When had she ever shied away from a challenge, or the truth? Never. And she wasn't going to start now.

Hesitantly, she slid her hand into his. Tehl's callouses caught along her smooth skin and warmed her frozen hand. She gasped, her gaze darting to his.

He shifted closer, brushing against Nali. He lifted their hands and placed hers against his cheek. Whiskers tickled her palm as he leaned into her touch. "Do I feel real to you?"

Sage stared at her hand cradling his face, another sob escaping her. He felt real, but could she trust it? His blue eyes beseeched her, begged her to trust him. Tehl had always protected her and told her the truth, even when she didn't wish to hear it. "Am I alive?

"Yes. Scarred, but not broken."

That truth hurt and yet it soothed. Awe filled her. "You're real." She stumbled around Nali and fell into Tehl's arms. Her nose stung as she pressed her face to his vest, but she didn't care. She pulled in a deep breath, his familiar scent of leather and pine invading her senses. No trick of the mind could imitate his scent. "I made it," she cried.

Heat suffused her as he crushed her against his chest, one hand pressed against her wet head. "You did," his voice rasped. "You made it." His lips pressed to the top of her head over and over as she clung to him. Her eyelids drooped, and she smiled against his vest.

"You did it, Sage. You're home." His arms tightened around her and he whispered it one last time. "You're home."

She was home. A sigh escaped her as her body went lax.

She was finally home.

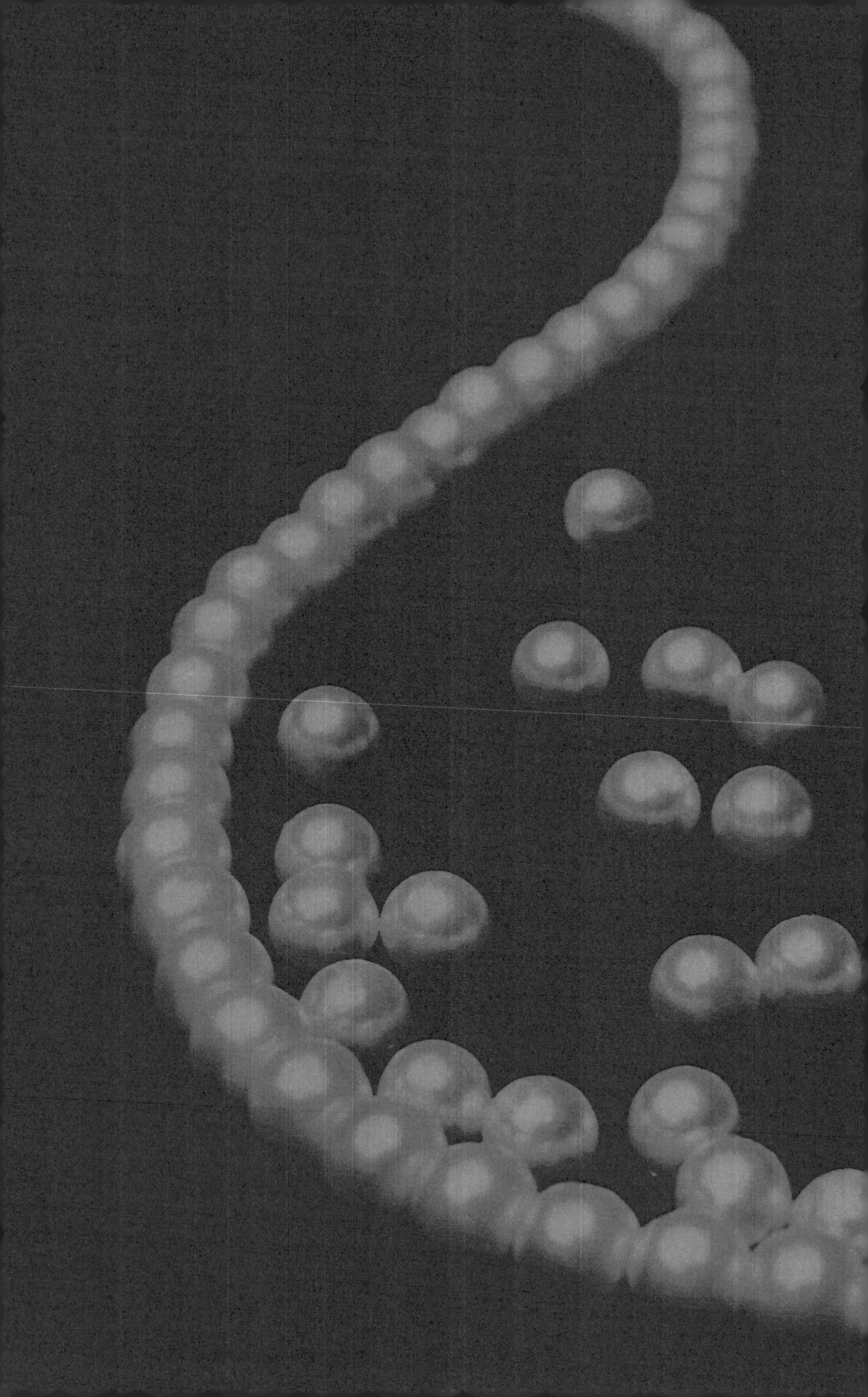

PART TWO
THE KING'S WARRIOR

PROLOGUE

FEAR IS A POWERFUL THING.

It can slap you in the face or sneak up on you, and then slowly drag you into the suffocating darkness that always seems to linger right out of sight.

It's crippling to know that it could strike at any moment, and steal the very breath from your body, the thoughts from your mind.

But there are worse things than fear.

Haunting memories. Pretty monsters. Self-destruction.

But they aren't all powerful. They can be conquered. Broken does not mean ruined.

There's strength in healing.

In love.

Sage thought she knew love.

She didn't.

Until Tehl.

ONE

TEHL

STARS ABOVE. SHE WAS HERE. In his arms.

Tehl buried his nose in his wife's hair, trembling. Sage was home.

He'd always been realistic, and, deep down, he'd felt like he'd never see her again—that he'd find her dead body somewhere. A tear dripped down his face, mingling with the dirt and sweat on his skin. Only now, as he held her in his arms, alive and breathing, could he accept that, deep down, he'd never really expected to bring her back for more than a proper burial.

"You're home," he murmured, his lips brushing the top of her damp head. His mind raced with questions, but he dismissed them, oblivious to anything but the woman in his arms.

"Home," Sage whispered into his vest, her voice weak as her body slumped against his.

He tightened his grip as she sank into him. "I'll take you home." Her family would be beside themselves when they saw her. "Let's go home."

But Sage didn't reply. Alarmed, Tehl craned his neck and peered down at her. Face slack, lips blue, she lay heavy in his arms, her parted lips releasing small unsteady puffs of breath.

"Sage?" he asked, shaking her. His own breath caught in his chest when she didn't stir. Something wasn't right. He hoisted her and shivered as the chill from her body seeped through his clothing.

"Zachael! I need you. She's too cold." Tehl turned on his heel and then froze at the menacing snarl that ripped through the air. He slowly turned back to the leren, making eye contact with the man-eater.

"Steady, boy," the weapons master breathed from somewhere behind him. "The beast is concerned for its mistress. Speak slowly and calmly to it."

Tehl's arms trembled as he held Sage away from his body like an offering, forcing his movements to be precise. "Easy. I'm not going to hurt your mistress, but she needs to be warmed or she'll die."

Sage shivered as he spoke, her whole body trembling, punctuating his statement. The beast's ears flattened, but it remained where it was. Tehl nodded; likely, that was all he was going to get from the creature, and he didn't have time to wait for more. Ignoring every instinct that commanded him to do otherwise, he slowly turned his back to the animal, his heart thudding in his chest. Zachael detached himself from his men and warily approached, his gaze pinned over Tehl's shoulder. The weapons master pulled his attention from the leren and motioned to Tehl.

"We need to get her dry as soon as possible," Zachael murmured. He laid a hand against Sage's chest, his face grave. "Her body is dangerously cold. There's no time to lose." The weapons master yanked his cloak from his shoulders and placed it on the ground.

Tehl dropped to his knees and gently laid Sage across the cloak. She looked so fragile and blue, as though she was already dead. His breath caught at the grim thought, and he steeled himself. Life was never certain, but surely it couldn't be so cruel as to give him a few moments with her and then let her die?

He shook his head, dismissing the idea as he began to unbutton her heavy, sodden vest. It did her no good for him to sit in fear. All that mattered was here and now. He hesitated when her shirt opened beneath his fingers, revealing creamy skin pebbled with goosebumps. He glanced at his men. Warmth and gratitude filled him despite the circumstances; his men had turned their backs and formed a protective barrier around him and his wife, respecting her privacy.

"Hurry up, son," Zachael admonished. "We don't have time to dally."

Tehl's numb fingers fumbled as he yanked off his cloak and dumped it unceremoniously on the ground. With care, he lifted Sage's torso, pulling the sodden top from her body before hastily covering her bust with his own cloak.

His jaw ticked when he caught sight of the monstrosity still wrapped around her neck, partially hidden by her hair. The collar's thorns had embedded themselves into her delicate skin, causing an angry red. It made him want to puke. The warlord had collared his wife like an animal. A rage unlike anything he'd ever known ignited inside him. A hard haze descended over his vision; the only sound he heard was the beating of his own heart.

The warlord would pay.

That *monster* would pay.

Tehl reached for the collar just as Zachael placed a hand on top of his.

The weapons master shook his head, sorrow in his eyes. "Not now. It's deeply embedded in her flesh. We'll need a healer to remove it. If you try now, you will cause more harm."

The collar glinted in the light, as though taunting him. How could he leave that *thing* on his wife?

"Think about your wife, what she needs most." Zachael seemed to read his thoughts.

His friend was right. His fury wouldn't serve Sage.

Tehl swallowed hard and nodded jerkily, scrubbing her damp hair with the corner of his cloak while Zachael yanked her boots and socks off.

Someone paused by his side. "For your princess, and my sister."

He glanced at Sam who averted his gaze from Sage, a bundle of cloaks over his arm.

Emotion clogged Tehl's throat as he handed his wet cloak to his brother and wrapped one of the dry ones around Sage's shivering form. He settled her on the ground and eyed the leather encasing her legs. There was no way he could get her out of wet leathers. Zachael pulled a blade from his sheath as another growl brought them both up short.

"Listen here, beast," Zachael said sternly. "I understand you're worried about her. We all are. But if you don't stop threatening and scaring everyone around us, you'll make it that much harder for us to help Sage. You're welcome to watch over her, just stop growling. It will all be okay." His tone brooked no argument.

Tehl stiffened as the beast chuffed, onyx fur teasing the edge of his vision. A tail brushed his back, causing his pulse to jump and his brother to curse. He blew out a breath as the feline settled beside him, surveying the scene.

"We need to cut her out," the weapons master said, dismissing the man-eater at their side. "Do I have your permission?" His blade hovered above her leather-clad hip.

"Do what you must."

Zachael eyed the beast and slowly began cutting the leather. The feline's body tensed beside them, but she didn't make any moves toward Zachael. His progress was slow, so Tehl drew his own blade, earning a hiss from the leren. Tehl held out his weapon on a flat palm so the beast could sniff it, praying it didn't bite his hand off. His fingers twitched as the feline locked eyes with him and sniffed. Its lips curled back slightly, but it didn't attack. He pulled his hand back gently.

"I'm going to help."

Grimly, Tehl set to the task of cutting the sodden leather, anxiety rising as Sage's shivers ceased. A bad sign, he knew.

"How far to the camp?" he asked as, at last, the stiff leather was pulled away. He set about working the cloak around her frozen toes.

"Not far, but it will be hard regardless…" Sam railed in response. Tehl nodded, tucking Sage's fingers underneath her arms and wrapping her up tightly.

"Let's ride." Immediately, his men mobilized.

"Blast." Sam frowned.

Tehl followed his gaze to Jasmine, who'd sunk to the ground and now listed back and forth, her eyelids heavy, skin ashen.

"Why hasn't she been taken care of?" Sam barked.

"We've done the best we could. She wouldn't let us near her, and she's clearly not well enough to redress herself on her own," James growled, glaring at the stubborn woman.

"I don't care what you have to do, but you get her warm and ready to travel," Tehl said before moving toward the copse of trees.

"I can handle this," Sam muttered, storming over to Jasmine. "Are you bloody stupid?"

"Ma-a-ay-be-e-e, bu-ut at least I-I-I am no-t-t-t ugly," she stuttered.

Sam yanked a blade from his waist and squatted. "Ugly is better than dead."

Tehl kept walking as stuttered curses burst from behind him. He ignored them. The bloody woman was too proud. She had to know she couldn't possibly do more on her own.

Tehl's men fanned out around him as they pushed through the last of the trees, their horses coming into view. They suddenly reared back and shied away; he stumbled and nearly fell. What in the blazes?

His gaze dropped to Sage's furry protector who licked her lips. Oh, hell no.

He stopped and met the feline's golden gaze squarely. "Our horseflesh is not for you to eat." It felt silly speaking to an animal, but, so far, she seemed to understand him. His mind flashed to the camp full of his men. "I'm taking your mistress to camp where we can heal her properly. None of my people are food. *None.* You hunt outside of my camp. If you hunt inside my camp, we will hunt *you.*"

The feline growled at his tone, but with a flick of her tail and a chuff, she seemed to acknowledge his demands.

Tehl walked faster and handed Sage off to Zachael as he swung up onto his own mount's back. The dark warhorse shied away from the feline lurking close by, but he didn't bolt.

"That's a good boy," Tehl murmured, stroking Wraith's silky neck. He took Sage from Zachael, who adjusted the cloak once more.

Just then, Sam stormed into the grove, carrying a now-unconscious Jasmine. Despite the anger and frustration on his face, he held Jasmine with the utmost care and deposited her gently into the weapon master's arms before mounting. Once he'd secured himself, he reclaimed Jasmine from Zachael. Settling her in his arms, he nudged his mount toward Tehl.

"Ride on!" Tehl shouted, nudging Wraith into a canter. The wind bit at his skin, blowing right through his damp clothing. He ought to have changed himself, or at least donned a dry cloak, but his mind had been on other things. He tightened his grip on Sage and ignored the chill.

The ride was miserable, as one emotion after another washed over him. Joy that Sage was alive. Anger at the state she was in. Fear that she might still not survive. It was miserable to be in his head.

Once or twice, he caught sight of flashes of black. He'd no idea how fast or far a man-eater could run. He doubted she could match the stamina of a horse, but then, he'd never had to find out before. He swallowed hard and prayed the creature wouldn't cause them any trouble.

When at last the tan peaks of his camp came into view, the anxiety inside Tehl loosened. The three-hour ride had seemed to drag on. Sage had survived the ride; she'd survive the healing.

A cry pierced the air at the approach of their party, and Tehl made out Hayjen as he stepped to the front of the awaiting group. Tehl nodded, meeting the man's anxious gaze, and slowed Wraith to a stop as Sage's uncle halted at their side and held out his arms.

"I have her," Tehl said, swinging his leg over the horse and sliding down. As soon as his boots touched the ground, he was moving, Sage's weight surprisingly light in his arms. There wasn't any time to lose.

"Lilja stoked the fire in your tent and had men bring water. It's heating now."

"Thank you."

"How is she?"

Tehl eyed Hayjen. "Not good. But she's alive."

A nod, as if he had already expected the news. "Rafe found Blaise. She's in rough shape herself."

"Then we have all three women."

"All worse for the wear." A pause. "He will pay."

The fury Tehl had been burying suddenly flared to life again. "That he will."

Hayjen moved ahead of him and held open the tent flap. A wave of hot air slammed into him as he stepped into the dim tent. Sweat beaded on his forehead and on the back of his neck. "I've got her, Lilja."

A small cry of alarm escaped from the usually-composed Sirenidae as she rushed toward them, her own skin covered in a sheen of sweat. "Sage?"

"She's alive, but her core is dangerously cold."

Lilja's expression hardened. "Lay her on the center cot." Her gaze flicked behind him. "Make sure to keep the tent flaps closed. We can't afford to lose the heat."

Tehl squeezed around cots piled with furs and blankets and did what he was told. It was hard letting go of Sage. His hands opened and closed as Lilja bustled around him, barking orders at Hayjen. He gazed down at Sage's pale face and knelt by her side.

"What can I do?" he asked.

"Grab that rock heating by the fire. Wrap it in a horse blanket so you don't burn yourself or Sage, and place it underneath her feet. If we don't get her toes and fingers heated up, she'll be in worse trouble."

Tehl moved to the fireplace, his breath coming in heavy pants. The air was stifling. He'd just plucked a stone from the fire when the sound of loud cries and startled shouting rent through the air.

"What the bloody hell is that?" Hayjen demanded, drawing his sword.

But there was only one thing that would make Tehl's men react like that.

"Prepare yourself, and don't make any sudden movements," Tehl said.

A shadow burst through the tent flap and skidded to a stop, hackles raised.

"Stars above," Lilja breathed, freezing, her hand pressed against Sage's chest.

The leren hissed and slunk toward Sage, her movements liquid. The beast leapt onto one of the tables, eyeing Lilja. Ever so slowly, Lilja removed her fingers from Sage and held out her hand, palm up.

"I mean you no harm, nor your mistress. She is my kin, and I offer you my friendship as well."

Tehl watched the exchange with wide eyes as the feline dropped from the table and silently padded toward Lilja.

"Love, that's a very large man-eater," Hayjen said softly, his tone holding a warning.

"She's just protecting her bonded. She won't hurt me, will you, darling?" she cooed.

Tehl sucked in a breath as the beast sniffed the Sirenidae's hand, bumping it with her nose.

Lilja smiled and brushed a hand along the feline's velvet head. "Hello to you, too." She turned from the beast and began to resume her work as the beast nudged Sage's face, giving her a gentle lick. Tehl gaped.

The Sirenidae glanced up and jerked her chin at him. "The stone."

He blinked a moment before hastily obeying.

Lilja tugged Sage to one side and patted the cot. "Wild one, she needs you."

The large beast nimbly climbed onto the cot and curled around Sage.

"Help me, Tehl. I need you to lift her. I'm going to pull this off. It's too damp to do her any favors." She motioned to the cloak.

Tehl averted his eyes and shivered as Sage's chilly flesh touched his own fiery skin. When requested, he let her back down, still staring in awe as the big cat accommodated Lilja, who tucked a fur around Sage.

"We need help!" Sam yelled, his voice drawing closer. His tone was oddly panicked. Sam rarely panicked.

Tehl pulled his gaze from his wife's pale face and glanced at the tent entrance as his brother burst in. His lips thinned as he got a good look at the source of Sam's distress. Jasmine's body hung limp in his arms. A pale leg escaped the confinement of the cloak, adorned with bruises, ugly red welts, and deep lacerations. Tehl's jaw clenched as the anger burning in his gut grew hotter. One brutality after another appeared in the warlord's wake, it seemed.

"Place her right here," Lilja commanded, sparing her niece a final look before rushing to Sam's side.

Tehl stood and tugged needlessly at the fur warming Sage, helplessness overtaking his features as he took in the dark smudges marring the skin beneath her eyes. She looked all but dead. He swallowed hard. "Lilja, what do I do?"

"Nothing," a husky voice rasped.

He hid his flinch as his gaze slid to what he had thought was a pile of furs. Swollen brown eyes peeked out at him from underneath a blanket. Blaise. She licked her cracked lips and slowly closed her eyes again, shivers shaking the furs around her. "She'll be fine."

"How do you know?" he barked.

A wry smile twisted the Scythian woman's battered face. "Do you really think the warlord would allow his prize to die so easily?"

Hatred washed over him like ice water along his skin. It was not a feeling he was accustomed to. "What did he do to her?" he hissed, dreading her answer.

Blaise cracked one puffy eye. "I'm sure he's given her an elixir to protect her from real harm. Her body will fight off the sickness and then heal itself."

A cough seized her, and Tehl quickly filled a cup with water and held it to her lips. Blaise drank weakly, water dribbling down her cheeks.

"Thank you," she whispered, her words garbled.

Tehl set the cup on the little wooden table and stared down at Blaise.

"There's no cause to worry?"

"There's every cause to worry." Blaise chuckled and then winced, her hand clutching at her ribs. "But not about her body. She'll fall into a deep sleep and wake up in a few days." Her gaze slid behind him. "You should be concerned for Jasmine."

"Thank you," he said, nodding and pulling the fur up higher over Blaise. Her eyelids slid closed, and her breathing evened out.

There wasn't anything he could do for his wife or Blaise, if what she had spoken was truth. He rolled up his sleeves, the fabric sticking to his damp skin, and turned to Lilja.

"What can I do?" he pleaded once more. Stars above, he needed something to keep himself occupied or he'd run mad.

Her worried magenta gaze met his. "Stoke the fire and pray."

TWO

THE WARLORD

SHE'D STABBED HIM.

The vixen had stabbed *him*. There was nothing Zane hated more than a traitor, and yet… he'd *liked* it. Reveled in it even.

Bubbles escaped his mouth, the river pulling him deeper and deeper into its watery clutches. Sage kept surprising him. He both loved and loathed it. Every time he thought he had her figured out, she surprised him, and not always in a good way. But that's what kept him coming back. She was a drug he craved, he needed—and he hated it. The dependency. The addiction to her goodness.

An emotion that he didn't want to acknowledge worked its way through him: worry. Not for himself. He'd survive. He always did. The river wouldn't kill him, but the death of his consort might.

He'd lived hundreds of years, and this was how he would lose the last person he'd ever cared for. It had been a mistake to keep her, but he couldn't help himself, much like the sun couldn't help but rise each morning.

His back slammed into a rock, but he welcomed the pain as it drowned out the voices inside him, howling in rage that his consort was dying and he was doing nothing. Even now, his limbs seemed heavier, dragging him deeper into darkness, his lungs screaming for air.

In freeing herself, Sage had killed herself. He'd seen others drown. It wasn't clean. It was brutal. Violent. He closed his eyes to the frigid swirling darkness around him. There was poetic justice in that. Their relationship had been brutal and violent in the best way. Only his queen would try to kill him and kiss him in the same breath. That was love. True love.

His lips curled back, the freezing water flooding his mouth. Love. The twisted emotion always managed to burn all his hard efforts to the ground. The darker part of him railed at the betrayal, but logically, it was bound to happen. Humans hurt the ones they loved the most. It was the reality of life. When you lived as long as he had, you saw it time after time.

Dark satisfaction filled him. At least his love didn't do it by halves. She'd dove in headfirst, and that's what had drawn him to her. If she was still alive when he found her, he'd never make the mistake of underestimating her again.

His black heart squeezed in his chest at the *if.* He grappled with emotions he'd long thought he was immune to: loss, sorrow; despair. He'd always been a master at power plays and manipulation. He never compromised. She made him softer, and he hated that, but not enough for him to let her go. She changed everything.

At first, he'd wanted to collect her fire and break her down and forge her into his own creation, but she'd fascinated him. She wouldn't break. By standing up to him, she'd fueled his obsession that he could only call love.

A love that she had for him, too. The voices quieted for a moment and seemed to purr. They knew the truth.

Sage loved him, too.

Though she tried to hide it, he'd seen it.

The moment the river tore her from his grasp, he'd seen it in her eyes. If she survived, she wouldn't be able to erase him from her soul. They were bound in ways that no one could imagine or understand. He was imprinted on her skin, just as she was imprinted on his.

Hands wrapped around his arms and lifted his body as his lungs began to burn. His men were just in time. For their sake, they'd better have found his consort.

Light filtered through his eyelids as they broke the surface. He sputtered and gasped for air, but didn't open his eyes as his warriors towed him to shore. Rock and sand scratched his bare back as they laid him down. He had never worried he would drown. His genetics made it almost impossible for him to die, and his warriors were the best of the best.

"My consort…" he rasped, his arms and legs numb.

"The river pulled her under, and we haven't been able to find her, my lord."

No, the voices inside him snarled. The river couldn't take her from him. She was *his*. His fingers curled into the sand beside his hips, rocks jabbing into his palms. Nothing would stand in his way. Not even death could take her from him. He wrestled his rage back. He could *not* lose it here.

"Blair?" he called, something thick lodging in his throat.

"He's still searching, my lord," a deep voice answered.

Ever-dutiful Blair. The man had proven to be beyond useful for all of these years. But Zane knew that his service wasn't given out of gratitude and loyalty. Fear was a funny thing. It motivated people in the most spectacular ways. Blair was the prime example of that. All it took was a casual inquiry after the man's family and he straightened up. But he didn't blame the man. Women had a way of enchanting the best of them.

"Find her," he rasped. His warriors nodded and melted into the surrounding forest.

His breath fogged around him as he slowed his breathing. He rolled his neck to the side, small pins of pain lodging behind his eyes as he stared at the deceptively calm river. How long could Sage survive the water? How long could she hold her breath? Cold dread settled in his stomach as his mind flashed back to her stabbing him. Her lips were already blue by the time he'd reached her.

One of the knots loosened in his chest. At least sickness wasn't an issue. He'd made sure sickness wouldn't take her from him. A small smile tugged at his lips. After her bout in the dungeon, he'd experienced how delicate she was beneath the fire. He'd forgotten how easily people died when they weren't protected. He'd given her the protection she needed. Sickness would never claim her, but accidents and suicide could.

Deep in his gut, unease pooled. He'd allowed himself to be ensnared by her, and now he was paying the price.

She was ours the moment she entered our throne room. The choice was not yours; it was ours. She belongs to us.

The voices never went away. But they went silent or calmed when she was around. Control was easier to accomplish. Her presence soothed all the chaos inside.

He smirked as feeling slowly crept back into his extremities. He wanted her with a fierceness he didn't know he possessed. He *needed* to claim her, but each time the voices urged him to *take*, he held himself in check. He wouldn't take that from her. She'd give it to him.

The temptation had been there every time he'd crawled into bed with her and wrapped his arms around her. At first, she'd been stiff, but at the end, her body molded to his and she sought him out in her sleep. He'd spent hours watching her sleep, caressing her body, relishing the cinnamon scent that drifted from her skin in intoxicating waves.

He'd always known he needed to produce heirs, but the women of his court always lacked something. However, in the stillness of the night with Sage asleep in his arms, he'd allowed himself to entertain the idea of heirs. Once the idea was planted, he could never free himself from it.

Sage, heavy with his child, was the reward. His future.

A future someone had tried to rob him of.

The warlord slowly sat up and placed a hand against the ground to steady himself. His consort was a brilliant woman, but she didn't have all the necessary skills to avoid detection so well.

She'd had help.

He rubbed the back of his neck, feeling the small wound. A toxin that could paralyze him for more than ten minutes was a rare thing. Whoever had given that to her possessed a dangerous weapon, and more so, they possessed dangerous knowledge. Someone had betrayed him.

He carefully pushed to his feet and strode toward his boots. There was a traitor in his midst. His gaze narrowed on his boots as his mind jumped to several options. He'd keep silent until the right moment, then strike.

You'll not hurt her.

No, he wouldn't hurt Sage. He'd punish her, for sure, and she'd beg him, but he wouldn't hurt her. Nothing would mar her skin.

He bared his teeth at the river, thinking about the state she'd been in when he'd finally caught up: cuts, bruises, scratches had covered every inch of her body. He'd hated that. Even though hunting her had been the most engaging event he'd participated in for years, it angered him that she'd abuse herself after all the effort he'd taken to heal her.

"Report," he commanded, his words sharp.

Blair appeared by his side and knelt. "She lives."

Just two words, but they calmed the voices inside. "Where is she?"

"She escaped."

He'd expect nothing less from his consort. "And are you tracking her?" he asked with a smile. The hunt was on.

"Yes."

"Very good."

"She's been retrieved."

The warlord stilled. That was not what he wanted to hear. "By whom?"

"By the crown prince of Aermia and his party."

The rage he'd been barely suppressing threatened to overwhelm him. The filthy cur had put his hands on *his* consort. The princeling would rue the day he stole what was his. No one took what was his.

Kill. Kill. Kill.

Tremors worked down his arms as he tried to get control of himself. He was dangerously close to losing control. Even when Sage had scorned him the first time, he'd not been this bad. He needed to calm himself. The stakes were much higher now. If he let emotion rule, he'd make a mistake, and he didn't have time for mistakes.

He blew out a breath and uncurled his hands. The Aermian boy was playing a game he couldn't win. A cruel smile tipped the corners of Zane's mouth. He'd relish taking everything from the pup of a prince as he claimed his consort once and for all. Aermia was as good as his.

The prince's actions accelerated his plans more than he liked, but it would be all the more satisfying to take Aermia and his consort as the prize in the end.

He turned to Blair, who still knelt at his feet, staring at the ground. If he were a lesser man, he'd kill him, but men like Blair were rare. His warrior didn't hesitate when telling him the news of his woman's disappearance. That was bravery.

"They're being followed?" he asked.

"Yes."

"Then leave them."

It was almost painful to say the words. The voices demanded he give chase and hunt Sage down, but he knew better. Recklessness always ended in failure. He'd plot and maneuver, and in the end, he'd be the victor. If he wanted her, he had to be patient.

In time, Sage would come to him, beg him to take her back.

And he would.

For a price.

THREE

TEHL

NEITHER WORKED.

All three women worsened through the night and the next day.

Tehl rubbed his bleary eyes and scanned the cramped room. Hayjen snored quietly in the right corner, his chin resting on his chest. Sam sat near Jasmine, bloodshot eyes staring blankly into space, while Rafe sat between Sage and Blaise, his face betraying his anxiety. His gaze flickered to Lilja, who buzzed around the room, humming a haunting tune. She'd worked tirelessly since the women arrived. Tehl didn't think he'd seen her sit down once.

He pushed to his feet and edged around the cot toward the Sirenidae. She paced to and fro in the tent, her brow furrowed, lips pursed. Something was on her mind, that much was obvious.

"You'll wear a hole in the floor," he said softly.

"It's better than sitting still while they die."

His spine snapped straight, and Rafe growled from his spot.

Lilja immediately halted and took Tehl's hand, an apology in her eyes. "I'm sorry. That was thoughtless of me. I shouldn't have said that."

Tehl squeezed her hand once and pulled back. He swallowed hard, choking down his fear before stating the thought he knew he shared with the other two men. "So…you believe she may die after all?"

She sighed and hung her head, her silvery white hair hanging limply over her shoulders. "I've done everything I can for them, but they need more care than I, alone, can give, and I'm running out of supplies." Lilja glanced at him from beneath her lashes. "I'm afraid we only have one option, and it has risks."

"We need to move them," Rafe guessed.

Lilja cast a look his way. "Yes." Her tone was resolute.

Tehl had been thinking the same thing, but there were so many factors he couldn't control.

"Of course, they may not be strong enough for the journey." She hesitated before continuing. "But if we don't get them the help they need, they'll die anyway." Lilja pressed her palms to her eyes and rubbed. "They will have a chance if we get them back to the palace, but if we stay here for too long, they will die." He glanced at Sage's still form, pensive.

"There's a storm brewing," Rafe added softly.

Tehl looked to the Methian with a raised brow. How did he know? The man stayed silent. Tehl glanced down to Sage and ran a thumb along her cheekbone. At this point, he didn't care how the man knew or what secrets he kept. Tehl was too damn tired for any more revelations, anyway.

"I sense it, too," Lilja said. "We must leave now, before it strikes."

"And how do you expect us to get them there alive?" Sam's voice whipped through the air. "They almost didn't survive the journey from the river to our camp. Do you really think they'll make it to the castle? It would be a death sentence."

Lilja placed a hand on Sam's shoulder. "She'll die without help. Can you hear her breathing? You know I'm speaking the truth."

Sam shrugged off her hand and pushed to his feet. He ran a hand through his disheveled blond curls and down his face, his gaze snagging on Tehl. "Will you risk Sage?"

No, Tehl wasn't *willing* to risk Sage, but he trusted Lilja. "We can't stay here. There's a frost every morning. We have to go." It was the only choice.

Sam scoffed. "But you're willing to risk Jasmine?"

He frowned. "What?"

His brother laughed bitterly. "Look at her!" Her wet cough punctuated his words. Sam frowned and tugged the fur higher on the girl. "The others might stand a chance, but Jasmine…it could be the end of her. She's too weak."

"We need to leave *for* her, brother. Her odds are no better if she stays. Think about it."

Sam shook his head, scorn heavy on his face. "And you know this, do you? Speak truthfully. We all know you aren't thinking about *her*. You care only for yourself and your own."

Tehl blinked, startled. Where was this coming from? Sam's words were filled with venom. He took another breath before answering, studying the color in Sam's cheeks, the dark lines at the corners of his eyes. All of them were anxious. All of them were tired. He couldn't remember the last time he'd slept a full night.

Tehl looked closely at his younger brother, noting the same ragged signs of exhaustion that surely marked his own face. When was the last time Sam had had a full night of sleep?

"Sam, you know that's not true," he said gently. "You know how much I appreciate everything Jasmine did for Sage. I owe her a debt for her sacrifice. Have I ever ignored such a debt?"

The fire popped and crackled in the silence as Sam stared at him. His brother's shoulders slumped, and he hung his head. "No, you haven't."

"And I'm not starting now. I have a duty to Jasmine as much as to Sage."

"You're right." Sam rolled his neck and straightened. "So, when do we leave?"

"Now," Rafe rumbled. "Or the storm will catch us."

Chills ran down Tehl's spine as the wind blew his hood from his face and rain dripped down the back of his shirt. He pressed his heels into Wraith's sides and urged his mount to move faster. The temperature had dropped steadily as they drew closer to Sanee. He cast a worried glance down at Sage. Her skin seemed almost translucent now. "Please don't die," he whispered, his voice lost to the howling winds and rain. She couldn't die now.

He leaned forward in his saddle and kept his gaze ahead as familiar landmarks began to appear, his heart beating in tandem with every stride Wraith took. They were so close. Just a little further and they'd be home. When the spires of the castle rose in the distance like ragged teeth from the cliff, some of the worry in his chest loosened. Just a little further.

His surroundings blurred around him as he thundered forward, closing the distance between him and his goal. The only thing to rouse him was the guard's cry that pierced the air when he neared the gates.

Tehl pulled hard on the reins, steamed breath pouring from Wraith's nostrils. His men surrounded him and Zachael held his hands out. Tehl let the weapons master take Sage from his arms. He swung his leg over his mount and slid to the ground. The impact reverberated through his stiff legs, nearly bringing him to his knees. He gritted his teeth, ignoring the pain and questions others barked around him, and took his wife back from Zachael. He brushed past his men and rushed toward the castle, the rain pelting him the entire time as if to mock him. To tell him he was too late.

He burst through the castle doors near the sparring ring and startled a few maids. Brusquely, he charged forward, tuning out their squeals and gasps. His wet boots squelched against the lush deep-blue carpets, water dripping from his cloak in a constant pattern as he forced his tired legs forward with each step. Heat suffused his side, and he spared a quick glance toward the beast following close by him. Ah, so it was not his own presence that had startled the servants after all. Absently, he smiled. By noon, there'd be all sorts of monster stories floating around the castle.

Gavriel materialized next to him, followed by Sam, Rafe, Lilja, and Hayjen. "I've sent a messenger ahead to alert Jacob and Mira of our arrival and to make ready."

"Thank you."

His cousin nodded and then stared at the beast. "Are you sure it was the best idea to bring the cat with us?" he asked, an eyebrow raised.

"There was no 'letting her come,' she just did. Be my guest to stop her."

Gav shook his head. "Let's hope she doesn't eat anyone before morning." A curse. "I'll need to warn Isa. There's no way I'll be able to keep her from the man-eater once she spots her."

"Maybe she'll eat some of the bastards around here," Sam said, adjusting Jasmine in his arms. "It would save us from ever having to deal with their idiocy again."

A small smile curled Tehl's lips upward. It was hardly the time to joke, but at least his brother was behaving a bit more like himself.

They cut through a room or two and used the servants' darkened corridors to reach the infirmary. Tehl led the way, the others trailing close behind him. Mira hustled around the cots, tying her blond hair onto the top of her head. Tears dripped down her cheeks as she rushed toward him.

"How is she?" She pulled up short when the beast growled. Her eyes widened, seeming to take up her entire face. "Is that what I think it is?" she squeaked.

"Yes."

Jacob took a careful step forward. The Healer showed more bravery than most men.

"She won't hurt Sage," Lilja murmured to the animal, daring to place a hand on the man-eater's head. "Jacob and Mira are friends. The Healer will help her."

Mira tore her gaze away from the feline and moved closer to pull back the cloak. She gasped. Tehl knew what she'd see. A woman pale and death-like, but more than that, a woman changed in a way not thought possible.

Mira grimaced, her eyes flitting once between his face and Sage's unfamiliar one. In that one look, he saw many questions, but she kept them to herself. She placed her hand on his wife's forehead and then immediately went to work. "Leave them on the cots and get out." She pulled away and gestured toward the cots near the fire.

All three men moved into action, depositing their charges onto the designated cots. Jacob bustled around his herbs, placing pastes, tinctures, and tonics on a table with wheels. He eyed them over the rims of his round glasses, his copper eyes pausing briefly on Rafe and Blaise before settling on Tehl.

"You brought her back."

Tehl brushed a wet strand of hair from Sage's face. "Have I really?" It was too early to tell.

Jacob pulled back the cloak and scanned Sage, his expression giving nothing away. "She's a strong girl. She'll make it."

"Can I assist in any way?" Lilja asked, stepping closer.

Jacob nodded. "I'd be pleased if you did, my lady." He turned his attention back to Tehl. "You need to leave."

Everything inside Tehl rebelled at the command. "I'm not leaving her."

"We need to keep this room free of all contaminants. That means all of you." Jacob scanned all the men glaring at him. "You're a hazard to their health. If the stars are willing, we'll save all of them, but I'm not taking the chance of you making them worse. Not to mention, only the princess is married. You are not anything to these young women. You'll ruin their reputations. Unless you plan to marry them all?"

"We've already seen them," Sam argued.

"But it wasn't *here*," the Healer reminded. "Appearances in the palace are different."

"Wise," Rafe murmured. He dipped his head and retreated, followed by Gav, and reluctantly Sam.

Tehl was Sage's husband. He wasn't going anywhere. She didn't deserve to be alone after everything she'd gone through. Tehl crossed his arms and stared down the Healer. "I'm not leaving her side."

The old man adjusted his spectacles, eyes gleaming. "You're wasting our time. I'm not saying you cannot come back, but you cannot be here now."

Tehl fumed. He was the damn crown prince. He had the authority to do whatever he pleased. How dare Jacob give him a command?

"How dare you—"

"Tehl," Mira said softly.

He glared at the blond healer. "What?"

She didn't flinch at his sharp tone. "You will do more harm than good right now. Do you want to help?"

"Yes," he gritted out.

"Then bring her mother."

He stilled. Her family. The last time she was sick, she had asked for her mother. Tehl pulled a surprised Mira into a hug. "Thank you." He released her and sketched a bow. "I'll fetch her, myself."

He placed a swift kiss on Sage's feverish forehead and spun on his heel. If he hurried, he could have her mother at the palace in an hour. He spared one last glance over his shoulder at the unlikely group and then shut the door behind him.

Four pairs of eyes latched onto him. Gav, Sam, Rafe, and Hayjen all stood just outside the infirmary in various states of agitation.

"I need to collect Sage's family."

Hayjen held a hand out. "I'll take care of that."

"I should be the one who goes," Tehl said, moving through the men. "It's my duty."

A large hand settled on his shoulder. "Your place is here, with your wife. I'll retrieve my sister."

Silence. Then, "You're Sage's uncle?" Sam asked. "I'll be damned."

Tehl ignored his brother and smiled at Hayjen. "Thank you." He didn't want to leave Sage alone when she was so vulnerable. He glanced to Sam as Hayjen disappeared around the corner. "Does Jasmine have any more family?"

Sam snapped his mouth closed and held up a finger. "We're revisiting this revelation that you kept from us." His brother gave him a dirty look. "No, just the children."

Right. Jasmine's niece and nephew.

"Where are they now?" Tehl asked.

"Here," Sam said, leaning one shoulder against the wall. "They're in the care of Isa's nursemaid."

"Wait a moment." Gav held up a hand. "As the only father among us, I advise against making the children aware of Jasmine's presence until she's well."

"You don't want the children to have to mourn her again?" Tehl asked. That was logical.

"Yes. They've only just begun speaking again. They've had enough sorrow in their lives." Gav shook his head. "They deserve peace, not upheaval."

"But do you really want her niece's last memory to be of the death of her aunt?" Rafe asked. "Speaking from losing someone as a child, the memory warps, but the guilt stays. You should give them a chance to say goodbye, or that little girl will blame herself for the rest of her life."

Tehl dropped his head, thinking over the situation. Either choice could harm the children, but he would do anything to have one last moment with his own mother. "We'll leave them be for now. But if things turn bad for Jasmine… They deserve a chance to say goodbye."

Gav pursed his lips, looking like he wanted to argue, but dipped his head in acknowledgment. "Speaking of children, I'm going to go find Isa and hold her for a while. I'll return in a few hours. Do you need anything?"

"Nothing but the good health of those women," Tehl answered.

Gav hugged him and slapped him on the back. "She'll pull through. Believe in her."

His cousin released him and slipped away into the darkness. Tehl stared after him, long after Gav disappeared, unspoken fears swirling through his mind. He blinked when his eyes grew dry and the darkness shifted.

"You need to sit down, son."

His father's voice disrupted his reverie, the king's face slowly taking shape in the shadows before him. His father hugged him tightly, but Tehl's body stayed frozen as emotion battered against him like the sea against the cliff face.

"You retrieved her?" Marq asked.

"We did," he choked out.

His father pulled back and stared him in the eye. "In what condition?"

"I'm not sure," he whispered. He snapped his mouth shut when a gurgle escaped the back of his throat, sounding suspiciously like a sob.

Marq clapped him on the shoulder and sank down to the floor; patting the space beside him, he held out a bottle of spirits. "The waiting is the worst. Tell me what's happened to my daughter."

Emotion lodged in Tehl's throat as he collapsed to the floor and took his father's offering. The liquor burned, but it gave him time to collect himself. "That's the problem. I don't know what's happened to her, only that she's different."

His father took the bottle and had a healthy swig before passing it to Rafe with a nod. "The experiences in our life tend to change us."

That wasn't what he meant. "She *looks* different."

His father stilled and released a shuddering breath. "All women change. It's part of nature."

"Not this change." The words tasted like ash on Tehl's tongue. Her change was partly due to his failure. His wife still looked like herself, but part of her was now alien, otherworldly, too perfect. "Everything has changed."

Marq stared at the back of his hands. "You're right. You're at a crossroads. This is where you decide your future."

"My future?"

His father speared him with his serious blue eyes. "Everyone's future."

FOUR

MIRA

IT WAS LIKE BEING INSIDE a nightmare.

She scrubbed her hands vigorously in the basin until her skin turned red from the abuse.

"Mira, are you ready?" her papa called.

She ducked her head and panted, nausea swirling in her belly. For the most part, blood and disease didn't bother her. She could look past it, but she couldn't look past the hideous contraption wrapped around her friend's neck or the way it dug into her tender flesh.

Mira gagged and grabbed the edge of the table to steady herself. She needed to pull herself together. Her papa's hands weren't as steady as hers these days, so she had to remove the collar. There was no one else to take her place; no one she'd trust with her friend.

Swallowing hard, she straightened and wiped her hands on her apron. She had a duty to do. She spun around and strode to Sage's side. She'd changed so much in Scythia. It was almost like looking at a stranger.

Lilja placed a shallow bowl with warm water on the cot and pressed into her space, making Mira's teeth snap together. She understood that Sage's aunt wanted to help, but her hovering was making Mira feel more on edge.

"How do you plan on doing this?" Jacob asked, lying clean tools across a linen-covered table.

"Originally, I planned on placing a small piece of wood underneath the collar to keep it from her neck and then slowly breaking pieces off." She leaned closer and pointed to where Sage's skin was attached to the metal. "But the longer I examine her neck, the more I think it will cause more damage. If I pry at the metal at all, it'll press the wood into her neck. That's a concern for infection."

"What about a towel?" Gwen offered, brushing a strand of hair from Sage's pale face.

She shook her head. "It's not strong enough. The metal will just rip through it and will offer no protection to her neck."

"What about someone's hand?" Lilja said.

"The chance of breaking someone's hand, due to the pressure, would be high." And extremely painful.

Lilja rolled her neck. "I'll do it."

"Can you handle the pain?"

A dark look crossed the woman's face. "I was bred for pain."

Mira blinked and narrowed her eyes. "I can't abide a martyr here. Can you keep calm if I happen to break one of your fingers?"

Magenta eyes met hers with absolute certainty lurking in them. "This will be a cakewalk."

It was unorthodox, but they didn't have much choice. The crown prince had made it abundantly clear that he wanted the monstrosity taken off her as soon as possible. Gwen shifted the bowl out of the way so Lilja could sit on the cot and wedge her fingers between the thorny collar and Sage's skin. Mira hissed out a breath when blood dripped down Sage's neck, slowly soaking the white linen beneath her head.

It was painful to watch. Mira plucked a file from her toolkit and began to delicately file at the collar. She winced as each of her movements caused Sage to bleed, but she dared not speed up her work. One wrong move and the file could slip, slashing open her friend's neck.

"You're doing great, love," Gwen breathed softly.

Mira bit her lip as she cut through one section of the collar. She wiped her forehead with the back of her hand, then moved onto the next strand.

It was slow going and her hands began to ache, but she soldiered on, keeping a close eye on Sage's blood loss. When she reached the last strand, she straightened and handed the file to her papa and shook out her hands. Only one last strand. It was the thickest one of all, and proved the most difficult to cut.

She held out her hand once the tingles had left her fingers, and Jacob laid the file back onto her palm with an encouraging smile. Mira focused on the last strand and began to saw. It was stubborn, but it, too, eventually gave up to her insistence. She dropped the file into the bowl of warm water and glanced at her papa.

"I need you to start to pull the collar away from her neck where it overlaps. It should break where I've been sawing."

Her papa shuffled to her side and began to delicately pry the shackle away from Sage's throat. Lilja's lips pursed, the only sign the metal was pressing uncomfortably into her fingers.

"That's it," Mira encouraged as the metal began to groan. "Just a little further, steady now."

No sooner had the words come from her mouth when the collar snapped, and one side gouged into Sage's neck.

"Damn it." Jacob pulled the offending metal from her neck.

Mira snatched a towel from the table and pressed it against the heavily-bleeding wound. "We need a poultice to pack it." She lifted the edge of the towel and peeked at the cut. "It's bleeding too much to stitch it now."

Her papa dropped the thorny chunk into Gwen's hands and swiftly moved to his herbs. For some reason, she couldn't pull her gaze from the collar lying on Gwen's palms. What kind of human being did that to another?

"He's not human," Lilja murmured.

Mira blinked, and then realized she had said that out loud. "On that, we can agree," she growled, glancing down to the crimson soaking through her towel. She frowned. That seemed like too much blood for the wound.

She lifted the edge of the towel and cursed. Not only had the metal cut Sage, but it had sliced Lilja across her fingers. She glanced up at the woman next to her. Lilja looked like she could be having tea, her expression was so calm. She stared at Sage's aunt, and a random thought passed through her mind: she'd never play cards with the woman.

"Papa," she called. "Make some for Lilja. She's been cut, too."

Lilja shook her head. "Don't worry about me. I'll heal."

Jacob moved to her side with a poultice. "Ready?"

"Yes."

"On the count of three. One, two, three!"

Mira pulled the towel out of the way and switched places with her father as he pressed the poultice to Sage's wound. He glanced at her and jerked his chin toward the tweezers. "Why don't you start on the other side? We won't be able to do the same thing. It's much more embedded on her right side."

She nodded, feeling sick. Gwen shuffled out of her way but never looked away from what she held in her hands. It seemed Mira wasn't the only one morbidly fascinated with the crown. She plucked her tool from the table and sucked in a deep breath to fortify herself. She could do this. It wasn't anything she hadn't done before.

Mira's stomach lurched painfully as she pulled the skin from around the metal. Gwen choked beside her.

"Gwen, I know you want to be here for Sage, but if you can't keep it together, you need to leave," Jacob said softly.

"I can do it," Gwen panted. "I'm not leaving my little girl."

"Then, take a deep breath, and, good hell, destroy that piece of trash."

Mira also inhaled deeply as she carefully worked on Sage's neck. She gritted her teeth as blood coated her fingers, causing the tweezers to move around in her hand. Quickly, she wiped her bloody hand on her apron and began her work anew.

From strictly a healing point of view, she was interested in how clean the damaged skin was. Normally, there would have been pus and infection, but there was nothing. What had they used to keep her neck clean?

She bit the inside of her cheek to keep herself calm. They had kept the collar clean but allowed her skin to grow around it. It was disgusting and inhuman.

A sigh of relief escaped her when she'd finally detached the last piece of skin. "I'm done," she whispered.

"Good," her papa said, glancing at her over his spectacles. "You grab your side, and I'll pull on this end, near Lilja's fingers."

She did what he asked and bile burned her throat as the thorny collar pulled away, somewhat stubbornly. Jacob cursed when it refused to budge in the very middle. He tugged lightly, causing the skin to stretch but hold. "We'll have to cut it away."

"Gwen, could you hand me the short dagger?" Mira asked, her voice hollow.

Sage's mum plucked the dagger from the table and placed it in her hand. She swallowed and held the collar from Sage's neck to cut away the attached flesh. Mira choked on bile as she cut away the metal. Jacob pulled away the collar, and she had to fight to not cast up the contents of her stomach.

Her friend's neck was a bloody mess, but that's not what bothered her. She dabbed at the blood, her stomach curling on itself. It was the impressions of thorns and roses carved into Sage's neck.

"Dear God," Gwen whispered. "My poor baby."

Lilja said curse words that normally would have had Mira scowling, but they somehow felt insignificant for what she was feeling. Woodenly, Mira placed the bloody dagger into the bowl of warm water and stood on numb legs.

Her papa bustled her out of the way and began to treat and dress Sage's wound. As if in a trance, she dressed Lilja's hand. All the while, Lilja watched her, but it didn't bother her. She couldn't feel anything.

Mira spun and forced herself to the wash basin. She dipped her scarlet-covered hands into the water and watched, detached, as the clear water battled with the blood and eventually lost, turning to a crimson pool of cruelty. For that's what it was. Mira was washing cruelty and depravity from her skin.

Rage unlike she'd ever known flooded her. This was not what the world was supposed to be like. Sure, she'd seen horrific things happen over the years as she trained to be a healer, but none of them had been this sadistic.

Something ugly formed in her heart. She'd never been one to take revenge, but there would be an accounting for what her friend had suffered. She wasn't a warrior in the truest sense, but make no mistake, when the time came to yank that bastard from the Scythian throne and destroy him, Mira would be there to witness him gasping his last breath, all the while laughing. And she'd make sure his lifeless body was left on the godforsaken battleground.

Monsters deserved to die like animals. Alone. Forgotten. Desecrated.

FİVE

SAGE

EVERYTHING HURT.

She was bloody tired of waking to everything hurting, but, this time, a smile touched her mouth. Pain meant she was alive—battered and bruised, but alive.

For how long? a hideous voice whispered in her head.

Her breath hitched as she battled the fear that threatened to swallow her whole. She was out of the warlord's grip. He couldn't get her now.

Sage shifted, her fingertips grazing soft fur on her right. Carefully, she cracked one eyelid and then pressed her face into Nali's silky fur. "Nali," she croaked.

A purr greeted her, rumbling through her body.

A voice cried out behind her, and a hand brushed along her arm.

"Sage?"

Tears sprang to her eyes. She'd know that voice anywhere. "Mum?" she replied, her voice catching on the word.

Slowly, she turned to the left, praying she wasn't dreaming. Words failed her as her mum's beautiful hazel eyes locked on hers. Surely it wasn't possible to create an illusion so beautiful?

It seemed impossible that her mum was here with her, but she couldn't help the hope that unfurled inside her chest like a flower in the sun. "Please, tell me you're real?" she said.

"Oh, baby girl!" her mum cried, tears tracking down her face. "I'm real. I'm here, love." Her mum brushed her hair from her face and peppered her forehead with kisses.

"I'm home?" It didn't seem real.

"You're home," a deep voice echoed.

Sage pried her eyes from her mum's dear face and glanced behind her. Pain washed over her at the little movement, but it was worth it.

Her papa's green eyes, so like her own, crinkled at the corners as he smiled down at her and ran a hand down her hair.

"Hello, baby girl."

It was too much. Sage squeezed her eyes shut, losing the battle with her emotions as sobs tore from her throat. It hurt just to look at them.

Large arms curled around her shoulders and pulled her into a tight embrace. Her lungs protested at the treatment, and pain ran up and down her arms and legs, yet she celebrated. She lived.

"It's okay, love. Papa has you," he crooned, his voice thick as he rocked her from side to side.

Sage clung to him like a little girl and wept. She'd made it home. Finally. Home. Tears dropped onto her face like rain, but she didn't care. Her pain was shared by her family.

"I love you," she said.

Her parents' murmurs of love became a chant in her mind as she let go and surrendered to the tears. When at last they abated, her papa didn't let her go. He whispered words of nonsense and love as her mum sang little songs quietly in the background. As Sage's eyes drooped and fatigue hit her, terror set in. What if this was in her mind? Would they still be here when she woke up?

"I don't want to go to sleep," she whispered into her papa's wet shirt.

"It's okay. You need to let your body rest," her mum answered, running a hand down the back of her head. "We'll watch over you. Protect you."

"Will you still be here when I wake up?" The words were small and vulnerable, born of suffering, fear, and uncertainty. Speaking them aloud sickened her, but she needed assurance, even if it was all in her mind.

A finger crooked underneath her chin and lifted. "Open your eyes, love."

She steeled herself and opened them to gaze up at her parents. Her mum leaned her head against her papa's shoulder and caressed Sage's face tenderly. "Nothing could tear your papa and me from your side. We'll stay."

"Promise?"

"I swear it," her papa said gravely, hugging her more tightly to him.

Her papa never lied to her. She released a deep sigh and rested her head against his chest, his steady heartbeat lulling her toward sleep. A small smile curled the corners of her lips as she breathed in. Fire, iron, and smoke teased her nose, a smell unique to her papa.

No dream could replicate that.

"Love you," she whispered.

"Love you most-est." Her mum's voice followed her into the dark and wrapped around her like the loveliest blanket on a chilly day.

Awareness slapped her in the face.

She jerked, her eyes snapping open. Her heart pounded as she scanned her surroundings. Nothing made sense. Everything was white, and it was bloody hot. Where was she?

Wait.

White walls.

Gleaming white walls.

The room blurred around her. How had he gotten to her? Had she never left the Scythian palace in the first place? A whimper escaped her. When would this torture end?

"Love?"

Her head snapped to the side. For a moment, she couldn't process what she saw.

A pair of worried green eyes stared back at her. "Baby girl?"

Recognition filled her mind. "Papa?"

His smile was full of relief. "Yes, it's me, baby. You're safe."

Safe? She was never safe. Safety was an illusion for the naive.

"What are you doing here?" she asked.

His brows furrowed. "Here?"

"In my mind."

Tears gathered in his eyes as he grabbed her hand. "I'm real, love. See the truth."

She forced herself to examine the white walls. Her stomach rolled, but the longer she stared, the more imperfections she noticed. The color of the walls wasn't white, but cream. Sage blinked and scanned the room. She recognized it. The infirmary. The Aermian palace. How did she get here?

She blew out a breath, ruffling the hair hanging in her face, and tried to sort through the fragments of her mind. Her brows slanted together when she tried to move her arm. It didn't move. She glanced to the left, and tenderness flooded her. Her mum slept, her cheek resting on the back of Sage's hand. The poor thing looked exhausted. Surely, her imagination couldn't conjure pain like this?

Her skin prickled, and she glanced back to her papa. "I'm here?"

Her papa stared at her, his eyes bloodshot. "You don't remember?"

Rain, crying, her mum singing. Her mind snagged on the last blurry memory. "Some."

He nodded, his face creased with worry. "The mind is a tricky thing."

That it was.

"I'm sure you'll have your memories back before you know it."

She already had her memories, ones she wished to lose. Ones that haunted her dreams. Her hand crept to her throat and she froze as her fingertips grazed gauze not metal. Gauze, *not* metal. The room spun, and she clung to consciousness with everything she had.

"Did you sleep okay?"

No, but she wouldn't tell him that. Her papa didn't need to know about the warlord's presence overtaking her nightmares. "Like a rock." She shifted carefully, pulling her arm out from underneath her mama. Tingles ran up her arm as she wiggled her fingers.

A chuff ruffled her hair, causing her to smile. Nali. If Nali was here, this had to be real. Tears pricked her eyes. She'd made it. Truly made it. "I love you," she said. Right then and there, she vowed to say that to anyone she cared for at any time she desired. Life was too short not to let the ones you cared for know you love them.

"I love you, too." She shared a smile with her papa before he glanced over her head, his smile hitching up one side of his face and making him look years younger. "She's magnificent."

That wasn't the response Nali usually gained. Most shied away from the massive feline. Sage combed her right hand through Nali's fur, earning a rumble of pleasure from the beast. "She's the best." The leren had protected Sage with her life. They had forged a bond that wouldn't ever be broken.

Sage scanned the room. The infirmary was exactly as she remembered it. White-washed stone walls were adorned with shelves full of plants and herbs, and the roaring fire Jacob was so fond of keeping crackled, bringing comfort to her mind. A wet cough sounded to her right, alerting her to others in the room.

Shame washed over her. She hadn't even thought about the others. "Blaise and Jasmine? Are they okay?"

The last time she had seen the both of them was at the river. Had they both made it?

"Both girls made it to Aermia. Blaise was allowed to leave today. As for Jasmine..." Jacob trailed off, his lips pressing into a thin line. "She's not well."

Her heart sank. Jasmine had been injured, and the water was beyond cold. Who knew how much damage that had done to her? The warlord's face flashed through her mind, how he prowled toward her, his wet body caging hers. Her stomach lurched, and she panted as she tried to push the memory away. They'd escaped, but at what cost?

"Sage?"

"Help me up, please." Her tone roused her mum, who shot up with wide eyes.

Gwen glanced around the room before her gaze settled on Sage. "You're awake."

Panic seized her lungs; everything was too confining, too small. All she could feel was the warlord's skin pressed against her. "I need to get up." Spots danced across her vision as hands levered her up. The room spun, and she clung to the cot, her nails digging into the canvas. He wasn't here. He couldn't touch her.

But for how long...

"Breathe, love," her mum soothed, her hand running up and down Sage's spine.

She would if the fist around her lungs would let go, if the monster would let her go.

"Look at me," Mira's calm voice commanded.

Sage's head snapped up, and her green eyes clashed with beautiful blue ones. Her friend knelt before her and reached for her hand.

"Breathe when I do." Mira pulled in a slow breath and released it just as slowly while Sage's papa wrung his hands beside her.

She tried, she really did, but she kept feeling the warlord's hand on her skin, his heated breath on her neck, his lips gliding across her cheek.

Mira pinched her chin between two fingers. "You're not there, Sage. Focus on me. You're in the castle. Leave that place. It has no hold on you."

Her eyes focused on her blond friend, Mira's words penetrating the fog in her mind. *He* wasn't here. Her breath came slowly, and the panic receded.

Sage squeezed Mira's hand, hardly believing her friend knelt before her. "I never thought I'd see you again."

Tears flooded the healer's eyes. "I always knew I'd see you again. We have too much mischief yet to cause."

Tears pooled in Sage's own eyes. "Stars above, I've missed you." With a choked sob, she threw herself at Mira. Her friend's arms wrapped around her tightly.

"I've missed you, too," Mira whispered into her hair.

"It's so good to see your face," Sage cried.

Mira pulled back and laughed, wiping her tears from her cheeks with her dress sleeve. "I'm such an ugly crier. Shame on you for making me cry in the presence of others."

"I won't tell anyone," her papa remarked. A pause. "Gwen is worse."

Sage smiled when her mum smacked her papa's arm and grinned up at him with adoration.

She glanced to the right, and her smile faded as she got a good look at the patient in the cot next to her. Jasmine's face was impossibly pale. Her honey-brown hair was soaked with sweat and clung to her head in clumps of Medusa-like strands. Black hollows marred the skin beneath her closed eyes, and harsh, struggling breaths passed her chapped, parted lips.

"Oh, Jasmine," she whispered. "How bad is she?"

"She's not well," Mira replied.

"That's not a real answer." Sage turned back to the healer. "The truth."

"Her injuries were serious, but it's the sickness that's settled in her lungs. There's too much fluid in them. Every breath is a painful labor for her."

"What can be done?"

"We're doing everything we can. Lilja has brought me special herbs I've been using to ease her breathing, but now we have to wait."

Sage swallowed. "Wait for her to live or die?"

"That depends on the fever and if Jasmine is a fighter," Mira said grimly.

A halfhearted laugh escaped Sage as she glanced back at Jasmine. "Fighter would be an understatement. She'll survive." She had to.

"I dearly hope so," Mira said, squeezing her hand and standing.

"She has to," she whispered, staring at the girl who had dared to help her—and at a greater cost to herself. "She has little ones who need her. Jasmine wouldn't let anything take her from them."

Jasmine's niece and nephew meant the world to her. There's no way her feisty friend would die from something as common as a fever. She couldn't. It wouldn't be right. Sage's mind turned to the twins. Where were they?

"I need to speak to Tehl." She turned back to her parents. "Better yet, take me to him."

"You've just awoken." Mira placed her hands on Sage's linen-clad hips, causing her to pause. "You're not well enough for that. I refuse to nurse you back to health again because of your bullheadedness."

Sage recognized her friend's stubborn stance from prior times. There would be no changing Mira's mind. Her gaze narrowed on the Healer, Mira's attire dawning on her. She wore only a shift. "Are you warming her?" Mira had done something similar for Sage when she was sick with fever.

"Yes," Mira replied. "Her fever is causing wretched shivers. I've had to place a thin cloth between her teeth, so she doesn't break them."

The heat at her back shifted as Nali repositioned herself behind Sage. Her gaze moved to the feline who eyed her through the slits of her eyes. "Maybe she won't need you anymore. I have something better."

Mira arched a blond brow. "You need your leren to keep yourself warm."

"I am in better health than Jasmine. Nali can help her more than myself."

"No."

The command in Mira's tone gave Sage pause. She peeked at the healer through her lashes. "You presume to give me commands?"

Mira raised a brow at her haughty tone. "I'm your healer and your friend. I will not let you jeopardize yourself because you feel guilty for the other girl. You are my priority."

Sage gaped at her friend. "I am healed."

Her friend snorted. "You're not healed. I bet you can't even stand by yourself."

She narrowed her eyes on the blond at the challenge, hating that she was right.

"What about a compromise?" her mum offered. "Nali can be split between the two of you."

"I think we're ignoring the most important being in this problem," her papa murmured. He lifted his chin toward Nali. "It's her decision. She hasn't done a damn thing except for what she wanted to for the last few days."

That was true. Nali only did what she wanted.

"Nali," Sage murmured, stroking her head and left ear. "Would you help Jasmine?"

The feline's eyes slid toward Jas. It still amazed her how intelligent leren were. It was almost as if she understood every word she said.

Nali's golden gaze moved back toward her, and she chuffed before lazily stretching and arching her back. She hopped down from Sage's cot, causing it to rock with her weight, and slunk around Jasmine's cot. The leren sniffed Jasmine's hair and sat staring straight at Mira.

"I think that's my cue to make room for her," Mira muttered. She rushed to Jasmine's cot and scooted the girl to the left side to make room for the massive feline.

With care, Nali climbed onto the cot, dwarfing it, and settled. Immediately, Jas moaned and turned toward the leren. Nali nuzzled the girl and then laid her head on her paws, her eyes shut.

"Well that settles that," Mira said, placing a hand on Jasmine's forehead. Her lips pursed as she pulled her hand away and tugged the blanket up over Jas.

"Any improvement?" Sage asked, already knowing the answer.

"None, but with Nali's help, that will soon change," Mira said brightly. Too brightly.

Sage glanced away from Jas to stare at her hands in her lap. How many times would she put Jasmine in danger? Would this time kill her? Her hands curled into fists, her nails biting into her palm. She couldn't break down now. Mira knew what she was doing. If it was within the Healer's power, she would do it. As much as it killed her, now was not the time to worry about Jas. The warlord would have plans already in motion. No doubt Zane would—

Her body stiffened, and her breath froze in her lungs.

Zane. She'd used his name. Stars above, she was going to be sick.

"Love?" Her mum's voice echoed around her, distorted.

"I'm going to be sick," she mumbled through numb lips.

She'd used his name, like a friend, like a lover. A bowl appeared in front of her right before she retched. Tears dripped down her face, her shame and disgust threatening to swallow her whole. After everything he'd done, she'd used his name? Maybe she was as depraved as he was.

Sage panted and her lips quivered as small sobs escaped her. Large arms wrapped around her, and she gagged. "Don't touch me," she whispered.

The arms immediately disappeared. "I'm sorry, baby girl." Her papa's voice was deep and near her ear, pain evident in his tone.

She squeezed her eyes closed as more bile flooded her mouth. Poison. She was tainted by poison. Even now, poison was leaking from her, tainting everything around her, hurting those she loved.

Her gasping breaths came harder, and stars danced across her vision.

"Sage?"

She shuddered and squeezed her eyes tighter. Why wouldn't Tehl go away? Why did he always come back when she was at her worst?

"Look at me, Sage," Tehl said more firmly.

No, she wouldn't. She couldn't. He was just a figment of her imagination.

"If you won't look at me, then breathe with me."

She dropped her chin to her chest and tried to slow her breathing to match his slow, deep ones. Each breath felt like she was suffocating. Her lungs burned, and her heart raced.

"I can't," she gasped out.

"You can, and you will."

His comment cut through all the vile emotions rolling inside of her. He was right. She wouldn't die right now. She had to calm down.

Sage started counting down from one hundred to calm herself. Painfully, she sucked in deep breath after deep breath, her inhales and exhales lasting five counts each. By the time she reached twenty, her heart had slowed, and her breath came in steady gusts.

Fingers brushed her knuckles in a fleeting touch, and she jerked backward, rocking the cot. She curled her hands around the edge of the cot to steady herself. She wouldn't risk anyone else by letting them touch her. Just being near her was dangerous enough.

"I'm sorry," Tehl said softly, his deep voice curling around her. "You need to open your eyes."

"Are you real?" she muttered.

"I'm as real as your family and that giant man-eater eyeing me."

His comment caused her lips to twitch. Tehl always told her the truth and protected her. If he said he was real, he was. If he said she should open her eyes, she needed to do it.

One at a time, she opened each eye and stared at the bowl in her lap, the scent of her vomit reaching her. She swallowed thickly as a masculine hand pulled it from her lap. Her eyes snapped shut. The last time they'd shared eye contact, she was being paraded around as the warlord's conquest. Guilt and shame weighed heavily on her.

"Come, now. Look at me."

Her mind flashed to the fuzzy memory of him reaching his hand out toward her while Nali stood between them. If he could face a leren for her, she could face her family and her fear for him. There wasn't room to be a coward. There was no place for it in her life.

Sage lifted her chin and forced her eyes open. He stared back at her, a black lock of hair dangling in front of his face. He watched her, but made no move toward her. She glanced to the side, her family observing her with worry. Slowly, she turned back to Tehl. What if this was all a dream?

One by one, she uncurled the fingers of her right hand from the cot and reached out. She expected him to move forward, but he held still. Her hand hovered in the air for a moment before she steeled herself and brushed the wayward lock of hair from his face.

Her breath stuttered out of her lungs as the silk of his hair slipped through her fingers. He was real. He was here. With her. His smile bloomed across his face, making him so beautiful her eyes hurt. Her gaze moved from his deep blue eyes to her scratched pale hand resting against his cheek.

He was beautiful, and she was beastly.

She snatched her hand back and held it against her chest and then held it out in front of her. Even though the skin was damaged, she knew it would heal into flawless smooth pale skin like her injuries had never happened.

Sage curled her hand into a fist. She was defiled, sullied, rotten, no matter how flawless she appeared. No one could remove the stain on her soul. The wounds that bled freely inside her soul would turn into ugly scars. Her eyes flickered to Tehl. She shouldn't be allowed to mar him by touching him. She wasn't fit to be in anyone's company.

His smile dimmed and the sadness that entered his gaze made her want to slap his face. She didn't want his sadness, his pity. She wanted his hate, his revulsion. That would make this whole situation easier. She could handle those emotions.

"Don't let him win," Tehl breathed.

His words were barely audible, but she heard them nonetheless.

Sage closed her eyes and dropped her head, sucking in a deep breath. He was right. What was important was the monster coming for them. They didn't have a second to lose. Each moment she let pass by, floundering in despair, was another life potentially lost.

Her brows furrowed as she pictured each horror that taunted her, each pain that she felt, as a single light in her mind. One by one, she extinguished them, a cool, disconnected feeling coming over her. As long as she kept herself numb, they *might* be able to get through this.

She slowly registered the overwhelming heat licking at her clammy skin, and the intense silence that hovered in the room like low clouds before a storm.

Sage waited patiently until all of the lights were firmly gone before she opened her eyes to meet Tehl's concerned gaze. Throwing her shoulders back and lifting her chin, she stared him down, uttering the words that threatened to lodge themselves in her throat.

"He comes. We need to prepare for battle."

SIX

SAGE

TEHL JUST STARED AT HER, with no reaction to her words. Did he not understand the significance of what she said?

"Did you hear me?" she asked softly.

Tehl blinked. "I heard you."

"And?"

"It's being taken care of."

One sentence. One measly line of information. "How?" she bit out.

An emotion flickered in his eyes before he shifted his gaze to the floor. "I have men working on this as we speak." He looked at her through his dark lashes. "Don't concern yourself about it. All you have to do is make sure you heal."

He had spoken the right words, and yet her gut rolled. He was shutting her out. Hiding things.

Sage slowly stood on wobbly legs, anger igniting in her belly. Her mum reached out for her, but she brushed her hand away and stared at the man kneeling before her. "You will not keep me in the dark," she said. "Stop hiding things from me."

Tehl blew out a breath. "I'm not hiding things from you." He rocked back on his heels and stood, towering above her. "Please get back into bed."

It was a reasonable request, yet everything inside her chafed at his words. "No," she said. "You will not tell me what to do!" The venom she heard in her own voice shocked her. "I refuse to be left in the dark," she said again. "If I had not been left in the dark about Rhys's disappearance, things might have been very different."

Tehl's face fell. She winced but didn't take back her words. It was plain that the words pierced her husband. They were ugly, but true.

"Love," her mum murmured, brushing a hand down her arm. "Tehl wants what's best for you, as do we all. Everything will be taken care of. Why don't you lie down and calm yourself?"

She flicked a glance to her mum. "I am calm." And she was. "You haven't seen me upset."

"What do you want to know?" Tehl asked, his voice soft.

She faced him and lifted her chin. "Everything."

A small smile tugged at his lips. "That's a very long list. Start with a smaller request, for my sake."

Her mind raced. What did she really want to know? "Has the border been protected?"

A nod. "Reinforcements have been stationed along the entire wall. No one will get through without someone seeing."

That was doubtful. If the Scythians didn't want to be seen, they wouldn't be. She'd experienced it firsthand. But something was better than nothing.

Sage glance at Jas sleeping fitfully. Where was her other friend? "Where's Blaise?"

"With Sam."

How nonspecific. *Again.* Her eyes narrowed on her husband. "She's not in the prison, is she?"

"No."

"*Where* is she?" Words were tricky things. You could make one believe the complete opposite of what your words actually meant with a flick of the tongue. Everything was in the details.

"She's in the war room with Sam. She's giving him information on Scythia."

Sage arched a brow at him. "Willingly?"

"Last time I checked," he said with humor.

Her breath caught, and some emotion leaked through. Stars above, he was handsome when he smiled. Her lips thinned at that thought. Smiles couldn't be trusted. Smiles hid a numerous amount of falsehoods, even if it was Tehl.

"I want to see her."

He dipped his chin. "I'll fetch her at once," he acquiesced. "Is there anything else you need?"

"Many things, but nothing you can give me."

His smiled slipped as a steely glint entered his blue eyes. "I'll only bring her on one condition."

Her jaw clenched. *Here it was, the bargaining tool.*

"You need to rest and stay here."

"You cannot cage me," she growled. She'd go wherever she pleased.

He held up his hands. "I would never cage you."

"You already have." Sage snapped her mouth shut, hating the biting words she'd thrown at him like daggers. Why was she acting this way? They'd moved past all of this.

Tehl winced. "I wish I could erase our past, but I can't. I can give you my oath that I will do whatever is in my power to make sure you never feel caged again, if only you would let me."

"Why are you keeping me here?"

"Because you're not healthy," Tehl muttered. "And I made a promise before all of this I'd see you healthy and whole." A pause. "And I need you."

That was unexpected. She blinked. "Why?"

"Because you are the key to helping us win the war."

Everyone always wanted something from her.

Skepticism must have shown in her expression, because he continued. "And because you balance me."

"How?" All she did was bring chaos into his life.

Tehl shifted on his feet as if uncomfortable, but never looked away. "I see the world a certain way, and the way you see it is completely different. Having you rule by my side will make Aermia better. *You* make me better." Her traitorous heart tripped at his self-deprecating smile. "I've been told I'm too blunt."

"I prefer blunt," she blurted. And she did. She'd had enough secrets and betrayal for several lifetimes.

"And that's why I'll tell you the truth, even when I think it will hurt you.

We both are brutally honest. It's a blessing and a curse."

Honesty. What a strange word. When was the last time she'd experienced something honest? Pure? Bitterness flooded her. She wasn't even sure she knew what purity was anymore. "Are you sure you know what honesty is?" They'd had their fair share of deceit between them.

"Sage," her mum chastised.

Tehl held a hand up. "It's okay. She's allowed to speak her mind." He moved closer, causing her pulse to spike. "My mum taught me of honesty, and you know how much I loved her. Would I besmirch her memory?"

She knew the answer. "No."

"No. If I make a promise to you, I will keep it." He scanned her face. "Now, will you compromise with me? I need your help for what is ahead of us, but we can't do that if you're sick. Promise me you'll get back into bed?"

Part of her didn't want to compromise, hated that she had to bow to his wishes, but her logical side understood he was right. Her legs shook beneath her, and, soon, they would collapse from her weight. As much as she wanted to jump into the thick of things, she wasn't at her best. Sage crossed her arms. "I will get back into bed if you bring Blaise to me."

"It will be done."

"Now." Specifics mattered.

"Now," he repeated. He slowly held his hand out, palm up.

Sage stared at it. It should've been an easy thing to take his hand, but it wasn't. *You're not worthy of touching him.* She'd made too many mistakes.

"It's just a hand."

If only he knew. It was so much more. She wasn't good anymore. She was poison.

"I won't leave until you take it."

She studied the stubborn slant of his jaw and bit her lip. He was as stubborn as she was. If she didn't take his hand, he'd stand there for the rest of the day. Her left leg buckled, and she locked her knees to keep standing. Sage puffed out a breath and steeled herself. Holding his hand wasn't as bad as possibly collapsing in front of him and allowing him to see how weak she really was.

Sage pulled her right hand from her chest and lightly placed her hand in his. She forced herself to stay still as his calloused thumb brushed over hers in a gentle caress, and then he leaned closer and placed a feather-light kiss on the back of each of her hands.

Tears pricked the back of her eyes. Each touch was tender and careful, like he was worried she'd run away. But really, it was the complete opposite. It made her want to jump into his arms and never leave. He was her safety, but she was his death. She'd hurt him if she allowed herself to get too close.

She pulled her hand from his and avoided his gaze, focusing on the blanket hanging over the edge of her cot. "Blaise?"

"I'll bring her to you."

"Thank you," she said.

"You're welcome, love."

The floor blurred as Tehl left the room. *Love.* He'd called her love. A fat tear escaped her left eye. Love was what started this whole mess. Love twisted people. Love was death.

SEVEN

TEHL

HE STRODE DOWN THE HALLWAY, relief and anger warring inside him.

When he'd walked in and she was awake with color in her cheeks, a knot had loosened in his chest. Blaise had spoken the truth. Sage had healed at a remarkable rate. He was both grateful and disgusted. Grateful that she hadn't died, but disgusted that the warlord still had an effect on her even though she was far from him.

His teeth ground together as he thought of how she'd panicked and then completely blanked out. It was like her light had gone out. All feelings and warmth just disappeared in a breath.

Tehl nodded to a servant who bobbed a quick curtsey before scurrying along. His brows furrowed as he glanced over his shoulder, and the servant disappeared around the corner. He'd been in such a black mood since Sage had been taken that hardly any of the servants looked him in the eye anymore. Another one of his sins to atone for. They didn't deserve his anger.

He tucked his thoughts away as he strode into the war room and skirted around the table, ignoring the heated argument and the bows that followed in his wake. There wasn't anything he could do to change his past actions, but, from today on, he could be better.

He caught his father's attention as their advisors began to argue again. The king rolled his eyes as Tehl sat down and clapped him on the shoulder.

"Son."

"Father."

It was odd having his father here after his prolonged absence. Odd, but not unwelcome. If they were to survive the upcoming war, they needed every man, especially their king.

Tehl focused on their advisors. Jeren was red in the face, but that wasn't new; the man was perpetually angry.

"What's going on? What's Jeren angry about this time?"

"Jeren is arguing for throwing the Scythian woman in the prison."

Tehl straightened and zeroed in on Blaise, who sat five seats down from him on his left. Her fingers clenched around the arms of the chair as Jeren said something particularly rude. Surprise flickered through him, though, when Rafe slid a hand over the top of her left curled fist. Her head whipped to the side, and she hissed at him quietly, pulling her hand from his. Interesting. What was that about?

"You can't expect us to believe that you'd help your enemy," Jeren accused, "and become a traitor for nothing. Why have you come here? To spy?"

"How long has this been going on?" Tehl whispered out of the corner of his mouth.

"Going on twenty minutes," his father answered.

"And why have you let it go on for so long?" The whole thing seemed a bit ridiculous. Blaise had already proven her loyalty.

"Because our advisers had a valid point that needs to be argued. *We* both know she's not here to harm us, but they don't. They deserve to have their say, and I'm curious how much it will take to crack her," his father murmured. "She seems most unflappable, but there's an undercurrent of rage flowing just below the surface."

"She won't crack," Tehl muttered, watching the drama unfold as the voices rose. "She was in our prison for months." They'd tried everything, and nothing had worked.

"But you didn't have him with you," his father remarked, glancing in Rafe's direction. "He seems…very protective of her."

Tehl studied the rebellion leader, noting how close he sat to Blaise. Rafe shifted in his seat, causing Blaise to glare at him and scoot closer to Sam. That in itself was interesting, but what intrigued Tehl even more was the dangerous expression Rafe was aiming at Jeren.

"He's angry," Tehl commented. That was an understatement. He looked like he wanted to rip the advisor's head off.

"Indeed," his father said softly. "Why do you think that is?"

His gaze slid to Blaise who sat so still she looked to be carved from stone, completely ignoring the giant of a man by her side. "She's rebuffed his help."

"Every man hates when a woman won't let him protect her," his father commented. "Especially when he considers her *his*."

Tehl's brows rose. Now, that was an interesting turn of events. Blaise and Rafe? Well, more like just Rafe. Blaise was doing everything in her power to ignore the rebellion leader.

"Who knows how much we can trust you?" Lelbiel commented, interrupting Tehl's thoughts. "We don't know you. How can we be sure you weren't part of the plot to hurt the princess?"

Blaise slapped her hands against the table and stood from her chair, her body vibrating with anger. "How dare you?" she hissed.

His advisor wrinkled his nose. "It was a valid question, my lady."

She leaned forward, her gaze locked on Lelbiel. "I would never, *never* hurt Sage. That woman has been through more horrors than all of you put together, but not by my hand." She scanned the table. "Some of you were even a part of those horrors," she accused. "I refuse to be lumped in with that sick monster on Scythia's throne. We may share the same bloodline, but he is *not* my family."

William steepled his finger and met Blaise's penetrating gaze. "We're not blaming you, my lady."

"It sounds like it," Rafe growled.

Blaise glared at the rebellion leader, and then focused back on William.

"I understand your frustration. We know what you've done for our princess." He held his hands out. "Please understand our position, though. How would you react if an enemy found their way into your inner circle? Not only that, but they were from the royal line and claimed to renounce their kingdom? It sounds a little far-fetched, doesn't it?"

Blaise chuckled and straightened, crossing her arms. "As much as an immortal king creating a perfect race of enhanced people?"

Silence met her statement.

Her gaze swept the table, and she paused on Tehl. "I am here because it is right to be. My people live in fear. Death and cruelty occur all too often." She pushed back her heavy, braided black hair and bowed at the waist. "I am here to help and serve Aermia in the dangerous time ahead. If the warlord continues to rule, both our peoples will cease to exist. His tyranny cannot continue."

"Agreed," Tehl said. "Are you prepared to fight against your own people? You will be branded a traitor. Think carefully. Words are easily said. Action is much more difficult."

She straightened, her lips thinning. "I have already been branded a traitor. The decision's already been made. The moment I cross into Scythia will mean my death." Her expression hardened. "And anyone who stands with that monster are not my people."

A quiet descended over the room at her declaration.

Tehl's father slowly stood and stepped down from his seat. Blaise warily watched him as he approached her. She crossed her arms over her chest and sketched a bow. "Your highness," she murmured.

"There's no need for that," his father rumbled, taking her hand. "You're as much a royal as I am, my lady."

Tehl hid a smile as Blaise blinked, clearly not expecting his gracious words. That was the thing about his father, he could charm almost anyone.

"I thank you," she said, still gaping at the king.

His father patted her on the hand. "You've made an immense sacrifice for my family. It will not be forgotten any time soon. Aermia will gladly accept your help, and, what's more, we'll support you after we rid the world of the warlord. Scythia could stand to have a leader like you on the throne."

Her eyes widened at the oath, and she glanced over his father's shoulder at Tehl for confirmation.

"It will be done." It was only fair they do what they could for her after the sacrifice she'd made and would still make. Logically, it was brilliant. If Blaise took the throne, they'd have an ally in Scythia for the first time in hundreds of years.

"Thank you," she said to his father. "I accept your offer."

Chills erupted on his arms. In that moment, they'd made history. Aermia had formed an alliance with Scythia. Never in his lifetime had Tehl guessed such a thing was possible. It was surreal.

His father released her hand and turned to the table. "Lelbiel, draft up an alliance. I'd like it in my office by tomorrow morning." He paused and scanned the table of men. "We've changed the course of history today. Now we have to prepare for it."

The men nodded around the table.

"We'll meet again tomorrow to discuss and sign the treaty." The king turned back to Blaise. "As long as that's acceptable to you?"

She looked startled at his attention to her. "It is."

The king smiled at Blaise. "It's settled then. Until tomorrow."

The Scythian woman blinked, and an answering smile adorned her face. It was all Tehl could do not to gape. He snapped his jaw closed and blinked several times. She was usually so stoic and grave. When Blaise really smiled, it transformed her into a completely different woman, and he wasn't the only one to notice. Rafe openly stared, his entire being homed in on her. But she seemed oblivious, smiling prettily at the king.

"I look forward to it, your highness," she murmured.

His father grinned down at Blaise and waved a hand at the table. "The rest of you are dismissed."

The men around the table reluctantly stood and filed toward the doors. Zachael stretched in his chair and stood, making his way toward Tehl. "Any change in Sage?" he asked, leaning a hip against the table.

"She's awake." That was the best news he had.

The weapons master clapped his hands together and smiled. "That's wonderful news. I knew she'd pull through. Our girl would never let sickness take her from us."

Tehl swallowed hard, loathing the way he felt thankful that the warlord had given Sage a draught and yet hating it at the same time.

Zachael eyed him and placed a hand on his shoulder. "Focus on your gratefulness, so your anger doesn't tear you apart."

He blew out a breath. "How do you always know what I'm thinking? It's uncanny."

"I've had a hand in raising you, my lord."

"That's the truth if I ever heard it," Garreth said, limping closer. "We basically lived in the training ring for years."

Tehl forced himself not to focus on his friend's shuffling gait. It hurt to watch each painful movement. No matter how much Garreth tried to hide it, the pain still showed through. "Brothers in arms." He held his forearm out.

"Absolutely," Garreth said, clasping forearms. "How is our princess?"

"Awake." He glanced over to Blaise, who had turned in their direction.

"She's awake?" she asked, concern plainly on her face.

"Yes, and she's asking for you."

"Then I better go to her." She turned on her heel.

He pushed from his chair and strode after her. "I'll escort you. I promised I'd bring you to her." This was not a promise he'd break.

Blaise glanced over her shoulder, a black brow arched. "In exchange for what? What deal did you strike with her to keep her in bed?"

Tehl scowled, holding his arm out for her. "Why must everything be an exchange?"

"Because you're both much too stubborn, from what I hear."

"Rumors," he muttered as she waved away his arm and followed him to the door.

"I'm sure," she replied sarcastically.

Their journey back to the infirmary lapsed into silence, but it wasn't uncomfortable. Tehl always cherished a companion who didn't need to fill the silence with chatter. Blaise seemed to be of the same mind.

"How is she really?" she asked when they neared the infirmary.

He wouldn't sugarcoat it. "Disoriented. Cold. Anxious."

Blaise opened and closed her mouth before staying silent.

Clearly, she wanted to speak.

"Just tell me," he sighed. "I prefer the truth, even if it is blunt and harsh."

"She won't be the same person as before," she cautioned.

He already knew that. "I know."

"The girl you married is dead. My uncle will have made sure of that. He—" She paused in the quiet hallway, squeezing her eyes closed. "He is an expert in breaking people and reshaping them into what he desires them to be."

"Sage is strong."

"She is, but he is old, calculating, and vicious. I'm amazed she was able to function at all when we escaped." Blaise hung her head.

A rock sunk in his gut. "What are you saying?"

She exhaled heavily. "I'm saying that every step you make needs to be a calculation, it needs to be for her benefit. If she gets in too deep, you have to pull her from the water. Your burden might be too much for her to bear now."

Understanding dawned. "You don't think she can rule."

"I don't know," she whispered, her dark eyes sad. "Maybe she will be able to. I only understand the warlord. What he's capable of." She sighed. "Nothing will be all right for a long time, if ever. Prepare yourself for that or let her go."

"Let her go? Like a divorce?" he asked, the words tasting like ash on his tongue. He'd never divorce her. She was his wife even if she was changed, suffering damage. They were bound, and he wouldn't abandon her.

"No, not a divorce. I meant you'll have to put her in a country home to live out her life in peace. She deserves that." A shrug. "If she can't handle ruling, that will be the best option for her, instead of letting her waste away in some tower in this castle. She'd be miserable there."

He hated the idea outright. Hated it. He'd grown accustomed to Sage, and, what's more, he loved her family. They'd become part of his own family while she was gone. If she was gone, it would tear another hole in his. He glanced to the side. None of that mattered. No matter how he felt about it, if it was the best thing for Sage, he'd do it. That was what you did for your family, and there was no one who deserved it more.

"If that's what she wants, I will do it. But I won't force anything on her."

Blaise studied him, her head cocked. "I was taught that the princes of Aermia were monsters. In my mind, I found it hard to imagine anything worse than the warlord." A dark smile. "Which is why he always hated me. But, after spending months in your dungeon, I realized one important thing."

"What was that?" he asked, not knowing where the conversation was going.

"That no matter how much the warlord tried to turn himself into the hero, he was always the villain. And no matter how much I tried to turn you into the villain, you were the hero." She held his gaze. "You're not what I expected, Tehl Ramses, and you treated me better than I deserve after what I did to that village." She swallowed hard. "I'm sorry for my part in hurting your people."

An apology. He didn't expect that.

"We have all done things we aren't proud of. It's how we fix those mistakes that is important. And, by my account, you've done everything in your power to atone for those things. You not only have my forgiveness, but my thanks," he said roughly. Sage would still be stuck in that hellhole if it hadn't been for Blaise and Maeve.

"I don't deserve it," she said, shaking her head.

"No one deserves forgiveness. That's what makes it so special." His mother had taught him that.

"I'll keep that in mind." She smiled at him and held her hand out. "Allies?"

He clasped her small hand. "Brothers in arms."

She flashed her teeth in a grin. "Sisters in arms."

Tehl smiled. No wonder Sage liked the fiery Scythian woman. She was a lot like his wife.

EIGHT

SAGE

SHE WANTED OUT OF THE bed and the room.

"Haven't you slept enough?" a familiar voice asked.

Sage glanced to the side, and she smiled. "Blaise."

The Scythian woman grinned at her from her chair. "I thought you were never going to wake up."

Slowly, Sage pushed herself up from her cot and brushed a strand of hair from her face. "It's the only thing I'm allowed to do, apparently," she grumbled.

Blaise stood and sat on the edge of the cot, patting her foot through the thick blanket. "You need to heal. That takes time."

"I know." And she did. Her legs had collapsed out from under her almost the moment Tehl left, and she'd been weak as a kitten since. Sage slid her hand over her friend's and squeezed before releasing it. "I'm so glad you're okay."

A wry smile. "Not much can hurt me."

Red flashed across Sage's vision. "There was so much blood." She shook her head to dispel the memory. "The last time I saw you, I thought you would die. How did you survive such a beating?"

Emotions rippled over Blaise's face. "There's not much I can't survive." A shrug. "I'm Scythian. I was bred to survive, and I've been through worse."

That broke her heart. Blaise caught her expression and shook her head.

"It is what it is."

That bastard had scarred more than just Sage.

Blaise glanced over her shoulder at Jasmine. "How is she?"

Sage glanced at her sleeping friend, frowning. Mira hadn't been able to hide her concern. If Mira was concerned about Jasmine, her condition was dangerous. "She's not well," she admitted. "But, with time, I'm sure she'll get better. Plus, Nali will help."

The feline's ear twitched at her name, but Nali otherwise made no move but to cuddle closer to the shivering Jasmine.

"She doesn't deserve this fate," Blaise growled.

"No, she doesn't," Sage whispered. Who knew how long Jasmine's body could survive such a fever? It had to break. It had to. A wave of sorrow and guilt moved through her. Sage ruthlessly shoved her feelings down. They wouldn't change anything. The best she could do was hope and pray.

Sage exhaled and focused on Blaise. "Have you been taken care of?"

"My care has been excellent."

"I can see with my own two eyes that you're fine physically," Sage said. "I meant, are they being kind to you?" Harsh words could be worse than a beating.

"By 'they,' do you mean the royals?" Blaise asked, picking at her nails.

"By the stars, you know how to skirt an issue," Sage muttered. "Sam would be proud."

"I'm sure after the few months I spent in the dungeon, he understands my gift of avoidance."

Sage rolled her eyes. If they beat around the bush, she'd fall asleep before she got the information she wanted. "Is the Crown forcing you to do anything you don't want to?" she demanded. "If so, I will march from this room and fix it right now." And she would as soon as her legs stopped shaking.

Blaise chuckled. "I'm sure you would, and it would be a sight to see, but don't worry yourself. Your royals can't make me do anything I don't want to."

"You don't have to help us." Sage exhaled and said what she'd been rehearsing in her mind for the last half an hour. "You are Scythian, and you're a wealth of knowledge, but you hold no allegiance to Aermia. I will not force you to help us, nor will I allow the Crown or council to either. You helped me escape that prison," she said thickly. "That I can never repay. You have my everlasting gratitude."

The Scythian woman cocked her head, her dark braids sliding over her shoulder. "You aren't the only one. You could've left me in the jungle."

"No, I couldn't have." No one deserved that fate. She would've killed Blaise before she allowed *him* to take her.

A shrug. "Anyone I know would have."

She scowled. "Then you've surrounded yourself with the wrong people."

"That matters not," Blaise said. "I am thankful nonetheless. You risked yourself for me. If the warlord had caught me, my fate would've been worse than death."

Sage breathed heavily, and bile flooded her mouth. She understood better than anyone what he would've done. Blaise would've suffered in an inhuman way.

"For that reason," Blaise soldiered on, "I give you my friendship and fealty."

Sage swallowed and shook her head. "You don't owe me anything. As far as I'm concerned, we are equal."

"I want to help. That monster needs to be destroyed."

The room spun, but Sage held on, gritting her teeth. "This is a serious decision. You'll have to fight your own people."

"So be it. The sacrifice will be worth the reward."

"It will be a thankless job." Sage's people would be suspicious of her. In their minds, Scythians were the monsters underneath the bed. Overcoming prejudice and deep-seated fear was no easy task.

"Indeed." Blaise grinned. "Your council wasn't too happy with me today."

Sage's brows rose. "You were at a war meeting today?"

"It was more of a trial."

"Surely someone stood up for you?" Sage gritted her teeth. Someone better have.

"A few, but the majority watched me with contempt and suspicion." Blaise waved off Sage when she opened her mouth to retort. "I'm the enemy who ended up in their inner circle. I would've been suspicious as well. I will win them over. It's only a matter of time. Despite their prejudice and wariness, they know how useful I will be to them." She flashed Sage a smile that looked so much like Maeve.

Maeve. Was the older woman okay? What kind of horrors would the warlord unleash on her? Shame washed over Sage for not thinking about her sooner. "Do you think your mother is all right?" she asked softly.

Blaise sucked in her cheeks and nodded. "My mother is wise and clever. I doubt he has figured out who helped you, but the entire court will be under scrutiny from now on. It will be very dangerous at court."

Sage shivered and rubbed her arms. Even thinking about Scythia caused her skin to crawl. Her brows furrowed as she glanced around the room, realizing it was quite empty. "Where are my parents?" They promised they wouldn't leave. It was unlike them to break such an oath.

"Your mum needed a bath, your father is waiting outside of the infirmary, and the healer is fetching Lilja."

Some tension drained from her body. "Oh."

Blaise shuffled to a stand and hugged her. "Colm seemed to think we needed privacy. I'll be back soon."

"You'll keep me apprised of what's going on?"

Her Scythian friend grinned wickedly. "Why, princess, are you asking me to spy for you?"

"It's not spying if you should be there in the first place," Sage called as Blaise moved toward the door.

"True," her friend said. "I'll let your father in."

"Thank you, Blaise."

She paused in the doorway and bowed her head. "My pleasure, my friend," she said before disappearing out the door.

A moment later, the door creaked open and her papa peeked in, his gray-streaked, brown hair tousled. "Hey, love, you have company." He pushed open the door, and Mira bustled in, followed by Lilja and Hayjen.

There was no stopping the tears that always seemed to be lurking in the corners of her eyes. "Lilja," she cried.

The Sirenidae rushed to her side and threw her arms wide, wrapping them around her. A citrus aroma surrounded her as Sage pressed her face into Lilja's silvery white hair. "Stars above, I missed you."

"I missed you, too, ma fleur," Lilja whispered, her words rough.

Huge arms circled both herself and Lilja, and her eyes sprung open. She lifted her head and smiled at Hayjen whose ice-blue eyes were surprisingly wet.

"It's so good to see you Sage," her burly friend rasped.

Lilja pulled back and pressed her long, graceful fingers against either side of Sage's face. "My heart is so happy to see those beautiful green eyes." She wiped her tracks of tears from her face only to have new ones appear. "Ma fleur, I dare say it's the most beautiful thing I've ever seen."

"I didn't think I'd ever see you again." The words hurt coming out, but they were the ugly truth.

Sage stared at Lilja's face, and, to her horror, another face imposed over hers. Her breath hitched when Lilja blurred into Ezra. Her heart began to race, and she couldn't tear her eyes away from the apparition before her.

"I'm sorry," she whispered. "I'm so sorry."

Ezra smiled, blood trickling from his mouth.

"Sage?" a distorted voice asked.

She tried to blink to dispel the nightmare, but she was frozen in place. He gurgled something that she didn't understand. If only she could help him.

"I'm so sorry," she sobbed, wishing the memory would release her.

Fingers dug into her shoulders and shook her roughly. She blinked hard and tore her eyes from Ezra, staring up into Hayjen's very-worried face.

"Can you hear me?" he asked softly.

Her bottom lip trembled as she nodded her head, *yes*. More tears flooded her eyes as she stared at her friend, not daring to look in Lilja's direction. She'd gone crazy. Specters of people haunted her everywhere she turned. There was no escape.

"Your eyes blanked, and we couldn't reach you. I'm sorry I shook you." Hayjen touched her cheek and knelt on the side of her cot, rubbing Sage's left hand between his. "Your hands are so cold."

Like her soul. Everything inside her was cold. If only it would numb the pain that plagued her. The guilt. The shame.

"Ma fleur?"

Sage slammed her eyes closed and held her right hand out to Lilja. The Sirenidae clasped her trembling fingers between her own. Maybe if she didn't look at her, it wouldn't happen again. She couldn't handle seeing Ezra again, reliving that moment. Each minute was a struggle to hold on. Memories crashed into her, one after another, threatening to drown her.

"I'm fine," she whispered. It was a pretty lie.

Lilja squeezed her hand. "What happened?"

Death. Her past sins and demons were catching up with her. "Memories," she choked out.

"Oh, Sage," Lilja said, her voice breaking.

Sage turned back to Hayjen and opened her eyes to stare into his sad face. If she was her normal self, she would've hated the pity and sorrow in his eyes, but, at that point, she was too tired to even care. He could pity her if he kept holding her hand and kept the monsters at bay. Pathetic, really.

Mira stepped next to Hayjen's right side and leaned close to place a bottle of warmed water underneath the blankets.

"Thank you," Sage said, grateful for the heat now suffusing her body.

"Anything for you, sis," Mira said with a smile.

Emotion clogged her throat for what felt like the umpteenth time. True friends were one in a million. They stuck around when things got bad, and, somehow, she'd managed to surround herself with so many wonderful people just like that.

"Look at all the visitors," a chipper voice exclaimed.

Sage peeked at the door, staring past Lilja's face at her mum, who bustled forward, her cheeks flushed, dark hair shiny and wet. She must have come straight from her bath without even drying her hair. Love and affection filled Sage. There was no one like her mum. She was the best.

Her mum pecked her papa on the cheek and then pushed in between Lilja and Hayjen. She cupped Sage's cheek and pressed a quick kiss to her forehead. "How's my favorite daughter?"

"I'm your only daughter," Sage said sarcastically, not missing a beat. Her mum had always said that since she and her brothers were children. She had her favorite daughter, favorite youngest son, and favorite oldest son.

It was nice to play at something normal, even if she felt far from it.

Her mum pulled back and cocked her head, frowning as she scanned Sage's face. "What's wrong?"

Everything. "Nothing." She forced a smile on to her lips.

"You can't lie to me, Sage Blackwell." Her mum stopped and grinned.

"Sage *Ramses*." Her smile dimmed. "You never have been able to. I can see it on your face. It's like you've seen a ghost."

Sage shivered. "Just memories."

Lilja's jaw clenched, her papa's fingers curled into fists, Hayjen stroked the back of her hand softly, and her mum hummed. Then Mira outright cursed.

"That bastard," Mira seethed. "If your family doesn't get to him first, I will."

Sage blinked. She didn't think she'd ever heard the blond healer curse.

"Get in line," Lilja whispered. The hard edge riding her voice caused Sage to shiver.

Mira scanned the group. "You're lucky to have such an amazing family."

"I am," Sage said.

Mira handed her a cup of tea. "I admit, I'm a little jealous. I never got to meet any of my aunts and uncles. They had died before I was born."

Sage slowly blinked. *Aunt and uncle?* What in the bloody hell? She glanced between her mum, papa, Lilja, and Hayjen.

Lilja stiffened and Hayjen stopped warming her hand, but no one corrected Mira. They just watched Sage as she processed the healer's words.

Lilja and Hayjen were really her family? How many more surprises could she take?

She sighed and settled on one simple word. "Why?"

Why had they kept this from her?

NİNE

SAGE

"I'M SO SORRY," MIRA MUMBLED miserably. "No one told me it was a secret."

Sage sat up straighter, swung her legs over the cot to face the group, and patted the healer's hand. "It's not your fault. You didn't know, and you're not the one who lied to me." Stars above, she hated secrets.

Mira's stricken face crumpled further, but she nodded and bustled toward her herbs, leaving the group in an awkward silence.

Sage eyed her family, reeling from the news. Why did they think they had to keep it a secret?

"Why?" she asked again, staring her mum down.

Her mum pursed her lips, but answered, "For protection."

What an opaque answer. "Protection from what?"

Her mum glanced to Hayjen but kept silent.

Sage's attention slid to her burly friend, and she scrutinized the person she thought she knew.

Lilja was clearly not her blood relation, so that left Hayjen. Her papa didn't have any siblings, and her mama's older brother died before Sage was born. Her eyes narrowed as she studied Hayjen. He looked close to her age, but she knew him to be much older, thanks to Lilja's special seaweed. He didn't exactly look like her mama, but the shape of his eyes, and the point of his nose hinted at…

Hayjen held her gaze, not looking away as she worked through each piece of the puzzle.

"So, you're my mother's brother?" she said softly.

He smiled and nodded. "I am. Older brother."

"By several years," her mum piped in with a smile.

Even though she knew what Lilja's herbs could do, her brain was having a hard time fathoming it. Hayjen looked like her mum's younger brother, maybe even her son, and yet he was older than she was. He looked like Seb. "Do my brothers know?"

"No," her papa said. "It's been too dangerous."

How long did they plan on keep the truth from her? "Were you going to tell me?" Was it just a happy circumstance that Mira said something she shouldn't?

"Of course," her mum replied. "We've always planned on telling you when the time was right."

"When the time was right?" Sage repeated. How convenient. "I would have said the time was right when you sent me to Lilja in the first place. Don't you think?"

"I asked her to keep silent," Lilja confessed.

Sage forced herself to look at the Sirenidae. Magenta eyes so foreign from her own gazed at her with affection. "Go on."

Her aunt patted her leg. "You understand why I hide myself, right?"

"You'd be hunted if others knew Sirenidae still existed." And they would. People were relentless when their anger and greed got a hold of them.

"Yes. People are greedy and desperate to live as long as they can and make the most out of the world they live in without consequence to others. But that's not the only reason we kept silent. It was to protect your family."

"Your family would've been outcasts," Hayjen said. "The old stories had a way of painting the Sirenidae people as monsters. No one would've come to the forge for anything. You'd have been forced out, and that's the best-case scenario."

Sage nodded. That made sense. It felt like years ago that she'd met Lilja, but hadn't that been her same response? Fear? "So, you lied."

Her mum nodded. "To protect those we love. It was a danger to them if we associated, and a danger to us." She leaned close and cupped Sage's cheek. "I was pregnant with you when they left the first time. We had more than just ourselves to worry about."

Hayjen squeezed Sage's right hand. "We didn't have another choice. The community knew your mum and me. I couldn't hide. It was too dangerous to stay when I didn't age any longer. So, I died."

"So, you died," she whispered, turning to her mum. "I saw you cry for him. You told me you missed your brother."

"And I did. He was my only family. He practically raised me."

"Couldn't you meet in secret?" Sage asked. Lilja's ship was perfect to hide people.

"We did for a while," Gwen explained. "But it became more dangerous after you and your brothers were born. We couldn't risk you remembering them. So," she sighed, "we wrote letters."

"Every couple of years I'd sneak to the forge and visit just long enough to see your mum and leave gifts," Hayjen said with a smile.

Her mind immediately went to the trunk that always sat at the end of her bed growing up, filled with trinkets and exotic gifts. So, that's how they afforded some of the things. Sage had always figured her parents squirreled gold away.

She glanced around the group. It still hurt that they hadn't told her the truth. They had lost so much time together. And if there was one thing she understood, it was that time was most precious. You never knew how much of it you'd have with someone.

"I would've kept quiet, you know," Sage said.

"Ma fleur, I know you would've," Lilja said, a tear sneaking out of the corner of her eye. "But, again, it was too dangerous. If anyone suspected a thing, your whole family would've been in jeopardy." Her aunt leveled her with a serious look. "You know, as well as I do, that information can be extracted."

Sage swallowed hard. She did. Everyone had a breaking point.

"Do you forgive us?" her mum asked.

"There's nothing to forgive. You were just doing what you thought was best. I don't necessarily agree with everything you did, but—" She shrugged.

"I don't know what I would've done in that situation. The only thing I'm upset about is all the lost time." She smiled at her family. "I would've loved growing up around the Sirenidae."

Lilja wiped her face and pulled her into a hug. "You're always welcome in my home."

"And what of the sea?" She'd love to go for another swim.

Her aunt pulled back with a grin. "As soon as you're well enough, I'll take you for a swim. The Leviathans are getting ready to have their pups."

If anyone else said that to Sage, she'd pass out from fear, but not Lilja. She had a wonderfully strange effect on the sea monsters. They acted almost as pets, and it was something to behold. She'd never forget swimming with the majestic creatures, or the peace of being in the embrace of the sea. Peace was something she severely lacked.

Her brows furrowed as a thought occurred to her. "Were any of the stories you told me of how you met true?"

"Some," Hayjen said. "If you have any questions, all you need to do is ask."

Her gaze dropped to his scarred wrists. "Were you a slave?"

"I was," he said gruffly. "Lilja saved me, though."

A chest-rattling cough interrupted them. She glanced over her shoulder at Jas. Even in the short period of time since this morning, she looked worse.

"Is there nothing you can do for her?" she asked Lilja.

"I've done everything I can. Her body is so weak."

Sage hung her head. "Will she die?"

"I don't know. Jacob, Mira, and myself are doing everything we can to undo what those animals did."

Jasmine being stabbed flashed through Sage's mind, momentarily blinding her. Dots moved across her vision and metal bit into her wrist while she screamed for her friend.

"Just breathe, ma fleur. The memories are just that, memories. They're not happening right now. They're not real."

"They're *very* real," Sage growled, her fingers clenching the sheet beneath her.

"They'll fade in time. I promise."

"How do you know?" None of hers had. Demons plagued her everywhere she looked, every time she closed her eyes.

"Because I've been there. I know what goes on and I *promise* you, it will fade. You'll heal."

A buzzing filled her ears as she blinked away the dots and focused on Lilja's sensual features. She couldn't have heard that right. "What do you mean you've 'been there'?"

"I was also held captive in Scythia, so I understand your pain."

Lilja said it so plainly. Like she was speaking about the weather, not the hell that Scythia was. Not like she'd just broken what was left of Sage's heart.

"When?" she rasped.

"At least thirty years ago."

Thirty years. Sage blinked. Lilja had known what was happening for thirty years and she'd done nothing. A blind rage filled her vision, and, before she knew what was happening, she'd slapped Lilja across the face. Her family gaped at her in shock, and she stared at her hand, wondering how it moved on its own.

Lilja touched her cheek and turned back to Sage, completely unruffled. "Anger is okay," she soothed. "It's okay to be angry."

It wasn't about anger. It was about betrayal. Her body began to tremble as she stared at Lilja. The creature in front of her had played human all these years and not stopped the monstrosities across the border. "You knew this entire time they were taking women? Hurting them? Using them as breeders?"

"Yes."

Bile burned her throat. She was just as guilty as the Scythians by doing nothing. "And yet you've done nothing?"

"That's not true," Hayjen spoke. "I was a slave headed to Scythia. My ship was full of women, and Lilja saved us all. We've been destroying their suppliers at sea for years, rescuing girls."

But they didn't save *her*. Her eyes slid to Jasmine. Or Jas. "This has been going on for years, and you've told no one?"

"Who would've believed them, love?" her mum asked gently. "They're pirates."

"The king would have," she spat. Marq never judged someone based on their appearance or their lot in life.

"Many went forward, but they were considered only rumors. They weren't important enough to garner attention," her uncle explained. "They needed proof. Solid witnesses."

"You're telling me that Poseidon's daughter wouldn't be received well by the king?" She shook her head at her family's startled looks. "Come now, don't be coy. I've done my studies and put the pieces of the puzzle together. Lilja could only come from the royal line. You had the power to make a change and you didn't." Sage stabbed a finger at Lilja. "You told me it was my responsibility to help if I was in the position to. You are a coward and a hypocrite." She cleared her throat to keep it from cracking, and gestured to her face. "If you had done as you asked me to months ago, this would not have happened."

"We can't change the past, love," her papa admonished.

"That I understand well." Her eyes began to well up. "But Lilja protected herself and the Sirenidae people, and, because of that, thousands have been tortured in…" Her breath hitched. "In unspeakable ways. Thousands more will die in the upcoming war."

"I'm so sorry you've been hurt." Lilja's voice cracked. "It kills me that you were hurt."

"Hurt?" she scoffed. "He didn't hurt me. He burnt me down to the ground and then formed me in the way that pleased him the most." She gagged while tears ran down her face. "How did you get out?" she found herself demanding. How had Lilja escaped that hell?

"I was given to a warrior and his men. One of them helped me escape."

A warrior helped her?

"Who?" What were the odds it was someone she knew?

"His name was Blair."

The nausea hit her, and she bent over the side of the cot, emptying the contents of her stomach. Blair, the man who'd tried to protect—but also hurt—her. The one with a pregnant slave at his side. She heaved again.

Mira slid a pot underneath her and held back her hair as she continued to retch.

"This is too much for her," Mira said sternly. "You need to leave."

Sage wiped the corners of her mouth and straightened, her bitterness and rage threatening to drown her. "He helped you escape?"

"Yes. Did you know him?" Lilja asked.

She cackled. "Oh, I knew him. He beat me regularly on our journey to Scythia. Even stripped me in front of his men."

Her mum gasped and began to cry, but Lilja didn't look away. Sage wanted her to, to be ashamed. To understand the pain and suffering she caused because of her inaction. "I can't abide to look at you," she said heatedly. "You are not my family, nor my friend. Get out, and don't come back."

"I will come back when you need me," Lilja said softly.

"Oh, you will," Sage said darkly. "War is coming, and I'll need your people to step up. They've hidden all these years, and it's time they faced the monster they've been hiding from and fight alongside the rest of us. You will aid me in that."

"Sage," Hayjen began, but she pulled her hand out of his.

"Get out."

He studied her, his lips pinched, and then stood. She ignored him as he placed a kiss on her forehead.

"Everything will turn out all right," he whispered. "We'll always be here for you."

Except they weren't. Where had they been when she was taken? How could she trust the words of cowards and liars?

Lilja stood slowly, not looking away from her. "I know what this is. I've done it myself. I will *never* abandon you, ma fleur. Never. I love you. When the time comes, I will come when you call."

What an ideal notion. "Lies."

"Sage," her papa said softly.

She turned to her parents. Even though she wanted them to stay and not leave her, she couldn't handle looking at them. They didn't deserve her anger and poison. "Please leave."

"Love, I'm not leaving you." Her mum's face hardened. "I'm your mother."

Sage turned to Mira, who stood by her side like a quiet sentinel. "They need to leave."

Mira stared down at her, searching her face before turning to her family. "You all need to leave. Your presence is upsetting her. I only agreed to allow you in here as long as you didn't disturb her."

"No," her mum argued.

"Yes," Mira said with a steely edge. "If you do not leave, I'll have you escorted out."

Her mum glanced at Sage for help.

"Please leave, Mum. I need—" She hiccupped. "I need to be alone."

Her mum tossed a nasty glare Mira's way and wrapped Sage in a huge hug. "I'll be right outside the door if you need me. I love you."

"Love you," she whispered back.

She watched as her family filed out of the infirmary, and she felt nothing, even though they all looked as if they'd lost. That was her fault. She knew it, and yet she couldn't stop herself from lashing out.

The old saying was true.

You always hurt the ones you love.

TEN

SAGE

"PLEASE, WAKE UP, PLEASE," SAGE whispered, brushing a strand of sweaty hair from Jasmine's gaunt face. She winced as another wet cough wracked Jasmine's fragile body. In the three days since she'd awoken, Jasmine had only worsened. Each breath she took was a struggle. Sage clutched her friend's limp hand and kissed her knuckles.

"You have to wake up, Jas. You have to."

"You need to go back to your own cot," Mira said softly. "I don't want you to get sick. You've only just recovered yourself."

It wasn't possible to obey Mira's request even if she wanted to. Her legs had long since gone numb while kneeling next to her friend's bed.

"How can I leave her when I've done this to her?" she whispered.

Mira knelt next to her, her hand resting on Sage's right shoulder. "This isn't your fault. She's here because you saved her."

"Have I really?"

No. In her heart, she knew Jasmine would die. Only instead of a quick death, it would be long and painful. She'd drown from the fluid in her lungs. An awful, brutal way to die.

"You need to rest."

"All I've done is rest." Sage swiped at her wet eyes. Or attempted to, at least. Sleep evaded her.

"No. I've hardly seen you sleep."

Sage slid her gaze toward the healer. "Except for when you drug me." That was the worst. It trapped her in the nightmares.

Mira's lips thinned. "I wouldn't have to drug you if you slept. You can't go on without sleep."

She turned back to Jas, ignoring Mira. She couldn't sleep. Every time she closed her eyes, *he* was waiting for her. No sleep was better than the nightmares she couldn't escape from.

She swallowed hard. The sick part of it was that she missed someone holding her at night. A curse tumbled from her lips as a tear slipped down her cheek. Maybe this was penance for her sins.

"This isn't your fault."

"Someone should pay."

"Yes, but not the innocent," her friend said. "You blame yourself for everything. Even the things you can't control. Sometimes, things happen that we can't control. That's just life."

"I'm no innocent. If you knew the things I've done…" She bowed her head. "I deserve to pay for my sins."

"Pay for your sins? Oh, Sage." Mira sighed. "My God would not punish you this way. He's known for love, not suffering. Why would he take someone you loved? Or punish Jasmine when she's helped you? That makes no sense. It would hurt the innocent. Only someone cruel would do that."

When Sage didn't respond, Mira muttered under her breath, "I think you need to leave the infirmary."

"What?" Sage whipped around.

"I agree with that," Jacob said, shuffling into the room.

"I'm not leaving," Sage said, holding Jasmine's hand a little tighter. Her place was at Jasmine's side. "Plus, you have all been telling me I can't leave for days."

"Three days," Mira remarked. "And you've caused mischief the entire time."

Sage ignored her as Jacob edged around the cot and leaned over Nali to rest a hand upon Jasmine's forehead. The leren cracked an eye and then ignored him, much like Sage wished to after his last comment.

"Her fever hasn't increased, but it hasn't lessened, either." His peculiar bronze eyes narrowed on her through his round spectacles. "You're making yourself ill by staying here."

"How can I leave her?" Sage asked, wiping a damp cloth against Jasmine's temple. "She deserves to have family at her side to watch over her." To protect her.

Jacob laid a wrinkly hand over hers and pulled the cloth from her hand. "And no one should have to watch someone they love die."

She glared at Jacob. "She's not going to die." Sage wouldn't allow it. Jas had too much ahead of her to die.

His eyes softened into something sad, yet knowing. "She's not well, Sage. I don't know how much longer she'll remain."

A sob caught in her throat. She hated lies, but, now, all she wanted was for him to lie to her. "Is there nothing we can do?"

"We've done everything we possibly can for her."

"Fix her, damn it!" she cried.

Nali's ears laid back, and she hissed at the Healer as Sage's tears blurred Jacob into a collage of color.

"I've done all I can. But you can help her, Sage," he said, frowning at the feline.

"How?" she croaked.

"By leaving," he pleaded. "Despair clings to you like a cloak. That will not help her. She needs peace and quiet. If you love her, you'll leave."

A bark of laughter burst out of Sage. What a clever way to get rid of her. "I see through your games, old man," she growled.

He was manipulating her, but she wouldn't challenge him and stay if she would hinder Jasmine's recovery.

She leaned close to Jasmine's ear. "Listen here, Jas. There are two precious children in this castle waiting for you. You will not abandon them a second time. You must get better. Don't let the monsters win. Don't let them take your family from you."

Sage pressed a kiss to her pale cheek and then stood on shaking legs. She pushed back her shoulders and stared down her nose at the Healer. "I'll go, but you'll keep me apprised of her health."

"Yes, my lady." He bowed. "There's an escort waiting for you outside the door."

She nodded and turned on her heel to leave.

A rumble stopped her in her tracks. Sage walked around the cot and placed a hand on either side of Nali's face. As much as she didn't want to part with her companion, Jasmine needed her more. "I need you to stay here and help her."

The feline's alert, golden eyes blinked as she stared at Sage.

"Stay, please."

Nali whined and bumped her nose against Sage's cheek. "I'll come back for you, but I need you to keep helping Jas. And no eating anyone," she added.

The leren gave her a good lick with her rough tongue and snuggled back down beside Jasmine. It was decided then. Sage scratched Nali behind the ear, receiving a contented purr before she moved toward the door, dread sitting in her belly like a lump of lead.

Sage hesitated, her hand hovering over the doorknob. This was what she'd been begging for over the last three days, and yet…a thrill of fear went through her. Once she stepped out of this door, she wasn't safe—or, rather, she left the illusion of safety behind.

Sage closed her eyes and prepared herself, pulling open the door. Her eyes snapped open, and she froze. Her papa and mum stood to the side speaking between themselves, but it was the big man grinning at her that caused her lungs to seize.

"Garreth," she breathed, not daring to move lest she disturbed the apparition. "I'm so sorry." Another senseless death on her hands. At least she could apologize for her stupidity.

"Nothing to be sorry about, love. Now, let's get you up to your room."

She still remembered the first time he had carried her to her room. She couldn't even walk and was so scared of what they'd do to her. It felt like a thousand years ago, not months.

"Love?" her mum asked.

Sage opened her eyes, not realizing she'd closed them. "Are you here to help me to my room?" she asked, ignoring another one of the ghosts haunting her.

Her mum's brow wrinkled. "We're coming with you, but," she said, gesturing to Garreth, "this nice gentleman will be the one helping you."

She gurgled and glanced between her mum and Garreth. "You can see him, too?" *Please say yes.*

Gwen's fingers tightened on her own. "Yes, love."

A cry gurgled in her throat, and she threw herself against Garreth. "You're okay?"

Big arms wrapped around her. "No one told you?" he rasped.

She shook her head *no*, his leather breastplate rubbing against her face. "I thought you died," she cried. "He told me you died."

"I'm okay, love. I'm okay," he soothed, running his hand over her tangled hair. "It's all right. I'm just fine." He pulled back and grinned at her. "See? Nothing wrong." He hoisted her up into his arms and smiled. "No man can keep me down."

She smiled wobbly and wrapped her arms around his neck as he began walking through the hall. Once again, the world had turned on itself. After being away from the castle, it felt foreign, not like her home. She turned her thoughts from the things around her and stared at the side of Garreth's face. New scars adorned his countenance, and his nose was slightly crooked.

"If you keep staring at me like that, I think the crown prince might take exception to it."

"Did Rhys give you these?" she asked as more warriors added to their ranks. Her fingers dug into the cloak that hung off his shoulders as she avoided the glances cast her way. Garreth glanced at her and moved faster, accentuating the limp she didn't bother asking about. It was the sick kind of thing Rhys would have done.

"He gave them to me." A smile. "Don't worry, princess, they add to my beauty, do they not?"

"They certainly do," she whispered. In truth, the scars were jagged and ugly, but, to her, they were a badge of honor, of survival. They'd both survived that monster. "My guess is that women fall all over themselves for you."

A snort. "They can't keep their hands off of me."

"Garreth," her mum chastised.

"Forgive me, my lady," he said, looking anything but apologetic.

"I see how you and Sam are such good friends," her papa remarked with a smile. "I'm sure you would've gotten along with our boys as well."

"Indeed," her mum grumbled, causing Sage to smile as they ascended the servants' stairs. "What's one more mischievous boy?"

"Thank you," Sage whispered.

"For what?" Garreth asked, his eyes on the stairs.

"For taking this route." She didn't think she could bear all the stares and whispers.

A slight smile. "You've never been one for fanfare."

"No, I have not."

"Although, I have to say I don't care for stairwells any longer."

That she understood. "Me, neither."

They reached the last stair and entered the royal wing. Some of the tension in Garreth drained as they moved down the corridor.

Her brows furrowed as they passed Tehl's room and moved toward her old room.

Garreth caught her look and answered her unspoken question. "The prince thought you'd be more comfortable in your own room."

Disappointment poked her. Of course, he wouldn't want her near him after everything she'd done.

He paused outside her old room. "Are you ready?"

"Yes." A lie, but what was one more?

ELEVEN

TEHL

"GOOD HELL," TEHL CURSED AS Sam was thrown across the ring. The Scythian woman's strength was incredible.

His brother hit the ground and rolled with the fall, popping back up. He staggered and shook his head before narrowing his eyes at his opponent. "That was cheap," Sam accused with a dangerous smile.

"War *is* cheap." Blaise sauntered up to the fence that encircled the training ring, her back to Sam. "If you see an opening, you take it, or you die." She wiped her face while Sam snuck up on her. "Scythians are stronger and faster than you."

Tehl leaned against the post, eyeing the woman. "You should never turn your back on the enemy."

"True, but he's not really my enemy now, is he?" she asked before spinning and meeting Sam's lunge head on.

The ring of swords echoed around them as the two locked in battle. Sam bared his teeth at her and pulled a dagger from his belt. Blaise kicked his leg out from underneath him as he slashed at her right leg, just missing her as she danced out of range, dagger and sword in hand.

It was a thing to behold. He'd never seen someone so fluid with a dagger and sword. She held the sword in one hand like it weighed nothing at all—for her, it probably did. What had started out as a training session between himself and his brother escalated when Blaise showed up in all her heathen glory.

His brother's schemes knew no bounds. It was brilliant, really, to invite her to spar with them each day. His men were already becoming accustomed to her presence. Tehl eyed the training yard, now surrounded with so many Elite he couldn't see past them. They, as well as he, couldn't pass up watching Blaise trounce his brother in fantastic fashion. It was amusing, to say the least.

"Kneeling before a woman, brother?" Tehl called. "Here, I thought I'd never see the day."

Sam spat blood on the ground and grinned at him. "If you've never knelt before a woman, then you've never lived. I'll gladly kneel before one."

Blaise snorted. "I doubt you'd know what to do with a woman."

Sniggers surrounded them as his men enjoyed the show.

Sam staggered to his feet. "I could show you better than I could tell you."

"Mmmhmm..." she hummed, eyeing him. Blaise strolled toward him, lashes fluttering. "You think you can handle me?"

"I know I can." Sam's words were careless, but the way his gaze tracked her wasn't. For every move the Scythian made, his brother countered it. Sam wasn't stupid. The key was staying out of her range. If she got a hold on him, he was done for.

She smiled and feigned to the right, but Sam was prepared. He blocked her, once, twice, and then, in a blink of an eye, he was on his knees with her sword held to his throat.

Tehl blinked. How in the stars had she done that?

The men around him stilled, each reaching for their own blades. Blaise scanned the ring, noting the hostile change in the men. Her expression blanked, but she didn't remove her sword from his brother's neck.

Tehl kept his pose casual. He knew she wouldn't harm his brother, and he wanted to show his men he trusted her. They needed to trust her if they wanted to survive in the upcoming battle.

Sam had concocted the idea three days before. The fastest way to integrate Blaise with his men was for her to train with them. Training was a dangerous thing. Accidents happened all the time, but if she trained with them, they'd begin to trust her. You had to have a measure of trust in your partner.

Blaise slowly lifted her left hand and ruffled Sam's wavy hair. "Do you yield?"

Sam grinned and lifted his chin to stare up into her face, exposing his neck even further to her. "What will you give me if I do?"

"Your life."

"That puts things into perspective." He flashed her a dimpled grin that knocked most women on their asses. "I concede to you, beautiful lady."

She shook her head at his antics and released him. Sam rolled his neck and grinned as she held her arm out to him as a gesture of goodwill.

That was a smart move. Sportsmanship was important to his men and she'd just honored Sam, even though they were born enemies.

Sam accepted her arm and stood, brushing himself off. "I didn't even see that last move."

"I'm faster than you. You have to be smarter," she said, sheathing her sword.

"Surely, you're not only going to challenge him?" a deep voice asked.

Tehl hid his smile as Rafe pushed through the Elite and leaned against the post. The rebellion leader couldn't keep away. Tehl had noticed a pattern in the last few days. Anywhere Blaise showed up, so did Rafe. It was an interesting turn of events.

She stiffened and glared at Rafe. "Surely you have something better to occupy your time, Methian?"

Rafe jumped over the fence, landing in a crouch. "Nothing would please me more than to spar with you."

"Do you really think it would be a fair fight?" she asked, cocking her hip. "I've been sparring for the last hour, and you're refreshed."

Rafe unclasped his cloak and laid it over a post. "By all means then, refresh yourself. I was led to believe you had much more stamina."

Tehl whistled as his brother clambered over the fence and dropped next to him. Rafe was playing with fire, but Tehl wanted Rafe to keep pushing her just so he could watch her grind him into the dirt.

"He's baiting her, the nutter," Sam panted, wiping the sweat from the back of his head. "I don't think I've ever been beaten this badly before."

"Indeed."

"Thanks," Sam said sarcastically. "I can always rely on you telling me the truth."

"True."

Sam shook his head. "She'll tear him to pieces."

"Why do you say that?" he asked, eyeing the two warriors in the ring like one might a pit of snakes. One wrong move, and the enemy would strike.

"She was holding back."

He'd noticed that himself. She'd pulled her punches a few times. "That was probably wise. I didn't wish you to be murdered."

"How touching," Sam deadpanned. "It was all I could do to keep up as long as I did. If that had been a real fight, I would've died in the first fifteen seconds. The warlord really did breed them for war."

"Bastard," Tehl cursed. Everywhere he turned, that monster was the cause of something that gave him trouble.

Rafe held his forearm out.

"I accept." Blaise slapped her hand against his and stalked back to his side of the fence.

She locked gazes with Tehl as she snatched a cloth from the fence.

"Insufferable dog," she growled. "He won't like what happens when he forces my hand. This was supposed to be a training, not full-out war."

"You can say no," he pointed out, handing her a ladle full of water from the bucket.

"And walk away after he challenged me?" she scoffed. "I don't think so."

"He challenged you?" Tehl frowned. He didn't remember that.

Blaise rolled her dark brown eyes. "Men."

Sam scoffed. "I will not be lumped in with him, thank you very much. He's as dense as a rock sometimes."

Tehl didn't bother defending himself. It was the truth.

She patted Sam on the cheek. "You, my pretty friend, should be in a class all of your own."

His brother beamed. "Thank you."

Her expression blanked. "It wasn't a compliment."

Sam pouted. "I'm hurt."

"I'm sure," she retorted, rolling her neck. She threw her shoulders back and straightened, a feral grin on her face. "I'm going to smear him across the dirt of the earth." With those parting words, she turned her back on them and moved to the center ring.

"She's going to slaughter him," Sam said with glee as Rafe prowled toward the center, his entire focus on the Scythian woman.

Tehl studied him and shook his head. "No, she won't."

Sam arched his brows. "She has every advantage over him."

"It's something in the way he moves, the way he carries himself. I believe they're evenly matched."

Sam narrowed his eyes on Rafe. "Perhaps you're right."

Zachael lifted his hands and nodded at Blaise. "Are you sure?"

"Yes." She secured her braids and sank into her fighting stance.

The weapons master dropped his hands, signaling the beginning of the match.

Neither lunged. They circled each other like one might a leren. Tehl's mind flashed to the beast who had attached herself to his wife. It was an apt description.

Rafe glided forward and lunged. Blaise danced out of his way and darted in, only to be blocked by the rebellion leader. Tehl sucked in a sharp breath when Rafe countered in a flurry of movements he couldn't keep track of, movements that flowed into another set.

Again, they circled before coming together in a series of clashes of steel and fists. Rafe hissed, and some of the Elite whooped as Blaise struck the first blood.

The rebellion leader held up one finger. "That's your one time." He smiled, but it wasn't nice. "You're fast, I'll give you that."

Blaise didn't respond. Her expression didn't even change.

In a wickedly quick move, Rafe attacked. Tehl's jaw clenched as steel scraped against steel in a teeth-rattling attack.

"Damn, he's not messing about," Sam said. "It hurts my arms just to watch her block those blows."

Blaise gritted her teeth and shifted forward, pushing the huge man back.

"Stars above," Tehl said, shaking his head. "How strong is she? He's double her size." It didn't bode well for Aermia if Scythia's army was made up of warriors like Blaise. They were way out of their league. His men needed more training.

He continued to watch the bout and winced as Blaise took a heavy blow to the chest. She staggered but recovered and slid under Rafe's guard to slap his stomach with the broadside of her sword as he wrapped a hand around her throat. They froze that way, face to face, both breathing hard.

No one cheered or spoke a word. It was almost a reverent silence for what they'd just witnessed. Sparring was an art, and Blaise and Rafe had taken it to another level.

"Yield," Blaise said, blushing.

Rafe smiled. "We're at a standstill, little leren. Concede."

"I will not," she said. "I will never bow to you."

"Never say never."

Blaise scanned his face and did something Tehl didn't expect—and neither did Rafe. She smiled. The rebellion leader didn't stand a chance. His mouth slackened, and his hands loosened. Poor sucker. Women were always tricksters like that. They never made much sense and were always surprising.

That was all the opening she needed.

Blaise slammed the butt of her dagger into the muscle of his thigh and threw her head into his face. Blaise pulled back and skirted out of his reach as he threw a blind jab.

Rafe seemed to swell in size as he pinned her with golden, watering eyes. "That wasn't pleasant," he said softly.

"It wasn't meant to be." She smiled and batted her lashes at him. "Are you ready for more, Methian?"

"Here it comes," Sam said with glee. "He's going to let loose."

A tremble went through Rafe, but he didn't lash out, he threw his head back and released a roaring laugh.

Blaise blinked, and so did Tehl. That was the last thing he expected Rafe to do.

He wiped his watering eyes and held out his forearm. "It's been a long time since I've enjoyed a bout. I thank you."

She stared at his arm, her fingers clenching around her weapons, and shifted, not taking his hand.

Take his hand, Tehl urged. If she couldn't get over her prejudice, how could she expect his men to?

"Take it," Tehl said under his breath.

Blaise cocked her head, her gaze flitting to him like she heard his words.

Rafe raised his brows at her hesitation. "What, little leren? Afraid to touch a Methian?"

Her jaw clenched, and her nose wrinkled. She exhaled and then approached Rafe. "Well met," she said clasping his forearm.

"Well met," Rafe said.

Tehl pushed from the post and began to clap. A bout like that deserved praise. Moreover, Blaise deserved a round of praise by accepting Rafe's hand when she clearly didn't want to.

She yanked her hand from Rafe's and turned her back to him. However, the rebellion leader never looked away from the woman strolling away from him to be congratulated by the Elite.

"If he stares any harder, her clothing will go up in flames."

Rafe jerked and glanced in their direction like he heard their conversation. Tehl crossed his arms and raised his brows at the rebellion leader.

A shrug was all he received in reply.

He wasn't getting off that easily. Tehl had questions that he wanted answers to.

TWELVE

SAGE

IT WAS JUST AS BEAUTIFUL as she remembered.

"Please, put me down," she said softly, soaking in the room that had changed her life.

The giant four-poster bed crafted from the pale aqua wood of the jardintin tree still dominated the room. White, gauzy curtains, draped from post to post, floated around the bed. Rich, dark blue carpets covered the stone floor, and deep-cushioned chairs were scattered around the spacious room in a sea of colors.

She slowly walked toward the bed and ran her hand over its silky white coverlet. The color bothered her. Before, she loved how crisp and clean it looked. Now, it was a symbol of how sullied she was.

Swallowing hard, she turned from the bed and, once again, took in the room. The large fireplace that occupied the wall adjacent her bed, its mantle comprised of purple shells, shimmering abalone, and the dainty starfish, still made her smile. That could never be taken from her, her love of the ocean.

Next, she looked past the fireplace to the two large doors of pale wood that overlooked the sea. Her heart lurched as she got a glimpse through the glass at the top. The ocean stretched for ages before kissing the setting sun that exploded into color after color. She'd missed the ocean with a fierceness that stole her breath. The sea was home.

"Love?" her mum called.

Sage turned and blinked at her parents. She'd forgotten they were still there. "What is—" She paused and stared at the dressing table and mirror. Distinctly male items were lying all over the surface.

Garreth followed her gaze. "The crown prince has been staying here," he said, answering her unspoken question.

She studied the room once more, noting little changes here and there. Male boots beside the bed. A broadsword on top of the dresser. A huge cloak thrown over the back of one of the chairs near the fireplace. Why had he stayed here? Was this a new development?

"How long?" she asked.

"Since before," Garreth said softly.

She swallowed hard and stared blankly at the room, not knowing how she felt about that. Part of her loved that he'd stayed there, but the other part wasn't sure if she liked him invading her space.

Her gaze was drawn back to the balcony doors. That was her special place. In her bones, she knew if she could just get out there, everything would be okay. The world would make sense again.

Sage rushed to the doors and flung them open, her heart pounding. A salty sea breeze ruffled her hair, the loose strands lifting in the air. Taking a step, her bare feet moved across the sun-warmed stone to the balcony. Gulls heckled and chased each other playfully. This was freedom.

The cool air kissed her bare arms and left a trail of goosebumps in its wake. She placed her hands on the balcony railing and closed her eyes to soak in the sounds of the crashing sea below. Home. This was home.

She sighed and opened her eyes. Nothing was as beautiful as the sunrise. The cool air brushed over her skin, and a shiver worked through her.

And, on the heels of it, a memory.

The sky painted with rich reds, oranges, and purples. His lopsided smile, while he held her tightly as the sun faded from view. Kisses to the top of her head. Affection.

Sage stared sightlessly at the ocean before her and shuddered. Even now, he was ruining her safe place. "Get out of my head," she whispered.

Still, she could feel the ghost of his arms embracing her. How could she think about such a thing after all he'd done? Her fingers turned white as she squeezed the railing. Part of her missed him, wanted the comfort and connection of his presence.

A soft curse left her lips. She was sick. Sick in the mind and heart. Heat burned behind her eyes, but she wouldn't cry. She'd done enough of that.

She inhaled the salty air and watched the gulls play, darting here and there to outrun their pursuer. If only she had wings to fly away. If she had wings, no one could reach her, nothing could touch her. Wings meant safety.

Her gaze dropped down to the waves below. Swimming was like flying. Lilja had flown through the water, riding the currents. It had been unlike anything she'd ever experienced. There was peace to be found under the waves, where silence reigned. How she longed for the peace. Her wings were waiting for her, if she only chose to grasp them.

A hand touched her shoulder, causing her to jump. She glanced up into green eyes like her own.

"Are you okay?"

Sage placed a hand over her papa's and forced a smile on to her face, even though the waves sung a siren song to her soul. "I'm tired." More than anything, she wanted to be alone. To think. "Mum?"

"Love?" Her mum stepped onto the balcony.

She glanced between the two of them. "You both look like you haven't slept in days. Go and get some sleep."

Her mum waved her away. "We're okay, love."

Sage reached out and clasped her mum's hand. "I need to bathe, and then I'm going to sleep. Please, please go and take some time. I'll be here when you get back."

"We don't need—"

"Gwen, I think Sage needs a little time." Her papa squeezed her shoulder and threw an arm over her mum's. "Let's go."

"But we promised," her mum argued.

"I have Garreth for company and protection if I wake up and you're not back. Right?"

"I'll be right here the entire time, my lady," he called from the doorway.

Sage smiled at her mum and hugged her. "Take your time."

Her mum brushed Sage's cheek. "You sure?"

"I am."

Her mum squinted at her, and then pecked her on the cheek. "We'll be back before you know it, my love."

Sage held it together as her parents disappeared from the doorway. Then her forced smile fell, and a sense of relief filled her as Garreth stepped into view.

"Do you need anything?"

She laughed. "I need many things, but all are things no one can give me."

Garreth hesitated in the doorway, shifting from foot to foot. "I'll stay in the room until your family or Tehl comes back, if you'd like?"

"No." She waved him away. She needed privacy to think.

"If you need me, I'll be right outside the door."

She nodded, hating his scars. "I'm sorry about what happened," she said, her voice small. "I'll never go anywhere without my escort again."

"Bad things happen. That doesn't mean it's your fault. It means there are horrible people out there."

That was the truth if ever she had heard it.

"I should be the one apologizing to you." Garreth stared at floor. "I didn't protect you like I should have."

"You did your best."

"Did I?" He shook his head. "I'm so very sorry, nonetheless."

"It seems we both like to blame ourselves for circumstances out of our reach," she said, hoping to soothe him. "I don't blame you." She faked a yawn and sat on the bed. "I'll call for you if I need you. Thank you for everything you've done."

"My pleasure, my lady."

Her pulse picked up as the door closed with a thud, leaving her alone. When was the last time she was left alone? "Stop thinking," she whispered to herself. She couldn't go back to that place. It was too easy to fall down the black hole of nothingness.

She stood, turning to the balcony, and moved to the railing. She stared at the ocean below. It was incredible that the waves made so much noise, when underneath the surface it was so still. The sea was the exact opposite of her. Inside was the rushing ocean crashing against the rocks, but on the outside, she kept herself still and placid. At least, she tried.

She lifted her arms out to the side of her body and relished the wind beneath her fingertips. Stars above, what would it feel like to jump? To have the wind rushing past her until the ocean met her and silence reigned supreme?

Sage glanced over her shoulder at the empty room and then to the waves below her. Her hands trembled as she lifted her nightgown up and swung a leg over the balcony. She froze as the thrill of fear went through her, but for the first time since she woke up, it wasn't because of a monster. This fear was within her control.

It would be so easy to slip off the railing and fly…

"Darling, could you come off the railing? It's giving me quite the scare," a deep voice asked.

"No," she whispered, not looking in the direction of her newest guest. Of all the times for him to visit, it had to be now.

"Well then, I guess I'm coming to you."

Large weathered hands clasped the stone railing. Marq swung a long, leathered leg over the stone edging and adopted her stance. She peeked through her fringe at the older man whom she held dear in her heart. Did he want to fly, too?

He didn't look her way but out toward the ocean. "I never tire of this view. Each sunset and sunrise are better than the last, and no two are alike. It gives me a measure of peace to watch it sink into the ocean's embrace."

The king finally turned to her, his steely, dark blue gaze sweeping over her. "I'm happy to see you."

She tried to speak, but the words lodged in her throat, and she trembled, causing alarm to show on Marq's face. She missed him. Missed his visits.

"Darling, I know it's not your intention to scare me, but I don't think you're quite well enough for this adventure. Would you mind getting down with me?"

"I can't," she whispered through her cracked lips. "I want to be free."

"You are free. No one is holding you here."

Lifting her head, she stared at the birds, the wind twisting her hair around her. "I want to fly."

"I know the feeling well. I have a floor to ceiling window in one of my towers that I used to stand in. I always admired the birds from there. I wished

I could fly, too."

She met his gaze. "Do you want to fly with me?"

"No, darling, I don't."

Her shoulders slumped. "Why?" How could anyone *not* want to be free?

"I remembered what was important." He held her gaze as he slid off the railing and back onto the balcony floor, and then held his hand to her. "I know it might not feel like it now, but you will fly. Maybe not in this way, but you will fly."

She glanced down at the water. It would be so easy to let go.

"Sage, look at me, darling."

Forcing herself away from the view, she watched him as he edged closer. "I need peace," she murmured. "Every move I make is plagued by monsters and horrors."

Marq smiled at her. It was a sad smile, but it didn't hold pity. "The monsters disappear as you slay them. That is up to you." He inhaled deeply and placed his hand over hers. "There will always be evil in the world, but it's up to people like you and me to protect the others."

"I'm not strong enough," she choked out. If she couldn't protect herself, how could she protect others?

"We can't always protect ourselves from calamity, but we show courage in how we deal with the aftereffects. Those, usually, are more difficult to conquer. I need you to be my warrior. You have it inside yourself, but you need to choose to fight. No one can force you to do that."

"I'm so tired," she said. She didn't have the energy to fight. She needed sleep.

"I know, sweetling. I know. But that is what your friends and family are for. Your fight is not alone. You are not alone, and you're not the first person to feel this way. You are loved." He swallowed hard. "Please take my hand."

She gripped the railing harder as she warred with herself. Flying would be the easy choice, but when had she ever made the easy choice?

"Be my warrior. Take my hand."

Her hand felt heavy as she pried her fingers from the balcony and placed it in the king's. He sighed and pulled her from the railing and into his arms.

Sage shuddered in his arms as he squeezed the air from her, his heart thundering against her ear.

"That's a good girl. You're so brave."

He pressed a kiss to the top of her head and shame crashed into her. Why did she do such a thing? It was beyond dangerous. There was a chance she'd have died if she attempted the jump.

"I'm sorry," she cried. "I'm sorry."

"It's okay, darling. You took my hand like a warrior. That's all that matters."

"I'm just so tired. I want the nightmares to leave me alone."

"I know. It'll get better. We'll fight them together. You'll never have to fight them alone."

With each memory, it was like she lost a little bit more of her sanity.

She leaned back and stared into the king's dear, wet face. "I think I'm broken."

He smiled, flashing his dimples, and cupped her cheek. "You're not broken. Maybe a little bruised and scarred, but whom of us aren't?"

That sounded familiar. Like she'd heard it before, but she couldn't place her finger on it. Exhaustion weighed heavily on her, and she leaned into Marq. If only she could sleep.

"Father?"

Sage pried her eyes open and blinked slowly as Tehl materialized next to her.

"She needs rest."

Marq transferred her to Tehl, his leather and pine scent wrapping around her as he hauled her into his arms and then placed her in the bed. She curled into a ball and snuggled into the covers. Maybe she would sleep. The bed was so soft.

Tehl's weight shifted and her eyes snapped open. Somehow, her fingers were clutching his shirt. His deep blue eyes met hers as he placed a hand over hers.

"Please, don't leave," she said.

"Never. I just need to remove my boots."

Marq leaned over the bed and brushed hair from her face. "Remember, you are my warrior. I'll be here if you need me."

"The king's warrior," she whispered.

He grinned at her. "It has a nice ring to it, doesn't it?"

THIRTEEN

TEHL

IN THE SPAN OF TEN breaths, Sage had fallen asleep, clutching his shirt and curled into a tiny ball, her face pinched as if she was trying to hide from her pain. Slowly, he pried her fingers from his shirt and shifted to sit up as his father pulled a blanket up over her.

She shivered in her sleep and burrowed further into the bed, her dark brown hair a striking contrast against the white pillow. It was surreal to have her here. He'd hardly dared to hope they would retrieve her; he knew it was a high possibility she'd never come home. It was a blessing that he was eternally grateful for.

Unable to help himself, he brushed his thumb across her worried forehead. Even in sleep, she looked terrified. His jaw clenched, and he pulled his hand back, meeting his father's gaze. This was the warlord's fault.

He glanced at his father. "How long has she been here?" he asked, moving to sit in the chair next to the fireplace. His father dropped into the other chair while Tehl pulled his boots off and dug his toes into the carpet. *Stars above, what a long day.*

"Garreth said only about an hour."

Tehl sighed, flexing his toes in his socks. Then he sat back, taking a real look at his father. His stomach dropped at the expression Marq wore. That look never boded well. He didn't want to ask what put that expression on his father's face, but he had to.

"What happened?"

His father dropped his head into his hands. "I had a conversation with Sage today that I never wanted to have with another human being." Each word held a weight. He lifted his head, a sheen of tears in his blue eyes. "I found her straddling the railing of the balcony." His voice cracked.

Chills erupted along Tehl's skin as his body flashed hot then cold, and a dull ringing filled his ears. His father's lips moved, but he couldn't understand them. They didn't make any sense.

"I don't understand," he muttered through numb lips.

His father scooted his chair closer and placed a heavy hand on his shoulder. "Sometimes, the world looks so bleak, a person only wants relief from the pain." He swallowed thickly. "It doesn't mean they want to leave the ones they love."

She didn't love him.

Tehl placed his head in his hands and struggled to breathe. Did she want to escape life that badly? She had so much to live for. So many people who loved her. "How did you get her down?" he managed to ask.

"I asked her to fight. She's always been a warrior, Tehl. She needed to be reminded that there were people who saw her strength, even if she couldn't see it anymore." His father sighed. "I don't think she actually wanted to hurt herself. She wanted peace and quiet. Her memories are haunting her."

Tehl nodded and pinched the bridge of his nose. The nightmares, he understood. The brutality of them haunted his own dreams.

"She's barely slept, and, when she does, it's more of a fight. She thrashes and cries out, but when she's awake, it's worse." Tehl rubbed his eyes. "She's a specter of herself. When a memory crashes into her, emotion cracks through for a few moments before it flickers away, and she curls back into herself." It was like watching the destruction of a beautiful painting.

His father pressed his lips together. "It'll take time for her to heal. Physically, she might be okay, but emotionally and mentally, she's not. It'll take time."

But how much time? He swallowed and glanced at the open balcony doors. "What if she doesn't get a chance to heal?" It was sheer luck that his father had been here. What if it happened again? What if she changed her mind?

"Do you remember when you found me in the tower?" his father asked.

He'd never forget that day. Even though he'd said some terrible things to his father, he hadn't meant them. All he wanted was to shock his father out of his rut. It broke him to watch his father wither each day and clearly long to be away from his family.

"Yes."

His father squeezed his shoulder and sat back in his chair, running a hand through his silvering hair. "That day, all I wanted was peace. When your mother died," he rasped, "a part of me also died. Each day was a struggle to breathe, to live. The pain was indescribable. Everywhere I looked, memories assaulted me. I saw her in everything and everywhere. It was exhausting."

He placed a hand over his mouth, his gaze going distant. "I never wanted to die. I wanted a measure of peace. That's all." His eyes focused back on Tehl. "Sage didn't want to die. I saw it on her face. She wanted an escape from the memories. That's it."

He shook his head. "My memories were of our wonderful life. Hers aren't. They're nightmares. I can't even imagine." A pause. "Has she told anyone what happened there?"

"No, not really." He only was privy to a few things because she screamed them while she slept. Mira had been very tight-lipped about Sage, and her parents didn't have any more information than he did.

"She needs to speak to someone," his father said, glancing over his shoulder at the bed. "She can't keep all of it inside."

Tehl followed his gaze to the precious woman sleeping fitfully in their bed. Lost. He felt lost. He wanted to be the person she confided in. "How do I get her to confide in me? I've never been good with understanding people and emotions. How can I help her?" That's all he wanted. To help her.

"By being there for her. The most important things you can do are support, listen, and love her. She needs all of those things."

He could do that. His father made it sound simple, but Tehl knew it was more difficult than that. He'd rather listen to someone than speak to them, anyway. As for love… He pushed from his chair and tiptoed to the bed, pulling up the blankets she'd shrugged off, so they now reached her chin.

He certainly cared for her. It had killed him while she was gone, but was that love? Or just devotion and caring for a friend? He didn't know, but he'd do his best to love her in the way he knew how. "I'll do my best," he vowed. He wouldn't give up on her.

"You will, son. You're a good man," his father said softly.

High praise that he'd hold close in times ahead.

Tehl turned as his father stood. Then, he pulled the king into a hug.

"Be patient and kind. Nothing will be easy. The time ahead of us will be brutal and bloody, and the only way either of you will survive is by supporting each other."

His father released him and pressed a kiss to Sage's cheek. "Sleep well, my little warrior, for tomorrow you'll have to fight." He straightened and strolled around the bed, pausing at the door. "I'll have Gwen and Colm stay in the room across the hall. Then, if she needs them, all you have to do is holler."

"Thank you," Tehl said, some of his fear dissipating. Neither one of them was alone.

"There's no need for thanks. Just take care of our beautiful girl."

"I intend to."

His father smiled and slipped out the door.

Tehl rolled his neck and glanced around the room. It felt different having her here. Everything looked the same, but there was a contentment to having Sage home.

A cold breeze drifted through the balcony doors, causing him to shiver and taking some of his contentment. He glared at them. They led to death.

He closed the doors and locked them. Then he pulled the royal blue draperies closed for good measure. They were a reminder of what could have happened today, and it was one more thing he didn't want to ponder.

The hearth was cool, and that needed to be taken care of given the way Sage was shivering. Tehl crossed to the door and cracked it. "Garreth."

His friend turned to him. "Yes, my lord?"

"Turn all servants away tonight. I don't want anyone to disturb Sage."

"It will be done."

"Thank you," he said, closing the door.

Tehl rubbed his hand together and began his ritual for bed. He started a fire, pleased that it lit so quickly, and fed kindling into it until it could support a few logs that would get them through the night. He then moved around the room, organizing his things.

His eyes drooped as he washed his face and loosened the ties at his throat. He'd hardly slept in the last few weeks and it had caught up to him. He brushed his fingertips along the stubble on his cheeks and jaw. He should shave it, but he didn't have the energy. His body was demanding sleep. It was a damn miracle he hadn't fallen asleep standing up.

He turned from the wash basin and glanced between the large chair and the foot of their bed. He longed to sleep in a regular bed, but it wasn't worth scaring Sage.

Tehl lugged the chair around the bed and sat by his wife's side, staring at her pale face. It was odd watching someone sleep, but it brought him a measure of peace. She was close and safe.

Even with the dark bruising beneath her eyes from lack of sleep, she was a beauty. It was like she'd popped out of a fairytale. A fairy princess. He smiled at the thought. How would she react if she heard him comparing her to a helpless princess?

His smile dimmed. Sage needed his help, but she wasn't a helpless princess. She was a king's warrior.

He brushed his thumb across the top of her hand, an unexpected swell of emotion rocking him. He could have lost her today.

An uncomfortable heat filled his eyes. "I don't know what he did to you," he whispered, "but understand I'll protect you with my dying breath. I'll protect you from yourself and from your nightmares. But, to do these things, I need you to fight. You're one of the most stubborn women I've ever met." He smiled and swiped at his eyes. "Don't let someone take what you love the most from you. He may have taken some of your time, but don't let him steal your future, because I'll fight for that, too. I'll fight for us."

FOURTEEN

TEHL

IN THE MIDDLE OF THE night, three things happened: the room lit up with a flash of lightning, followed by a tremendous crash of thunder, and then Sage screamed.

He had lurched up from a full sleep as if slapped across the face, grabbing the dagger at his waist, heart threatening to beat right out of his chest. *What in the hell?*

For a second, he sat panting, his eyes wildly searching the darkened room for danger. Had someone gotten inside?

Another round of lightning and thunder brought another scream and lit the room in a ghostly light for one blinding moment. Their door thudded open, light pouring into the room. Tehl blinked furiously, his fingers tightening around the dagger in his hand.

"Are you and the princess all right?" Garreth asked, his body a silhouette in the doorway.

Tehl shook his head, trying to clear the spots from his vision, and glanced at Sage. She trembled in the bed, her eyes wide, gaze unseeing. A nightmare.

"She's dreaming," he whispered, horror pricking his skin at the utter terror on her face. "I need to wake her up."

"Do it gently, or you'll make it worse," Garreth admonished. "Do you need any help?"

"No." He didn't want anyone to see Sage at her worst. She'd hate that. She deserved her dignity and privacy. "Thank you."

"It's nothing, my lord." Garreth stepped into the hallway and closed the door, casting the room into darkness once again.

Tehl sheathed his dagger and smoothed a hand over Sage's arm. "Sage? You need to wake up."

She jerked, her eyes wild, more cries pouring from her throat. She rocked away from him and struggled against the covers wrapped around her legs.

"Let go," she whimpered.

He eased from his chair and circled the bed, avoiding pieces of furniture, the hairs standing up on his body as she cried out again. The sound unhinged him, cut him to the heart. No one should experience that kind of fear. What had the warlord done to her? What caused this sort of fear? He pushed aside his thoughts and focused on the terrified creature in his bed.

"Sage? You need to wake up, love," he crooned, barely making out her terrified features in the dark, only illuminated by the dying embers of the hearth and flashes of lightning. "No one will hurt you. You're okay."

But she didn't hear him. Didn't see him. No recognition registered on her face.

"Trapped," she cried, wrenching the blankets from her body and then tearing at her nightgown.

"Love." He reached out and paused, remembering the last time he touched her during a nightmare.

She'd attacked him with a ferocity that bespoke of an unfathomable pain and rage, but that's when they barely knew each other. Maybe she'd react differently this time. He'd have to move carefully.

He reached a hand out and brushed her cheek. "It's only a dream, love. Look at me."

Sage slapped his hand away. "Hot, so hot," she moaned, her sweaty hair whipping around her face.

Momentary shock rendered him motionless as she yanked her gown over her head. He jerked and glanced away from her as heat rushed through him.

So much skin.

Stars above, how was he supposed to wake her now?

Tehl glanced at her from the corner of his eye as she wrapped her arms around her legs and rocked side to side giving him a peek of what she hid behind her billowing shirts and tight leather vests.

He whipped around and stared at the wall, cursing his body. The circumstances were terrible for him to feel anything for his pretty wife. One flash of creamy skin, and his mind had blanked. Was he so weak? No, he wasn't. It was just a physical reaction. It didn't mean he was a bad person. If he acted on it… Disgust curdled in his belly. He couldn't even finish the thought.

He pinched the bridge of his nose and forced his mind to the problem at hand. How could he soothe her when she was so wild and naked? A memory surfaced of his mother singing to him when he was a child. That had always calmed him when he'd been scared. If only he could remember the words. If he couldn't, he'd just have to make up his own. Tehl exhaled heavily. Singing was not his talent, but he'd exhaust all options before trying to hold her down again.

Clearing his throat, he began to hum gently, still not looking in her direction. Hopefully his rusty voice wouldn't make it worse. He inhaled and began to sing softly.

Darling, darling, there's nothing to fear.
The sun is rising, so there's no need for tears.
I'll hold you and protect you in the dark of night.
The shadows can't touch you, so there's no need for fright.

Darling, darling, there's nothing to fear.
The dawn is approaching, and the sky is clear.
I'll fight your demons and all of your foes,
I love and adore you more than you'll ever know.

Darling, darling, there's nothing to fear.
The night gives way, for the new day is near.
I'll tell you my secrets to keep you awake,
Nothing can hurt you, so there's no need to quake.

Darling, darling, there's nothing to fear.

The sun is rising, so there's no need for tears.

He sang the verses over and over for what could have been minutes or hours. His throat was hoarse when a hiccupping sob, different from the feral cries, came from behind him.

"Sage, love?" he called, his voice rusty.

"Tehl?" she whispered.

He glanced over his shoulder, keeping his gaze on his wife's face. Her haunted eyes met his, tears slipping from the corners of them. She looked wrecked.

"You were having a bad dream," he explained.

She slapped her hands over her eyes and sobbed anew. "I'm sorry," she cried. "I'm so sorry."

Tehl shifted around and averted his eyes as he pulled a sheet up over Sage's body. She may not be concerned over her modesty, but he was.

"There's nothing to be sorry about." He reached out again to comfort her, but hesitated. She hated comfort after a nightmare. His jaw popped as he clenched his teeth and pulled back. Time to give her space.

He moved to stand when her hand touched his arm.

"Please, don't leave me."

He glanced at her in surprise. "I'm not leaving you. I'm moving to my chair."

She shuddered, tears still slipping free, and held up the covers. A clear invitation.

He tried not to gape. That had never happened before. She'd always clammed up and pretended he wasn't there. She'd regret this in the morning. Sage hated others seeing her at her weakest.

Tehl patted her hand. "You don't need to worry. I'll be right next to you in the chair."

"Please," she begged, her voice breaking.

Only one word, but it broke something inside him. He could give her this. She might resent him tomorrow, but he'd be damned if he turned away from her when she needed him the most and her plea was well within his power to grant.

Tehl placed his hand over hers and lowered the blanket. He crawled over the bed and lay beside her, brushing her tears from her damp face. "It's okay," he murmured, even though nothing was okay. "I've got you."

Her deep emerald gaze mapped his face slowly, as if she searched for something, and another sob burst free as she snuggled into his arms. He stiffened and held absolutely still as she burrowed into him, her face now pressed to his chest, sobs bursting from her in a rough, tortured way.

He slowly slid his arms around her and hugged her to him as she shook in his arms. He kissed the top of her head and whispered comforting words while staring out of the balcony door windows.

This was the first time he'd ever held a woman like this. It should have been a wonderful moment, but a hollowness filled him. The warlord had taken this from them. He trembled, trying to keep his emotions in check. This was not how it was supposed to happen. It was unfair.

Sage hiccupped, her fingers knotting in his shirt as her body shuddered. He'd kill the warlord for what he'd done. He'd suffer.

His wife whimpered, pulling him away from his morbid thoughts. Blinking, he loosened his grasp, knowing he'd been holding her a little too tight. The leader of Scythia would experience justice, but not tonight.

Tonight, Tehl focused on Sage. She needed him.

He began humming the lullaby while brushing his nose along the crown of her head, her cinnamon scent filling his nose. That brought him a measure of comfort. Everything was different, but at least she smelled the same. That was a constant, and it somehow grounded him.

Tehl rubbed one hand up and down her back, continuing to hum. Her tremors slowed, and, soon, she fell quiet. He wondered if she'd pull back, but she didn't—if anything she pressed closer. The storm quieted except for the patter of rain against the windows.

His arm began to ache, and he shifted to his back, trying not to disturb her. He expected her to stay where she was, but Sage cuddled up to his side. Tehl slowly lifted his arm, and she pressed her cheek against his shoulder, her hand laying on his chest.

He swallowed and stared down at the small hand over his heart. Was it wrong to enjoy the sensation of skin pressed to his? He hated the circumstances. Hated it. But he'd always wanted companionship.

Carefully, he lifted his right hand and placed it over hers. He sucked in a breath when she laced their fingers together and sighed, her breath ghosting over his neck.

"Thank you."

Her words were so soft, he almost didn't hear them.

"It's nothing."

"No, it's everything," she murmured. "You've helped me and gained nothing in return."

It didn't feel that way. He had his wife in his arms for the first time, willingly. That felt like a great boon when, only months ago, he thought she'd stab him before sharing a bed with him.

"It's my duty." What a fib. It wasn't his duty. It was his privilege.

She hummed and scooted closer. "Don't let them get me."

His throat tightened at her words. "Never."

His arm hurt.

Tehl shifted to relieve the pain and scooted closer to the blazing warmth. His hands caressed silky skin, and he smiled, completely content. When was the last time he woke up so relaxed?

Blinking his eyes open, all his lethargy evaporated. Green eyes watched him from underneath dark lashes. He glanced to his hand, which played along Sage's spine.

Her very naked spine.

He started to pull his hand back when Sage halted him, her hand grasping his bicep.

"It's okay," she murmured. "It was nice."

He swallowed, out of his depth. Who was the creature in his bed? He didn't understand this Sage. His Sage would've yelled and threatened to stab him for taking such liberty without her express permission.

His mouth bobbed when she pressed closer, a contented sigh brushing across his neck hotly. He shifted, not knowing where to put his hands as little details began to filter in the longer he was awake.

His eyes dipped, and he jerked, his gaze moving over her head, not daring to glance down at the beautiful naked body pressed against him. The sheet had slid down at some point in the night to expose her upper half.

Tehl took a shallow breath through his mouth as heat rushed through his veins and her scent swirled around him. This was not happening. He'd be the biggest cad in the world to react to her after the god-awful night she'd had. It was wrong, and yet his body had other ideas that had him scowling.

"It's okay, Tehl. We're married," she whispered.

He stilled. It felt like a trick. A dirty, dirty trick. What did she really want?

Tehl kept his gaze averted but still stroked her skin. He couldn't help it. She was so soft, and he never thought he'd get the chance.

"You've been through hell," he rasped. "I won't take advantage of you, even if you wished it."

The words were easy to say, controlling himself was infinitely harder. He placed a kiss on the crown of her head and ran his fingers through her hair. There. Those were safe touches, weren't they?

He cleared his throat while concentrating on the storm outside. "Are you hungry?" he asked. She had to be hungry. She'd hardly eaten anything in the last couple of days.

Her body grew rigid in his arms, and yet he didn't dare to look down. There was too much to tempt him. Too much to look at that he didn't have a right to. Yet.

His breath hissed out as she pulled away from him and abruptly sat up, flashing him the side of one breast and her entire bare back before he snapped his eyes closed and sat up with his back to her.

That wasn't an image he'd ever forget. He shuddered as the sheets rustled and he placed his head in his hands. What was wrong with him? He'd slept with her before. Why was he having such a hard time now?

"I'm famished," she said, her voice wooden, nothing like it had been a minute ago.

His brows furrowed as he dragged a hand across his mouth. Did he offend her? Had she noticed his reaction? "I'll ring, so we can break our fast," he said brightly, even though he was worn out and confused.

"Appreciated," her hollow voice answered.

"You're welcome."

Brilliant. Now she was down to one-word sentences. He'd done something wrong.

He stared at the pale plastered wall across from the bed, feeling very lost and young. Somehow, he always managed to muck everything up. It was one mistake after another.

Unbidden, the image of her bare body flashed through his mind, causing his teeth to snap together.

What was that all about? Sage never let him see a scrap of her skin before she disappeared. The only time he saw her tempting curves were when she dressed in one of Lilja's dresses for dinner, a dress that appeared to have been poured over her body.

Again, he asked himself, who was the strange creature in his bed? Sage was here with him, but not *his* Sage. It was like he didn't know her at all.

His heart sank.

They were back to the beginning. They were two strangers.

He knew her return wouldn't be without its difficulties. He understood she wouldn't come back as the same person, but it still hurt. They hadn't been the best of friends, but at least they knew where the other person stood, who they were.

But now he hadn't a clue.

Tehl rubbed a hand across his heart where their hands had rested all night.

Despite all the negatives, maybe there was some good as well.

Sage had never initiated physical contact unless it was needed. Today, she wanted affection from him just because she enjoyed it.

Some of his concern melted away.

That was a step in the right direction.

It would take time to get to know each other, but they'd gone through it once already. They wouldn't make the same mistakes this time.

For better or worse, she was his, and he was hers.

FIFTEEN

SAGE

HE DIDN'T WANT HER, THAT much was clear.

She gazed out the windows at the turbulent ocean, white frothy tips capping the stormy waves. That's exactly how she felt inside. Everything crashed against each other in a raging mess. The wind howled, and Sage wanted to rush onto the balcony and howl, too, if only it would relieve some of the rejection trapped inside her.

Her fingers brushed along the thin, fine linen covering her lap, worrying at the material.

Last night hadn't been what she'd expected. She knew the nightmares would come for her. They always did. The worst of it all was waking up and searching for *him*. Wanting the warmth and comfort he'd provided her even though the warlord was the reason she fought terrors each waking moment.

And yet…she wanted him.

Her fingers knotted in the fabric as shame and revulsion churned in her belly. What kind of sick person missed their torturer?

She breathed through the nausea and peeked over her shoulder at Tehl. She'd done him a disservice last night. He'd done everything in his power to care and comfort her while she'd been pining for another. No wonder he wouldn't look at her this morning. She was a whore. She was even dressed as a wanton woman.

It wasn't clear to her where her clothing disappeared to in the night, but she was sure it wasn't Tehl's doing. That was apparent by his stiff demeanor and how he held himself back from her. She'd been naked—and in his arms—and yet, he'd done nothing, said nothing.

Did she say something last night to turn him away? All she remembered was his voice and her being so hot and not wanting to be alone. She stared at his back with more shame washing over her. Months ago, she'd have been outraged he'd come to bed without a shirt, but it was she who'd stripped and just about thrown herself at him.

Pathetic. Disgraceful. Desperate.

She turned back to the balcony doors, her toes skimming the cold stone floor. A chill ran along her exposed skin, but she didn't move to cover herself. It was just skin.

She chuckled, the sound hollow and haunting even to her. She'd been a prude before she'd been taken. If there was one thing she'd learned in Scythia, it was that modesty was subjective.

"What's so funny?" Tehl's deep voice washed over her.

"Life," she replied.

"It has a way of surprising us."

More like stabbing her in the back.

She stood and clutched the sheet tighter around her and moved to the balcony doors, resting her palm against the cool glass dotted with condensation and rain. "That it does."

"I love rain."

That was personal. Why was he offering an olive branch? He hadn't done anything wrong.

Sage blinked and spun, the sheet flaring around her legs. Tehl still stared at the wall, but there was less tension in his body. "What do you love about it?"

He leaned back, placing his palms on the bed, and squinted at the ceiling. "It's clean. It washes away filth and rubbish, leaving behind beauty."

"And here I thought you liked it because it was dark and glum, like your personality." Her eyes widened as she realized what had popped out of her mouth. In that moment, she wished she could snatch her words from the air and cram them back into her mouth. He was making conversation, and she was acting like a cornered viper.

Tehl's body began to shake and a roar of laughter escaped him. Her jaw dropped. When had she heard such laughter like that? It was the sound of freedom and joy.

She ached for that joy, that freedom, but she'd settle for being near someone capable of such emotion.

He wiped at his eyes and shook his messy, inky hair, glancing in her direction before pinning his gaze on the far wall, his back to her again.

She made him uncomfortable. Sage cinched the sheet tighter along her body, and her toes dug into the rug beneath her feet. "I'm covered, and I'm sorry."

Slowly, he turned, his brows furrowing. "Why are you sorry?"

"I was rude." She waved a hand, heat filling her cheeks.

His confusion melted into a heart-stopping grin as he flashed two dimples that had her heart in her throat. "Don't be sorry. I've always enjoyed your feistiness. You seem more like yourself when you are…"

"Ornery?" she quipped with an arched brow.

"Fiery. You've always been full of life."

She swallowed. As opposed to the darkness that slowly ate at her now. "I see."

His hands curled into fists, and his smile disappeared as he studied her face. "Can I be honest with you?"

"Yes. I prefer it." She was so tired of deception. Lies.

"As do I." He inhaled deeply and met her gaze squarely. "I'm awkward. I'll always be awkward, but I'll always tell you the truth. I don't know where we go from here. I don't know how to help or be what you need."

There was no help for her. But how could she explain that to him?

"But I'll do my best, and, for that, I need you to tell me what you need, what's on your mind."

She clutched the sheet tighter. Could he handle her monsters? It was a burden she didn't want to level onto anyone.

"Can you handle the truth?" Because she couldn't. She wanted to hide from it. From the things she'd done.

"Sometimes, the truth is ugly, and it hurts, but we have to deal with it."

"We?" she whispered, hardly daring to hope.

Tehl stood and moved around the bed, halting a handbreadth away. "You and I. It will always be you and I against the world. I meant my vows."

Her vows. She'd already broken them in a way that couldn't be fixed.

"I've done terrible things," she whispered. The compromises. Ezra. The warlord.

"Mistakes are part of being imperfect. No one is perfect, Sage, no one. If you expect that from yourself or anyone else, you're inviting disappointment and heartache." He held out his hand to her, palm up. "You don't have to tell me what happened, today, tomorrow, or next week, but you can't hide from what's going on, and you can't hide it from me."

"You can't handle the darkness," she whispered, staring at his hand. "It's too great." Painful.

"Nothing is too great when you work together with those that love you."

Her gaze snapped to his face. "I don't deserve it."

"No one really deserves love, but that's what makes it so special. I need you to fight. Fight for yourself, your family, your friends, our kingdom, us, for the children we might have in the future. I need you to fight with everything you have to not let him win." Tehl seemed to swell in size as he squared his shoulders. "I will fight for all of these things with or without you, but it will be easier to have you by my side. You are a champion, a warrior." He looked her straight in the eye. "You are not the victim. You're a survivor."

His words seemed to wrap themselves around her and sink into her skin. She wasn't a victim.

Sage was a survivor.

Her wounds were brutal, ugly, and dark, but she'd survived them.

But she wasn't the only one to survive such horrors. Her mind flashed to all the pregnant women at the feast table. How many women had been used? Were still being used?

Sage hugged herself, shaking as she fought her way back from the image in her mind. She had to fight for them. Live for them. Survive for them.

If she didn't, who would?

SIXTEEN

SAGE

FIGHTING WAS EASIER SAID THAN done.

Three days had passed quicker than she expected. Breakfast had been quiet affairs before Tehl disappeared for the day. He checked on her several times during the day and left her with news on the world outside their room. Each time he left, she longed to go with him, but even she knew her body lacked the strength that was needed.

Against Mira's wishes, she'd begun to train in her room. She couldn't stay here forever, and there wasn't time to waste. The times were too dangerous.

Sage scowled at her trembling limbs and sank to the floor. The months in Scythia hadn't done her any favors. Her body may have been healed from the drugs they'd given her, but she'd lost so much of her strength.

Sage cursed and plucked her dagger from the floor. She held her breath and threw the dagger. It sunk into the bedpost with a dull thud. A small smile tipped up her mouth. At least she hadn't lost her aim. There was her silver lining.

"Stop fouling up the furniture." Her mum glared at her from over the top of her embroidery. "You'd have thought I raised you in a barn."

The urge to stick her tongue out at her mum tugged at her, but she managed to curb it. Barely. "Sorry, Mum," she wheezed, brushing a sweaty strand of hair from her face.

Her mum arched a delicate brow. "If you were sorry, you'd stop doing it."

It was only the third time today. The bed would survive. Her restlessness, not so much. It eased some of her panic to have a dagger back in her hand, to control something. It was satisfying to see it hit her mark each time.

She lay on her back, sinking into the plush rug. Even though she was exhausted, it had been great to work her muscles. There was comfort in routine.

"You should get back into bed. You've overdone it today."

Sage waved a hand at her. "I've done nothing today." It was the truth, but her body complained anyway.

"You've visited Jasmine, spoken to Blaise, and trained against my wishes."

In the scheme of things, it wasn't much. "I can't stand staying still. My mind never stops." Every time she stopped, unwanted memories plagued her. She shook her head. It was better to wear herself into the ground.

"I know, love."

"I need to fill the…" She paused. "The void."

"I understand that, but you shouldn't push yourself too hard. It's only been a few weeks."

Almost three weeks. It felt like a lifetime and a blink of an eye at the same time.

Time was distorted. The world sped by while she struggled after it. But each moment she let slip by was a moment lost to the warlord.

She shivered, the sweat cooling on her skin. She wasn't a betting woman, but she'd bet her sword the warlord would strike soon. He'd lost the element of surprise. That wasn't something he'd take rolling over.

"Sage?"

She blinked and craned her neck to see her mum. "Yes?"

A deep crease wrinkled her mum's forehead as she gazed at Sage. "Where did you go, love? I called your name three times."

"I didn't hear you." Too lost in her worries.

"You didn't answer my question."

Sage gritted her teeth and rolled her head to the right, staring up at the ceiling. "To a place where there's nothing but rage, pain, and darkness."

Her mum laid her embroidery on the floor and then lay beside Sage, her dear face pillowed on her crossed arms. "You're not alone."

"So people keep saying." It was one thing to hear it and another to believe it.

"And you don't believe that?"

"Mum." She sighed. "I don't know how to deal with all of this."

Her mum placed a hand over hers. "Then tell me."

"I can't," she whispered.

To say the words out loud would give them more power to hurt. The warlord had done enough damage. Sage wouldn't let him hurt anyone else.

"Love, you need to let it out."

Probably. Sage met her mum's hazel eyes. "You kept Lilja and Hayjen from me to protect me. I can't speak of these things. It's to protect you."

Her mum cupped her cheek. "It's my job to protect you, not the other way around."

If only they understood that danger that was coming for them. Blaise and Lilja were probably the only two who truly understood the evil that would descend on their world.

Guilt pinched her.

She'd treated Lilja cruelly the last time she'd seen her. True to their word, Lilja and Hayjen hadn't come back. Sage wanted to reach out, but not today. Today, she'd train and plot.

"It's like you're miles away," her mum murmured, a hitch in her voice. "How do I help you?"

"Mum." She swallowed. "You can't help me or save me."

She smiled sadly as tears filled her mum's eyes. Sage reached for her hands and squeezed.

"It's okay, though. I'll be okay. The best you can do is support me. I need your support. I need someone to believe in me." Even though she didn't believe in herself.

"I've always believed in you, and I always will."

"I know. That's what I need the most. The days ahead will be brutal, Mum. The only way we'll survive it is if we stick together as equals. You will always be my mum, and I will always be your daughter, but I need you to support me as a leader of Aermia. I need you to push me when I falter, because it will happen."

"I can do that."

"Thank you," she said. "I need you to contact Lilja."

Gwen wiped her eyes and nodded. "I can do that."

"It isn't to make up," Sage warned. "I need her." Lilja would be a major key in the upcoming war.

"What do you plan on doing with your aunt once you have her?"

"Persuade her to do her duty."

"You want to use her?" Her mum's voice held disapproval.

"No, not use her, utilize her." Sage wouldn't manipulate the Sirenidae. Lilja would choose to help. She'd understand what was at stake.

"She's a person, not a tool."

"That may be the case, but she's necessary." Aermia needed the Sirenidae to defeat Scythia.

"Don't turn into someone you're not."

Sage smiled at her mum. "That's what I have you for."

Her mum didn't crack. "Stay true to who you are."

"I don't know who I am." That was probably the most truthful statement she'd uttered in days.

Sage shied away from her mum's probing gaze and slowly sat up, her head pounding as the room swirled around her for a brief moment. "I need a bath," she muttered as her stench hit her.

Her mum stayed quiet before a ghost of a smile touched her mouth. "I wasn't going to say anything, but you stink." She pushed to her knees and pulled Sage into a hug. "Don't think I don't see your distractions for what they are. When you want to speak, I will be here. Don't hold it in too long. It only makes it worse." Gwen kissed her cheek and stood, shaking her simple skirts out. "I'll start on that bath."

Sage closed her eyes and lay back down on the floor, listening to her mum hum a song as she started the bath. Water splashed, and the scent of cinnamon and mint wafted from the bathing room.

Footsteps padded back into the room along with the quiet swishing of skirts. "The bath will be ready for you in a few minutes. Would you like me to help?"

"No!" Sage swallowed and gentled her voice. "No, I'm all right. I can do it myself." The last thing she wanted to do was expose her body to her mum. The changes still shocked her sometimes. Her body seemed like a foreign entity.

"I'll be in my room just across the hall if you need me."

Translation: if she heard anything abnormal, she'd storm into the room.

"Thank you, Mum."

"Welcome, love."

The tension in her shoulders leaked away as the door closed behind her mum, leaving her alone. Since the king found her a couple days ago, it seemed like everyone watched her more closely. Maybe it was all in her mind.

Her gaze traveled to the balcony doors, and the shame sickened her, causing her hands to clench in the carpets.

What in the blazes had she been thinking? Clearly, she hadn't been using her mental faculties at all. What she'd almost done was unforgivable. She truly hadn't wanted to die; she just wanted to be free from the pain.

Sage rubbed at her chest where the constant pain and rage threatened to choke her. This was her new reality, and she needed to deal with it. If she didn't, it would consume what was left of her, and there were people depending on her.

Forcing herself from the floor, she staggered to her feet. If she let herself dwell on it, she'd only descend deeper into the darkness.

Sage unbuttoned her vest and moved into the bathing room. Steam caused her clothing to once again stick to her skin as heat and herbs enveloped her.

She peeled off her leather vest and glanced up at the huge tub. The vest fell to the floor from her numb fingers as a memory assaulted her, a hexagonal pool imposing itself over her reality.

"That's it. Just relax," he crooned. "I'll take care of you."

A warm, sudsy cloth started on her hand and carefully moved up her arm. Sage kept her eyes closed, blocked out everything happening to her, and focused only on the warm water and the comfort it gave her. She checked in when he washed her stomach and the tops of her thighs, but his hands never strayed to her important bits.

His hands moved to her head, and she hummed, soothed by the soft touch of his hands through her hair. His hands stilled.

"You like that?"

"Mmmhmm... My mum used to wash my hair and brush it for me. I love it," she said, not knowing why she gave a stranger that information.

"I'll remember that," he rumbled and began washing her hair again.

A few times, she hissed as he untangled her matted locks, but, for the most part, it was the best thing that had happened to her in a very long time. It was the last good memory she'd have before she died. "Thank you."

"My pleasure," he hummed.

"Sage?"

She gasped and stumbled away from the huge tub. Her back met the vanity behind her, rattling the glass bottles on top.

Tehl stood in the doorway, his shoulders almost touching either side. "Are you all right?"

Far from it. His concern made everything worse. Genuine worry pulled his brows together into a frown when he shouldn't be concerned but outraged by her thoughts. She glanced back at the tub, her sins weighing heavily on her. The longer she stared at the bath, the more certain she became that she wouldn't get in it.

"I'm fine," she rasped.

"Are you getting in the bath?" he asked.

"No," she shook her head, her braid whipping side to side. A quick scrub from the water basin was all she needed.

He stepped into the bathing room and stood next to her, staring at the bath. "It seems like you were going to take a bath." Tehl gestured to the oils next to the pool of water and sniffed heavily. "Cinnamon certainly isn't my scent."

She hunched over as another memory slammed into her.

"Cinnamon," he growled. "How is it you haven't bathed in days and yet you still smell like cinnamon?"

A hand brushed over her head as she panted and forced herself to look away from the smooth stone floor beneath her feet to Tehl.

"You're not there." Tehl bracketed her face with his hands, forcing her to look into his eyes. "You're here with me."

Tears of frustration spilled down her cheeks. "He's everywhere." Escape was nowhere to be found and utterly elusive.

"There's no one here but you and I." His gaze darted to the bath. "Would you like help?"

Horror seized her. After the debacle three days ago, she didn't want him anywhere near her when he could glimpse her skin. "No!"

He studied her face and brushed his thumbs along her cheekbones. "You need a bath."

"Are you saying I stink?" she quipped as her stomach rolled.

He flashed his teeth. "I didn't say that."

It was odd to be joking with him while on the verge of a mental breakdown.

"Can you bathe yourself?"

It was on the tip of her tongue to lie and say she could. But they both knew she wouldn't get in the bath. Chances were that she'd run a wet rag over her body as quick as possible and then avoid this room like the plague.

Tehl must have read her face, for he squared his shoulders and pulled her into a hug. She shuddered and reluctantly wrapped her arms around his muscular form.

"It just so happens that I need a bath, too, and it's always hard to scrub my own back. Maybe we could help each other out."

"What?" she gasped as he swung her up into his arms. "No, Tehl." She couldn't do this.

"Hush," he soothed. "Nothing untoward. I want nothing from you."

He stepped into the tub and plopped down, sloshing water over the edge. Her eyes flew to his face as warm water soaked through her clothing, and panic clawed at her throat.

"You don't understand," she whispered.

"Trust me," he said softly before arranging her to sit between his legs.

Her mouth bobbed when he placed a wet hand against her forehead and gently guided her head back against his chest.

It wasn't a matter of trust. Sage trusted him. He was with her the entire time in Scythia.

It was the memories it invoked. As much as she wanted to say each one was torture, they weren't all bad, and that's what she hated the most.

Her mind flashed to right before she'd left the Scythian castle.

The warlord knelt by the bath, watching her with an intensity that made her gut clench. How long had he been watching her? She crossed an arm across her chest and one to the juncture of her thighs. "Wh-what are you doing?"

"Watching my consort bathe, as is my right."

She shrank deep into the tub, wishing to disappear from his heated gaze.

"My lord, you're making my job difficult. No doubt you wanted her to relax during her bath?" Maeve said.

"Indeed," he murmured. He smiled, all seduction, and skated his fingertip across the top of one of her breasts. "So beautiful."

Everything cried out at the violation. There was nothing she wanted more than to slap his hand away, but she didn't. She let him touch her. She had to.

Her breath caught, and her fingers clenched against each of Tehl's knees.

The warlord hadn't forced her to let him watch her.

She'd allowed it.

She'd let him touch her in ways her rightful husband hadn't.

Sage bowed her head and inhaled the scented steam from the water, her mind tearing her apart with guilt.

Tehl's hand brushed over the crown of her head and down her spine as she fought to ground herself in the moment. It was just her and the crown prince.

He said nothing, but his presence completely surrounded her, making her feel sheltered and cherished. That somehow made her feel even dirtier. She didn't deserve to be sheltered and cherished.

She stared at her reflection. He didn't deserve a wife who was unfaithful. Tehl was a good man. He should be married to a good woman as well.

A tear dropped from her cheek, sending a small ripple through the bath water.

Whore. It was an ugly word, but correct in its description.

Scythia whore. That's what she was.

He deserved the truth, and she couldn't keep it from him any longer.

SEVENTEEN

SAGE

IT HAD BEEN ON HER mind since she'd awoken.

Every time she glimpsed Tehl's face, the guilt and shame almost drowned her.

He'd never abandoned her while she was in Scythia. What had she ever done for him? Lied and cheated.

Sage quashed her sorrow and forced the words from her throat that had been suffocating her since the moment she'd found herself in the infirmary.

"I've been unfaithful."

Tehl's hands froze on her back; the only sound was their breathing echoing in the room.

She expected him to push her away, but he surprised her. His arms wrapped around her middle, and he pulled her snug against his chest, burying his face in her hair.

His breath skated along her neck heatedly. "You are not accountable for his crimes." His tone brooked no argument. "Never forget that."

He didn't understand. She'd made choices. She bit her lip hard and shook her head. "You don't get it."

Tehl lifted his head and placed his chin on top of her head. "Sometimes when a man takes what isn't his," he said hesitantly, "a woman can be made to feel like it's her fault, but it's never her fault. It's his and his alone."

Pain lanced her heart as hot as a blade straight from the forge.

Tehl thought the warlord had raped her. What had happened was worse.

"He didn't rape me."

Tension drained from his body as he hugged her close.

"Thank God," he whispered, just as she said, "I said yes."

His entire body went rigid, his arms turning to bands of steel around her.

The words tasted vile upon her tongue. The truth wasn't always sweet. It was a double-edged sword. Sometimes, it was painful.

"I'm sorry," she rasped, blinking rapidly to keep the tears at bay. If only she'd been stronger, smarter, better.

Silence reigned, so stifling that Sage couldn't breathe.

She longed to rush from the room, but that was the coward's way out. She couldn't run from her problems. Facing what she'd done was part of her punishment.

Just when she thought she couldn't stand the silence any longer, he spoke.

"What did he do to you?" he whispered.

Everything and nothing.

Her lips trembled as he pressed a kiss to the back of her head. Heat filled her eyes, and the room distorted around her. Why did he touch her like this after she'd betrayed him?

"I don't blame you," Tehl said.

"You should," she said wretchedly.

"I won't, and I don't."

Sage wrenched around to look at him, water splashing over the sides of the tub as she got a good look at his face. He schooled his expression as he met her gaze. Ever calm.

"Why?" she cried, slapping the water with her hands. "I deserve it!" Why couldn't he see that? Why was he being so nice to her?

His brows slashed together as his blue eyes darkened. "What you had to do in that hellhole to survive doesn't matter." He cupped her cheek, his angry expression at odds with his gentle touch. "The only thing that is important is that you're home."

She jerked completely around, kneeling between his legs, her finger curling around the tub edges, the stone pressing sharply into her palms. "How can you say that? You don't even know what I've done."

"What would you have me do?" he asked, holding his hands in the air. "Condemn you for someone else's actions?"

"You deserve a faithful wife."

"Don't I get a say in what I deserve? Do you think either of us deserves to be in this situation?" He pinned her with his narrowed eyes. "Since the beginning, we've fought. Fought against each other, fought our enemies. Now, we're going to fight *for* each other." He stabbed a finger at her. "I know you better than you think. You seem to think the weight of the world rests on your shoulders and that you're responsible for everyone's actions around you. You're not." Tehl ran his wet hands through his inky hair. "I refuse to watch you take responsibility for that monster's actions." He eyed her and blew out a breath. "What did he do to you?" he asked brokenly.

"He made me fall in love with him."

There. The words were out. The ones that haunted her for months.

Part of her wanted the warlord, and it sickened her.

Sage gagged but composed herself.

Her husband didn't shout, curse, or rage. A sort of sorrow rippled over his face, and he glanced away, rubbing a hand over his mouth.

"How did he manage that?" Tehl glanced in her direction. "He hurt you. How is it possible you fell for him?"

Sage swallowed down a sob threatening to burst from her chest. His questions were fair, but it was like being dragged over hot coals to hear the words from his mouth.

"The only thing I can say is that he broke me down until I had nothing left."

Tehl scoffed. "I can't believe that. You're the most stubborn woman I've ever met."

"When I fought," she hiccupped, "he hurt others."

"And that's *love*?"

"I don't know." She dropped her head into her hands. "But no matter what I do, he's always in here." Sage rapped her knuckles against her temple. "I can't escape him. He was right," she gasped. "I'll never escape him."

Tehl scooted forward and pulled her into his chest. "That's not love, Sage. That's control. That's depravity. True love isn't like that. He can't force you to love him. He's playing sick games with your emotions. He can't claim you—you were already claimed."

If only that was the truth.

She shuddered, clutching at his shirt. "Not fully."

"What do you mean?"

"He married me." Nausea caused the room to tilt. The words alone made her ill.

"What?" Tehl said confused, his brows knitting together. "That's not possible. You're already married."

She'd thought so, too. "It is."

"How?"

"He had me examined." Another violation to lay at the warlord's feet. "Then claimed me as his consort. He knew our marriage wasn't consummated."

A nasty curse burst out of Tehl. She flinched back, but he caught her face between his two hands, his eyes darting all over her face. "Did you consummate his claim?"

"No. He didn't, we didn't..."

Sage's mind darkened. What if the warlord *had* taken advantage when she was unconscious? What if there was some truth in her nightmares and it wasn't just her dark imagination?

His shoulders slumped. "Thank God." Tehl placed a hand over his eyes, hiding his emotions from her.

Everything about this moment was wretched.

She couldn't feel smaller or dirtier if she tried. Her lips trembled, but she forced them together and pushed to her feet, sloshing water everywhere. She'd lost another part of herself by revealing the truth, but he needed to know.

"I'll go," she rasped.

Tehl's hand curled around her wrist, stopping her from leaving the tub. Sage stared at him while he stared at their hands, her clothes dripping water in a constant symphony of soft plops.

"Sit down."

"I should go." It was too hard to stare at his beautiful face after everything she confessed.

"Please don't." He tilted his head back and stared up at her through a fringe of dark lashes. "The only place you should be is here." A pause. "With me."

Her heart squeezed, and her corsets seemed extremely tight. How could he mean that?

He gave a little tug on her wrist and she found herself slowly sinking into the water. What did she do to have such a man in her life? How was it possible that someone so noble was real?

Her pulse picked up its pace when he placed his hand on her waist and pulled her close, her thighs bracketing his. Tehl reached out and pulled the leather thong from her hair and began to unwind her braid.

Her stomach flipped. She knew where this led.

"Wh-what are you doing?" she stuttered.

"Taking care of you. *My* job."

He ran his fingers through her hair and then plucked a vial of soap from the stone edge, pouring a generous amount in his large palms before lathering it.

Entranced, Sage watched his slow but precise movements, completely out of sorts.

He paused and gestured to her hair. "May I?"

When was the last time someone had asked what she wanted? She didn't deserve his kindness, but she wanted it all the same.

Selfishly, Sage nodded, unable to speak past all the emotions lodged in her throat.

Tehl ran his hands along her scalp and began to massage. Her eyes slowly closed as he methodically scrubbed her hair, leaving nothing untouched. He pulled her hair over her right shoulder and lathered bubbles to the tips.

Tears prickled behind her lids. There was something so intimate about another person washing your hair. Anger and sadness battled with each other. This was another thing the warlord had stolen from her. Her memory resurfaced.

His hands moved to her head, and she hummed, soothed by the soft touch of his hands through her hair. His hands stilled.

"You like that?"

"Mmmhmm… My mum used to wash my hair and brush it for me. I love it," she said, not knowing why she gave a stranger that information.

"I'll remember that," he rumbled and began washing her hair again.

A few times, she hissed as he untangled her matted locks, but for the most part, it was the best thing that had happened to her in a very long time. It was the last good memory she'd have before she died. "Thank you."

"My pleasure," he hummed.

She breathed through the onslaught of images and forced her eyes open to stare into deep blue eyes, not the obsidian ones of her dreams.

"I can see he haunts you." It was a statement. No judgement.

"He's everywhere."

"Even here?" Tehl gestured to the tub.

Especially here.

She bit her lip and nodded, waiting for his reaction.

His lips pursed, and his jaw clenched, but they were the only signs he was angry.

He slowly released his breath and began lathering her hair again. "Then we'll make new memories. Happy ones."

"You want to make new memories with me?" Hope fluttered in her chest, unbidden and unwanted. Hope destroyed.

"I do."

"After everything?"

He met her gaze squarely. "Yes."

It seemed too good to be true, but Tehl said he'd always be honest with her. She glanced to the side of the tub, his gaze too much to take in, when her attention snagged on the soap. The crown prince had shown over and over that he was worthy of every good thing life had to offer. Since Sage had entered his life, she'd made a right mess of things.

There was one thing she could do for him. It was small and wouldn't make up for all of her sins, but it was something. "Is it all right if…" she hesitated and gestured to the soap.

Tehl cocked his head, studying her. "You don't have to. This was just for you. This moment is not about me."

She wanted to. To give back to him after everything he'd done. Even if it was as small as washing his hair.

"I want to."

It was only three words, but they held a weight that settled between them.

"If you wish." He winced. "I didn't mean I don't wish it. Only that if you *want* to… I mean, I'd like that."

Sage smiled at his rambling.

His awkwardness was still there. That comforted her in a way she hadn't expected. It was normal. Normal was something she'd lacked for a long time.

She leaned forward and wobbled, her knees slipping. Tehl's hands gripped her waist, steadying her. Her pulse jumped, but she avoided his gaze and ran her soapy fingers through his dark locks.

He sighed, his breath ghosting over her cheek.

It was a simple task, but it was somehow more intimate than anything she'd ever experienced. They were two beings caring for each other who expected nothing in return. It was beautiful. She blinked repeatedly to keep the ever-hovering tears at bay.

She worked at the muscle at the base of his head, and Tehl groaned, slumping further into the tub, his eyes fluttering shut. Her nerves disappeared a little more with his attention not focused on her.

Sage tracked how his obsidian hair slid over her pale skin. It was a dichotomy of opposites.

He was the dark to her light, but really it was the opposite.

He was the light to her darkness.

She cupped her hands in the warm water and rinsed his hair, making sure to avoid his eyes, then openly stared at her husband.

The strong line of his square jaw highlighted his sharp cheekbones. She found herself tracing the bridge of his nose and the delicate skin underneath his down-swept lashes. He was so different from her and yet so beautiful.

Her fingertips skimmed his top lip and the dimple in his right cheek. She continued to follow the length of his neck to the hollow at the base of his throat.

Tehl swallowed, and her eyes flew back to his face.

Brilliant blues met her gaze. They snared her, warmth spreading through her as he gazed back unflinchingly.

"It's okay to touch," he said, his voice gravely.

Their breath mingled as they stared at each other.

Her gaze dropped to his lips.

It felt like a lifetime ago since she'd kissed him.

Without really making the decision, she leaned close and pressed her lips to his. That's all it was, a press of lips, but she felt it to her toes, and it unlocked a torrent of emotion.

His breath deepened like he was struggling to draw in enough air. Her fingers brushed against the length of his neck, his skin hot and damp.

She stopped breathing when his hands traveled from her hips and wrapped around her waist, like bands of steel, his fingers tangling in the wet strands of her hair.

"I wasn't prepared for this," he whispered against her lips.

His lips brushed hers again, soft, gentle. He kissed her like he was trying to memorize the moment, their lips melding and drifting away. Cherishing.

Kissing had ceased to mean anything to her in the prior months. *He* had done that.

Her lips trembled. She wanted to forget all the former kisses. If she could have one wish, it would be to erase every depraved kiss stolen from her.

Sage surged forward and kissed Tehl with an intensity that had her head spinning.

"Sage," he growled, his arms loosening around her waist.

"Make the hurt go away. Help me forget," she whispered, nuzzling his lower lip. She pressed closer for another kiss when his hands cupped each of her cheeks, holding her back.

"Love," he whispered. "Not like this. He has no place here. This is just you and I."

Tears dripped from the corners of her eyes. What was she doing? Who had she become to use someone who cared about her?

"I'm sorry."

"It's okay, Sage."

She shook head. "No, it's not."

Tehl pulled her close and pressed his forehead against hers. "One day, we'll get there. But it won't be because we're trying to forget." Her eyes flew to his, and he gave her a small smile. "You're not the only one who wants to erase those memories."

"Then why?"

He kissed each of her cheeks, her nose, her forehead, and her chin before answering. "Because it won't be because we're in a rush, or because of fear, or the need to forget, or the need to claim."

She shivered at the word 'claim', and he rested his forehead against hers, not looking away.

"It will be because we can't bear to be apart. It will be because we desire to show honor and love to each other. It will be beautiful." His smile became sinful. "And hot and perfect, because it's us." He brushed a droplet of water from her cheek with his thumb. "We will have what our parents had."

In that moment, she believed every word of his fairytale.

It was a beautiful fantasy Sage would cling to, so she could survive reality.

EİGHTEEN

SAM

"AGAIN! YOU'RE NOT FAST ENOUGH," Sam barked.

Bodies slammed against each other, Maisy, a pale blur as she tried to take Ruth down.

Ruth lost one of her daggers. She spun, ripping from something from the holster at her hip. A dart.

One that held a serum that burned like the devil.

Maisy's eyes widened and then narrowed, blocking Ruth's blow as she stabbed at her.

Ruth ducked under Maisy's arm, spinning beneath her grip as she drove her knee into the side of her.

"Better," Sam muttered, studying the two girls. Both were fast, but Ruth was scrappy. She had a dangerous edge to her that Maisy didn't.

Ruth attacked. *Chop. Chop. Block. Punch.*

Maisy met every blow, her forearms slapping against the other spy, and he could see she didn't expect the bigger girl to match her for speed.

Even though Ruth was taller, she was just as nimble. She'd been training as a warrior since she was a child. Her trainers had stripped her reaction time from her, so everything was pure reflex. Because they had taught her how to read movements, she was always several steps ahead.

Every time Maisy countered one of her blows, Ruth was ready for her, already disengaging and striking elsewhere.

Maisy grunted as another knee took her high in the thigh.

The dart flashed silver in the light as Ruth held the dart high, and Sam could see the choreography of Ruth's final move as she lured Maisy into a combination that would lead to her writhing in pain.

"Halt!" he called, raising his hand.

Both girls froze, breathing heavily.

Sam scanned the familiar faces of his spies. "That is what we're looking for. You need to be speed itself and anticipate your partner's next move. If you don't, then…"

Maisy rolled her right shoulder back and straightened. "Then you'll be dead."

"Precisely," he murmured. "The Scythians are faster and stronger than you. You need to be smarter about your blows." He met the gazes of his trainees, one by one. "We can't afford mistakes. It'll mean your life and others."

It was a sobering thought that kept him up almost every night, that and the very sick brunette wasting away in the infirmary.

"Dismissed."

He turned on his heel and strode toward the back entrance of his makeshift sparring room. He paused and tugged his shirt from a peg on the wall and pulled it over his head, and then tied his laces as his pupils filed out of the room.

At some point, it was probably a food storage area, but it suited his purposes just fine with its high ceiling, many accesses, and being utterly forgotten. No one had stumbled into his little hideout in well over four years.

Maisy caught his eye for a moment before he glanced away. It hurt to look at the girl. Her every mannerism reminded him of her sister. A sister who had disappeared months ago in Scythia. He'd sent the girl's only family away and now she was alone. Not alone, she'd never be alone. His girls were his family. They may not share blood, but they shared a bond many would never experience.

He sighed as she pushed to her feet and marched in his direction, determination in every step.

"Sam?" she asked, shifting from foot to foot.

He smiled at her and pointedly glanced to her feet. Her shuffling stopped, and she stilled. That was the funny thing about Maisy. In the field, she had no tells, but around those she trusted and loved, she was an open book. She couldn't hide a damn thing.

"Any news?" Her dark eyes were hopeful.

Eyes that she shared with her sister. But that was the only thing. Whereas Maisy was fair and willowy, Lissa was swarthy and all curves. That's what made her the perfect insurgent for Scythia. Lissa could pass for their people, but apparently not well enough. She'd gone silent over six months ago.

Sam crossed his arms and pressed his lips together, hating that he had to tell her the truth. He wanted to lie to her, give her a pretty lie that would help her sleep at night. But he didn't. "There's been no news, Maisy."

Maisy's shoulders slumped, and she swallowed a few times. "I expected that answer."

It was the same answer he'd given her week after week. It broke his heart each time he told her the truth, and a little more hope died in her eyes. Honestly, it was admirable that she still asked. Most shut down and mourned their loved ones.

The girl nodded and pushed back her shoulders, her expression hardening. "I want to go in."

Sam nodded and took his time answering. "I know you miss your sister, but it's not safe for you."

"And it was for Lissa?"

"Lissa was in a different situation, and you know it."

"The situation has changed."

Sam leaned a shoulder against the wall. "You couldn't blend in if you tried. You wouldn't fit in."

"That's the point. I don't need to fit in. They're taking women, *Aermian women*, women who look like me."

'Woman' was a stretch. Maisy was beautiful—but she was still a girl, with an air of innocence surrounding her. It was one of the reasons she was such a damn good spy. No one suspected her cherubic face to be listening in.

"That may be true, but I need you here."

"My sister needs me!" Her voice echoed in the room.

He'd been waiting for this moment. All his girls hit a wall when they'd lost someone. Maisy had kept it together for longer than he'd expected, but she was starting to crack.

She dashed angry tears from her cheeks. "How can I stay here when they're doing God-knows-what to her?"

His heart clenched, and he pulled her into a hug, patting her back. Since he'd released the information about what was happening to the women in Scythia to his network, his girls had been on edge, and he didn't blame them. It was a person's worst nightmare.

"As I laid in bed last night, I wished she was dead," Maisy hiccupped, "if that was the only way to spare her the horror of those monsters. What kind of person does that make me?"

Sam pulled back and cupped her face between his hands. "It means that you're a caring, merciful person, and you don't want those you love to suffer."

She blinked her big, watery eyes up at him. "I miss her."

"Me too," he whispered and placed a kiss on the crown of her head, hugging her again.

He didn't offer platitudes or promises. There weren't any promises in their line of work, but he could hold her together while she crumbled until she was strong enough to put herself back together.

Her sobs quieted, and she pulled back, wiping her face on her sleeve.

"You okay?" he asked softly.

"Yeah." She stared at his shirt. "I'm sorry about all of that." She waved a hand at his splotchy shirt that looked like a dog had slobbered all over it.

"It's nothing."

She shuffled from foot to foot. "Is there anything you need from me tonight?"

"Are you working at the tavern later?"

"No."

"Then go and get some sleep."

Maisy nodded and spun on her heel, snatching her cloak off the ground. She clasped it around her neck, hiding her trousers beneath. She paused at the door and looked over her shoulder. "You get some sleep, too, Sam."

"I'll try."

She lingered for a moment and then disappeared out the door, leaving him to the cold silence of the stones. The silence seemed accusing. It rang in his ears, reminding him of all the people he'd lost to Scythia.

He dragged a hand over his face, his scrub scratching at his palms. When was the last time he shaved? Hell. When was the last time he bathed?

From the smell of him, it had been a while.

He scanned the area one last time and blew out the remaining candles, casting the room into complete darkness. It engulfed him, seeming to caress his skin like an old lover. At one time, he'd been terrified by the darkness, but now he was more comfortable in the shadows than the light.

Slipping out the doors, Sam wove through a maze of hallways and staircases by touch. His fingertips ran along the stone walls as means of a guide, though he'd had the way memorized for years. It was an old habit that he'd started as a child. A way to ground himself in the dark, so it didn't feel like the darkness was swallowing him whole.

Sam ghosted from the bowels of the palace and snuck through the darkened kitchen. Cook snored in the corner on her cot, her mouth wide open. He pulled her blanket up over her shoulder before silently creeping away.

The older woman was a grim and gruff, but a gem nonetheless. She knew of his comings and goings and kept her mouth shut. His lips hitched up. Every now and again, she brought him little pieces of information.

He rounded a corner, the infirmary coming into view. Despite himself, his pace picked up. He hadn't been by to check on the village girl yet.

Immense heat greeted him as he entered the room on silent feet. Mira stared blankly into the blazing fire while Jacob snored softly in his rocking chair. Sam paused when he got a good look at the third person in the room. Colm sat hunched over, his eyes closed, head nodding. The poor man hadn't slept much in the last two weeks.

The man-eater, he had since learned was named Nali, cracked open a golden eye and chuffed at him, before closing it again. They'd made friends over the last few days. He'd filched a haunch of ham and a few steaks for the beast, which she'd sincerely appreciated, if he went by all the purring. If only women were that simple: bring them some food and they'd be your best friend. Unfortunately, they were a lot more complicated.

Sam halted next to the cot and placed a hand on Colm's shoulder. The older man immediately straightened and blinked his eyes as if to clear the sleep from them.

"Sam?" he said roughly.

"Yeah."

Colm patted him on the hand and slumped back into his chair. Mira glanced tiredly over her shoulder at them, before turning back to the fire.

"What are you doing here? You should go and get some sleep," Sam said.

The older man stared at Jasmine for a long moment. "She doesn't deserve to be alone. To be without family." He reached out a hand and ran it along the crown of the girl's head. "She helped my Sage and for that, I owe her, and anyone who Sage considers family is also mine." He pulled his hand back and rubbed it across his eyes. "I'll care for her as my own."

Sam stared down at Colm's head and hoped he ended up as good a man as Colm. His kindness and loyalty were something he admired.

"I'm going to sit here through the night. I'll make sure she's not alone. Go get some sleep in a bed with your wife," Sam said.

His friend gave him a wolfish smile, despite the fatigue clearly riding him. "Never been one to pass up a night in bed with my wife." His smile dimmed as he stared up at Sam. "You'll look over her?"

It was more than just a question. It was Colm asking if he would handle the responsibility the older man had deemed his own task.

"I will," Sam said.

"Okay. I will see you in the morning." Colm leaned close and placed a kiss on the village girl's forehead. "You need to wake up, little miss. There are many people waiting for you." He straightened and clapped Sam on the shoulder before strolling out of the room.

Sam pulled the chair closer and plopped down into it. He rested an elbow on the arm of the chair, and leaned his cheek against his fist, watching the pale girl before him. "How is she?" he whispered.

Mira sighed. "No worse, but no better."

If she became any worse, she'd die.

He shied away from that thought. For some reason, this girl mattered to him. Of course, he cared about all human life, but there was something intriguing about her. Not to mention, she'd be a wealth of information. Information that could win the war.

A drop of sweat trickled between his shoulder blades. How did the healers stand the heat? He loosened the ties at his throat. It was almost suffocating. Jasmine shivered. There was only one person in the room who wasn't practically melting.

He reached forward and plucked her clammy left hand from the cot and held it between his. "Today was an interesting day," he spoke softly. "You probably would've enjoyed it immensely. I got slapped by a fisherwoman today."

"You probably deserved it, too," Mira muttered.

Sam grinned and rubbed Jasmine's hand between his to work some heat back into her cool skin. "It depends which side of the story you heard, but I had a handprint on my face for several hours. Tehl, Gav, and—would you believe it—even Blaise, got in on the teasing."

His grin fell when Jasmine shivered so hard her teeth clacked together. He placed her hand underneath the blanket and fussed with the edge, despising the fact that he could do nothing but wait to see the outcome.

"Now that's a spectacle I would've liked to see," a rusty voice said.

Sam glanced to Jacob. The older man had stopped snoring when he'd come into the room. Cunning old coot. But they had more important things to speak about than his public slapping.

"I'm sure you would've enjoyed it." Sam eyed Mira and then glanced back to Jacob pointedly.

Jacob's unique bronze eyes traveled to Mira. "Darling, why don't you go get some sleep?"

"I'm not sleepy," she said, her words slightly slurring.

The Healer's expression hardened. "What is my rule about exhaustion?"

"Exhaustion—" A yawn. "—breeds mistakes."

"Exactly. You've pushed yourself beyond your limits. Please go and get a few hours of sleep."

Mira stared at her adopted father for a few moments before acquiescing. "I'll go and find my bed for a few hours, but then I'll be back," she said, pushing from her chair. She pressed a kiss to Jacob's weathered cheek before checking on the village girl and giving Nali a good scratch on the top of her head.

Sam watched with a smile, as she eventually wandered out of the room after making sure everyone was okay. Jacob was a lucky man to have such a daughter and healer at his side.

"She's remarkable."

Jacob stared at the closed door. "I am a lucky father, and, as a Healer, there's no one better to replace me when I die."

He scoffed. "You'll never die."

A bark of laughter slipped out of the old man. "And you'll settle down with a quiet-spoken girl someday."

"Who says I won't?" Sam crossed his arms and smirked at Jacob. "I might marry your own daughter."

Jacob sniggered. "If you think Mira is quiet-spoken, you haven't spent enough time around her."

"Isn't that the truth? She's got a bit of sauce to her, doesn't she?" he joked.

"That she does, but it's tempered by her sweetness."

"Indeed." Sam shifted in his chair to get comfortable and asked the question he'd been thinking about all day. "Have you discovered what was in that ring?"

"There wasn't much poison left in the ring to test. Gavriel and Lady Lilja have been helping. I think we might have come up with a similar poison, but I can't be sure. I have no one to test it on."

That posed a problem. If they could replicate the poison from Sage's ring, then it would give them an advantage in the war. From what he got from his sister-in-law's few words was that it worked as a paralytic. If needed, he could get his hands on a Scythian to test, but it would be dangerous.

Then there was the other option. Blaise. He could ask her to help with the experiment, but he didn't want to. She was their ally. What if something went wrong with the poison? They couldn't risk her death. But…she truly was the easiest route. All he had to do was walk down two corridors, up three flights of stairs to her, and ask.

He exhaled harshly. "I'll find you a subject."

"The sooner the better."

"You'll have your test subject by the end of the week."

"You're not going to do something terribly dangerous, are you?"

Sam smiled wickedly. "Why, no, I'm just going to do a little fishing."

"Fishing, you say?" Jacob asked, rocking in his chair.

"Yes, fishing."

Now all he needed was the proper bait, and Ruth would be just to their taste.

NINETEEN

SAGE

"I'M READY TO LEAVE THIS blasted room," Sage said, glancing away from the velvety night sky.

Tehl glanced up from the book he was reading, his forehead all wrinkled. "What was that?"

A little bit of warmth seeped into her heart at how mussed and disoriented he appeared, like he'd been yanked from a completely different world. "What are you reading?"

He placed his book on his lap and shrugged. "A little bit of nonsense."

That she did not expect. Tehl was always so practical. Very few times had she ever seen him show a shred of whimsy. "You? Prone to a little bit of drivel, are we?" she teased.

"Everyone needs an escape once in a while," he reasoned.

His comment was offhand, but it was like cold water had been thrown over her. She was the reason he needed an escape. Each night, he barely slept, because she woke him with her thrashes and crying. Not once did he complain.

"I'll leave you to it," she murmured, turning back to the window.

"No," the crown prince said softly. He placed his book on the table next to the fire and gestured to the chair across from him. "I'm quite finished. Why don't you come and sit with me and tell me what's on your mind?"

She arched a brow and plopped into the other chair. "Why do you think there's anything on my mind?"

Tehl snorted and crossed his legs at the ankles. "You've been pacing for a good two hours, Sage."

She hadn't even noticed. Her mind had been a whirl with so many things, she'd hardly noticed how the night deepened.

Sage glanced at the fire and stared at the glowing embers, trying to figure out where to start. There were too many things to speak about and not enough time. It made her anxious. He wiggled in his chair to get more comfortable as the silence continued, and she peeked at Tehl from underneath her lashes. That's one thing she appreciated about him. He didn't have to fill the silence, and, yet, it didn't feel uncomfortable when they didn't speak.

"I'm ready to leave this room."

Tehl nodded but didn't look her way and continued to stare into the fire like it held the answers to every problem in the world.

Sage continued. "I'm strong enough to leave this room. I have been for a few days."

"I agree with you."

She blinked. Well, she hadn't expected that. She'd expected an argument. "I'm glad."

He turned to her and pinned her with his deep blue eyes. "Physically, you are healthy enough to leave this room, but are you prepared for what is outside that door?"

No, she wasn't, but she didn't have time to wait for that. No one did. "I have to be."

"The choice is yours," he said, "but I want you to consider the cost. Little things trigger you. I won't always be with you, and that leaves you vulnerable to the prying eyes of others." He held up a hand when she opened her mouth to retort. "I don't care what others say, but I do care about how it will affect you. What affects you, affects me. Are you prepared for that?"

It was difficult letting Tehl help her when an episode overwhelmed her. But to have others witness her weakness? The thought alone made her shudder, but she knew she couldn't hide forever.

"I know what it will cost me, but the cost is worth it. I'm needed."

"You are needed, but we don't need to shove you in the middle of everything. I can make arrangements to ease you back into palace life."

"We don't have time for that." Her throat tightened with the fear that rose up from her belly. Every moment they dallied, was a moment they lost.

"What do you know of what's coming?" Tehl asked, his voice grave.

"If we do not band together, it will be the end of us all."

Her ominous words hung in the air, heavy, and as dark as black waves crashing against the bluff.

The crown prince rubbed a hand across his mouth. "What do you suggest we do?"

"That's precisely what I wished to speak to you about. In our acquaintance, we have two individuals who are the bridge to allies we desperately need if we are to win this war."

Tehl gazed at her thoughtfully. "You mean Lilja and Rafe?"

That surprised her. She suspected he knew about Lilja, but not about Rafe. "That's right. I'm astonished you know about Rafe."

"He didn't tell me willingly, but we've reached an understanding all the same."

"Good. It will help if he hates you a little less."

Tehl chuckled. "I think you'll be surprised how well we get along these days."

"Are you friends?"

"In loose terms." He leaned closer, clasping his hands together and hanging them between his knees. "So, you're proposing an alliance with a mythical race, which hasn't been seen in hundreds of years, and with the kingdom that just tried to overthrow our crown?"

She scowled at him. "Well, when you put it that way, it sounds idiotic."

He held his hands up. "It's not idiotic—insane maybe, but not idiotic." His lips twitched as if he was fighting a smile.

Sage gaped. "You're teasing me."

"Yes. What of it?"

Who was this man? Her Tehl rarely got the end of a punchline. *Her Tehl.* Some heat crept into her cheeks. When had she started thinking of him that way? "Nothing, just a delightful surprise."

"You think I'm delightful?"

Of course, he'd hone in on that. "As delightful as a burr in my boot," she retorted.

Tehl grinned at her with a twinkle in his eyes. "There she is. I was wondering where my fiery wife had gone."

Sage waved a hand at him as he leaned back into his chair, bumping his elbow into the table near the fire. Her eyes narrowed at the book sitting precariously on the edge. The foolish man would burn his book if he wasn't careful.

She popped up from her chair and rescued the book, tossing it onto the bed, before sitting back down.

"That's no way to treat books," Tehl commented.

"Neither is burning them."

"It wasn't going to burn."

"Says you."

The bickering made her smile. It was comfortable. It felt like home.

He mirrored her smile before sobering. "So, how do you propose we unite three kingdoms?"

"We need to approach Lilja and Rafe separately. I think Lilja will be the easier sell."

"Because she's been helping our people all this time?"

Sage ignored that comment. How much had she helped if she was hiding? "Because she's my family, and I know..." She forced the words out: "She's a good person." She knew it was the truth, but Sage was still hurt. "She's old enough to understand the stakes. Convincing Lilja will be the easiest."

"And Rafe?"

"He holds sway. How much—" She shrugged. "I don't know."

"He seems too highly educated to be someone lowly."

Those were her thoughts, too. Rafe was too arrogant to be common. "Those are my thoughts too, in a way, but he doesn't give much away. And he's an excellent liar."

"Indeed, he is. He's helped us so far, more or less, and after..." Tehl paused, pursing his lips. "After our broken delegation in Scythia. I'm sure he's already reported to Methi."

She ignored his comment about the delegation. As it was, the memories were trying to creep up on her, but she wouldn't let them. "That will work to our benefit. They will already know how dangerous the threat is if they do nothing. Plus, if Aermia falls, so does Methi," she said. It was the sad, grim truth of it.

"When would you like to meet with them?"

"I've already sent for Lilja."

Tehl nodded. "I can approach Rafe tomorrow."

"I would like us to meet with them in private, if it's acceptable to you."

He blinked. "Together?"

"Well, we are to rule together, are we not?" she asked, a little stung.

"It's not that I don't desire that, it's just… You've always kept to those you view as yours, and I to mine."

"I think it's time to change that. We can't afford miscommunications; the stakes are too high."

"I agree. What time would you like me to be here to meet with Lilja?"

"After dinner perhaps."

"Would you like me to take dinner with you?"

The request was shy, so sweet that it made her feel both happy and unworthy. Happy that he'd want to eat with her. Unworthy that he'd spend his time with a soiled creature.

"I'd like that. Maybe we should send for dinner for Lilja and Hayjen as well. Negotiations are always better on a full stomach."

"You are quite right."

They lapsed into silence, each lost to their own thoughts. Sage watched him from the corner of her eye, marveling at how lucky she was to have such a friend.

"You're my friend."

Tehl startled, his eyes widening. "Where did that come from?"

"The proper response is 'Sage, you're my friend as well.'"

"Sage, you're much more than my friend. You're my consort."

His words echoed in her ears, and her fingernails sunk into the arms of the seat. "Don't call me that." Her words were full of venom and darkness. She was no one's consort. Never again.

Tehl reached between their chairs and brushed his fingertips along her left hand. "I won't call you that again."

"Ever," she whispered.

"Ever," he promised. "Release the chair, love, or you'll hurt your hands."

She didn't move.

"I'd hate for you to damage your hands. Think of all the daggers you won't be able to throw."

Sage gritted her teeth and focused on her husband's face. "That's not as funny as you thought it was."

He graced her with a lopsided grin. "True, but it got you back to the present, didn't it?"

It did. "Thank you," she said, forcing her hands to release their death grip on the chair.

The warlord seemed to haunt her every waking hour, but there was one thing in particular she'd been dreaming about that terrified her, even in the bright light of day. One nightmare she could put to rest if she did one simple thing.

"I'm having Mira examine me tomorrow."

Tehl jerked, his mouth bobbing. "Sage…"

She held up her hand. "My mind has been made up. It needs to be done."

His gaze took a tender edge, and he clasped her right hand between his own. "I don't expect that of you. It's not needed. I trust your word."

Tears clogged her throat. "I was drugged many times. I don't know what happened to my body." Her voice cracked. "I'd like to think I would know, but the truth is I don't. And despite everything *he* said… He's a mad man, not to be trusted." She swallowed heavily. "Our children could be called into question; that is reason enough."

His nostrils flared. "They'll accept any child from you if I accept it."

"That's what makes you a good man, but I can't live with that. Also—" She squeezed her eyes closed, keeping her tears at bay. "I need to know for myself. I can't keep imagining the worst."

His jaw worked as he thought about it. From the surly expression on his face, he clearly didn't like it. "Do you want me to go with you?" he asked, hesitantly, looking in every direction but at her.

Her heart squeezed, and the world shifted around her. Of all the things he could have done or said to make Sage love him. It was that. Clearly, it made him uncomfortable, and, to be honest, she was, too. Not to mention that it wasn't done. Men didn't accompany women to examinations, let alone princes. But he knew it would be hard for her, and he didn't want her to be alone. That was true companionship.

"No, thank you."

He nodded, still not looking her way.

Sage scooted to the edge of her seat and placed a hand on his cheek, causing his gaze to clash with hers. "I am lucky, indeed, to be married to such a fine man." She dropped a small kiss on to his left cheek and leaned back.

Tehl reached up and held her hand to his cheek. "We'll make it through this."

"Together."

"Together," he whispered back.

TWENTY

SAGE

"YOU'RE PACING."

Sage cast a glance Tehl's way, and then she continued her route across his study. When he'd suggested they meet Lilja in his study, she'd jumped at the chance. But the longer she was away from something familiar, the more jittery she became.

She shook out her hands and bounced on the tips of her toes as she stopped in front of a huge wall lined with books. Her hands itched to pull out the old tomes from the shelves and crack them open, just to see what secrets they held. Her nose wrinkled as she peered closer at the ones at her eyeline. *Royal House of Aermia* and the *Laws of Aermia*. Maybe those held *too* many secrets.

Her gaze flitted up the bookshelf, her attention snagging on a deep blue book with faded gold filigree adorning the spine. It looked out of place among the sea of brown, tan, and black spines surrounding it.

Without meaning to, she stretched for it, but it was well beyond her reach. Sage stepped up onto the bookshelf and extended again, barely missing her mark. A gurgle sounded behind her, and heat swamped her back as a solid arm slid around her waist.

"I look away for one moment and you climb things," Tehl growled. "What part of 'take it easy' did you not comprehend?"

Sage scowled at the books and wiggled in his grasp. "I was trying to reach a book."

"Clearly." A sigh. "Which one?"

She tipped her head back and pointed to the elusive blue book. "That one."

He chuckled, ruffling the hair at her neck. "I should have known."

Tehl reached over her head and deftly pulled the book from the shelf with ease. She glared at his hand as he pulled her from the bookshelf and held the book out to her. Tall people sure had it easy.

She plucked it from his hand and stepped away from him. "Thank you," she said mulishly.

A snort. "Don't sound too grateful," he retorted, his voice drifting away.

A sigh escaped her. She wasn't unthankful; she was tired of others doing things for her when she could do them for herself. But she needed to be reasonable. They were just helping. Turning on her heel, she strode to Tehl's desk and crowded next to him until he looked up at her with a raised brow.

"Thank you."

He studied her for a moment and dipped his chin. "You're welcome." He pointed his quill at her treasure. "Are you going to open it?"

Sage brushed her hand gently across the cover and opened it with care. A smile graced her face as she read the title.

Gifts from the Sea.

Of all the books to pick up, she'd picked one about the sea. She turned another page, the musty scents of aged paper and old ink greeting her like old friends. How long had it been since she'd read a book? It seemed like such a luxury.

Her gaze bounced back to the practical tomes adorning the shelves. "This doesn't seem like it fits."

"It doesn't." Tehl shuffled a few papers to the side and leaned back in his chair, his gaze distant as he stared out of the adjacent windows toward his balcony. "My father spent a great deal of time in this room. My mother snuck in here to work on her correspondence." A smile. "Misery loves company. But when she didn't have work, she came and read. My parents didn't need to talk, they just enjoyed being in the company of each other."

Her gaze darted down to the book in her hands. "This is your mother's?" she asked.

"It is."

She held it out to him, feeling uncomfortable. She didn't mean to touch something that was clearly precious to his family. He looked up at her and gently pushed it back toward her. "You take it. It's collecting dust on that shelf anyway. My mum gained joy from trading books with others. I'm sure she would have given it to you herself if she were here. Plus—" He glanced at the bookshelves and to the chairs clustered next to the open balcony doors. "It would do Father's heart good to find you here reading sometime."

That sounded like an invitation. "And you wouldn't mind?"

"You're quiet enough." His lips curved into a smile. "I've found I like company when I'm being forced to do something I hate."

Her lips tipped up. "Misery loves company?"

"Something like that."

A knock.

Sage straightened and placed her book carefully on the desk.

"Enter," Tehl called.

Garreth opened the door. "Lilja and Hayjen are here for you."

"Send them in."

She braced herself as Hayjen strolled into the room. His face was placid, but his ice blue eyes held a wealth of emotion that she promptly ignored. Emotion had no place in this conversation. Lilja commanded Sage's attention as she swept into the room, her citrus scent teasing the air.

Tehl stood and gestured to the chairs and refreshments near the balcony. "Please sit."

Sage jumped when a hand settled on the small of her back. She glanced up into Tehl's heartbreakingly handsome face. "Yes?"

"You ready to sit down?"

"Yes."

She allowed him to guide her to the chairs and sat much less gracefully than the Sirenidae, now staring at her with fathomless magenta eyes, had.

An awkward silence settled over the group as Sage stared at her friends-turned-family. The ones who'd lied to her. She blew out a breath. Today wasn't about personal feelings. Today was about bridging divides.

"You know why you're here," she said.

Lilja nodded. "You want a meeting."

"We do," Tehl rumbled.

"They won't help," her aunt said. Her tone was matter-of-fact.

"They will," Sage said. There wasn't any other choice.

"In hundreds of years, they've done nothing, despite my entreaties. What makes you think they will now when they wouldn't listen to one of their own?"

"Ezra." Saying his name hurt her.

Lilja's brow furrowed in confusion. "Who's Ezra?"

"A Sirenidae I met in Scythia." Sage bowed her head. "He was my doctor."

"Your doctor?" Hayjen asked. "As in he worked with the warlord?"

"Something like that," she murmured. "I thought he was my friend…until he tried to drown me."

Tehl sucked in a sharp breath.

"I was bathing one day when he appeared by my side."

The memory rose to the forefront of her mind, unbidden.

Ezra knelt beside the pool, his face looking infinitely sad as he leaned toward her.

"Wh-what are you doing here?" she screeched, blinking water out of her eyes. "Get out!"

He dipped his finger into the water and drew a pattern. "You're too good for our world, Sage. You shouldn't be here."

She took a tiny step away from him. Something in his voice was off. It sounded as if someone had died. "Thank you. If you give me a moment, I'll get dressed and come out to you."

His lips tipped up, but he didn't look up from his water drawings. "Do you remember when we spoke of peace?"

Chills erupted along her arms. Something wasn't right. Why was he bringing that up now? She glided back another step, eyeing the stairs that led out of the pool. She darted a look to the open door. No guards. Could she make it out of the pool, to the outer door? Unlikely.

"Yes," she said, slowly twisting toward the Sirenidae. She jerked when her gaze clashed with his.

"I want to give you peace," he whispered, and something akin to determination altered his expression. "I'm going to help you end your suffering."

She balked and opened her mouth to scream, but he lunged. Water closed around her face as he shoved her under. What the bloody hell? Her feet touched the bottom, and she propelled herself to the surface.

Gasping for air, she pushed toward the stairs, panic building in her breast. All she needed to do was make it to the stairs. Her foot landed on one stair, then two, and then three. Hope blossomed. Maybe she would make it.

A shriek flew out of her as a hand grabbed her ankle. Her palms slammed against the stone, and her chin cracked against the step's edge, clicking her teeth together. Dark spots dotted her vision, and the room swirled. She dug her fingers into the stone as she was pulled back and kicked at his hand.

"Let GO!"

He jerked harder, and her nails broke, her hands slipping. She sucked in another breath and screamed, the sound piercing the air, and echoing around the empty room.

She scrambled forward when the hand released her ankle, but she didn't make it far. Ezra's arm wrapped around her torso, and his hand slapped across her mouth, cutting off her screams. He towed her back into the pool, kicking and screaming.

"Don't do this," she pleaded from behind his hand.

"I'm sorry..." His voice broke. "I have to save you from him. I won't let you be used. You deserve peace after everything you've suffered. I'm going to grant you at least that."

Her eyes widened. He was really going to do it. Ezra was going to drown her.

She pulled in a deep breath through her nose when he kissed the top of her head and pulled her under. All sound disappeared except for Ezra's soft humming. She struggled against him, bit at his hand, raked her broken nails down his arms. But he didn't budge. Panic filled her as her lungs burned, begging for air. She flung her head back and crashed it into his face in a blind panic. She needed air. Now. But even that didn't help. It earned her a hand around her throat.

Unable to hold her breath any longer, she sucked in a breath and choked. Her body spasmed at the invasion in her lungs. It burned. Stories said drowning was peaceful, but those were lies. Her body seized, trying to get rid of the fluid. She tried to claw her way to the air, the surface of the pool just above her, taunting her. She gazed at her hair floating around the pool and closed her eyes. This was how she would die.

Suddenly, something slammed into her, breaking the vise around her torso and throat.

She touched her throat, flinching at the rough texture, her story dying off. She could still feel the echo of his hands around her throat.

Sage met Lilja's pained gaze. "He didn't want to hurt me. He wanted to spare me the pain of what he knew was coming." She swallowed. "There were many times I wished I had died then."

Tehl cursed under his breath as Lilja's eyes became watery. But Sage continued.

"That's everyone's future if we do not band together and fight. The Sirenidae are naïve if they don't think Scythia will come for them. If Ezra was working with him, what makes you think others won't to save their families, their friends?" She let the question hang in the air before she continued. "I know what I would do for my family. Anything. No one is safe until he is gone."

"We don't disagree with you," Lilja said softly.

"Good, then you'll arrange a meeting," Tehl said.

Hayjen and Lilja exchanged a glance before looking between the two of them.

"We will do our best, and you'll have your meeting, but I can't make any promises that they'll listen. However, know this, we'll be on your side."

"Will that make a difference?" Tehl asked.

Her uncle cast a sharp look his way.

The crown prince held up a hand. "Your support means something to us, but, when it comes to negotiation, only those who possess power matter."

Blunt as ever. Tehl wasn't wrong. Sage arched a brow at her silent aunt as if to say, 'do you want me to tell him or will you?'

"That won't be an issue," her aunt supplied. "I may be banished, but I'm still a daughter of the king."

Tehl blinked but otherwise didn't react. "Well, that's… fortuitous."

"Indeed," Sage said.

Lilja pinned her with an unreadable look. "We will arrange the meeting within the next two weeks in exchange for something."

Of course, she wanted something. The woman was a bloody pirate for heaven's sakes.

"Next week," Tehl cut in. "Time is against us."

She nodded gracefully. "Within the week." Her attention turned back to Sage. "I'd like to have a conversation with you in private."

That worked perfectly. Sage also wished to speak to her aunt in private. "Then it's agreed."

Tehl held out his hand, and Lilja clasped his forearm.

"We're in accord."

"We are."

The Sireniade turned her attention back to Sage. "Can we speak now?"

"Yes." She turned to Tehl who watched her. "Would you like us to go someplace else?"

He shook his head. "I'm in need of a bout or two." He jerked his chin at Hayjen. "Would you like to join me in the ring?"

Her uncle smiled, and it was a bit feral. "I always enjoy a good bout." He pushed from his chair and smacked a kiss against his wife's cheek as Tehl stood. The crown prince moved around his chair and placed a hand on Sage's shoulder, squeezing.

"If you need me, send for me."

"I'll be fine," she said softly.

"I know." He said it simply. Like he believed it to be the honest truth.

Sage smiled at him and reached up to give his hand a squeeze. "Once we're done, maybe you could bring your book back?" The question hung in the air.

He blinked. "I'd like that."

"Okay." She fought a blush as he stared at her like he was trying to see inside her mind. The fact was that she didn't want to be alone, and she enjoyed his company. When she was alone, her monsters liked to come out and play.

He released her and strode across the room, each step purposeful, and flung open the door. Hayjen followed him, and a rush of nervousness and anger slammed into Sage as the door quietly clicked shut.

Sage turned to her aunt and cocked her head. "You've gotten me alone. What do you want?"

TWENTY-ONE

LILJA

HOSTILITY AND ANGER RADIATED OFF Sage. It was evident in every line of her niece's body. Even the way she tilted her head spoke of her readiness to fight. It pained Lilja to see her like that, but she knew it well. She'd been there herself. It had been years, but some days, it felt like yesterday.

"I want nothing from you," she said softly.

Sage tossed her head with an unladylike snort. "You and I both know you don't want nothing. Stop lying to me, or is it such a habit by now that it comes naturally?"

"That was earned," Lilja said. "It's natural to be angry when someone keeps the truth from you. I can't change the past, but I can apologize. I am sorry."

Her niece gazed out the windows. "I know you're sorry, but it doesn't make it okay."

"You're right. Apologizing is only half of it. Taking the steps to correct the misdeed is what matters."

Sage nodded and bit her lips as if to keep from saying what was on her mind.

"Ma fleur, tell me what's troubling you," Lilja asked gently.

"I can't understand why you did nothing. The women," Sage choked, her green eyes flashing. "They are suffering so much and yet you kept silent. I don't understand why you didn't say anything to me months ago. I would have believed you. I would have pressed the crown."

"You weren't ready."

"Not ready? No, you weren't ready to let go of your freedom."

A spark of anger flared in her chest, but Lilja tamped it down. Sage was hurt, lost, and looking for someone to blame for the atrocities she'd gone through. She needed to be calm. She could handle her niece's rage and pain. She needed someone like Lilja to help her, because they were more alike than she knew.

"There was a time when I felt the same as you. When I came out of Scythia, I was more broken than a person should be." Lilja looked at her hands, still able to feel the weight of her tiny daughter in her arms. "I lost more than just myself in that hellhole. I lost my daughter."

Sage's eyes widened, and Lilja's breath hitched. Even now, after all these years, a pain unlike anything she'd ever known welled up inside her. "They took my first and greatest love from me, and left me a broken, wretched carcass. When I finally escaped, I sought solace in my family." She smiled bitterly. "They helped for a time, but when I came out of my sorrow and demanded vengeance, no one lifted a finger. They claimed it was too dangerous to leave the sea. They also thought to use it as an example of what would happen if anyone disobeyed their laws."

"Those bastards," Sage spat, her green eyes sparking with anger.

"Indeed," Lilja said. "They were supportive as long as they didn't have to leave their bubble of safety. It was there and then, that I left. I refused to reside with a people who were so apathetic that they wouldn't fight for those they loved."

"What did you do?"

"I fought. I caused mayhem. I mourned. Then, I found my purpose."

Sage leaned closer. "And what was that?"

"I only had so much power at my disposal. So, I did my best to protect those who could not protect themselves, and I made sacrifices."

"So, you pirated."

"I did."

"Not for selfish gain, but to keep others from Scythia."

"Yes." Lilja scooted forward in her chair. "I didn't tell you this to excuse the choices I've made in life. I'm imperfect and I make mistakes, but I also stand by the choices I make. The reason I have explained my story, ma fleur, is so that you know you're not alone. You will *never* experience what I experienced. I will fight for you with my dying breath. I will not turn a blind eye to your rage, pain, and sorrow. I will stand beside you and support you when you need it. You will never be made to feel like this was somehow your fault, and your horrors will not be turned into a life lesson." She held out her hand to Sage. "I will always hold my hand out when you're drowning, because that's what you do when you love someone. That's the meaning of true family and friendship."

Sage stared at her hand, her eyes becoming glossy. "What was her name?" she whispered.

Soul-wrenching pain stabbed her. "Gem."

"Gem," Sage said softly. Slowly, she stretched out a hand and placed it in Lilja's. "I won't ever let another girl face what you and I went through. I'll fight for them. I'll fight for Gem."

Lilja squeezed her niece's hand, relief washing over her. Sometimes a person could lose themselves to bitterness and rage. But Sage hadn't surrendered herself to the darkness; she was just lost.

"As will I."

Lilja tugged on Sage and stood, pulling her into a hug.

Sage stiffened for a moment then embraced Lilja in return, until her lungs felt like they would burst.

"How do I survive this?" Sage whispered against her shoulder. "How do I come back from this?"

"One day at a time, ma fleur." Lilja pulled back and clasped Sage's face between her palms. "Each day will be a fight, but it will get easier. I promise."

Her niece nodded. "I can fight."

Lilja smiled. "I know you can." She pulled her into another hug and then stepped back.

Sage met her gaze squarely. "I'm visiting Mira." Her gaze dropped to her toes. "I need to be examined."

Lilja cursed, her rage almost choking her. So help her, if that fool prince asked that of her, she'd tie him to a rock and drown him, or maybe drop him in leviathan-infested water. "Did Tehl ask that of you?" she asked calmly.

"No." Sage shook her head. "He told me it wasn't necessary, but I need to know."

"Sometimes knowing isn't always better."

"True, but this might help the nightmares, and if there is a child…"

Lilja clasped and squeezed her hands. "We'll love it no differently."

Sage nodded, a tear dripping down her face. "I need to know. Will you come with me?"

Stunned, she stared at her niece and again pulled her into a hug. "Of course, I'll come with you. But wouldn't you rather your mother was there?"

"My mum has been through enough. This is one thing she doesn't need to know, unless Mira finds something. I don't want to worry her more than I already have." She pulled back and wiped at her face. "You, my dear aunt, can handle it. You will stand by my side?"

Lilja nodded. "I will."

She wouldn't let Sage suffer alone. She would give her what no one else did.

Vengeance.

TWENTY-TWO

SAGE

SHE WAS GOING TO PUKE.

"Ma fleur, it's going to be okay."

Lilja ran her hand over Sage's arm in a soothing motion, but it did nothing to calm her nerves. She wanted to object to everything about the situation. The longer she lay on Mira's table, the more she wanted to bolt from the room.

"You don't have to do this," her aunt said in a hushed tone.

Sage stared up at the ceiling. If only that was true. Much rode on the outcome of the examination.

Mira walked through the door, and Sage's stomach lurched. The blond healer closed the door, shutting off Jacob's quiet humming from the main section of the infirmary.

Mira moved to her right side and grinned at her. Sage gave her a wobbly smile and groped for Lilja's hand. Long fingers clasped hers, and her heart slowed just a touch. She wasn't alone. Everything would be okay.

"Sage. I'll be gentle, and it'll be over before you know it." Mira hesitated, her face a mask of concern. "Are you sure you want me to…?"

"Yes."

She really wanted to shout 'no,' but she didn't have a choice. The examination had to be done. She hadn't thought about it when she was in Scythia, but her flow had never come. It became glaringly apparent when she'd been lying in bed several days prior in the infirmary.

Sage focused on the white-washed ceiling as Mira moved around to the end of the cot.

"Please scoot down to the end," Mira's calm voice said.

She complied and blew out a breath as the healer gently touched her knees.

"Please let your legs fall to the side."

Sage gritted her teeth and closed her eyes, obeying Mira's command. Lilja squeezed her hand in support which she squeezed in return. Breathe. That's all she had to do. Breathe through the violation that was necessary because of *him.*

She bit her lip as Mira began the examination. Her eyes teared up at the slight pinch, but it wasn't the worst thing she'd ever experienced. Red flashed through her mind. Pain. Blood. Helplessness.

"Almost over," her friend said softly.

Sage swallowed hard and focused on the swirls inside her lids. This was for the best. Not knowing was the worst. If she was with child, then she'd deal with it, but she couldn't stand the nightmares that came each night when she imagined the worst. Dreaming of the warlord taking what wasn't his while she slept and couldn't move. She inhaled deeply to keep the contents of her stomach *in* her stomach.

Her right hand moved from the table to her belly. She'd made the decision the day before that she'd love and adore the child with every single breath she took, despite how it was begotten. Children were innocent, and she'd not condemn an innocent for the sins of the damned.

"All done." Mira straightened and pulled the sheet over Sage's legs.

Sage forced her eyes open and lifted her head, meeting the deep blue gaze of one of her dearest friends. Mira broke into a huge smile, and Sage's breath caught.

"You're intact, Sage. There's no child. There's been no ravishment."

A choked sob escaped her, and she lay back, tears streaking down her cheeks. No child. No violation. Zane had kept his word.

She cried louder, hating that she'd used his name unbidden. That she was thankful he'd kept his word.

"It's okay, ma fleur," Lilja murmured, stroking the hair at her temple.

Sage untangled her left hand from her aunt and pressed the heels of her hands to her eyes, hoping to stop the flow of tears. Relief. She felt sheer bloody relief.

Mira placed a hand on her right shoulder. "It's over, Sage. It's over."

It was far from over. But it was one less nightmare that would plague her each night.

Glass shattered, startling her. She met Mira's widened eyes as Jacob cursed loudly from the other room.

"Missy, everything is all right," Jacob said loudly.

"Who the bloody hell are you?"

Sage bolted upright, almost cracking her head against Mira's. "Jasmine."

TWENTY-THREE

JASMINE

SHE SWIPED AT HER EYES and tried to make sense of where she was. Her throat ached something fierce, and she longed for a drink of water. But what she wanted more were answers.

Her fingers slipped along the petite dagger she'd snatched off the table near her side. An old man held both hands up placatingly as she shifted to the side, eyeing the basin she'd thrown at him.

"It's okay, missy. My name is Jacob."

She blinked the sweat from her eyes and held the dagger out in front of her. Her arm shook, and each breath was wheezed and horridly painful. Her eyes felt like they were full of sand, and her lids weighed a million pounds. All she wanted to do was lie down and go to sleep, but fear had her holding the blade higher.

Had the Scythians gotten her again? The little old man didn't look Scythian, but that didn't mean anything. All it meant was that they'd captured an old man who looked to be Aermian, although there was something about his eyes. They shone like copper behind his spectacles. She'd not seen eyes like those before.

"I will only ask one time. What do you want with me?" she rasped. He opened his mouth, but she shook her head. "Think carefully of your answer, or I might be tempted to slit you from your navel to your gullet."

"I'm Jacob, Royal Healer of Aermia."

She scoffed. Why would the royal Healer be tending to her? Likely story. "Listen here, you old coot—"

"Jas," a familiar voice whispered.

Jasmine froze then peeked over her shoulder at the one person she had been to hell with. "Sage?"

The green-eyed beauty slowly approached her like she approached a dangerous animal. "I'm here, Jas. We're both safe."

"Safe?" she asked.

Sage gave her a wobbly smile. "Yeah, relatively."

Jas's time in Scythia had taught her that nowhere was safe. People only experienced the appearance of safety. She shakily gestured to the old man edging around her cot. "And him?"

"He's harmless. Jacob is the palace Healer. He and Mira." Sage gestured to the blond woman with huge blue eyes behind her. "They've been taking care of you. You're very ill."

Stars above, her fatigued body agreed with that statement. It was worse than when she'd been thrown from her horse when she was thirteen. Everything pained her, but it was her labored breathing that bothered her the most. It was like breathing with a wet rag stuffed inside her mouth.

A growl startled her, and she stared down at the beast in which her fingers had found purchase. She gaped at the large golden eyes staring at her. A leren. A bloody leren. Flashes of the man-eater surfaced in her mind.

"Nali?" Jasmine asked.

The beast chuffed and settled down while Jasmine tried to process everything around her. The room began to spin, and she placed her hand with the dagger on the cot to steady herself. She lifted her head to stare at Sage. "The twins?"

Sage smiled. "They're here. In the palace."

The blade slid from her fingers and clattered noisily to the floor. All that mattered were the children. The room spun, and Jasmine smiled as everything dimmed.

Her family was safe.

The second time she woke, it was much more peaceful.

Jasmine opened her eyes and stretched, a huge yawn cracking her jaw.

"Jasmine?" a soft-spoken voice called.

Glancing to the right, she locked eyes with the lovely blond she vaguely remembered. "Who are you?"

The blond smiled at her, flashing white straight teeth. "I'm Mira. I'm your healer." She abandoned her herbs on a sturdy wooden table, wove through the cots, and paused by her side. "How are you feeling?"

Like someone had punched her in the chest repeatedly. "I've been better."

Mira knelt by her side and held out her hand. "Will you permit me to check your temperature?"

She snorted, the motion causing her throat to scream in pain. "I think we passed pleasantries and manners by now if you've been tending to me," she rasped. Her brows furrowed. How long exactly had the healers been taking care of her. "How long have I been here?" she asked, as Mira lay cool fingers against her brow.

"Almost three weeks."

Jasmine flinched. Three weeks? "As long as that?"

The healer pulled away and placed two fingertips on the underside of her wrist. "You've been very ill, Jasmine. It's a miracle that your fever broke."

The severe expression of the healer's face chilled Jasmine. She must have been at death's door.

"How surprised are you that I'm awake and speaking to you right now?" She studied the blond's features carefully. Reading people was a particular skill of hers. Most of the time, she could tell when someone lied to her.

But the healer didn't shy away from her question. "I didn't think you'd survive. You sustained grievous injuries on your way to Aermia. Then, being exposed to the elements and taking a swim in the chilly water so late in the year did nothing for your health. The sickness settled in your lungs, and we've battled it ever since."

Jasmine rubbed a hand over her chest. Her breaths now weren't exactly painful, but they weren't comfortable. Her thoughts turned to her niece and nephew. She *needed* to see them. "Am I contagious?"

"No. Otherwise, the princess would not have been allowed to visit you."

"Sage has been visiting?"

"Every single day. You actually just missed her. The crown prince summoned her, or she'd still be here by your side."

She was beyond lucky to have such a friend to care and watch over her. Jasmine eyed Mira as she tucked the blanket around her feet and bustled to the fireplace, pulling a kettle with care from the heat. She didn't doubt that this woman had much to do with her survival. The infirmary was clearly her domain. It was evident by the way she moved with confidence.

"Thank you," Jasmine said.

The healer glanced over her shoulder and smiled. "There's no need to thank me. I did what anyone else would."

"That I highly doubt. And I would be grateful to anyone who brought me back to my littles." She paused. "Can I see them?"

Mira slipped around the cot with a cup of tea in her hand and sat in the chair next to Jas. She placed the cup on a little side table and wiggled an arm underneath her shoulders. "Can you sit up?"

Jasmine nodded, but she gasped out a breath when pain slammed into her.

"Yep, those are the broken ribs. Luckily for you, you've slept through the worst of it."

If this wasn't the worst of it, broken ribs must be something truly heinous. She gritted her teeth and sat up slowly with the help of Mira. The healer plucked the cup of tea from the table with her other hand and held it to her lips.

"Drink up. It will soothe your throat and help with the pain."

Jas obeyed and blew on the liquid before taking a swallow. It burned a little, but it soothed her dry, scratchy throat, which was a godsend.

After a few more gulps, Mira pulled the cup away, and she licked her lips. She hadn't forgotten that the healer hadn't answered her question. If she wouldn't get the children sick, there was no one who could keep them from her. She'd drag herself from the damn room if that's what it took.

"My children," she stated. "I want to see them."

The healer nodded and placed the cup back on the table before lowering her back to the cot. "I promise you will see them soon."

"Do they know I'm here?" *Alive.*

"No, they do not."

Anger was her first emotion. "Why?" she bit out.

Serious blue eyes peered into her own stormy gaze. "We didn't know if you'd make it. I did everything in my power to bring you back to your little ones. There was talk of letting them know you were here, but, in the end, it was decided no. Could you imagine if we let them see you and then you died?" she murmured.

Jasmine's anger melted away. That made sense. These people were only looking out for Jade and Ethan. She reached out and clasped the blond's hand. "Thank you. I understand the decision you made. But what about now?"

"I think it will be best if you gained more strength before we brought them in."

Her heart screamed 'no,' but her head told her it was a good plan. The children wouldn't suffer in her absence. She'd be the only one to suffer, but she knew she wasn't strong enough to care for them now, nor let them leave her again. They'd never leave her sight again.

The next week passed with long, boring bouts of silence and naps. Each day, her body gained strength. She'd come to enjoy her visits with the Royal Healer, Jacob. He had an interesting mind and an even more interesting sense of humor.

She looked forward to her daily visits with Sage. Her friend tried her best to be positive, but darkness clung to her like a cloak. Jas couldn't imagine the horrors that had been rent on her during their time in Scythia. Her own short visit to the warlord's chamber would haunt her for the rest of her life, and that was only a handful of minutes. Sage had been there for months.

Jasmine glanced down to her shoulder and ran her finger over the long thin scar that she'd carry until she died. What kind of scars did her friend carry?

She closed her eyes and paused in her rocking. Over the last week, nausea would strike at the oddest times and leave just as quickly. The worst part was that she didn't have an appetite, so all she did was dry-heave. Then there was the fatigue. It was like she couldn't keep her eyes open. All she wanted to do was sleep.

Her stomach churned, and she leaned forward, her head between her knees, and panted. Sometimes if she breathed just right, she wouldn't dry-heave.

A weathered hand appeared underneath her nose, and, with it, the bitter scent of peppermint. "Thank you, Jacob," she croaked. She inhaled deeply through her nose while the Healer ran a palm across the top of her back.

"My pleasure, missy."

He continued his ministrations until the bout passed, and she straightened in the rocking chair she had absconded from the elderly man. Jacob moved around her chair and eased himself into the one across from her.

"How are you feeling today?" he asked.

Jasmine waved a hand at him. "Better and stronger each day."

He pierced her with his unique gaze and then tapped his right temple. "How about up here?"

She shrugged a shoulder. "I'm tired. Honestly? Awful." She paused and glanced toward the door for eavesdroppers.

"You can speak freely here."

"I know, but I just don't want anyone overhearing one word." She turned back to Jacob and heaved a sigh. "I feel guilty."

"Why?"

"Because I didn't suffer what Sage did." She shook her head and stared into the fire. "I can see the torment clinging to the princess, the pain. But I didn't experience that. The worst I suffered was fear. Fear of not being able to come back. Fear of not seeing Jade and Ethan again." She swallowed. "The men weren't bad. They had strict rules—but those were to protect me. They never hurt me."

In the past week, she'd found herself even missing them. They weren't bad men. They were just stuck in a bad situation.

The side of her face prickled the longer Jacob stared. "What?" she asked tiredly, turning to the Healer. "You clearly have something on your mind."

The old man steepled his fingers and closed his eyes. He sighed and then scooted his chair closer to her. Jasmine frowned as he pulled her hand between his. "Jasmine. Those men weren't good people."

Her frown deepened. "Just because they're Scythian doesn't make them bad people. That's prejudice of a nasty kind, and I'm surprised to hear such generalities from you."

"That's not what I meant, missy."

He stared at her with a sorrow that made her breath catch. "Then, what do you mean?"

His face creased, and his lips flattened. "Jasmine, love, I have some news that might distress you."

Her mind flashed to the twins. "Are the twins okay?" she asked, squeezing his hand.

"The twins are just fine. It's you whom I'm worried about."

"Pah, I'm just fine."

His face creased even more. "Love, I believe you are with child."

"What?"

"You have all the signs," he said gently. "Fatigue, nausea, lack of the flow."

She flinched, and her gaze dropped to her belly. "It's not possible," she muttered while staring at the little bulge she'd not given a second glance at until now.

"I'm so sorry, Jasmine."

She yanked her eyes from her belly. "It-it can't be possible. I've never…" Bile flooded her mouth, and she swallowed, feeling sick. "I can't be!" Her voice was shrill even in her own ears. "They never touched me." He squeezed her hand, but she barely felt it.

"Are there any timeframes, any days, you cannot remember? Sometimes, certain drugs…"

His voice became fuzzy as she stared blankly at the fire, its heat not warming her in the slightest. She did have missing periods of time. Every night was a blank after dinner. She slept well through the night, and nothing ever disturbed her. That she knew of.

"But they protected me," she said, her voice wobbly. "They cared for me."

"Jasmine. Those who love and care for us, don't take without asking. They don't steal from and harm those they love."

Her lip trembled. "I can't believe it."

"We can do an examination whenever you wish." His lips pressed harder together. "But it's my opinion that you are, indeed, with child."

She pulled her hand from the Healer's and laced her fingers together. "As soon as Mira returns, she'll do the examination and prove you wrong."

She folded her arms. They'd see.

"So?" Jasmine asked, sitting up.

Mira stepped away from her and washed her hands in the bowl behind her. Slowly, the woman turned to her, her face desolate, no expression at all.

Her stomach dropped. "No." Mira blinked and moved to touch her arm, but Jasmine yanked her arm away. "No!"

"You are, indeed, with child, Jasmine."

"But they took care of me." How could they do this? Heat filled her eyes as a big ugly sob erupted from her chest. Chills broke out along her arms as her body flashed hot and then cold.

Mira wrapped her arms around Jasmine, pulled her into a hug, and began to rock her. "It's okay. We'll get through this. You're not alone."

Alone. She was alone. She had no husband. No memory of the creation of the being that was now growing inside her without her permission.

Darkness began to creep into her vision, and the room spun as ice crept through her body. Someone was screaming, a horrible, ugly, gut-wrenching sound of pain and sorrow, but she couldn't lift her head to see who it was.

Huge arms wrapped around her, and she turned into the warmth, trying to burrow into it. Hoping, praying that it would keep the stabbing chill of betrayal from completely freezing what was left of her broken heart.

TWENTY-FOUR

SAM

HE TIGHTENED HIS ARMS AROUND the woman breaking apart in his arms. Her gut-wrenching sobs tore at his heart. "It's okay," he soothed, staring over Jasmine's head at Mira, who looked like she was about to break into tears herself.

Jasmine jerked away from him, almost clipping him in the chin, her tear-stained face turned upward. Something in his chest clenched when her glazed, blue eyes met his.

"They destroyed me," she cried, her eyes rolling into her head, and she slumped into his arms.

"What in the bloody hell?" he whispered, staring wide-eyed at the woman in his arms. "What happened?"

"It's not my place to say," Mira hiccupped, her eyes liquid. "Keep her head elevated."

"Like hell, it isn't," Sam barked, rearranging Jasmine so her neck wasn't crooked. He narrowed his eyes at the healer. "So help me, Mira. I'll shake it out of you if I have to. No one cries like that unless an atrocity has happened." His stomach dropped. The only thing Jasmine had really spoken about were the twins. "Are her children all right?"

"The twins are fine, but…" Mira swallowed and shook her head. "Bring her to the other room where we can warm her by a proper fire. I'll explain more then, once I've had a chance to care for her."

Sam rose and followed Mira out of the room. Jacob rocked in the rocking chair, his white hair sticking up in every direction like he'd been running his hands through it. He watched them enter the room, his mouth turned downward. Sam placed Jasmine down gently and stepped aside, so Mira could make her comfortable. He crossed his arms and shifted on his feet, feeling restless. He hated being in the dark.

"For the second time, I ask, what is wrong?"

Mira cast a glance to her father, and they stared at each other, a silent conversation passing between the two of them. Jacob broke first and met his gaze.

"I'd hoped to be wrong," the old man rasped. "She's been sick for so long, but the nausea, fatigue, and lack of appetite…"

A ringing filled Sam's ears. Most other men wouldn't understand what the healer was alluding to, but not him. He'd met many girls with the same symptoms over the years. "She's with child?" he croaked. It hurt even saying it.

"Yes," Mira said softly while tucking a blanket around the unconscious Jasmine.

He dropped his head to stare at his boots, sorrow for the woman washing over him. The injustice in the world never ceased to amaze him. No one deserved ravishment, to have their choices stolen from them in such a brutal manner.

"She told you what happened?" he asked.

"No, she doesn't have any recollection of the conception at all." Jacob muttered a dark oath. "She defended the men who held her captive. She didn't believe me, so she asked for an examination." He shook his head. "I should have waited. It was too soon."

"She would have noticed, father," Mira said, placing a hand on Jasmine's forehead before sinking down into the chair next to the cot. "We had no choice."

A rage unlike anything Sam had ever experience ignited in his chest. How dare someone touch a woman without her consent. It was one of the most disgusting things he could think of.

His hands twitched by his sides, wanting to strangle someone. This was why men killed for women. This reason right here. They provoked a deep-seated feeling of possessiveness that called for men to protect them.

Mira eyed him, her face hardening. "You reek of unchecked anger. You need to calm down."

"I've got it under control."

"Not from where I'm sitting," she retorted. "If you want to truly help Jasmine, you need to calm down right now, or I'll bar you from the infirmary."

Sam scoffed and smiled arrogantly, even though all he really wanted to do was beat someone into a bloody pulp. "I'm a prince and the spymaster. You couldn't keep me out of here if you wanted to."

Mira pushed from her chair and threw her shoulders back, a steely glint in her eyes. "Listen to me and listen well. You've been in here every night since Sage and Jasmine arrived. Don't think I didn't see you lurking in the dark." She stabbed a finger at Jasmine. "She has been through hell, and she doesn't even know it. From this moment on, she'll need stability and a calm environment. Pregnancies with too much stress will cause damage to the babe and could kill her. She's delicate enough without you bringing a barrage of messy emotions into her life. So, you either calm down and help, or you get the hell out. You better believe me when I say, I'll cut you open before I let you hurt this girl."

He swallowed and forced his anger down. Mira was right. "I'm sorry. I am angry."

"As we all are." Mira tossed her hands in the air, a tear leaking from the corner of her eye. She scrubbed at it angrily. "Which is why I'm going to leave the room until I can regain my composure, and I suggest *you* do the same as well." It was more of a command, not a suggestion.

Mira strode to her father's side and dropped a kiss on his whiskered cheek. "I'll be back soon."

Jacob cupped her cheek. "Take your time. I'll stay here with her."

"I know, but I don't think she should be alone with men right now, so I'll hurry."

The healer nodded, his gaze returning to the fire.

"Sam?"

He glanced at Mira. She snatched a leather pouch off the long table covered with jars of herbs.

"You speak of this to no one."

"I'm as silent as the grave." He'd not breathe a word of it. Once it was out that she was with child and not married, well… He ground his teeth and hissed out a breath. The way of the world was not kind to unmarried pregnant women, no matter how they'd become that way. Again, his rage flared up.

Mira waved her leather bag at him. "You fancy throwing daggers?"

Stabbing something would most definitely help. "May I accompany you?"

"You needn't ask. Come along," she called, moving through the infirmary door. "Let's stab something. Maybe I can exercise the anger and disgust out of my system."

He followed her but didn't reply. Sam already knew the truth. There was no way to rid oneself of those emotions. He'd tried for years. The best he could come up with was to forge it into something else.

The time would come for him to unleash his rage on the world, but it wasn't this day.

Today, he would hone his self-control, so he didn't hurt the little, broken brunette in the infirmary.

TWENTY-FIVE

TEHL

"THERE'S BEEN AN ATTACK ALONG the northern border, near Nagali," Garreth reported. He leaned over Tehl's desk and handed him the missive.

"Our northern border?" Tehl asked, his brows furrowing.

He'd been waiting for the warlord to strike, but this was rather anticlimactic. Why had he attacked there? What used to be a lush farm area was nearly a desolate wasteland. In fact, it had been that way for over two hundred years. There were only a few stubborn Aermians who stayed in the area. But it was a rough way to live between the sand storms and the attacks from predators.

Tehl cut open the missive, scowling further at the letter. There wasn't much information. Basically, only what Garreth had reported. "Is there no further news? Nothing at all?"

"I'm sorry, but no. The only other piece of information I was able to glean from the messenger was that there were few casualties."

"That's good news," he muttered.

"But there were disappearances."

Sage, who had stayed silent until that moment, sat up from the chair she'd been slumped in. "How many?" she asked sharply.

"Ten."

"All women?"

"No. They took three men."

Sage pushed from the chair and strode to the window overlooking the balcony, but not before Tehl saw a flash of pain cross her face. He stared at his wife's back for a moment before glancing at Garreth. "Has Sam dispatched anyone?"

"Yes. We'll have word within a few days."

"All right. Thank you, Garreth."

The Elite bowed to him and exited the room, a slight hitch to his gait. Tehl stared at the missive as the door closed silently behind his friend. "What are you up to?" he muttered.

"He's playing a game," Sage said.

Tehl scowled and glared up at his wife, who'd moved across the room like a wraith. "You're as bad as Sam."

A ghost of a smile flitted across her mouth then disappeared as she leveled a serious look on him. "This wasn't a random attack."

Tehl leaned back in his chair, the leather creaking. "There's nothing out there."

Sage shrugged and sat on the edge of his desk while fingering the feather of his quill. "Make no mistake." She tapped the missive with her knuckles. "He struck here for a reason. He does nothing without a purpose."

He met Sage's haunted green gaze. "What are we really up against, Sage?" She'd said very little about the warlord. Only that he was dangerous.

Her face crumpled, and she turned away from him to pace from one side of the room to the other. "He's calculating. Each move he makes serves a purpose to further his agenda. To say he's intelligent would be like saying the sun is bright." She scrubbed a hand over her face. "The warlord is charismatic, charming. His enthusiasm makes you want to believe what he believes. And if that wasn't enough, he's…" She swallowed, her gaze darting to him. "Well, you know, handsome." Her hands curled into fists.

Tehl pressed his lips together, hating that just speaking about that monster brought her such pain. "You know I wouldn't ask unless it was important."

She chuckled, the sound bitter. "It's more than important. It's dire. I don't have a choice."

"You always have a choice." Even as he said the words he knew they were a lie.

"I've never heard you tell such a bald lie before, Tehl." Sage flopped into her chair and slung her legs over the arm of it. "This was just the beginning." She rolled her head to the side, staring at him. "It will get worse from here. We don't know his angle right now, but we know where this leads." A pause. "War."

War. It was only three letters long, but it held a sinister edge to it and left a bad taste in his mouth. "We need to meet with Rafe tonight."

Sage nodded and closed her eyes. "It needs to be private. I have questions that need to be answered, and he owes me." She cracked one eyelid to peer at him. "I also need to speak to him privately."

He bristled a little but tamped it down. He trusted Sage…and now he trusted the rebellion leader, too. "All right."

"All right?" she arched a brow at him.

"Yes."

"That's different," she whispered. "What's changed?"

"Rafe has proven himself honorable when it comes to you." That and he seemed to have turned his attention to a certain Scythian beauty.

Her eyes narrowed. "What do you know that I don't?"

"Nothing that needs to be said."

"You're keeping secrets from me?"

He frowned at her. "It's not my secret to tell."

Her lips twitched. She was teasing him. He blinked. It was odd, but he liked it. He'd seen her tease and play with others, but she'd never engaged him before. "Maybe if you're nice, I'll tell you."

Her jaw dropped open, and her eyes narrowed further into slits, causing him to stifle his grin.

"You don't want to play this game with me."

Oh, he most definitely did. Each day was filled with its own anxieties, worries, and dangers. But he'd seize each opportunity to invite laughter and light in. It was a rare gift. One he'd not take for granted again.

Tehl arched a brow at the rebellion leader as he strolled into the room like he owned the place. His arrogance never ceased to surprise him. Rafe pulled the lid from the decanter and gave it a heavy sniff before pouring it into an ornate goblet and throwing it back.

"Help yourself," Tehl said dryly.

"Long day?" Sage called from the balcony. She turned from the sunset and abandoned her vigil, strolling into the room.

He sighed, his body relaxing as she moved away from the drop. Sage had been standing at the balcony for so long, Tehl hadn't been able to focus on the letters scattered across his desk. His mind kept imagining her swinging a leg over the railing and disappearing from view. She'd never mentioned her conversation with his father, nor her attempt, but she spent enough time on their balconies that he could never forget what had happened.

Sage gave him a funny look, and he shook himself, realizing he'd been staring for quite some time. He pulled his gaze from his wife and met golden eyes watching him with amusement. If he had been prone to blushing, he would have done so. He knew what the rebellion leader thought. That he was gawking at Sage.

Tehl scowled and crossed his arms over his chest. Even if he was staring, it was his right. She, by law, belonged to him. If he wanted to gawk at his wife, he bloody well would.

Rafe cocked an eyebrow at him as if saying, 'Really? We're back to this?'

Tehl rolled his shoulders and placed his hands on the desk. The rebellion leader was right. There was no need to be so defensive. Rafe eyed him for a moment more then turned to Sage with a warm smile.

"Nothing I can't handle, little one."

Sage winced but quickly wiped the expression from her face. "We're about to add to your burden."

"Is that so?" He leaned against the bookshelf, his gaze bouncing between Tehl and Sage. "Out with it," he said, reaching for the decanter again.

"We need you to deliver a message to your people."

He froze for only a moment before slowly pouring more spirits into his goblet. "Oh?"

"We need your people to align with us."

Rafe took a measured sip. "That is a huge undertaking. I'm not sure I can guarantee much of anything. I don't hold as much power as you think."

Sage scoffed, her eyes narrowing. "Cut the lies. You and I both know you hold a great deal of power. I'm not sure what your station is, but I know you can arrange for us to meet with the crown of Methi. Not only that, we need you to do it quickly and quietly."

"How quickly?" Rafe questioned.

"Within the week," Tehl said.

The rebellion leader barked out a laugh. "You expect me to arrange a meeting with the Methi crown within the week? It's impossible. Travel and negotiations would take months."

"We don't have months," he said. "Scythia has attacked again."

Rafe growled. "When?"

"Within the last several days."

"The causalities?"

"Minor, but still disturbing," Tehl answered. "We don't know when Scythia will strike again, but we know this is just the beginning. It will only get worse from here."

"And you expect Methi to aid you without an incentive?"

"If Methi does not support us, they will be next."

"That sounds like a threat, little one."

Sage shook her head. "Not from Aermia. There won't be any Aermia left. All there will be is Scythia. The warlord is coming, and it's not just for us. If Aermia falls, so do all the kingdoms."

"Methi is not without its own defenses."

"True," she mused, perching on the arm of the leather chair. "But if you think your prowess in battle and your mountains will protect you, you are a fool. When he sets his mind to something, he will gain it."

"And you believe he's set his mind on Methi?"

Her face hardened, even as it paled. "He wants it *all*." The way she said the words sent a chill down Tehl's spine as her gaze emptied of all emotion. She turned her blank gaze from him to the rebellion leader. "We will all perish if we do not unite."

Rafe studied Sage, his expression grim. "It will not be an easy thing to unite the world."

"It's not easy to escape the depths of hell, and, yet, here I am," she said, holding her arms out to her sides. "And it was only done with the help of all the races. Aermian, Sirenidae, Methi, and Scythian. If we do not work together, we will all perish."

"I will do my best."

Sage stared at him before glancing out of the window at the darkening sky. "I know you will."

Rafe swallowed another sip of spirits and placed his goblet on the bookcase, nodding to Tehl. "There is no time to waste, it seems. I'll send a missive immediately."

Sage chuckled and glanced over her shoulder. "Don't pretend you don't have your people nearby."

The rebellion leader's lips curled into a satisfied smile. "You were always my best pupil."

"No, just your favorite."

His expression softened. "That's true as well."

Tehl watched Rafe and Sage stare at each other, and he smiled inwardly. Their friendship had healed. He'd been threatened by the rebellion leader when he'd acted so dishonorably with Sage, but, now, it was clear there was nothing but the kind of love friends shared.

His wife pushed off her chair and strolled to his side. Tehl tipped his head back to stare into her face. She leaned close and pressed a kiss to his cheek. A jolt went through him at the simple touch that made him want to yank her into his lap, but she pulled back and slipped her hand into his.

"You remember what I asked earlier?" she murmured.

Tehl stared at her lips for longer than was polite as her words sunk in. He blinked. She wanted to speak with Rafe in private. He nodded and pushed from his chair.

"I have many other engagements this evening before I seek my bed. So, if you'll excuse me," he said.

Rafe tugged on his vest. "I'll follow you out."

"I wish to speak with you," Sage said.

"If you insist," the rebellion leader said, settling back against the bookshelf.

Sage squeezed Tehl's hand once and let go. Tehl surprised himself by snatching her retreating hand and bringing it to his lips to kiss the inside of her wrist. Her eyes widened as he lingered.

The devil inside him, that he kept a tight leash on, grinned in delight. “I’ll see you tonight.” He breathed across her skin, and a little shiver visibly worked through her that made him want to cheer.

“I’ll see you tonight,” she said, a little breathy.

He smiled, dropped a kiss on top of her head, and tried not to strut toward the door.

One step forward. Many more to go.

And he looked forward to each one of them.

Life with Sage wasn’t simple. It was exhilarating.

TWENTY-SIX

SAGE

THE DOOR CLICKED SHUT BEHIND Tehl, leaving her alone with Rafe for the first time in months. She glanced at him and then away. His golden eyes always saw too much, and today wasn't about her. It was about him.

She rubbed her forehead and then gestured to the chairs. "Would you like to sit down?"

"If it will make you more comfortable, little one."

Sage nodded and stalked to her favorite chair. The buttery leather seemed to give her a hug every time she slid into it. Rafe prowled to the other chair and sat, dwarfing it much like Tehl did. She studied him for long moments, and he let her. His deep wine-colored hair was longer than it had been when she'd met him. It was the lone braid at the front that surprised her.

Dark, beaded hair curtained around her face…

She gritted her teeth and dug her fingers into the chair arms to ground herself. *You are not there. You are here, in Tehl's study.*

"Are you all right?" Rafe's deep voice asked.

Sage opened her eyes, not realizing she'd closed them in the first place. He stared at her, concern clear in his reflective eyes. "I'm fine."

"No, you are not."

She glared at him. It was easier to be angry than accept his pity. "Why haven't you visited me?" she demanded. It had been bothering her for the last week. She'd even sought him out, but couldn't find him before she grew so tired she had to retreat back to her room.

"I figured you needed time," he said softly. "After the last time we spoke… I wasn't sure if I was welcome."

She glanced away from him. He'd hurt her before, but it paled in comparison to everything she'd experienced in Scythia. It actually made her feel ashamed. She'd been petty and vindictive at times. "I'm sorry," she said, turning back to him.

Rafe blinked slowly and blinked again; she'd surprised him. Rarely did the man ever show surprise.

"You don't owe me any apologies," he said softly.

"I do." She straightened and lifted her chin. "I let my personal feelings get involved in decisions that would change the kingdom. You were doing the best you could. I see that now."

A pained expression crossed his face. "Little one, don't justify what I did. It was wrong, no matter the circumstances, and I hurt you. That still pains me."

She waved a hand at him. "There are worse things in life." The statement was flippant even though her heart sped up. She understood true evil beings now. Rafe was not an evil being. He was human. He made mistakes just like herself.

"I don't deserve forgiveness just because there is a bigger monster out there."

It was uncanny. He'd always been able to read her.

"Tehl and I spoke about this the other night. No one deserves forgiveness, and that's what makes it precious. It's a gift. Please let me make it right between us." The telltale heat began behind her eyes.

Rafe pushed from his chair and knelt in front of her, placing his palms on either side of her face. "I'm sorry to my very bones, Sage, for what has taken place between us. If you need my forgiveness to move on, I forgive you. Even though there's nothing to forgive."

Some of her guilt eased at his word.

He continued. "It's I who should be begging for your forgiveness." He pressed his lips together and glanced away. "I'm ashamed of the way I acted. I'm not that type of man."

He turned back to her, and she placed her right hand over his, on her cheek. "Please let there be peace between us."

"Until my dying breath," he said. His thumb swiped something from her cheek. "I also must atone for my broken promises. I promised you that I'd protect you, that I'd make Rhys pay."

She stiffened as an assortment of images assaulted her.

"I'm to blame." He said it with so much pain, it snapped her out of her spiral.

Sage pulled his hands from her cheeks and held them in her hands. "No one is to blame for that animal's actions, except himself."

"Is he…" A hesitation. "Did he hurt you?"

Her skin cooled as another memory crept up on her.

Rhys leaned down until the tip of his nose brushed hers, as if they were lovers. Fear paralyzed her as she stared into the mud-brown of his eyes.

"If you weren't property, I would've torn you apart already." His eyes ran over her face, an unholy glee in his gaze. "Maybe I already did."

One of the warriors pushed a flask against his mouth and another pinched his nose. He fought harder, spewing the brew everywhere. Sage watched in horror as liquid and drool dripped down his chin, and he mouthed, 'You're mine.'

Not like he could have. "No."

Rafe scanned her face. "You never could lie to me. Don't start now."

"He's dead. Does it really matter?" she asked dully.

"He's dead?" Her friend squeezed her hand. "Did you kill him?"

"No, that honor was taken from me."

"Murder is not honorable."

"But vengeance is." She shivered and stared over Rafe's shoulder blankly. "He should have been made to suffer, experience the pain and suffering he'd brought on others. But he was gone in the blink of an eye."

"What happened?" Rafe asked, his voice soft and smooth.

"The warlord," she said flatly, as one of her nightmares rushed to the forefront of her mind. "Rhys brought me before the warlord." She could remember how beautiful and untouchable he'd looked sitting on his throne with his imposing leren sitting on either side. "Rhys had warned me to keep my mouth shut." She smiled bitterly, focusing for a moment on Rafe. "But you know, I was never one to keep silent. I spoke out and was rewarded for such the perceived embarrassment." Sage touched her mouth where Rhys had backhanded her. "I found myself on the floor, then a hand reached out to help me up..."

"Take it, please," his smooth voice said.

With no other option, Sage slipped her hand into his. He lifted her from the floor, and she swore she heard her bones creak. She met his gaze and dipped her chin as she pulled her hand away. "Thank you."

A nod. He scanned her face slowly, taking all the time in the world. Then, he moved down the rest of her body, stopping here and there to examine a scar, a cut, a bruise. Was he admiring his man's handy work? Looking for ways he could hurt her? She held herself stock-still as he walked around her as if he were inspecting chattel.

"What happened to her clothing?" he murmured, only loud enough for Rhys to hear.

"The other woman needed medical attention. Sage had to use her shirt as punishment for insubordination."

The warlord hummed and paused by her side.

"Is she still pure?" The question lingered in the air.

"Of course, my lord. We wouldn't dare touch what is yours."

She forced herself to hold still when he caressed a scar along her hip and then her wrist.

"How did she come by the scars?"

"She and I had...a disagreement, if you will," Rhys replied smugly.

Her stomach churned at his lies.

"And the rest? She's been beaten badly."

"All deserved, I can assure you. She brought them on herself. She never stopped fighting."

Another hum. "What do I cherish most in the world?" the warlord asked conversationally.

"Perfection." Rhys's response was automatic.

"What comes second?"

"Our line."

"True," the warlord answered, circling her again. "And who bears our lines?"

"Our women," Rhys drawled.

Sage turned her head to follow the prowling warlord. All his pacing had her on edge. He stopped between Rhys and herself.

"Do we ever hurt our women?"

"No," the monster replied, his mud-brown gaze darting from her to the warlord.

He glanced at her arm, and the warlord's lips thinned just a touch. Slowly, he began circling her again. This time, she turned to keep her back from him. She was finished with his inspection.

A small smile tipped up his sensual lips. "I wondered when you would give up your submissive pose. You don't have it in you to bend to someone else's will."

She bared her teeth at him, countering his movements. "You know nothing about me."

"On the contrary, I know everything." The warlord slid behind Rhys and whispered, "You shouldn't have marred her. You know how I feel about that, and yet you disobey me."

One moment, Rhys was staring smugly at her, and, the next, he was gurgling on the floor, scarlet liquid slipping from his neck.

Her body flashed hot and cold, and a high ringing filled her ears. A tremor rippled through her body as Rhys gasped and writhed on the floor. Even as death claimed him, he managed to choke out something that would surely haunt her dreams.

"I'll always be on your skin," he coughed, and the light in his eyes dimmed.

She blinked. No.

Sage scrambled toward Rhys and dropped to her knees next to him. Carefully, she held a hand over his parted lips, shaking. Not one breath. "No," she uttered as she frantically grabbed his wrist to feel for a pulse. Nothing. "No, no, no, no, no, no!"

Her eyes darted back to his face, and she gagged at his empty, unseeing eyes. He was gone. Dead in a matter of heartbeats.

No pain. A clean death. No suffering.

An ember of rage caught flame in her gut. How dare he die! "You bastard!" she screamed and slammed her fists on Rhys's unmoving chest. "You don't get to die! Breathe, damn it."

Still, his chest didn't move. He was dead.

He didn't deserve a quick death. He didn't deserve death at all! He deserved to rot and suffer in eternal hell like she did every day. A wail came out of her that didn't seem physically possible. "Death was too good for him!"

Sage pulled her hands back and held up her shaking palms. They were red. Covered in blood. She retched, bile burning her throat and flooding her mouth. In a frenzy, she scrubbed her hands over her pants and half-corset, sobbing. She didn't want him on her. Pushing up from her knees, she tried to stand, only for her feet to slip in the gore. Again, she gagged and scrubbed harder, but only succeeded in making it worse. Her body now looked like a garish painting of red, brown, and black.

Even in death, Rhys seemed to win.

Sage blinked back to the present, the room a blur of colors around her. "The warlord took him from me. The warlord was observing, completely calm, utterly unaffected by the murder he'd just committed. I cursed him. You know what he did?"

Rafe shook his head.

"He shrugged, shrugged like it was nothing, and said Rhys deserved to die for his actions." Sage shook her head. "He didn't deserve to die. He deserved to suffer. When I told him that, he said the reason he'd executed Rhys was because he'd touched me. For that, he had a price to pay, and that I was too valuable to ruin." She laughed hollowly. "No, that was the warlord's right. He wanted to ruin me himself."

"I am so sorry, little one," Rafe whispered brokenly.

Sage focused on his golden eyes, her body numb. "Sorry doesn't fix what happened."

"No, it doesn't," he said sadly. She gasped as he yanked her off the chair and pulled her into a rib-crushing hug. "I promise to do my best, as will my people."

"I know you will."

Rafe pulled back, rubbing his hands up and down her arms. "Stars above, your skin is like ice." He glanced around the room, spotting what he was looking for. He tugged a blanket off the back of his chair and wrapped it around her shoulders. "I hate that you went through that. Hate it."

The only thing she could do was nod. She hated it as well, but there was nothing for it. What was done, was done.

"The only consolation I can find is that he's gone. Rhys can't hurt you anymore."

She chuckled, the sound dark and haunting. "Maybe from the mortal world, but he haunts me most nights." She glanced out at the balcony to the night sky, stars just barely appearing. "Rhys was a rabid dog compared to the monster that's ruling Scythia." She turned back to a grave Rafe. "He cannot succeed, Rafe. We cannot allow it. The warlord kills everything in his path."

"He won't."

"Will you fight with me?" she asked.

"I will fight with you. I vow it."

He held his forearm out to her. Sage reached a shaking hand out and clasped forearms.

"I missed you, friend," she said.

He squeezed her other hand. "As I missed you."

TWENTY-SEVEN

RAFE

HIS SMILE DROPPED AS HE exited the study. He nodded curtly to the Elite stationed outside the door, both relief and worry at war inside him. Sage's words whirled in his mind as he strode down the wide hallway, turning to his left, and jogged down the steps, ignoring the stares he always seemed to draw. It was the eyes he knew. In Aermia, they were unique, but in his kingdom, he was one of many.

Many who would fight in the upcoming battle.

Rafe had always known his actions would lead to war. That much wasn't a surprise. His people had been preparing for Scythia's attack for over fifty years. But now that it was upon them, he found himself anxious. Before, the people in Aermia were just another part of the plan, but now? Now they had names and faces. They were friends. Friends he'd watch die because of the blackguard on the Scythian throne.

Sage's empty green eyes flashed through his mind. The warlord had damaged Sage. A deep-seated fury brewed in his gut. No one hurt those he loved. The abomination that called himself lord would die.

He barely noticed when a maid scampered out of his way, her eyes wide as he stalked by. Even after everything Sage had gone through with Rafe, she'd never given up. She'd fought. Rafe could always see her fire brewing right underneath the surface. But today? He rubbed at his chest as he pushed through the exterior doors leading to the training ground. Today, he'd truly seen how broken she was. Her fire was still there, but it flickered and sputtered, hardly alive.

It was his fault. He should have tried harder to find Rhys. But even as the thought passed through his mind, he knew the truth. If it hadn't been that traitor, it would have been someone else. No one can control everything, no matter how much he tried. It just wasn't possible.

Rafe passed through the gate and jogged down the slope into Sanee, weaving through alleys and then running across roofs. He squatted on the edge of a tavern roof and listened to the medley of music, shouting, and crass jokes below. He whistled a five-note song. An answering tune floated softly through the air.

He dropped from the roof, landed on his feet, and rolled to absorb the impact.

"I hate it when you do that," a male voice commented from the dark. "You're going to break your neck one of these times, and I will be blamed for it."

Rafe straightened and swept his cloak back. He could have dropped from three times that height and been just fine. "You've seen me attempt much more dangerous feats."

Badiah stepped from the darkened corner and pulled his pipe from his mouth, shaking his head. "And I'm not completely over those experiences. You scared ten years off my life."

He leaned a shoulder against the tavern and smiled at the shorter man. Even after all these years, Rafe had no clue how old Badiah really was. There were a few lines around his eyes and mouth to indicate he was older. "I'm sure you have many more left yet," he said.

Badiah puffed on his pipe, eyeing Rafe. "I've not seen much of you lately. How is our girl?" he asked softly.

He pressed his lips together and shook his head. "She's not the same as she once was."

Sadness crossed his companion's face. "But at least she's out of his grasp. He can't hurt her anymore."

"The damage is already done."

"Then we kill him," Badiah said without inflection. "That girl deserves peace, and we will give it to her."

"We will." Rafe reached into his pocket and handed the wiry man the note. "Deliver this as fast as you can. It's time."

Badiah straightened. "It'll be done. I'll have news for you soon."

"Thank you."

His companion nodded and turned on his heel, disappearing down the alley. It still amazed him how easily the man blended into his surroundings. Rafe tugged his hood up to cover his face and went the other direction.

There was much to do and little time.

War was brewing.

TWENTY-EIGHT

SAGE

SHE SAT ON THE BED, staring at the fire.

Today had been more emotionally exhausting than she expected. Speaking to Rafe about what had occurred with Rhys in Scythia had been liberating and draining. The flames danced, casting shadows on the wall that writhed and twisted together in mesmerizing patterns.

"How did your conversation go with Rafe?" Tehl asked quietly.

She glanced over her shoulder as the bed sank behind her. The crown prince sat with his back to her, rubbing the back of his head. "It went about as well as I expected."

He grunted but didn't say anything further.

Sage stared at his back for a beat before turning to the fire. Her eyelids drooped, but she didn't want to sleep. Sleep opened her to the horrors she'd rather forget.

"I forgave him," she blurted.

"What?"

She scooted onto the bed as Tehl twisted to look at her. "It was time," she said, picking at her linen shirt. "I've come to realize that friendship is one of the most important things in the world. And Rafe's been my friend for a long time. He's fought for me, and that means something."

"That's well-done, Sage."

His reaction was curious to her. Rafe and Tehl never saw eye to eye, but, after today, she'd say they were…friends? She peeked at him through her lashes. "I'm surprised how amicable today was."

Tehl stretched his leg out on the bed and leaned back on his hands, brows furrowed. "Why wouldn't it be?"

"You weren't the best of friends before."

"We came to an understanding and then fought together for something important." He shrugged. "That bonds people."

"That I—"

A knock interrupted her.

Tehl pushed from the bed and opened the door. Sam nodded to Tehl and strode into the room without an invitation.

"That is the second time someone has walked into *my* room like he owns it," the crown prince muttered.

Sage hid her smile at his grumpy tone.

Sam plopped into a chair by the fire and held out a note. "I know it's late," he said wearily. "But Lilja sent news."

She froze. This was it.

"A meeting has been set for tonight. I'll escort you to the place."

Sage sprung from the bed and begun to tug on her boots. Lilja had done the impossible. They had a meeting with the Sirenidae. Her movements were quick as she strapped her daggers to her body. There was no time to lose.

"Have you notified anyone else?" Tehl asked, clasping his cloak around his shoulders.

"Lilja said it was only to be both of you and myself. The Sirenidae are skittish enough. It could damage our chances if we arrived with a large party."

Tehl pulled her cloak from a chair and held it out. Sage paused for a moment then turned so he could help her with the cloak. A small burst of warmth suffused her at the simple gesture of kindness. She'd seen her papa do that for her mum her entire life.

"Thank you," she said, her fingers brushing his as she clasped it closed.

Sam yawned and slowly rose from the chair, his movements stiff.

"What have you been up to today?" she asked. "You're moving like an old man."

Her brother-in-law winced. "I've been training with Blaise."

"Truly?"

"She walloped me today. I'll be feeling it for quite some time."

Sage sniggered. She'd have loved to see that.

Tehl pinned his brother with a serious look. "Did Lilja say anything else?"

"Just to prepare a convincing argument."

Sage nodded and moved toward the door. "Tehl and I have been working on it since we spoke with Lilja."

"Good."

She yanked open the door and stepped outside, followed by the two princes. They jogged through the quiet corridors of the sleeping palace. Sage sighed when they exited the palace, inhaling the crisp night air. There was nothing like being outdoors. The knot in her chest loosened when she was outside.

It meant freedom.

Sage opened her eyes and trailed behind the princes. Hay and horses surrounded her when they entered the stables.

"Horses?" she asked. The docks weren't too far away. The walk would be easy. "They're not really inconspicuous."

Sam led a dapple-gray horse from the stall. "Lilja isn't in the port. We'll travel about an hour and meet her."

"Am I to ride with you?" Sage asked turned to Tehl.

He smiled and brushed his hand along the silky face of a mare. The bold face with the uneven stripe made for a striking contrast. With twinkling eyes, he led the mare to Sage.

"This is your mare."

Sage blinked at him and then the horse. He'd purchased her a horse? She reached a hand out and let the tall mare sniff her palm. A smile curled her lips as the curious mount lipped her shirt and then headbutted her in the chest, almost toppling her.

"She's spirited, isn't she?" she said, planting her feet, while stroking the mount's velvety nose.

Tehl ran a hand down the mare's neck. "Just like her owner."

She smiled, loving the animal already. Her family had always owned a horse, but Sage had never owned one herself. "What's her name?"

"She doesn't have a name."

Sage scowled at Tehl. "Why doesn't she have a name?"

"I thought you'd like to do the honors." He avoided her gaze as he said it, focusing on the horse.

Her heart warmed as she stared at her husband. Tehl was clueless sometimes when it came to emotions, but he made up for it by being observant and thoughtful.

Sage placed a hand on his arm and smiled at him when he looked at her. "Thank you so much. I love her."

He nodded and coughed into his hand. "I'm glad." His attention turned back to the mare. "What will you name her? She's gone quite some time without a name."

She patted the horse's neck. "I'm not sure. I'll figure it out soon."

Tehl handed the reins to her and then opened the stall for the huge black war horse that had been staring at them since they'd arrived. He strode right up to Sage and blew air into her face before sniffing around her pockets. Her husband scowled.

"Listen here, Wraith, you don't need apples all the time. Leave the ladies alone."

Wraith sidled up to her mare, who eyed him suspiciously.

Tehl chuckled and led Wraith from the stable. "Easy there, boy, or she'll bite you again."

"Again?" Sage asked.

"Wraith thinks himself the boss." He nodded to her mare. "Your mount taught him otherwise." He glanced at her. "Do you need help up?"

Sage eyed the tall horse. She could manage. Barely. "I can do it."

Tehl said nothing for moment, staring from her to the mare, before turning his back and mounting Wraith.

She turned to her own horse and brushed her hand along the mare's muscular shoulder. "Hello there, pretty girl," she whispered, stroking the horse. "My name is Sage, and you and I are going to be best friends."

Sage placed her foot in the stirrup and swung up onto the horse. "Easy, girl," she murmured as the mare pranced before settling down.

She glanced to the left. Tehl and Sam spoke quietly between the two of them.

Sam straightened and nudged his mount with his heels. The beast responded immediately. Tehl glanced at her. "Are you ready?"

Excitement vibrated through her. It had been ages since she'd ridden. "Let's go."

She couldn't wipe the grin from her face if she tried. Sage pulled on the reins and slowed next to Sam. He grinned at her and swung from his horse.

"You enjoyed your ride?" he asked taking her reins from her.

"It was invigorating."

Her mare was made to run. Her movements were so fluid, it was like flying. Sage had felt utterly free. Tehl stepped close as she swung her right leg over the horse, his large hands settling on her waist, lowering her to the ground. Sage grabbed his forearms to steady herself and smiled up at him.

"So, you like her?" he asked.

There was a hint of uncertainty to his voice. Sage popped up onto her toes and pecked his cheek. "I love Peg."

"Peg?"

"Yeah," she said, turning back to her mare. "Riding her was like flying so I thought Pegasus was an appropriate name, or Peg for short."

Tehl stepped around her and scratched Peg between the ears. Her mare leaned into Tehl. Sage hid her smile. It seemed that Sage wasn't the only one who loved him.

She stiffened as she stared at the crown prince.

Stars above, she loved the man.

He glanced at her and frowned. "Is something wrong?"

"No," she said shakily. Could he see it on her face? "Just worried about tonight."

He shifted, shadows covering his face, hiding his expression from her. Tehl reached out and brushed her cheek with one finger. "You'll do just fine. You always do."

Sage exhaled and stuffed her new-found feelings deep. She'd deal with them later.

TWENTY-NINE

TEHL

HIS BROTHER GROANED. "THE SHIP didn't look this far away. My arms are killing me."

Sage smirked at Sam. "That's all you got?"

"Why don't you take a turn, if it's so easy?"

"I'll leave that in your capable hands," she murmured, reaching out to touch the water.

Tehl snapped a hand out and caught her. She glanced at him questioningly. He lifted his chin to the sleek dark fin slicing through the water.

Sam followed his gaze and scowled. "Of course, we have to take a row boat through leviathan-infested waters," he muttered with a curse.

Sage pulled her hand from his and smiled. "They won't hurt us. They're here for Lilja."

"Lilja?" he asked.

"They are her…companions of sorts."

Sam blinked. "Like a pet?"

"No. A leviathan is no one's pet."

"Can she control the beasts?" Tehl asked.

"No, but she can give them her request, and they choose whether or not to follow."

"So, she communicates with them?" he pried. The idea intrigued him.

"In a way," she answered, staring out at the waves.

The moonlight disappeared as they neared the boat. He stood and held a hand out to Sage. She placed her hand in his and carefully stepped up the rope ladder hanging over the side of the ship.

"Be careful," he said softly.

"Always."

He watched as she nimbly climbed the ladder.

"Now seems like the perfect time to make a comment about what a nice looking—"

Tehl glared at his brother. "Finish that thought, and I'll throw you into the water."

Sam held his hands up with a grin. "I was going to comment on nice *form*." He wiggled his brows. "Where was your mind, dear brother?"

On the woman above them.

Tehl rolled his eyes at his brother and tied the dingy to the ship before climbing up. Hand over hand, he ascended the ship and hauled himself over the railing. Sage stood next to Hayjen and Lilja.

The older man turned to him and held a hand out. Tehl clasped his hand then turned to the Sirenidae. She wore one of her complex knotted dresses with her silvery hair straight down her back. He'd never seen her hair not in a braid. "You look well."

Lilja inclined her head. "Thank you," she said as Sam joined them. "They will arrive shortly, but I need to warn you about the Lure. When they arrive, you'll be tempted to go to them, touch them."

"What?" Tehl demanded.

"How?" Sam asked.

"Pheromones. The seawater reacts with their skin, making them almost irresistible," Hayjen muttered. "It's disconcerting the first time. We wanted to make you aware of this before it happened."

"As if they needed something else to make them more desirable," Sage grumbled.

Lilja flashed a smile at her niece, but it melted into determination. "They're here."

Tehl scanned the darkened water lit with moonlight. Nothing. "How do you know?"

She tapped her ear. "The leviathans' song changed."

"Intriguing," Sam whispered as the group lapsed into silence.

Tehl strained to hear something, but all he heard were the waves lapping gently against the hull. The ship creaked ominously, and a long-fingered hand curled over the deck railing edge. Startling magenta eyes peered up, over the edge. A moment passed, and then the Sirenidae catapulted herself over the railing and landed with grace. She flipped her wet, white hair over her shoulder and stood in nothing but a sealskin suit.

Lilja glided forward and handed the girl a robe. "Mer."

Mer slipped the robe on and hugged Lilja. "Aunt." She released Lilja and rushed to Hayjen, who threw his arms wide and pulled her into a hug.

"Hello, Mer," Hayjen said gruffly.

The girl pulled back and turned toward him. Tehl's knees weakened. She was beautiful, but not his taste. Despite that, he felt the need to be closer to her, to touch her skin. He managed to tear his gaze from the girl and forced his feet toward Sage.

She glanced over her shoulder at him as he pressed himself against her back and wrapped his arms around her.

"What are you doing?" she whispered.

"If I do not hold on to you, I might throw myself at her," he panted harshly.

Sam cursed. "Bloody unfair."

The Sirenidae offered an apologetic smile. "I'm sorry." She backed away. "I'd introduce myself, but I'll wait until I'm dry." She whistled softly and planted herself in front of the railing.

Even from here, Tehl wanted to grab her and hunt for the intoxicating scent. He yanked his eyes from the Sirenidae and pressed his face into Sage's neck, pulling in deep breaths. She shivered in his arms, and his hands began to wander. Tehl curled his hands into fists. Stars above, this was brutal.

Sage gasped. Tehl peeked over her shoulder as two males swung over the railing, both tall and muscular in a wiry sort of way. His gaze narrowed on the sealskin loin cloths. Lilja held out robes for each of the men.

His wife shifted in his arms and arched into his body. He blinked and stared down in shock as her fingers wove through his own and pressed them harder against her body. The older Sirenidae surveyed the boat, pausing briefly on Hayjen, and then turned back to Lilja.

"Daughter," he said, his voice like thundering waves.

Lilja dipped her chin. "Father." She glanced to the other man. "Cousin."

"It's been a long time," the younger man said.

"It has, Lareme."

Tehl's shoulders drooped with relief as the burning need to get closer to the Sirenidae lessened. He lifted his head and made to step back when Sage's fingers tightened.

"Not yet," she whispered, her tone panicked.

Tehl paused and cuddled her close.

The Sirenidae king turned in their direction, his white brows raising. "It's been a long time since I've met someone able to fight the Lure."

Sam stumbled next to his side. "It packs a punch."

Lareme chuckled. "That it does."

Sage sighed, released her death grip on his hands, and stepped out of his embrace, her legs a little wobbly. She sank into a curtsey. "Thank you for agreeing to meet with us, my lord."

"We weren't given much choice." The king cast a dark look toward Lilja. "My daughter is quite persuasive when she desires to be."

"Then we are thankful for that as well," Tehl said, moving to his wife's side. He held his forearm out. "Welcome to Aermia."

The king eyed him and then slowly clasped his forearm. "Well met." He cocked his head, studying Tehl's otherworldly eyes, his white braids framing his face. The king released him and Tehl felt like he'd gone through a test, but he had no clue if he'd passed or not.

Next, the king slowly turned his focus to Sage. A spark of pride filled Tehl at how his wife raised her chin and met the king's gaze without flinching.

The king eyed her. "You've caused quite a bit of commotion. More news has reached my ears about Sage Ramses than any other person in the last six months. You wreak havoc everywhere you go."

"I bring change," Sage corrected, not batting an eye.

The king's lips twitched. "I can see why Lilja loves you. You're just like her."

Tehl glanced at Lilja in surprise. The last part didn't sound like a compliment, and he wasn't the only one to notice, but Sage took it in her stride.

"Thank you. I always hoped to be a strong, capable woman who protected the ones she loves."

"Loyal, as well," the king murmured. "An admirable quality."

Sage dipped her chin but didn't answer.

The king turned on his heel and prowled back to the ship railing. "Let's cut to the chase. I know what you want, and we cannot give it to you."

Mer gasped and glared at the king, but she kept silent.

"You promised to listen," Lilja said softly.

"There's no need to draw it out if we all know what you want."

"Then why meet?" Sage asked. "If you already had decided, why meet at all?"

"I desired to meet the future rulers of Aermia."

"We won't be ruling if you don't unite with us," Tehl said. "War is brewing, and, if you don't stand with us, Aermia will fall. The kingdoms need to unite if we are to defeat the warlord. There's no other way."

The king shook his head. "It's too much risk. My people aren't warriors. I won't have them slaughtered for the sake of another kingdom."

Tehl schooled his face as Sage's jaw clenched next to him.

"You're being short-sighted. The fall of Aermia might not affect you now, but it will."

"The damage would be minor. The Sirenidae people are completely self-sufficient, and the warlord can't reach us," Lareme said. It was a bald statement, said without pride. It was spoken like a fact.

An eerie laugh erupted from Sage. A chill ran along Tehl's arms as he turned to his wife. It was devoid of humor.

"You're a fool."

Tehl blinked at his wife. Of all of the foolish things to say…

The king's magenta eyes narrowed on her. "Pardon me?"

Sage took a step forward. "You heard me." She flung her arm out, pointing at the sea. "You've hidden yourself from the world for so long that reality is now out of your reach."

"And what reality is that? Please, enlighten me, young one."

"The world is ending as we know it. Change is inevitable. It is our choice, though, whether it's for better or worse."

"Such ideals," the king said softly. "You only see what is right in front of you. I lived many generations and have come to this knowledge; crowns rise and fall. It's the way of life."

"And the annihilation of the Nagalian people? Was that a way of life?"

"It's the past."

"No." Sage shook her head. "It's our future. Do you really think the ocean will keep you safe?"

"No one can breach our depths."

"Maybe not now, but, mark my words, if Aermia falls, so will the Sirenidae." She glanced down at her boots. "I'm sure you're aware that I spent time in Scythia."

"I am," the king said gravely.

"In my time there, I met a Sirenidae."

The king stiffened.

"His name was Ezra," Sage continued. "He cared for me but followed the warlord's bidding."

Tehl crossed his arms and glanced at Sam, who was busy cataloguing the Sirenidae.

"Not possible," Lareme scoffed.

"The warlord has many ways to control people. It is the epitome of arrogance to think yourself infallible to his machinations. Ezra was not a bad person. He was doing his best to protect his family, and he was not the only Sirenidae in his service. Your people are not safe. Some have been enslaved for years."

Sage bridged the space between herself and the king. Tehl admired his wife as she braced her feet and stared up at the imposing king defiantly. She pushed her hair over her shoulders exposing her neck. "Do you know how this happened?"

The king kept silent as he stared at the healing wounds of Sage's neck.

"This is the product of the warlord. He collared me with a broken crown made of metal thorns. I wore that cursed collar for months." She gingerly touched the wounds. "This will be the fate of your people. Slavery and cruelty."

The king stared down at Sage, his expression unreadable. "I'm sorry for what you've experienced. But one does not justify the many. I have a duty to my people."

Sage swallowed then nodded. "True. It's one kingdom, but it'll mean thousands of lives. I hope you can live another hundred years carrying the deaths of thousands on your shoulder, because it will be you condemning them to slavery when it was within your power to help."

"You have a barbed tongue, young one," the king said.

"The truth is painful."

The king chuckled, but it wasn't happy. "Well spoken." He held his arm out. "I'm sorry we cannot do more."

Sage inclined her head and clasped his forearm. "You say *cannot*. I say *will not*, but I thank you for listening. It was interesting meeting some of my kin."

"Kin?" Mer piped in.

"Lilja is my aunt," Sage said, stepping back from the king.

The Sirenidae king's attention snapped to Lilja. "Daughter?"

"What she speaks is true. Sage is our kin."

The king frowned. "I am sorry. Truly, I am."

"So are we," Tehl said, striding to Sage's side. "Thank you for meeting with us. I hope you'll reconsider your decision. This is a battle no one race can win. We have to stand together."

"I wish you both the best."

The king nodded to each of them and strolled to Lilja. He kissed her forehead. "You're welcome to come home."

"My home is with my husband, family, and people. *I* will not abandon them and disappear into the sea. It's without honor."

Tehl's eyes widened at the jab.

The king stared at his daughter silently then pulled off the robe and handed it back to Lilja. "Then we are at odds."

"It's nothing new. Farewell, Father."

He sighed and turned away. He spared them one last glance before stepping onto the railing and diving off, disappearing into the black water below.

Lareme stared at the dark water and then back to them. "My uncle is a wise man, but, sometimes, it takes time for him to think things over."

"Time is short," Tehl said.

The Sirenidae nodded and hugged Lilja. "I'll do what I can," he said, handing his robe over. He smiled at them and took off running, launching over the railing.

"Show off," Mer muttered. She slowly turned to Sage. "I'll change his mind."

Sage smiled ruefully. "I don't think there's much that can change his mind."

Mer smiled, every bit of it devious. "If I can't change his mind, I'll lead the people myself."

"Mer," Hayjen growled.

She waved a hand at the burly man. "Someone has to do something if he will not." Mer clasped Sage's hands and then his. "It was wonderful to meet my extended family. Know that you're not alone. Even if he won't fight, my sword is with you."

She skipped over to Lilja and Hayjen, hugging each of them fiercely. "Love you both. Send for me if you need me." She waved and disappeared off the side of the ship with a complex dive.

"The little imp will be the death of me," Hayjen grumped. "Why can't she do anything the safe way?

Lilja patted his cheek. "That was safe."

Tehl tuned them out to stare at the dark sea. Sam appeared on the other side of Sage and leaned heavily against the railing.

"That could've gone better," his brother said.

"He's blind to the danger," Sage whispered.

"Ruling is difficult," Tehl began, "Every decision made could mean someone's life. He's ruled longer than we have lived, longer than our grandparents lived. I don't agree with his decision, but I can understand it."

Sage peered up at him. "It doesn't make it right."

"No, it doesn't."

Tehl rubbed her back and tried to see if he could perceive anything in the deep water. It was a heavy blow for Aermia, but now he could only put his hope in Methi.

War was on the horizon.

Now they had to stand up and fight.

THIRTY

TEHL

"THAT MAKES THREE MORE STRIKES in the last ten days!" Jeren exclaimed. "We have to do something."

"Steps have already been taken. Soldiers have been sent out to defend the affected areas," William said sharply. "But they're too late each time. The Scythians attack and then disappear like smoke."

"Can you show me the areas that have been attacked?" Sage asked.

Lelbiel and the gruff Noah rolled open the huge map of Aermia and pointed to the four towns that had been hit. Tehl took a closer look even though he knew it wouldn't make much of a difference. He'd studied the map with his father and brother for most of the night prior. It didn't make sense. There wasn't a pattern.

Sage rounded the table and pushed between Noah and Lelbiel, her eyes narrowing. "The attacks are scattered."

"Indeed, my lady," Zachael answered.

She placed her palms on the table and scanned the map again. "What has been taken in each place?"

"Not much," Sam said, leaning back in his chair. "They didn't touch the weapons or gold. There have been abductions, but even that's not consistent. They left most of the women during the last two attacks."

Most was the key word. Women were what the Scythians consistently stole.

Unmarried woman. Sage flicked a look his way like she heard his thoughts.

She glanced back to the map and pointed to the most recent attack. "What happened there?"

"They burned the town to the ground. It's the most populated area that they've attacked so far," Garreth said.

"They're escalating," the king commented while stroking his neat beard. "The question is, to what? We already know we'll have war, but why the attacks? For misdirection?"

"No," Lilja said. "That's too simple to him. This is one move of many. We need to look at these like they are chess pieces."

"So, he's playing with us," Rafe said.

Tehl turned to Blaise, who stared intensely at the map. She'd stayed silent almost the entire time. "Blaise, what do you think?" he asked.

Deep brown eyes snapped at him. "I think this is just the beginning. He's testing you."

"To see how we'll react?" Tehl concluded.

The Scythian woman nodded. "He's a master when it comes to planning. The warlord has lived long enough that he can usually predict an outcome. Your choice in how you approach these attacks will decide which move he makes next."

"So, he doesn't know what he's doing next?" Jeren asked, his face a mask of confusion. "You just said he plans everything."

Blaise chuckled. "Oh no, he knows what he's doing. He never has just one plan, but many. So many, they're like the strands of a spiderweb."

"So, we're back to our original question. What do we do?" William said tiredly.

"We could send an Elite team to track the Scythians," Noah suggested.

"No. It would be a death sentence. Those men wouldn't come back alive. I've lost enough men to know that," Sam said bitterly.

"I agree with the spymaster," Sage added. "I've run free through our forests all my life, but their jungle? It's nothing like our forests. I would've died the first day if not for the warriors. The Elite wouldn't survive."

"We can't leave our people unprotected," Garreth said, staring hard at the red dots on the map.

"We're not doing nothing." Tehl pushed from his seat and circled the points of each attack. "The attack areas have no rhyme or reason." He traced a path between the attack sites. "All of these villages have been near the Mort Wall. So, we evacuate our people nearest to the wall and bring our soldiers back."

"You'd leave our border vulnerable?" William demanded.

"Our border is already vulnerable. We have our soldiers spread too thin and that's why the Scythians are getting through undetected. We need to shrink our protection zone."

Zachael and William both leaned closer. The weapons master brushed a finger along the Aermian-Nagalian border.

"The Scythians will not come through the deserts of Nagali. It would take too many resources and too much time. We can pull our men from that part of the border and station them along the Aermian-Scythian border and across the north end of Aermia. That way there will be extra support in the fiefdoms of the north."

"That's wise, but it still feels like we're giving the Scythians ground," Garreth said.

"No, we're protecting what's most important. The north end is scarcely populated as it is," the king commented. "I approve of this plan. Tehl?"

"It's a sound plan. Sage?"

Sage nodded. "Tighten the noose. We can't afford to let them sneak right through our boundaries."

Garreth stood and bowed, exiting the room with William, Zachael, and Sam in his wake. By the end of the day, they'd have everything in place.

Tehl glared at the map. What was the warlord up to?

THIRTY-ONE

SAGE

"THIS SEEMS FRIVOLOUS," SAGE CALLED from the bathroom.

"We have no choice."

She gathered up the slight train of the dress and bustled out of the bathing room. Tehl sat on the bed, his head in his hands.

"Are you all right?" she asked while trying to adjust the pins stabbing her in the head.

Some days, she longed to cut her hair off. It would be so freeing to not carry all the weight around. Her lips pulled down as she stared into the mirror above her vanity. She still hadn't gotten used to the creature that looked back at her in the mirror. Lifting a hand up, she placed it on the mirror just to remind herself that she was indeed real. She wasn't a specter, even though she felt like one.

A soft hiss pulled her attention to the man also reflected in the mirror. He stared from the bed with unabashed male appreciation. Her body warmed as his gaze wandered down her body, so strong it was like a physical touch.

"Sage," he began, and then cleared his throat. "You look lovely."

That was one of the things she loved about Tehl. He was honest. She eyed the corseted, peachy silk dress and tugged at one of the straps that kept falling down her shoulders. "If only these straps would stay up," she muttered.

"I believe, love, they're supposed to fall off the shoulders."

"And how would you know?"

"I'm not blind. Many ladies wear dresses like that. Now, stop fussing with them."

She growled and let them slide off her shoulders. It wasn't that revealing, but it felt exposing. Her hand clasped at the front of her throat as she realized the problem with a sickening lurch. Her neck looked too empty. A choker would've looked beautiful.

"Sage?"

"Will I ever be free of him?" she whispered, staring into the mirror in horror. She'd hated the collar the warlord had forced on her and yet… part of her felt comfortable with it on. It grounded her, because she knew what her place in the world was. Who she was.

The foreign creature in the mirror didn't know who she was.

Tehl stepped behind her, and his hands slipped around her waist, pulling her into a hug. He rested his chin on her shoulder and stared at her in the mirror, his blue eyes fathomless.

"He's not here. He has no place here."

His breath brushed her ear as he spoke, his scent curling around, settling some of the fear in her gut. Sage pulled her hand from her throat and laced her fingers with his, drawing comfort from his touch.

"I need a necklace."

It was such a simple statement. To anyone else, it wouldn't have meant anything, but to Tehl, well…she knew he understood. Her ladies in waiting had tried to get her to wear necklaces since she'd arrived, but she'd turned them down, not able to think about having anything around her throat.

His gaze dropped to her healed throat. There weren't any scars, but she still felt the collar's weight, the bite of pain, the warm metal heated by her skin.

"There's nothing more satisfying than to see my collar on your skin. Beautiful," the warlord whispered.

She sucked in a deep breath, focusing on their laced hands and the man behind her. She wasn't there. She was here, in Tehl's arms. Safe.

"You don't need jewelry to look beautiful."

"The dress needs it." She needed it. To prove that she could. She wouldn't let the warlord control her life.

Tehl detangled himself from her without a word and strode into the wardrobe. She sagged against the vanity and closed her eyes, counting her breaths. It was just a necklace. That's it.

"What about this?" Tehl rounded the vanity and held a simple silver chain with a deep, blue gem for the pendant. "I thought you'd like this one. It's simple."

It was simple. Any other woman might have been offended at the simple offering, but not her. It was exactly the type of thing she'd pick out for herself. Understated, but of high quality.

He held it out further. "Go on, take it."

She didn't want to take it, but with trembling fingers, she plucked the necklace from Tehl's hand. The cool dainty chain slid through her fingers as she held it up.

"Put it on," he urged.

Another simple action. But simple actions these days turned out to be some of the most difficult.

Clumsily, she unclasped the necklace and lifted it to her throat. Her hands shook, but Tehl didn't help her. He just smiled at her encouragingly.

Her stomach lurched as she clasped the chain. She stared at the necklace, the sapphire nestled in the hollow of her throat.

He grinned at her like she'd single-handedly slain an enemy. "The chain is lightweight, so if you can't get the clasp, you can pull on it and it'll break."

She swallowed hard. This man. Sometimes, he destroyed her. "Thank you."

"My pleasure." He offered her his arm. "Are you ready?"

"Ready to eat." She placed her hand on her stomach. She'd hardly eaten anything all day.

"Me too," he grumbled. "I'm starving to death."

Sage eyed him and took his arm. "That I highly doubt."

Tehl made a face. "They fed me greens and fruit today."

Her mouth watered. "That sounds delicious."

He scowled. "A man needs meat." A pause. "And gravy."

Spoken much like her brothers. Sage smiled and patted him on the arm. "Let's find you some meat before you waste away." *Big baby.*

"I don't appreciate your tone, wife."

Sage hid her smile. "I don't know what you're referring to."

He snorted. "Mmhmmm…you may be spending too much time with Jasmine."

Her fiery friend had a quick wit that made Sage laugh more often than not. Her smile dimmed. Jas had not been her normal self for the last few weeks.

"I'm worried about her," she found herself saying as they exited their bedroom.

Tehl sobered and squeezed her arm. "She'll heal. It takes time."

That was something she understood keenly. "The twins make her better."

Jade and Ethan were the light of Jasmine's day. As soon as she was healthy, the twins had been taken to her. Sage choked up just thinking about the reunion. They'd not left Jasmine's side since.

"Children tend to do that. Speaking of which… Isa told me you were taking her riding."

Sage rolled her eyes. "I told her I'd take her to meet Peg."

"Well, you better say that to Gav. He's kept her from the stables."

"Because of her mother."

"Yes."

Sage frowned. She could understand being afraid, but riding was a part of life he couldn't keep Isa from or it would hobble her.

"I'll make sure to speak with him."

"The sooner the better or he'll come looking for you. His temper is something fearsome."

Her lips pursed. She'd need to have a talk with Gav. He'd been standoffish since she'd gotten home, and it bothered her. A lot.

She and Tehl descended the stairs, and she plastered her court smile onto her face. Thoughts for another time.

What in the hell was happening?

Sage tried to keep the horror and embarrassment off her face. Not for herself but for Jas. Her friend was currently in a group of men, smiling coyly and flirting. It was worse than flirting. She didn't even have a name for it.

"She's drawing attention," Tehl muttered underneath his breath.

Sage scanned the room and grimaced as Rose and her posse were giggling behind fans while watching the catastrophe. "I don't know what's gotten into her. Jasmine would never act like this."

"You're sure you don't know?" Tehl asked quietly while eyeing the spectacle.

A retort was on the tip of her tongue, but she swallowed it. She didn't really know. They survived something extraordinary together that had bonded them, but, other than that, Sage didn't know much about her. But Jasmine didn't strike her as a flighty, frivolous type of woman.

She studied her friend and frowned when Jasmine ran her fan up the lapel of a young man with sandy-blond hair. The hair rose on Sage's arms at the hungry look the man cast her and the secret smiles passed to his friends.

"I need to stop this," she whispered scooting back from the table.

Tehl stood and held his arm out. "I'll accompany you."

They descended the dais and strolled toward the group. Jasmine smiled widely at Sage and curtsied. The vultures surrounding her friend bowed and engaged Tehl in conversation almost immediately.

Sage sidled up to Jasmine and wound her arm in her own. "Walk with me?"

"Gladly," Jas said, smiling at the sandy-haired fellow, and allowed Sage to moved her away.

"You make friends quickly," she said, smiling at those they passed.

"They're not really my friends. I amuse them. The wild girl from the village."

Startled, Sage stared at her. "Are they laughing at you?"

"Stars above, no." Jasmine waved a hand at her, her smile sharp and bitter. "They just want to bed me."

"You look stunning." And she did. Earlier in the day, she'd taken a stormy blue, green dress to Jas for tonight. She had so many, and the color had reminded her of her friend. She was right. The color did make her eyes shine like jewels. Jasmine was slightly more endowed than she was, so the sweetheart cut showed more of her assets than Sage would've been comfortable with, but to each their own.

Jasmine snorted. "I look like a china doll dressed up like this."

Sage smirked, knowing the feeling well. She still wasn't comfortable wearing such expensive clothing, but she'd stopped fighting her ladies-in-waiting as long as there were not jewels on the dresses. She drew the line there. "You fit right in."

"I fit in with all the strutting peacocks, eating and drinking like we're not on the verge of war," Jasmine said in a disgusted tone.

If Sage hadn't experienced the court before, she would've thought the same thing. The people may have seemed carefree, but there was an underlying tension that thrummed through the air. Everyone was scared, but they had to go on with their day-to-day lives.

"Not everything is as it seems."

Jasmine flashed her a brilliant smile that would make any courtier proud in its veneer. "That is the first truthful statement I heard tonight." Her gaze wandered to the wolfish blond.

Sage followed her gaze and kept her face blank. "He's not as nice as he looks."

"Maybe I'm not looking for nice."

She turned to Jas, brows raised. "I don't want to see you hurt, or the twins," she tacked on.

"He won't get near the twins," Jas murmured. "This means nothing."

"Okay. Don't get yourself in too deep. I'm always here for you."

"And that's why I love you." Jasmine steered them toward the group of men.

Tehl glanced at Sage, giving her a half smile.

"Speaking of deep, your prince can't keep his eyes off of you. I'm glad he's worthy of your love."

Startled, Sage gaped at her friend. "Who said anything of love?"

Jasmine chuckled. "It was written across your face and his when he found you."

She blushed. Could Tehl see it, too?

"My advice?" Jas said softly. "Life is too short to waste on misunderstandings. One thing I learned in that godforsaken place was to cherish every day you have with those you love. Don't be a coward." She lowered her voice to a whisper. "I've seen you stand up to horrid monsters. You can take the first step and seize your happiness. You deserve it."

Wise advice, indeed, albeit scary. Even thinking about saying those three little words out loud caused her heart to speed up.

"What about yourself? If you're giving advice, you might as well be able to take it yourself."

"Love is not in the cards for me. I have two little ones I have to raise. I don't have time for that."

"And the blond?"

Jasmine smiled. "A diversion."

"Be careful," Sage whispered as they neared the group.

Her friend squeezed her arm. "Always."

Jasmine released Sage's arm and smiled at the group. "What sort of things have you all been speaking about?"

"Things that will shock your womanly sensibilities," the blond commented.

"That I can't believe. There's not much that can shock me."

"Joshua and I were speaking of hunting," Tehl interrupted as awkward as ever.

Sage grinned at Jasmine and slipped her arm into the crook of Tehl's elbow. At least she knew the wolf's name. "And what do you hunt?"

"A number of things, my lady," he said, a small smile tugging at his mouth as he stared at Jasmine.

Sage smiled at him, but it was more of a baring of teeth. The bastard couldn't have been more suggestive if he tried. "You should try your hand in the training ring."

He laughed, the sound haughty. "I'm much too busy for such things."

Sage tensed. "Such things as protecting your kingdom?" She smiled at Tehl, despite the blank expression on his face. "My lord, my husband, spends a *great* deal of time there."

She hid her smug smile as Joshua's smile slipped.

"Forgive me, I meant no offense." He sketched a bow.

"No offense taken." Sage waved him away and cuddled closer to Tehl's arm. "I find myself quite exhausted after the day's events, my lord."

Tehl eyed her. "It has been quite harrowing." He smiled blandly at the group. "Good evening."

Murmured goodnights followed them as Tehl towed her away from the group, his steps brisk. Swamp apples. The crown prince was not happy. "Will you tell me what I did that angered you, or will you brood all the way back to our room?"

"You can't help yourself?" Tehl sighed. "You just made an enemy of a duke's son."

"He was a pompous windbag who looked at Jasmine in a way I didn't like."

"I'm sure Jasmine could have handled it on her own, love."

She frowned. "I'm not so sure." She peeked up at Tehl. "I'm worried about her, and he's a snake in the grass. I can feel it."

He paused at the bottom of the stairs and tipped his chin down to look at her. "Don't worry. Sam is watching over her."

"Sam?"

"Yes. Sam knows of Joshua's tricks. He won't allow anything to happen to Jasmine."

Somewhat soothed, Sage followed Tehl up the stairs.

At least she wouldn't have to deal with the fool.

THIRTY-TWO

JASMINE

SHE GAZED PAST THE BLOND duke's shoulder, blankly staring at the deep blue velvet curtain. Had the twins been put to bed already? Of course, they had. It was past their bedtime.

His lips traveled down her jaw to her neck. Her gaze traced the silver scrolls on the draperies, feeling nothing.

"You're so beautiful, love," he muttered against her skin.

Love. How cliché. She doubted he even knew her name.

Jasmine squinted, her brow furrowing. Damn. She didn't know his name, either. What was it? Jesse? James? Josh… Joshua! That's what it was. Not that it mattered. She wouldn't remember his face an hour from now. She never remembered any of them. They didn't matter. None of this mattered.

Joshua pulled back, his grey eyes smug as he pressed her back into the stone wall. "As soon as I laid eyes on you tonight, I was enchanted."

She sighed. The last thing she wanted was to hear him speak. She wanted oblivion, the numbness and condemning silence that came with hands upon her skin.

Jas ran her hands up his silk vest and seized his lapels in her hands, crushing the dainty, expensive fabric. A snort almost escaped her. The pink silk was the most ridiculous thing she'd ever seen on a man.

He grinned wolfishly and pressed his palms on the wall above her head.

"You're not much for talking, are you?"

"Talking is overrated," she whispered.

"On that, my fair lady, I must agree," he said, bridging the gap between them.

Her eyes closed of their own volition as Joshua attacked her mouth in what she thought was supposed to be a kiss. It was more of a mauling.

She shifted her face to the side, and Joshua happily continued to kiss whatever skin he could get to. A shiver worked through her when he breathed near her ear.

"You like that, do you?" he rasped.

It tickled.

His hands left the wall and made their presence known low on her hips. Jasmine stared into the darkness wishing she could just disappear. Maybe if she concentrated hard enough, she'd disappear into the wind like the seeds of a wishing flower. Forever scattered.

A sigh escaped her, and his lips curled into a smile. "Like that?"

No. She couldn't feel anything. Her soul was numb. There wasn't a flicker of disgust or heat. Just a gaping maw of nothingness. It was a pressing of skin together. Nothing more.

His hand drew circles on her hips and then skated forward. Every muscle locked up in her body as his fingers grazed her belly. Her breathing became shallow as she fought the heat behind her eyes. Her fingers curled into fists, and she blinked repeatedly. He didn't notice the slight swell, but she felt it keenly. No matter how much she tried, there was no forgetting. Nothing could undo the crimes. The knowledge of what had been taken.

Jasmine squinted as light flooded into the cove, and she glanced away, trying to clear her vision.

"If you do not wish to be betrothed by morning, I suggest you leave now," a cultured voice said with humor.

She got control of herself and avoided Samuel's gaze. No matter where she went, he seemed to pop up. He wasn't her caretaker. If only he'd leave her alone.

Joshua jerked away from her as if burnt and turned to grin at the man she could scarcely escape.

Sam leaned against the wall, the picture of relaxation as he took in the scene. Jasmine tugged her gown into place and dropped her eyes to the floor as she felt for any hair that might have escaped its confines. It was time to go. She wouldn't wait around for the lecture that would surely come. Just because he knew her secret didn't mean he knew her, or what was best for her.

"I appreciate the warning," Joshua said, his tone light, if not a little thwarted. "I'll take my leave." A finger brushed her cheek, causing her to look up.

Grey eyes crinkled when he smiled at her. "Goodnight, love."

"I'm not your love," she said, brushing out her skirts. She'd never be anyone's love.

"I always did like my women feisty," he murmured. "Until next time." He bowed and disappeared from view.

Good riddance. There would be no next time.

She rolled her neck and winced as she thought about the long walk to her room. The heeled shoes Sage had lent her were killing her feet. Why would anyone wear these torture devices when flat, soft boots were available?

She shook out her skirts one more time and brushed by the male still staring at her, ignoring him. If she never had to look at his smug face again, it would be too soon. Her cheeks heated as she remembered sobbing herself into oblivion in his arms. Never again. She'd never allow herself to be that vulnerable with a man again. The heat behind her eyes said otherwise.

"Not even a 'thank you' for getting rid of the toad?" he asked.

"I could have gotten rid of him without your help, thank you."

She gritted her teeth as footsteps approached behind her. She would not break down here. No breaking down. None. She was stronger than that.

"I really deserve thanks… unless you were trying to trap him into marriage."

The comment brought her up short. Her tears dried as anger took its place. Jasmine forced a chuckle out. She couldn't let him get to her. The prince enjoyed getting a rise out of others. She wouldn't give him the satisfaction.

"He wouldn't have married me over a few kisses, and I certainly wouldn't have married him." She'd never marry.

Men like Joshua didn't care for others. They took, and she had children she had to worry about. Children… Her gaze dropped to her belly. She swallowed thickly and stared straight ahead as she powered down the hallway as fast as she could, the heels rubbing against the blisters on her feet.

"Well, you and I both know you've been kissing your fair share of men recently."

Skidding to a stop, she whirled around to glare at the prince. "Excuse me?"

He smirked and sauntered closer. "You've collected quite the harem from what I've heard."

"That is none of your business," she hissed, glancing around. There were too many corners for her liking. Anyone could be listening. "Keep your mouth shut and leave me alone."

"I would leave you alone if you stopped leaving messes everywhere else," he retorted. "You have no idea how many of your little 'escapades' I've had to cover up in the last few weeks. You're being careless."

"I never asked you for that." She never asked him for anything. Being in debt to someone was not her cup of tea. "I can take care of my own affairs. Now, if you'll excuse me."

"No, I will not excuse you," he said, stepping closer, his blue eyes snapping with anger. "Things aren't roses and sunshine right now, but you need to abandon this path of self-destruction now before you get hurt."

She chuckled. The hurt was already done. No one could hurt her now. They'd have to get past the ice that encased her. "You know nothing about me."

"On the contrary," he whispered, his blue eyes darting between hers. "You'll be thrown from the palace and be forced to take care of the twins alone if your extracurricular activities are discovered."

"Sage wouldn't abandon me."

"There are some things that are too great. Do you think a woman considered having loose morals would be allowed to remain in the princess's inner circle?"

Jasmine flinched as if he'd slapped her. His words stung. A woman with loose morals. His face fell as her eyes filled with tears.

"I didn't mean it that way," he said softly.

"Yes, you did." She was ruined, but it hurt for someone else to say it. She wiped her cheeks and smiled at him. "Thank you for the speech. I will keep that in mind the next time I tumble someone," she snarled before spinning on her heel. A large hand curled around her arm and spun her about.

"What are you—"

Sam backed her against the wall, his nose touching hers. Her heart pounded as he pressed more of his body along hers. What the hell?

"Is this what you want? What you've been looking for?" he murmured.

No, it wasn't. She didn't want to feel, and, anytime she was around the prince, all she did was feel. Her numbness melted away, leaving behind rage, pain, betrayal, and disgust.

His hands ghosted down her sides to her hips, and he nuzzled the side of her jaw. "I'll gladly give you what you seek." He pulled back and looked her in the eye. "All you have to say is 'no.'"

Jasmine stared at him with hate but hated herself more. He was like all the others. She'd heard about the prince's conquests. She placed her hand around his neck and smiled seductively at the prince, even as a voice in the back of her head told her not to do it. But she ignored the warning. She'd made her bed, and now she had to lie in it. Sam was known for his exploits and never staying with one woman. He was exactly what she was looking for.

"I'd like to see you try," she taunted.

His lips curled. "Challenge accepted, my lady."

She closed her eyes, expecting him to paw at her like every other man had, but he didn't. He breathed with her, chest to chest.

"Look at me," he said with a hint of iron in his voice.

Jasmine opened her eyes, and he brushed a finger along her top and bottom lips before leaning close and pressing a chaste kiss to her mouth. She didn't close her eyes, and neither did he. They stared at each other. What was this madness? This was the blessed numbness she wanted.

Samuel brushed a kiss along her cheekbone and then along her jaw. She tipped her head back to stare at the ceiling and sagged into the wall, the cool stone seeping through her gown, guilt pricking her. She pushed it away. What was one more sin to add to her already long list?

Cool air kissed her ankles, but she hardly cared. She closed her eyes and tried to forget everything around, imagining the cool forest on a morning hunt. How she missed the forests, the worn, smooth wood of her bow in her palm.

"Check mate," the prince whispered.

Her brows furrowed, and she opened her eyes, blinking.

"This is highly irregular," a prim voice snapped.

Jasmine's attention snapped toward the voice. Five well-dressed women glared at her with varying degrees of disgust.

A buzzing filled her ears. She'd been ruined publicly, and she didn't feel a thing.

THIRTY-THREE

SAM

SAM STARED AT JASMINE'S BLANK face. Not a flicker of emotion while the women declared their degrees of shock. In that moment, he second-guessed himself. Had he done the right thing?

Sam knew what image they painted. Jasmine rumpled, his hand hoisting her skirts up as he pressed himself against her. It was the image he wanted. The image that would change his life forever.

He'd kept an eye on Jasmine since her breakdown. She put on a good show for everyone, but it was all a lie. He knew an actor when he saw one. The only time she lit up was when she was with the twins. She was a remarkable mother, and that's what had sealed his decision. He knew how her story would end if she didn't marry before the babe began to show more than it already was. Even now, he could feel the hard, proud little bump pressing against his stomach.

Jasmine had tried to help Sage when she didn't even know her, and that had cost her everything. He wanted to give her something in return, and this was the only way he could think of doing that. She was hell-bent on destroying herself. If she wouldn't protect herself, he had to.

Slowly, he lowered her skirts to the floor and smiled boyishly at the older women, wrapping an arm around the stiff Jasmine. He flicked another glance at Jasmine, praying she didn't ruin the ruse he'd orchestrated.

"Hello, ladies."

"My lord, we did not mean to intrude," the baroness said, her tone sharp and disapproving. Her lips thinned as she frowned at them, not hiding her thoughts whatsoever.

"That's quite all right," he said grinning. "We were celebrating our betrothal."

He kept his smile in place as her thin, graying brows practically climbed to her perfectly coiffed hair. "Betrothed?"

"Indeed," he said gaily, hugging Jasmine closer.

The old crones tittered between themselves, and the baroness pressed forward, reaching a hand out. "My congratulations," she said, her ember-like gaze sliding to Jasmine at his side. "You are one very lucky woman."

Jasmine said nothing. *Thank the stars.* Silence he could work with.

Sam tucked her underneath his arm and pressed a kiss to the baroness's hand. "I'm afraid it grows late, and I have to share the news. Ladies."

He winked at them, causing the older women to blush as he steered his new fiancée away from the gossip-mongers. The news of their engagement would be spread all over the palace by morning. It would be an affair to remember, but that was okay. A quick marriage would fade from mind, but a bastard child? Not so much.

They rounded the corner, and Jasmine yanked her arm from his and spun to face him. "What the hell was that?" she hissed, her stormy eyes wild.

Anger. He could handle anger.

Sam wove around her and picked up his speed. She was about to explode. Words would be had, but he needed to get her away from hearing ears for that conversation. She'd ruin everything if she lost control now.

"Don't you dare walk away from me."

"I'm not walking away from you." *He was leading her away from the harpies who would love to tear her apart.*

She stomped behind him. Sam eyed the empty hallway. Good enough. He spun, snagging her wrist and pulled her into one of the secret coves.

Jasmine yanked her arm from his grasp and glared at him. "Don't touch me."

He held his hands up and took a step back.

"What was that?" she demanded. "What have you done?"

"That was me saving your life." He leaned a hip against the wall. She was justifiably angry, but, in the end, she'd understand he was doing what was best for her and the twins. He wouldn't allow another girl to be destroyed by the Scythians when it was within his power to do something.

"My life? You just *lied* to those women."

"I didn't lie to them."

"You told them we're *betrothed.*" She said the word like it was something dirty.

"We are."

"No, we are not."

"Yes, we are," he said slowly. "What do you think those women would have done if we weren't, hmmm? I'll tell you. Word would have spread, like wild fire, of our little tête-à-tête." Her face paled. "You would've been well and truly ruined in the court's eyes. It's a dangerous game you've been playing. You've been lucky so far."

"So, you made up a lie?" she said flatly.

"No, I saved your reputation and just provided for the twins and yourself for the rest of your life."

"I won't go along with this," she whispered.

He chuckled, hating each moment he played the bad guy. That's what he got for trying to be the knight in shining armor. "You will. You will not make a fool out of a prince of Aermia, and you certainly won't turn away the best life you could offer to the twins. We have but one choice. To marry. If you won't do it for yourself, you need to do it for the children. They don't deserve to suffer for the outrageous mistakes of other men."

Sam held firm as one tear dripped from the corner of her eye.

"And what do you expect to get from this arrangement?" she asked.

That was not the question he expected. "Nothing."

A bitter laugh followed as she wiped away the lone tear. "Nothing? No one does anything for nothing."

That was the bold truth, he knew. He sighed. "I need a wife and a family. I'm not as respectable as I should be, I am told." She'd believe that. It wasn't quite true, but it was close enough to the truth for now.

"A wife in truth or in name only?"

"In name only." For now.

She scoffed. "What of heirs?"

His gaze dropped to her belly. "The one you carry will be sufficient." He'd give the child his name. She deserved that much after everything she'd given for Aermia. His stomach twisted as he remembered her tear-streaked face. He'd make those bastards suffer; they couldn't expect to get away with causing her pain.

Her hand fluttered near her belly, and she glanced away, her bottom lip trembling. "I hate you."

So be it. "Good. It'll make the next part easier," he whispered.

THIRTY-FOUR

SAGE

SHE STARED AT THE MIRROR and slowly pulled the pins from her hair. A necessary evil she was told. They helped form a beautiful visage, but she wasn't sure it was worth the pain. Her gaze flicked to Tehl's reflection. The crown prince had his back to her as he began to tug his shirt over his head.

Nervousness ran down her spine, like ants marching across her skin, as she watched him. She admired the burnished skin he revealed and a blush touched her cheeks. She was staring at him like a wanton woman. She jerked her gaze back to her own reflection as he looked over his shoulder as if he felt her gaze.

Internally, she cursed herself. What in the blazes? He'd always been handsome, but since her revelation at the coastline, she'd found her attention lingering on him far longer than it should have. *Wanton, indeed.*

She pulled the last pesky pin from her head and shook her hair free, so it fell in waves down her back. Thank goodness only warm candlelight illuminated the room or he'd have seen the blush scorching her cheeks.

"You're quiet tonight," Tehl said softly as he tugged his belt from his waist then placed his daggers on his side table.

"There's a lot on my mind."

He turned and slung a hip against the bed. "Like what?"

Like how she loved him. Her breath hitched at the thought. It still baffled her how she hadn't seen it before, and how it had slapped her in the face, leaving her elated and terrified. "I'm worried about Jasmine," she said instead.

Coward, her inner voice whispered.

He frowned and stared at the fire. "She's going through an adjustment period. Healing takes time. She'll be okay."

"I don't know." Sage turned, kicking the train of her dress out of the way. "Something happened, and now she's changed."

Tehl turned to her, a line of tension entering his shoulders. "That's to be expected after a trauma."

His words were soft, but they still felt like a blow. He wasn't just speaking of Jasmine. Sage spun and placed her hands on the vanity, her eyes squeezing shut. He spoke the truth. She wasn't the same girl. Hell, she didn't even know the girl she used to be. The old Sage had died in Scythia, and a creature of nightmares and vengeance had been born.

Large hands settled on her shoulders, and only years of practice kept her from jumping. She hadn't even heard him move.

"I didn't mean to upset—"

"You didn't," she cut him off, peeking at him from under her lashes. Hunched over like she was, he towered over her. A little thrill of fear went through her, but she pushed it away. This was Tehl, and he'd never hurt her.

Sage straightened and reached back to place her right hand on top of his. "You're right. Trauma does change people." And she was sorry for it. "But Jasmine changed right before she was released from the infirmary. She went from her bright, sarcastic self to…" An image of Jasmine's empty blue eyes floated to the forefront of her mind. "It's like part of her died."

Tehl squeezed her shoulders, and she blinked, focusing on his deep blue eyes.

"It hurts to watch someone you care about suffer and battle demons that you can neither see nor protect them from," he rasped. Her fingers clenched around his at the emotion leaking through his voice. "You can't take away the pain, but you can be the best friend possible."

Like he had. "Sound advice," she murmured. "Thank you for being my friend."

His fingers tightened for a moment. "It's been a pleasure being your friend."

She snorted. "Let's not get carried away. The sleepless nights are no walk in the park."

"That's true. But, in being your friend, I've gained much more. Losing a little sleep is well worth it."

Her heart picked up speed. This man. "And why is that?"

He smiled, causing her breath to hitch. "I gained a friend of my own." A shrug. "I've never had many. Sam and Gav are family. There are the men… but it's different with you."

A heartfelt confession so honest that it made her want to weep. Sage ignored the heat gathering behind her eyes. "I don't think I could put it any more eloquently."

Tehl rolled his eyes. "Now that, I don't believe. You and I both know I'm terrible with words."

"That you are." She smiled at him, and he returned the expression, both grinning like idiots. Her smile faded first. "But, in all honesty, I mean it. Your friendship is a gift I could never afford."

His smile faded into something more serious as he dropped his gaze. His thumbs ran along the tops of her shoulders and underneath her hair, causing her to shiver. He paused, a little line forming between his brows. He ran his thumbs up the sides of her neck. Goosebumps rose along her arms at the soft touch.

She watched his eyes flicker as his left thumb brushed the heated chain of her necklace. He caught her eye in the mirror. Her breath caught, but not in fear. Her pulse picked up as she saw the look in his eyes. *Desire.*

She'd seen that look on men. On *him.* But all those men only saw one part of her, or what they believed her to be. Tehl *knew* her. He'd seen all the ugly and yet…he still looked at her like she was the most beautiful thing in the world.

"Do you want me to take it off?" he whispered.

She blinked. Then blinked again. He meant the necklace. She wanted to slap herself when a nervous giggle slipped out. "Please."

He slowly swept her long hair over her left shoulder and fumbled with the latch. Sage hid her smile when he cursed underneath his breath and glared at the necklace. After two more tries, he unlatched it with a growl.

"Stupid design."

She hissed when the chain caught some of the hair at her nape.

"I'm sorry," he muttered before dropping a kiss to the back of her neck.

She froze, his heated breath leaving her skin. She stared at his reflection and he stared back, both of them silent. She couldn't even hear his breath.

"It's okay. Half the time, I want to cut my hair off." There. She'd said something to dispel the awkward silence.

"No."

"No?" She arched a brow.

Tehl gently placed the necklace on the vanity, his heated chest brushing her arm, and then straightened. "I love your hair. It's shiny and smells nice. I even find myself sniffing it sometimes. Cinnamon. I smell it all the time…" He sucked in his cheeks, embarrassment clear on his face as he rambled.

"So, I shouldn't cut it?" she asked, throwing him a line.

He puffed out a breath. "No." Even though he was obviously embarrassed, he didn't look away. He didn't hide from her. Honesty. She'd always treasured it, and Tehl encompassed it.

Sage turned her cheek and kissed his fingers still cupping her shoulder. "Then I shan't."

Tehl shifted behind her, his body grazing hers, causing everything to heat. Her lips parted as he leaned close and placed an open mouth kiss on the top of her shoulder, never losing eye contact in the mirror.

Part of her wanted to run and hide, but that part was small. Her fear and nervousness had no place here. This was Tehl. Her awkward, honest, kind husband who carried the weight of the kingdom upon his shoulders and managed to look out for everyone around him.

His lips found her throat, and then his teeth grazed the tender skin there, and he never looked away from her. Each move was slow, like he was waiting for her to pull away from him. But that was the furthest thing from her mind.

His touch didn't cause bile to burn her throat, or disgust and shame to drown her. It soothed and yet burned her all at once.

"So beautiful," he murmured against her skin, his callused hands drifting down her arm and across her torso, catching on the fine fabric of her dress.

Sage trembled and slowly spun in his arms. She tilted her head back, and Tehl stared down at her. She knew he would step away if that's what she wanted. He wouldn't push anything. But she didn't want him to step away; she wanted him to hold her. To love her.

Slowly, she moved, sliding her hands up his arms, and pressed her palms against his chest, feeling the rapid thud of his heartbeat. She looked up. His mouth was closer, his breath whispering over her forehead. The throb of his heartbeat increased its tempo beneath her hand. She licked her lips, and a thrill went through her as he watched her movement, obviously transfixed.

She looped her arms around his neck and pressed up onto her toes as his arms banded around her waist. Her belly trembled as the words she'd been rehearsing in her head tumbled from her lips. "Let me love you."

Four little words. That was it. But it changed everything.

Emotions flitted across his face, too fast for her to catalogue them as he held perfectly still. Sage's heart pounded, and a whooshing sound filled her ears. What if he rejected her again? Could she handle it? Surely, it would break what was left of her.

She dropped her eyes to the small spattering of hair on his chest, afraid of his answer. The silence felt condemning, suffocating.

A finger slid underneath her chin and lifted, forcing her to meet his deep blue eyes. He searched her face, his fingers caressing the soft underside of her jaw. Whatever he was looking for, he found. His lips curled, and his mouth drifted closer.

"No." Her heart stuttered. "It will be my pleasure to love you," he whispered before kissing her.

Lips brushed against lips, and, as she took a breath, she stole his. Tehl cupped her cheeks with both his hands and pressed closer, his mouth opening over hers as he tasted her, a faint hint of his tongue flickering over her lips. *Stars above.*

Her hands flexed against his neck and as he pulled back to brush his nose against hers, an odd sound rose in her throat, one that sounded suspiciously like a sigh. His gaze flicked to hers as if to make sure she was all right.

Sage swallowed and smiled. "I trust you."

He didn't ask for the words, but she needed to say them all the same. She trusted him more than she trusted herself most of the time.

A groan erupted from his throat, and then his hands were on her, lifting her onto the vanity, her back pressed against the mirror. She leaned forward, her hands sliding over the smooth skin of his shoulders. How had she gotten so lucky?

He shuddered and caught her face in his hands, and then his mouth swooped across hers in a kiss that caused her to go up in flames. Her fingers wandered into his silky black hair and a rumbling sound vibrated from his chest.

His hands skimmed down her waist and slowly began to lift her skirts.

"This is enough," he rasped, between kisses. "This is all I need, love. You can say no."

"It's not nearly enough," she said, tugging on his hair, so he met her gaze. "This is my choice. *Our choice.* This is our future."

Tehl curled his hands against the back of her knees and pulled her forward until the insides of her thighs caressed his hips, and he settled her there. "For so long, I've wanted you more than I've wanted anything."

His tender words caused a fat tear to sneak out.

He cupped her face and gently stroked her cheeks as he stared into her eyes. "I don't want to hurt you. I want to make you happy."

She pulled his left hand from her face and kissed his palm. "That's what I know: you will never hurt me," she whispered. Her other hand went to his nape, and she pulled his head down, so his mouth went back to hers. "You are mine, and I am yours."

He brushed his lips across hers. "I'm happy to call you mine and to be yours."

"Then make it so," she breathed, her cheeks heating.

"I intend to, love," he whispered.

A knock.

They froze, staring at each other.

"Maybe they'll go away," Tehl whispered, kissing her neck.

Another knock.

Disappointment filled her as he growled.

"Who in the hell would be calling at this hour?" he all but snarled.

"It's likely important," she said softly.

Tehl pressed his forehead against hers. "So is this."

"I'm not going anywhere."

His disgruntled expression caused a small giggle to escape her. He blinked, and the corners of his mouth curled.

She couldn't remember the last time she giggled.

A third knock.

Tehl glared at the door. "Stars above, I'm coming." He turned back to her and arched an eyebrow before kissing her hungrily, and then, leaving her breathless, he pulled back.

"Are you ready for this?" he asked, tugging her skirts down and holding a hand out for her.

Sage tried not to blush as she accepted his hand and glanced at the vanity. He followed her gaze and squeezed her hand, pulling her attention back to him.

"This is the beginning, you know," he said softly.

"The beginning?"

"The beginning of us."

THİRTY-FİVE

SAGE

"HELLO, PRETTY GIRL," SAGE CROONED at Peg. The mare nickered a hello and butted her in the chest affectionately. She grinned and stroked Pegasus's velvety nose. "I don't have any treats for you." Peg ignored her and nosed around her pockets.

"Are you ready?" Gav asked, his face shadowed by the hooded cloak he wore.

She craned her neck to look at her friend. "Yes."

He stared at her for a beat then nodded. "Make sure to tell her about your shadow."

"Nali," she breathed. That sneaky beast. She turned back to Peg and gave her another pat on her chest. "Don't worry about the kitty-cat out there. She'll not harm you." Peg snorted in answer.

Sage led her out of her stall, the earthy smell of hay and horse fading as they moved out of the stable. Zachael, William, Rafe, and Marq sat on their horses, only lit by the soft moonlight. She glanced at Tehl. He had already mounted Wraith, his mammoth of a horse, and leaned down to speak quietly with Gav. She watched them, feeling a little left out, and fiddled with the clasp of her cloak.

Since she'd come home, Gav had been different. He'd been quieter, more withdrawn. She couldn't help but think she'd done something to upset him, but, for the life of her, she couldn't imagine what it was. He hadn't spent enough time around her for Sage to offend him. But those were thoughts for another time. Tonight, they had to seal an alliance with Methi. Rafe had arranged a meeting. Aermia's future rested on the decisions made tonight.

Pegasus jerked and shied to the side, yanking her from her thoughts. Sage pulled on the reins and planted her feet, reeling the mare in as she reacted to the huge feline. "It's okay, Peg. Nali won't hurt you." The whites of Peg's eyes showed as she backed up another step. "It's okay."

Warmth suffused her back as two hands reached around her to hold Peg.

"Get back, Sage. It's okay. I got it."

She blinked at the anger in Gav's voice. Why was he so angry? Peg was still getting used to her.

"This is dangerous," he growled, elbowing her out of the way.

Her eyes narrowed on him, and she pushed the hood from her head to scowl at her friend. What was wrong with him? She hadn't done anything wrong. It was natural for a horse to be afraid of a predator. Plus, it was her responsibility to care for her mount, and Peg needed to learn to trust her.

Sage ducked underneath Gav's arms and curled her fingers around the mare's cheek piece once again. "She's mine. Now, move."

"Why are you so bloody stubborn?" his voice raised.

Peg jerked again. Gav was making it worse. His agitation was affecting her horse. Sage let go of the cheek piece and pulled on the reins. "You're frightening her. Calm down and back away," she growled.

He gritted his teeth and glared at her. "No. It's not safe."

His words penetrated her confusion. She'd never seen him lose his temper, and he certainly had never spoken to her in such a manner. It was the horses. The horses set him on edge, because of his wife. Sage moved her hand to his arm and squeezed, her heart going out to him.

"It's okay," she said softly. "I'm okay. I'm not going to get hurt."

Gav squeezed his eyes, a tremble moving through his body.

"I've got her," she said.

He nodded and slowly released her horse. Gav stormed to his dapple-gray mount and swung up into the saddle. Sage watched his hands clench and unclench on the reins. She glanced at Tehl, who was staring at his cousin with sympathy. The poor man.

Sage turned to Peg and ran her hands along the mare's neck. "You're okay, sweet girl. Are you ready to go on a ride?" she whispered. The horse's ears flicked forward at the word 'ride.' "That's right. We're going on a long ride." She gathered the reins in her left hand, placed her left foot in the stirrup, and climbed into the saddle without a fuss. She leaned forward and patted the mare's neck. "Good girl. Now let's ride."

The wind whipped Sage's hair around her face, and she grinned, wanting to whoop with joy. Riding Pegasus was unlike anything she'd ever experienced. It was true freedom. The moon painted the road and surrounding trees in soft whites, like the world had been gilded in silver.

The thundering of Peg's hooves kept pace with her heartbeat, almost as if they were one creature. Rafe reined in his mount and slowed ahead of her. The ride had gone too quickly. Peg's sides heaved as they slowed and took another offshoot from the road. The trees grew in arches over the path, like they were bowing to the heavens above them.

The men closed around Marq, and Sage shivered as the path darkened, only to be broken up by small puddles of moonlight. She scanned the area around them and froze as something dark darted through the trees. Her hand crept to the dagger at her waist. A flash of golden eyes. Her shoulders slumped, and she glared at the darkened forest. "Bloody cat," she whispered.

"What was that, my dear?" the king asked, his voice barely above a whisper.

"Nali."

A huff. "She's quite the protector."

"That she is," she murmured, focusing on their surroundings again, the hair on the back of her neck standing on edge. She had the feeling she was being watched. Sage tipped her head back and scanned above them thinking of the snake that had almost killed them in Scythia. They were too confined.

Her left hand clenched around the pommel of her saddle, and she focused on her breathing while squeezing the reins in her right. Panicking would do no one any good. She counted down her breaths from one hundred and sighed when the pathway opened to a small meadow with what looked like a rundown cottage.

Rafe paused and slid off his horse. "We leave the horses here."

"Here?" Zachael asked, his salt-and-pepper brows furrowing.

"You will thank me for it."

Rafe met Sage's gaze, his amber eyes practically glowing in the moonlight. What was he trying to tell her? She stared at the stone cottage. It wasn't small by any stretch of the imagination, but there was something off about it. It looked to be abandoned, and yet… the roof was in fine condition, as was the masonry. This place was used often.

She nodded to Rafe and swung off of Peg. Why did he want her to know it was in use? And what about the horses? Was there something that would spook them? She froze, the reins hanging limply from her fingers. What sort of predators did the Methians bring with them? At that moment she was beyond thankful that Nali had accompanied them. There wasn't a thing that feline couldn't detect.

Brushing the hair from her face, she pulled her hood up, shielding her face. It would be best to disguise the fact she was a woman. Not all men appreciated an outspoken woman.

Tehl stood to her right, his arm brushing her shoulder, and Gav to her left. Rafe scanned their group and nodded before striding out into the meadow confidently. Her lips twitched. The man wore arrogance well. Many would see it as stupidity, but she knew his capabilities. He'd catalogued every potential danger before his feet had even touched the ground.

Nali stalked from the trees and pushed in between Sage and Gav, her lips pulled back and the hair along her spine slightly on end. Gav missed a step and moved to make more room. Sage studied her feline companion, and then scanned the trees. There was clearly something Nali didn't like out there.

Rafe stopped in the middle of the meadow, allowing them to catch up. Sage paused, her cloak swishing around her boots as a group of tall, cloaked figures emerged from the other side of the clearing.

She placed a hand on Nali's head as a chilling growl rumbled in the feline's throat, never taking her eyes from the hooded warriors. And that's what they were. Warriors. Sage still remembered the first time she met Rafe. Each move he had made was fluid, calculated, predatorial. These men moved the same way.

They halted several strides away, and the whole forest seemed to hold its breath.

Marq stepped forward and pushed his hood back, his head held high. "Well met, my brothers."

"Well met, my brothers," the tallest warrior said. "I have to say, I'm surprised that you risk yourself." It wasn't a taunt, but a simple statement.

"Times are dangerous, and my people need me. I'll do whatever is necessary to help them. As is my duty."

The shortest warrior stepped around the warrior who spoke first and pushed back her hood. Sage's breath caught in her throat as one of the most beautiful women she'd ever seen stepped forward. Her long hair was deep-wine in color, streaked with silver, and braided into an intricate rope that draped over her shoulder. Lines bracketed her mouth, and her eyes said she laughed often, but it was the color of her eyes that struck Sage the most.

They were amber. The exact shade of Rafe's.

The tall warrior pushed back his hood, revealing himself to also bear a striking resemblance to Rafe. He indicated the woman with a quick movement of his hands. "My mother, Queen Osir."

Sage's fingers curled into fists. That lying weasel. Rafe had kept more secrets. She stared at his hood, and Rafe slowly glanced in her direction as if he felt her gaze. He pushed back his hood, not glancing away from her. There was an apology lurking in his gaze. She puffed out a breath and looked away from him. They would be having words later. The bastard was royal. A damn royal spy.

Marq stepped forward and held his hand out. Queen Osir scanned him from head to toe, her shrewd eyes missing nothing. It was an examination, and, by her smile, she hadn't found him wanting.

She stepped forward and placed her hand in his. "My lord," she murmured.

"My lady." He placed a chaste kiss on the back of her hand and straightened. The two royals stared as if sizing each other up.

The Methian queen swept her arm out toward the cottage. "Shall we?"

King Marq dipped his chin. "After you."

The queen's lips twitched, a ghost of a smile. "So polite," she murmured. Sweeping aside her cloak, she strode purposefully toward the cottage.

"Brave," Gav said under his breath. "To turn her back."

"I am among friends, no?" she called, pausing several strides ahead.

Gav's eyes widened.

Marq strolled by her side. "Indeed, my lady."

She huffed a small laugh as both Aermian and Methian men circled them. "Uneasy friends."

"New friends."

Sage stayed put and ran a hand over Nali's fur. Apparently, Rafe had inherited his acute hearing from his mother. Curious.

Tehl paused, waiting for Sage to catch up. She rolled her shoulders and followed the group.

Here went nothing.

THIRTY-SIX

SAGE

SAGE STEPPED TO THE DOOR, and Nali darted in front of her, blocking the way. Tehl paused just inside the threshold, watching. Gav moved closer to her side, and scanned the darkened forest.

"What is it?" she whispered. Something had set off the feline.

Nali sniffed the air, and her ears laid flat against her head. She back-pedaled and nudged Sage from behind. Sage cast one last look around the meadow and allowed Nali to herd her inside. Her hand crept to the dagger at her waist as she entered the cottage. Whatever the danger was, it was outside.

Sage shuffled to the side to make room for Gav as Nali pressed against her leg, her hackles still raised. She brushed her hand along the leren's neck, and surveyed the room from beneath her lashes.

Her suspicions had been right. Someone had been using this house for quite some time, though it looked rundown from the outside. Furs covered the stone floor, and a fire roared in the hearth. Large comfy chairs were set in a rough circle around the room.

Sage's people spread out as one of the Methian men yanked the heavy, tan draperies closed and took the cloak from the queen.

Queen Osir placed her hands on the back of a large, brown leather, winged-back chair. Long scars ran down her arms in crisscross patterns that made Sage shudder. They looked painful. What had done that to her?

The queen scanned the group and then paused on Sage, before sliding to Nali. "A bonded couple," she murmured. "It's a pleasure to see a leren. It's been so many years."

Sage sank her fingers into Nali's fur, as the queen rounded the chair and approached them slowly. The leren growled softly and bared her fangs. "Easy," she whispered. It wouldn't do to have her feline attack a potential ally.

The queen paused. "I mean neither of you harm. I'm partial to felines. They hold a special place in my heart." Her piercing amber gaze wandered back to Sage. "There's no need to hide what you are. You won't find enemies here because of your sex."

Sage pushed her hood from her head and met the queen's probing gaze. "Not everyone has those ideals."

A sharp smile touched the queen's mouth. "Then they are stupid, indeed."

An answering smile tugged on Sage's lips. She liked the queen already. "As you say."

"I've heard much about you, Sage Ramses. Since you've entered the fray, you've changed much in Aermia." The queen drew in a deep breath, her expression turning grave. "I've also heard of your trials in Scythia. I am most sorry for what you've suffered."

Sage's throat tightened, and she swallowed down the grief and anger that always seemed to hover just at the edge of her control. "It's in the past."

"No, experiences like that are never in the past. They may fade, but we carry them for the rest of our lives. They shape who we are. Who are you?"

"Whatever the Crown needs me to be."

A ghost of a smile followed from the queen. "You have many names. The Rebel's Blade, Crown's Shield, Enemy's Queen." That one made Sage wince. "King's Warrior. But I don't think just one of those names could encompass who you truly are."

"And who do you think I am?" she asked warily.

"You, my sweet, are the end of our worlds."

She jerked back as if slapped, and Nali snarled. She'd done everything in her power to avoid that exact thing.

"It's not a bad thing. It's exactly what we need."

"The world needs shaking up," Marq commented, casting Sage an unreadable look. He gestured toward the chairs. "Shall we begin?"

"Yes. Time is against us." The queen nodded to Sage and took her seat, followed by Marq.

Tehl brushed his fingers along her knuckles, raising an eyebrow as if to say, 'Are you okay?' She nodded and trailed behind him to take a seat to his right. Nali placed herself on Sage's other side and leaned into her leg.

"We'd like to thank you for meeting with us on such short notice," Marq said.

The Methian queen waved a hand at him. "There's no need to mince words. War is upon us, and we'll fight beside you."

Sage blinked and peeked at Tehl who stared, his brow furrowed. That was blunt, and she wasn't the only one to notice, but her king just smiled, completely composed.

"I'm glad to hear that. I, myself, hate to skirt around an issue. Aermia is grateful for your assistance."

"We're always willing to help a neighbor, but in this case, it also helps Methi."

The king cocked his head, studying Queen Osir. "If Aermia falls to the warlord, so does the world."

"True, and that's why we will defend it like it is our own home."

"I wish everyone had your views," Tehl commented.

The queen's eyes narrowed. "They are fools. If there's one thing I've learned as I've grown older, it's that older doesn't always mean wiser. Many years of life breeds apathy."

"True." The king crossed his arms. "I can see what you stand to gain with this alliance, but what I truly want to know is what you'll want in exchange."

The queen grinned at him, her eyes twinkling. "That's always the question, isn't it?"

"It's the way of the world. No one does anything for free, especially those who rule. We can't."

"Spoken like a true king." She tipped her chin up and tapped her fingers on the arm of the chair. "We want access to the seas around Aermia. The schools have migrated from the Maekin Sea to your part of the world."

"We will allow you access to our waters at certain times of the year when the fish population is high. If we over-fish, then we both will be in the same boat." The king cracked a smile. "Pun intended."

The queen chuckled and shook her head. "Agreed, and you are not what I expected."

"My wife said the same thing when she met me."

"I was sorry to hear of her death." She placed a hand over Marq's. "I, too, have lost a mate. So I understand your suffering."

"Thank you. I'm sorry for your loss as well. No one should have to experience that type of pain."

She nodded and pulled her hand back. "We have one more condition, and I'm afraid it's non-negotiable." Queen Osir's face turned to stone. "You seem like a good man, but even good men are prone to envy. I am about to show you something the Methian people have guarded with their lives. I warn you now, if you hurt those we love, we'll kill you."

Marq's brows rose. "I think there was a compliment somewhere among the threats. Clearly, our alliance puts someone you love in danger, so I'll ignore the threats. What is it that you want?"

She blew out a breath and glanced to her son, who'd stood like a stone statue at her side. "It'll be easier to show you. Raziel?" She held her hand out, and her son helped her from the chair, as the men around the room stood. She eyed the group. "If you attack, we will. You have been warned."

Marq glanced at Tehl and Sage. "I assure you, my men will keep control of themselves."

"As you say."

Queen Osir swept from the room, disappearing into the darkness outside. Gav, Zachael, and William surrounded the king.

Rafe stopped halfway to the door and turned toward the Aermian group. "Don't be afraid. This is not a trap."

"Says the son of the Methian queen," Sage growled, glaring at Rafe.

"I'll explain later."

"Yes, you will," Tehl said softly. Sage glanced at her husband. She wasn't the only one stung by Rafe's secrets if she went by his expression.

Marq stared at Rafe and then exited the home, his men encircling him. Sage followed, Nali on her left, Tehl on her right.

"You run if it's dangerous," Tehl whispered.

She shot him a sharp look. "I'm not going anywhere."

The crown prince stared at her. "Bloody stubborn woman."

Sage grinned, and stepped out into the moonlit glen, her eyes immediately searching for danger. Nali's ears flattened, and the hair along her spine stood on edge again. "What is it, girl?"

Nali pressed closer to her thigh as the queen whistled, the sound piercing the air. For a moment, there was complete silence, and then, it was as if the forest had exploded. Sage's breath froze in her lungs, as huge winged creatures burst through the trees, and landed in the glen between the Methians and Aermians.

"Wicked hell," Tehl whispered.

Sage placed her hand on Nali's head as the feline snarled at the menacing interlopers.

"They will not hurt you," Queen Osir called.

Sage would've retorted if she could have spoken at all. It wasn't possible to turn away from the spectacle even had she wanted to.

The creature in front of them crouched and growled at Nali, its tail, white with black speckles, whipping back and forth as its brethren pressed closer to its side. A name came unbidden to Sage's mind. Fiilee. Felines as huge as horses with leathery wings. A creature from story books. Was every myth rooted in truth?

The fiilee's dark gray wings flared as it snarled again at Nali, causing the other three at its side to snarl. The hair rose on Sage's arms. They were huge and terrifying. She barely noticed when the leren moved in front of her, each step slow. They made Nail look like a kitten.

Queen Osir moved through the fiilee like she wasn't strolling through a herd of the most dangerous creatures to ever be recorded. She placed a hand on the creature's white speckled shoulder, and whispered a few soft words. The light blue eyes of the fiilee flicked to the queen and back to Nali. Sage tensed, and clenched her fingers in the leren's fur. There was no way she would let Nali fight with that thing.

"There's no need to be afraid. They will not harm you."

"They don't look very friendly," Sage called.

"They, like your leren, only wish to protect us." The queen stroked the beast's white and gray fur. "Now that they know you're not a danger, they'll leave you in peace."

"You speak to them?" Tehl asked.

"More or less. Our ancestors were able to devise a way of communication. They're highly intelligent."

"And deadly," Zachael commented.

"I see now why you were so worried," Marq said. "They provide you a source of protection that none have had since the dragons were wiped out."

The queen lifted her chin. "You know of the origin stories?"

"I do, and I promise we mean these creatures no harm. It's truly a privilege to see one alive and well, let alone three. They will give us an advantage."

"Scythia is an enemy like none we've known. To survive, we will need every resource at our disposal."

The fiilee slowly closed its giant wings and leaned into the queen.

Crown Prince Raziel stepped forward and placed a hand on the darker fiilee to the right. It was broader across the chest, and its spots were so many that it looked more black than white. He ran his hand along the arch of the wing where fur faded into leather. "An aerial advantage will mean everything."

A deep purr rumbled out of the beast, vibrating into Sage's chest. How magnificent! Even though the raised hair on the back of her neck told her to stay far away, she still wanted to sink her fingers into the fiilee's fur.

The Methian crown prince smiled at Sage, his eyes dancing. "If you'd like to meet the living legends, step closer."

She cocked her head and took a step forward, but Tehl slid in front of her, his body blocking her view. "What are you doing?" she hissed, a little put out.

"Keeping you from being eaten," he retorted.

Sage rolled her eyes and glanced at Rafe, who watched the exchange with a calculating glint in his eyes. The man saw way too much. "Do you think Rafe would let me get hurt?"

Tehl's shoulders lowered, and he glanced over his shoulder. "No."

"Then, step aside."

He surprised her by doing just that and then looping her arm through his. "Where you go, I go."

She hid her smile. It wasn't the time to moon over her husband. Tehl led them forward, no hesitation in his steps. He stopped an arm's reach away. "Is this close enough?"

Sage shook her head and met Raziel's familiar amber eyes. "Can I touch him?"

The Methian prince stroked the beast behind the ear, earning another purr of contentment. "Skye would like that."

"Hello, Skye," she said softly, staring at the fiilee with awe. The beast perked up, his light blue eyes practically glowing in the moonlight.

Tehl squeezed her hand once as she took a step closer and then followed her.

Sage held her palm out for Skye and locked her legs as he snuffled her hand. Her heart nearly stopped when a huge rough tongue darted out and wrapped around her wrist before retreating.

"That's his way of saying hello."

"It's a pleasure to meet you," she murmured as Tehl held his hand out as well. Skye sniffed him and then bathed his hand in saliva in the same welcome.

A booming laugh pulled her attention as Marq grinned at the queen's fiilee who'd licked him from chin to hair line, saliva clear on his face. She smiled, and then glanced at Tehl when he cursed. He rocked back a step as Skye butted him in the chest, releasing a rumbling purr that Sage felt to her toes.

"He's quite friendly, isn't he?"

"Only to those he deems worthy of his friendship."

"What does he do to those he doesn't care for?"

Raziel's smile turned sharp. "They disappear."

"Lovely," Tehl said, scratching the huge feline behind the ear.

Sage placed a hand on Skye's shoulder and ran her fingers through the thick fur along his spine. It was much thicker than Nali's. Speaking of Nali…

She glanced over her shoulder and spotted the leren. Nali sat just out of reach, eyeing Skye and then Sage like she was a traitor.

"All's well. He won't hurt you," Sage assured.

Nali huffed and flicked her tail.

"Stubborn beast," Sage muttered as she turned back to Skye. There was something about the fiilee that made her want to wrap her arms around it. So, she did. Warmth suffused her as Skye sniffed her head and nuzzled close. "You're just a big sweetheart, aren't you?"

"He's a pain in the ass," Rafe grumbled, sidling up to his brother. "Since he was a cub, he's always caused mischief."

"Zeefa was always worse, brother."

"Zeefa?" she asked.

"My companion."

Her brows furrowed. Companion?

"My fiilee."

Her gaze narrowed. When she got him alone, she would rip him apart, the dirty, secret-keeping liar.

"We will need to introduce your men to the fiilee before battle. They need to get acquainted with our companions." The queen's voice floated toward them.

"It will be arranged."

Sage released Skye and turned toward the two rulers.

"It's been a pleasure to meet with you, King Marq."

"And I you, Queen Osir. May the wind favor your return home."

The queen grinned and swung up onto her fiilee's back, sitting just behind its shoulder blades. "Thank you and safe travels. If you have need, you know how to reach us." She straightened, looking everything like the heroine of a story book on the back of her mythical steed.

Marq stepped back as the fiilee's wings spread, readying for flight.

Sage turned to Raziel and held her hand out. "Well met."

He glanced to Rafe and back to her before clasping her forearm. "I would have enjoyed calling you family," he said with a glint in his eyes.

Sage squeezed his forearm a little harder than necessary. The man had a little bit of the devil inside him. He obviously knew of her past with Rafe. "Don't be so sure. I'm a tough woman to live with. Too much independence." Heat suffused her back.

"She's a challenge, but well worth it. Life is never dull."

Raziel gazed over her head at Tehl. "Of that I'm sure."

Tehl slipped his hand into hers and led her away from Skye. Nali huffed as they approached her, her tail flicking in annoyance.

"Oh, stop pouting," Sage said. "You know I love you best."

Marq, Zachael, Gav, and William joined them and watched as the warriors mounted the fiilee.

Queen Osir smiled. "Until we meet again."

Marq lifted a hand and the fiilee launched upward, their huge wings stirring the air around them. Sage brushed her hair from her eyes and watched until she couldn't see them any longer.

"You have much explaining to do," the king said, turning to Rafe.

"You understand why I couldn't tell you."

"I do, and that's why I'm not angry. But I am curious as to how a Methian prince ends up in my kingdom, on my council."

Rafe winced and swept a hand toward where they'd left the horses. "A story I'd be happy to tell when we're at the palace."

"All right." The king patted Rafe on the shoulder. "Don't think you can avoid me. I have two sons and a nephew."

Sage smiled and glanced at Tehl and Gav who exchanged smiles that were a bit evil. "I can't wait to hear this story as well."

Rafe sighed. "How angry are you?" he asked as they strode after the king.

"She hasn't started yelling," Gav said. "That's a good sign."

"Yet," she said.

He had so much explaining to do.

THIRTY-SEVEN

TEHL

SAGE STUMBLED INTO THEIR ROOM, and Tehl shut the door behind them. He hid his smile as she yanked her boots off and tossed them across the room before crawling into their bed.

"You're not going to change?" he asked, pulling his belt and sword from his waist.

A grumble.

"What was that?"

"Too tired," came the muffled reply.

He chuckled and splashed water on his face from the wash basin. He was exhausted and yet… something buzzed in his veins. Something all Sage's doing. Tehl ran his wet fingers through his hair and smiled to himself. During what he'd remember as Rafe's confession, she'd cuddled into his side, her head on his shoulder. It was the best feeling. For the first time since his mother died, he'd felt like he was home.

He tugged his shirt off. Everything had changed tonight. The Methians and their fiilee were a godsend. "I half expected you to climb onto Skye tonight and fly away," he joked. "You couldn't stop touching the beast. I'm sure you made a friend for life." A light snore caught his attention. "Sage?"

He spun and leaned against the dresser, crossing his arms. Sage had sprawled out in the middle of the bed, her dark hair fanned out around her, lips parted in sleep. Tenderness flooded him at the sight of his woman.

His woman.

A streak of possessiveness went through him. She was unequivocally his, and he found that he liked it. A lot.

He shook his head and pushed off the dresser, rounding the bed. He grinned as a stubborn strand of tangled hair lay across her face, dangerously close to being sucked into her mouth.

"What am I going to do with you?" he muttered, and exhaled a soft laugh. Another snore answered him. He brushed the hair from her cheek, shaking his head. Sage was a beautiful disaster.

Tehl blew out the candle and gingerly crawled into the bed. He stared at her face, bathed in soft firelight. For once, she didn't look like she was in pain, her expression clear and at peace. He wished she'd stay that way. But inevitably, the nightmares would strike. He couldn't remember the last time either of them had slept the night through.

He reached out and traced one of her eyebrows and then the bridge of her nose, her skin like silk. Tehl froze as her lashes fluttered, but she didn't wake. She snuggled into his chest, her sigh heating his cheek.

This woman. She changed everything.

He brushed her shoulder and then curled his arm around her waist, her body molding to his. She had suffered horrors and, yet, she'd given him her trust. Something he'd not take lightly. This was the feeling his father had talked about, and now that Tehl had it in his arms?

He pulled her a little closer, his fingers splayed across her back. He would never let her go.

This was everything.

THIRTY-EIGHT

SAGE

AWARENESS SLOWLY CREPT IN, AND with it, the feeling of being suffocated. She cracked her eyes open and discovered the source of her affliction.

Tehl had thrown his leg over hers and was currently wrapped around her like an octopus. She lifted her head a smidge and squinted at the windows. It was too early to tell what time it was. Sage lowered her head and stared at the ceiling. What had woken her up? Usually, it was nightmares, but those left her with a pounding heart and bile in her mouth. She suffered neither of those things.

She turned her head and stared at Tehl. Stars above, there was so much love in her heart for that man. Her husband was a diamond in the rough. Her gaze dropped to her belly as his hand moved, his fingers caressing the skin between her trousers and shirt. Sage glanced back at his face, her breath catching.

He stared at her, sleepiness clinging to him in way that was beyond appealing.

"Nightmare?" he rumbled.

No. More like the best dream she'd had in a long time.

He shifted closer, his fingers brushing the skin of her belly, causing it to swoop. All she had to do was say the words. It would be easy to give in to his curious touches without saying what needed to be said.

His brows furrowed. "What's wrong?"

"Nothing," she whispered, twisting her hands together as anxiety fluttered through her. She'd been planning what she wanted to say. But now that the moment was here? She wasn't ready.

"That's a lie if I ever heard one."

Sage winced. "Life keeps surprising me. I made a vow when I woke up in the infirmary, but it's proving more difficult than I anticipated."

"How so, love?"

Her heart fluttered at the endearment. "It's hard to explain."

"You've never been one to beat around the bush. Out with it."

All the things she wanted to say tripped over in her head, but nothing escaped her lips. Tehl smiled at her and squeezed her hip as if encouraging her. But, somehow, she'd lost her voice. Why was this so hard to say?

"Could you close your eyes?"

"What?"

"Close your eyes, please."

He arched a brow at her, but did as she asked.

Sage stared at him, her pulse picking up speed as she collected her thoughts.

"When I met you," she began haltingly.

"You mean when I caught you," he said, cracking an eye.

She smacked him on the arm and gave him a hard look. Tehl grinned and closed his eyes once again. She pulled in a deep breath and tried again. "When you caught me in that alley, I thought you were the vilest knave on the surface of the earth."

His brows slashed together, but he kept his eyes closed.

"Then, I was forced into the company of your friends and family. I still didn't like you, but I figured someone who was surrounded by such wonderful people had to have redeeming qualities."

"Charming," he muttered.

"Hush, you," she chastised. "Let me finish. Then I was sold to you." His eyes flew open, and she held her hand up. "You gave me the choice. *You*, not them. I appreciated that, even if I didn't show it at the time. We've fought each other, invisible enemies, and the ghosts of our pasts." Specifically, hers.

"In Scythia, you kept me sane," she whispered. "You were with me every step of the way. You protected me, urged me to never give up, and, even when I ignored you, you never abandoned me. You kept me from dying there, from giving in."

"Sage," he murmured, his sapphire gaze drawing her in, robbing her of her breath. His fingers caressed her cheek. "I wish you never were there in the first place."

Her eyes slid closed as she gripped his wrist, and held his palm to her cheek. "As do I, but we can't change the past, no matter how much we wish to. I'm just so sorry that it took me this long to realize what it all meant."

"Realize what?" His question was quiet, and had an edge to it.

She brushed a finger over his stubbled jawline and leaned forward, gently brushing her lips across his. Easing back, she boldly met his gaze. She'd never been a coward, and she wouldn't be one now by having him close his eyes.

"You were the one my mind chose to protect me. Not my mum, Lilja, or Gav. *You.* All along, I'd cast you as the monster, but you never were. You are the hero to my story. You are my epic love."

His eyes widened, emotion tightening his features. "You love me?"

She nodded, as tears gathered at the corners of her eyes. "I have for a long time, but Peg sealed it."

He grinned, his gaze suspiciously shiny. "I knew you'd love that damn horse. She is the equine version of you." He pressed his forehead to hers and closed his eyes. "Since the moment I met you, I wanted you." He puffed out a breath. "I couldn't understand why. You were the enemy, mouthy, and as prickly as a porcupine. But I liked you."

He opened his eyes and pulled back, apparently searching her face for something. "Are you sure it's me you want? I know things can be confusing for you at times," he asked.

"I'm more sure about loving you than I've been about anything else in my life."

He stilled, and his eyes seemed to burn her. His hand curled around the back of her neck and he pulled her close, his lips brushing hers. "You slay me. Lead, sweet wife, and I will follow. Everything I am is bound to you until we depart this world."

She blinked hard as he repeated part of their vows. "Until we depart this world," she whispered across his lips.

That was the breaking point.

His lips crushed hers, fierce and demanding. It wasn't gentle. It wasn't skilled. *It was everything.* He kissed her like his life depended on it. She looped her arms around his neck and kissed him with every fiber of her being.

Her hands sank into his hair, as he deepened the kiss. Warmth swept through her middle when his fingers slid down her neck and over her shoulder. He pulled her hard against him and turned. Sage gasped as he came down on top of her, his weight pressing her into the bed.

As the room started to spin, she tore her mouth from his and panted for air. He instantly claimed her jaw, lips trailing up to her ear, then along the side of her neck.

"Lucky," he murmured. His teeth grazed her skin and she shivered.

"What?" she breathed, staring blurrily at the low fire.

He pulled away and pushed himself upright. Kneeling between her thighs, he stared down at her with glazed, burning eyes. "Lucky. I'm the luckiest man."

She swallowed hard, trying not to cry. *She* was the lucky one. She traced a pattern along his muscular thigh. "We both won."

He scanned her face and leaned down again, bracing himself on his elbows. "Sage." He clasped her cheeks between his palms and stared at her. Slowly, he kissed her, his lips tender, but edged with a desperation they both felt. "Let me love you?"

Heat flashed through her body, and a flush crept into her cheeks. This wasn't something she had to think about. She knew her answer already.

Sage curled her hand around his neck. "Yes."

He pulled in a deep breath, some of the tension in his body dispelling. Then he was kissing her again. Slow, deep, drugging kisses she never wanted to surface from. He found the buttons of her vest and undid them, brushing aside the leather. His mouth drifted to her chin, and Sage arched her neck as he kissed down her throat to the hollow between her collarbones.

A memory slammed into her.

She sucked a deep breath when his hand slid down, fingers brushing across the tender skin under her jaw then trailing over her abused neck.

She turned her head to the side to break the kiss. The warlord's mouth traveled across her jaw and along the side of her neck, following the path of his hand. His fingers caught the edge of her robe and pushed the fabric off her shoulder. The cold air made her shiver, and her eyes slammed open as he nipped at her collarbone.

Sage gasped, and squeezed her eyes closed. The warlord had no place here. He didn't get to ruin everything. He didn't get to be part of this.

"Love?" Tehl asked, nuzzling her cheek. "Are you all right?"

She forced herself to breathe normally and opened her eyes, guilt almost drowning her. Even now, the warlord invaded her mind. "I'm sorry," she croaked.

He gave her a tender look. "You have nothing to be sorry about."

Tehl began to pull away, but she seized his arms to keep him from escaping. The warlord would not ruin this. She wouldn't allow it.

"No."

"No?"

"No," she said pulling him close to kiss him. "This is about us."

Her lips curled into a smile as his glazed eyes met hers. His finger caught in the linen of her shirt, exposing her shoulder. She shivered from the touch of cool air and as his mouth moved across her bare shoulder, his fingers skating over her body. Her skin heated, and she blushed as she ran her own hands along his arms and shoulders.

This was how it was supposed to be. Mutual love and desire. The need for his skin on hers.

She dragged her fingers up his neck and through his dark hair, her teeth nipping at his lips. He rumbled his pleasure, which had her lips curling against his. There was something gratifying about pleasing the one you loved. Heat scorched her cheeks as she contemplated her next move and then followed through.

Sage reached between their bodies and slid her hands over the hard planes of his abdomen and up his chest. Stars above, he was perfect.

He stilled and then sat up. The firelight haloed his dark form, shadowing his expression from her. He reached for the hem of her shirt and paused, asking an unspoken question. Sage gathered her bravery around her and sat up, pulling the vest and shirt over her head. Goosebumps broke across her arms as her body was exposed to him.

"No corset?" he whispered, his voice rough.

Sage crossed her arms over her chest and glanced toward the balcony windows. She shrugged one shoulder. "They're uncomfortable and not practical when fighting."

She jumped when his hand circled her wrists and gently pulled her arms away from her body.

"Don't hide from me. You're stunning."

She peeked at him from beneath her lashes and was almost burned by the heat in his gaze. "Such beauty should *never* be hidden from your husband." His eyes drank her in as he leaned closer and placed a kiss over her heart. "Never."

He lowered himself onto her, and, again, his mouth found hers. His fingers moved to the button of her trousers, no hesitation this time. She inhaled sharply as he slid the fabric down, and his fingertips grazed her thighs as he traced the lines of her body. Her breath hitched at his teasing touch. An unexpected giggle escaped her when his fingers explored the back of her knees.

He halted, and grinned. "You're ticklish, love?"

"Maybe." She wouldn't give him that information.

A dangerous glint entered his blue eyes. "We'll come back to this," he growled as his fingers began their journey again, running over her hips, the curve of her waist, her chest, and then back down. Each touch was deliberate, like he was trying to memorize every inch of her.

He kissed her again, his mouth hot and relentless. The world narrowed to just Tehl and her, and all she could do was hold onto him and remember to breathe.

All thoughts fled when the last vestige of her clothing disappeared along with his. Her breath hitched as Tehl stared at her, awe apparent on his face.

"I've never seen anything so precious and beautiful," he whispered. He nuzzled her neck, his tongue darting out to trace her throat.

Any nerves she had disappeared with his soft, honest words. Sage smiled as he pressed a tender kiss to her cheek.

"So perfect," he murmured.

She relaxed and brushed her fingers along her husband's sides, marveling at his strength. His breathing picked up and the world fell away when he pressed his body against hers, his touch growing wilder. She sank her fingers into his inky hair and yanked his mouth to hers, demanding more.

No doubts. No pain. Just love.

"I want you more than I've ever wanted anything," he panted against her lips. "This is everything."

"Everything," she echoed, when he guided her legs around his waist and they melded into one. Her fingers dug into his shoulders, and her eyes widened, breath completely leaving her.

He kissed her softly, cradling her in his arms. Tehl stroked her face, her lips, her eyebrows. He trembled and rested his forehead against hers, as if he was fighting to restrain himself. His dark lashes fluttered against her cheeks, and then deep blue eyes met hers.

"Only me," he whispered.

"Only you," she whispered.

His smile was blinding, and then, he *moved*. For a moment she wasn't sure if it was pleasure or pain, or a blend of both. All she knew was that it changed everything. Her awareness narrowed to nothing but him, his love, his touch, his kiss, and their bodies together.

Tonight was theirs.

THIRTY-NINE

TEHL

THERE WAS SOMETHING WRONG WITH him. Tehl couldn't look away from her.

Sage slept in his arms, her warm, naked body pressed to his. The fire burned low, and the light was muted, painting her pale skin a soft golden hue that he wanted to taste. Again.

He felt whole. Happy. And nowhere near sated. Even now, he wanted her again, to lounge in bed with her for days like they should have done at the beginning.

She sighed in his arms as he adjusted to her, and ran his hand along her spine, reveling in the silky skin. The differences between them intrigued him. Where he was calloused and rough, she was soft. His gaze flicked down the bed to the tangled sheets and discarded clothes. His lips twitched. She didn't wear a corset. That would prove to be distracting now that he knew.

He glanced back at his wife. Her whole being was distracting.

Sage snuggled into his chest, her long strands of hair a crazy mess around her head. He stifled his chuckle. Once her hair escaped its confines, it turned into an entity of itself.

"You're staring," she said, not opening her eyes.

Tehl pressed a kiss to her forehead, his gaze drifting to said hair. "It's alive."

She thumped his arm and opened her eyes, smiling. "It can't be helped."

He swallowed, emotion rocking him. Who knew his wild, rebel wife would bring so much joy into his life? She had her flaws, granted. She was stubborn and held a grudge. But he'd take the good with the bad. The good out-shadowed all the bad.

She blinked. "What are you thinking?"

He ran his hand along her shoulder and scanned her face. "Did I hurt you?" It had been on his mind since he'd woken. The first time was always painful for a woman, and he didn't want her to have any regrets.

A smile darted across her lips. "I dare say it was quite the opposite. Most enjoyable night I've had ever."

His body tightened as she ran her foot up his calf. "You aren't sore?"

She blushed at his blunt question. "Yes, and no." Her fingers brushed his chest. "I didn't expect it to be like that."

"Yes," he murmured. It could drive a man wild. No wonder Gav was so distracted after he married. Fingers brushed his thigh, causing his hands to press harder into her spine. Stars above. He was in so much trouble.

"I wouldn't mind if we…" Her cheeks heated again.

He grinned and traced the blush with a finger. She was brash most of the time, but, add sex into the mix, and now she was shy. "I would love to touch you," he groaned. "But your body needs time to heal, and I would like to care for you before reality knocks at our door."

"Care for me?"

"Bathe with me." It wasn't really a question. "Let me care for my wife." It was something his father had beaten into him. He and Sam were to always care for their wives.

Sage shifted against him, watching him with lazy abandon. "I would love to bathe with you." She slapped a hand against her belly as it growled, and she gave him a silly smile. "Sorry."

He grinned and swiftly kissed her lips. "Food is on its way, love. I'll draw a bath." He popped from the bed, and Sage hissed. He spun with a raised eyebrow and followed her gaze to the red smear on the sheet. She jerked the blanket over it, hiding it from his view.

Tehl rounded the bed and sat next to his wife, who refused to look at him. "Don't be ashamed. This is not shameful. It's wonderful. Thank you for giving yourself to me. Your innocence is something I will always cherish."

She peeked at him over her shoulder. "You're so blunt and then, every once in a while, you say just the right thing."

He smiled and opened the drawer of the side table, pulling out a handkerchief. Corner by corner, he moved the fabric out of the way to reveal the treasure he had hidden there. Two silver cuffs sat in his hand. His heartbeat picked up as Sage leaned close and ran a finger along the decorative cuffs he'd made for her.

"I made them for you, since the other ones were lost."

"How long have you had these?" she whispered.

"I started working on them as soon as we returned."

"Why wait until now to give them to me?"

He cleared his throat and stared at his wife. "Because I wanted you to *want* to wear them. I wanted it to be truly your choice."

Sage smiled. "I want to wear them." She held out her wrists. "Will you put them on?"

The nervousness in her belly evaporated. She wanted this as much as he did. Sage gasped as he turned the cuff over, so she could see the inside.

"What's this?"

"I thought you'd like it." He touched the horse with wings engraved on the inside. "Peg makes you feel free. I wanted you to be able to carry her wherever you go. And know that even though we are bound, you will never be caged."

A fat, salty tear dripped down her cheek as he slid both cuffs into place.

"Thank you. I love them." She wiped the tear away and held her arms out to stare at her cuffs. "I'll wear them with pride." Sage threw an arm around him and kissed his left cheek. "Where are yours?"

He pulled his cuffs from the same drawer, eager to wear them. Sage plucked them from his hands and slid a cuff onto each of his biceps. They stared at each other for a moment, both grinning.

"Why are you so smiley?" she teased. "You happy to have your cuffs on me?"

"Beyond pleased." He kissed her shoulder, not able to help himself. "Maybe it's because my wife shared my bed," he tacked on, feeling lighter than he had in ages.

"My bed." Sage smiled impishly. "You should share my bed every day. It'll improve your diplomatic skills. Really, it would be best for our kingdom."

Apparently, she had no idea how appealing that was, and how much he wanted to pounce on her. "You tease," he accused and forced himself to leave the bed. If he didn't, they'd stay there all day.

"Only for you," she called as he entered the bathing room.

He glared at all the clothing that hid her body from his view. It seemed like a travesty to cover such beauty.

"Stop pouting," she said, rolling her eyes. "You're the one who said we needed to be responsible."

"I'm regretting that decision now," he muttered. Her answering peal of laughter had him smiling.

She tossed her braid over her shoulder and winked at him. "Men, you all are always so predictable."

He growled and wrapped an arm around her waist, pulling her back into his chest. "I'm not the only one who enjoyed our time in the bath." Her skin pinked. He grinned wickedly. He knew she enjoyed teasing him and now he had the perfect weapon with which to tease her.

Sage opened her mouth to retort when there was a knock at their door. She scowled. "It was only a matter of time."

"Indeed."

He let her go, and she pulled open the door. "Sam."

His brother entered, and closed the door behind him as Sage moved back to Tehl's side to strap on the rest of her daggers. Sam eyed the two of them and then the bed. He froze and glanced away, a secret smile on his face as he met Tehl's eyes, his gaze dropping to the cuffs circling Tehl's biceps.

His brother arched a brow. All Tehl could do was smile. He had a wife in truth now. Everything was as it should be. His grin widened. Nothing compared to what he shared with his wife. It was as close to magic as he could imagine.

"So who's demanding our presence this morning?" Sage asked, buckling her last sheath around her thigh.

"Morning has come and gone. It's late in the afternoon."

Tehl's eyes widened as Sam grinned. Ah hell.

"What have you been doing all day?"

Sage blinked, and her mouth bobbed, at a loss for words.

"Enough," Tehl said, casting an apologetic glance at his wife. "What do you need?"

Sam's smile melted, his expression blank. "There's news."

"Has another village been attacked?" Sage asked.

"No, but Scythia's army has been spotted."

"How far from the Mort Wall?" Tehl demanded.

"A day's walk from the Potam River."

So close. "Our soldiers need to be moved there immediately."

"Gav has them moving already. A camp will be set up shortly."

Tehl snatched his sword from the side table and buckled the belt around his waist. "We depart within the hour."

"The men are assembling now." Sam stared at the floor. "There's more."

"What is it?"

"I married last night."

Tehl blinked. "That's not funny."

"Do you think I would joke of my marriage?" Sam asked seriously.

Why in the world would he get married? Then it occurred to him. His hands curled into fists, and he glared at his brother. "*Who* did you compromise?" He took a step forward, but a hand stopped him. Tehl glanced down at his wife. She wasn't looking at him, but her narrowed eyes were focused on Sam.

"It's done," she said. "There are much more pressing matters to deal with. His marriage hardly matters in the light of other things." She stepped closer to Sam and hugged the bastard. "My congratulations."

Sam stared over her shoulder at him as he hugged Sage. "Thank you," he said softly.

His brother didn't even look sorry. "Mum would be so disappointed."

Sam's face tightened, showing a flicker of hurt before he schooled his expression.

Sage released his brother and stepped back. "Who is the lucky woman?"

Sam focused on Sage. "Jasmine."

Tehl sucked in a sharp breath. "Out of all the women…" He broke off when Sage slapped Sam.

Sage poked Sam in the chest. "Shame on you! She's a good person." She heaved in a deep breath. "I know I'm missing other pieces to the puzzle, but I'm too angry to figure out what they are right now. Leave, before I get the feeling back in my hand and I'm tempted to slap you again."

Sam nodded, a red handprint on his left cheek. He strode to the door.

"Sam," Sage called. He paused by the door and glanced back at her. "I'm upset, but I still love you."

Sam glanced to Tehl and then back to Sage. "Love you too, sis."

Tehl rounded on Sage as soon as the door shut. "Why were you so easy on him? What he's done is deplorable. It's shameful."

"Your brother is a good man. Every decision he makes is calculated."

True. After all these years, his brother had been discreet enough that he never had to marry any of the girls he dallied with. Why now? "You think he compromised her on purpose?"

"It's a thought, but I don't know why."

"My brother is not one to be easily understood." He shook his head. "It matters not now. The deed is done." He drifted closer to Sage and stared down into her face. "I won't ask you not to go."

"If you did, I'd ignore you."

"This is your battle as much as mine. But I wish…" That they had more time. His gaze dropped farther, to her flat belly. His hands curled around her hips and pulled her close. "Last night could have resulted in a child."

"I'm sure that's not the case," she argued.

"But it's a possibility. War is never quick or easy. If you show signs, you will leave the battlefield, understood?"

She stared at her belly and then met his gaze. "If there is a child, I will leave."

He bent and kissed her lips, thankful she was being reasonable. "Prepare yourself, love. I'll be waiting for you with Peg."

Tehl pressed one more quick kiss to her lips and forced himself from their room. He couldn't think about how easily Sage could be hurt in the coming months. He would trust her and protect her to the best of his ability.

No one was taking her from him. Sage was finally his.

Together, they'd rid the world of the monsters.

FORTY

SAGE

SAGE STARED OUT AT THE ocean, her body slowly going numb. Scythia approached. He was coming for her. She knew it was only a matter of time before he hunted her down. Her gaze dropped to the waves crashing below, their siren call still there, but much less appealing.

She hissed and spun, storming inside. Even now she could feel the tell-tale panic trying to claw up her throat. Her reflection caught her attention, her steps pausing by the mirror. Every time she looked at herself, she saw the warlord. The product of his tampering.

Her hand wandered to her bare throat. He had no power over her anymore. She was free, and despite the changes to her physique, she was still herself. Cool, emerald eyes stared back at her, as cold as the light armor covering her arms and chest. If was ironic, really. The armor protected her body, but it was her mind that needed the protecting.

"Sage?"

She jumped and glanced at the door. Blaise stood in the doorway, watching with evident concern. The Scythian closed the door softly and leaned against it.

"He won't win," Blaise stated.

"Who are you trying to convince? Me or yourself? You and I both know we're not ready for war."

"Aermia is ready. You aren't."

She grimaced and turned back to the mirror, hating that Blaise was right. She wanted to pretend none of it ever happened. She wanted to forget.

"You can't pretend he's not out there. You can't wish him away. You need to fight, or he wins."

"I'm not strong enough." There. She'd said the words that had been haunting her for weeks. She was scared to be near the warlord. What if he messed with her mind again? Could she even trust herself?

Blaise moved to her side and stared at the mirror. Sage stared at her friend's reflection, eyeing the painted, swirling patterns that adorned the exposed part of Blaise's right arm. It was beautiful in a terrifying way. Blaise had always been stunning with her olive skin and dark hair, but the paint added a touch of danger.

Her friend pulled a small container from her pocket and plopped it down on the vanity. "Sit," she ordered. "And face me."

Sage turned and sat slowly, staring up at Blaise. "What now?"

"You sit still, and you listen."

Blaise leaned over her and opened the little container, pungent herbs filling the air. She dipped her thumb into the black sludge and pulled it back. She gave Sage an inscrutable look and lifted her chin up.

"Many years ago, my ancestors created the Tia paint. It was a rite of passage, if you will. Close your eyes."

Sage closed her eyes and shivered as Blaise smeared cold paint from her forehead to her eyes, and then down to her cheek.

"Keep them closed." Blaise shifted and began drawing on Sage's face again. "Birth is a miraculous thing. It's always been difficult for women as a whole. Only the strongest survive such a brutal experience. When the time came, the medicine women would paint an expectant mother's face. It was said to help her fight, to embolden her in the face of such pain and the possibility of death."

"I'm not with child."

"The tradition evolved. When war between clans erupted, as it always does, the men started to wear the face paint as a symbol of what they were fighting for: their women and children. It wasn't simply war paint, but a mark of their devotion and dedication to those they loved."

She spun Sage around. "Open your eyes."

Sage opened her eyes and stared at the painted woman in the mirror. Dark charcoal lined her eyes, causing the green to pop. Three bold lines slashed through her left brow and down to her cheek. Black dots followed the underside of her right brow and extended from her eye in three separate lines. Her gaze zeroed in on her obsidian lips. The creature in the mirror didn't look like her, and yet, when she smiled, so did her reflection.

Blaise placed her hands on Sage's shoulders and squeezed, pulling her attention from her reflection.

"You are not the woman he held in his cage. That Sage is dead and gone. He forged you into something else, not his pawn, but his demise." Blaise smiled, but it wasn't nice. "You are his greatest mistake. You are not his consort. *You* are his judgement, his enemy, and his ultimate destruction."

"I am not his consort," Sage whispered. "I am his destruction."

"You are his death."

"I am his death."

"My mother would have never risked her plans for you if you weren't important. She believed you would bring change. I believe that as well." Blaise hugged her from behind and rested her chin on Sage's shoulder. "We are sisters in arms, you and I."

"Sisters in arms," Sage murmured. "I will fight."

"And I will stand at your side. That monster will regret ever hurting those we love."

The ember of rage that always seemed to smolder in Sage's gut, ignited. She was his greatest weakness.

To eradicate the darkness, she had to become darkness.

He'd never see her coming.

FORTY-ONE

THE WARLORD

THEY THOUGHT THEY WERE SO clever. They were children really, playing at being warriors. They had no idea what the future held.

Zane smiled as he watched the Aermian army scurry about like ants as they built their camps.

Ignorant.

They were ignorant of his spies. Ignorant that their greatest enemy walked among them. A leren among babes.

He stilled and glanced over his shoulder, as awareness tingled over his skin. A sixth sense that she was near. He narrowed his eyes on the approaching party. The crown prince lead the group, but Zane didn't care. He only had eyes for one person. The goddess in armor and war paint.

"Sage," he whispered, all covetousness and possession. His consort stole his breath away, her beauty so bright it felt like it burned him where he stood.

He kept his head bowed as the group passed him, his fingers brushed her cloak for one second before he receded into the bustling camp. He could steal her away now, but that would be too easy.

His consort has challenged him, and he loved a good fight. No, he wouldn't take her this day. He'd wait for her surrender, and it would be all the more sweet.

Zane adjusted his cloak, and grinned.

Soon enough she'd bow to him. All he needed was a little patience. His consort would grace him with her presence soon enough.

Then he'd destroy her world.

CONTINUE THE SERIES WITH

REIGN OF BLOOD AND POISON

ABOUT THE AUTHOR

Thank you for reading *Queen of Monsters and Madness*. I hope you enjoyed it! If you liked this book, please review it BECAUSE the review rating determines which series I prioritize. If you want the next book in this series soon, review this book. Thank you!

If you'd like to know more about me, my books, or to connect with me online, you can visit my webpage WWW.FROSTKAY.NET, check out my facebook group FROST FIENDS, or follow me on Bookbub to receive news about my new releases.

You've just read a book in my AERMIAN FEUDS series. Other books in this series include *Reign of Blood and Poison*, *Warlord's Shadow*, and *Siren's Lure*.

www.ingramcontent.com/pod-product-compliance
Lightning Source LLC
Chambersburg PA
CBHW020352310726
48979CB00015B/2560/J

* 9 7 8 1 6 3 8 7 7 0 1 6 9 *